A DARKNESS UNTO THE DAWN

A DARKNESS UNTO THE DAWN

• *A Novel* •

R.A. St. James

August Crow Publishing

Published in the United States by August Crow Publishing

ISBN hardback:- 978-1-7361079-0-4
ISBN paperback:- 978-1-7361079-1-1
ISBN eBook:- 978-1-7361079-2-8

www.augustcrowpublishing.com
www.rastjames.com
www.nowbeginstherevolution.com

Author's Note

Police brutality against African-Americans is a real problem, and has been since the abolition of slavery. It is impossible to stay abreast of current events in the United States and not be aware of the constant stream of news reports detailing atrocities committed by police officers against unarmed, and often innocent, Black men, women and children. It is some of these events that inspired this novel.

However, I am well aware of the fact that most law enforcement officers are good people who dispense the duties of their job in a fair, caring and unbiased manner. I want to make it clear that this novel is a work of fiction and is not meant to be interpreted as a blanket indictment against all police officers. I also do not condone nor encourage anyone reading this to take the law into their own hands.

These injustices need to be fought, but let's fight them in the courts and at the ballot boxes, via protests and petitions, and by never forgetting the price paid by those that have fallen in the struggle for equal rights in this country.

R.A. St. James

If you would like get on the mailing list to receive special bonus chapters, to be updated about new releases or to leave comments or questions for the author, please go to:

AugustCrowPublishing.com

or

RAStJames.com

If you would like to stay up on news stories and articles related to matters important to the African-American community, please subscribe to:

NowBeginsTheRevolution.com

For Monk –

Who filled my shadows with sunshine when I didn't even know I was in the dark

Book 1: BLACK MOON RISING

Chapter 1

Fireworks. Thunder, lightning and various colors of the sunrise. Fireworks. That was always his first memory of the event. It was as though Zeus, the God of Thunder, was at war with his son Apollo, the God of the Sun. Strangely enough, Apollo was also the God of Plague. That seemed particularly appropriate because death followed the fireworks.

The boy in the passenger seat looked down at his freshly-pressed white shirt, a 9th birthday gift. He brushed some lint off it. Then he noticed the traffic light. The light was red and it suddenly filled his field of vision. This red light was the first hint that something was about to happen, even though it was just sitting there. Doing nothing. But the boy found himself staring at it intently.

As he blinked his eyes, time slowed down. For a moment, he couldn't hear anything. There were no traffic sounds. There were no engine sounds. Even the fan, blowing warm air as a substitute for the A/C that had stopped working two summers ago, was silent. Then, from somewhere at the end of a long tunnel, he heard a voice. The voice broke through the silence and sped towards him.

"There you go, pops, windows spotless! Can a brother get a dollar?"

The boy's father leaned towards him, shifting his weight so he could reach for the wallet in his back pocket. At 5'9", Lucian Carter wasn't a particularly tall man. However, this movement reminded the boy of a great tree that was about to topple over but somehow righted itself at the last moment. His father's large, callous-covered hands unfolded the worn leather billfold.

The man, covered in grime and with a Windex bottle hanging from his belt, reached for the dollar bill. The boy barely noticed. His attention was still fixed on the traffic light. It began slowly changing from red to green, as though one color was bleeding into the next.

Someone behind them beeped, impatient. The boy's gaze shifted back to the dollar bill, which somehow magically floated out the window. It took forever to transfer from his father's hand to the stranger's. The man looked at it and scowled.

"That's all you got? Come on, man, let me get another one. I gotta get uptown. This won't even cover my bus fare."

"Sorry, that's all I can spare," the boy heard his father say as he shifted his weight again. The giant sequoia threatened once more to fall to earth but stopped mid-tilt. The wallet slipped from his hand and fell onto the floor. His father reached between his legs, recovering it. There was another beep from one of the trailing cars.

"Nah, motherfucker! You gonna have to do better than that!" screamed the man. A large silver gun suddenly materialized, filling up the entire space of the window opening. His father immediately froze.

"Listen, brother, you don't have to do this. You can have the money," he said, his deep voice calm and steady as he raised both hands to his shoulders. His left hand still clutched the wallet. The man outside lowered the gun as he snatched the billfold and ripped it open.

"You got a whole lotta money in here! Why you lie to me? Huh?" he asked as he took a step back and raised the gun to the window again.

"Look. I'm just trying to live my life and take care of my family," said his father, the slightest hint of defiance in his voice. His hands were still raised as he stared straight ahead, refusing to look at his assailant. The boy mimicked his father, once again focusing his attention on the traffic light.

"Man, fuck yo' life!" yelled the gunman.

His father quickly leaned forward and turned, putting his body between the weapon and his son. There was another beep, further behind them this time. And then, as if on cue, came the fireworks. The thunder was deafening inside the close confines of the small sedan. The boy saw the lightning in his peripheral vision. As it kicked from the barrel of the gun, he momentarily saw spots before his eyes.

In that briefest of milliseconds, the boy thought to himself that the spots reminded him of those little flashing lights he sometimes saw after a hard sneeze. Those little lights that danced and jittered at the outer edges of his vision, making him feel that he was on some kind of strange space tour. Of course, he had never been to space, but he imagined that it must feel somewhat like what he was feeling right this moment. Everything was slow and fluid, the atmosphere at once both beautiful and deadly.

The starburst that followed the explosion wasn't so much a splash as it was a painting. It was as though an invisible brush was deftly adding streaks of liquid red to the dash and the inside of the windshield. The liquid was thick and rich, but thin enough that he could still see the green light shining through the glass. The colors mixed to create a new hue: grayish blue.

The boy was frozen. He continued to stare at the light. He couldn't tear his eyes away from it. He didn't want to see what this painter, this violent Van Gogh standing outside his father's car, may have done to his nice white shirt. He certainly did not want to see what the man may have done to his father. He felt—rather than saw—the man with the gun turn and run. He heard the screeching of tires as the cars behind them peeled off, looking for refuge from this crazed display of color and light.

And then, the silence again. He could feel the color dripping; dripping off the glass, dripping off the dash, dripping off him. But he couldn't hear it. He didn't even feel any moisture or wetness, even as he felt chunks of some foreign matter sliding down his face. Something hung from his chin and then fell into his lap.

After what felt like years, he was finally able to pull his gaze away from the traffic light. He turned his head ever so slowly and risked a glance at his father in the driver's seat. The tree that was his father was still there, but was now leaning heavily to the right, its descent halted only by the seatbelt. The tree was still there, but it was now incomplete.

The boy's father, the top part of his head gone, stared back at the boy. There was still some light in his eyes, but the light was fading fast. In its place was a darkness. The darkness began to blossom, spreading over the iris, covering the white and then erupting, like a volcano, reaching desperately for the boy—

Ish woke up and leaped out of the bed in one fluid motion. His breathing was hard and ragged, his body covered in sweat. He bent low into a combat stance, ready to face any and all attackers, but no one was there. He slowly realized where he was—alone, in Los Angeles, in a hotel room on the 34th floor. As he stood up, his breathing began to return to normal. He grabbed a towel from the bathroom and tried to wipe himself down before giving up and jumping in the shower.

After his shower, he walked over to the balcony. The view was spectacular. He had turned on his iPod and Ice Cube's "The Predator" was playing in the background. He held a tumbler of *Jura Camas an Staca* scotch. It was thirty years old, the same age as the man holding the glass. His name was Ishmael Carter. Everyone called him "Ish".

Ishmael Octavius Carter was born May 1, 1986, in Chicago to Adriana Lima and Lucian Carter. Adriana's parents were native Brazilians who had moved to the U.S. before Adriana was born. Lucian was a Louisiana Creole. Ish's mother was beautiful and statuesque with bronze-colored skin. His father was chocolate-brown and handsome.

Due to his mixed heritage, Ish was racially ambiguous. He had greenish-hazel eyes, black wavy hair and dusky copper-colored skin. People often asked him 'what he was'. Black? Puerto Rican? Indian? Pakistani? It didn't help that he often spoke in languages other than English. His mother grew up speaking Portuguese and his father French and Creole. Ish's family could often be heard communicating with each other in any of the four languages.

This could have made Ish an outsider in the communities that he grew up in, but with his chiseled good looks, natural ability for sports and easy charm, he was quite popular with the other kids, male and female alike. Those were simpler times. Sometimes he wished he could return to them.

His phone vibrated, and he pulled it from his pocket and looked at the screen. It was Chad. Again. He muttered a curse in Pashto and pressed 'ignore'. That was at least the eighth time tonight. Chad never did have much patience, but tonight he would have to wait. Ish needed a minute.

He grabbed the remote and flicked on the TV. It opened to a news channel showing breaking news of another unarmed African-American who had just been shot and killed by a police officer somewhere in

Oregon. It showed a stream of faces of other recently deceased black men and women who had died at the hands of the police. He shook his head in sadness.

He had recently returned from his final tour of duty in Afghanistan, and his life was in shambles. His daughter was dead. His wife was in jail—and wanted to stay there regardless of what he might be able to do to get her out. And to top it off, he had to come home to this shit—the news full of stories of cops killing brothers in the street like it was a fucking turkey shoot. He knew that one of the reasons these stories were affecting him so intensely was because of his daughter's death. Not just the fact that she was gone, but the way it happened.

He grabbed the bottle of *Camas* and poured himself another double. At $500 a bottle, he had already gone through about $250 worth before he dozed off, but he barely felt any effect at all, from either the alcohol or the price tag. The fact that he was 6'3" and 225 pounds helped with the metabolization. And any effect of the cost was cushioned by the fact that the software company he co-founded had a contract with the Department of Defense worth a minimum of $18.2M a year. But still, he knew he needed to cut this shit out.

He needed to get back to his company. There was too much to do and too many details to focus on over the next 24 hours for him to be taking such liberties. But this was the best way he knew to take a little bit of the edge off before jumping back into the fray. Over in Afghanistan, whenever he began to really feel the stress, whenever he began to feel that darkness start to take over his soul, he would sometimes put on the gloves and go six or seven rounds on the heavy bag. Occasionally, he and the other guys would even do a little sparring for fun. But the hotel didn't have a heavy bag, and as wound up as he was feeling right now, he wasn't sure he would be able to pull his punches enough to avoid seriously injuring whatever sparring partner might be placed in front of him.

The problem was the faces. He couldn't get the faces out of his head. And that included his daughter's. Every time he recalled his daughter's face, he now also saw the face of Derek Wellsby, LaTonya Fisher, Terri Cross, Rakim Debuque, Tyrone Williams, Marcus Payton, and the list went on and on.

They represented a variety of demographics. They were men, women, young, old, law abiders, criminals, parents, children, rich, poor and everything in between. But the two things they all had in common was that they were African Americans and that they were killed in cold blood, while unarmed, by white police officers. Some started as traffic stops, some as response to a reported disturbance, some as 'stop and frisk', but they all ended the same way: with a dead Negro on the ground and a fucking cowardly white cop standing over them.

Shit, he thought to himself, shaking his head again. It's not like any of this was new. Blacks have been victimized, beaten and assassinated by white people since the first slaves were brought to this country 400 years ago. Yeah, we got rid of slavery, and Jim Crow and segregation, and blacks were now highly paid lawyers, doctors, entertainers and even politicians. But we've always been victims. And no matter how much we've marched about it and talked about it and cried about it, all too often our cries for justice have been ignored.

The difference now is that just about everyone carries a video camera in their pocket, called a cell phone. We're all Spike Lee. We're all Lee Daniels. We're all Ava DuVernay. So now we sometimes have proof, with scenes that play out in full-color video over millions and millions of smart phones, PCs, laptops and TV sets.

Finally, liberal white America is coming to the realization that life is not as peachy keen as they might have once thought. In other words, fifty years after the death of Martin Luther King, race relations in this country are still fucked up. But now there's a new movement. Now there is a new cry for justice and people are listening. But movement is slow, and the faces weigh heavy on the soul. Not just the faces of the dead, but the faces of their survivors, interviewed on Fox and CNN and ABC, tears streaming and voices cracking as they try to answer ridiculous fucking questions like, "How does it feel to know that your innocent son was gunned down by a police officer?"

The problem is the same as it ever was. There were too many people standing on the sidelines, shaking their heads but not doing anything to truly attack the problem head on. And he counted himself among that number. It felt like he had left one war in Afghanistan for a different one back here in America. But at least in the Middle East, he was doing what he had been trained to do—fight. Maybe it was time for him to start bringing some of those skills to this war. Maybe it was time to bring the fight home.

Chapter 2

Ish was in Afghanistan. He had landed there for the first time just three weeks prior, and every day it had been hot. But not just your normal old everyday hot. It was as though the devil had soaked the earth in gasoline and then pissed all over it, setting the entire world on fire. Ish was told when he arrived here that "you get used to it", but whoever told him that was, so far, proving to be a serious goddamn liar.

They were riding in the back of a Humvee with the windows open. The army had started equipping some vehicles with A/C, but unfortunately Ish hadn't been blessed enough to get assigned to one. Rolling with the ballistic-resistant windows down was probably not the best idea when they were in an area notorious for sniper attacks, but today they all felt like they'd almost prefer getting shot in the head to roasting alive in the belly of a large tin can. Almost.

He was rolling with a motley crew. Rough around the edges was an understatement. Some of the guys hadn't proven to be all that friendly, but there were two that he immediately hit it off with. These two soldiers went by the names 'Blade' and 'Bird'.

Blade's real name was Nathan Bartholomew. He was a handsome, diminutive dark-skinned black man, about 5'7" and thin, but sinewy. Ish hadn't yet gotten the story on where the nickname 'Blade' came from, but he knew the man carried several knives on him at all times, and he figured that had to have something to do with it. Though he may have been deadly with a piece of steel, the man was also a social butterfly, constantly chatting and laughing with the other guys.

Damon 'Bird' Johnson, on the other hand, was a feather of a different color. Bird could often be found chilling quietly, reading a book or looking around with a half smirk on his face, like he knew something everyone else didn't.

He was also African American, an East Coast native, about six feet tall and 230 pounds. His body looked a bit softer than it should for a soldier, but he was extremely strong and had great endurance. He wore black horn-rimmed glasses, and around camp he constantly sported an old, black t-shirt with a picture of saxophonist Charlie 'Bird' Parker on the front. That's how he got his name. It was a combination of the t-shirt and the fact that the only music he ever listened to was 1950s-era bebop jazz.

Ish noticed that the man sitting across from him was staring in his direction. It was the newest member of the group, having just rotated into the squad a couple days before. He looked as if he could have been a little younger than Ish, but there was already a weariness to his features. That weariness was offset by the child-like glint of his steel-blue eyes, making his age harder to peg. He sported a neat, blond crew-cut and matching goatee that implied he spent a little too much time in the mirror.

The man had been officially introduced as Lt. Justin Gilroy, but everyone called him Jag. Ish assumed it was one of those personally chosen 'bad ass' nicknames that many Spec Ops soldiers like to give themselves, like "Madman" or "Smasher". It wasn't until much later that Ish learned that his full name was Justin Anthony Gilroy—his initials, J.A.G., being the source of the moniker.

"So, where you from?" asked Jag, finally breaking the silence. His accent was subtle, but clearly Southern.

"L.A," Ish muttered in response, not really in a mood to talk.

"L.A? Like South Central L.A?"

"You assume I'm from South Central; why, because I'm black?" Ish replied, a bit of challenge in his voice.

"Hey, brother," said Jag, smiling and holding his hands up in a gesture of surrender. "I didn't mean nothin' by it. Just trying to break the ice. Besides," he continued, "my ex-old lady grew up in South Central. You know Shondra Maynard?"

"We don't all know each other," said Ish, scowling at him like he was some kind of idiot. He didn't know what this white boy's issue was, but so far, he didn't like him.

Jag laughed. "Yeah, I guess it is a pretty big city," he said.

Though the heat was a relentless as ever, the sun was starting to go down. Blinding rays had been angled directly at the back of the truck for the last half hour. Ish pulled his shades down from his helmet and put them over his eyes, as much to block out the sun as the conversation. Jag took the hint and let them ride in silence for a while.

"So, tell me," he finally said, apparently unable to remain mute any longer. "How did an L.A.-raised, African American brother man like you learn to speak so many damn languages?"

"Practice," said Ish.

"Huh," said Jag, appearing intrigued. "English, Spanish, Urdu, Pashto, Kurdish. What is it, seven altogether?"

"Actually, it's eight," said Ish wearily.

"Damn," said Jag, smiling. "You alright, man!"

"What about you?" Ish asked, deciding that if he couldn't get the man to shut up at least he could turn the conversation away from himself. "Where are you from? You definitely don't sound like you were native to L.A."

"Nah, I'm actually out of Tennessee," he said. "I met Shondra in college. That was my first taste of dark meat, and it was the sweetest piece of ass I've ever had in my entire life! I've been chasing the black berry ever since. Let me tell you, what they say is true. Once you go black, you never go back!"

Ish just stared at him for a moment, dumbfounded that this guy would actually say something like that out loud, and to a person of color that he just met. Ish shook his head in wonder. "Unbelievable," he mumbled.

Before Jag had a chance to say anything else, an explosion turned their boredom to misery. The door on the right side of the Humvee disintegrated, and both Jag and Ish were thrown thirty feet into the hot sand. Ish was unsure how long he laid on his back, the sun glaring down on him like a spotlight. The first things he noticed was the silence and the clouds floating overhead.

One cloud looked exactly like an angel, wings and all. It appeared to be flying, flapping these huge, feathered appendages in slow motion.

He was certain that if he just listened more closely, he would be able to hear them as they beat against the air. Suddenly, the sky went dark and it began to rain. But then his focus changed, and he saw that the darkness was Jag's face, leaning over him and blocking the light. The rain was the sweat dripping off the other soldier's nose and splattering down into Ish's face.

"You alright, South Central?" he asked. Ish couldn't believe that the man was still smiling.

"Yeah, I'm okay," Ish said, though he wasn't sure that was true.

"Everybody alright?" asked someone from the other side of the truck.

"Roger that," said someone else.

Miraculously, no one was hurt. The IED they hit had damaged one side of the truck, but all the tires looked intact and the engine was still running. This was their lucky day. Ish got up, grabbed his rifle off the ground and, with his back to the vehicle, scanned the horizon for hostiles. He saw no movement. They were adjacent to some fields, but the ground looked newly planted. There was nothing for anyone to hide behind. There were a couple of small structures in the distance, too far away to tell if they were actually occupied.

"Alright," said the commander. "Let's all get back in the truck and get the hell out of here before—"

Ish's ears barely had time to register what sounded like a single firecracker before a sledgehammer slammed into his chest. He found himself on his back again. This time there wasn't the soothing silence he had experienced before. This time his ears were assaulted with the chaos and madness of men fighting for their lives.

"Sniper! Second floor, nine o'clock!" someone yelled. Automatic weapons were firing all around him. As he scrambled to his feet, he remembered wondering exactly which floor they were referring to and what the time had to do with it. Something slammed into his chest again. Because he was leaning slightly forward this time, he was able to remain on his feet. He swung his weapon around, confused, not sure which direction to shoot and which direction to move for cover. He braced for the next round that he knew could strike him at any moment.

An M-4 rifle opened fire next to his right ear. Before he could look to see who it was, someone had grabbed him by the back of his uniform. He was dragged, arms flailing, to the other side of the Humvee.

Once they were safely behind cover, the soldier turned to him. Ish was surprised to see that it was Jag that had rescued him. The man was still smiling.

The firefight lasted only twenty minutes. Afterwards they were able to get their vehicle back on the road and return to base without further incident. Ish had taken two direct sniper shots to the chest, but his body armor had saved his life. He had two painful bruises and a possible cracked rib, but he'd live to fight another day. The only other injury from the attack was a facial laceration one of the other soldiers suffered from a ricocheting shell.

Once Ish was done being looked over by the medic, he returned to his bunk, only to find Jag waiting there with two cold beers and his apparently permanent smile.

"Glad you made it, South Central!" he said, holding one of the beers out to Ish.

Ish shook his head in amazement and couldn't help but return the smile. Perhaps this guy wasn't so bad after all.

Chapter 3

It was called "Murph", named after Navy Lieutenant Michael Murphy, a Navy Seal that heroically gave his life to save his men during a firefight with Taliban fighters in Afghanistan in 2005. A couple of years after his death, CrossFit athletes around the U.S. began doing it on Memorial Day to honor the fallen soldier. It was Murphy's favorite CrossFit workout when he was alive, and it was a beast. It began with a 1-mile run, followed by 100 pull-ups, 200 push-ups and 300 air squats, and finished off with another 1-mile run. All while wearing 20 pounds of body armor.

Ish was introduced to it when he first arrived in Afghanistan. They had a full gym setup, but the men were always looking for other creative ways to change things up and deal with the boredom of downtime. One thing was undeniable: it was impossible to be bored while performing the Murph workout. Ish had seen guys pass out, vomit all over themselves, shit their pants—there was even a couple of hospitalizations for heatstroke.

But Ish loved it. He loved how alive it made him feel, and he loved the competition. He held the camp record with a time of just over thirty-nine minutes. He was halfway through the final one-mile run, and it was looking as though he might be able to shave as much as twenty seconds off his best time when he noticed that the chaplain had appeared and one of the other soldiers was pointing him in Ish's direction. Instinctively, he knew something was terribly wrong. Abandoning his workout, his breathing labored, sweat pouring off of his body, he walked over to meet the man.

The conversation was brief, and as the clergyman walked away, Ish felt frozen to the spot of ground he was standing on. He couldn't get his legs to move. He could feel a motion inside his head, like great metal gears were spinning at a blurring speed, running calculations and then calculations on those calculations, trying to find a solution for a puzzle he wasn't sure he even understood. In his peripheral vision he saw Bird approaching.

"What's up, Big Man?" asked Bird, smiling.

Ish didn't answer or even acknowledge that he knew anyone was speaking to him. Bird's smile faded as he took a step closer to his friend.

"What's wrong?"

Ish's head swiveled until his eyes were focused on Bird.

"I'm not sure," he said. He looked around him and ran a hand through his hair. "The chaplain just delivered a message. Something has happened to Sumatra. She's in the hospital, in critical condition."

"Jesus," whispered Bird. "I'm so sorry, man. How did this happen?"

"He didn't know any more than that."

"When are you leaving?"

"Huh?" said Ish.

"I asked when you are leaving."

"Ummm, I don't know. They're trying to arrange a transport now. I need to, uh, get to a phone; try to reach Layla, my mother, someone."

Bird put his hand on his friend's shoulder and they embraced, holding each other for a few moments. "Thanks, brother," said Ish. His voice was monotone, almost mechanical, but his eyes, though tear-less, were twin seas of emotion, betraying feelings that he had spent the majority of his time in the army learning to hide.

Ish went in search of a phone, and twenty minutes later he finally found one. First, he called Layla. There was no answer, and he was forced to leave a message. The next call was to his mother and then to Chad. Again, no one answered.

A feeling of panic was starting to rise in him. It started in his bowels and snaked its way toward his throat. He forced it back down with a fierce determination, took a deep breath and dialed Layla's number again. The phone rang seven or eight times, and then just when he thought it was about to go to voicemail again, there was a click. Someone breathed into the phone. There was a crackle of static and a hiss of white noise.

"Ish?" said a voice that sounded a thousand years away. It was Layla.

"Yeah, it's me," said Ish.

"Oh my god. I'm so sorry," said Layla.

"What the hell happened? How is Sumatra?" he asked. His voice was calm and level, concealing the anguish he was feeling inside.

"She's gone."

"What do you mean 'she's gone'?"

"She's gone."

"Gone where?"

"She's gone."

"Talk to me, Layla. What happened?"

"She's gone."

"Jesus."

"And now I have to go, too. Goodbye," said Layla as the line went dead.

Ish tried calling back several times, but each time the call went to voicemail. His next call was to Chad.

"Ish! Thank God," said Chad, his voice sounding on the verge of cracking. "I've been waiting for you to call."

"What the hell happened?" asked Ish.

"I'm so sorry, man. I still don't know all the facts, but I'll tell you what I do know."

The news Chad delivered broke Ish's heart into a million pieces. Three hours later he was sitting in the back of a plane on his way back to California. It was a twenty-hour flight, giving him plenty of time to think, though that was the last thing in the world that he wanted to do. He knew the end result of the tragedy that had occurred, but he didn't know any of the details. For the entire twenty hours, he battled against his mind, struggling to stop it from filling in those details, from making accusations, from plotting revenge. None of these thoughts were useful when he had so little information behind the message that Chad and the pastor had delivered.

There was no alcohol served on the plane, and several times during the flight he felt an uncharacteristic yearning for a drink, to the point that there were many moments when he was sure he was about to become totally unhinged if he couldn't find a way to relax.

During these times he leaned his seat back, closed his eyes and listened to his breathing. He had started meditating years ago while taking a psychology class. At the time, he thought it was a lot of nonsense, but he kept at it. He started off small, with low expectations; just dipping his toes in the water, as it were. But he began to slowly see results. It allowed him to be more in control of his stress levels, and by extension, his life. It wasn't easy, but it was simple. And like any learned skill, the more he practiced it, the easier it became.

He had started moving away from it when he came to Afghanistan, though he wasn't exactly sure why. Maybe it was the safety he felt from the camaraderie of his close friendships with Jag, Bird and Blade. Maybe it was the idea that he needed to retain just a little bit of an edge; that getting too 'relaxed' might be a liability in such a dangerous and uncertain place. All he knew was that he hadn't meditated in months, and now he was grasping for it, as though it were a tiny life preserver in an enormous lake that he had been tossed into after not having swam for years.

As Ish walked off the plane and into the LAX terminal, he was shocked to see his mother standing there, waiting for him. He walked up to her and before he could say anything, she wrapped her arms around him and held him tight, burying her head in his chest.

She was only a couple of inches shorter than he was. Tall and regal, she had a golden caramel complexion, matching light hazel-colored eyes and short, curly gray hair. Normally, she greeted her son with a smile so dazzling it rivaled the sun. But today she wasn't smiling.

"Mama," he said after she finally released him and took a step back. He was going to ask her how she knew he was coming, but he thought he already knew the answer: Chad.

"I'm so sorry about what happened to Sumatra, son," she said. Her voice was heavy with sadness, and he could see the pain in her face. The stunningly beautiful woman that he had always thought of as ageless was aging right there before his eyes.

"Thanks," he said. "How've you been?"

"I've been tired, son. Very tired," she said, her head dropping a bit. "Darkness has touched our lives yet again, and I'm waiting for the Lord to once again show us the light."

Ish and his mother had never really seen eye-to-eye on religion. He was raised as a Christian. He grew up in the Methodist churches of Chicago and L.A. But he had a scientific mind, and as a teenager he began asking questions that his pastor had a hard time answering. Why were there no dinosaurs mentioned in the Bible when we have fossils as proof that they once roamed the earth? If Adam and Eve were the beginning of humanity, doesn't that mean we're all the product of incest? If God is perfect, how is it he created a world so messed up that he had to destroy it all and start over? And why did he need Noah to help him?

He overheard some of the 'church ladies' talking one day. They called him an 'upstart', a 'heathen', a 'troublemaker'. None of that bothered him. He knew the risk when he made the decisions to ask the questions. But he knew that he couldn't call himself a true believer if he had doubts. His questions were a way to strengthen his own faith, not weaken the faith of others.

What had finally turned him off of religion for good was one Sunday when he was sitting in church, watching them pass the offering basket around for the third time that service. As it passed him, the pastor was telling everyone how badly in need they were of a new roof for the church. He told everyone that the new roof was going to cost over $75,000 and urged everyone to try to donate $100 today.

As Ish heard him speak these words, his baritone voice booming and echoing like the voice of God himself, he thought about the Rolex watch he had often seen the man wearing, the beautiful 3,000 square foot house that his family lived in and the brand-new twin Jaguars that the pastor and his wife had sitting in the parking lot. He thought about the people in the congregation that he knew were fighting bankruptcy under the weight of astronomical medical bills, that couldn't afford to buy their kids new school clothes and that had taken the bus to the service that morning because either they couldn't afford a car or couldn't afford to fix the one they did have.

He thought about all these things for the rest of the service. By the time the pastor had dismissed them, he had made up his mind. He left the church that day, both figuratively and literally, and never went back.

But his mother was ever devout, even in the shadows of the most tragic turn of events. They had had many talks since that day he walked away from the church at fifteen years old, and she was always confident that one day he would find his way back to the Lord. He didn't share that confidence. But he loved and respected his mother, so he tried to avoid debating religion with her because he didn't want to upset her. But today he just couldn't help himself.

"Mama, God didn't have shit to do with this," he said, his eyes locked on hers. "If he did, my daughter would still be alive."

He saw the pain in her face deepen as she turned away from him.

"I'm parked in the lot, son," she said softly. "Come on, I'll drive you home."

They drove in silence for a while as his mother deftly navigated the heavy L.A. rush hour traffic. She was an older lady, but she definitely did not drive like one.

"I'm sorry for cussing at you," he said.

"It's okay," she said, and they were quiet for another couple of miles.

"How many of the details do you know?" she finally asked once they were on the freeway.

"Just the basics," said Ish.

"You still haven't spoken to Layla?"

"I did, but only for a moment. Have you seen her?"

"I was over to the house yesterday. She's having a hard time of it, as you can imagine. Be gentle with her. She's fighting her own battle in more ways than one."

"I know, Mama. I know."

Ish let his head sink back into the headrest of the SUV and tried to relax. He could feel the muscles in his jaw starting to tighten. Oddly enough, he rarely experienced this in combat. When his own life was on the line, he was always in what could best be described as a Zen state. But when those that were closest to him were in trouble, he felt the tension acutely. It had happened a couple of times in firefights when one of his crew had gone down but never when he himself was under fire.

"So how have you been, Mama?" he asked.

"I've been fine. The Lord has seen fit to keep me blessed."

"How's your blood pressure?"

"It's good. Sometimes I forget to take my medication and it gets a little uppity, but my doctor says that I'm in fine health for someone my age."

"Good," said Ish. "And my aunties?"

"They're fine. They went with me yesterday to see Layla. We took her a casserole, a baked chicken, some collard greens and macaroni and cheese. I think the company was more nourishing for her than the food was. It doesn't look like she's been eating very well lately. But that's to be expected."

They drove the rest of the way in silence. Ish felt guilty, because it had been a few months since he had had a good, long conversation with his mother. But right now, all he could really think about was getting to Layla and finding out what had happened.

Part of him didn't want to know. He didn't want to have to face the pain head on. He felt like he was on the way to a root canal with a dentist that was all out of Novocain. There was a part of him that wanted nothing more than to tell his mother to turn around and take him back to the airport, where he could take the next flight to wherever in the world it happened to be going. But that was impossible. He could never turn his back on family.

He felt the car stop moving, and when he looked out the window, he saw that they were sitting in front of his house. All the windows were shuttered, the blinds drawn. It looked dark and foreboding. This was his stop.

Chapter 4

Ish didn't have keys with him, so he rang the doorbell. When there was no answer, he thought to try the doorknob and was somewhat shocked to find the door unlocked. The house was dark, all the blinds drawn. Sunlight flooded into the foyer from the open door, but its effect on the gloom was minimal. There was a heaviness to the air that he could only describe as dread.

The last time Ish had felt this kind of apprehension was in Afghanistan when the squad was running a special recon in groupings of caves in the lower mountains. They were being super careful, as they always were, using night vision goggles and moving at a snail's pace while they monitored the area for booby-traps. They had reached the center of the main cave when it happened. There was an explosion that felt like it might bring the entire mountain down on them.

In the storm of dust that was created, their night goggles were useless, and they were completely blind. As the echoes from the boom started to fade, Ish realized that someone was screaming in anguish. In their blindness, a couple of the other soldiers called out to the wounded man, trying to console him and let him know that help was on the way. Abruptly, the screaming stopped.

When the downed man was screaming, the squad had something to navigate to, an immediate point of destination to focus on. Once the screaming stopped, no one wanted to move or speak, for fear that whatever had stopped their comrade's voice might stop their own. In that moment, Ish knew that a good man was down and that he needed help, but he didn't know how to get to him or what might be waiting for him once he did. The sense of foreboding that he felt in the silence of that cave was very similar to what he felt now walking into his own house. In the cave, once the dust settled and they were able to regain some visibility, they found the downed soldier. He had been ravaged by shrapnel; a large piece was embedded in his chest and eventually pierced his heart. It was suspected that his moving around had caused the metal to shift, and that if he could have only sat still, he might have lived.

So here Ish was, standing in the doorway of a house that was no longer a home, feeling lost in the dark and knowing that inside someone was injured and afraid, and that just like the fallen soldier, too much movement on the part of the injured could be fatal. He set his bag on the floor and closed the door behind him.

"Layla?" he yelled. He stood where he was for a few moments to give his eyes a chance to get accustomed to the dark. "Layla? Are you here?"

He heard a rustling sound coming from somewhere on the second floor. He made his way to the stairs and slowly ascended. His hand rested on the banister, sliding along it with each step, and try as he could to avoid it, he couldn't help but envision the last time he had seen Sumatra. It was right before his last trip to Afghanistan. She was sliding down this very banister, pigtails flying, her laughter bouncing off the walls. He had yelled at her about how dangerous it was, and when she got to the bottom she began to weep. He was already late for his flight and barely had time to give her a kiss and a hug before he ran out the door. That face, with the large hazel eyes streaming tears and full of pain and disappointment would forever haunt his dreams as the last time he saw his daughter alive.

As Ish reached the second-floor landing, he heard the rustle again. There was a stale, musty odor in the air. Layla had always been a meticulous housekeeper—always straightening up, vacuuming, putting things away—so it felt particularly strange to walk into their house and have it smell anything less than spotless. At the top of the stairs he paused and listened again. Sumatra's bedroom was to the left, and he looked longingly at her door but knew he was in no condition to enter her room. Instead, he turned right and headed towards the master bedroom. The closer he got to the room, the stronger the mustiness became.

The bedroom door was open. A small amount of sunlight seeped into the room from the gaps in the blinds. He could see where someone had tried to hang sheets over the windows to make the room even darker, but the job was done haphazardly. Standing in the doorway, Ish was shocked. While the rest of the house he had seen so far didn't appear to be too much out of place, their bedroom was in utter shambles. The floor was littered with all manner of Chinese takeout boxes, half-eaten cans of tuna, empty soda cups, liquor bottles and an assortment of other types of trash. There were several large dark stains on the carpet, including a spot of what appeared to be vomit.

The wreckage extended to the dresser and side tables, which were also covered in trash and rotting food along with some empty pill bottles. In the middle of all this chaos was Layla, lying on an unmade bed, her head resting on a dirty pillow devoid of a pillow case. Her eyes were closed, and she appeared to be sleeping, but her body was jerking in small spasms, perhaps fighting some personal demon in a dreamland far, far away.

"Layla?" said Ish gently as he walked towards her, but her eyes stayed closed. He went to the nearest blind and partially opened it, bathing the bed in soft light. He hardly recognized the woman the light revealed. One side of her face was slightly puffy, with a faint purple tint to the skin, and there was a deep cut above one eye. He could tell they were at least a few days old. It looked like the cut was infected. Her hair was wild, covering her head in odd, shifting angles like a storm looking for a place to land. She opened her mouth slightly to gasp, and he could smell the sourness of her breath. Her lips were dry and cracked; in some areas the skin was so dry that it had split open and bled, the dried blood replacing the shiny lip gloss that she normally wore. The overall effect was bordering on the grotesque.

She was almost unrecognizable. This was not the woman he had last seen with their child. The Layla he knew had always maintained the appearance of the consummate glamour girl. Almost six feet tall with long, luxurious black hair, high cheek bones and flawless chestnut-brown skin, she was a woman so strikingly beautiful that she mesmerized all those that came upon her. This woman looked like a crack fiend.

He touched her arm and called her name again. He began to gently shake her. Suddenly her eyes flew open, as though she were some kind of android and someone had just flipped her power switch to the 'on' position. Though she appeared to be instantly wide awake, she didn't immediately make any attempts to rise. Slowly her eyes began to drift around the room, drawn to the light. She frowned at it, as though it were some dangerous intruder, but then kept examining the room until her eyes came to rest on Ish's face.

"Ish," she said. There was more disappointment in her voice than surprise or relief.

Layla pushed herself up on one elbow, ran her hand over her face, then sat up on the edge of the bed.

"I'm glad you made it back in time for the funeral," she said groggily.

"Layla," said Ish patiently as he took a seat on the bed beside her. "What the hell happened?"

"Didn't you get the message? She was 'accidentally' shot by a police officer."

"How does that happen?" he asked, incredulous, using every ounce of strength he had to stop his voice from escalating to a scream. "How does an eight-year-old accidentally get shot by a police officer?"

Layla shook her head. She looked like she was about to laugh. She tried to force a smile but failed as a sob shook her body. She took a deep breath and shook her head again.

"I'm sorry, Ish," she said. "I tried. I—" Another sob shook her body. She took one more deep breath and then sat up straight. "I'm okay," she said, but when Ish put his arm around her shoulder, she broke down. She buried her head in his chest and cried, her tears soaking his shirt and breaking his heart. He mourned not only his daughter's death but also his own shortcomings, and how he had failed to protect the two most important people in his life. He began to rock her back and forth, trying to soothe her and telling her everything would be alright, though he knew it was a lie even before the words left his lips.

They sat like that for nearly twenty minutes before Layla gently pushed him away and sat up again.

"I need to go to the restroom. I'll be right back," she said.

She went into the bathroom and shut the door. That fact concerned Ish, because almost from the beginning of their relationship they had developed the habit with each other of using the bathroom with the door open. He wondered if she might be in there trying to harm herself;

taking pills or maybe cutting her wrists. But she had had plenty of time to do that before he arrived if that were her plan. He decided she probably just needed a few minutes of privacy to get herself together. As the minutes stretched on, it took considerable effort on his part not to knock on the door or call out to ask if she was alright. Finally, she emerged, tears dried, hair a bit neater and pink gloss helping conceal her ravaged lips. She returned to her place on the bed beside Ish.

"Are you hungry?" she asked. He shook his head no. She scanned the room, a stunned look on her face, as though noticing the trash for the first time. She dropped her head, looking embarrassed. "Sorry, I don't think there's anything here to eat anyway. I need to do some grocery shopping. And cleaning."

"Don't worry about all that; it's not important. What is important is your health. Are you okay? Do we need to go see someone? A grief counselor? A doctor? A psychiatrist?"

"I'm okay, Ish," she said, touching the back of his neck with her hand. "It's just been a lot to deal with, with you not being here."

"I know. But I'm here now. Are you ready to tell me what happened?"

"Yes. I think so," she said. She paused a minute before continuing. "It happened on a Friday," she said. She cleared her throat, at the same time shifting her weight in a way that placed a couple of additional inches between her and Ish. He wasn't sure if it was conscious or unconscious.

"It was a hectic day. Sumatra was let out of school early that day, and I had a ton of running around to do, so when Fatima came by, I asked her if she wouldn't mind staying an extra hour or two while I stepped out to run some errands."

"Fatima? Who's Fatima?"

"She's the woman that replaced Carmen. Didn't you get the letter I sent you about that?"

"Ummm." He shook his head. "I don't think so."

"I definitely sent you a letter. Or maybe it was an email," she said, rubbing her face and looking confused.

"No, I never got that. But I thought you were very happy with Carmen."

"I was for a long time, but the quality of her work had started to slip. She just wasn't keeping things as clean as she used to, and I was spending way too much time cleaning up behind her."

"Oh. Okay."

"Anyway, when I left, Sumatra was playing in the back yard, and Fatima was sitting on the deck, watching her. I was gone for about two hours. As I drove back up to the house, I noticed a police cruiser parked next door in front of Rasheed's house. I remember thinking, 'Great, the only other black person in the neighborhood is being visited by the police. I can hear the gossip already.' As I was pulling into the driveway, I saw the cop, who was already out of his car, walking towards Rasheed's house with his gun out, yelling. I couldn't hear what he was saying because the windows were up, but before I could even turn the engine off, he started firing. I could see the gun flinching in his hand from the recoil, the smoke curling up into the air. By the time I opened the car door, I saw Rasheed scrambling to his feet near one of his bedroom windows."

"He had his hands out in front of him, and there was already blood on his shirt. I heard him say 'This is my house, man! I wasn't breaking in! I was just replacing one of the screens!' But the cop fired again, and Rasheed took off across the yard towards our place. A shot hit the ground in front of him and he changed direction, and started running towards me. I didn't know what to do, so I jumped back in the car, shut the door and ducked down. I heard several more shots. I don't even know how many. Five? Six? Maybe more. I don't know. The last one hit the car, and then there was silence," she said, her voice cracking on the last word.

She had stopped talking, and there was a faraway look in her eyes. Ish knew that she was in a fragile state, and as much as he wanted to rush her, to say something that would get her to continue, instinctively he knew that it was best to let her go at her own pace.

"Would you like a glass or water or something?" he asked. She nodded. Ish walked downstairs to the kitchen. When he returned with her water, she was standing by the window, wiping at her eyes with a tissue. A stray shaft of light was shining through the blinds and onto her face. Even now, in the worst condition that he had ever seen her in, she was still one of the most beautiful women he had ever known. That made his heart ache all the more.

"Here's your water."

"Thanks." She took a few sips, pulled the hair away from her eyes and back behind her ears, and walked back to the bed. Ish followed her and they both sat.

"It seemed like the silence stretched on forever," she said. "I was afraid to raise my head. And then I heard a scream. At first, in all the confusion, I didn't know who it was or where it was coming from. Then it hit me: it was Fatima screaming, and it was coming from the rear of the house.

"Ish, I don't know how I got from the car to the house. I don't remember opening the door or running across the yard. I must have run past Rasheed's body, but I don't remember. It was as though I was instantly teleported from the Range Rover to the back yard, like something out of an episode of Star Trek. When I got to the back yard, she was...she was..." She began sobbing.

Ish got up and grabbed her another couple of tissues. He put his arm around her shoulder again and gave her time to pull herself together. A few minutes later she was ready to continue.

"She was lying on the grass. She was wearing a long white skirt with gray and pink lines with a matching shirt. But for some reason, my eyes must not have registered the gray or pink, because she looked like she was wearing all white. My first thought when I saw her was that she looked like an angel. I walked towards her—floated, really, because I couldn't feel my legs—and as I got closer to her, I saw the blood. It created a halo around her head. Her eyes were closed, and I didn't need to put my ear to her chest or feel for a pulse to know that she was gone. But I got down on my knees beside her and checked anyway. Somewhere I could hear her calling out to me, saying goodbye. It was a tiny voice, and it sounded far, far away, but I knew it was her.

"I don't know how long I sat there, cradling her in my arms. It might have been two minutes; it might have been an hour. It was like I was lost in some terrible dream, and I kept telling myself that I would wake up any minute. What finally woke me was the sound of more screaming. At first, I thought it was Fatima again, but then I realized that it was me. I was screaming. I was wailing like a mad banshee! I heard some man speaking, and when I turned around and looked up, I was staring into the face of the cop—the cop that had just killed my baby." Her brow furrowed into a frown. Her eyes got colder, and her mouth twisted into a scowl.

"Before I knew what had happened, I was on top of him. This cop must have outweighed me by at least 80 pounds, but he was helpless before my wrath. There was raw terror in his eyes. I was a whirlwind—punching, gouging, kicking, stomping. More screaming brought me out of my trance, but this time it was his screaming. He sounded more like a woman than me or Fatima ever could. He was covered in blood, sobbing, snot coming out of his nose as he begged for me to stop. You would have thought that would have been enough for me. But it wasn't." Her eyes were glazed over as she relived the memory.

"I saw his gun in his holster and I reached for it. He was so battered and terrified that he didn't even try to stop me. I pointed that gun at his head and I pulled the trigger, and pulled the trigger and pulled the trigger, over and over again. But nothing happened. He had emptied his clip shooting at Rasheed. I stood over him, sobbing and shaking, until Fatima came and gently pulled it from my hands. The next thing I knew, I was tackled by another cop. They beat me for a bit before finally cuffing me and throwing me into the back of a patrol car."

"What happened when you got to the police station?" asked Ish.

"Pretty much what you'd expect," said Layla. "I don't remember much, but I do remember them telling me that Sumatra had been taken to the hospital and declared dead, and that Rasheed was in serious but stable condition. The cop's condition was somewhere between those two. He was in ICU with a fractured skull but expected to survive. I vaguely recall them reading me my rights and asking me if I did it. What I clearly do remember is saying, 'You're fucking right I did it', but the rest is kind of a blur. I must have called Harry at some point, because he showed up the next morning and arranged for bail. I was out two days later."

"Right," said Ish. "It must have been him who sent the message to me."

"Have you spoken to him?"

"No, I haven't spoken to anyone since the chaplain approached me. Except for my mom. And Chad. He's the one that filled me in on the basics."

"He's a godsend, and I owe him a serious apology," said Layla. "He's come by a couple of times since I was released, but I wouldn't let him in. I think one time I screamed at him from the window like a crazy person. Probably cussed him out. Everything in my world has been fuzzy since Sumatra left. It's like she was the lens that I viewed life through, and when she left, something happened to the focus ring on that lens. Now everything is blurry, all shadows and light, smoke and fog. I'm blind without her." She began weeping again.

Ish wanted to put his arms around her again, but it felt redundant. More than that, it felt like a weak and inadequate gesture. How do you console a woman that's just lost her only child? Especially when you're grieving over the same loss yourself? He almost laughed out loud at the absurdity of it. What stopped him was the anger. A rage was crawling up his throat, choking him as it tried to escape, eager to unleash destruction upon the world at large. But he knew he couldn't allow that to happen. He couldn't face the resulting consequences of that kind of irresponsibility. He forced himself to take a few deep breaths. He closed his eyes, let his body relax and felt the rage sink back into the deep, dark depths from whence it came, the world once again safely beyond its reach; at least, for now.

"So, what's the status on your case?"

"Harry was confident when he came to see me that they'd soon drop the charges. He was wrong. I think he must have temporarily forgotten that I'm black," she said and chuckled. "He knows it now. They're indicting me. He seems rather lost."

"Harry's a great corporate lawyer," said Ish. "He's more than competent to deal with company matters like copyright infringement and licensing agreements, but he doesn't know shit about criminal law. Not to this degree. I know some people that can either help or point us in the right direction. I'll call Harry later today and let him know that we'll be handing this off to someone with more experience."

"I'm sure he'll be relieved to hear that," said Layla, smiling slightly. It was the first time Ish had seen her smile during their entire conversation. That should have made him feel better, but instead it just caused his sadness to deepen even more. Maybe because it reminded him of how often she used to smile and how beautiful that smile was. He had always thought of Layla as the epitome of joy. But now, even though she had broken a smile, he knew there was absolutely no joy in it, and there may never be again.

"So, the funeral is Friday?" asked Ish.

"Yeah, I think so. That sounds about right," she muttered.

You 'think so'!? he wanted to yell at her. *Our fucking daughter is dead, and you 'think' you know when the funeral is???* But he bit his tongue. Literally. It was all he could do to stop the words from erupting out of his mouth. On a gut level he was angry, he was hurt and he was dying for someone or something to lash out at, and she was the nearest target. But intellectually, he knew that she was so close to the edge right now herself that the slightest bit of additional drama could push her over. In fact, a part of him wondered if she might already have gotten so close to the abyss that there was no coming back no matter what he did. Kind of like in those sci-fi movies where the spaceship gets too close to a black hole and gets sucked in, never to be seen again.

"Who made the funeral arrangements?" he asked.

"Ummm, I think it was your mom," she said, her face frowning in concentration. "Yeah. It was your mom. She asked me if it was okay. She said something about how I looked like I was a bit overwhelmed." She smiled again, and it reminded Ish of the way drunks smile when they're deep under the influence.

"Yeah," Ish said, taking another look around at the debris-littered room. "If she came in and saw this, I have no doubt that she'd assume you were a bit overwhelmed." He turned back to her and touched her arm. "How are you really? Are you okay?"

"Ish," she said, "I'm so fucking far from okay that I don't even know what 'okay' is anymore." Her eyes had suddenly cleared, and she was staring hard at him with complete lucidity. The intoxication of grief that had been fogging her brain seemed to have evaporated into thin air. For the first time since he had stepped into the room with her, he actually recognized her as the person he knew.

He had no idea how long this lucidity would last. There were a million questions he wanted to ask before she drifted off again, but he decided to ask the only one that really mattered: "What can I do to help?"

"I think I'm beyond help," she said. A new frown began to spread across her face, and she slowly turned her head to stare at him again. "How long are you going to be here anyway? Four or five days?" It was more accusation than question.

"Six days. I leave out again Monday," he said.

"Six days! What the hell do you think you can do for me in six days?! Huh?" Her voice was starting to rise as she sat taller, shoulders back and chest forward. Her breathing increased, and she looked like a bull getting ready to charge. Then she stopped, took a very deep breath and slowly let it out. Like a helium balloon with a slow leak, she gradually and evenly deflated until she seemed half the size she had been just moments before, folding into herself like human origami.

"I'm sorry," she said.

"For what?" he asked.

"For everything."

"Don't worry about it. We'll get through this. Together. I'll tell you what," he said, trying to sound as optimistic as possible. "Why don't you jump in the shower while I straighten the place up a bit, and then we can go grab something to eat?"

She nodded her head silently, touched his face, and walked into the bathroom.

Chapter 5

The next couple of days were a lesson in chaos, and some of the most stressful of Ish's adult life. The first 48 hours was spent monitoring Layla. Ish never let her leave his side for anything other than bathroom breaks. They stayed in, and he cooked for her. Ish was an excellent cook, and the food he prepared was natural, wholesome and nutritious. It appeared to be excellent medicine for her, because each meal brought a little bit more color back into her eyes, a little bit more life back into her soul.

Bringing life back into the house was another job altogether. He had tried to reach Fatima, but she neither answered her phone nor returned his call. Layla thought she remembered her saying something about leaving the country. Finally, against Layla's wishes, he contacted Carmen, and after explaining the situation, she agreed to come back, at least until he could find someone else. It took her three days of hard labor to bring the house back to the state it had been in before the tragedy.

Six days was not enough time. After taking the first two days to make sure that Layla was somewhat stabilized and that Carmen was capable of managing her, Ish spent most of the rest of his time in meetings. There were office visits with Layla's attorneys, interviews with potential new housekeepers, private meetings with stress management specialists, etc. His goal was to get as much in order as he could before he had to return to Afghanistan. Ish's mother and Chad had both offered to help any way they could, and he knew they were completely sincere, but he felt he needed to handle as many of the details himself as possible for his own peace of mind. Besides, staying busy helped keep him from focusing too much on his own grief.

The day of the funeral was particularly bright and sunny, which felt not only odd, but downright insulting. If he were a Christian, he probably would have raised his fist at God and cursed him for his sense of irony. But he wasn't, so he just tried to convince himself that the reason it was so bright and warm was that Sumatra was in heaven, smiling down at them all. Which, he noted to himself, was even odder. He wasn't a Christian, yet he still believed in some version of heaven. If his mother knew, she would have thought there was hope for him yet.

The funeral party was small. Most of the relatives there were from Ish's side of the family. There was his mother, his aunts, a few cousins, and of course Chad, along with a few other close friends. Layla's mother and father had both passed several years ago, and she'd never associated with any of her extended family members. She didn't even know who they were, let alone how to find them. The people who were there to support her were friends and a couple of sorority sisters from her college days.

All of Ish's army friends sent their condolences and expressed their deepest regret on not being able to be there. The exception was Ma'am, Bird's sister, who was currently enlisted in the Marines. Ma'am was the epitome of the strong black woman stereotype. A track and field star in junior high, she was a large, muscular woman with glowing chocolate-colored skin and long, luxurious dreadlocks, and she was as tough as any man Ish had ever met.

Her real name was Athena, but for years she had gone by the name Ma'am. She got her nickname in her first year of high school. One day, while walking down the street, two grown men started harassing her, called her "man" because she looked so masculine. She ended up beating them both to a pulp right there in the middle of the street and forcing them to call her "ma'am" instead. Several people in the neighborhood witnessed it, and everyone started called her "Ma'am" from that day forward.

Shortly thereafter, like so many inner-city youths, she tried crack for the first time and instantly became hooked. She spent most of her high school years as a full-blown addict, living on the street, tricking for money and getting harassed by cops. She got clean when she was twenty-one and joined the marines, and had been straight ever since.

Ish had gotten to know her through Bird. They first met when they were all on leave at the same time and had rendezvoused in Germany for a few days of rest and relaxation. The two of them immediately hit it off and had been fast friends ever since, staying in touch through the years.

Ma'am was on leave herself and was at the airport on her way home to New York for a few days when she heard the news of Sumatra's passing. She immediately changed her ticket and rerouted to L.A. Ish almost didn't recognize her in the black pantsuit. Every time he had previously seen her, she had been in either fatigues or khakis. She looked good; more feminine than he would have expected.

Most people would have described the funeral service as 'lovely' or 'beautiful', but Ish had never understood the logic in using such positive terms for something so tragic as the passing of a loved one. It was tragic when an 80-year-old loved one died; it was ten times more tragic when that loved one was only eight years old. So, when people came up to him after the service to tell him how 'lovely' or 'beautiful' it was, it was all he could do not to physically attack them. Fortunately, since it was a funeral, he didn't have to try to pretend to smile, and the attendees seemed to understand, on some gut level, that it was best to give him some space.

Layla was surprisingly composed. Three of her girlfriends had rallied around her the entire day before, helping her pick out a dress and shoes, working on her hair, etc. Their presence seemed to infuse new courage into her. Ish had expected her to breakdown, if not in the church then certainly at the grave site, but she didn't even shed a tear. At first, he was thankful that he didn't have to try to grab her, screaming and flailing, or stop her from jumping onto the casket. But then he started to worry about exactly how—and when—she was going to express the grief that he knew must still be bottled up inside her.

"How are you holdin' up?" asked Ma'am afterwards as people were making their way back to their cars. He was so absorbed in his thoughts that he didn't notice her right away.

"Huh? Oh, hey, Ma'am. I'm doing okay. Thanks for coming."

Ma'am nodded in response. An awkward silence filled the air between them.

"Bird told me what happened. I'm so sorry, man. And a cop! That's makes it even more horrible."

Now it was Ish's turn to nod in response. He glanced across the parking lot, where Layla was standing in a small group of women. He was waiting for her to tell him she was ready to leave.

"When do you have to head back to the job?" she asked.

"Monday evening."

"Well, if there's anything I can do, you know I'm here for you, brother."

"I know you are," he said and hugged her. "Where are you staying?"

"I'm at the Marriott by LAX."

"Ma'am, we've got plenty of room. You're more than welcome to camp out at the house. Layla would love to have you," he said, though he didn't really know if that were true. Layla liked Ma'am, but he wasn't sure how much company she was going to be able to tolerate the next couple of days.

"Thanks, Ish, but I'm good. I fly out to New York tomorrow night."

"Well, at least have dinner with us."

"Sure. Text me the info." They hugged again, and Ma'am headed back to her car. Ish walked over to the two limo drivers that were waiting for them and let them know they'd be ready to leave soon.

As he approached Layla, the group was just beginning to break up. Everyone was sharing hugs, and those that had come in one of the limos were getting themselves situated inside the vehicles. Everyone else was headed to the parking lot. It was just Layla and Ish. He looked at her and smiled. Even in the midst of all this sadness and despair, the natural beauty she exuded never failed to take his breath away. She tried to return the smile, but it was a strained effort.

"Are you ready to go?" he asked as he put an arm around her waist and gently drew her to him.

"No, not yet," she whispered. She walked back to the burial site, grabbed a flower from one of the bouquets, and sat down on the grass beside the casket. The two limos full of people waited patiently for her, understanding that this was something she needed to go through. It was an hour before she finally rose and joined them.

Ma'am rang Ish's doorbell at 7:00pm sharp, on time down to the second. She was wearing her marine dress blues, which was closer to what Ish would have expected her to wear to the funeral. Ma'am was a soldier through-and-through. Some people adapted to military life, some people were born for it; Ma'am was definitely the latter. But while she adhered strictly to the discipline, she still managed to bring a little bit of street swagger into her expression. That was Ma'am.

"How's Layla?" she asked after Ish took her coat.

"She's having a rough time of it, but she's coping. I don't think she's going to be joining us for dinner. She's upstairs resting,"

"That's understandable," she said.

Carmen appeared in the hallway. "Excuse me, Mr. Ishmael. Dinner will be ready in twenty minutes."

"Thanks, Carmen," he answered before she turned and left them alone again.

"'Mr. Ishmael'? I didn't know you were rollin' like that. Mexican maid and everything! You get a lot fancier treatment at home than out in the bush, huh?" asked Ma'am, smiling and poking him with her elbow.

"You know, that woman has worked with us for over five years, and I've told her a thousand times to just call me Ish, but she won't do it," said Ish, feeling uncharacteristically embarrassed. "And by the way, she's Guatemalan, not Mexican," he said, returning her smile.

Ish walked into the dining room and Ma'am followed him. He grabbed a half-empty glass of wine off a side table. "Can I offer you a glass of—" he began. "Oh, sorry," he said. "I almost forgot."

"Don't worry about it; it's cool," she said.

"Can I get you some water or juice?"

"No, I'm fine for now, thanks," she said as they both took a seat at the table.

"Will it bother you if I—" he asked, tilting his glass of wine in her direction.

"Not at all. I hang out with a bunch of the hardest drinkin' muthafuckas in the Middle East every single weekend. Trust me, I'm used to it."

Ish nodded. "So how many years clean are you?" he asked.

"Nine. Nine long years. Seems like only yesterday I was bustin' up bars and doin' God-only-knows-what for a rock. Those were wild times, boy."

"Yeah, I was just thinking about some of the stories I've heard you tell. Wild times is putting it mildly. Do you ever miss it?"

Ma'am paused, cocking her head to the side and looking up at the ceiling as if searching for the right answer.

"I don't know if 'miss' is the right word. They say once you're a' addict you're always a' addict. And that's true. But once you decide to give it up—once you decide to really and truly give it up—your mind state changes on a molecular level. You still yearn for it from time to time, but it's not the same as missing it. It's like getting out of a really abusive relationship. You might miss the dick from time to time, but not enough to go back to lettin' a muthafucka kick yo' ass every night."

Ish raised his eyebrows and nodded his head. "I get it," he said. "I've known so many people that were consumed by their addictions; good people that were taken way too soon. What do you attribute your success to?"

"What do I attribute my success to?" replied Ma'am, her eyes sparkling. "Well, one day I met someone. A man."

Ish nodded. "Yeah, I know a lot of people that have had someone come into their lives that helped them see that there was another path."

"But this wasn't just anyone. Wasn't just any man. This was our Lord and Savior, Jesus Christ."

Ish was surprised. He never knew that Ma'am was particularly religious. He thought his face was impassive, but Ma'am must have picked up on something.

"You don't believe me?" she asked.

"Hey," he said, raising his hands in self-defense. "Far be it for me to try to tell you what you did or didn't experience. I try not to get in between people and their religions."

Ma'am smiled, but there was a seriousness in her eyes. "You're Special Ops. I know you've been in some fucked up situations, inches from death. You never once encountered God in a foxhole?"

"I can't say that I have. But I haven't been looking for him. And I suspect he hasn't been looking for me, either."

"You're so wrong, my brother," she said tenderly. "God loves you, and he watches over you every day."

Ish felt the anger rising up in him again. He wanted to scream at her, asking her where God was when the policeman was shooting his daughter in the head with a .40 caliber semi-automatic, but he controlled it. The last thing he wanted to do was fight with his friend on the day of his daughter's funeral.

"Tell me," he said, "how do you know that his man that came to you was Jesus?"

"Well, what happened is that one night I was out on the stroll, fiendin' for a rock and tryin' to get straight. This dude picked me up and drove into this dark alley. I was supposed to be giving him head, but his shit wouldn't get hard, and he started getting pissed off, tryin' to blame his plumbing problems on me. The more I tried to help him along, the more pissed he became. Next thing you know this dude is punching me in the face. But that was a mistake. I'm a tough bitch and I got mad skills from the shoulder going way back, so I start touchin' this muthafucka up, rainin' fists down on him. This fool is bleeding all over me, all over himself, all over the car—then I hear a police siren somewhere in the distance, and I freak out. If cops drive up and see this, I'm fucked, and I still need to get my fix. So, I try to get out of the car. I'm tuggin' at the door, but there's blood all over my hands and I can't get it open. Then I feel something stick me. I thought this fool was out, but he done woke up and stabbed me! I finally get the door open, roll out onto the ground with this knife sticking out of my side, and he starts the car and screeches away."

"I'm lyin' there, in the filth and mud, trash all around me, and I can feel my lungs collapsing. My breathing is getting more and more difficult, I'm spitting blood all over the ground, and I lay back, ready to let it all go. Then I see this figure walking towards me out of the shadows. He smiled, and the entire alley lit up like Christmas. He kneeled down beside me and told me that everything would be alright. That my time was 'not nigh'. That's what he said—'not nigh'! Then he touched my face, and all the pain left my body. I heard the knife clatter to the ground and suddenly I could breathe."

"Wow," said Ish.

"I know, it's hard to believe if you weren't there to see it with your own eyes. I didn't believe it myself at first. I assumed I must have been hallucinating or something. But the blood that I had spit up was still there. This happened. From that night on, I pledged to change my life. I never used crack again. Never used any drugs again, not even aspirin. I never touched another drop of alcohol. Never turned another tricked. I'm not saying I'm a perfect Christian, but God gave me another chance, and I'm just trying to make the most of it."

"Well, this is certainly an interesting conversation to be having on this, of all days!" exclaimed Layla, who, having appeared out of nowhere, was standing at the door, scowling.

Chapter 6

Neither Ish or Ma'am really knew how to respond. It was Ish that finally spoke.

"Hey, babe. Are you joining us for dinner?"

"Dinner? If I had an appetite, I just lost it!"

Ma'am turned away from her, looking uncomfortable.

"What do you mean?" asked Ish.

"I mean my baby girl's body is barely in the ground, and you're sitting here in my home talking about the blessings of God?"

"Babe, I know you're upset, but I think you're overreacting a little. Ma'am was just telling me a story. She didn't mean any disrespect."

"Really?!" yelled Layla. She grabbed a chair and violently pulled it out so that she could join them at the table. "Did you both forget that I was in the house? Did you both forget that my daughter was just fucking murdered in our backyard, not thirty feet from here?!"

"Layla!" screamed Ish before turning to Ma'am. "I'm really sorry about this."

"Layla, you're not thinking straight. Let's go upstairs and discuss this in private," he said.

"Why? Because Ma'am is here? You didn't seem to have any problem discussing family business with her before I came down. No need to change now!"

"What is wrong with you?" asked Ish. "I know you're hurting, but that's no reason for you to be rude to our guest."

"Fuck our guest!" yelled Layla. Carmen poked her head out of the kitchen, looking nervous and confused, then quickly retreated back to the safety of her dinner preparations.

"Ummm, I think I'd better be going," said Ma'am.

"Hold on, Ma'am," said Ish before turning his attention back to Layla. "Alright, you want to talk about this here? Let's do it. But before we do, you need to understand something: you don't have a fucking monopoly on grief! I lost a daughter, too!"

"Ish, this isn't the way to handle this," said Ma'am. Ish looked at her with fire in his eyes.

"Ma'am, let me deal with this—"

"No!" Ma'am replied, cutting him off. "First you stop me from leavin', now you're tellin' me to butt out. You can't have it both ways. If I'm gonna sit here and listen to all this bullshit, at least I'm gonna have a say!" The three of them glared at each other.

"Your wife is hurting. You're right. But it's more than that. Grief is like a poison. It can get into your bloodstream, infect all your organs and alter your brain chemistry. You may think she's acting crazy, but now is not the time to be fighting with her. Now is the time to comfort her. The only cure for this poison is love. Grab this woman, wrap her in your arms and show her that love is stronger than pain." Ish felt his anger start to recede a bit, and he looked somewhat sheepishly at both women. Layla still looked like she could spit nails.

"Did you hear what I said?" asked Ma'am. "Quit standing there looking like a goddamn retard! Grab this woman and do it like you mean it!"

Ish hesitantly got up and walked towards Layla. "Ish, leave me alone," she said, but he kept coming. When he reached her, he kneeled down and attempted to embrace her, but she began fighting him off. "I said leave me the fuck alone!" she screamed. She started swinging at him. He was able to slip the punches, but in the struggle, she fell against a side table, knocking over a glass vase of flowers and several dishes, some containing salsa and salad dressing. They shattered on the marble floor, splattering the three of them, but Layla did not stop fighting and Ish did not stop trying to comfort her. They slipped in the spilled mess, almost falling several times.

Finally, Ish was able to get his arms around her as she beat on his chest with her fists. After a few minutes she stopped resisting and burst into tears, sobbing and wailing, face buried in his shoulder. Her body shuddered with the power of her grief, and taking Ma'am's advice, Ish just held onto her as tears silently fell from his own eyes.

He didn't know how long they stood like that, but eventually both of their tears slowed, and they tenderly kissed each other.

"You two have a seat," said Ma'am kindly. "I'll go get something to clean this up." Ish and Layla sat at the table, staring into each other's eyes while Ma'am went into the kitchen to look for some towels.

* * *

Leaving Layla to return to his unit was one of the hardest things Ish had ever done; maybe even harder than being notified of his daughter's death or attending her funeral. At least with the death and the funeral, there was a finality to it; a clear understanding that nothing that he did was going to change what was now the reality. But in leaving Layla he was left to wrestle with the questions of exactly what the current reality was. And what the future held in store.

Thanks to Ma'am, Ish was able to somewhat reconnect with Layla the night of her outburst, but they only had another three days together after that. Most of that time was spent holding each other and offering comfort. Some of the time was spent talking to her new lawyers about her case and all the possible outcomes.

He learned that she had been bailed out before she had been arraigned. The arraignment was scheduled for Tuesday morning, when they expected her to be formally charged with assault on a police officer. They might even go for attempted murder, considering the officer's injuries. Bail would probably be increased, but of course money wasn't an issue, so they didn't foresee any issues keeping her free during the trial. He wished more than anything that he could be there with her for the proceeding, but he would already be on a plane halfway across the world.

For her part, Layla didn't seem at all worried about the possibility of going to prison. She said that no challenge that prison could present could possibly compare with the challenge of losing her little girl at the ripe old age of eight. Ish had spoken to Carmen before he left and explained the situation to her. She agreed to help watch over Layla and to let him know if anything looked out of place. He got the same promise from Chad and his mother. Even the lawyers had said they would notify him if they noticed any advanced signs of stress or odd behavior from their client. But all that did little to reassure him. He had already lost one of his girls. He was terrified at the prospect of losing the other.

* * *

'Welcome back, Ice-Man!" said Jag as Ish walked into the barracks. 'Ice-Man' was the nickname that Jag had created for Ish, an homage to his ability to stay cool under pressure. Most people still just called him 'Ish', but Jag always had a way of putting his unique twist on everything.

Ish barely had a chance to put his bag down before someone was shoving a cold beer into his hands. The guys were all happy to see him but were clearly tip-toeing around the idea of mentioning his daughter. They were probably confused as to what was appropriate to say and what wasn't. Bird was the first one to come to him privately to try to discuss it, but Ish waved him off. He felt somewhat bad about doing so, but it was just too soon.

A day after his return to Afghanistan, Ish received a message from one of Layla's attorneys. During the arraignment hearing, she had ordered him to refuse bail and had remanded herself into custody. She told them she felt safer in jail than on the street. Ish was beyond enraged. He didn't know what the hell that meant, and neither did they, and there was no way for him to reach her by phone.

He told them to do whatever they could to secure her release. They agreed but were not optimistic of their chances for success if she refused to leave. He knew he would lose his mind if he didn't let it go. So, with a heavy heart, he left it in their hands with instructions for them to keep him abreast of any changes.

Ish quickly stepped back into his combat soldier routine. It was the only way he could maintain his sanity. But everything was different now. The flashes of rage that he had often felt since hearing of his daughter's passing were becoming more and more frequent. It was like a flashing strobe light that had started off slow but began blinking faster and faster until it was one constant, unbroken beam. He tried to contain it, but it was a beast that overwhelmed his every effort. He started snapping at his friends for no reason and making moves in the field that were often reckless if not full-on suicidal.

It all came to a head one day when they were out on a routine assignment. The mission that day was simply to pass out bags of rice, salt and candy to some local villagers and their children. Everything was going as planned until Ish noticed a young man peaking at them from around the corner of a building. Something about the man was off, and without thinking much about it, Ish yelled at him. The man took off running, and Ish gave chase.

He didn't bother to alert the rest of guys as to what he was doing. Jag and Bird both saw him take off, and after alerting the captain, they ran after him. The young man ran into a large field, heading towards the mountains. Ish was right behind him, but he was slowed down by his 90 pounds of gear.

"Mines! Mines!" he heard someone yell from behind him. It sounded like Blade. Something in the back of his mind told him that meant he should probably stop, but he didn't. He didn't even slow down. Focused as he was, he not only ignored the yelling behind him, he also failed to register the meaning of the red flags and red stones spread out in the field before him. Suddenly there was a thunderclap, and the man he was chasing disappeared in a cloud of smoke and raining soil and body parts. Landmines.

Just as he began to stumble to a halt, something heavy hit him from behind and knocked him, face first, into the dirt. It was Bird, who was now on top of him, bear-hugging him from behind. "Stay down! I got you!" he yelled. Ish tried to wrestle free from him, but he was too tired and shocked to put up much of a fight. As he stopped struggling and began trying to catch his breath, Blade appeared. He and Bird grabbed Ish, one on each shoulder, and began dragging him to safety, carefully retracing the path they had taken to get to him.

No one said much to Ish after they got him safely out of the minefield or on the ride back to base. Once he had calmed down, he had to marvel at how lucky they all were to have been able to avoid stepping in the wrong place and suffering the same fate as the man he had chased. When he got back to his bunk, Jag, Blade and Bird were waiting for him. Other than them, the room was empty.

"What. The fuck. Is wrong with you?" asked Bird. He stood up to meet Ish, but Ish brushed against his shoulder as he walked around the man and sat down on his bed. Bird turned around, his eyes following him, his face twisted in disbelief.

"You're not even going to answer me?!"

Ish looked at him nonchalantly. "Sorry," he said and laid back on his pillow.

"'Sorry?' That's it? That's all you have to say?" Ish stared at him impassively. Bird and Jag watched the interaction with guarded interest.

"Listen," said Bird, "I can't imagine what you must be going through, but you almost got us all killed out there today! It's one thing for you to put your life in jeopardy, but it's another to drag the entire squad in with you!"

"I didn't drag anyone in," said Ish. "No one told any of you to come running after me."

Jag shook his head. "Come on, Ice-Man. Now you're just talking like a goddamn idiot. You're definitely outside your head, 'cause the Ice-Man I know would never do something so fucking stupid and inconsiderate." Ish glared at him. "I'm telling you the truth, brother," he continued, "and you know it. You know sure as a goose shits on Sunday that there was no way we were going to let you run off and not go after you."

"He's right, man," said Blade. "'No man left behind'." He tried smiling, but no one returned it, so he gave it up. They all sat in silence for several minutes.

"I'm going to get some grub," said Jag, breaking the silence. He seemed irritated and annoyed, but eager to put some distance between himself and the tension that was thick in the room.

"I'll join you," said Blade.

"Me, too," said Bird, then turned back to Ish. "Can we bring you anything?" he asked. Ish shook his head.

"Okay, man," he said. "Just try to keep in mind that, as tragic as Sumatra's passing was, it was God's plan and she's in God's hands now." Ish bolted upright in his bunk.

"What is it with you people and God?" asked Ish. "First your sister and now you. I've heard enough talk about your fucking God. Layla had it right. Your God is as fucking useful today as he was the day my daughter was killed! So, fuck your God."

"I know you're grieving right now—" began Bird.

"No, this isn't about grieving, it's about logic. I'll never understand you fucking Christians," he spat. "At least other religions make a little more sense. A Muslim gets to go to heaven with 72 virgins. A Hindu gets to come back as a wealthy man instead of a fucking dung beetle. The beauty of those systems is that you don't know whether or not they deliver until after you die, and no one can report back from the dead. Brilliant!" He stood up and began to pace back and forth, slowly getting more and more animated.

"But Christians are supposed to get rewarded right here on earth! Right? Live a good life, follow the 'Jesus' example, and your prayers will get answered. Bullshit! Some of the most devout Christians to have ever walked into a church still get cancer, still live in poverty, still get pissed on by the rest of society! And many people that aren't Christians are living a charmed life! There's no fucking logic to it! Practicing Christianity is no guarantee of success, and not practicing is no guarantee of failure, so how is it so many of you fools continue to believe in this goddamn fairy tale?" He stopped pacing and turned to face them, his face a mask of disgust, challenging either of them to dispute what he'd just said.

Bird took a deep breath. "You get some rest, brother," he said wearily as he stood up. "If anything looks good, we'll bring you back a plate." Jag, Bird and Blade quietly walked out of the room, leaving Ish to glare after them. Only Blade glanced back.

Ish walked out of the barracks a couple of hours later and found Bird sitting alone. He sat down beside him.

"Hey, man, I want to apologize," said Ish. "I was completely out of line."

"Don't worry about it, brother. None of us blame you. At least, not for that," he said, smiling slightly. "We do, however, blame you for almost getting our asses blown off."

"I know. That was...that was...I don't know exactly what that was."

"What's going on in your head? Are you feeling like you're ready to die?"

"You know, that's the weird part. I don't. Sumatra is gone, but Layla needs me more than ever. What I'm feeling is not a desire to die. I guess it's more like a slight lack of desire to live. Maybe I just wanted to see my baby girl again."

"In heaven?"

Ish shrugged. "Yeah, I guess."

"But I thought you didn't believe in heaven?"

Ish took a deep breath and stared down at his shoes. "Yeah, I guess it's complicated. Maybe it's not God that I don't believe in. Maybe it's just Christianity that I have a problem with; the Bible, the hypocrisy, the rituals. I suppose that would make some people want to revoke my 'Negro card'. But the truth is I've always felt like an outsider, so this shouldn't be any different."

"Jesus was an outsider," said Bird. "When you get right down to it, we're all outsiders here on earth. But we're all insiders in God's eye."

"Well, I don't know about all that," said Ish as both men chuckled. "But I just wanted to drop by to say I'm sorry for what I said earlier and to let you know that I won't be running off half-cocked anymore. I feel grounded again. I've regained my peace."

"I'm glad to hear that. But tell me, how did you do it? How does a man who doesn't believe in God find peace? Not that I'm saying I don't believe you. I'm genuinely curious."

"I guess you could call it a form of meditation. I laid down and let my mind go. I thought a lot about Layla. And Sumatra. I tried to imagine what she would think of me if I got myself killed doing something stupid and left her mother here to face life alone. The last thing I would ever want to do is disappoint her. So, I asked for the strength to carry on. And here I am."

"Asked who for the strength?"

"The universe. The 'powers that be'. The whatever-it-is-out-there that controls all this chaos."

Blade chuckled again. "That sounds a lot like prayer, my brother."

"Here you go!" said Ish, laughing. "Man, you Christians have a hard time letting go!"

"I'm not trying to hard-sell you," said Bird. "I'm just concerned about your immortal soul."

"So, you're just trying to make sure I'm good with God when the day comes that I arrive at the pearly gates?"

"Exactly."

"I appreciate that, Bird. I really do. But tell me something: If you and I hit an IED tomorrow and find ourselves standing before God, how exactly are we going to explain to Him why we were over here, seven thousand miles from home, shooting teenage boys in the face when the Bible clearly fucking says, 'Thou shall not kill"?

Bird didn't have an answer, and the two men simply stared into the distance, sharing the silence. After a minute or two, Ish turned to Bird and wrapped him in a strong embrace.

"I've got to go find the others and apologize to them, too. I hear there's a movie tonight. They're showing "Scarface". You want to go check it out?"

"Yeah, I'll meet you there."

Ish walked away in search of his other friends. As he moved through the camp, he reflected on the conversation he'd just had and all the sins that being a soldier had caused him to commit. If there really was a God, Ish hoped that he wasn't keeping count.

Chapter 7

"Hey, Ice-Man," said Jag. "What do you hear about this new captain?"

"Not much," said Ish, "other than his name is Stanwick and he was originally with Mobility. Why? Have you heard something?"

"Not really. But I met him a couple of years ago. We were doing a joint mission out of Kabul, and I got to spend a little time with him. Something about him rubs me the wrong way. He makes my asshole itch."

"What the...?" exclaimed Ish, laughing. He sat up in his cot. "What the hell does that mean?"

"It's hard to explain, but you know how sometimes you get that Spidey-sense tingle when you're around certain people? That sense that you always need to keep a clock on 'em, even if it's just out of the corner of your eye? I get that from him." Jag lit a cigarette and took a deep pull from it, then turned his head to blow it away from Ish.

"This army is full of those types," said Ish, "so that's nothing new."

"Yeah, but I typically don't find that kind of shit floating around in Spec Ops. You know what I mean? We got a code for a fucking reason, man."

"I don't know about all that. If there's one thing I've learned in my life, it's that it pays to keep an eye on everyone."

Jag pretended to be hurt. "Are you saying you don't even trust me? Come on, Ice-Man, we're brothers!"

Ish smiled in response, and Jag returned it.

"You know if it wasn't for you, I might not even be here. So, don't go getting all bitchy on me," said Ish.

The communications sergeant rushed into the barrack.

"Captain Stanwick is here!" he said. "Wants everyone to meet him for a drink in twenty."

"A drink?" said Ish. "That's a hell of a way to introduce yourself to the group."

"I told you there was something a little off about this guy," said Jag. "As a matter of fact," he said, lowering his voice, "he's actually got a bit of a reputation."

"Yeah?" said Ish. "What kind of reputation?"

"They say he's got a taste for young tang. And that no means yes, if you know what I'm saying."

"Dude, I have no idea what the hell you're talking about, and I speak eight languages. Try it again in English."

"You've heard of the saying 'all is fair in love and war'? Apparently, this guy likes to combine the two. They say he does almost as much fucking as he does fighting. The problem is that he usually has to drag his partner to the dance. And doesn't seem to care too much how old they are, either."

Ish took a moment to consider the implications of all this. If these allegations were true, it certainly wouldn't be the first deviant that he had encountered in the military. But Jag was right. Usually, in Special Ops, you were able to avoid the worst of the worst.

* * *

They drove out from the base in two vehicles. Stanwick was in the lead Hummer; Blade and Bird were with him. Ish was in the second vehicle with Jag and a couple of other guys. The terrain they were traveling on was particularly rough. They were trying to stay off the roads as much as possible to reduce the IED risk. After a couple of hours of being jarred around in the rear of the truck, Ish felt bone sore.

Before they mounted up, Stanwick had reminded them that their primary goal was WHAM: 'Winning Hearts and Minds'. Unlike what you see in some Hollywood movies, most of the activities Special Op teams like Ish's engaged in were training foreign troops and offering assistance to the local citizenry. You don't 'win hearts and minds' by terrorizing and killing innocent civilians. It's not as though firefights were uncommon, just less desirable by all involved.

Today an elder had asked to meet with them. He had some complaints about the way some of the soldiers had been treating his fellow villagers. He also hinted that he might have some Taliban intel to pass along.

The trucks pulled into the center of the village, and Ish gratefully hopped out, happy to have his feet back on solid ground, at least for a little while. Stanwick and one of the other officers greeted the elder while the rest of the soldiers scanned the fields and surrounding hillside, searching for signs of any hostiles.

Stanwick signaled, and Ish followed him into the elder's home. Very few of the natives spoke English, and Ish, the most advanced linguist in the group, often served as interpreter. The old man greeted Ish in Pashto and smiled. Ish returned the greeting as they shook hands. The old man, whose name was Omar, appeared happy to see them but also tentative and slightly nervous, which was to be expected.

Omar invited them to sit on a pair of stools, and Ish began translating for Stanwick. The village spokesman was upset that a soldier from their compound had beaten one of the local teenagers. Stanwick tried to explain that the boy had been chased after he threw rocks at a passing army truck, and that any injury he sustained would have been the result of him resisting capture. He added that the teen should consider himself fortunate that the soldiers hadn't felt the need to open fire. They debated the particulars, going back and forth, each trying to defend his position, with Ish as the middleman.

A few moments later, Ish heard a rustle from the back of the house that caused both him and Stanwick to instantly tense. They relaxed when a young girl entered the room. She couldn't have been more than ten or eleven years old, but she was stunningly beautiful. She was thin, like most Afghani females, with long jet-black hair and brilliant emerald-green eyes that almost glowed in the dim light of the room. Though there was little real physical resemblance between the two, seeing her immediately made Ish think about his own daughter, and he almost winced from the pain in his chest that accompanied it.

While both Ish and his commander had relaxed when they realized that the noise they had heard wasn't evidence of any kind of threat, Stanwick's demeanor had changed. The only way to describe it is to say that he seemed somehow energized. Ish and Stanwick continued their conversation with Omar, but Ish noticed Stanwick's eyes kept darting over to the girl, who was sitting at a table preparing some kind of food. He was obviously distracted and several times had to ask Ish to repeat certain statements. After about fifteen minutes the girl, perhaps recognizing the attention and becoming uncomfortable, rose and walked out of the front door.

Shortly thereafter the meeting ended, with Stanwick promising to talk to his men about being more considerate in their dealings with the younger villagers. Omar then pointed out an area on a map where he believed a group of Taliban had set up camp. Ish and Stanwick returned to the vehicles they had arrived in, and after the rest of the men mounted up, they began the journey back to base.

They had traveled about a mile or so when they spotted a young man crouched down by the side of the road ahead. When he saw the trucks coming, he paused for a moment, then stood up and darted into a house a few yards away.

"That looks like the same joker that was throwing the rocks last week," said Stanwick over the radio. "Let's hold up a minute. I want to have a quick chat with him."

Both trucks pulled up in front of the house the boy had disappeared into. Everyone stepped out onto the road, each man facing a different direction and scanning the area for threats.

"Everybody look alive," said Stanwick as he checked his M-4. "Bird, take a couple guys with you and check out the rear. Ish, on me," he said as he began moving toward the house.

Stanwick banged on the door with the butt of his rifle and waited a few moments. When no one appeared, he tried the handle. The door was unlocked, and he slowly pushed it open. Ish and Stanwick both took a moment to listen for any signs of trouble before quietly creeping into the house. The front room was empty.

"Come on out!" yelled Stanwick. There was no answer. He looked at Ish and raised his eyebrows inquisitively. He nodded at the doorway to the next room, indicating that Ish should go through first.

When Ish entered the next room, he found the boy huddled in a corner. With him was the girl who he and Stanwick had seen at the elder's home. Neither appeared to be armed. Moments later Stanwick was standing beside him, the two large soldiers making the tiny room feel claustrophobic. A smile appeared on Stanwick's face, and his breathing quickened

"Ask him what he was doing on the side of the road."

Ish had to repeat the question three times before the boy would answer. In a nervous stutter, he told Ish that he was planting some flower seeds.

"Right," said Stanwick sarcastically. "Tell him we're watching him." After Ish translated the warning, Stanwick stepped aside and waved his gun towards the door. "Get on out of here, boy." The boy didn't move. "Get, I said!" The boy then leaped up with his hands in the air and ran from the room. "We're clear," said Stanwick into his radio. "The kid is on his way out."

After the boy had left the room, Stanwick leaned his machine gun against the wall behind him and turned to face the girl.

"Hi," he said, beaming a large smile at her. "What's your name?" She didn't answer, her face a mask of fear. He tilted his head at her in impatience. She nervously shook her head in response, her luminescent eyes darting back and forth between Ish and the captain. Ish opened his mouth to speak to her in Pashto, but Stanwick raised his hand, silencing him before he could get the words out.

"What," said Stanwick again, "is your name?" The girl finally responded, in several words of Pashto.

"She said—" began Ish.

"It's okay," said Stanwick to Ish, cutting him off again. All the while his eyes never left the girl. "I think she and I can find a way to communicate without your help." He pulled a bandana out of his pocket and wiped the back of his neck. "As a matter of fact, why don't you wait outside. Tell the guys I'll be out shortly, after I'm done questioning her."

At that moment Ish realized how hot and stuffy the room was, and suddenly he wanted more than anything to be back out in the open where he might catch a breeze if he were lucky. But he didn't want to leave the girl; this girl that strangely reminded him of his own daughter.

"Captain, how are you going to question her? She clearly doesn't speak English."

Stanwick looked at him as though he couldn't believe he was still there. "Didn't I just give you a fucking order, soldier?"

As they turned to face each other, they were nose to nose, their bodies consuming much of the space in the compact room. They stared at each other, neither man speaking. Ish felt a bead of sweat trickle from his neck down his back. Stanwick's eyes darted to the rifle he had leaned against the wall moments ago. He shifted his weight, casually moving his right arm so his hand rested on his sidearm. It was a subtle message, but Ish received it loud and clear.

"With all due respect, sir," he said, his voice calm and even, "I don't feel right leaving you here alone. It's not safe. We haven't even searched her for weapons or explosives."

"I'll search her myself. That will be all." His eyes bore into Ish's in a way that dared him to say anything else about the matter. Ish glanced back at the girl one final time, then slowly walked out of the room.

"So, where were we?" he heard Stanwick say as he walked through the front door and joined his waiting squad.

Chapter 8

Once Ish reached the other men, Jag was the first to approach him.

"What's going on? Where's the captain?"

"He's still inside. There's, ummm, a girl in there. The daughter of the elder we just met with. Cap wants to question her."

"Okay," said Jag, confused. "What's wrong?"

Ish turned his back to the other men and Jag stepped closer to him. "The girl doesn't speak any English," he said in a lowered voice. A look of understanding spread across Jag's face. It was quickly replaced by a mix of resignation and anger.

"I was wondering when this shit was going to finally happen," he said. "I suspected all along that the stories I heard about him were true."

"Shit," said Ish. Jag was looking at him expectantly. Bird and Blade walked up and joined them.

"What's going on?" asked Bird. Ish filled them in on the situation. Bird looked back toward the house's front door.

"So, what do—" began Bird. He was interrupted by a scream from the house. It sounded like the girl. The soldiers turned as a group, focusing their attention on the front door. Essentially, they now consisted of two groups. First, there was Ish, Blade, Bird and Jag, and the remaining five men of the squad comprised the other group. For a moment no one moved, then Blade and a man from the other group broke off and ran into the house. While they were gone, Ish and the other guys looked around nervously—at the house, at the surrounding area and at themselves.

Moments later Blade and the other man emerged from the home. Blade looked shaken while the other man, Smith, seemed unperturbed.

"Everything's fine," said Smith, taking a seat in the rear of one of the trucks and grabbing some jerky from the storage compartment. Smith and Stanwick had served together the previous year. "Cap will be out soon. Knowing him, I give him about two minutes," he said and laughed. Several of the other men laughed with him. Ish walked over to Blade and placed a hand on his shoulder. Bird and Jag followed.

"How old do you think that girl is?" asked Blade.

Ish just shook his head in response.

"This shit ain't right!" said Blade. His voice was urgent, but at the same time he was trying to whisper, so that the men in the other group wouldn't hear him.

"I know," said Ish. "Try to calm down. Let me go try to talk to him again."

When Ish walked back through the front door, he was immediately hit with the musk of sex and perspiration. As he entered the back room, he saw Stanwick standing, buckling his pants. The girl was lying on the ground atop a pallet. Her eyes were wide open, frozen and unblinking in death. There were red welts around her throat. A blanket was haphazardly thrown partially over her, leaving one naked breast exposed. There was a large, crimson stain in the center of the blanket over the area that covered her crotch.

"What the fuck did you do!?" shouted Ish.

"I thought I told you to wait outside!"

"You just raped and killed the daughter of a village elder! Are you fucking insane?"

"Don't worry about it," said Stanwick as he zipped up his pants, grabbed his rifle and began walking out of the room. "If the boy says anything, they'll blame him. He probably wasn't supposed to be seeing her anyway. I could tell by the way he looked at me when we caught them together."

Stanwick was moving fast, and by the time he had finished talking, they were walking out the front door.

"Let's move it out!" said the captain. Before he could take another step toward the lead truck, Ish grabbed his arm, spun him around and landed a right cross to the side of the man's head.

The power of the blow spun Stanwick around in the opposite direction into one of the other men. The soldier caught him before he could fall to the ground while two other men grabbed Ish from behind. Ish could have easily broken free from them, but he could see Bird, Blade and Jag tensing to make a move. He shook his head slightly, instructing them to hold back.

"Have you lost your goddamn mind!?" yelled Stanwick once he was back on his own two feet. The side of his face was red where the punch had landed, and there was a trickle of blood at the corner of his mouth.

"You're the one that's lost his mind if you think I'm just going to stand by while you rape and murder an innocent child!" yelled Ish in reply.

"What's he talking about, Cap?" asked one of the men that was holding one of Ish's arms. His name was Chavez. He was the Medical Sergeant.

"He's talking nonsense about shit he doesn't understand," said Stanwick, wiping at his mouth.

Ish finally wrenched himself free from the two men holding him, but he stood where he was. "What is there to understand? When we entered the house, a young girl was alive and healthy. Fifteen minutes with you and now she's naked and dead. Do the math."

Stanwick didn't reply. He simply stared at Ish while he straightened his clothes as though he were deciding exactly what he wanted to do with him. Ish noticed that Bird, Blade and Jag all had their weapons in their hands, their fingers on the triggers. They looked tightly wound, as though they could snap at any moment. The rest of the men were either staring at the ground or at the captain, their faces a mask of either embarrassment or some degree of bloodlust.

Ish looked at Chavez, who was standing beside him looking confused. "Don't take my word for it," he said to Chavez. "Go in the house and see for yourself."

Stanwick stared at Chavez, silently daring him to go into the house. Chavez looked away. "What transpired inside that house is classified, and no one is to enter without my express permission," he said, looking around at all the men. His gaze returned to Ish, and Stanwick walked up to him until they were nose-to-nose again.

"You know I could court-martial your ass for that little stunt, right?" he said, smiling. Ish remained silent. "But we're light on qualified replacements for a man of your skills. And I like you. *Ice-Man.* You're a good soldier. Just maybe a little bit high strung." He chuckled. "So, I'm going to give you the break of a lifetime and pretend that what just happened didn't really happen."

He made a move to pat Ish's shoulder, but the look Ish gave him caused him second thoughts, and he brought his arm back down to his side. "Let's get home, have a drink, and forget this little squabble ever took place. We're moving out!" he said as he turned and headed towards the front vehicle.

A couple of the men quickly followed Stanwick's lead. Some of the more unsure ones, like Chavez, began a slow, awkward shuffle back to the trucks, leaving Ish, Bird, Blade and Jag standing together in a circle.

"Let's head out," said Ish through clenched teeth.

Moments later both trucks were moving, putting distance between themselves and the scene of the captain's crime.

After dinner Ish walked out into the fresh night air. He was outside but still protected by the heavy walls that surrounded the compound. Bird, Blade and Jag were sitting at a table off to the side. Jag had a strained look on his face and was saying something to the other two but stopped short when he saw Ish approaching.

"What's up, fellas?" asked Ish solemnly.

"That was some crazy shit we witnessed today," said Blade. He said it casually, in the same way he might have said, 'How about those Lakers?' or 'Can you believe that rain last night?' But there was a hint of bitterness in his voice.

"'Crazy' doesn't even begin to describe what that was," mumbled Ish.

"I've never seen anything like it. Not even close," said Bird.

"Then you ain't lookin' hard enough, son," said Jag, "cause that kind of bullshit is more common than most people would ever believe."

Bird looked irritated. He hated when Jag called him 'son'. He had complained about it several times, and Jag always apologized and promised to try to stop, but being from the South, it was just part of his vernacular. Jag didn't even recognize the racial connotations of the word and its potential to offend, but everyone else at the table did. They all pretty much just gave him a pass—except for Bird.

They were silent for a few minutes, each lost in some private thought or contemplation. Jag craned his neck to look around for any eavesdroppers and then addressed Ish.

"Listen, Ice-Man. I guess I should be the first to tell you. I've decided to pack it in. In three months, when our tour is up, I'm out."

"What? What are you talking about?" asked Ish.

"I mean I'm civilian-bound, chief." His head was low, and he had to look up to meet Ish's eyes. "That mess we saw today was pretty much the last straw for me. I don't have the stomach for this business anymore."

Ish couldn't hide his surprise. "Wow," he said. "I always figured you as a lifelong soldier."

"In my heart I'll always be a soldier. But this ain't soldiering. I signed up to protect America from enemies foreign and domestic. Not to stand guard for murdering pedophiles."

"So, what are you going to do then?"

"I don't know. I'll probably spend a few weeks at home doing some serious R&R, and then maybe I'll come back and snag a mercenary gig. Or maybe I'll just go work on my uncle's milk farm, even though he's kind of an ass-hat, and he and I don't really see eye-to-eye on anything other than the direction of the next sunset. But..." He shrugged as if to say, 'It is what it is.'

"Well, man," said Ish, "we'll definitely miss you."

"Actually," said Bird, his voice low, "Blade and I are leaving, too. We feel like shit, leaving you here all alone. But this is no longer our war. And I know you feel it too. I've seen how your spark has dimmed over the last couple months. I know a lot of that had to do with Sumatra's passing, but I saw signs even before that. And today—today I wanted to kill that motherfucker. I feel that if I stay, I run the risk of losing who I am. Or at least, who I want to be."

Ish nodded. "So, you, too?" he asked Blade.

"I didn't have the greatest childhood," said Blade. "But my mama taught me to know the difference between right and wrong. The problem is that people like Stanwick believe that 'might makes right'. And it's thinking like that that has made America one of the most hated countries in the world. Even when we leave our families and risk our lives to protect their freedoms, they still hate us. And when we're doing shit like what Stanwick did today, who can blame them? There are better ways to make a difference. And a hell of a lot easier ways to make a living. Besides, Bird and I came in together. I guess it's kind of fitting that we leave together."

"I totally understand," said Ish. "You have to do what's best for you. For each of you. I love you guys like brothers. And if there's ever anything I can do to help, you know all you have to do is let me know." They all nodded in acknowledgment, then they spent a couple of hours shooting the shit before bed.

The next day, Ish ignored each of his friends for the most part. There were some mission briefings that they attended together, but it was a slow time, and he spent most of it doing chores like laundry or reading in his bunk with headphones. He was trying to ignore it, but he was battling what felt like a mild depression. Or maybe it was not so mild. Depression wasn't something that he'd had much experience with. They called him 'Ice-Man' for a reason.

Ish had never really dreamed much in his life. But ever since Sumatra died, he was experiencing dreaming on an almost nightly basis. The dreams were so vivid they almost seemed four-dimensional. Sometimes they were comforting, but most of the time they were terrifying. Most of the time, he would have much preferred to be awake and in combat with the Taliban than to have to do battle with the demons that attacked him in his slumber.

After Stanwick killed the Afghan girl, the frequency of the dreams accelerated. More and more often, the captain was a character in these dreams. Sometimes he was the devil. Sometimes he was a monster—a six-headed alien or a giant lizard. But, as is the bizarre nature of dreams, sometimes Stanwick appeared helpless, in the form of a woman or a lamb or some other small animal. In one dream, Stanwick appeared as a dandelion, which Ish picked and then blew away, laughing as the petals floated away and were ignited by the sunlight, exploding in the air like fireworks.

Sometimes it wasn't Stanwick that found him in his dreams, but the Afghan girl. Sometimes she chased him, begging for him to rescue her from her murderer. Sometimes she came to him like a succubus, sexually teasing him and tempting him to follow her to some place dark and dangerous. Ish started sleeping less and less. He counted himself lucky that there wasn't much going on in the field during this time. As the days wore on, the lack of sleep began to take its toll, and he sometimes found himself stumbling around like a zombie. Bird, Blade and Jag had all approached him, trying to engage him in conversation, trying to find out what was going on with him, but he always told them that everything was fine.

It was at the end of one of these slow days that an idea popped into his head; a wild, crazy, dangerous idea.

Chapter 9

The next day at chow, Ish saw Stanwick sitting at a table by himself and walked over to him.

"What's up, Cap? Mind if I sit?"

Stanwick looked at him, his face a mixture of suspicion and surprise. After a few moments, he began to relax and his face broke into a smile.

"Sure, why not," he said.

Ish sat, put a forkful of food into his mouth and then looked up from his plate, squinting into the distance at nothing in particular as he chewed.

"I wanted to apologize, Cap, for my reaction the other day," he said without turning to look at his commander.

The captain took a long drink of whatever it was that was in his cup. It smelled like whiskey.

"Don't sweat it, Ice-Man," he said. "In the heat of war, shit happens. Emotions can sometimes run high. You've got a soft spot for hajji. I get it. They're like stray dogs. You want to adopt 'em, take 'em home and give 'em a bowl of warm milk." He took another sip from his cup.

"But let me tell you something," he said, leaning closer to Ish, his voice sinking into a low growl. "You can't afford to get soft on these motherfuckers. Otherwise, you'll end up going home in a fucking body bag, and they won't give a fuck. If it were up to me, I'd treat 'em like stray kittens—put 'em all in a burlap sack and throw 'em in a river some fucking where."

Ish nodded his head and put another forkful of food in his mouth, but his appetite had vanished. He struggled to chew threw clinched jaws, forcing himself to smile.

"You're right," he said. "I should know all this by now, but sometimes I think I forget where I am, and I think these are actually people that we're fighting."

"Exactly. When you get right down to it, they're nothing but wild animals. I mean, shit, what kind of a rational human being blows himself up to win a fight? How fucking crazy do you have to be?"

Ish chuckled. "Well, I just wanted to let you know that it's an honor to serve with you, and to thank you for not throwing the book at me, even though I fucking deserved it." He extended his hand, and the captain shook it. Ish noticed that Bird, Blade and Jag were sitting on the other side of the compound, eating their own meals. They were staring over at him and the captain. Their faces were blank, but he could imagine how confused they probably felt.

Ish took another couple of bites of his food. "I'll tell you what," said Stanwick. "Just to show you that bygones are bygones, why don't you come by my bunk around 22:00. Me and a couple of the other guys are going to be breaking open this beautiful single malt I just picked up."

"Now you're speaking a language we can both understand," said Ish, his smile broadening. "I'll see you then." He grabbed his tray and began walking back toward the kitchen. As soon as he passed through the doors Bird, Blade and Jag fell in step beside him.

"How's it going?" asked Blade.

"Not bad," said Ish, turning his head slightly. He dumped his partially-eaten meal into a large trash can and walked over to the dessert counter. The three men followed him.

Ish stared at the dessert options as the three men flanked him.

"I don't know if you deserve any dessert today, Ice-Man," said Jag. "You didn't eat all your din-din."

"Yeah," said Ish distractedly, "you're probably right." He turned and began to leave the mess hall, hoping that his crew would get the hint and let him alone. They didn't.

"Ish, hold up," said Bird. "You got a minute? We'd like to chat with you."

"Not really. I'm kind of busy," said Ish, not slowing his stride until Bird stepped in front of him and stopped, blocking his path.

"Look, my brother," said Bird, holding his hands up, "I know you're pissed at us for bailing out, but this is no way to deal with it. We deserve better than this. We're just trying to live our lives the best way we know how."

Ish glared at him for a moment, then his features softened.

"You've got it all wrong. I'm not pissed off at all. I totally support what you guys are doing. I just, umm, have some other things that I'm trying to take care of right now."

"Yeah, we saw you gettin' all buddy-buddy with Stanwick," said Jag. "I don't mean to sound like a jilted school girl, but if you're not pissed at us, how do you explain the fact that you've been avoiding us like the plague for the past week?"

"Jesus Christ," said Ish, his voice hard with frustration. "This isn't about you guys, alright? It's some personal shit that I've got to take care of on my own. You don't need to be involved with this."

"You sound like a man in trouble," said Blade. "Part of the code is that we don't leave a man in trouble. Ever." Ish was about to answer but saw another soldier headed in their direction, probably on his way to grab food. Ish tilted his head to the side, pointing to a deserted area of the compound near the fence. He began walking, and his three friends followed. When he felt like he was safely out of earshot of anyone else, he turned to face them.

"The reason I've been putting distance between you and myself is that I'm about to get involved in some serious shit—something that could result in a prison sentence. I don't want any of you in a position where you could be mistakenly implicated. And the less you know about the details, the safer you'll be."

"Well," said Jag, raising his hands above his head and stretching, "I ain't exactly a rocket scientist, but I've been in enough threesomes to know how to put two and two together. You don't have time for us, but you're cozying up to Stanwick. You must be planning some kind of retaliation for the dead girl." Bird and Blade both looked at each other, their mouths hanging open from the shock of the realization that what Jag had just said made perfect sense.

Ish didn't respond to the accusation, as though he didn't even hear it. But he didn't need to answer; they all knew it was true.

"So, what's the plan?" asked Bird.

"The plan," said Ish, "is that you all walk away and forget you ever heard any of this."

"That's not going to happen," said Blade. "We're a team, and we'll win or lose as a team."

"This is a one-man operation. It doesn't take a group of people to do what I'm planning."

"Well, it's not exactly like we've had time to discuss it," said Jag, looking around at Bird and Blade, "but I think I speak for all of us when I say that is no longer an option." His two friends nodded their heads.

Ish again refused to answer. "So out with it," said Bird. "What are you planning? What's your angle?"

Ish could see that it was futile to continue to fight with these guys. They were right. They had always done battle as a team. They were even there for him emotionally when he had learned about Sumatra's death. But if things turned out the way he knew they were likely to and they all paid the price for it, he didn't know if he would ever be able to forgive himself for letting them take part. But his options were now limited. It was either let them be a part or run the risk that they would foul something up trying to help him against his will. He took a deep breath, filling his lungs with warm Afghanistan air, and then let it out in a large sigh.

"The plan is simple: I get Stanwick to willingly leave the base with me, get him to a remote area and make him disappear."

"The fucking bastard deserves worse than that," said Blade. "But it's a start."

"True," said Bird. "But how are you going to deal with witnesses? Getting him off the base is not all that difficult, but getting him off without anyone seeing the two of you together is something else entirely. Once the investigation starts, whoever he was last seen with is going to be suspect number one."

"I haven't exactly figured that part out yet. And to be honest, I don't know if I really care whether or not they catch me."

"That's your depression talking," said Bird. "The signs are all there. I've noticed it for a while now, but I never really wanted to say anything. I figured if it got bad enough, I could sit down with you and try to help you talk through it."

"I'm not depressed," Ish scoffed.

"Bullshit," said Bird. "I didn't get $80k in debt getting a psychology degree for nothing. I know depression when I see it. Under the circumstances, it's completely understandable. There's no shame in it," he said, putting his hand on Ish's shoulder.

"Before you two start making out, let's get back to the plan," said Jag. "Do you have a timetable for this?"

"Not really," said Ish. "It depends on how things progress with him and me. He's invited me to join him later tonight for a drink with a couple of other guys. I'll have to play it by ear; see how it goes."

"Understood," said Bird. "Just promise that you won't make a move without us. Stanwick is a crafty fucker, and you stand a better chance of pulling this off smoothly with our help."

Ish's nod was almost imperceptible, but not quite. Satisfied, his three friends walked off and finally left him to his thoughts.

Ish showed up at Stanwick's bunk at 10:10pm. Two other soldiers were already there. Stanwick must have started early, because he was already showing signs of being buzzed, and the liter bottle of scotch was now one-fourth empty. Ish also smelled weed, but no one was currently smoking.

Ish's mother had always told him that you never show up at dinner party empty handed. This wasn't exactly a dinner party, but Ish had brought a sizable bag of beef jerky with him nonetheless and presented it to his host, who graciously accepted. The army sometimes supplied dried meat, but it was nowhere near the quality of what Ish had brought. This was one of the many 'gray market' items that you could purchase around the base if you had the cash and the right connections, both of which Ish had.

As they sat around drinking and snacking on the beef, they began swapping war stories. Some centered around battles in the field, others centered around battles back home. There were stories of victories and defeats, friends gone but not forgotten and women who were either the sources or the victims of various broken hearts.

At about 3:00am Ish started fading. Both of Stanwick's friends had to be up soon for an early briefing and had stumbled out an hour ago. Stanwick and Ish were left alone, both puffing on the nubs of cigars they had been chewing on for the last forty-five minutes. Ish wasn't a smoker, but Stanwick had passed them around and he felt obligated.

Thankfully, they weren't cigarettes, and since you didn't have to inhale, it was easy to fake.

"Ice-Man," said Stanwick, his voice showing just the slightest signs of slurring, "you're a good man. I read your file before I arrived to take over this command. I was impressed. Confused why a millionaire pretty-boy like yourself would lower himself to eating MREs and shitting in a tin can, but impressed. Hell, I'm still impressed. Though, I have to admit, I was a little disappointed about how things went over the girl, but I shouldn't have been surprised. I knew from what I read that you were principled and headstrong."

Ish nodded in agreement, mentally forcing his body to ignore the fatigue that was settling into his bones.

"But to be honest, I like that. I have enough 'yes men' around me. It's refreshing to know that there is someone around that might call me on my shit and that has the balls to actually stand up for something they believe in." He took a deep drag on his cigar, held the smoke for a couple of seconds, and then slowly blew it out.

"What I need to know, Ice-Man, is whether or not I can count on you. I need to know whether you and I are going to be comrades out there or combatants. Because if we're going to be constantly scratching up against each other, it'd be better for you to just move on to a different outfit. I have too much respect for you and what you've given over here to be a party to you destroying your career over some bullshit."

"I read your file, too," said Ish, acknowledging the slight look of shock on Stanwick's face. "Yeah, I know. It pays to be connected. What I learned is that you are a man that I can learn a lot from. You're a man that's been around the world and back; a man with a reputation as an expert strategist. I'm here to do a job—destroy the enemy. I think you can help me better do that. That's all that's important."

Stanwick let those words sink in for a few moments, then held up his almost empty glass. "Cheers!"

For the next couple of weeks, Ish and Stanwick spent more time together. When they left the base on missions, Ish rode in the same vehicle with Stanwick, leaving Bird, Blade and Jag to ride together in a separate one. Several times they encountered the village elder, either walking along the road or standing beside it, conversing with other Afghani. Stanwick usually nodded at him in greeting. The elder never nodded back, his eyes simply starring like two ice-cold daggers into the face of the man who had killed his daughter. If Ish had ever wondered if the old man knew the truth of what happened to his child, that question was now answered.

Ish felt sorry for the man, but more than that, he felt guilty. He was at least partially responsible for what had happened. Certainly, his options had been limited, but he couldn't help but feel that he should have figured out some way to save her. Even the vengeance that he was planning in her honor started to feel hollow to him, as though it just wasn't enough. Then one day he had a new idea.

Chapter 10

After discussing his idea with the guys to make sure they were all on board, Ish came up with an excuse during one of their missions to ride in the truck with his crew and to break from the caravan for a quick 'solo' recon mission. During that break they stopped by the elder's village and Ish had a short but emotional conversation with him. Initially, the man was suspicious, but within fifteen minutes they came to an agreement that allowed Ish to feel some inner peace for the first time since learning of his own daughter's death.

As the days and weeks passed, Stanwick gradually relaxed more and more around Ish. He even began pointing out to Ish females that they encountered along the way, often making crude comments about their anatomy, the way they were dressed or what he'd like to do to them if he ever got the chance. Ish mostly just chuckled and nodded.

Two months after Ish's confrontation with Stanwick over the murdered girl, he arrived back at his bunk to find a note. It was from a soldier who was known as the 'go to' person for importing contraband. Ish had spoken to him three weeks prior and placed a very special order with him. The order had finally arrived. After picking up the package, he had a quick meeting with Bird, Blade and Jag, and then went to see Stanwick. He found him pouring over some inventory documents.

"What's up, Cap?"

"Ice-Man!" exclaimed Stanwick, putting his pen down and taking off his glasses to rub his eyes. "I'm just trying to get this paperwork finished before the next supply run. They always wait till the last goddamn minute to give me this shit."

"Well, if you're feeling up to it later, I've got a special treat I'm willing to share with someone that can appreciate it."

"Yeah?" said Stanwick, a grin beginning to spread across his face. "Whatcha got?"

Ish looked around to make sure they were alone and then reached into his knapsack and partially pulled out a bottle, revealing it to Stanwick like it was one of the crown jewels.

"Wait...this can't be...*Camas an Staca*?" he whispered. His eyes glittered as he licked his lips. You could sense the saliva gathering in his mouth. Pavlov would have loved him. Ish just nodded in response, returning the grin.

"This stuff—!" Stanwick began before catching himself and lowering his voice back to a whisper. "This stuff retails for $500 a bottle! And that's when you can find it in stock!" He was giggling with glee. "Where the fuck did you get this?"

"It pays to be connected," said Ish.

"No, what pays is to be serving with a millionaire. You are a generous man!"

"Well, this is not the kind of scotch that you drink alone. And it's definitely not for the common man. You're the only person within a thousand miles of here that has refined enough tastes to appreciate an elixir of this caliber."

"This is the real deal?"

"Real as a heart attack."

"Did you want to break it open now?"

"With these hooch-swilling goons walking around? We'll have everyone and their mama standing in line with an empty cup begging for a taste or wondering where we got it."

"You're right, you're right. How about I book the strategy room for tomorrow night? That way we can guarantee we won't be disturbed. Say around 20:00?"

"Perfect," said Ish as he carefully placed the bottle back into his bag.

Ish arranged for a clandestine meeting with Bird in the latrine an hour before he was to meet with the captain.

When Ish walked into the restroom, Bird was already standing at one of the urinals. Ish knelt down and made sure there were no feet visible in any of the stalls, then he opened each door individually, just to be sure that they were alone. When he was done, he walked up to the open urinal on Bird's left and unzipped his fly, even though his bladder was empty.

"Everything a go?" asked Bird without turning his head to look at Ish.

"So far, so good. You guys all set?" Bird nodded.

"Just make sure that the distraction is as over-the-top as possible. And don't forget to use the 'abort' signal if you need to."

"We'll see you soon," said Bird as he zipped up his pants, washed his hands and walked out.

Ish arrived at the strategy room at 8:00pm sharp. He brought with him a large container of hot Cajun chicken wings, a 6-pack of beer and two iced steins, in addition to the prized bottle of scotch.

"These are beautiful," said Stanwick when he saw the wings. "But do we really need the beer?" he asked, obviously anxious to get his first taste of the *Camas*.

"We need something to clean the palate between the wings and the scotch."

"Right you are," said Stanwick. "Good thinking."

What Stanwick didn't know was that Ish had previously coated one of the steins with a chemical that was almost completely tasteless—GHB, aka the 'date rape' drug. The taste would be further masked by the spices in the wings. The captain would never know there was anything in the glass other than beer.

They had finished two beers each and half the wings when Ish started to notice that one of Stanwick's eyes was getting lazy, but the commander was impatient to taste the scotch. After Ish broke the seal, they both sniffed it from the bottle and let the aroma swirl around the membranes of their nasal passages, already intoxicated by the very idea of what they were about to partake in. Ish had been worried about the slight possibility that the bottle could be counterfeit, but one sip and he knew that his money had been well-spent. It was like sipping liquid gold. As Ish turned his wrist to deliver the second sip into his mouth, he took a sneak peek at his watch. It was 8:55. He was doing good on time.

At 9:25, Stanwick almost fell out of his chair, splashing scotch across the front of his shirt. By 9:45 the captain was laying on the floor, curled up in a fetal position and out cold. Ish grabbed another chicken wing and sat back to wait for the signal. He had a slight buzz, but he hadn't had nearly as much of the *Camas* as Stanwick had. And then there was the GHB. Surprisingly, that had been even easier to get than the rare scotch was. Apparently, GHB was not an uncommon order. Ish didn't want to think about what the other soldiers were using it for.

At 10:01 Ish heard what he had been waiting for—the voices of Jag and Bird, loud and aggressive. There was something about accusations of theft and a commotion that sounded like tables being turned over. Several other voices joined the mix. Ish could imagine the other soldiers trying to get between his two friends.

Moments later there was a soft knock at the door. Ish opened it and nodded silently at Blade. Blade had driven an MRAP vehicle up to the back door of the building. "All clear," he said.

They grabbed the captain by his arms and shuffled him into the back of the vehicle. No one was around. If anyone had seen them, they simply would have said that he was drunk and they were trying to get him back to his bunk without anyone noticing. But thankfully, they were alone. Once inside, they zip-tied his hands and feet, gagged him and covered him with a tarp. Ish stayed in the back of the vehicle with the captain while Blade drove it back to its usual position.

Now they had to play the waiting game again. Blade, Bird, Jag and Ish had all been assigned to a group executing a night raid on what had been reported as a Taliban munitions stash. It was to be two trucks, with four men each. Ish and company would be in the second truck, with the first truck containing the second group of four. They were supposed to move out at 10:30, which gave Jag and Bird roughly half an hour to kiss and make up and then grab their gear. Sitting in the driver's seat waiting for half an hour would have looked suspicious, so Blade went to grab his own gear, leaving Ish alone in the back of the truck with the captain. Ish prayed that he had gotten the dosage of GHB right and that the captain wouldn't wake up before they were ready for him to. So far, he hadn't moved a muscle.

Thirty minutes later Ish's body tensed as he heard someone open the driver door and climb in. "We have a green light," said Blade. Ish heard Jag saying something to Blade through the driver window. Moments later he was in the passenger seat and Blade was turning on the ignition. The back door swung open and Bird climbed in.

The look on Bird's face was grim. "How did it go?" asked Ish.

"Fine."

The lead vehicle started moving, and Blade navigated their vehicle to follow suit. Ten minutes later they were outside the walls of the base and traversing a steady trail into the mountains. It took two hours for them to arrive at their destination, a goat herder's shack in the middle of nowhere. Three men from the lead vehicle approached the building on foot, and moments later reported back that the structure was empty. Ish had known that it would be. The intel was phony, having been cleverly arranged by him as a stray broadcast picked up by communications.

One of the men from the lead truck walked back, approaching Blade on the driver's side.

"There's nothing up here! All this fucking way for nothing! Let's pack it up and head back to HQ."

"Roger that," said Blade.

Fifteen minutes from base, Jag got on the radio to the other truck.

"We're going to take a swing around the perimeter and give it a once over."

"You really think that's necessary?" radioed someone from the lead truck. "I've got a card game I'd like to get to while everyone still has some money left."

"You go ahead; we got this."

"Roger that," came the response. "We'll catch you on the flip side."

Blade started a trajectory that began with them staying within 200 yards of the base wall, but as he drove, his arc gradually grew wider and wider. By the time they had gotten halfway around the base they had changed direction entirely and were heading towards a grouping of low hills a few miles away.

When the truck finally came to a stop, they were in an area enclosed on three sides by cliffs. There were trees that created a slight canopy, partially obscuring the truck from anyone that might be perched on the cliff or some other elevated point.

"Jag. Let's make sure we're alone," said Ish.

"On it." Jag grabbed a night vision scope, ran to the top of a nearby hill and began to slowly canvas the area. "Just us and the snakes!" he called down a few minutes later.

Stanwick was still out. Bird tried rousing him but he was out cold.

"I think you might have over-medicated," said Jag as he looked on from the passenger seat.

Ish had anticipated that, and had brought a couple of ammonia inhalants. He removed the gag then broke open an inhalant and waved it under Stanwick's nose. Within thirty seconds the captain came to.

"Where the fuck am I?" he asked, his eyelids still heavy and his voice slurred.

"You're at your trial," said Ish.

"My what?" he asked, already sounding slightly more coherent.

"Let's get him out of the truck," said Ish. He and Bird each grabbed an arm. They dragged him to a spot a few feet in front of the truck's headlights and pushed him down to his knees.

Stanwick's eyes were looking less drowsy with each passing second.

"What the fuck do you assholes think you're doing?!" he yelled, his voice a combination of anger and fear.

"We don't have time to get too dramatic," said Ish, stepping to the lead position facing Stanwick. "You're here for one simple reason: to pay for what you did to that village girl as well as all the other innocent girls and women that you've harassed, raped and murdered in your position as a soldier in the United States army."

"You goddamn cocksucker, are you fucking kidding—" A well-placed front kick from Ish slammed into Stanwick's solar plexus. He rolled over onto his side, gasping for air.

"If you're going to speak, you'll need to check your tone. Another outburst and we'll be forced to gag you again." Ish nodded at Bird and Jag, who grabbed Stanwick and helped him back to an upright position. He was still struggling to get air back into his lungs and looked like he was going to pass out again. Ish waited for his distress to begin to ease before he continued.

"As I was saying before you interrupted, we have tried you in absentia and found you guilty of war crimes. This is your sentencing hearing, and the sentence is death."

Stanwick began laughing hysterically, which didn't help his breathing efforts, but it seemed he couldn't stop himself.

"Let me get this straight. You fucking assholes are deeming to pass judgment on me?! Under what authority?"

"Under the authority that we are moral human beings and that to allow what you did to go unpunished would be the same as committing the crime ourselves."

Stanwick looked around him as though he was just realizing the direness of his position. He looked at the walls of the cliff and at the darkness that encircled them. You could tell by the look on his face that he finally understood that no one would be coming to rescue him.

"Alright, alright," he said slowly. "I confess. Yes. I did rape and kill that girl. And yes, I did rape—and in some cases kill—several others. You have every right to want to bring me to justice. Give me a pen and paper, and I'll write out the confession right here, and you can deliver me to the MPs for a proper trial."

Ish shook his head. "It's too late for that, Stanwick. Why do you think we're out here in the middle of the night, risking our lives and our own freedom instead of having simply reported you? We know how the army works. We knew that the chances of charges even being brought against you were slim to none. And our military careers would probably have come to an abrupt end, adding insult to injury. No, we needed to do this ourselves. It was the only option."

"So, you're just going to shoot me like a dog in the street and leave my body out here in the middle of the fucking desert?" His voiced was on the edge of full-scale panic.

"You know," said Ish, "even though it's better than you actually deserve, that was our first thought. However, after careful consideration, we came up with a much more just way to deal with this situation."

Stanwick's already pale face blanched two shades whiter as his lips began to tremble from the fear of what those words might mean.

"Listen, chief," said Stanwick, his eyes pleading. "Let's not make any rash decisions. You and I are friends. Drinking buddies! I understand that some of the things I did were unacceptable, but let's let the authorities handle this! Whatever you're planning, don't do it!"

Ish ignored him and looked at his watch. It was almost time. A whistle from Jag confirmed it.

"Touchdown in two!" yelled Jag from his lookout post as he began walking back to them.

"What the hell does that mean?" asked Stanwick, his head swiveling back and forth from Ish to Bird to Blade, begging for an answer.

When everyone refused to answer him, it triggered something in Stanwick. Moving at a speed that was surprising for a man still recovering from a heavy dose of drugs and alcohol, he was on his feet in a flash and headed for the darkness beyond the lights. He only got seven or eight yards before Bird and Blade grabbed him and dragged him back. They returned him to his knees and held him as Ish grimly stared past them, into the darkness.

Like phantoms materializing out of thin air, the village elder, along with four other Afghani men, suddenly appeared.

Ish walked over to greet them. "As-salaam alaikum," he said, his right hand over his heart as he nodded at each man.

"What the fuck is this?" asked Stanwick. "What the hell are they doing here?"

Ish walked back over to stand before him. "You have committed crimes against more people than I want to think about. Unfortunately, we can't have every one of the victims represented here. So, we decided to settle on inviting the family of your most recent victim. Or, at least, the most recent victim that we're aware of."

"Inviting witnesses. What a nice formality," said Stanwick, his voice heavy with sarcasm.

"They're not really witnesses," replied Ish. "These men will actually be the ones dispensing your punishment." He nodded curtly at Jag, Blade and Bird, who began walking back to the truck as the Afghani men moved in.

"Wait," said Stanwick. "You're not—you're not giving me over to these fuckers, are you?"

"Your latest crime was against this man's family," said Ish. "Who could be better qualified for deciding on your punishment?

"What are they going to do?" asked Stanwick.

Ish stopped and turned to face him. "I don't know," he said, "but I would expect it to involve a lot of pain and take a long, long time."

"God damn it, I order you to—" began Stanwick before one of the village men struck him in the back of the head with the butt of a rifle, knocking him unconscious. Two others grabbed him and dragged him off into the darkness. Ish heard a horse snort and now understood how they were able to travel so silently.

The elder turned to him and gave a slight nod. Ish felt he should say something, but he didn't know what, so he simply returned the nod and joined his men at the truck.

Bird was standing guard and looking somewhat concerned.

"What exactly do you think they're going to do to him?" he asked.

"I don't know," said Ish, "but it can't be any worse than what I would have done."

Without another word the four men mounted up, turned the truck around and headed back to the base. The next day Stanwick was reported missing, and a DUSTWUN (Duty Status Whereabouts Unknown) was issued. Soldiers from all over the region began an intensive search that lasted several weeks. Not surprisingly, no trace of Stanwick was ever found.

Chapter 11

The announcement was made that the passengers were free to release their seatbelts, but Ish didn't move. He was almost oblivious to the activity all around him. People were grabbing bags from the overhead compartment, trying to quiet crying babies, bumping into each other as they jockeyed for a position closer to the door. They were anxious to leave, so ready to get on with their lives. But Ish knew there was only darkness waiting for him, and he was in no hurry. Besides, he was sitting in a window seat and wasn't in anyone's way. So, he waited, putting off the inevitable for as long as possible.

When there were only a few passengers left on the plane and he still had not moved, he noticed two flight attendants whispering and pointing in his direction. He was wearing dark shades and a camouflage jacket, both of which he had worn the entire flight. In this post-9/11 age, it was a look that had the potential to be intimidating, especially on a passenger who looked like he could have been Middle Eastern and didn't seem to want to leave his seat.

Ish finally unbuckled his seatbelt, grabbed his bag and wordlessly left the plane under the watchful eye of three stewardesses and a lone man still sitting in the back of the plane, who Ish was sure must be an air marshal.

He didn't have any checked luggage, so he was able to bypass baggage claim. As he walked out of the terminal, he paused for a moment to look up at the sky. It was a beautiful Southern California spring day. The sun here was warm and embracing as opposed to the

Afghan sun, which always felt mean and abusive. But inviting as it was, it did little to lighten the gray and blue that blanketed his soul.

He jumped in the back of a cab and gave the driver his Newport Beach address. He really didn't want to go there. Now that Sumatra was gone and Layla was locked away, he didn't know how he would be able to stand moving around in that house for the next few days, let alone sleeping in it. But there were things that needed to be taken care of. He had already made arrangements to have a moving company meet him there the next day, complete with packers to box everything up. But there were certain items that he could not entrust to them. In addition to weapons and ammo, there were some precious sentimental pieces, like a ceramic bear that Sumatra had once made for him for his birthday.

He pulled his phone out of his pocket and speed-dialed a number. "Hi Carol, it's Ishmael Carter. I'm fine and yourself? Great. I just touched down and I'm on my way to the house. Yes. Right. I'll be there all day tomorrow with the movers, so feel free to bring the paperwork by at your convenience. Tell the buyers that they can take possession a few days early if they like. Right. By Monday afternoon I expect to be completely cleared out. The cleaning team is coming Tuesday. I'll have my copy of the keys dropped off at your office Wednesday morning and you're free to turn them over to the buyer whenever you like. You too, take care."

Selling the house felt like a crime. So much of his life he had dreamed of living in a house exactly like this one. It had become a symbol of his success and validation that some of his dreams were finally coming true. But what are you supposed to do when the manifestation of your dreams has become the scene of your nightmares?

* * *

Ish stood at the front door of the house and watched the moving truck drive away. All of his belongings as well as Layla's and Sumatra's were now on their way to a rented storage space until he could decide where he was going to settle. It probably wouldn't be Newport Beach. The grief he now associated with this city was too heavy to bear. And it probably wouldn't be Redondo either, even though his mother and aunties all lived there in the houses he had bought them. He needed more distance than that. He didn't want to be anywhere near the ocean for the foreseeable future.

He had already made long-term reservations at a hotel in L.A. It was a beautiful building, and he had secured a room on the 34th floor. The altitude was important. It gave him a feeling of separation, of being slightly removed from the horror that he faced every day he woke up.

Ish threw a leather overnight bag into the back of his black Mercedes Benz and pulled out of his garage for the last time. Traveling north on the 405 from the stability of his old house to the transience of his awaiting hotel room felt symbolic. He was leaving a painful past behind him and moving towards what was an uncertain future. His dashboard indicated he had an incoming call. He tapped a button on the steering wheel to accept it.

"Hello?"

"What's going on, Ish?"

"Hey, Chad. Not much. Just finishing up at the house."

"I'm sorry, man. I know that had to hurt, as much as you loved that house."

"It was time."

"So, how's it feel to finally be a civilian again?"

"I don't know. In a way, I kind of miss it already," said Ish.

"I thought this is what you wanted?"

"Maybe. At this point, I'm not really sure whether I quit or was kicked out. Maybe both."

"What do you mean?" asked Chad.

"Nothing; it's not important," said Ish. "What's up?"

"Now that you're back in town, I thought you might want to talk about your plans for returning to work. It might even turn out to really be therapeutic for you; help keep your mind busy."

"No amount of work is going to be able to make me forget all of this."

"I'm not saying that you can forget," said Chad. "I just think that working a few hours a day might at least give you a daily break from thinking about it."

"Are you shorthanded?" asked Ish.

"Not really," said Chad. "But you know there's always more than enough work. And we still have to finish up that code for the JPL project."

"I thought you were handling that?"

"I am. But it's your specialty. You could get it done in a third of the time it takes me."

Ish felt frustrated but tried to hide it. He didn't want to offend his friend. "Okay, I'll tell you what, I'll swing by the day after tomorrow. How's that?"

"Beautiful," said Chad. "I know it feels like I'm pestering you to return before you're ready, but I think once you get back here and have something else to wrap your mind around, things won't seem so bleak."

"You're probably right. See you in a couple days," said Ish as he hung up. But his words didn't match his feelings. The only thing he really wanted to wrap his mind around right now was caramel-colored, came in an expensive bottle and wasn't sold to people under the age of twenty-one. He changed course and headed toward his favorite liquor store. It was in West Hollywood and was one of the few places that sold the brand of alcohol he preferred. He hoped they were stocked up.

Safely back in his hotel room, a box of *Camas* bottles resting on the dresser, Ish leaned back on the bed, drink in hand, and tried to get comfortable. But he couldn't. He felt jumpy and exposed. He was never much of a whiskey drinker before he went into the service. But early on, during his first tour of duty, they had stormed a house and came across a stash of top-shelf scotch. He couldn't even remember the name of it. He just remembered that it helped calm his frayed nerves; that it gave him a place of refuge to get away from the violence he faced every day, even if only for an hour or two. And that scared him a bit. He wasn't used to having crutches in his life. Especially when he felt that he was so physically prepared for this particular adventure. But seeing it up close and personal was another story.

When you watch war movies, even the most violent, modern war movies, you only see so much. Even when a film shows an arm blown off or a leg missing, you don't get the full impact of what that truly represents until you witness it in person. Most war films fail to capture the clouds of flies and mounds of maggots that plague your every move, or how the blood of the dead and wounded mixes with the soil to form a brick-colored mud. Films don't show how, as you walk through that mud day in and day out, it leaves a dark-red stain along the edge of your boots, like the ring left in a filthy tub that someone had just used to wash away the vilest of sins.

Movies are also quite poor at imparting the odors of war. People who are dying tend to involuntarily lose control of their bladders and bowels. Mixed in with the acrid stench of gun powder and burning fuel was the unmistakable smell of piss and shit. Men who were writhing in agony while being attended to by medics who were desperately trying to save their lives had the added insult of having to wallow in their own waste. Thankfully, most were in too much pain to feel any shame. But the images burned themselves into Ish's psyche. And the drink helped him cope with the things that the army didn't prepare him to cope with.

It was 6:00am before he finally stopped drinking and fell asleep. Most of the next day was a daze. On the third day, the phone calls began. Most were from Chad, and they came like clockwork every two hours. He no doubt was concerned that Ish hadn't yet appeared at the office as promised and was worried about his wellbeing. But Ish refused to answer. He refused to even listen to the voice messages or read the texts. He knew that Chad would be trying to talk him into leaving the solitude of his hotel room. Maybe just to meet for lunch. Or coffee. Or a drink. Drinking was definitely on the agenda, but right now he wanted to do that alone.

The next several days were a blur—a blur of single malt scotch, nightmares and the occasional room service meal. Ish noticed that the box of bottles was almost empty. He would need to make a liquor run soon. But not quite yet. He poured himself another drink from the last remaining bottle and flicked on the TV.

He started flipping through the news channels. There was a story about Marion Bristol, an unarmed eighteen-year-old African American shot to death by a police officer in Missouri. On another channel was a story about Jamal Houston, another unarmed black teenager who was killed by a cop in Illinois. He kept flipping. There was a piece on Fred Gregory, then another on William Sullivan—two more unarmed black men killed by cops. There was a football game, a show about the state of the stock market and some kind of reality dating show, but Ish keep flipping back to the channels detailing how young black men were an endangered group in America.

Houston. Gregory. Sullivan. Houston. Bristol. Gregory. Eventually, it became one endless stream of death, smiling prom pictures and video footage of grieving family members. Finally, Ish stood up on shaky legs, howled and threw his tumbler at the screen with all his might. Sparks shot out the back of the TV as the glass from the shattered LCD blanketed the carpet in front of it.

When he woke up the next morning, the day felt different. Somehow both brighter and darker at the same time. As he looked around the room, he knew it was time to get his shit together. As housekeeping was cleaning up the glass, he went to the front desk and paid for the TV. He told them not to replace it while he was still using the room; just in case. He had the valet pull his car around to the front of the hotel. Instead of driving to the liquor store, he headed in the other direction. It was time to go see Chad.

Chapter 12

On the long, slow drive to Santa Monica, Ish reflected on a memory he had of the beginning of this path. The music had the entire house rattling to the beat. There was a sea of people, many of which he didn't even recognize, dancing, drinking, eating and smoking. Some were getting more familiar with each other than he felt particularly comfortable with, especially since they were doing it on his new furniture.

He, Layla and Sumatra had moved into the Newport Beach 'mini-mansion' 8 months prior but had delayed the housewarming party until tonight. Most of their time since the purchase had been spent working with decorators, architects and contractors getting the place exactly the way they wanted it. Layla had borne the brunt of it, spending a lot of time trying to choose amongst a sea of fabric swatches and tile samples, while Ish and Chad worked on getting the new offices of their software company, Macrolox, up and running.

Also adding to the delay of their celebration of the new house was a massive amount of partying. Ish hardly had any time for partying in college, and for the first four years after they opened the doors of Macrolox, he and Chad were too busy working to party.

But now they had built a staff of highly qualified professionals and were finally expanding into the kind of luxurious offices a company like theirs deserved. He and Chad were finally able to breathe, dialing their normal 80-hour weeks back to a reasonable 50. He suddenly realized that it was time to take a moment to enjoy some of the fruits of his labor; to see what he had been missing. Not only did he have more money than he had ever dreamed of, he probably had more money than anyone he knew had ever dreamed of. The first few weekends after he and Chad had closed escrow on the new office building were pure madness. They'd leave Sumatra with Ish's mother, and the three of them, plus whatever pretty young thing Chad happened to be seeing that month, would proceed to drop money at clubs all over So Cal and Vegas. But soon Ish and Layla realized that not even the dopest club could take the place of time spent with their daughter, and they gracefully bowed out and left Chad to party on in their stead.

When Chad found him this particular night, Ish was sitting in the back yard off in a corner by himself. He was staring absently at the pool full of beautiful people laughing and screaming just a few yards away.

"You alright, dude?"

"Yeah," said Ish, snapping out of his daze. "I'm just relaxing for a minute."

"Man, this party is ridiculous! Look at all these honeys!" said Chad, grinning in appreciation. "Oh, by the way, I meant to tell you. I got a call just before I got here. The new servers were installed this morning, and everything has been tested and is rock solid. We're golden."

"That's good news," said Ish. "That makes it a little easier to say this. I've been thinking about taking some time off. Do you think you can run the office by yourself for a while?"

"Ummm, yeah, sure. You and Layla want to get out of town for a couple of weeks or something?"

"Not exactly. I just enlisted. In the army."

Chad froze, his beer halfway to his mouth, a shocked and confused look on his face. Then he erupted into laughter and chased the sound with the gurgle of a long pull from his bottle of Guinness. Ish could tell by the bright shine in his eyes that he was a little bit tipsy.

"You're funny, man."

"No, I'm serious."

"Dude, you have a major fucking contract with the Department of Defense. You're kind of already in the army."

"It's not the same. I want to do something more significant. Look at all this," said Ish, waving his hand in the direction of his pool and house. "I live in a country where all this is possible for someone like me. We recently elected the first black president of the United States.

Yeah, we got Osama Bin Laden, but there are still others like him out there, plotting on destroying us. I feel that I need to be out there defending our country and our way of life. It feels selfish to do anything less. Besides, with my language background and, as they say, 'ambiguous racial profile', I'm a natural choice for duty in the Middle East. The recruiter almost started drooling, watching me sign the enlistment form."

Chad looked dumbfounded. He shook his head back and forth in disbelief. "Have you told Layla?"

"Not yet," said Ish, sighing heavily.

"When are you planning to do it?"

"Tonight."

"You know what," said Chad, taking another long, lazy swallow of beer, "I can't talk to you about this right now. It's already killing my buzz. Plus, I don't want to be anywhere in the vicinity when you break the news to Layla, because when she blows up, you're going to feel like you were already in the army, dodging artillery fire or some shit. I'll catch you later, dude." They bumped fists and Chad stomped off, swaying slightly, just as Layla walked up.

"What's that all about?" she asked.

Ish looked up at her from his chair and was mesmerized. She was wearing a white linen casual top with matching pants that was just tight enough to be sexy but loose enough to be comfortable. As usual, she wore no makeup other than a bit of lip gloss, but her skin glowed. Her hair, which she had been growing out a bit lately, was long and wavy, cascading around her shoulders. The light from the pool backlit her head, creating a halo effect. As he had so many times before, he couldn't help thinking how much she looked like an angel.

"It's complicated," he said. "This isn't the place to talk about it. Maybe we should go upstairs, where we can be alone."

Concern clouded her face. "Ish, we have a house full of people and a party to host. What is this all about?"

He could hear the stress in her voice already, and he hadn't even said anything. But she knew him better than anyone, with the exception of his mother and maybe Chad. And he knew that she could tell that whatever he wanted to talk to her about was going to be something serious. Several times in the last few months, when they were lying in bed together in the dark listening to the quiet, she had told him of this fear that she had that things were too good, her life was too perfect, and that certainly disaster and tragedy was just around the corner. It shocked him the first time he heard this, because it was so out of character for her.

Layla had always been a glass-half-full girl, a shining example of resilience and optimism. Nothing ever really appeared to bother her. Whether it was her getting laid off from her third job or finding out that she might have breast cancer (which turned out to be a false alarm), she always smiled and bore it, with an 'and this too shall pass' attitude. But the good fortune of the government contract and the possibility of never having to worry about money ever again seemed to overwhelm her senses. It was like she had suddenly discovered a unicorn and wasn't sure whether it was friendly or some vicious, rabid beast just waiting for her to get close enough to pounce.

"You're right," he said, standing and wrapping his arms around her. "We do have a party to host. It's nothing that can't wait till tomorrow. How about we invite my mother over for lunch and we can all chat then?" He kissed her softly near her ear.

"Okay," she said hesitantly as they began to walk back into the house. She was clearly still concerned but was willing to put her concerns on hold for at least a few hours. He hoped she could maintain that patience until he could get his mother there so that he could tell them both together.

* * *

Ish made them lunch—grilled ground lamb burgers and vegetable kabobs with homemade pineapple salsa and blue corn chips. Layla had been sulking around all morning, which was completely unlike her. He knew that she was trying her best to not confront him about whatever it was he needed to tell her, but it was obviously eating at her.

Ish's mother came over while he was still cooking and spent an hour playing with Sumatra. She was almost four years old now and loved nothing more than hanging out with Grandma, talking her ear off or playing hide-and-seek.

Ish set the table, got Sumatra situated and made sure everyone had everything they needed before he made his own plate and sat down. Layla was picking at her food, and his mother picked up on the tension.

"So, what's going on, son?"

"Mama, I've been thinking a lot lately, about everything, and I decided to enlist in the army." Layla's fork fell out of her hand, bounced off her plate and tumbled to the floor. She didn't try to pick it up. She stared at Ish, mouth agape.

"What did you just say?"

"I joined the army," he said, his voice steady.

"Are you out of your fu—" she began, then glanced at Sumatra and Ish's mom. "Are you out of your mind?" she demanded.

"I know this is a shock, but I feel it's the right thing to do."

"Ish!" she said, exasperated. "I don't even know where to begin." She shook her head in wonder.

"Ishmael, why are you doing this?" asked his mother.

"Things are changing, Mama. We finally have a black president of the United States. I have the perfect life. And there are people out there that would like to take it all away. I don't feel right letting others fight that battle alone."

"What brought this on? Where did this idea even come from?" she asked.

"I guess I first started thinking about it a couple of months ago. Do you remember Evan? Used to live over on Glasper Street?"

"You mean Miss Oliver's boy?"

"Yeah. He came home. He did two tours in Afghanistan. Had both legs and an arm blown off."

"That's right. I think my sister was telling me something about that."

"I heard through the grapevine that he was in an assisted living facility in Sherman Oaks. I went to see him and I was surprised at how emotional I was. Evan and I were always cool, and we hung out from time to time, but we were never really close. But seeing him in that wheelchair, with the look of death in his eyes, saddened me and pissed me off all at the same time. There are people out there that would like to see us all in that condition—blown to hell. Or worse. People that want to fly more planes into more buildings. I can't stick my head in the sand and hope that someone stops them before their violence gets to me and mine. The fact that I've found a way to financial success shouldn't mean that I don't have an obligation to help defend this country and the great things that it represents."

"Son," said his mother, her voice calm and steady, "everyone has a job to do in this world. A role in the greater scheme of this reality. No man—or woman—can be everything. You're a fighter; you always have been. But you're not a soldier."

"I can be a soldier."

"I didn't say that you couldn't be a soldier. I said that you're not a soldier. That's not your role in this reality. As I said, you've always been a fighter. You were always that person that stood up for the underdog, against all odds. So, I understand your desire to join this particular fight for justice, but you're already performing that role with the creation of this encryption program of yours."

"It's not the same," said Ish. "It's about standing beside those on the front line. It's about honor. That's something that you instilled in me when I was a kid, and it's been ever present in my life."

"I did teach you to value honor, but there's a thin line between honor and martyrdom. And you have too many responsibilities to be a martyr."

"I'm fully aware of my responsibilities, Mama. But I have money now—enough money to take care of everything that needs to be taken care of."

"Yes, you do have a lot of money now. But even with all that money, being a martyr is the one thing that you still can't afford."

Ish didn't immediately reply. He sat back in his chair and stared into the distance, eyes unfocused. He didn't know what to say to his mother to make her understand, and he was bracing for the tornado of rage that he knew must be brewing within Layla, who was intently watching them.

"Thank you for the meal," said his mother as she pushed her chair back from the table. "I'm suddenly not very hungry. I suspect that you and Layla have some things to discuss. If you like, I can take Sumatra with me for a few hours."

"That's not—" began Ish.

"That would be great," said Layla quickly, cutting him off. "Just give me a couple of minutes to get her stuff together." She got up and walked out of the room.

"Ishmael, I know you want to handle this your own way, but if I could give you just a bit of advice?"

"Yeah?"

"When you talk to her, don't just talk. Listen. And not just with your head, but with your heart as well. Recognize that overnight you have turned what was a dream life for her into a sort of nightmare. Understand that she's hurting. And that while she's going to try to talk you out of this, she knows you well enough to know that you've already made up your mind. And that means she's not just in pain, she's also in mourning."

"Mourning? Mama, just because I'm joining the army doesn't mean I'm never coming back. Most American soldiers that go into combat come back alive and well."

"Her mourning isn't over the idea that she might lose you. Her mourning is over the fact that she's already lost what, for her, was a perfect life. You've taken her paradise and replaced it with uncertainty. I hope that she can one day learn to forgive you."

* * *

"Well?" said Layla, after she and Ish had walked his mother to the door and watched her drive off with Sumatra.

"I know you're upset—"

"Ish, how can you do this?! Our life is here! Your daughter, not even four years old yet, is here! How can you just abandon us to run off and get yourself killed?"

"Haven't you heard anything I've said? You're right. Our life is here. And I have an obligation to go fight for that life."

"Why do you think you have any obligations to fight for this country? Are you forgetting this is the same country that brought your ancestors here as slaves in the first place? Are you forgetting that even after all this time, we still, to this day, have a race problem here in this country?"

"Things are changing, Layla. We need to keep an open enough mind to change with them."

"Things are changing? Why, because you have money now? Because, as you keep mentioning, we finally have a black president?

Do you honestly believe that just because there is a black man in the White House, you're no longer a nigga in this country? They consider him a nigga, too. Don't get it twisted, Ish. Things have not changed as much as you wish they had."

Ish sighed. "I don't know that I'm ever going to be able to get you to understand this. And I know I won't ever get your blessing on this. But I hope that one day you will at least find a way to forgive me."

"So, what are we supposed to do while you're gone, Ish? Are we supposed to stay here, on 'death watch', waiting for you to either come back in a body bag or minus some major body parts, like your friend? What the fuck am I supposed to tell your daughter when she asks why you did this?"

Ish bowed his head. His heart was hurting. What Layla didn't know, and what he couldn't really explain to her, was that the ache in his heart started the day he made the decision to enlist. Leaving his family for the army was not what he wanted to do. But it was what he felt he needed to do. His father had always told him that the definition of a man was someone who not only knew the difference but heeded to it.

"If something were to happen to me, I would hope that what you would tell her is that her father was a man of honor and conviction. That, at heart, he was a good man who always followed his conscience and did what he thought was right, regardless of the consequences. That's how I've always lived my life, Layla. And that's the legacy that I hope to leave to my daughter, regardless of the outcome of my service to this country. Leaving her money and property and stocks and bonds doesn't mean shit compared to teaching her how to be a human being governed by honor and courage."

For a moment they just stared at each other, then Layla fell into his arms and began sobbing. For a long time, they simply held each other and cried together. No more words were necessary.

* * *

Ish arrived at the Macrolox office early, before anyone else. He walked around, examining the cubicles, touching the wall paper, smelling the newly laid carpet. He could see how the average person might view this as a dream come true. But as fantastic as it was, it wasn't what he had ever dreamed about. He never thought that he would ever accomplish something like this. Nor did he think that he couldn't accomplish it. He never really thought much at all about what he would be doing the rest of his life, post-college.

Ten years ago, if someone had pushed him, as his mother sometimes did, to give an answer for what his life would look like in ten years' time, he would have said that he'd probably be working in IT for some Fortune 500 company. Never would he have guessed that he'd actually be writing code for his own company. The issue was that money had never really motivated him. Both his parents had taught him a healthy respect for it, and after his father passed, it was frequently in short supply, but he was never 'turned on' by it. He thought of money as simply a tool. It was necessary in certain situations and to accomplish certain tasks, but it was never the holy grail of all existence.

"Hey, dude." Ish jumped, startled out of his reverie. It was Chad.

"What's up, man."

"What are you doing?"

"Just taking it all in, I guess."

"I tried to call you yesterday."

"Yeah, I saw. Sorry. Layla and I were having a moment."

Chad nodded his head. "So. You ready to maybe tell me what's going on?"

Ish chuckled. "What's funny?" asked Chad.

"Sorry. It's just that this feels like déjà vu. I've had this conversation with Layla and my mother several times now and I feel like the scene just keeps getting rewound and replayed."

"I wish I could have been there for one of the original performances, but unfortunately, I wasn't. And since we're supposed to be partners in all this, I'm going to have to ask you to repeat it again."

"Okay. Long story short. I feel like I need to contribute something more to our country, so I decided to join the army and do my part on the battlefield."

"Is this about Evan?"

"Not really."

"What do you mean 'not really'? Ish, ever since I've known you, you've been taking on other people's problems, fighting other people's fights. We're creating something grand here. Something remarkable! This is your company! I need you here to help run it."

"It's our company, Chad."

"But it was your work that was the genesis. Your program is what got us here. I can't do this without you."

"Yes, you can. You have to. And it's not going to be permanent. I'll be back in a couple years, and I'll be checking in as regularly as I can. In the meantime, you can have my salary. I have enough cash in the bank to easily take care of Layla and Sumatra while I'm gone. They won't want for anything."

Chad shook his head in disbelief. "I just don't understand, Ish. What do you think you can do in combat that's going to eclipse what we're doing here at Macrolox? You want to go into the field and fight terrorist one at a time when our encryption protocol is fighting terrorism on a worldwide scale. It doesn't make any sense!"

"I'm sorry, man. I wish I could make you understand, but I can't. At least, not right now. I've got two months before I ship out. I'll be here every day until then, helping you as much as I can. We've got a great team, Chad. We spent a lot of time carefully hiring them all. That said, this should be a piece of cake. If you run into any issues while I'm gone, brief me when I call in and I'll give you whatever help I can."

Chad just stared at him, his face etched with concern.

"Come on," said Ish, slapping him gently on the arm, "I'll brew us up a pot of the dark stuff. I've got a lot to get done today." Ish walked toward the kitchen, leaving Chad gazing at the floor in astonishment.

Chapter 13

When Ish walked into the office, Chad was leaning over the computer screen of one of their programmers, a black male, twenty-five-ish, sporting a goatee, large diamond-like earrings and a hoodie. As Ish walked up to them he couldn't help but feel a compassion for the young man, and the danger he, perhaps unwittingly, faced on a daily basis as he traversed the streets of L.A., dressed as he was. Most people casually observing him would never guess that he was an extremely bright rising star in the tech world or that he earned over $100,000 a year working for Macrolox. Many would see him simply as a potential criminal; a threat to be assessed and, at the very least, kept under a watchful eye.

Ish knew this firsthand, the same way virtually all black men in America knew it. He had grown up under the oppression of constant suspicion. He often carried a leather messenger bag, but he knew that if he was going into a store and didn't want to risk a confrontation, it was always safer to just leave it in the trunk.

The people who would have asked him to leave his bag at the counter on his way in, or who would have relentlessly followed him around the store as he browsed, would never have stopped to consider the possibility that he might actually be wealthy. The fact that he was a multi-millionaire was not something they would have found easy to believe, even if he had shown them his bank balance. And most of those who would have been convinced would have assumed the money came from drug sales or some other illegal enterprise.

Ish patted both men on the back as he walked up, interrupting their conversation. "Ish!" said Chad, surprised to see him. Chad tried to smile, but Ish had known him long enough to know that it was forced. He was clearly concerned and irritated that, even though Ish had been back from Afghanistan for almost a week, he had not heard from him, despite what must have been at least thirty attempts to reach him by phone.

"Mr. Carter, good to have you back!" said the programmer. His name was Rayquon Denson. Ish and Chad had always told everyone at the company to address all personnel by their first names, but some people had so much reverence for the company leaders that they ignored that directive. Rayquon had come in as an intern, working closely with Ish for the two months before Ish deployed. He felt that he owed Ish a huge debt for supporting him, training him and eventually giving him a job. But the truth was that by the time he came to Macrolox, he was already a brilliant programmer. Ish had helped smooth out some of his rough edges, but the guy was destined for greatness no matter where he went. Ish and Chad had always considered it a blessing that they were able to swoop him up before one of the other tech companies did. Ish was glad to see he was still here four years later.

After a minute or two of exchanging pleasantries with Rayquon and a couple of the other people in the office, Ish excused himself, and he and Chad retreated to the War Room.

The War Room was a secure conference room they had specially designed for private meetings and where all delicate matters were discussed. It was located at the far end of the building behind two steel reinforced doors that required both a handprint and retina scan for entry. Not only was it windowless and completely soundproof, it housed state-of-the-art technology to guard against all known types of both conventional and radar-based eavesdropping devices. In addition, it was also swept for electronic bugs at least once a week.

This type of security might raise eyebrows or create undue curiosity in most businesses, but everyone who worked for Macrolox knew that the company's maiden success was a contract supplying the Department of Defense with super-encryption data software. They were in the business of keeping secrets, and being a DoD contractor meant that they could not afford to take any chances or allow any lapses in security. To some, this might have felt like overkill, but corporate and political espionage was much more common than most people ever realized.

Once he had locked the door behind them, Ish turned to face his friend. Chad sat on the edge of a table with his arms crossed. He looked like a pouting child.

"Dude, where the hell have you been? You were supposed to be here four days ago!"

Ish took a deep breath, grabbed a chair and sat down. "Is there any fresh coffee?" he asked, a slight smile spreading across his face. Chad nodded at the machine, and Ish rose and fixed himself a cup while Chad watched in silence.

"Look," said Ish as he sat back down and took a sip, "I apologize. I'm sorry. I know you were only trying to help. But I'm going through a rough time right now, and you wouldn't have wanted to be around me the last couple of days. Trust me on that." He took another sip of the dark-brown liquid and could already feel the caffeine coursing through his system, reversing some of the effects of the binge.

"Don't worry about it," said Chad, his voice losing most of its edge. "I understand. I mean, I can't really imagine what's it's like for you, because I've never been there, but I know loss is hard. I just want you to know that I'm here for you."

Ish nodded his head. "Thanks, man."

"So!" said Chad, clapping once and rubbing his hands together like an evil villain from an old silent movie. "You're all coffee'd up, got the java buzz happening; are you ready to get to work?"

"Well," said Ish. "Yes and no."

Chad leaned forward from his position against the edge of the table, his face now deadpan. "What do you mean 'yes and no'?"

"I need another two weeks or so."

Chad sighed and dropped his head in exasperation.

"I know, dude," said Ish. "I know you need the help, but I just need a few more days to take care of me. I spoke to Layla the other day and it didn't go well. I'm wired, and I'd like to get away for a few days and decompress. Maybe I'll go to Catalina, disconnect from the grid and give my system a chance to recharge. Maybe do some fishing."

"You're right, man," said Chad. "I'm being selfish. Do what you need to do. We'll hold the fort down till you get back." Both men rose and embraced warmly.

Back in his car, Ish started the engine but didn't put the car into gear. He sat gazing into the distance, thinking about whether or not Catalina was really where he wanted to go. The isolation might be good for him. But then again it might just increase the sense of void that he was feeling; the sensation that he was drifting through space, like an astronaut whose tether had suddenly snapped.

Ish chuckled to himself. It was hard to believe that he had become such an introspective, sentimental guy. He was a completely different person eight years ago—the classic 'strong, silent' type; stoic, resolved and unflappable. But the birth of Sumatra had changed everything. His connection to her connected him to the rest of the world. Once she was born, he was no longer an "I". He was now an "Us", and the "Us" included not only Sumatra and Layla, but all of humanity.

Of course, Layla was where it all began, but he was always aware of the differences between his love for his wife and his love for his daughter. Being with Layla was like finding the only other puzzle piece in the world that fit his puzzle piece. He adored her for everything that she was, from the top of her head down to the bottom of her feet. But for all the closeness that he felt to her, they were still two individuals, with separate histories and bloodlines. Having a child with her changed his entire universe.

Before his daughter was born, he only saw the light of the sun. With Sumatra's arrival, he also felt its warmth. He had always been a compassionate person, always quick to help others, even at the risk of putting himself in peril, but he still always felt like an outsider. No one would have ever guessed that by looking at him. He was captain of the football team, loved by all his teachers and the object of more female crushes than he could ever keep track of, yet he still always felt different.

But Sumatra was the catalyst that altered all of that. She fulfilled something inside of him that he never even knew was missing. Sometimes he would sit in the recliner in her room at night with the lights out and just watch her sleep. Sometimes in those quiet moments in the dark, he would silently weep from the love that he felt for her, though he never let Layla or Sumatra see it.

Yes, after Sumatra's birth he was unequivocally different. It was as though she, through the alchemy of love, had rearranged all his molecules from the inside out. He looked the same and he talked the same, but he was not the same. Layla recognized it, and so did his mother. But now his daughter was gone, and where did that leave him? Would he simply revert back to—

The phone rang, startling him and breaking his reverie. The volume on the stereo was turned up, and the ringtone filled the car with sound. Ish pressed the 'answer' button without even thinking to look to see who it was that was calling.

"Hello?" he said.

"What's up, Big Man?" asked a cheerful voice.

"Blade! What's going on, little brother?"

"Not a whole lot. Just checking in to see what kind of trouble you're getting yourself into," said Blade in his normal jovial, fully-amped style.

Blade was the most positive, silver-lining-finding black man that Ish had ever met. And even though he was barely 135 pounds soaking wet, he was also, pound-for-pound, one of the toughest. Ish would never forget the time they were interviewing some locals in a tiny village back in Afghanistan. One of the residents in the home, a huge, hulking guy, was looking antsy, and Ish was trying to keep a tab on him out of the corner of his eye while at the same time trying to concentrate on the person they were conversing with. A kid burst into the room with some kind of bundle in his arms, and when they all turned and drew down on him, the antsy guy made a run for it. Blade immediately gave chase.

Ish and the rest of the guys quickly followed, but lost them through the maze of buildings and had to backtrack. By the time they finally caught up with the two of them, Blade had found his weapon jammed and they'd had a ten-minute mano-a-mano fisticuffs brawl. Blade was less than half the guy's size, and he wore the evidence of that with a broken nose, swollen jaw and an eye that was already almost completely closed. But the guy he chased ended up with two severely broken arms and a mouthful of broken teeth. He should have said a prayer to Allah that the small black man had chosen not to pull one of the several knives he always kept on him. After all, he didn't get his nickname from his boxing skills. But whether armed or unarmed, Blade was like a small nuclear bomb—a tiny package that was always dangerous and capable of causing mass destruction. And he'd smile at you the entire time.

"I was just sitting here, thinking about Layla," said Ish. "I'm just trying to clear my head a little; figure out what the hell is going on with her."

"I can tell by your voice that whatever it is, it isn't good", said Blade. "Is there anything I can do? You know my cousin has some political clout with the prison systems out there."

"I appreciate it, brother, but what she's dealing with is internal. No politician can help her right now. What are you up to? I heard you had touched down. Where are you camping these days?"

"I'm in Baltimore for a minute, visiting my sister. Of course, I know you've heard what's going on down here. Man, it's crazy! Every night the streets are filled with people protesting, marching, holding rallies. I've never seen anything like it. You'd think this was the first time an unarmed Negro had been shot by police! Like we don't know that's almost a sport here in Baltimore! But I guess this was the last straw. People just ain't having it no more."

"You out there, too?" asked Ish.

"What, marching? I've walked around and checked it out, but that's not really my bag. Plus, I'm trying to get settled and find a job and whatnot, you know. So, what are your plans for the immediate future, Mr. Millionaire?" asked Blade, laughing.

"You know, I need to get back to work myself. But this thing with Layla has me so stressed out right now, I'm just struggling to keep my sanity."

"I can believe it. And I heard about that discharge bullshit. Fuck them; it was time for you to move on anyway. Have you heard from Bird or Jag?"

"They left a couple of messages, but I'm sure they're busy adjusting to their new lives. I'll catch up with them soon," said Ish.

"Well, now that you've got some time, you need to get in a little R&R yourself before you get too busy again," said Blade. "Hey, I've got a great idea! Why don't you come to Maryland and kick it with me for a few days? My fam would love to meet you, after all I've told them about you. And my sister is a bomb cook! Some soul food, some good drinks, clear your head. It'll be good for you, man."

"You know what? That might be just the ticket," said Ish. "You're right, I really need to get the hell out of this city for a minute. I'll tell you what, I'll tie up some business here and try to get there by Thursday evening. Cool?"

"Perfect! Let me know when you touch down, and I'll scoop you up."

"Cool. See you then," said Ish.

Chapter 14

The silver Mercedes inched forward, slowly moving through the throng of protesters that had flooded the streets. Ish looked at his watch and Blade started tapping out a nervous rhythm on the steering wheel, craning his neck back and forth, looking for some sign of an opening in the crowd.

"Wow, I'm really sorry, man," said Blade. "Something told me we should have left earlier. I knew the streets were going to be a mess, but I never imagined it would be this bad."

"Don't worry about it, brother. We'll get there," said Ish, leaning back in his seat. "I'm just glad I got to chill with you and your people for a couple of days. You were right. Your sister is a bomb cook! Thank you again. This was exactly what I needed."

"You know you're welcome anytime, man. My sister loves feeding people that love to eat!" said Blade, laughing. But his face quickly got serious again as he stared through the windshield, his frustration showing.

"If I could just get past these next couple of blocks, I think it'd be pretty smooth sailing," he said. Suddenly he saw an opportunity. A lull in the crowd had created a clear path to a side street. Blade spun the wheel and revved the car forward, almost hitting two teens who tried to kick the car as it drove by.

"Here we go!" said Blade, now smiling broadly. "We should be able to run these side streets all the way to the terminal." He pulled out his phone and routed the trip on his navigation app. "It says we'll be there in twenty-two minutes, which will give you plenty of time to catch your flight."

Half an hour later, they found themselves in what appeared to be a deserted industrial area. The airport was nowhere in sight, but they could see planes flying low overhead, so they knew they were close. Blade pulled the car over to the curb, his anger written all over his face.

"Goddamn it! According to the map, we should be sitting in the airport parking lot right now. Shit! Sorry, man; let me try a different app," said Blade, stabbing at his phone with his fingers.

"Don't stress, little brother. I'm in no rush," said Ish. "If I miss the flight, it's no big deal. I'll just catch the next one." That's when he caught sight of the police cruiser in the side mirror slowly creeping up behind them. "We've got company," he said as the cop car came to a halt and turned on its red and blue flashing lights.

"I don't have time for this shit right now," said Blade, looking in the rear-view mirror, as he placed his phone on the dash.

"Just relax," said Ish.

The driver door of the police car opened and a white officer wearing the standard blue uniform and mirrored shades stepped out. He was between 5'11" and six feet, barrel-chested and with bulging biceps that strained against the short sleeves of his department-issued shirt.

Ish was looking straight ahead and couldn't see the man as he walked towards their car, but he heard the snap as the officer released the strap on the holster of his service weapon. That's when he noticed that there didn't seem to be anyone in any of the buildings on this street. There were also no cars, either at the curb or in any of the various parking lots that he could see. It appeared that they were completely alone—just Ish, Blade and the officer.

Ish was glad to see Blade put his hands on the steering wheel as the officer approached. He was probably taught at a young age the same way Ish had been. In their relatively short time together, Ish's father had always made a point of drilling into his son's mind that there were more dangers in the streets than just criminals. Yes, drug dealers and gangs and addicts were never in short supply, but he also made sure that he was fully aware of the fact that the police also posed a threat. He taught his son to respect the law but also to be wary of it. No sudden movements, turn off the radio, keep your hands in plain sight at all times; these were just a few of his father's rules for survival.

"Good afternoon, gentlemen," said the officer, stopping just short of the driver door and leaning forward to peer into the car, his right hand resting on the butt of his gun. "Nice Benz. Are you experiencing some kind of car trouble?"

"No officer," said Blade. "We're just a bit turned around and stopped for directions. We're trying to get to the airport."

"The airport? The airport is just half a mile east of here, son. Are you sure that's where you were going?"

"Um, yes, sir," said Blade, chuckling slightly, "that's where we're headed. Following this app, I don't know if we'll ever get there, but that's where we're going."

"Uh huh," said the officer. "I'll tell you what, let me see your license and registration and we'll have you back on the road in two shakes of a lamb's tail."

"No problem," said Blade as he lifted both hands off the steering wheel and then paused, with them hanging in midair. "I'm just going to reach into the glove compartment?" The officer nodded and Blade retrieved the registration.

"My license is in the wallet in my back pocket," he said to the officer, and the officer nodded again. Blade pulled his license out and handed both documents to the policeman.

"Nathaniel Bartholomew," said the officer, reading off the driver's license. "Tell me, Mr. Bartholomew, why is it that the registration says this car belongs to a Mr. Vincent Goldberg?"

"It's actually my sister's car."

"You have a sister named Vincent?"

"No," said Blade, chuckling slightly again, "my sister's name is Virginia. It's her car, it's just registered in her husband's name."

"Well, isn't that convenient. A young black man like yourself is driving a brand new $80,000 car that's registered to another man, but actually happens to belong to your sister. I'm sure that's all 100% true, but how about you both step out of the vehicle until we can get this all cleared up?" The officer stepped back away from the driver side door.

Ish calmly reached for the door handle and was about to open his door, but stopped when he realized that Blade wasn't moving.

"Officer," said Blade, taking a big breath and tightening his grip on the steering wheel, "I know you're just trying to do your job, but I'm trying to get my man here to the airport and we're already extremely late. Is there some other way we could do this? You said the airport is only half a mile away. Maybe you could follow us there so that I could let him out and then you could run the registration from there?"

"What the fuck do I look like?" asked the officer, his voicing rising. "This isn't a goddamn caravan. I told you once, and I'm not going to tell you again. Get the fuck out of the car!" He took another step back and pulled his weapon out of the holster.

"Just relax, little brother," said Ish under his breath as they both exited the vehicle.

"Put your hands on your heads and walk backwards to the trunk."

Both men silently did as they were told. Once at the trunk, the officer holstered his weapon and patted them both down. They were both facing the Mercedes with their backs to him. He emptied both their pockets, placing the contents on the trunk. Suddenly something caught his eye and he froze, grabbing Blade's keys and holding them up.

"What the hell is this?" he asked, pointing to the item that was attached to Blade's keyring.

"It's a Ranger coin," said Blade.

"I know what the fuck it is. How the fuck did you get it? Did you steal Mr. Goldberg's Ranger coin as well as his car?"

Blade turned around and looked at him, his face twisting with rage.

"He's a Ranger," said Ish. "We both are. We served together. Let's all just relax. We're all on the same side here."

"I wasn't talking to you," said the officer.

"This is some bullshit," said Blade.

"What'd you say to me, boy?" asked the officer, leaning forward.

"I said 'this is some bullshit'. We haven't done anything wrong. We're just trying to get to the airport, and you're on some racial profiling trip and are about to cause us to miss the flight, for no good fucking reason."

"Both of you turn the fuck back around. I'll get to the bottom of this."

Both Blade and Ish began to comply, but Blade stopped when he saw the officer was reaching for his cuffs.

"Are you arresting us?" he asked, incredulous.

"I told you to turn your black ass around!"

"No, if you're going to cuff me, you're going to at least tell me what the fuck we're being suspected of doing," said Blade.

The officer quickly took three steps back, pulled out his weapon again and pointed it at Blade.

"Both of you! Turn around and put your hands on the trunk!"

"Fuck that! I ain't doing shit!" said Blade.

"Blade!" yelled Ish. "What the hell are you doing? It's not worth all this. Do what he said and let's get through this so I can catch my plane!"

"You aren't going to be catching any plane today, nigger. Your ass is going to jail! Now shut your mouth and grab that trunk!"

Ish slowly did as he was told, but Blade was frozen in place by his outrage and defiance. Without warning, the officer grabbed the pepper spray off his belt and blasted it into Blade's face.

"Oh, shit!" said Blade, rubbing at his eyes, coughing and gagging. The officer grabbed him and slammed him into the trunk.

"You just added resisting arrest and assault on a police officer to your GTA charge, Tupac," the officer hissed and slammed him into the trunk two more times. Blood was streaming down Blade's face from a cut that had opened on his forehead, mixing with the tears from his eyes and the mucous coming from his nose.

The officer grabbed Blade's wrist with one hand, twisting it behind his back, and punched him in the kidney. Blade winced in pain, and despite being almost completely blind, easily twisted out of the wrist lock, spinning around and shoving the cop back with both hands. The officer stumbled and quickly reached for his gun.

"No!" screamed Ish. The words had barely escaped his lips when the first three bullets struck Blade square in the chest. The next two were meant for Ish, but by the time the officer pulled the trigger, Ish was no longer in the same place. He had already sidestepped the officer, quickly closing the distance between them as the two slugs whizzed by him, just centimeters from his face. In one smooth motion, he grabbed the officer's arm with one hand while the other swung in a slight ascending arc, smashing violently into the cop's windpipe. The crunch of bone sounded almost as loud as the gunshots. The officer fell to the ground, gagging and clutching at his throat, blood streaming from his mouth as he instantly began to suffocate.

Ish turned to check on Blade, but it was too late. Unlike the cop, he was probably dead before he hit the ground. This man, who had survived scorpion stings, snake bites, snipers and suicide bombers fighting in a foreign land to protect the freedom and rights of all Americans, was just murdered by one of the very people he had fought to protect. It was beyond ironic. Ish stood and looked down at the two dead men laid out before him. The grief he felt for Blade's passing felt like a giant stone had been dropped on his heart. But this wasn't a time to mourn. He scanned the area around him. He couldn't see anyone. It appeared that no one had heard the shots. Despite not considering himself to be a religious man, he said a quick prayer for his fallen comrade. He then grabbed his bag out of the backseat, dried his eyes and calmly began walking in search of the airport.

Chapter 15

The bar was fairly empty, so Ish and his group were able to claim a table in the back, away from the rest of the patrons. On the way to the table, he had quietly slipped the waitress a $50 to make sure that she didn't forget about them. The tip had worked. The trays of tequila shooters, beers and single malts—and ginger ale for Ma'am—were flowing like clockwork. No one was in danger of having a dry throat.

"I still can't believe he's gone," said Jag. He threw back another shot of tequila and sipped from his beer. His eyes were heavy, but it was also apparent that he was still in full control; still monitoring the area, his eyes constantly sweeping back and forth over the room, the same way they had done whenever they were in hostile areas in Afghanistan.

"Me either," said Bird, shaking his head. "I had plans to come see him at the end of the month. It's crazy. All that time we spent dodging bullets from snipers and avoiding IEDs, and he gets taken out by a cop. A fucking cop!"

"Shit, it don't surprise me none," said Ma'am. "I mean, have you been watching the news lately? It's starting to feel like we a' endangered species 'round this muthafucka. Like we was born with targets on our backs. That's why I stay hot," she said, patting the breast pocket on her jacket that Ish knew concealed a small .380 semi-automatic. "Let a cop try some funny shit with me and it'll turn into Kabul up in this bitch!"

They all chuckled, but each of them knew she was serious. Ma'am was not a person to trifle with. She was equal to—on a good day, maybe even better than—every man at this table. No one had more heart or more courage than she did. And her fierceness was unmatched. She literally put the 'war' in warrior.

"I still don't understand it," said Chad. Technically, Chad was bi-racial, the product of a white mother and a Chinese father. But in many ways, he identified with the African-American culture as much as any of them did. Born and raised in Los Angeles, he and Ish had gone to the same junior and senior high school, both of which were about 90% black.

The first time Ish had seen Chad, he was part of a breakdancing squad performing at a school talent show. Ish knew a girl in the troupe, and after the show they all went to Flip Burger to eat. As they chatted, Ish was amazed that this half-Asian kid knew as much about rap and R&B as he did. He turned out to be a real 'hip-hop head'.

People used to sometimes call him 'wigga' or 'jigga', the result of combining 'white' or 'jap' with 'nigga', when they'd see him sauntering down the hall in his baggy jeans and Wu-Tang jersey. It was not exactly a term of endearment, but he would just laugh it off. Some people accused him of being a poser; of cultural misappropriation, if you will. But once you got to know him, you knew it wasn't a façade. Chad was the real deal. It was shortly after they first met that Ish discovered just how real.

* * *

"What's going on?" Ish asked a girl as he walked up to the crowd. He was wearing a high school varsity jacket and jeans, and had a backpack slung over one shoulder.

"The Black Student Union is protesting," she said.

"Protesting what?"

"Didn't you hear about what happened last week? Mrs. Farmington called Darnell a 'damn nigger' in the middle of Biology 101!"

"What? Oh, shit!" said Ish, putting his fist to his mouth in astonishment. "That's crazy! So, what's the BSU trying to do?"

"Trying to get her fired! The principal hasn't done anything. He won't even talk about it. This is ridiculous. Someone's got to do something."

"I hear that," said Ish as he raised up on his toes to get a better view over the crowd of activity.

"Wait a minute," he said. "What is Chad doing up there with the Black Student Union?"

"Who's Chad?" asked the girl.

"Chad. The Asian dude."

"Oh, is that his name? I didn't know. But he's a member, if you can believe it." Ish looked at her blankly. "I know, I was confused, too. But hey, they say it's all about diversity these days. I think they elected him treasurer last week."

Ish decided to hang out for a while to find out what exactly was going on. A few minutes later Chad began walking through the crowd, passing out flyers. They read: 'Mrs. Farmington has an issue. Are we going to let teachers at this school to use racial slurs against us? Hell NO! She Must Go! Join us by signing our petition.'

"Hey, dude, what's up?" said Chad when he saw Ish. He reached out to shake Ish's hand, but instead of using the typical 'conservative' handshake, he grabbed Ish's hand up high in a manner used mostly by blacks and Latinos. Ish was amused but returned the handshake. "Ishmael, right? I met you after the talent show a couple weeks ago."

"Yeah, I remember," said Ish. "So, I hear you're a part of the BSU."

"Yeah, I know some people think that's a little strange. But love has no color, my brother. We all deserve to be treated equally. People using color as a barrier to justice is bullshit. I'm just trying to be part of the solution instead of part of the problem."

"I feel you," said Ish. "So, how's it going so far? You guys making any progress?"

"To be honest, I don't know. We decided that a petition was the best way to go, but I'm not so sure about that. I think we need a more drastic action."

"Like what?" asked Ish.

"I think we need to set it off. Break some shit! Burn some shit! Something to make them really listen to what we're trying to say!"

"Maybe you're right," said Ish, nodding his head in approval. "But I don't know. Politics isn't really my thing. I'm just trying to do my time, get decent grades and get into a nice college."

"Dude, you can't just stick your head in the sand! We all need to be involved! The more we stand together, the more weight we have to throw around."

There as a commotion somewhere in the crowd. It appeared that a skirmish had broken out between one of the black protesters and a white student. Chad shoved the flyers into Ish's hand and ran towards the noise.

Chad disappeared into the mass of people, and after a few seconds Ish followed after him. In the center of the crowd was Chad, a black girl and a large white guy. The white guy looked like he was probably a senior. He was about 6 feet tall, with the physique of a college linebacker, shocking red hair, a matching red mustache and piercing blue eyes. The girl had a medium-chocolate complexion, cornrows and a pretty face. She was about three inches shorter than the white guy, but did not seem to have any problem getting in his face. Chad, skinny and even shorter than the girl by a good inch and a half, was standing between them.

"You people just don't get it," the white guy was saying as Ish walked up. "You're the ones that cause all the trouble. Before they started busing all you 'brothers and sisters' in from the hood, this was a great school. Now it's a fucking shit hole. I'm embarrassed to say I even attend here."

"No, you don't get it," said the girl. "We're not asking for anything special. We just want to be treated with the same dignity and respect we would receive if we were white students. This is not a hostile takeover. This is simply a cry for justice. We are not the enemy."

Even though it was clear from the look in her eyes that she was furious, the girl spoke calmly and with patience. Anyone observing them could easily see who was the more intelligent, more rational, of the two. But it was also clear to Ish, scanning the faces that encircled them, that the white guy had some support from some of other white students in the crowd.

"Come on, Mike," said Chad to the white guy. "You need to relax, dude. We're just trying to get our message out there. Calling Cassandra a bitch is uncalled for. We respect the fact that what we're saying doesn't resonate with you, but ask that you at least respect us as human beings and fellow students. Cool?" Chad smiled at the guy—his offer of an olive branch.

"Yeah," said a white girl from the other side of the crowd. "They're not hurting anyone. It's free speech, man."

"Totally," said a white guy in another section of the group. People started nodding their heads in agreement. Even some of the kids that Ish initially thought were supportive of the red-haired boy were nodding. There were a couple of fellow white kids who actually stepped away from him, as though to make it perfectly clear to the rest of the students that they were not part of his team. The scales had shifted, and the agitator was clearly in the minority.

Mike looked around him, his mouth twisting into an ugly curl, a result of his surprise and frustration at being so outnumbered.

"Fuck you!" he said to Chad, then turned to the crowd. "And fuck all you other nigger lovers, too!"

That was all it took. Chad exploded into action. Ish had never seen anyone react so quickly. He doubted that Chad's brain even had time to process what his emotions had already triggered. Mike's words were still hanging in the air when Chad threw the first punch.

Chad was passionate and fully committed. The problem was that he was obviously not a fighter. In fact, it looked to Ish as though this might be the first punch he had ever thrown in his life. He was off balance, his weight was on his front leg and his hand wasn't even fully closed into a fist. Mike saw the awkward, looping punch coming from a mile away and was easily able to step back out of the way. Little did Chad know that the guy actually did him a favor. If he had connected, he might have broken his hand.

Mike, on the other hand, was not handicapped by a lack of experience. He threw a punch in response that had the power of a sledge hammer. It wasn't particularly fast, but when it slammed into Chad's jaw, it knocked him to the side like a ragdoll. Chad's body collided with the girl's, and they both fell to the ground. Mike was moving to pounce on the two grounded BSU members when Ish stepped in front of him.

"That's enough," he said, his voice even and calm. "You've made your point. Just let it go before someone gets hurt."

Incredibly, Chad was up in a flash and already trying to get around Ish to get to the guy who had just knocked both him and his partner down with one punch. *Where does this guy get his balls?* Ish wondered. He'd never seen anyone so ill-equipped to fight yet so eager to do so.

"Get out of the way, Ishmael!" said Chad, pushing against Ish's outstretched arm. "This guy is a fucking racist, and it's about time someone taught him a lesson!"

"Come get it, fucker," said Mike. He didn't try to get around Ish, but he also wasn't making any attempt to walk away.

"Chad," said Ish, "I know how you feel. But this is not the time, this is not the way, and you are not the guy. Step back and let this go."

"What are you saying? I ain't no punk!"

"I'm not saying you're a punk. But this dude has at least 60 pounds on you. Live to fight another day."

At that moment a murmur began in the crowd. A teacher was walking across the compound towards them, and some of the students decided it was a good time to begin to disburse. Chad still didn't seem convinced.

Ish locked eyes with him. "Do you want to get suspended today and have to explain that to your parents? Let's walk away, Chad."

"Yeah," said the girl, who has gotten up off the ground and was brushing her clothes off. "Remember that our goal is to keep this non-violent."

"Yeah, non-violent," said Chad, a look of sheer disgust on his face. He looked at Mike, at the girl and then at Ish before stomping off. Ish and the girl followed, leaving the white boy to glare at them as they retreated.

Ish followed Chad and the girl for a couple of minutes until they came upon a small group of students seated at a lunch table outside the cafeteria. Everyone in the group was holding a stack of the same flyers that Chad had been handing out, which Ish was still clutching.

"What happened?" asked one of the students, a short, slim black girl. She had large hazel eyes and wore her hair in a giant curly afro that framed her pretty face like a halo. Ish recognized her. Her name was Isabelle. She was on the cheerleader squad, and he had been flirting with her on and off all year.

"That dude Mike Walters tried to start some shit," Chad growled.

Isabelle looked at the girl who had walked up with Chad for an answer, but the girl just shook her head.

Isabelle then noticed that Ish was also holding a handful of flyers.

"Hey, Ishmael," she said, smiling. "Are you joining the BSU?"

"No," he said, handing the flyers to Chad. "I was just holding on to these for a minute."

"You should think about it," she said.

"Maybe," he responded absently. He was staring at Chad, who was sulking on the bench.

"So, what was all the commotion?" she asked again. No one said anything.

"Cassandra?" she said, addressing the girl who had been with Chad and Ish during the altercation.

"Mike wanted to start a fight," said Cassandra. "He punched Chad."

"And I would have taken care of it if Ishmael hadn't gotten in the way!" said Chad.

"Chad, we've talked about this," said Isabelle. "We won't get anything accomplished if we start striking out at them. First you wanted to burn down the teacher's lounge, and now this."

Ish chuckled. "You wanted to burn down the teacher's lounge? Shit! That's bodacious, man."

"I didn't say burn it down," said Chad. "I simply suggested setting a couple of trashcans on fire to create some smoke and water damage. I just think we've been begging them to take us seriously for far too long. We need to at least touch them in their wallets if we want to get them to pay attention."

"You know that's not our way," said Isabelle. "If that's the direction you're moving in, maybe you need to start your own group."

Chad stared at her, clearly annoyed, but he didn't respond.

"I've got to get to class," said Ish, breaking the awkward silence.

"Yeah, me too," said Chad. He and Ish were in the same history class, and it was starting in ten minutes. "I'll get some more flyers printed and meet you guys at Flip Burger at four."

He and Ish walked off to class together. They were silent for a few minutes.

"You know, for a small guy you have a lot of spirit," said Ish. "But the next time you toss a punch at someone, you should close your fist a little tighter. A broken hand is no joke."

"I don't fight unless I have to," said Chad.

"Yeah, you don't seem like you have a lot of experience in that particular pastime," said Ish. "But if you're going to go around standing up for girls' honor like that, you might want to take a few self-defense classes or something."

"Didn't I hear you won some kind of boxing award?" asked Chad.

"Golden Gloves," said Ish.

"That's right! Hey, man, maybe you could give me a few lessons?"

"Uh, that's not really my thing. But you could come down to the gym and join one of the classes. Though you might want to try a martial art class, rather than boxing."

Chad stopped walking and locked eyes with Ish.

"Martial arts?" He sneered. "What kind of racist shit is that? What, because I look more like 'Bruce' Lee than Muhammad 'Ah-Lee' I should join a karate class instead of boxing?"

"No," said Ish, smiling. "It's just that you're not exactly the biggest kid on the school yard, and so I think you might do well in aikido. It's a great style that trains a smaller opponent to use a larger opponent's size and strength against them. There's a school over on Manchester that just opened that's really good. I've been taking a few classes there myself."

"Oh, okay," said Chad, sheepishly returning the smile. "Thanks. Maybe I'll look into that."

Chapter 16

"What don't you understand?" asked Ma'am, jarring Ish out of his daydream. "That America don't like black folk? I know you got a little flavor, Chad, and no disrespect, but listening to the music and wearing the clothes don't make you black. For you, this is a uniform that you can take off whenever you like. You can run home, throw on a cardigan and some hush puppies and no one would ever suspect that you was 'down with the brothers'. We don't have no uniforms. This skin is our uniform, and we have to live in it every muthafuckin' day."

"Then why aren't you doing something about it?" asked Chad.

"Like what?" replied Ma'am.

"Like...well..." said Chad, stammering. "I don't know. Work to get some laws passed to make people accountable for stuff like this. How did they do it back in the 50s and 60s? March. Protest. Do whatever it takes to make people listen."

"It's not like people haven't marched," said Bird. "People are marching and protesting all over the country. All the establishment does is apply enough Band-Aids to get people to shut the fuck up and they move on."

"The problem is bigger than that," said Ish. "The real difference between black people now and black people back during the height of the Civil Rights movement is that so many of us have gotten so comfortable that we don't feel enough incentive to join the fight. The most damaging thing white America ever did against the struggle for our civil rights in this country was allow so many of us the opportunity to become middle class. When everyone was poor and we were all dealing with the shame and anger born of sitting in the back of the bus and entering hotels through the rear entrance, it was easy for a few key people to get us all coordinated and working towards the same goal. But when you have a nice corporate job, a new Honda in the driveway and a few dollars in the bank, it's a lot harder to find the motivation to call in sick for a week and run off to join a protest."

"That's a bunch of bullshit!" said Jag, his southern twang especially thick now that he had a couple of drinks in him. "I mean, I'm just a white boy from Tennessee, so I should probably just keep my mouth shut on this, but I love all of you like brothers—and sisters," he said, nodding at Ma'am, "and I've had a few tonight so I'm just gonna add my two cents to the mix."

"Oh, here we go," said Bird.

"Hold on now," said Ish. "He's got as much right to join the discussion as anyone here. Let's hear what the man has to say."

"Thanks, Ish," said Jag, pausing to take another long drag from his beer. "Listen. Let's look at this from a military perspective. When we were in-country and found out we were being tracked by a sniper, what did we do? We didn't complain to the local village elders or send a letter to our congressman asking if there was anything he could do. We systematically beat the grass to flush them, gained the more advantageous position and took the motherfuckers out. We should be acting, not just reacting."

"So, what are you saying?" asked Bird. "Are you suggesting we instigate a military action against the LAPD? Are you serious? What the hell would that prove, other than to get everyone involved killed or thrown in prison?"

"Oh, don't be such a pussy, man," said Jag, smiling.

"What the hell did you just say to me?" asked Bird, beginning to rise from the table.

"Whoa!" said Ish, spreading his arms out. "Everybody dial it back a notch. We're here to say our farewells to Blade, not get into a fucking fistfight over some nonsense." Bird slowly lowered himself back into his seat, but he kept staring icily at Jag, who was still smiling and seemed unconcerned by Bird's reaction.

There was quiet around the table. Everyone appeared to be lost in their own thoughts, as though they were trying to digest the situation that had just unfolded before them.

"Hey, Bird," said Jag, still smiling. Bird refused to answer.

"Bird!" he said again.

"What!"

"Did I hurt your feelings, honey? I'm sorry. You know I love you. Let me buy you a drink. What are you drinking? Shirley Temple? Mai Tai?" asked Jag, his smile getting broader. Bird looked off into the distance, clearly trying to ignore him.

"Come on, baby. Are you going to make me say it? Okay, I apologize. Better? Now come on over here and give Daddy some sugar." Now everyone else at the table was smiling too, except for Bird. But it was clear he was struggling not to join them.

"Okay," said Jag, "I think we need some cuddle time. Y'all give us a minute." He got up, stepped over to Bird on the other side of the table and grabbed him in a bear hug from behind.

"Get the hell off me, fool!" said Bird, but he was already laughing.

"We need some more tequila over here! Hey, waitress lady—" Jag called, but by the time he stood up he could see that she was already on her way with a tray full of amber-filled glasses.

"All jokes aside," said Ma'am after the laughter had died down and the waitress had left, "maybe that's not such a crazy idea. Maybe it's time to take the fight to these racist muthafuckas instead of just waitin' for them to bring the fight to us."

"Sis," said Bird, "you're not really thinking about actually implementing some of this foolishness, are you? We all know there are always going to be soldiers that fall in the line of battle, but I'm still trying to deal with the loss we came together today to mourn. I don't need to be worrying about you out there provoking cops and trying to go 'wild west' with them. It's a losing proposition."

"Sometimes I think you spent too much time at them white colleges, little brother," she said. "Sometimes it feels like you're a little too reluctant to rock the boat. I remember when you was gettin' in trouble for writin' protest articles in the high school newspaper. You were all 'afro this' and 'black power that'. I'm not sayin' you've gotten soft, but I think Ish has a point. You fill a wild dog's belly full of food, and it's a lot easier to get him to roll over."

"Ain't nobody rolling over," said Bird, waving his hand dismissively. "All I'm saying is that there's a way to effect change in this country, and picking fights with police officers is way down on the bottom of the list!"

"Whose list?" asked Jag. "I don't know that it would make much of a difference in the end, but I could say the same about the tours of duty we all just got back from. What the fuck difference did that make? We were over there, eating, sleeping and shitting in hostile territory, trying our best to get the job done and come back not just alive, but with all our fucking arms and legs, and what difference did that make? None that I can see! But I still did it, because I believed in the cause. I believed that taking a stance meant something, and I would have been proud of my efforts even if I had come back in a fucking body bag."

The table went quiet again. The tension was palpable. Everyone seemed edgy and on guard.

"Hey," said Chad, breaking the silence, "how about we all raise a glass to Blade?" Everyone at the table grabbed their drink of choice, stood up and turned to face Chad.

"Unlike all of you, I'm not a military man," he said, taking a moment to look each of them individually in the eye. "That was never my calling. And I admit that I didn't know him as well as you did. But I consider myself extremely fortunate to have been accepted by a group as special as this, and I find it a high honor to be included in this farewell to one of our fallen. Let's raise a toast to Blade, and may the bastard that killed him rot in hell."

"Cheers!" they said in unison, and they each tossed back their drink.

They all returned to their seats, and flipped their empty glasses upside down on the table.

"It's clear that I'm the real minority at this table," said Bird. "I mean, I know that these atrocities are real and ongoing, and I've even had a few bad run-ins with cops myself. But obviously, there has to be both bad ones and good ones. Don't you think the bad ones must be the exception rather than the rule?"

"Little brother," said Ma'am, "you always led a sheltered life. And you've been lucky. You was always lucky. Goin' to a white school and hangin' out with your little white friends. Always in the 'white' place at the 'white' time."

Bird shook his head in disagreement.

"Me, on the other hand," continued Ma'am, "I've been in the trenches. You want to know what cops are really like? Then you should watch how they act when no one else is around; when they dealin' with people that they think no one cares about. When I was livin' on the street, still usin', I got my ass beat on numerous occasions by numerous cops. Raped a couple of times, too. Shit, most of the time I didn't even fight back. I was at a point in my life where I didn't care whether I lived or died. Sometimes I woke up in jail. Sometimes I woke up in the hospital. Eventually I was back out in the street, doing it all over again."

"Sis, you don't have to do this—"

"Yes, Bird, I do. You think I'm ashamed of my past? I've been clean for nine years now. That journey made me who I am today. But the point I'm trying to make here is that we ain't talkin' about a 'one bad apple' situation. There's a lot of fuckin' bad cops out there. Maybe they're like lawyers. They start off thinking they can save the world, but before you know it, they go from steppin' in shit, to wadin' in shit, to becomin' shit."

"Hey, my dad is a lawyer!" said Chad.

"Let's not make this personal," said Ish.

"Why all the drama?" asked Jag. "We're just drinking and having a friendly conversation. It's not like we're going to go out tomorrow and start popping people in blue uniforms. You ladies need to relax. No offense," he said, smiling at Ma'am.

"Jag," she said, "you've been actin' like this whole thing is a joke, but the truth is people are still dyin' out there in them streets, every day, at the hands of them wearin' those blue uniforms. Maybe it is time some of them start gettin' popped."

"They already are," said Bird. "Didn't you hear about those two cops that got blasted in Vegas last week? Assassination-style. They were sitting in their patrol car, in a parking lot, eating lunch. Somebody sprayed the car with an Uzi through the back window."

"Serves the muthafuckas right!" said Ma'am.

"How would you know?" asked Bird. "I think we can all agree, at the very least, that not every single cop is bad. Hell, a lot of the people me, Ish and Jag served with became cops once they were discharged. And a lot of them are people I would trust with my life! So, who knows if these two cops actually did anything worth being killed for?"

"This is the age of the internet," said Chad. "Nothing is secret for long. It would be easy enough to research their service records; find out whether they were into anything foul."

"What would be the point in that?" replied Jag. "These dudes are already dead. Who cares? It's not the dead cops that you gotta worry about. It's the live ones."

"I'm just saying," said Chad, "that it's not like it's impossible to figure this stuff out. Let's take, for example, this cop that murdered Blade. It would probably take me less than an hour to hack the police database and access his entire file."

"Again, professor, that would be a waste of time and effort. We all know Blade was clean as a church lady's drawers. And besides that, he took the bastard out himself, so that's another closed case."

Ish cleared his throat and sat up straighter in his chair. "I don't know if this is the right time to get into all this, but there are some things about that situation that didn't make it into the news reports." He looked around him to make sure that no one else was in earshot before he continued.

"You all, each and every one of you, are my most trusted friends in the world. Bird and Jag have watched my back more times than I can count. Chad, in addition to helping me create financial security, has always been like the brother I never had. And if I were to ever have a sister, I would wish that she were exactly like Ma'am. So, I feel like I can tell you all anything."

"What the hell are you trying to say?" interrupted Jag. "Spit it out, man."

"I was with Blade when this shit went down. We were on our way to the airport."

"Holy fuck," whispered Jag. "Let me guess. You were the one that took out the cop?"

"Yeah," said Ish.

"I knew it!" said Jag. "I saw the pictures. There's no way Blade could have taken those hits and continued moving, let alone done that kind of damage. He was a tough motherfucker. And fast. But he wasn't that fast."

"What the hell happened?" asked Bird.

"Like I said, we were on the way to the airport. We had to detour because of all the protesters. The fucking GPS got us turned around, and we ended up in an empty industrial park. Cop pulled up behind us. Got into the 'white man vs. nigga' act pretty much right off the bat. Wouldn't believe the car wasn't stolen. Saw Blade's Ranger coin and accused us of stealing that, too. I think what happened is that he knew we really were Rangers and got scared thinking we might come after him later or something. I think that from that moment forward he had no intention of letting us leave that street alive." Ish paused to take a deep breath and blow it back out.

"Anyway," he continued, "he started beating on Blade. Peppered him; slammed his head into the trunk. Finally, Blade shoved him. That was all it took. Before we knew what was happening, he had opened fire. If I had been a foot or two further away, I never would have got to him."

"Jesus Christ," said Bird.

"The news reports said that an 'anonymous witness' called it in, and stated that they saw the cop's unprovoked attack. Were you the caller?" asked Chad.

"I was," said Ish.

"And there were no other witnesses?"

"I don't believe so, but I guess I'll find out soon enough. Either way, the cops will come knocking at some point simply because my prints are all over the car. Of course, they can't prove that I was in the car at the time of the stop, but I'll definitely be questioned."

"This just keeps getting better and better," said Bird sarcastically. "What are you going to do if this thing goes sideways?"

"Just leave the country, man," said Jag. "You've got the money. Why even entertain this bullshit? You can live anywhere in the world you like."

"A crooked cop tries to kill him, kills one of our own, and *he* should leave the country?" asked Ma'am. "Ain't that a bitch! We've been runnin' for too fuckin' long. That's how we ended up where we are today!"

"Hey, I didn't say 'run'. But why wait around for the cops to come after you over some trumped-up charge when you don't have to?" asked Jag.

"Nobody is running," said Ish firmly. "I would never leave the country with Layla still behind bars. And besides, Ma'am is right. We have been running too fucking long. I need to face this head-on. In fact, I'm flying back to Baltimore tomorrow morning."

"Why in the world would you do that?" asked Chad.

“Because I don’t have a permanent residence here. I sold the house as soon as I got back stateside, which is why I’ve been living in hotels ever since.” Chad began nodding his head, already understanding where he was heading with this. “So, they’ll have trouble tracking me down based on the address on file with the DMV. And the longer it takes for them to find me, the more of a suspect I’ll become to them. Better I find them before they find me.”

“Makes sense,” said Ma’am. “So how you gonna play it?”

“His sister and I have hired a lawyer. We’re going to walk into the station bright and early Thursday morning and serve them for illegal arrest and murder.”

“One thing is for sure,” said Jag smiling. “Your balls are as big as they ever were! That’s some gangster-ass shit, man!”

“Ish,” said Bird, his voice heavy with concern, “are you sure you want to do this? It sounds risky as hell.”

“What’s my alternative? I need a legitimate reason for contacting them before they come looking for me, and this is as good as any. Besides, it’s not a ruse. They did illegally arrest him and they did murder him, and the fact that the cop died in the process is not payment enough for what they did to this man. I owe it to his sister and the rest of his family to do whatever I can to try to get them as much justice as possible.”

“You don’t have to do this alone, Ish,” said Ma’am. “I know we don’t have to say it, but I’ll say it anyway: we’ve got your back. What can we do to help?”

Chapter 17

When Ish stepped off the plane in Maryland, the heat and humidity wrapped itself around him like a cloak. Afghanistan was hot, but this humidity was something else altogether. His first thought was that he needed to handle his business as quickly as possible so that he could get back to the relative cool of the L.A. beach region. But then he remembered why he was here. This was nothing to be taken lightly. There were some serious matters that needed to be explored and attended to, and he wasn't completely sure how much control he would have on the outcome.

Blade's sister, Virginia, offered to meet him at the airport, but he declined the offer. He didn't want to inconvenience her. Besides, he needed a few minutes alone to just breathe in the air of the city; to get used to its smells and vibrations. Sitting by himself in the back of a cab would give him a little bit more time to do that. It was something he learned in the Middle East. One of the guys he served with on his first stint taught him the technique. He called it 'osmotic acclimatization'. He said the more in tune you were with your surroundings, the more likely you were to know when something in those surroundings were out of place. He said it could save your life. And he was right.

There were several incidents in which Ish had been out on patrol or clearing the rooms of some dwelling and got the feeling that something wasn't quite right. Those few seconds of hesitation had allowed him to avoid booby-traps, snipers and a suicide bomber or two. Of course, he wasn't expecting anything like that here in Baltimore, but as his father used to always say: "If you stay ready, you don't have to get ready."

Ish had wanted to make reservations at a hotel, but Virginia wouldn't hear of it. She told him that the spare room he had stayed in when he had come to visit Blade was ready and waiting for him, and she wouldn't take no for an answer. He hadn't wanted to offend her, so he eventually gave in and accepted, even though he knew being so close to them would increase his feelings of guilt over Blade's death.

"Hi, Ish! It's so good to see you!" said Virginia. Ish was barely out of the taxi, and she was already walking across the driveway to meet him. Virginia was a fine specimen of a woman. Her dark skin and high cheek bones hinted that she was of purer African heritage than many black Americans. She wore tight black jeans, a pink t-shirt tied at the bottom and a matching pink wrap around her long, curly hair. About medium height, with a tiny waist, she moved with the grace and elegance of a ballerina. However, her ample hips, thighs and bust indicated that dancing was probably not what she did for a living. At least, not ballet dancing. She was actually a teacher—a physics professor at a nearby college. Her husband, Vincent, was an accountant.

Vincent stood at the front door and watched as his wife made her way to the taxi. He was about ten years older than Virginia, which would put him at about forty-five. He was prematurely balding and about thirty pounds overweight, but he wore it well. Ish was sure that when people saw them together, they wondered what this beautiful black woman was doing with this paunchy Jew. Most of them would probably assume that he had money and that it was more of a financial arrangement than a romantic one. But they would be wrong.

First of all, Vince didn't really 'have' money. He made a decent living, but he was far from wealthy. With their dual income, they were able to live in a nice house and drive nice cars, but this was no 'sugar daddy' situation. This was a romance of the highest caliber. Vince and Virginia were very much in love. They had first met five years ago at a local fundraiser event. It wasn't until they bumped into each other at the grocery store a couple of weeks later that he asked her out for coffee. They had been together ever since.

Still, Ish couldn't help but wonder what it was like to be someone like him, married to an African American woman. And not just any African American woman, but one who was getting as much attention from men, black men, as Virginia undoubtedly was. Was he insecure? Did he worry that one day some chocolate-skinned brother would swoop in and sweep her off her feet? Ish hoped not. He had always been a realist, but he still liked to believe that love eventually conquered all.

"How was your flight?" asked Virginia after giving him a warm hug.

"It was fine. That is, until I walked off the plane and into this sauna that you people call 'summer'!" he said, smiling.

"I know. It's been like this all week! Come on inside and let me get you a glass of this mint lemonade I just made."

"How've you been, Vince?" asked Ish, as the two men warmly shook hands.

"Pretty good. Well, as good as can be expected, considering the circumstances."

Vince hadn't known Blade for very long. Most of the time that he and Virginia had been together Blade had been overseas. But they bonded well during the times Blade came home on leave and had been surprisingly close. In fact, in one of their last conversations Blade confessed to Ish that he actually liked Vincent better than any of Virginia's past boyfriends. It's not that they were bad guys, he' d said. Virginia had too much self-respect for that. But he always got the feeling that they were more into her for her physical beauty than for her soul. He said that Vincent didn't appear to be like that at all. It made him feel like he could worry about her a little less, knowing that someone like Vincent was watching over her.

Listening to Blade talk, you would have thought he was the older of the two, but he was actually the baby of the family. They had another brother somewhere in New York, the oldest of the three of them, but no one had heard from him in years. Virginia had hired a private investigator to try to find him, to let him know about his brother's funeral, but hadn't had any luck.

After he had stored his bag in the guest bedroom, Ish joined Vince and Virginia in the dining room, where three glasses of lemonade were waiting. The house was tastefully furnished. Virginia's woman's touch was evident everywhere, but Ish had initially been a little surprised to see so much African art. There were paintings and sculptures, some of which Ish recognized as Tanzanian. But there were also a few Jewish pieces, including a Star of David and a menorah.

"First, let me say once again how sorry I am that this happened to Blade. Nathan," he added. "I feel especially bad because if he hadn't given me a ride to the airport that morning, he'd probably still be alive today."

"It's not your fault," said Virginia, touching Ish's arm. "But I'm still confused as to what he was doing in that area, so out of the way, to begin with."

"That I don't know the answer to," Ish lied. "But no matter why he was there, he didn't deserve to die. And even though he was able to take the cop out before he passed, that's still little compensation for his loss of life. That's why I'm here. The lawyers that I've hired are some of the best around. I think they can help give you some closure, by making the police department pay for what has been a history of this kind of thing happening not only in Baltimore, but all across the country."

"Thank you very much, Ishmael," said Vincent, sitting with his arm around his wife's shoulder. "Virginia and I very much appreciate your generosity. When are we to meet with the lawyers?"

"Actually," said Ish, "that's one of the things I wanted to talk to you about. A good friend of mine, Chad Yang, has some connections with some of the principals in the #BlackForLife organization. They have a protest planned for tomorrow, and Chad's arranged for a few of their members to march with us up the front steps to the police department. There is sure to be a couple of camera crews there, and the lawyers think that the publicity will be good for the case. Are you okay with that?"

Vincent and Virginia looked at each other, and some silent communication seemed to take place.

"I just want justice for my brother," said Virginia. "I don't care what we need to do to get that justice. And like Vince said, thank you for doing this."

"It's the least I can do. Blade—Nathan—was a great guy. We were tight the way squad members are always tight, but it went beyond that. I don't have any brothers, but through the years I've developed a close, brotherly bond with a few guys. Chad is one, and your brother was another. He helped keep us alive over in Afghanistan, not just because he was good with weapons, but because he was funny, and loving, and had a heart the size of a tank. I miss him more than I can really express to you right now."

Virginia cooked dinner for the three of them. A healthy meal of baked chicken, scalloped potatoes and green beans and mushrooms in a port wine reduction. She was a good cook. After dinner, Vince went into his office to finish some work, and Virginia and Ish retired to the living room with a glass of wine each.

"So, Ishmael, tell me a little about my brother and what he was like over there in Afghanistan."

"Well, we were in war. Like any war, it was not pretty. It was a dirty, dangerous, daunting place to survive, where life seemed to have even less value than in the worse American ghettos," said Ish.

"Nathan had always had a temper, but small as he was, it's hard to imagine him holding his own in that type of an environment," said Virginia.

"Your brother was a fighter and a natural-born soldier," said Ish, chuckling. "He was living proof that sometimes big things come in small packages. I remember when I first saw him, saying to myself, 'Who is this little guy and how the hell did he get here?' But he quickly erased any doubts that we had about whether or not he was man enough for the job. He was tough as steel. His nickname fit him to a 'T'."

"I've often wondered how he came about that name. I asked him about it once, but he said he didn't want to get into it. What's the story?"

"Well," said Ish, pausing as he tried to decide if this is something that Virginia really wanted to hear. "By the time I met him, he had already acquired the nickname, but early on he did something that clearly showed why it was so appropriate. There was a situation during our second week in country that happened when we were out on patrol. We had run across a bunch of IEDs, bombs planted along the roads, that we needed to either defuse or detonate, both of which took longer than expected. We ended up deciding to pitch camp and head back to base the next morning.

"A couple of hours later, the lookout woke us to alert us to movement on the horizon. A group of Taliban fighters had discovered us, and next thing we knew, we were in a major firefight. It was like monsters in a bad video game. No matter how many of these guys we dropped, another sprang up to take their place. We started getting low on ammo, and they started closing in. But we kept fighting. And the closer they got, the more careless they got. We made every shot count and started turning the tide." Ish paused to refill his glass and refilled Virginia's while he was at it. She appeared to be hanging on his every word.

"By the time we had dropped the last bad guy, we were down to our last clip of ammo. We had maybe twenty shells left. The sun was just coming up, and we were exhausted but relieved. We had hardly had any sleep and were anxious to get packed up and back to base as soon as possible. One of our last tasks before moving out was to check the bodies for possible intelligence—maps, plans, etc. Plus, we wanted to grab as much extra ammo as we could get for our trip back to base. Your brother and I were searching the bodies together. We were almost done when two of the last bodies that your brother was about to frisk jumped up and grabbed him."

Virginia's reflexively grabbed the arm of the sofa, her face etched with anxiety.

"These two guys were both splattered with blood, which made it look like they had been shot. In reality, they had been wearing bulletproof vests, which protected them, and they both had lain down when they were hit and stayed there, not moving a muscle, for at least two hours! They must have been deployed as a final 'Hail Mary' once the group saw that they were close to being defeated, because one of them was wired with explosives. Can you believe that? Anyway, the one that was wired tried to detonate the bomb as the other grabbed Nathan's leg in a death grip."

"But there was some issue with the detonator, and the bomb didn't go off. I had a gun on them, but they used Nathan as a shield and I couldn't get a shot off. I knew it was only a matter of moments before the bomb guy fixed his malfunction and blew the four of us sky high. Suddenly, I saw Nathan reach down into his boot and pull out a knife. For the next few seconds all I saw was the blur of his arm and the silver of that blade as it glinted in the sun's early morning rays. By the time he was done, he had slit the throat of the one on his leg and gutted the other, in spite of the fact that he was wearing a vest, from one side of his body to the other. I mean, this dudes' intestines were literally pouring out onto the desert sand."

"Ugh, my God!" said Virginia, putting her hand to her mouth and leaning back in her seat in horror and disgust.

"I'm sorry," said Ish. "That was definitely too much information."

"No," said Virginia, recovering somewhat, "I asked. Please continue. I'd like to hear the rest of it."

"Alright," said Ish, pausing to take another sip of his wine. "Well, that was pretty much it, except for the most amazing part. During this dazzling display, which couldn't have taken more than ten seconds, not only had he taken the two attackers out, he had also cut the wires to the detonator! It was, without a doubt, one of the most remarkable things I had ever seen. That was Blade. To this day I've never seen anyone that could do what he could with a sharpened sliver of steel."

Chapter 18

The next morning Ish was up early. He went for a six-mile jog to clear his head and get ready for the day that lay before him. He walked out the door at 6am, but the temperature and the humidity were already bordering on brutal. He was sweating profusely before he had even run the length of the first block. Yet there were already some protesters in the street. It was likely that many of them had been out all night. He finally started to understand just how committed these people were to fighting to get their voices heard and their cries for justice answered.

After a quick shower and a protein shake, Ish dressed and prepared to meet with a couple of representatives of #BlackForLife. Chad wasn't a member of the organization, but he was very active in the civil rights community. He had a lot of friends in a variety of different groups dedicated to justice and equal rights for minorities. Some were centered on racial justice, while others geared more towards the rights of gays, lesbians, trans-gender and women in general.

The Baltimore chapter had agreed to be present during Ish and company's 'march to the station', but they wanted to meet first to lay down some ground rules. After graciously declining Virginia's offer of breakfast, Ish called for an Uber ride and headed to a downtown coffee shop for the meeting.

* * *

Ish was the first to arrive. He found a cozy table in the back of the shop and ordered an *Americano.* Five minutes later two women walked in the front door, and somehow Ish immediately knew that they were the women from #BlackForLife. He stood up to wave them over, but they had already seen him and recognized him as well.

Both women appeared to be in their mid-thirties. One was black, and the other, the taller of the two, appeared to be Puerto Rican. The black woman wore glasses and had her ebony hair in an afro. She had full lips and chubby cheeks, but her body was rail thin. She was tastefully dressed, pairing jean shorts with a silky beige, armless top. She looked like a college professor on summer break. The taller woman had long, auburn hair pulled back into a ponytail. She wore dark blue slacks and a loose-fitting plum-colored t-shirt. She was quite a bit heavier than her colleague but shapely. Both women were beautiful in their own way. Neither wore makeup, and neither needed it.

"You must be Mr. Carter," said the taller woman as she reached out to shake Ish's hand. "I'm Marquita Valdez, and this is Khadija Syed. We represent the Baltimore chapter of #BlackForLife."

"It's a pleasure to meet you both," said Ish. After ordering coffee and tea for the ladies, he patiently waited for them to start the conversation.

"Mr. Carter—" began Khadija.

"Call me Ishmael, please," said Ish.

"Ishmael," she continued, "Chad briefed us a bit on your case, and we hope that we can be of some assistance."

"We would very much appreciate that," said Ish. "It's a horrible tragedy for the family, and I'm really just here to support them and help them deal with the legal aspects of the case."

"Understood," said Khadija. "However, we first need to make sure that you're aware of some of the rules governing the #BlackForLife movement and are willing to abide by them." Ish nodded for her to continue.

"The most important thing to keep in mind is that #BlackForLife is a nonviolent movement, both in word and deed. Not only do we not engage in any kind of violent or overtly aggressive action within our organization, we also don't call for or endorse violent actions by others. We believe that to be involved in those types of initiatives would undermine any political power we have accrued and would ultimately dilute the messages that we're trying to get the public at large to get behind. Much of our power is derived from the goodwill that our nonviolent stance creates."

"The ability to simultaneously be both non-threatening and a force of change to be reckoned with: I understand," said Ish. "We have no intention of trying to circumvent what the #BlackForLife organization represents. Our personal objective is to expose this case to the court of public opinion; to raise its visibility and make it more difficult for it to be swept under the rug or have it become another casualty on the wrong side of a scale of justice slanted against minorities."

"Well stated," said Marquita, smiling slightly. "If you don't mind me asking, can you tell us what your relation is to the Bartholomew family?"

"I'm a family friend. I served with Nathan in Afghanistan. As is often the case with people that you are in battle with, we became close. As a matter of fact, I was actually in Baltimore visiting him on the day he was killed."

"Yes, I think Chad mentioned that," said Khadija. "I'm sorry for your loss. I read the news reports, but they were a bit skimpy on facts. All we really know is that Nathan was killed by the police officer but delivered a fatal blow to the officer before he died. Do you have any other information about what happened that day?"

Ish took a moment to gather his thoughts. These were the types of questions he was going to be repeatedly asked in the upcoming days and weeks. He didn't like the fact that he had to obscure the truth about what had happened that day, but he knew very well that there was often a world of difference between justice and the truth, and that sometimes justice was the only thing that mattered.

"I wasn't there," he said. "Nathan drove me to the airport that day and his encounter with the cop happened sometime after he left the airport. So, I don't know much more than what the news agencies have reported, based on what the as yet unidentified witness claimed to have seen happen. What I do know is that Nathan was no criminal. He was a man of honor. It's true he was a soldier, and a damn good one, but he was not a man given to unwarranted violence. If he struck out at this police officer, it was as an act of self-defense. And that's the basis of the family's unlawful death claim—that he was killed defending himself against police brutality."

“Fair enough,” said Marquita. “Well, if you have no other questions, I guess we should go meet the family and the attorneys.”

Ish paid the check, the ladies thanked him and they all got into Khadija’s SUV and headed to the lawyers’ office to meet Virginia, Vincent and the attorneys.

By the time Ish, Marquita and Khadija arrived at the offices of Lambert, Garrison & Tuttle, Virginia and Vincent were already seated and waiting in the lobby. After introductions were made all around, they were greeted by the receptionist and ushered into a conference room. A few moments later the attorney arrived.

“Good morning,” he said, shaking everyone’s hand. “My name is Leonard Garrison and I’ll be the lead counsel on this case.” He was a handsome black man, medium height, forty-ish, with and athletic build and close-cropped hair. He wore a neatly trimmed mustache, had eyebrows that were too perfectly shaped to be natural and smelled of some complex but tastefully applied cologne. He wore a tailored pinstriped suit, brilliantly shined shoes and a Rolex watch. However, in spite of how well-groomed and cultured as he obviously was, he did not at all come off as pretentious.

Ish had grown very adept at reading people. While interacting with the populace in Afghanistan, it was a necessary survival skill. During missions in the various towns and villages that they worked in, if you couldn’t get some sense of the basic character of an individual at a quick glance, you would not survive for very long. That was not a war in which the enemy soldiers all wore a specific uniform. Sometimes the only thing that separated a friend from a foe was a twitch or a sideways glance. Miss—or misinterpret—the clues and you could end up getting your remains scraped into a body bag. Or worse. So, his intuition had become well-honed and was field-tested. And his intuition told him that Garrison was down to earth, honest, and worthy of trust. He started to relax a bit.

“So,” said Garrison after everyone had taken a seat. “I’ve already spoken at length to Mr. and Mrs. Goldberg and Mr. Carter regarding the finer details of the case. I won’t rehash all of that right now. But the broad strokes are this: Mr. Bartholomew was stopped by Officer Newhall. We assume that the stop was the result of either a minor traffic violation or simply for ‘driving while black’.

"There was no weapon recovered at the scene," he continued, "so we know that Mr. Bartholomew was unarmed, and that he was both pepper-sprayed and beaten before being shot to death. We also know that, at some point before he died, he apparently delivered a strike to the officer's throat, crushing his windpipe and causing him to die of strangulation. Most of this was also corroborated by the as yet unknown witness who called 911."

Garrison read on Virginia's face the anguish caused by his retelling of the events and respectfully paused to give her a minute to gather herself. Vincent, who was again sitting with his arm around her, pulled her close and allowed her to bury her face in his chest. After a moment, she dabbed her nose with a tissue, squeezed Vincent's hand and sat upright again, head high and shoulders back. She was once again in control. She nodded for Garrison to continue.

"Obviously, it would be pointless to only go after the officer. For one thing, he died in the encounter, which complicates matters for us. But more to the point, as agreed by Mr. and Mrs. Goldberg and Mr. Carter," he said, taking a second to visually address each as he said their names, "our real objective here is not simply to make them pay financially. Our true objective is to change the system and the way it, quite often, unjustly deals with minorities; specifically, blacks and Latinos. Yes, we are asking for $65M in punitive damages, but as we all know, if you can't touch these people in their wallets, it's hard to get them to take you seriously. Any questions so far?"

Garrison waited. Everyone else at the table shook their heads 'no'.

"Very well," he said. "The basis of our suit is that Mr. Bartholomew was a victim of wrongful death at the hands of the Baltimore Police Department. The defendants in the suit are Officer Newhall individually and the department as a whole. I have already had our investigators get to work. What they've discovered so far is that Mr. Bartholomew—"

"Mr. Garrison—Leonard—" interrupted Virginia. "If there are no objections, I think I would feel more comfortable if we all addressed each other by our first names. If you don't mind."

"Certainly," said Garrison, looking at each person at the table to see if anyone took issue with the suggestion. No one gave any such sign. "What we've discovered is that—Nathanial? Nathan?" He looked inquisitively at Virginia.

"Nathan is fine," she said.

"What we discovered is that Nathan had no criminal record to speak of, beyond a couple of unpaid parking tickets years ago," said Garrison. "He was also a decorated war vet. All that works in our favor. One thing that might work against us is the fact that he did have a reputation for fighting in the street. He was apparently never arrested for it, but it was well known that he wouldn't shy away from a scrap."

"What does that have to do with anything related to this case?" asked Virginia.

"Well, in cases like this, it's not uncommon for the lawyers for the other side to use such information to paint a portrait of someone who not only enjoyed fighting but was constantly looking for one. The quintessential 'angry black man', if you will," replied Garrison.

"My brother was always small for his age. Perhaps you don't understand the implications of that, but in the neighborhood we grew up in, any sign of weakness, physical or mental, made you a target. My brother spent his formative years defending himself against bullies. If he had not been willing to fight back, he probably would not have survived. He probably would—" she stopped, a sob caught in her throat.

"Mrs. Goldberg—Virginia—" said Garrison softly. "I do understand. I grew up in a pretty rough neighborhood myself. But you have to understand that on the battlefield of the courtroom, a lot of people, particularly white people," he said, looking apologetically at Vincent, "use tactics of character assassination against minorities to prejudice the jury against them. To be honest, it usually doesn't take a lot to get the jury to buy in, especially if that jury is majority white, as is often the case."

"I'm sorry," said Virginia. "I know you're just here to help. I guess I'm still a little overly sensitive."

"No apology necessary," said Garrison. "It's to be expected. Listen," he said, closing the folder that was open before him, "how about we save the rest of this discussion until after we return from the police station? I think having that behind us will lessen the stress just a bit."

They all agreed and headed out to rendezvous with a group of protesters near the precinct.

By the time they arrived at the pre-agreed checkpoint, about ten blocks from the police station, the crowd was already over 200 strong. Several carried long banners inscribed with the words '#BlackForLife',

'No Justice, No Peace' and 'Justice For Nathanial' in letters six inches tall. Ish was visibly moved and had to turn away from the crowd for a moment to inconspicuously wipe some moisture from the corner of his eye. It was one thing to see these protest crowds from a distance or on the screen of a television or computer monitor. But seeing it up close and personal, especially when they were rallying around someone who you personally knew, was another thing altogether. There was a power and electricity in their unity. And everyone knew it. Most were already sweating under the blanket of the blistering heat and smothering humidity, but instead of being beaten down by it, they seemed to be energized.

Garrison was passed a megaphone and stood in front of the crowd. He had left his blazer in the car and rolled his shirtsleeves up. Standing there on top of an abandoned overturned shopping cart, he looked like a union organizer. There was a faint smile at the corner of his lips, a smile that exuded confidence and an eagerness to get to the business at hand. There were several news cameras and reporters in the crowd, but you got the impression that he was not even aware they were there.

"Good morning, everyone," he said, his booming voice echoing off the nearby buildings. "Thank you so much for coming out. My name is Leonard Garrison. I am lead counsel for Nathanial Bartholomew and family. As you know, the reason for this march is to bring attention to the tragedy that befell Mr. Bartholomew at the hands of the Baltimore Police Department, and our serving of a complaint against said department for excessive force and wrongful death. Understand that the serving of this complaint today is mostly symbolic, as the majority of the documents will be served at the courthouse. Again, thank you for your support, be safe and God bless." He gracefully stepped down off the cart and handed the megaphone to Khadija.

Khadija whispered something to Marquita, turned to the crowd as if assessing their readiness to begin, and started walking. The crowd fell in step behind her.

"What do we want?" she yelled into the megaphone.

"Justice!" answered the crowd.

"When do we want it?"

"Now!"

They kept this call and response going all the way to the police station. The crowd picked up members along the way. By the time they reached the station, Ish estimated they were being backed by at least 400 people. A line of police officers, decked out in full riot gear, stood in front of the station as a human barrier, blocking any further progression of the crowd. Khadija handed the megaphone back to Garrison.

"Thank you so much for your time and energy," he said to the mass of people before him. "I'm going to go inside with the family and handle a little business. Your service has been enormously appreciated!"

Ish, Vincent, Virginia and Garrison turned as a group and walked up to the line of officers. A burly white officer standing immediately in front of Virginia looked like he wanted to spit on her, but instead he nodded to the officer next to him, and several of the officers parted and let the group of four through. They opened the doors to the station and disappeared inside.

Chapter 19

Once inside the police station, Garrison asked to speak to the commander. They were led to a room. It had the stark look of an interrogation room, but with a larger than expected table and too many chairs. Ish assumed it was their version of a conference room.

After a few minutes, three men entered the room and closed the door behind them. They introduced themselves as Chief Amster and Detectives Danning and Colleti. They offered everyone coffee but all declined.

"Chief Amster," said Garrison, "I, along with the family of Nathanial Bartholomew, am here to officially serve you a notice of complaint for unlawful arrest and wrongful death as the result of Mr. Bartholomew's encounter with one of your officers." As he spoke, he reached into the breast pocket of his shirt and withdrew a folded letter, which he handed to the Chief.

As the Chief of Police read through the paperwork, Ish noticed that the two detectives were both staring at him. Garrison must have picked up on it as well.

"Excuse me, Chief," said Garrison after a few moments. "I don't mean to interrupt you, but I'm just curious: why are these two detectives in this meeting with us?" The Chief looked up from the letter, and then slowly pushed it aside. He leaned back in his chair with the posture of a man who had grown weary of his job. He had thinning white hair, a white mustache, and a gut that hung far over his belt. His face was a ruddy complexion, and there was a hint of redness to his nose that suggested that maybe he drank too much. His eyes were vacant and unfocused as though he wasn't really taking in everything before him.

"You're right," said the Chief, with a barely detectable trace of a southern accent. "I was going to wait until after we dealt with all this, but we may as well get to it. Colleti?"

Detective Colleti cleared his throat. He looked to be of Italian descent. He had thick black hair that he wore parted down the middle of his head. Perhaps in his mid-thirties, he was getting a little soft in the middle, but you could tell he had probably been a high school or college jock. While the Chief's eyes appeared distant and barely engaged, Colleti's, intense and laser-focused, were the exact opposite. He opened a file that he had brought into the room with him.

"You were introduced as Ishmael Carter," he said, still staring intently at Ish. "Is that Ishmael Carter of 1737 Capri Lane, Newport Beach, California?" he asked, reading the address of the home that Ish no longer owned.

"Yes, that's right," said Ish.

"We've been looking for you, Mr. Carter. We had some L.A. officers go by your house several times, but no one ever seems to be home. We have some questions for you."

"What kind of questions?" asked Ish.

"For one thing, we'd like to know why your fingerprints were found all over Nathaniel Bartholomew's car, including the trunk, and where you were the day he died."

"Wait a minute," said Garrison. "We didn't come here to get interrogated. We've served you with notice and our business here is done."

"Are you counsel for Mr. Carter?" asked Detective Danning.

"Yes, I am," said Garrison, beginning to raise his voice, "and there will be no more questioning until—"

Ish raised his hand. "It's okay, Leonard. I'd be happy to answer the detectives' questions. Why don't you take everyone back to the office? I'll meet up with you later."

"Ishmael, I don't think that's wise—" began Garrison before Ish cut him off again.

"Don't worry, Leonard," he said. "It'll be okay."

Garrison paused. The look on his face said that he wanted to protest more, but he finally relented and escorted Vincent and Virginia from the room. Within moments Ish was alone with the Chief of police and the two detectives.

Ish leaned back in his chair and interlaced his fingers together. He mentally assessed each of the three men. None of them seemed particularly menacing or dangerous. But Danning had a bit of a wild look in his eyes. His clothes were wrinkled, and he looked like he probably could use a shower. There was a scar on his left cheek that you could barely make out under what appeared to be about three days of beard growth. His brown hair was long and wavy, sticking up all over his head as though he had just crawled out of bed. Some people went to salons to get that look. Ish was pretty sure it came natural to Danning.

Yet, in spite of how little attention he paid to his appearance, his eyes were the eyes of a man both dedicated and calculating. Ish instinctively knew that if he were to ever match chess moves with this man, it would be wise not to underestimate him. Even his appearance was not something to be taken at face value. Maybe it was just the way he was. Or maybe it was a clever ruse, created to distract people and cause them to make careless mistakes that Danning could then capitalize on.

The cops appeared to be waiting for Ish to initiate the conversation. He considered remaining silent and forcing their hand, but he was already tired of looking at the drab paint on the walls of this room. He wanted to get this business concluded and behind him as quickly as possible.

"So, officers," he said, "how can I help you?"

Danning dived right in. "Where were you on the day that Nathanial Bartholomew died?" he asked.

"That depends," he answered.

"On what?" asked Colleti.

"On what time of the day you're asking about."

"Let's say between the hours of 10am and noon," said Danning.

"At 10am I was sitting in the Baltimore airport terminal. At approximately 11:06 I was boarding a plane to Los Angeles."

"And when—" started Danning.

"Let's cut to the goddamn chase here," interrupted Colleti. "We have reason to believe that you were present when Officer Newhall stopped Bartholomew."

"What gives you that impression?" asked Ish.

"Because we don't believe that what happened to Newhall could have been done by Bartholomew, especially when he had already been blinded by pepper spray. Besides," continued Colleti, "as we already mentioned, your fingerprints were all over the goddamn car!"

"That doesn't surprise me," said Ish. "I was here visiting Nathan for a few days. We drove all over the city in that car, and that was also the same car that he drove me to the airport in."

Chief Amster had yet to speak. He was apparently content to simply observe his detectives at work. Before Colleti could speak again, Danning leaned over and whispered something in his ear. Ish couldn't hear what was said, but the frown on Colleti's face indicated that whatever it was, he didn't like it.

"Alright," said Colleti to Ish, his voice heavy with resignation. "I guess that's it for now. But understand something," he said, scooting his chair a few inches closer to Ish and lowering his voice. "I know you were there, and I'm pretty sure you're the one that took out Newhall, and that you're also the source of the mysterious 911 call. As soon as I find a real witness that ties you to that location, I'll be bringing your black ass in on charges of murder." Ish just nodded in response.

"You're free to go," said Danning.

"Uh, one more thing," said Amster, finally speaking up. "I understand that you served in Afghanistan with Bartholomew. Special forces, wasn't it?"

"That's right," said Ish matter-of-factly as he pushed his chair back and stood up to leave.

"They say special forces training turns ordinary men into walking lethal weapons. Is that true?"

"I'm not at liberty to say," said Ish.

"Meaning, you could tell me but then you'd have to kill me?" said Amster, smiling slightly.

"Something like that," said Ish, returning the smile. He exited the room, leaving the door open behind him.

As Ish walked from the conference room and through the station towards the main doors, he felt the eyes of every officer in the precinct glued to his every step. Some of their faces were masks of disgust bordering on rage. He wouldn't have been surprised if one of them had tried to tackle him right there.

Once outside the police station, Ish called an Uber to come pick him up. He was told it would be a twenty-minute wait. As he stood in front of the station, waiting, he was well aware of the unusual amount of undue attention he was getting in the form of mean stares and sideway glances from various officers entering and leaving the precinct. He thought about calling Uber back and having them pick him up a few blocks away, but that seemed overly cautious. As hostile as the vibes he was getting were, he felt it unlikely that any of these police officers would actually approach him or that anything would come of it if they did.

Eighteen minutes later he was sitting in the back of a black Jaguar sedan with dark tinted windows. He decided not to return directly to the law office or the Goldbergs' home. He didn't feel like answering a bunch of questions right now, questions that he knew were certainly going to be asked. Besides, a little time alone would help him to re-center himself and decide on his next move. He really hadn't spent much time planning this trip beyond the march to the police station. He would play it by ear. The goal was to make himself available to Garrison and Virginia for anything that he might be able to help with. Once he was no longer needed, he'd head back to L.A. and decide on the next course of action.

The driver was able to recommend an excellent restaurant in the vicinity. After a leisurely, decadent lunch of lamb chops, kale salad and a steamed apricot puree on toast, Ish checked in with Garrison. The lawyer had nothing to report, but wanted to know what the police interrogation was all about. Ish tried to de-escalate the entire situation, telling Garrison that the cops were simply concerned because his fingerprints were on Nathan's car. Which, while not the complete truth, was at least the majority of the truth. Ish declined Garrison's offer to look into the matter more closely, and they agreed to touch base in a few days after Garrison had finished the initial court filings for the case.

Next, Ish let Virginia know that he was out of the police station and would be back at the house around dinner time. He hunkered down at a beautiful downtown coffee shop to people-watch and unwind. While there, he made some calls to his friends in L.A. to update them on the progress he was making. He was able to speak to Bird and Jag, but had to leave messages for Chad and Ma'am. He made a note to try them again in the morning.

Dinner with the Goldbergs wasn't as uncomfortable as he had thought it would be. Vincent and Virginia accepted his 'fingerprint' explanation without many questions. After all, it wasn't unreasonable that the cops would have dusted the car for prints, and it also wasn't unreasonable that his would have been found there.

Ish was a skillful cook and offered to make dinner for the three of them, but Virginia was so grateful for all he was doing for her brother that she wouldn't hear of it. After dinner, they all watched a movie on cable together. It was some kind of romantic comedy. Ish didn't remember much of the plot or even who the stars were. His mind was a thousand miles away, wondering how Layla was doing, and what he might be able to do to secure her freedom.

He didn't sleep very well that night. He tossed and turned, his dreams morphing into various nightmares and horror stories. At 5am he finally decided he'd had enough of this losing battle and might as well get up and get an early run in before the temperatures became too unbearable.

He walked out of the house at 5:15am, wearing a loose-fitted t-shirt, track pants and Nike cross-training shoes. The guest key that Virginia had given him, allowing him to come and go without disturbing them, was in his pocket, along with his driver's license. It was still a good 40 to 50 minutes before sunrise, and the streets, though not entirely empty, were more sparsely populated than he had seen them since he arrived back in town.

Two miles into his run he came across a park with a small pond in the middle of it. Staring at it gave him an unusual sense of peace, so he stopped running and took a few minutes to walk around it and stretch his hamstrings out at a park bench that he happened upon. After fifteen minutes, he decided that he had procrastinated long enough and started jogging again, heading out of the park.

Ish was at the outer edge of the park, running through one of its parking lots, when a police cruiser drove past him down the street. Almost immediately, it slowed and then made a lazy U-turn. Ish kept jogging towards the street, staring straight ahead but keeping track of the cop car in his peripheral vision. The cruiser's overhead red and blue lights began flashing, and the car pulled into the parking lot driveway and stopped directly in front of Ish, blocking his pathway to the street beyond. Two officers got out of the car. Both were white, appeared to be in their mid-to-late twenties and had short, brown hair. They were also both about 5'10" tall, but one had a very slight frame while the other was extremely muscular. Seeing them together, Ish immediately thought of Steve Buscemi and Arnold Schwarzenegger. Except these guys weren't actors.

Ish took a deep, calming breath and waited for the cops to address him.

"What are you doing in this park?" asked Buscemi.

"I'm just out for an early jog, officer," said Ish. "Is that a problem?"

"It is when you're breaking the law," said Schwarzenegger.

"What law?" asked Ish.

Buscemi pointed at a sign a few feet away. "The park is closed daily from sundown to sunup. In case you haven't noticed, the sun's not up yet. That makes you a trespasser. Let's see some ID."

"No problem," said Ish as he began to reach into his pants pocket.

"Hold it!" said Schwarzenegger. "Keep your fucking hands where I can see them!"

Ish froze, doing as he was told.

"Hey, man," said Schwarzenegger to his partner, a big smile starting to spread across his face, "I don't need to see this fucking guy's ID. I know who he is. This is Ishmael Carter. I had no idea when we rolled up on him, but now that I see him in the light, he looks exactly like his picture on Colleti's investigation board."

Buscemi froze, his mouth hanging open. "You mean this is the guy that...?" Schwarzenegger nodded his head slowly. "Shit," said Buscemi, starting to develop a smile of his own. "This must be our lucky day."

Ish knew he was in trouble. Both cops were at least 15 feet away from him, and a good ten to twelve feet from each other, flanking his left and right sides. Unlike the situation with the cop who had attacked Blade, there was no way he could get to them before they could draw on him.

"What is this about?" he asked calmly.

"This is about you being a cop killer," said Buscemi as he pulled a taser gun from his utility belt.

Ish knew it was pointless to try to reason with these cops, so he simply shifted his body into a fighting stance and prepared for their assault.

"Looks like this nigger wants to rumble," said Schwarzenegger, circling to his left.

"Maybe he wants to kill us like he did Newhall," said Buscemi, scowling as he raised the taser and pointed it at Ish's chest.

The fact that the one officer had pulled a taser instead of a handgun and the other still had yet to pull a weapon told Ish a couple of things about their plans. First, they didn't want to attract too much attention. And second, they wanted to spend a bit of time working on him. If they had just wanted him dead, they could have shot him point blank. Maybe they meant to kill him, maybe they just meant to rough him up, but whatever their intentions, it wasn't going to be pretty. Considering the fact that they had just accused him of killing one of their colleagues, he seriously doubted that they were going to be content with a simple beat down.

Ish began backing up, trying to put some space between him and the two cops. Schwarzenegger pulled something off of his utility belt, and with a flick of his wrist was holding a 21-inch telescoping steel baton. There was a bloodlust in his eyes. Ish angled his body toward Schwarzenegger, who was slowly closing the distance between them, but he kept Buscemi in his peripheral, as the taser was the more immediate threat. Ish knew that for the taser to be most effective, both prods had to hit him in the upper torso. As he turned his body toward Schwarzenegger, he was consciously giving Buscemi a smaller target, with the hope that he might be able to dodge the taser attack altogether.

But the cops apparently had some experience with this. Schwarzenegger leaped forward and feigned a swing with the baton. The distraction was enough to cause Ish to momentarily take his eyes off Buscemi, who used the opportunity to fire. One prod hit him squarely in the chest. The other entered his left bicep. It wasn't ideal placement, but it was enough to cause the left side of his body to lock up.

As the current surged through him, it felt like all of his muscles were on fire. He involuntarily bit his tongue and felt the blood explode into his mouth. He went down on one knee, and as he was falling back, he felt the steel of the metal baton graze his left jaw. Somehow, he was able to get his right arm to move and positioned it in front of his face to protect himself from the next blow. Instead of using the baton, Schwarzenegger kicked him instead. He felt the cop's steel-toed boots smash into his ribs. Meanwhile, Buscemi began punching him in the face.

But the taser surge had ceased, and with his muscles starting to release, Ish was able to strike back. He grabbed Buscemi's shirt and hammered the cop with two elbow strikes. The thinner cop howled in pain and stepped back, but the more muscular one kept up his boot attack. Ish rolled to his side to protect it from further abuse, but the next kick hit him in the solar plexus, and he felt all the air escape from his lungs. He tried to curl himself into a ball to protect himself as much as he could, but the next strike he felt was Schwarzenegger stomping on his head.

Wrapping his arms around his head was poor protection from the stomping, and Buscemi had returned and was also kicking him repeatedly in the back. After the fourth head stomp, he felt himself beginning to lose consciousness. He thought of Sumatra, and wondered briefly if she was in heaven, watching her father get beaten to death. At least he was consoled by the possibility that he might soon be reunited with her. Just before he passed out, he heard a voice say "Hey! What are you doing to him?" And then all the pain was gone.

Chapter 20

When Ish opened his eyes, all he could see was white. His first thought was that this must be snow. He must be outside somewhere in the midst of winter. Yet, there was no landscape to speak of; no trees, no mountains, no hills, not even clouds. Then he started to discern shapes. He thought that they could be stars, except that they were dark instead of bright, and they were round and in a uniform pattern that would have been unusual for any star pattern he had ever seen.

His focus gently evolved, and soon he could see that what he was looking at were holes. What he initially thought was the sky was, in actuality, the ceiling. Gradually, a sound began to reach his ears. It was a rhythm, and initially all he could detect was the rhythm; a pulse, with no timbre that he recognized. But after a few minutes he was able to decipher the pulse. It was a beep. Turning his head to the side, the sky/ceiling shifted, and he was staring at the green and red lights of a machine. He swallowed, and it felt as though he had licked a sheet of sandpaper. He closed his eyes again and was thankful for the darkness that gracefully engulfed him.

In the folds of the darkness, Ish felt a warmth on his right side. He tried to ignore it, but it was persistent. Once it became obvious that it wasn't going to go away on its own, he forced his eyes to reopen, curious as to what it was that was so insistent on getting his attention. What he saw was a hand. The warmth that he felt was body heat from that hand. Obviously, it belonged to someone who was unaware of his extreme desire to simply be left alone.

Ish's eyes focused on this intruding hand and followed it up the arm it was attached to. At the end of the arm was a face, and the face seemed familiar. Chad. The face belonged to Chad. Why was Chad bothering him when he was trying to sleep? Ish took a deep breath, and suddenly he was flooded with an awareness of memories. He realized that the machines that he had just seen were typical of hospital rooms, as was the rhythmic beeping he had initially heard. He must be in a hospital. Then he remembered the cops. Schwarzenegger and Buscemi. And then their stun gun, baton and boots. Yeah, the boots he remembered quite well. He felt a growing pain in his chest, which reminded him exactly what his interaction with those boots had been.

"Chad?" he said. His voice sounded distant and unfamiliar. He tried to clear his throat and broke out in a fit of coughing. Someone put a straw in his mouth. Instinctively, he sucked on it, not caring what it was he was about to consume as long as it was liquid. It was water. At least, that's what it tasted like.

"Welcome back to the world of the living," said Chad. He was smiling, but there was a sadness in his eyes.

Ish stared at Chad for a few seconds. Neither spoke. Ish slowly turned his head and took in the room. Chad was the only other person present. The room was, indeed, predominantly white in color. There was a green chair beside the bed. And there was a small table with an orange top. But other than that, everything was white—the walls, the ceiling, the floor and even the bedding. Everything, that is, except Ish and Chad.

"Where am I?" he asked once he had finished taking a visual inventory of the room.

"Mercy General," said Chad. "Do you remember what happened?"

Ish frowned. His mind started to flip through his memories, trying to remember what had transpired directly before this moment. It was like crawling around the floor of a pitch-dark room, looking for a lost key, knowing that if you couldn't touch at least some piece of it, you'd probably never find it. But then a flicker of light appeared out of nowhere.

"A couple of cops beat the shit out of me," he said. There was some sense of relief in his voice. Bad as the memory was, it was better to have bad memories than no memory at all. "But I'm a little fuzzy on the details of how I got here."

"A group of people came across the scene where the two cops were attacking you," said Chad. "Everyone whipped out camera phones, and the cops panicked and took off. You were out cold. They called an ambulance, which brought you here." Chad stood up and took his jacket off before continuing the story.

"After Virginia hadn't heard from you all day, she tried calling you and heard your phone ringing in your room. That's when she began to worry. She starting calling around to local hospitals that evening. She got lucky with the first one she called. She had my contact info from the funeral and didn't know what else to do, so she called me. I was on a plane at midnight. Been here ever since."

Ish shook his head in disbelief. "How long have I been out?" he asked.

"You were in a coma for two days. Brain swelling. The doctors are pretty amazed at how quickly you've been recuperating since you came to. You actually woke up yesterday morning. You and I already had this conversation once. But the docs said it's normal for you to experience a bit of short-term memory loss, so I'm not surprised that you don't remember."

Ish didn't speak for the next ten minutes. His frown had returned and was hardening by the minute. Chad had known him long enough to know that it was best to give him some time to process the situation on his own terms. He finally fixed his gaze on Chad.

"Those fucking cops tried to kill me," he said. "They accused me of killing the cop that killed Blade. Apparently, I'm a 'person of interest' in the investigation. I need to get out of here."

"And do what?" asked Chad.

Ish gave him a hard look. "Thanks for coming, Chad. You know how much I appreciate it. But it's time for you to go back to L.A. You don't need to get involved with what I'm about to get into."

Chad didn't know what to say. He looked lost.

"Alright then," he said finally. "The doctors say you'll be here at least another five or six days for observation. I'll let you get some rest, but I'll stop by to check on you tomorrow on my way to the airport." They embraced warmly, and Chad walked out of the room, leaving Ish alone with his thoughts. No protest, no argument. Knowing Chad as he did, he couldn't help thinking that their exchange had gone a bit too smoothly for his liking. Something was up.

* * *

The next morning came and went, and Chad never appeared. On the one hand, Ish was glad that he had gone. He had always been protective of his childhood friend. And Chad had a habit of acting recklessly sometimes. But on the other hand, he missed him. The road that he was about to plunge down was a dangerous one, and he wasn't completely sure he'd have another chance to see his old friend before...before what? He had no idea where this would all lead. They say revenge is a dish best served cold, but he didn't feel like waiting for his to cool down.

For most of the last two days he had been contemplating what his next step would be. Even with as much thought as he had given it, he still didn't exactly have a concrete plan. What he knew was that cops like Schwarzenegger and Buscemi had been doing what they'd done to Ish to innocent black people since the days when the first blacks were captured and transported to this so-called land of opportunity. He'd personally lost everything because of it—his woman, his child—everything.

Obviously, he couldn't cure the world. He wasn't going to be able to bring every dirty cop to justice. But what he could do was track down these two cops and serve them some personal justice of his own. So, his first move was to figure out what their real names were and pay them a visit. What he was going to do to them once he did catch up to them was something he was still working out in his head. But it wasn't going to be gentle. And he didn't want Chad associated with it.

The attending doctor came into the room that evening to let Ish know that they would be releasing him the next morning. The short-term memory loss seemed to have pretty much cleared up, and they didn't expect any other lasting effects from the short coma and head injury. Three ribs were cracked, and those would be sore for a few weeks to come, and there was some deep bruising along his spine that would also be some source of extended soreness, but overall, they considered him to be quite lucky. Even the cuts and abrasions on his face were clearing up remarkably quickly.

Virginia had come for a visit a couple days before, shortly after he had awoken to find Chad in his room. She brought him a change of clothes and his wallet and cellphone. Their conversation had been awkward and painful. He could see how the stress of what had happened to him had affected her, especially so soon after her brother's death.

"Ishmael," she had said, wringing her hands together nervously from a metal chair next to his bed. "Do you think this was retaliation for us bringing the lawsuit against the department?"

"No, not at all," replied Ish. "If that were the case, they would most likely have gone after you rather than me. I'm just paying the bills. You're the one actually suing them. I was just in the wrong place at the wrong time. Don't worry about it."

But he could tell that she was worried. There was guilt written all over her face. She felt responsible for what had happened to him, and he wasn't sure how to convince her otherwise. Telling her that he was the one who had actually killed the cop who killed her brother, or even that the cops suspected him of such, was not going to help the situation. It could only serve to make her more of a target if the cops ever realized that she knew the truth of what had happened that day.

The next morning, Ish was up early. After getting dressed and signing the necessary paperwork, he grabbed the rest of his belongings and headed for the exit. What he saw before him in the lobby of the hospital caused him to freeze mid-step; there stood Chad, Jag, Bird and Ma'am.

Ish embraced each of his four friends then took a step back to examine them as a group. They obviously all knew the question that was on his lips, so he didn't voice it, given that they were in public.

"I have a suite at the Sheraton," said Chad, reading his mind. "We can talk there."

Without another word, the group walked out the front doors of the hospital and into a rented SUV that the valet had waiting for them. Once they were all inside and on the road, with Chad behind the wheel, Ma'am was the first to break the silence.

"You don't look too worse for wear. How do you feel?"

"I've been better, but I've been worse," said Ish.

"I prayed for you," she said. "For a minute there we thought those muthafuckas had killed you. But it's alright. We're here now." Ish smiled in response, but she didn't return it. Her face was grim and determined. Ish had a pretty good idea of what was going on behind the mask.

When they arrived at the hotel, Chad self-parked the vehicle, and everyone maintained silence all the way up to the room. The suite, which was on the eighteenth floor, was enormous. It was tastefully furnished in a bronze-on-white color scheme. There were modern art paintings on two of the walls in the living room area and a medium-sized conference table in the center of the room. A 50-inch TV took up much of a third wall. The final wall was floor-to-ceiling glass that delivered a stunning view of downtown Baltimore. Closed doors on each side of the room led to what must be bedrooms.

Ish put his bag down on a table next to the TV and took a seat at the conference table. There were decanters containing water, coffee and orange juice. Everyone took a moment to grab a glass or cup of their beverage of choice.

"So," said Ish, looking around the table at his friends. "What, may I ask, are you all doing here?"

"Don't ask stupid questions," said Jag. He was absent his normal shit-eating grin. Ish realized that there were very few times that he could remember having conversations with Jag when his face wasn't plastered with that ever-present smile. That was just a part of who he was. He was the guy who never took anything so seriously that it made him break character, but that always got the job done anyway. But something had changed. In that moment, his old friend appeared to be a different man.

Instead of responding to Jag, Ish looked at Chad and waited for him to answer. He was fairly confident that whatever was happening had been instigated and organized by Chad.

"When I left you at the hospital," began Chad as he looked down and self-consciously picked some lint off his shirt sleeve, "I felt enraged. You have to understand, Ish, that I've been fighting this battle for going on 15 years now. While you were overseas, fighting foreign terrorists, I was here, fighting domestic ones." Ish took a deep breath and nodded for him to continue.

"Obviously, police brutality was only a part of it, but it was probably the most infuriating part. In the 21st century, you'd expect the political machine to move slowly in response to things like pleas for equal pay or more affordable education. But how can it be that black people in America are still being hunted, beaten and killed as though they were nothing but animals?" The question was rhetorical, but he still let it hang in the air for a few moments. No one at the table felt the need to answer it.

"Chad," said Ish, "I understand that you're upset. But this isn't your fight."

"Why isn't it?" asked Chad, his voice heavy with challenge.

Ish was speechless. He stared hard at Chad but did not know how to answer this simple question. He knew that emotions were raw right now, and that saying the wrong thing could hurt and offend his old friend, which was the last thing in the world he wanted. His gaze softened, and he leaned back a bit in his chair and took a sip of coffee from his cup.

"I apologize," he said finally. "I know you've been involved in the fight for civil rights since we were back in high school. And I truly respect your dedication and commitment. But what are we talking about here? Are you ready to attack cops for your cause? Are you ready to go to prison, maybe even the grave, for what you believe in?"

"Yes, I am," said Chad. "You know, when you told me you were enlisting in the military, I thought that the reason I chose not to follow you was that I was afraid. Yeah, I said that I needed to stay here and take care of the company, and that I didn't like what the U.S. was doing over there, and that my parents would never forgive me if I died in battle. And all that was true." He took a breath and scanned the faces of the other people at the table, as though he had forgotten they were there and had just realized that he and Ish weren't alone.

"The thought of being in gun battles with foreign people in a strange land terrified me. But what I've grown to realize is that it's not that I was afraid of dying. I was just afraid of dying for something that I didn't believe in. I believe in this. Even though my skin is yellow instead of black, I believe that I'm a part of this, and that this is something important. Important enough to die for. That's something that I think even my parents would understand."

Ish felt anger welling up inside him. He wanted to cuss his friend out, to insult him in a way that, just moments ago, he would have done anything to avoid. He wanted to tell him that he was no soldier; that he was just a fucking nerd with a 'nigga fixation' and that he needed to turn around and take his sorry ass back to L.A. But then he realized that these thoughts weren't the result of anger, but the result of fear.

He was afraid for his friend. He was afraid that Chad was about to ruin his life fighting in a war that he would never truly be equipped for. He was afraid that he would one day have to sit down with this man's parents and explain to them why he hadn't stopped their son from making the biggest mistake of his life; how he had failed him as a brother and as a friend. And he was afraid because he knew that nothing he could say was going to change Chad's mind. Chad Yang had chosen his path, and with or without Ish, he was going to follow it to the end.

"Let's forget, for a moment," said Ish, "that you're no soldier and are way out of your league here, Chad. But the rest of you?" he said, waving his arm at the other people at the table. "You're all experienced soldiers. How did you all get mixed up in this mess?"

"I asked them—" began Chad.

"He didn't need to ask us," said Ma'am, cutting him off. "When a friend is in trouble, you don't need to wait for them to ask for help. If you were pinned down from heavy weapons fire in some valley in Afghanistan, do you think any of us would wait for you to ask for help?"

"This is different," said Ish.

"No, it's not," she answered.

"In Afghanistan, you weren't breaking the law," said Ish.

"Depends on whose fucking law you're talking about," said Jag. The smile had returned to his face. "We might not have been breaking U.S. laws, but we were breaking somebody's fuckin' law! I think the Afghanis probably have laws against cocky foreign soldiers coming into their country and shooting their people to shit. But that's just a guess."

Ish was at a loss for words again. He stared at Bird, who so far was the only one at the table that hadn't weighed in. Bird shrugged his shoulders and nodded his head as if to say, 'What can I say? They're right'. Ish wanted more from him, but he accepted that for now.

"So, what exactly are you all proposing?" he asked the group. "Are you here to help me go after these two cops?"

"Yes, but it goes beyond that," said Chad. There was a rise of excitement in his voice, and he leaned forward in his chair. "This is way bigger than just going after two dirty cops."

"Explain," said Ish.

"Okay," said Chad. "We could take revenge on these two cops. We could even make them disappear. But what exactly would that change? Very few people would know exactly why they suffered the fate they suffered. Their families would cry for them, and the department would look for someone to pin it on, but they'd be not only quickly forgotten, but quickly replaced. Two new cops would take their spots, and there is no guarantee that they would be any better, any less corrupt."

"I suppose that's correct," said Ish.

"So, what we have to do is take this offensive public. We need to make sure that everyone understands that what will happen to these two cops is retribution for their crimes against humanity. Police officers across the nation need to be put on notice: abuse innocent people and become a target yourself."

"Wow," said Ish, taken aback. "That's, uh, that's deep. And not at all what I was expecting. What you're talking about is, um, kinda crazy. We're five people. How in the hell would we be able to pull off something like that?"

"Well, you see—" began Ma'am.

"And how the hell was Chad able to get you all down here with such a ridiculous plan? What about your jobs? What, are you all on fucking vacation?"

"Actually, that's not far from the truth," said Chad, smiling. "You see, they all work for us now."

"What do you mean they 'work for us'?"

"I knew it was irrational to expect that they could all just take time off from their jobs, so I offered them all jobs at our company. They are now all official employees of Macrolox Inc. Brilliant, right?"

Ish could not help but chuckle. He shook his head.

"You people are all insane," he said. "I need to hit the head."

After he returned from the restroom, instead of going back to his seat, he opened the sliding glass doors and walked out onto the balcony. Standing at the rail, he stared across the horizon, deep in thought. A few moments later Bird appeared beside him. Neither man immediately spoke, both appearing to be absorbed in the spectacular view. Bird broke the silence.

"I know what you're thinking right now, Ish," he said softly. "I remember what you were like when you first found out about your daughter's passing. How reckless and foolhardy you were, almost to the point of being suicidal. But you were still careful not to deliberately put any of our lives in danger, so I know that has to be eating at you right now; the idea that we're unnecessarily getting involved in a fight you'd rather just fight by yourself."

Ish didn't respond, instead continuing to simply stare out across the city.

"Look, I get it," said Bird, turning around and leaning his back against the rail. "But you have to understand that we wouldn't be here if we didn't think it was the right thing to do."

Ish finally turned and locked eyes with his friend.

"I have enough blood on my hands, Bird," he said. "I've become part of a culture of death and have done my fair share of the killing. Some of it I regret, and some of it I don't, but the one thing that I have learned is that no matter how many people you kill, there are always more that need killing. And yet, none of it makes very much difference at the end of the day. So, what bothers me is that you're all about to throw your lives away on a worthless cause that's not going to matter much in the greater scheme of things."

"Worthless? My brother, this cause is far from worthless. We have potential to save some lives. Maybe we can stop another Blade from dying. Maybe we can stop another unarmed black teenager from being gunned down in cold blood."

"Do you really believe that?" asked Ish. "I mean seriously: do you really think that anything we do to a handful of cops is going to make a dent in what has been 200 years of institutionalized racism by the police forces of this country?" He returned his gaze to the horizon. "If you do, then that proves that you've been listening to Chad too much, buying into his propaganda."

"You're being a bit disrespectful," said Bird. "We're not children."

Ish squeezed the railing with both hands in frustration. "I'm not saying you're children, Bird. And I'm not trying to be disrespectful. I'm trying to save your fucking lives. Literally save them, so that you don't waste them trying to make a difference in a fight you can never win."

"I get it," said Bird, nodding his head. "You're afraid. Afraid for us, maybe even afraid for yourself. But you haven't even heard what Chad has to say. We listened to him for two days before we all accepted his offer. This isn't some spontaneous, spur-of-the-moment decision. Plus, the fact that I'm here should tell you something." That last comment caused Ish to shift his gaze back from the landscape to his friend.

"You know that I'm by far the most conservative one in the group," continued Bird. "Shit, I'm damn near a Republican. But don't let Ma'am know I said that, or she'll kick my ass. The only thing she hates worse than a white Republican is a black Republican." Both men chuckled.

"My point is, if Chad was able to convince someone as right-leaning as I am, then you know that whatever he said must have been really heavy." Ish looked down at his feet, contemplating what his friend had just said. "Because the bottom line," said Bird, "is that regardless of whether I'm a Democrat or a Republican, I'll always be black, and I'll always be proud of my racial heritage. And as far as I'm concerned, an attack on one black person is an attack on all black people. If I can help fight that in any way, I'm willing to do whatever it takes. So, before you make any more decisions about our futures, at least come in and listen to Chad's plan."

Ish didn't speak for a long time as he stood staring at the ground. Bird was patient, knowing better than to interrupt the process. Finally, Ish looked up. "Fair enough," he said. Bird opened the door, and Ish followed him back into the hotel room.

Ish and Bird both took a seat.

"Alright," said Ish to Chad. "I'm listening."

Chapter 21

Chad cleared his throat and licked his lips before taking a big sip of water. There was the flush of excitement in his cheeks. He looked like an eager third grader about to give his first book report before the rest of the class. As nervous it he might have appeared, Ish knew firsthand that Chad was an excellent speaker and teacher. He'd seen him lead many meetings and workshops, both in school and at Macrolox. Part of his awkwardness was natural, but a part of it was also exaggerated; an excellent way to reduce the barrier between teacher and student, employer and employee, and make him that much more relatable.

It worked brilliantly. The staff of Macrolox were some of the brightest, most innovative group of people that Ish had ever met, and were all constantly being courted by some of the largest tech companies in the world. But the Macrolox turnover rate was almost non-existent. Most of their current payroll of thirty-four people (thirty-seven now, with the addition of the three soldiers seated) were original hires. A couple of programmers had left to start their own companies or pursue some other type of entrepreneurial interest, but it was a very rare occurrence. A lot of that also had to do with Chad's skill at hiring; he had an eerie knack for reading people and knowing who to hire and who to pass on. It was no surprise to Ish that Chad had been able to bring their three friends together for such a wild, unlikely project.

"Let me start at the beginning," said Chad. "Hearing about Blade's death was a shock. As I've said before, I didn't know him as well as any of you did," he said, looking around the table, "but I spent a decent amount of time with him and I considered him a friend, as I do all of you. So, his murder filled me with sadness and just really pissed me off. After the night that we all got together in his honor at the bar, I couldn't get over these feelings. I'd be at the office, writing code or reviewing a contract, and suddenly I would find myself thinking about it again, over and over. And then when Virginia called and told me that you were in the hospital, it was like déjà vu. I thought we were about to lose you, as well." Chad paused. He sniffed and cleared his throat again, clearly fighting to keep his emotions in check.

"I was on the next flight, and was stoked to find that you were going to be alright. But that anger wouldn't go away. And looking in your face that day in the hospital, listening to the words that came out of your mouth, I knew that you weren't going to just let this go; that you were going to fight for justice. And I wanted to be a part of that fight. And I figured that the rest of the gang would probably want to be a part of it, too. So, I went back to L.A. and invited everyone to a dinner meeting at the office."

"You should have been there, Ish," said Ma'am. "He did the shit up tight! Lobster, shrimp—them giant shrimp. What do call them again?" she asked, turning to Chad. "Pawns?"

"Prawns," said Chad.

"Yeah, there you go. That shit was delicious! Very classy," she said, nodding her head for emphasis. "I was impressed."

"I get that," said Ish.

"Anyway," said Chad, eager to get back to his story, "the purpose of the meeting was to present this idea I had. A way to possibly effect massive change all across the country.

"I've given this a lot of thought," he continued as he grabbed a leather messenger bag off the floor beside him and began digging around in it. He pulled out an iPad and entered a six-digit code to unlock it. "I have a slide presentation here that lays it all out—"

"I don't need to see all that right now," said Ish a little impatiently. "Just give me the broad strokes."

Chad paused, clearly a bit deflated at not being able to show Ish the product of all his planning.

"Okay," he said. "As I mentioned before, simply going after those two cops is not going to change anything. It might make us all feel a little less angry, but that's about it. What we need to do is make them an example, and make sure that the whole world knows what happened to them, and why. We need to put cops on notice: if you violate the rights of minorities, you will have a higher power to answer to, and answer you will."

"And how exactly do you plan to tell the world about this grand deed? Take out an ad in the New York Times?" asked Ish.

Chad gave him a look that said 'don't be silly'. "A website," he said, somewhat smugly.

Ish's eyebrows arched as he pondered the idea. He was starting to see where Chad was going with this. It was still a crazy idea, but there was a certain logic to it.

"Let me make sure I understand this," he said. "We"—he looked around the table and waved a hand in the direction of the other people seated—"go after these two cops, and we broadcast their fate on a website, to create a sense of fear and cautiousness in all other cops?"

"It's a little more complicated than that," said Chad, "but that's the basic idea."

"And what are you suggesting should happen to these cops? We smack them around a little bit? Make them run through downtown naked? What?" asked Ish. There was an edge in his voice, a sense of frustration.

Chad didn't answer. He looked across the table at Blade, Ma'am and Jag.

"What are you looking at them for?" asked Ish. "This is your fucking plan, isn't it? Answer the question."

"You know the answer to that question, Ish," said Chad. "It's go big or go home. They have to go. Besides, don't act like you weren't already planning to take them out. I saw it in your eyes in the hospital room. These cops were dead the moment they drove off and left you still breathing, lying in a pool of your own blood in that park. The only question is whether we can make something epic out of this tragedy."

Even though Ish knew Chad was right, he couldn't believe what was happening right now. The people in this room were his most loved and cherished friends. How could they have all gotten to this point, willing to become murderers and fugitives? How does a group of people from such disparate backgrounds come to terms with something like this? How could they all be willing to forfeit their lives so easily with no guarantee that any of it would make a bit of difference in the long run?

Ish walked back to the sliding glass door and looked past the balcony and into the distance. He weighed his options, trying to figure out if there was a way out of this for him. After a few minutes, he turned around to face the others.

"Chad, I need to speak to the team alone. Please give us a few minutes."

"Alone?" said Chad. "If what you have to say involves this project, I deserve to be here." Jag nodded his head in agreement.

"Go for a walk, Chad," said Ish. His hands were in his pockets, and he appeared relaxed, but there was no mistaking the tone in his voice. This was not up debate.

Chad looked as if he wanted to protest further, but thought better of it. He gathered up his iPad, put it back in his messenger bag, and with the bag slung over his shoulder, walked out of the room.

After the door slammed shut behind him, Ish returned to his seat. He rubbed his hands through his hair and took a deep breath.

"What the fuck are you all doing?" he asked. No one answered. Bird looked away while Jag nonchalantly cleaned his nails. Only Ma'am actually met his gaze.

"Isn't one of you going to tell me how it came to be that you're following a civilian into a domestic war against the American police force?"

"You need to get off your high horse," said Ma'am. "He may be a civilian, but everything Chad said is dead on. None of us really wanted to have him involved in this any more than you do, but your boy knows what he's talkin' about. And if it weren't for him, none of us would be here right now. Every mission needs an organizer. He's ours. Besides, he's so fired up he's goin' ahead with this with or without you."

"He can do it without me, but he can't do it without all of you," said Ish. The implication was clear. He was asking them to bow out.

"Ice-Man," said Jag in his familiar, relaxed drawl, "you're acting like my Gramma Betty. I understand you want to do the mother hen dance and all. It's your nature. I get it. But what do you think you're protecting us from? None of us are married. None of us have kids. I had a crappy construction job, Ma'am was working security and Bird—well, okay, Bird's professor gig was pretty sweet—but we're all here because this thing is bigger than any of us as individuals."

"It's a suicide mission," said Ish.

"Maybe it is. But how many suicide missions did we run in Afghanistan?"

"He's right," said Bird. "Why do you believe putting our lives on the line in the Middle East for a government that barely protects us at home is any more noble than what we're planning here?" Ish didn't have an answer to that question, so Bird continued.

"We all joined the military to make a difference. We all knew when we joined that we might not make it back safe and sound. And we did it anyway."

"Death is one thing," said Ish. "Prison is another."

"Man, you're so blind right now," said Jag. "You seem to forget about all our people that have been captured and imprisoned in the name of war. I'll tell you, I'd sure as hell rather spend the rest of my life in a prison in Tennessee than a week in a prison in Kabul."

Ish stood up and leaned against the back of the chair. He searched the face of each of the people sitting at the table. His head hurt. His mind was a mass of confusion. Again, he didn't know what to say. So, he grabbed his bag and, with everyone silently staring at him, walked out of the room.

As he walked down the hall towards the elevator, Chad was leaning against a wall, talking on his cell phone. He quickly hung up as Ish hit the elevator button to summon the car.

"Ish, where are you going?" Ish didn't answer. He continued to stare straight ahead. The elevator doors opened, and he stepped inside.

"Ish! Where the hell are you going?" asked Chad again. They stood face to face, Ish in the elevator, Chad in the hallway. The door closed. As soon as Ish arrived in the lobby, he went out to the front of the hotel, where several taxis were waiting. He got into the back of the one that was at the front of the line and gave the driver Virginia's address.

The taxi's air conditioner was either not working well or the driver was opting to save gas by keeping it on a warmer setting, because the inside of the car was warm and muggy, a drastic difference from the coolness of the hotel room Ish had just left. As they weaved through the traffic of downtown Baltimore in the stifling heat, Ish tried to relax. He felt trapped, like a caged animal.

In the service, he had never really ever wanted to be in command. He was a natural leader, and people had been following his lead since elementary school. But leading a football team and leading people into war were two totally different things. He didn't mind taking the responsibility for losing the big game, but taking the responsibility for people losing their lives was something he was never going to be comfortable with.

Suddenly he felt exhausted and defeated. In some ways he regretted that he had ever gone back to Baltimore. All he wanted to do was try to help Blade's family find some sense of closure and maybe a bit of justice. And now his closest friends had followed him into a hornet's nest, and he had no idea how to get them out of it unharmed. His cell phone buzzed. It was Chad. He ignored the call.

He was relieved to find the Goldberg house empty. He was in the mood for neither sympathy nor more questions. He took a hot shower and changed clothes. Then he lay down for a few minutes. He had a headache, but he wasn't sure if it were a result of the stress of his current predicament or an aftereffect of his injuries. Forty-five minutes later he was up. His head felt a bit clearer. He made calls to both Virginia and Garrison. Neither had anything new to report, but both were happy to hear that he was out of the hospital, and they each offered their help for anything he might need.

One of the most valuable skills Ish had learned in his special forces training was how to quickly get a read on a situation; to rapidly calculate all possible options and to be able to choose the best one. Whether you were pinned down in the middle of a firefight or trying to control an angry mob of dissidents, there often wasn't a lot of time to make a decision, and the result of that decision could be the difference between life and death. Ish spent the next thirty minutes carefully weighing the odds for and against the various options available. He came to a decision. It was time to move.

Ish called for an Uber, then called Chad.

"Hey, man," answered Chad. "You alright?"

"I'm cool. Where are you?"

"I'm still here at the hotel."

"Is everyone else still with you?"

"Bird is outside, taking a smoke break, but yeah, everyone is here."

"Good," said Ish. "Tell them to hold tight. I'm grabbing a ride and I'll be there shortly."

"Okay," said Chad. "Is there a message I should give them?"

"No, just tell them I'm on my way, and we'll speak when I get there."

"You got it," said Chad, and they both hung up.

The Uber was a Mercedes, and the A/C was blasting on high, making the ride back to the team's hotel much more comfortable than the cab that Ish had taken to get away from them. It was mid-afternoon on a weekday, so traffic was relatively light. As he got closer and closer to his destination, Ish felt a calm begin to fall over him. It was much the same way he had dealt with dangerous battle situations in the Middle East. Once he knew the plan and what direction he'd be moving in, all fear and nervousness disappeared from his mind. It was how he came to be called 'Ice-Man' by Jag.

Ish's father had often told him there was "no use crying over spilt milk," because from the time he was a baby he had a reputation for whining and throwing fits whenever something didn't go the way he wanted or expected it to. For the longest time, Ish didn't understand what his father was trying to tell him until he had the opportunity to literally experience it for himself.

One Saturday morning when he was six years old, Ish got up earlier than usual and decided that he was now old enough to make his own cereal. With his parents still sleeping, he crept into the kitchen, grabbed a chair and used it to climb up to the top shelf of the refrigerator and grab the milk. It was in a glass bottle that had only been recently opened and was almost completely full. Getting it out of the fridge without falling and breaking his neck was a great accomplishment. But the process of pouring the milk into his bowl of Cap'N Crunch proved too much for him. He lost control of the heavy bottle and dumped all the milk all over the counter and floor. Moments later his father appeared in the doorway.

Ish was afraid that his dad would be furious, but instead he calmly hugged his son and told him not to worry about it, that accidents happen. Ish watched his father mop up the mess, and as he finished, Ish began to cry. His father asked him why he was crying, and Ish pointed to his bowl of dry cereal and the empty milk bottle and told his father there was no more milk left. His father asked him to explain how his crying was going to put milk back in the bottle. He answered that he didn't know, but he kept sobbing. His father told him to sit there and think about it, and walked away.

For twenty minutes Ish sat at the table, crying and looking at the empty bottle of milk. When his tears finally started to dry up, his father walked back into the room and said, "The bottle is still empty. Don't cry over the things you can't change. Tears are for pain. Pour that cereal in the trash while I cook you some breakfast."

It was a poignant lesson, and it was one that stuck. He was only six years old, but from that moment on Ish vowed to try not to waste his energy worrying about things that were beyond his control. It was a philosophy that had served him well for most of his life. His friends had made up their minds. The milk wasn't yet spilt, but the bottle was teetering and it was too late to try to catch it now.

Chad answered the door and let Ish into the hotel room. Bird, Jag and Ma'am were sitting at the table in the same seats they were in when Ish last saw them. There was an air of reserve and caution in the room. Everyone was aware of the seriousness of this meeting. Ish closed the curtains to the balcony and then joined Chad and the others at the table.

"Okay, let's get down to business" he said as though he had never left. He was now in tactical command mode. "Let's go over the top-level logistics of the operation. Chad, you said you had some plans. The floor is yours."

"Thanks, Ish. So, the first thing I'll need to do it set up a cloaked server so that when the authorities try to trace the signal back—"

"Hold up," interrupted Ish. "Before we get into all that, I'd like to know who the initial target of the operation is going to be."

Chad looked around at everyone, slightly confused. "Um, I thought we had decided that. I thought it was clear that we'd be going after the two cops that attacked you."

"And when we do that, who you think is going to be suspect number one? Maybe the ex-military black guy that they just beat the shit out of a couple of weeks ago?"

"I thought there was no report filed?" asked Ma'am.

"There wasn't," answered Ish, "but that doesn't mean people don't know. I suppose it's possible that these two officers never spoke a word of what happened that morning to anyone else, including their families and fellow cops, but I wouldn't want to bet my fucking life on it."

"Oh, shit," said Chad, lowering his head. "I didn't even think of that."

"Obviously," said Ish. "Look, we need to treat this like a military operation. And just like a military operation, we can't afford to be lax when it comes to calculating all the angles. Not if we all expect to survive this."

"I apologize," said Chad.

"No, it's us that should apologize," said Jag. "We're the ones with battle experience. Overlooking details like that is inexcusable. I think the excitement of the thing got us all a bit overly riled up. Don't worry, Ice-Man," he said, earnestly. "It won't happen again."

"Good enough," said Ish, nodding at him in acknowledgment. "So, Chad, let's take it back from the top. What's your basic game plan?"

"Well, since the two cops that assaulted you are now off the table, I suggest we hack into various police databases, comb the files for evidence of serious wrongdoing, and compile a list of viable targets. I've actually already started hacking into PD systems in a few of the major cities—L.A., D.C., Atlanta, New York and Miami—in anticipation of locating future prospects. Getting in—and getting out again without anyone being the wiser—is child's play. But the process of reviewing millions of digital pages is beyond tedious, in addition to being extremely time consuming. So, I'm in the process of writing some code that will crawl the data and pull what we need."

"Are you using the ART34 string?" asked Ish.

"Yes, but I'm having some trouble getting it to parse correctly. That was always your baby. Maybe you can pull an all-nighter with me, like we used to do in the old days, and help me debug it?" he asked, grinning.

"Okay, but I'd feel better doing this back in the offices as opposed to here in the field. Let's all get on the next flight back."

"I don't mean to interrupt this geek convention," said Jag, "but what should we be doing while you two are playing Bill Gates?"

"I was just getting to that," said Ish, grinning slightly. "We're going to need a bunch of gear that you can't find at Sports Chalet. Night scopes, sniper rifles, flash bang grenades, etc. I'll get together a list. I know you all have your own contacts, and I'll add a few of mine. You might have to zigzag the country a couple of times, but I don't think you'll have any problems securing what we need. Chad will get you set up with company charge cards to handle your plane tickets and other expenses. We'd better order some lunch. I'm hungry, and we've got a lot to talk about."

Chapter 22

The Macrolox offices were quiet. Most of the employees had left for the day, but Ish and Chad weren't worried about being disturbed. They were secluded safely behind the impervious doors of the War Room. Even still, Ish always felt better discussing delicate matters when he knew the rest of the offices were empty.

He took a sip of his coffee and grimaced. But looking at the cup made him smile. It had been a birthday gift from Layla five years ago. It had a picture of the rapper Notorious B.I.G. on one side and the phrase 'It was all a dream' on the other. He leaned back in his chair and rubbed his eyes, which had been burning for the last hour. He and Chad had been back in L.A. writing code for the last three days. He looked up at the clock. It read 1:53am.

"You look like you're about done," said Chad from a desk on the other side of the room.

"I just need a booster. This coffee reminds me of my Great-aunt Candice after she divorced Uncle Earl—cold and bitter." They both chuckled. "Is there any more?"

"I could use some myself," said Chad. "I'll put on a fresh pot." He walked over to the file cabinet that served as their 'coffee room' and began grinding a fresh batch of beans. After hitting the 'brew' button, he came over and sat down in a chair next to Ish, who was lost in thought.

"Are you okay, man?" he asked.

"Huh?" said Ish, his trance broken.

"I said are you okay? You've been zoning out all day."

"Oh, yeah. Just thinking about Layla."

"Oh, shit!" said Chad. "Today's her birthday, isn't it? I totally forgot! I'm sorry, man."

"No worries. Really," said Ish, waving off his friend's concern. "I can't even call her to wish her a happy birthday. I was hoping she'd be out by now and we could celebrate in person, but she's still refusing to leave, regardless of what I do."

"Wow. I'm sorry. I didn't know things were that bad."

"The only reason I'm really even doing this, all of this, is for her, and in memory of Sumatra. But I can't even tell her about it, even if I could reach her, because all the calls are monitored." Ish put his hand up to his chin and gazed off into the distance again.

"I know how hard that must be making this for you," said Chad. "I kind of feel the same way. The people that I'm doing this for will, if all goes well, never know that I was a part of making it happen. And not that I'm looking for gratitude or have any desire to play the hero in this story, but you know it's always been important to me that the people I care about know that I'm standing up with them."

Ish nodded his head in understanding then looked up thoughtfully.

"You know," he said, "it's funny, but I just realized that as long as I've known you, I've never asked you how a young Asian kid developed such a love for black culture in the first place."

Chad chuckled. "It's kind of a long story."

"I've got nothing but time, brother," said Ish.

"Alright. Let's see. Um, I guess it all started with dance, really," said Chad. "I remember I must have been about seven or eight, and my parents took me to Venice Beach one weekend, and on the boardwalk were these kids breakdancing. Man, that was the most remarkable shit I'd ever seen in my life! And there were these little kids doing it, too. Soon as I got home that night I ran to my room, put a book on the floor and tried to spin on my head. Almost broke my damn neck! The chiropractor thought I was insane!" They both laughed.

"No, I'm serious! After I explained to him what I was doing, he told my parents that they might want to consider taking me to see someone. He thought I might be engaging in 'self-destructive behavior'. I talked them out of it, but it was funny."

"Yeah, I can just see Mr. Y looking at you and wondering just what the hell it was you were trying to do. 'Is this kung-fu, Chad? This does not look like traditional kung-fu. You are going to hurt yourself, my son',” said Ish, imitating Chad's father's thick Chinese accent. They were both laughing so hard now that tears were coming out of Chad's eyes. The coffee was ready, so Chad grabbed the carafe and poured them both a cup.

“But I kept at it, man. I didn't stop. It fascinated me. And then the music! Oh my god, the music! The first album I ever bought was Nas' *Illmatic.* On cassette, no less. I had to hide it from my parents, and I could only listen with headphones on my little Walkman, but I wore that tape out! I just kept getting deeper and deeper into it after that.”

“What were your Asian friends saying about all this?”

“Most of them were family, because there weren't a lot of Asians in my hood, but they didn't understand. But I didn't care, because as much as I loved all the music, the side benefit was that girls started really digging me! Black girls, white girls, even the occasional Asian girl. Suddenly, I was cool!” They laughed again.

“Yeah, an Asian dude into hip hop wasn't something you saw every day. I remember that first time I saw you, at that talent show. You definitely stood out,” said Ish.

“True. But you know it wasn't all love. I got a lot of grief from it, man. Got in a lot of fights, which means I got my ass kicked a lot!” said Chad, shaking his head. “But I couldn't give it up. Somehow it had gotten into my blood. It frustrated my parents, but I was getting straight A's, so they didn't really stress me too much.”

“How did you go from break dancing and listening to rap to marching with signs and staging sit-ins?” asked Ish.

“It was the natural progression of things, I guess. I saw black people as part of my tribe, part of my ‘cultural identity', if you will. When I started learning about slavery and Malcolm X and Dr. King in history class, I was seriously bothered by it. But I thought all that was just part of America's dark past. It wasn't until I was a little older and started to learn about how black people were treated in the present that I started to really get pissed off. Like, how store owners would follow us when I went in with my black friends but not when I went in alone and how black kids I knew were getting constantly harassed by the police for no reason.” A dark shadow passed over Chad's face.

“I guess the final straw was this incident that happened with a good friend of mine, a dude named Chauncey. Man, Chauncey was one of the nicest, coolest and most talented kids I have ever known. He had mad dance skills, and much of my early break dance moves I learned from him. But he wasn't limited to the b-boy stuff. When the jocks weren't around, this dude was doing jazz moves, ballet moves, tangos! He could do it all. One day we were walking down Crenshaw, just minding our own business, when these two cops drove up and said he fit the description of some guy that had just robbed a liquor store. They started pushing him around and one of them hit him in the mouth with his billy club. He spit blood and teeth out all over the ground, and for a second everybody froze. Then Chauncey took off running. I guess he could see where this was all going. They drove after him, and the next time I saw him was two days later, in the hospital. They had crushed his legs between the car and a brick wall. One had to be amputated." The shadow deepened.

"He never walked again. He could have, with a cane or a prosthetic, but his heart was broken by the fact that he would never dance again, and he turned his back on all of it. A few months later, he and his family moved away, and I never saw him again. I sent several letters to the new address, somewhere in Texas, but I never got a response. Ever since then, I've tried to be involved in every civil rights action group I could find, hoping that I might be able to make a small difference somewhere along the way."

Ish nodded his head in silence. Each man sipped his coffee, allowing the gravity of the story to hang in the air between them, each acknowledging its importance without either of them having to say a word.

The next day Bird, Jag and Ma'am checked in with Ish: they had everything except for the remote sniper navigation system. But Ma'am had a lead. Jag and Bird had tickets for the next flight back to L.A. Ma'am was headed to Philadelphia to follow up on the navigation lead.

Ish and Chad had worked until 3:00am. When Ish got into the office the next morning at about 8:00, Chad was already there and had good news.

"I think we did it!" said Chad.

"Hold up, let me at least grab some coffee first," replied Ish.

"Right here," said Chad, smiling as he reached behind him and returned with Ish's Notorious B.I.G. mug filled with piping hot java.

"How did you know—" began Ish.

"I saw you drive in on the monitors," said Chad, talking quickly. "But that's not important. What is important is that we cracked it! I spent about an hour debugging the code this morning, and it all came together. For the last two hours the program has been probing police databases all over the country, starting here on the west coast and slowing working its way east."

"My man!" said Ish, giving him a high-five and then pulling up a chair. "Anything look promising so far?"

"That's the best part," said Chad. "We got our first hit right here in L.A. About two years ago a cop out of Hollywood stopped a twenty-two-year-old black male motorist for not using his turn signal. One thing led to another. The cop's report said that he felt his life was in danger, so he emptied his 9mm into the driver. No weapon was found at the scene, and the driver never even exited the vehicle. Two bystanders caught the whole thing on phone video, but the grand jury failed to indict. The civil suit by the family was dismissed. If ever there was a bastard in need of consciousness realignment, it's this dude."

"Cool," said Ish, rubbing his chin in thought. "Bird and Jag are on their way back, and Ma'am should be here in a couple of days. We'll get together as a team and brief them once they're all back on the ground."

"I've also been thinking about how we're going to cover our identities in the videos," he continued. "Ski masks are the obvious choice, but I don't think they create the right impression. Makes us look like criminals, if you know what I mean," he said, grinning slyly.

"That's true," said Chad. "There's a ton of different kinds of masks we can get. The way people get dressed up for Halloween these days, pretty much anything is available. Everything from Michael Myers to Spider-man to Nixon and everything in between."

"Yeah, and that's kind of the problem," said Ish. "So many choices, it's hard to choose one. Let's stick with the ski masks for the time being, and put the question to the rest of the team. Perhaps they have some suggestions."

"Good idea," said Chad. "I've already got some ideas for the script I'd like to run by you."

"Let's get to work," said Ish.

Chapter 23

Ish, Jag, Bird and Chad were all waiting in Macrolox's War Room when Ma'am texted that she had arrived and was buzzed in. After hugging everyone, she made herself a cup of tea and joined the rest of the group at the massive table.

"So," said Ish. "It appears that everything is almost ready. We've acquired all the gear we need, and it's sitting in rented storage facilities."

"How far away is the site?" asked Chad.

"Actually, it's in several different sites, spread out across the city but all within an hour's drive from here. We chose public storage places in good neighborhoods and where there were no cameras that would be documenting our coming and going. That's one fewer clue for anyone in law enforcement that might be investigating this."

"Speaking of investigations, where are we at with targets?" asked Jag.

"Chad, would you like to speak to this?" replied Ish.

"Sure. As you guys all know, we can't afford to make a mistake in this process. If we're going to go after a crooked cop, we need undeniable, indisputable proof that he is what he appears to be. This isn't a court of law, where decisions are made based on 'reasonable doubt'. Ish and I have written a program that can hack into pretty much any police database in the country, analyze the employee and internal affairs files on thousands upon thousands of police officers, report that data back to us and exit the system, all without anyone knowing we were ever there." He stood smiling and looking around the room. Everyone stared back at him, seemingly unimpressed.

"This is a big fucking deal, guys. How about a little applause?" asked Chad. Everyone smiled and clapped weakly. "Okay, okay, settle down. Seriously, this program we've come up with"—he looked over at Ish and shook his head in wonder— "is some high-tech shit. Anyway, we've had it running the last few days, and we've gotten a ton of hits based on keywords and meta tags and some other technical stuff that I won't continue to bore you with. But we wanted to take it further, to be extra sure, so I bumped the names against all known news feeds as well as YouTube and a bunch of other video sites, and we have our first four candidates. One is here in L.A., the others are New York, Nashville and Baltimore. We're skipping Baltimore for now, for obvious reasons. That leaves L.A., New York and Nashville."

"So, what exactly do we know about these cases?" asked Bird.

"Everything," said Chad. "We know what the news outlets reported, we know what their bosses and IA people thought, and we have actual video evidence of every single incident. We even raided some law office databases and grabbed some of the legal briefs and notes."

Jag whistled. "Wow. You boys don't mess around."

"Thanks, Chad," said Ish, taking over. "The plan here is that we all get briefed on the cases, and we all vote on whether or not to move forward. It's not a 'go' unless the vote is unanimous. Agreed?" he asked, looking around at each member of the crew. They all nodded their heads.

"But before we even get to that, I want to confirm with each one of you one more time that you're all sure you're ready to do this. Jag?"

"Ice-Man, I look at it as just trading one war for another one. Instead of shooting foreigners in a foreign land, that may or may not be bad guys, I get to go after someone in my own country that I know for sure is dirty. It's a slam dunk as far as I'm concerned. I'm in."

"Ma'am?" asked Ish.

"What he said," she said, and everyone laughed.

"What about you, Bird? How are you doing?" asked Ish.

"It's a difficult thing. I think it was easier when I was in Afghanistan, shooting at people that looked so different from us. Like Jag said, they're foreigners, but more than that, they're just foreign. Unfamiliar. Different. I think it made it easier for me, as a practicing

Christian, to come to terms with the dark side of it. Doing the same thing here on American soil against people that look like the people we grew up with is harder. But I prayed on it, long and hard. And I believe that God wants me to be a part of this. Count me in."

"Good," said Ish. "Let's get started on the briefing, but before I go on, I'd like to take a minute to touch on something both you and Bird just mentioned," said Ish, pointing at Jag.

"While Chad and I were here working on debugging this code, we had a lot of time to chat about the details of this project, drilling down into some of the specifics of what we're trying to accomplish. One of the things we realized is that when you break it down, this is about making all cops feel accountable for their actions, not just the murderers and the assassins. That means we have to go after a variety of different types of offenders. That being the case, death is not a just verdict for every offense. As with anyone that commits a crime, the punishment should fit said crime. In other words, we need to take an 'eye for an eye' approach to this if we truly want to call it justice." Ish paused to let his words sink in.

"Makes sense," said Jag, nodding.

"Alright then," said Ish. "Let's get started. The three cases that we are about to brief you on involve three different crimes: assault, rape and murder. Chad?"

Chad hit the light switch, enveloping the room in darkness before an image appeared on the 52-inch plasma screen that covered one wall. The image was the profile picture of a white male with short, wavy black hair and blue eyes. He had a slight mustache and was wearing a police uniform.

"This is Officer Dexter Pogue. Dexter is a bully. He likes to beat people up." The profile image dissolved and was replaced with a New York Times article with a headline that read 'Cop Accused of Excessive Force Has Long History'. "This cop," Ish continued, "has been accused of excessive force forty-seven times. He's only been punished once, and that was just a three-day suspension with pay for punching an elderly lady in the face." The next image showed a police department document listing recent complaints against the officer.

"We have this video of one of his more recent offenses," said Ish. The still image of the police document was replaced with video that showed Pogue punching a black teenager in the jaw. The teenager's hands were cuffed behind his back, and when he fell, landing on his face, the officer brought his knee down on the teen's neck. As the boy struggled, the officer punched him repeatedly in the back. The video ran for three minutes.

"This kid ended up in the hospital with a broken jaw and eye socket, a damaged kidney and multiple other injuries. The family tried to sue, but the case was thrown out."

"How is that possible?" asked Bird. "Didn't the judge see the video?"

"He did," said Chad. "But the cop said it was 'self-defense'. He said the boy spit on him and resisted arrest."

"Damn," said Ma'am.

"Forty-seven complaints and this dude has never lost a case? Who the fuck is his lawyer, Johnnie Cochran?" asked Jag.

"Most of the cases never get to court," said Chad. "Even the complaint he was suspended over was handled in-house. No suit was ever filed. Remember, these cops tend to prey on people that society doesn't really give a fuck about and that don't have the financial means to fight back. When you're struggling to put food on the table every night, you don't have a lot of money left over for lawyers to fight cases that you know you're probably going to lose anyway."

The room felt cold. Each member of the team, with the exception of Ish, was carrying the tension of the moment in their faces, their eyes hard, brows furrowed. Ish, true to his 'Ice-Man' moniker, was the only person who looked unaffected. But inside he was as bothered as everyone else was. Maybe even more so. He kept glancing out of the corner of his eye at Jag. Jag was notorious for cracking jokes to reduce the drama, sometimes in completely inappropriate ways, but he seemed to be taking this seriously, as if it were personal to him. Even the comment about Johnnie Cochran didn't really appear to be meant as a joke.

"Let's move on," said Ish, nodding at Chad, who pressed a button on the remote, cycling through to the next image on the screen.

"Next on the list is Detective John Ratcliff," continued Ish. "Mr. Ratcliff has a problem with the concept of 'No Means No'. According to his file, he's been accused of inappropriate sexual conduct while on duty nine times, and actual rape three times." The image on the screen was of another white man, this one in a gray business suit. He was handsome, with blond hair, blue eyes, high cheekbones and a square jaw. He looked more like a runway model than a cop.

"None of these accusations ever saw the inside of a courtroom. Most of them never even made it to IA. Detective Ratcliff seems to have friends in high places. Here are some documents showing some of the favoritism he received." Several documents appeared on the screen, one after the other. Most of them were memos of one type or another that was evidence of someone higher up in the department squashing the allegations.

"The incident that really caught our eye with this guy happened two years ago. He was investigating a burglary and paid a visit to the ex-wife of a 'person of interest' in the case. There is no video tape of the actual event, but there were video cameras in the hallway of the woman's apartment." A video, without sound, began to play on the screen.

"The video clearly shows Ratcliff arriving at the apartment at 2:46pm. You see the woman here opening the door for him, and she appears normal, not stressed or injured in any way. Even without audio, it's clear from their body language that he's trying to get into the apartment and that she's trying to prevent him from doing so until he forces the issue." The woman on the video is seen reluctantly stepping aside as the officer enters and closes the door behind him.

"Fast forward to about twenty minutes later, at 3:05pm, Ratcliff exits the apartment. As you can see, he appears to be buttoning and zipping up his pants as he walks off. Five seconds later," said Ish, pointing at the screen, "we see the woman exit the apartment, stumbling into the hallway, her clothes ripped and disheveled, apparently screaming for help. Even in this low resolution, you can see the blood and bruises on her face, which clearly weren't there just twenty minutes before."

"Needless to say, Ratcliff denied everything. Initially, he said he never even entered the apartment; that he only spoke to her at the door for five minutes. Once the tape surfaced, he admitted that he'd had consensual sex with her, but that when he told her he was married she flew into a rage and attacked him. He said he pushed her away and she fell into some furniture."

"That's a lot of fuckin' falling," said Ma'am.

"The especially sad thing about this case is that the woman was three months pregnant at the time. She lost the baby. One doctor went on record as stating that he believed it was from injury sustained during the attack. Shortly thereafter, she tried to commit suicide, but her family got to her in time. For the last two years she's been in and out of institutions for drug and alcohol abuse, problems she didn't have before the attack."

Suddenly, Ish felt bone tired. Discussing these horrific travesties wore on the soul. It was like opening up the wall on your multi-million-dollar house only to find that it was riddled with mold. The weight of the discovery was physically sickening. The expense and complexity of the reparation was overwhelming. But inevitably, you forged ahead.

"Finally," he continued, his voice heavy, "we have our last candidate of the day." The picture on the screen was yet another white man, this one also wearing a policeman's uniform. This man was no model. He had stringy black hair, mean, tiny eyes, and a long, crooked nose that looked like it had been broken multiple times. He was attempting a half-smile, but what he produced was a cruel, curved gash in a hard, unyielding face, the skin peppered with pockmarks and scars.

"This is Officer Thaddeus Janssen. His crime: murder in the second degree. Of all the files we've reviewed so far, Janssen's was the most astonishing. This guy is the Teflon Don of the police force. The guy has had over 60 complaints filed against him for police brutality alone. He's shot and killed 8 people in the line of duty. Seven of them were black men. All of them were unarmed."

The screen began showing image after image of various newspaper headlines: 3 Killed In Police Drug Raid; Officer Accused Of Killing Innocent Man; Verdict For Officer Janssen: Not Guilty.

"As you can see from some of these headlines, Janssen has spent a fair amount of time in court answering for his crimes. The problem is that he's never been punished. He's never lost a case. Never received any kind of sanction for his behavior. This guy has never even been suspended."

"How is that possible? What's his angle?" asked Bird.

"He's an earner," said Chad. "I've read through a ton of paperwork on this guy, and the one thing that keeps coming up is what an asset to the department he is. The guy's a fucking 'Dirty Harry'. He holds the record for arrests, holds the record for the amount of drugs confiscated, holds the record for convictions. And we're not talking about just the record for New York City. We're talking the record for the entire state of New York. Never mind that he's been accused of all these instances of misconduct. Never mind that twice he's led raids on the wrong addresses. Never mind that he's gunned down eight—eight!—unarmed civilians. It's like he has a guardian angel."

"Well," said Ish, "that's about to change. Last spring, he stopped a thirty-two-year-old black man for failure to use his blinker. The guy had his five-year-old daughter in the back seat. After reviewing his license and registration, Janssen asked the man to get out of the car. When the man asked why, Janssen refused to give him a reason. According to the five-year-old and the other witnesses at the scene, including the one that took this video," said Ish, pointing to the screen, which showed a frozen shot of a police officer standing next to a car, "Janssen simply yelled 'get the fuck out of the damn car before I put a bullet in your black ass!'

"When the man opened the door and attempted to comply, Janssen punched him in the face. The man retreated back into the car, put both hands on the steering wheel, and began sobbing and shaking, clearly confused and terrified. Janssen then pulled his weapon and pointed it at the man's head, causing him to panic and attempt to put the car in gear. Janssen's report stated that he then felt his life was in danger, so he shot the man nine times. Nine. Right there in front of his daughter."

Ish nodded at Chad, signaling him to start the video.

Chapter 24

The video showed exactly what Ish had just described. The audio was muffled, but the words "fuck" and "black ass" were crystal clear, as were the nine shots that Janssen fired into the car's front compartment as it began to roll. It moved about six feet before coming to a halt. You could also hear the five-year-old screaming in the back seat. It was the most haunting sound Ish had ever heard. He didn't think he would ever forget it.

As the video finished, Chad turned the screen off and hit the wall switch, once again flooding the room with light. Ish thought that each face sitting before him looked perturbed, but each in a different way.

"I'm just curious," said Ma'am. "What excuse did Janssen give for the altercation?"

"He said the man reached for his gun," said Ish.

"Figures," she mumbled in reply.

"Anyone have any issues with these three targets?" asked Ish. No one spoke up so he continued. "Okay. So, as I mentioned once before, the ultimate plan is to announce our mission and intentions to the world via a website—without giving the actual names of the targets—then to hit all three one after another, hopefully with no more than a few days between each mission. That means the operations will have to all be extremely tight and well-planned."

"We'll also need to document the events, so we'll be using multiple video cameras to record footage that can then be uploaded to the website. It's imperative that people know that our group is responsible; otherwise, it's all kind of pointless."

"Speaking of that," said Ma'am, "ever since you sent us that text asking for suggestions for the masks, I've been giving it a lot of thought. You're right; it is important that people know we're the ones responsible for all this, so we need to have a brand. And our masks will be seen as part of our brand, so we can't just choose any old Mickey Mouse kind of shit, right? So, I was thinking maybe some Guy Fawkes masks."

"Who the hell is Guy Fawkes?" asked Jag.

"Wait, I think I know this one," said Chad. "Isn't that the masks people were wearing in that movie *V for Vendetta*, with the Star Wars chick?"

"Princess Leia?" replied Jag.

"No, the younger one," said Chad, snapping his fingers. "Ummm, Natalie Portman!"

"Was that before or after Princess Leia?" asked Jag.

"Well," said Chad, "it was kind of both before and after, because Princess Leia was in the first movie, and the Natalie Portman movie came later but actually took place earlier in the storyline—"

"I don't mean to interrupt this George Lucas nerd-fest," said Ish, "but could we let the lady finish?"

"Right," said Chad, turning to face Ma'am.

"Thanks," said Ma'am. "Back to the question of who Guy Fawkes is. First, yes, those were the masks used in the *V for Vendetta* movie. But Guy Fawkes was a real person. He was part of a group of people in the early 1600s that plotted to kill the king of England. In the movie, 'V' was a character that was a' anarchist, a freedom fighter and a vigilante. Kinda like us. Here's a pic of the mask," she added, showing everyone a photo on her phone. It was a smiling white face with a thin mustache and goatee and dark, prominent eyebrows. "They're pretty commonly used by protesters all over the world. But I was thinking maybe we could spray paint ours brown."

"You know what," said Ish after looking closely at the pic, "I think that's brilliant, Ma'am!"

"Thank you," she said, smiling.

"Yeah," said Chad, his mind spinning. "We can put these over the ski masks and throw on some dark hoodies, shades and gloves, and no one will even know what race we are, let alone what we look like."

"Perfect. So that's settled," said Ish. "Any other questions?"

"There is one more loose end we need to discuss," said Chad. There was a mischievous sparkle in his eye. Ish knew the look well.

"What's that?" he asked.

"A name! We need a name for the organization. I can't believe we haven't thought about this before."

Ish nodded his head in agreement. "You're right. A name will also help immensely in branding our message to the public. Any suggestions?"

"I've been racking my brain on that all day," said Chad. "It's a lot harder than I thought it would be."

"Anybody else have any thoughts?" asked Ish.

"How about the African American—" began Bird.

"Nope," said Chad. "Even though they don't know who we are, I think the name should be inclusive of the entire group, and I'm not African American."

"How about we just replace 'African American' with 'black'?" replied Ma'am. "You may not be African American, but you pretty much pass for black." Everyone laughed.

"I think we can do better than that," said Ish. "We're not races, we're people."

"People..." said Chad, gazing thoughtfully at the ceiling. "Yeah, how about The People's...something."

"That's a start," said Ish. Everyone started warming up to the idea and tossing different words back and forth: Army. Militia. Force. Then Jag came up with a winner.

"Revolutionary," he said.

"Yeah, I like that!" said Ma'am.

"People's Revolutionary...People's Revolutionary...," said Chad, mumbling to himself.

The wheels in Ish's mind started turning. Like a well-oiled Rubik's Cube, it began to shift and spin, clicking and whirling as the pieces of the puzzle began to fall into place. Suddenly, he sat up straight and looked around at everyone.

"The People's Revolutionary Organization for Police Reform. P.R.O.P.R. 'Proper' for short."

"Yeah!" said Chad. "That's it! PROPR. That sounds dope!" Everyone was nodding and high-fiving each other. They had found their name.

After all the congratulating was over, it was time to get down to business regarding some of the logistics.

"Chad, get online, please, and let's find out what our domain name options are," said Ish.

Chad grabbed a MacBook, fired it up and began typing. "Shit. PROPR.com is taken," he said. "As well as PROPR.org and PROPR.us. Let me try a few more things." He spent the next 20 minutes typing while everyone waited patiently, checking their phones or reading over files to fill the time. Finally, he looked up, dejection etched on his face.

"The only thing available that even comes close is to spell out the entire name: PeoplesRevolutionaryOrganizationForPoliceReform.com. That's one long goddamn URL."

Ish shook his head. "There's got to be something better than that. Let's forget about the name for a minute and focus on the purpose. What are we trying to do?"

"We're trying to put the police on notice," said Bird.

"We're trying to tell the people that change is possible," said Jag.

"We're trying to let America know that war has been declared," said Ma'am.

"You're right, Ma'am. I like that," said Ish. "We're trying to let America know that war has been declared."

Chad began typing some more. After a few minutes, he shook his head. "I haven't found anything yet. Keep it coming."

"How about...the revolution..." said Ish. "No. How about NowBeginsTheRevolution.com?"

Chad's fingers flew over the keys. "Yes! That's available. Is that what we want to go with?" He looked around at everyone.

Everyone gave some form of affirmative: a nod, a thumbs-up, a grunt, but it was unanimous.

"I think that's it," said Ish.

"Cool," said Chad. "Give me a few minutes. I need to create some untraceable dummy accounts before I register this." Again, his fingers flew over the keyboard. Fifteen minutes later he raised his head again. "Done."

"Great," said Ish. "Moving on: As I also mentioned before, the punishment should fit the crime, so we've got three different methods of attack that we need to plan. The bully is overdue for a good old-fashioned beat-down. The rapist needs to understand exactly what it's like to be sexually violated. And the murderer: he took a life, he owes a life." He paused to give room for any objections. No one voiced one, so he continued.

"Let's take a minute to go over the rules of engagement," he said. "First and foremost, no innocents are to be harmed in these maneuvers. In each mission we will have a single specific target, and that individual is the one and only target. If we screw up this part, it not only negates any progress that we could have made, it puts us back ten steps from where we started. Does everyone understand the seriousness of that?" he asked, looking around the table. Heads nodded in affirmation.

"I don't want to be the one pissing in the lemonade here," said Jag, "but that might not be as easy done as said. I mean hey, we pretty much got the same directives before we were dropped into the Middle East, and we all know how that sometimes turned out. We've killed women, children, old people; bombed churches and hospitals; mowed people down at weddings. In the heat of battle, sometimes shit falls apart. You know that as well as anyone, Ice-Man."

"Yeah, I know, Jag," said Ish. "But we've got to be better than the U.S. Army. We have more on the line. In Afghanistan, we were simply reacting to a threat. Here, we're trying to start a revolution. I've got to know that you're all 100% in on this; that you're willing to sacrifice your lives for it, if necessary." Ish stopped talking and waited for his statements to sink in, and for someone in the group to respond. Again, no one did. He took a sip of his coffee and waited a few more seconds.

"Anyone have anything to say?" he finally asked.

"The reason we don't have anything to say, if I can take the liberty to speak for everyone," said Bird, "is that, with the exception of Chad, we're all soldiers. No one has ever asked us if we're willing to die for a mission. Not even the recruiters that signed us up wanted to walk down that alley. Because we all know, whether it's spoken about or not, that every time we step out onto the field of battle, there's more than a fair chance we won't be coming back. We're all soldiers, so we all understand.

"Before I got on that plane headed to Baltimore to meet you at the hospital," continued Bird, "I kissed my mom and my uncles and cousins, and called as many of my other relatives and friends as I could, the same way I do each time I deploy, because I knew that might be the last time. And my guess is that everyone at this table did something similar. So yeah, Ish, we get it. We know the stakes. We accept the challenge."

"Glad to hear it," said Ish. "Chad has an iPad for everyone," he continued as Chad began passing out the devices. "These contain all the data we have on the targets. The password is your six-digit birth dates. Before we leave this room, you'll need to access them, change your password and set-up the fingerprint touch ID. From that point forward, you'll need to always use both the pin and your thumbprint to open them. They're all running our encryption software, so we feel confident that these devices are as secure as any devices on the planet. You have the rest of today and tomorrow to acquaint yourselves with the briefs, and then tomorrow night we'll meet at Chad's house for dinner. I'm manning the grill."

"Cool. What can we bring?" asked Jag.

"Whatever you like. Or nothing at all."

"I'd like to run into L.A. and pick up a couple of bean pies, maybe some cobbler or something," said Ma'am. "I've been having a taste for a little soul food ever since we touched down."

"That'd be great," said Ish. "If there's nothing else, we're adjourned till tomorrow."

Chapter 25

Ish walked into the kitchen from the patio, carrying a plate of steaks he had just taken off the grill. Chad's house was beautiful. It was furnished in a clean, modern style that hinted at Italian influences. Expensive art was everywhere, an eclectic mixture of African and Chinese pieces. Oddly enough, they looked good together. Chad had bought the house three years ago, and Ish realized that he had only been there twice. There was a time when the two of them spent as much time at each other's places as they did at their own. He felt a pang of guilt that his military service had prevented him from being more involved in his friend's life.

Bird, Chad and Jag were sitting in the adjacent dining room, each with a beer in their hand.

"Baked potatoes will be ready in five, so everyone, feel free to grab a plate," said Ish.

"Great! Let me hit the head first," said Jag. Chad pointed him in the direction of the bathroom. Two minutes later he returned.

"Can I get you another beer?" asked Chad.

"Yes, but first, what the fuck is that smell?!" he asked, his face frowning in disgust as he attempted to cover his nose with his arm.

"That's chitlins!" said Ma'am from her seat at the table. She was sitting in front of a plate piled high with the pungent meat, which she had just taken out of the microwave. It was one of the treasures she had picked up when she went looking for bean pies. "Ain't you never had chitlins before?"

"Fuck, no!" said Jag. "Are you sure they didn't sell you a bad batch? That don't smell like anything suitable for consumption!"

Ma'am stared at him, astonished. "That accent you got ain't British," she said. "How the hell did you ever escape the South without ever eatin' chitlins?"

"I grew up in the South, but I guess we were what you'd call 'uppity'," he said as he sat down, still trying to cover his nose from the odor. "We didn't even eat hamburgers. Filet mignon, quail and rack of lamb were my mama's favorites when it came to meat. She used to often say 'just because we live in the South doesn't mean we can't be civilized.' She would have given everything she and Daddy had in savings to get rid of our accents. My mama had some issues. But Daddy was a through-and-through country boy, and we all took after him, so there was only so much Mama could do with that."

"Poor baby. You don't know what you missin'," said Ma'am, grinning broadly.

"I'm sorry, but I'm going to step outside for a few. Check on the taters," said Jag, looking a bit queasy as he walked out to the patio.

The rest of the group broke out in laughter.

"How'd you ever make it through three tours with that one?" said Ma'am to Ish. "I don't remember ever seeing quail on the menu in any of my mess halls. As a matter of fact, sometimes we were reduced to eatin' shit that I wouldn't feed a fuckin' dog."

"In addition to being a demolitions expert," said Ish, "Jag had a unique talent for finding the best food within a hundred-mile radius. We may have had to deal with the same heat and dirt and bugs as everyone else, but we always ate well."

"That is the truth," said Bird, laughing.

A few minutes later everyone was seated at the table, enjoying their meal. They each had steak, but Bird and Ma'am also each had a side bowl of chitlins.

"Jag, can you pass the hot sauce, please?" asked Ma'am.

"No disrespect," said Jag, pointing at the grayish meat as he reached for the bottle of Tabasco, "but that is disgusting! Seriously, how the fuck can you two eat that shit?"

Bird and Ma'am didn't seem at all insulted. They looked at each other and smiled.

"Let me tell you something, whiteboy," began Ma'am.

"Whoa, you're opening with the race card?" replied Jag, smiling.

"Let me finish," she said, "and you'll understand the racial element. You see, what you don't understand is that this dish is part of black American history. This is part of our heritage. If it wasn't for chitlins—and pig's feet, hog maws and all the other nasty bits of the pig that masta', your ancestors, didn't want, my people may never have survived slavery. For a lot of folks, it was either learn to eat that or starve. If we had refused, we might not be here today. That's real talk."

"I understand all that, but this ain't fuckin' 1847. Let me let you in on a little secret," he said, leaning towards her conspiratorially. "Slavery is over. You can fucking eat steak now!"

"You still don't get it," said Ma'am. "Black people have survived in America for so long because we have had the ability to take negatives and turn them into positives. We took what the white man threw away, the entrails of pigs, and we made a meal from that shit that sustained us and gave us the strength to be able to survive to fight another day. So now we hold onto that part of our history. It's a similar situation with the word 'nigga'. The white man used it to degrade us, to strip us of our dignity. But over the years we claimed it for ourselves. We took ownership of it. For better or worse, it's ours now. And we use it anyway we want to and dare whitey to try to take it back. It's all about empowerment."

Ish felt like he should jump in and say something, but there was something interesting going on here, so he leaned back, slowly chewed his steak, and watched the scene play out before him.

"You're right, I still don't get it," said Jag. "I know I can't say the 'n' word, and maybe there's some logic to your thinking there. But I have no desire to eat pig guts, so what kind of power do you think that's really giving you? Let me tell you something," he continued, "trust me when I say white people are not at home, behind closed doors wishing they could eat chitlins! What a lot of them are doing behind closed doors is using the 'n' to describe your kind. Yes, they might not be saying it to your face, but trust me, they're saying it. So, explain to me, exactly, how you're gaining power from any of that?"

Ma'am put her fork down and bowed her head, as though she were praying for strength. But before she could answer, Bird jumped into the conversation.

"Brother Jag, you just don't understand the real meaning of power. Power, real power, is not something that others give you. Real power is the power that you take; the power that you give yourself. In the greater scheme of things, it doesn't matter what White America does behind closed doors. It doesn't matter what they think of the food we eat, the words we use, or the way we walk, dress or wear our hair. Though, let me just say, we don't all agree on the use of the 'n' word," he said, glancing at Ma'am, who rolled her eyes in response. "But bottom line: we are survivors. And the simple act of survival, especially against the kind of tyranny we suffered under, gives us a kind of power that no one can ever take away."

Jag nodded his head slowly, as he took a bite of his steak and chewed it, apparently ruminating on all he had just heard.

"I think I see where you're coming from," he said after taking a drink from his bottle of beer. "But as the only white guy in the room, I have to say that it makes me a little depressed to know that after all these years, fifty years after the civil rights movement, we're still so separated by race."

"You must have grown up wearin' rose-colored glasses in whatever Southern town you was raised in," said Ma'am. "Because the simple truth of the matter is that this ain't never gonna go away. People like to surround themselves with the familiar. Humans self-segregate. We tend to shy away from those that are different from us. It's natural and it's always gonna be that way, because we're always gonna be different."

"I understand what you're saying," said Jag. "But we're human beings. We've sent people into space. We should have evolved past this kind of petty nonsense. The problem is that people tend to treat race the way they treat politics. Once they've aligned themselves with a particular side, they blindly accept and defend whatever that side seems to stand for, regardless of how bat-shit crazy it might sound. A prime example is this shit that's going on with Pop Greer."

"You talkin' about the rape allegations?" asked Ma'am.

"Rape allegations?" asked Chad. "Wait—are we talking about Pop Greer, the black actor and comedienne? 'America's Favorite Dad' Pop Greer?"

"One and the same," said Jag.

"Holy shit! I haven't heard anything about this. I used to love *The Greer Show*! Someone accused him of rape?"

"Not just someone. Fifty someones," said Bird.

"Damn," said Chad. "I can't even wrap my head around that. Pop Greer raped 50 women? I can't even believe that's possible!"

"And see, that's the problem," said Jag. "There are a lot of people that don't believe it's possible. And a lot of those people are other black people who feel the need to give him the benefit of the doubt. Why? Simply because he's black. He's black. They're black. They're from the same click, so they blindly rally to support their own. They lose the ability to be objective. It's the same with the political parties. People that label themselves as Republican tend to support whatever the Republican party puts out there, regardless of how completely fucking ridiculous it may be. Democrats are no better."

"I think you might be condemning the brother a bit prematurely," said Bird. "The evidence isn't all in yet. And the majority of these allegations are ten, fifteen, twenty years old."

"See, this is what I'm talking about!" said Jag, slapping his hand down on the table. "Fifty women come forward screaming rape, and we're supposed to believe that all of them are lying? That this is just, what, some great conspiracy meant to bring down a cherished black celebrity? Conspiracy created by who? And to what end? If we were talking about a white guy raping fifty black women, none of these people that support Greer would have any doubts at all that the white guy was guilty."

"I'm not saying I know the truth," said Bird. "I'm just saying that anything is possible. People like to dismiss conspiracy theories out-of-hand, but throughout history there have been some powerful people doing some crazy shit behind the scenes."

"I can't even discuss something like this with you if you're going to go there," said Jag. "People are always looking for the boogeyman. The boogeyman don't exist."

"Oh, there are boogeymen out there. Trust me, I've seen 'em," said Ma'am. "But I think I have to side with Jag on this one. I didn't want to believe it either, but when fifty different women of all colors, shapes and sizes accuse one muthafucka of the same goddamn crime over a period of decades, nine times out of nine that muthafucka is as guilty as sin!"

"Yeah, okay," scoffed Bird. "How did we get on this topic anyway?"

"Well, I was trying to make a point," said Jag. "My point is this: until we as a society stop seeing people as part of a group and begin to see everyone as an individual, we're never going to be able to rise above racism, classism, elitism and all the other 'isms that keep us at each other's throats. Until then people will continue to hide behind flags, to throw stones from the shadows and then run back to the angry mob for protection."

"Shit!" said Ma'am, smiling. "I never knew you was this deep, Jag. You're kind of turning me on!"

"Yeah, I'm a sexy motherfucker," said Jag, returning the smile as he inhaled another mouthful of steak.

"Hey, hey! Back up, playboy. That's my sister," said Bird. He was half smiling, and Ish got the impression he was only half joking.

After dinner, they retired to the living room. It was a massive enclosure, decorated in white and brown; white walls and ceilings with a white marble floor to accent the brown, distressed-look leather furniture. There was a TV screen so large that it covered most of the wall it was attached to. A basketball game was playing on it, but the sound was muted. Beneath it was a spread of various electronic devices. Tasteful lamps, end tables, throw rugs and knick-knacks completed the scheme. Everyone had grabbed their beverage of choice and was relaxing, leaning back into the plush sofa or a matching chair, absorbed in their own thoughts.

"Chad, where are we at on the website?" asked Ish.

"I actually finished that last night. I wanted to surprise you."

"Is it already set up on the onion router?"

"Absolutely. And *Syncription* is fully installed. Not even God could trace this back to us."

"Excellent. So, everything is ready to go for tomorrow?" asked Ish.

"Yes. The lights and the background arrived earlier today. I tested everything this morning, and we're golden. By the way, I think it was a stroke of genius to change from the ski masks to the Guy Fawkes masks. They're going to look amazing on screen."

"You're welcome," said Ma'am. There was a sense of satisfaction to the way she said it, or maybe it was just a tone of confidence, but it reminded Ish that she was the kind of person that people constantly underestimated. She was from the street, and her word choices, speech patterns and general appearance never let you forget that. But she was also extremely intelligent. Those who underestimated her did so at their own folly.

"We're really doing this, aren't we?" said Bird to Ish later when they were in the room alone.

"Yes, we are. Are you sure you're okay with that?"

"I've told you yes several times. Why do you keep asking me the same question over and over again?"

"Because I know that you're a loyal dude. Maybe loyal to a fault. I've fought beside you. Killed beside you. But I know that ultimately, you're a little different from the rest of us. You operate from a different, uh, 'political perspective'. I wouldn't want your sense of loyalty to back you into a corner and have you commit to something that you will ultimately regret. I'm not trying to be disrespectful. On the contrary, I'm trying to make sure that you have as many opportunities as possible to change your mind, if that's what you want to do."

"But you're not asking these questions of any of the others?" asked Bird.

"No, but they're different. Chad, Jag and Ma'am are idealists. They believe in the objective without much consideration for the logistics. You, on the other hand, understand that the devil is in the details. That's what makes you so valuable to this mission. You keep in mind the logistics of what we're trying to do."

"Did you just call me a Republican?" asked Bird.

"Not in so many words," said Ish, laughing softly. "But I guess that's one way to put it."

"Let me make myself clear, once and for all," said Bird. "Regardless of the fact that my sister has committed herself to this project, if I didn't want to be here, I wouldn't be. If I didn't believe in what PROPR is trying to do, I wouldn't be here. I'm not one for pissing my life away on some bullshit errand. The fact that I'm here means you have my full support. I hope you can accept that, because I don't want to have to keep proving myself to you every time you start to feel paranoid."

Ish smiled. "Understood, my brother. I stand corrected."

Chapter 26

Ish's phone was vibrating with an incoming call. His standard initial reaction to phone calls as of late was annoyance; the phone usually meant more stimulus to a system already at overload. He pulled it out of his pocket and looked at the screen. It said 'unknown caller'. Historically, he would have ignored such a call, but ever since Layla had been locked up, he knew that any one of these 'unknown callers' could be her.

"This is a collect call from an inmate at a California correctional facility," said a robotic sounding female voice. "Please press one on your touch-tone phone if you wish to accept the charges."

Absentmindedly, Ish put his hand on his chest, right over his heart, bowed his head and took just a moment to breathe. There was a tiny, painful nugget of warmth there, kind of like the feeling you get when you stub a toe really hard on a heavy piece of furniture.

His pulse began to quicken, and the nugget of pain began to spread, flooding through his body and mind. This was something he thought he had learned to control; that kind of emotion had been purged from his system long ago, shortly after boot-camp. With the places he had been and the things he had since done, these kinds of feelings were things he considered to be outside his emotional budget. They were something he could no longer afford. Anger, outrage, hatred—those were things he could connect with in abundance. They served the greater purpose, which was keeping him alive. This was something else, something he thought he had, at least temporarily, outrun. But losing his girls had crippled him, and now it had caught up with a vengeance.

Ish quickly recovered and entered the number, releasing the call. The flood eased back just a bit.

"Hey, you, it's me," said Layla.

Ish paused. He loved this voice. He was never sure what to expect next when they talked, so he just savored the moment and the comfort it created. He felt the flood ease back a bit more, and his hand moved away from his chest.

Layla's voice had a warm, lilting quality to it, rich like amber, and radiant like the sun. And like the sun, Ish could feel it healing him a little, second by second. But by the same token, he knew that if exposed to it, unprotected, for too long, it had the power to leave him burned, raw and overly sensitive just from want and longing. He needed to be careful.

It hurt to even think like that. He could remember this voice in his ear, singing quietly while they danced to old Minnie Riperton albums in their living room years ago. Or whispering sweet nothings to him while they walked hand-in-hand along Santa Monica Pier at midnight, watching the moon play over the waves. This voice was ingrained in his dreams. It was also this voice, shrill with panic and fear after the death of their daughter, that often haunted his nightmares. So, he waited, trying to delay letting go of the warmth but afraid that he could burst into flame at any moment. The truth was that no matter how things had changed, he loved this woman more than life itself, and he always would.

"I thought this might be you," he said. "How are you?"

"Ish, I'm good, I'm good. I'm...good," she said, her voice buttery sweet but somewhat distant and unfocused. "I called because Sumatra reminded me that I should probably keep you in the loop."

"Sumatra?" said Ish. "Umm...babe...Sumatra's gone."

"Yeah, I can see how you might think that," she said. "I thought so too at first. But she's not really gone. She comes and sees me when she can."

"Okay," said Ish, not knowing how else to respond.

"She really does help keep me from going totally off the deep end. She...she—" She stopped abruptly, as though she had lost her train of thought and was trying to reconnect with it. "Anyway, for the most part everyone just kind of stays out of my way. And I stay out of theirs. But still, sometimes you just can't..." she began, and then paused again.

Ish closed his eyes and took a deep breath. The flood was coming back. She was all over the place.

"What is it? What's wrong?" he asked.

"It's nothing. It's just that they're thinking about moving me to another facility, upstate somewhere, and we felt I should tell you before you heard about it from someone else. It's supposed to happen sometime within the next two weeks." She whispered like it was a secret, as though she wasn't aware that the phone call was surely being recorded. The flood was back to full strength. He rubbed his chest again. Damn, he wanted her out of there.

"Moving you? Why? Did something happen?" he asked, his voice starting to rise.

"I had a meeting with the warden and a couple of other jail officials yesterday. I told those people that I didn't want to go. I told them over and over again. I told them, I told them. I told them...," she repeated again, her voice trailing off as though she was slowly drifting away from the phone. "But they told me I had to go anyway. I told them to leave me alone, but they weren't listening. So, I figured, if they we're going to use their ears, what good were they?"

"What the hell are you talking about, baby? What did you do?"

She started whispering again. "Maybe if he had been wearing glasses, I would have at least felt he was using them for something." Layla took a deep breath. "Anyway, you really don't need two. Kind of redundant, if you ask me," she said, her voice returning to one that he recognized.

"Layla," Ish began.

"Like I said, they weren't trying to hear what I was saying," she continued. "This time I thought they might really let me out." She began to fade out again. The flood began a resurgence. He tried to take a deep breath, but he simply couldn't. His chest felt constricted. She resumed, her voice returning to the whisper. "They were all smiling so nice and pretty. Ish, there was a brother there. Yes, there was a brother this time! I kind of felt sorry for him. But the one that was running the show was this Asian dude. Smug prick, leaning back in his leather chair, smiling and nodding. He started talking about how my bail had been posted weeks ago, and that they needed the cell for other prisoners, and he knew I'd be much more comfortable in my own home as I waited for trial. Yada, yada, yada.

"I told them I still wasn't leaving, so the guard started trying to drag me out, and I started kicking and flailing, so this motherfucker picked me up and body-slammed me onto the floor! I have to say, it hurt like hell for a minute. Everyone was stunned, just looking at me while I tried to get my breath back. Then the guard started reaching down all apologetic-like to help me up. Before he knew what was going on, I had grabbed this fool by the head and had my teeth wrapped around his ear."

"Oh, Layla," said Ish, sighing.

"You know, I always assumed an ear would be pretty easy to bite off. They're a lot tougher than you might think. And the blood! Ha! I don't think those stains are coming out anytime soon. He might as well just burn that uniform."

Ish leaned back slowly. The flood roared through his system, beginning to feel like a full-on tornado. "Damn, Layla" he said between clenched teeth, realizing he was beginning to lose control. He rubbed his eyes and slowly blew out a long, tight, pain-filled breath. His mind was whirling. He did not recognize this woman. She had completely lost touch with reality. He was aware that she had been acting strangely since Sumatra's death, but he chalked that up to grief response. This was something else. This was verging on full-out mental collapse.

She didn't speak, but he could hear her breathing on the phone.

"Listen," he said. "Please. You have got to stop doing this. You could have been out of there a long time ago. We could be together, fighting this from the outside."

"I told you it's not safe out there," she said, the amber in her voice fading into a tired, dirty brown, the clarity disintegrating to a mumble. "It's not safe. It's just not safe out there. This is where I am supposed to be. They're killing black folks. If you're not careful, Ish, you could be next. I could let them start the release process and you could be dead before I hit the street. Your money? Your title? Your education? Not even your service protects us. Nothing protects us. We have to protect ourselves, and until we can, we will keep getting gunned down."

Something about the way she said that last sentence gave him pause. It hinted at the possibility that she had not completely descended into madness. He couldn't quite explain it, but there was a sense of hope in it. It was the kind of hope that he recognized from their previous life together and that he had often wondered if he'd ever be blessed enough to hear again. He felt as if this was the real reason she had made this phone call; as if this was the message she had been, maybe subconsciously, trying to express to him all along.

"You want me to come home, Ish?" she asked. "Then do something. Do something to make me feel safe. Something big. Something big enough to make me feel there's still a place for people like me in this bullshit society. If you can do that, then maybe we can have something to talk about. Maybe we can talk about a future."

Ish was shocked. It was as though she could read his mind, as though she knew exactly what he was planning. Actually, he shouldn't have been surprised. He and Layla had always had this strange, almost psychic connection, like they were attached by the roots to each other's souls. It wasn't just the quirky ways that some couples can finish each other's sentences. It was deeper than that. Still, hearing aloud a reference to that which he was secretly already working towards filled him with a rushing sense of panic. But also, of something that felt like hope.

"In the meantime," she continued, "you should know that they say women sometimes don't survive these facility moves, especially if they've been labeled a 'trouble maker'. If something happens and I don't make it, remember this: I did not go easily. Comfort yourself with the fact that I was a warrior to the end. Never forget that."

Ish was not a man who had ever felt the need to prove himself to anyone. He moved with ease and confidence in his skin and in his life. Sumatra and Layla were the only people on the planet who had ever had the ability to make him feel insecure and vulnerable. But that's exactly how he felt right this moment. Yet saying goodbye to this woman and letting her die in prison was never going to be okay for him. Keeping in mind the fact that their conversation was likely being closely monitored, a thought occurred to him.

"Do you remember when I convinced you that you could have snow in the summer?"

He could hear the sarcasm in her voice as she sighed softly. Of course, she remembered. It was at the Slauson Swap Meet—South Central L.A.—one Saturday afternoon. It was the middle of summer, the temperature was in triple digits, and she was working at a food truck. Ish was a regular. He had seen her there many times. Their eyes would often meet, but they'd never had a conversation. He could feel her watching him whenever he was around, shopping for clothes or new sneaks, and a few times he tried to start a dialog, but nothing ever came of it. She would humor him a bit and move on to the next customer. He finally stopped trying, but he made it a point to walk by her spot and flash a smile and a nod at her anytime he was there.

He remembered how she was always in motion while she worked. While other workers lazed around or left the truck to go shop, she stayed diligent and busy and would handle every single customer gracefully and with respect. He remembered her laugh and the way she never complained as she wiped sweat away from her brow and fanned herself with paper plates. He remembered how she hid her body with modest attire from the prying eyes of the men around her. But he could see how graceful and athletic she was just by the way she moved around the truck. The physical pull that he felt towards her was maddening, but he continued to give her space.

Then, this particular day, after three months of Saturday afternoon visits, he had come to the truck and noticed that she looked especially weary and was moving slower than usual. He felt compelled to approach her. He ordered a burger, and as he waited, put on his most charming demeanor.

"If you could have anything right now, what would it be?" he asked.

She looked up at him and smiled. "What are my parameters?" she answered.

"No parameters; whatever you want, I will do everything in my power to get it for you next weekend. However, it has to be the one thing that is guaranteed to make you relax and smile," he said.

He could tell that she thought he was completely full of shit, but without a pause she said "Snow. I would want snow."

"Snow?" he asked, smiling and looking around like he wasn't sure she was talking to him. "In Los Angeles? In the middle of a July heatwave?"

"You said anything," she said, teasingly. "And I want snow."

"Huh," he said, slowing stroking his chin while pondering the dilemma. "Okay. Let me see what I can do."

Their journey began there. That next weekend he borrowed a friend's twin-engine plane and flew her five hours away to Timberline

Lodge, Oregon, the only area in the U.S. that typically still has ski-worthy snow that late in the season. He had paid her manager to cover her shift at work and spent two hours talking her into getting into that plane with him. He let her photocopy his ID and his pilot's license and leave it with her best friend. And then, he delivered on his promise. He gave her snow.

They spent the day snowmobiling and sledding, talking about movies and music, and sharing dreams and fears. He remained a gentleman the entire time, and she remained a lady. They both arrived back home late the next day slightly sunburned, deeply relaxed and on the way to falling head over heels in love with each other. Their lives would never be the same. They married six months later.

"Yes, Ish," she said, "I remember when you gave me snow."

"Then you know I would do anything to make you happy. I would move heaven and earth to make the impossible possible. I can do this," he said.

"That's sweet, babe, but even you can't get blood from a stone."

"Is that what you want? Blood from a stone?" he asked. "If that's what it takes to make you happy, I'll get you your blood. I'm working on something right now that will do exactly that. Something major. Something even more surprising than snow in July. Something as shocking as watching a stone bleed."

"Ish, what are you talking about?"

"I can't go into details right now. I just need you to trust me. But what I can tell you is that this will be revolutionary, and the revolution will be televised."

"What are you—" she began.

"Look," he said, "I don't know how safe I can make this world for you. I'm not even sure I know what 'safe' means anymore, for black people in America. But if I'm successful in this new project, it may help create a world that is at least a little bit 'safe-er'. Maybe if I can make this work, we can at least feel a little bit of justice for some of the death that we've had to suffer, and from that justice we might just be able to find life again."

There was a long pause. Neither one of them spoke. It was as though they were both afraid of what they would say next, as though a spell had been created that the wrong words could break. Suddenly, a robotic female interrupted the silence: "You have three minutes left until this call expires." Those were the words.

"Goddamn it!" she muttered. "Ish, I don't understand what it is that you're trying to tell me, so I can't tell you whether or not it would make a difference; whether or not it would make me actually want to come home. But if it's as big as you're hinting, I might be open to discussing it. Maybe. But try not to get your hopes up. I've been enough of a source of disappointment for you. For both of us."

"You have never, ever been a disappointment to me," he said, "so don't even go there. Just do me one favor. Promise me that you'll try to hold it together at least until I can get through this. No more crazy shit. No more ear appetizers. No more antagonizing the jail staff. Promise me that you'll survive. Please. Just survive. And I'll get you your bleeding stone."

"I believe in you, Ish, you know that," she said, her voice cracking. "And I'll do my best, but it's hard to make promises in here. It's hard to make promises without hope, and that's the first thing they try to strip from you after they seal the doors up behind you. Hope. But you did bring me snow in July, and if anyone can change the world, it's you. I've got to go. Be you, baby. Love."

And then she was gone, leaving Ish with his frustrations and a silence that was loud enough to drown out the world. If he ever had any doubts that what he was about to do was the right thing, they had all just disappeared like so much snow in July.

Chapter 27

They all met back in the War Room at Macrolox. They had brought in black drapery material and used it to cover the walls, creating a backdrop free of any recognizable elements. Chad seemed uncharacteristically nervous as he set up the lights for the video shoot and crawled around double- and triple-checking connections. Jag, Ma'am and Bird were trying to help, but Chad was committed to doing most of it himself. Ish was rehearsing his script, running it over and over in his mind, hoping that he hadn't forgotten anything important. He and the rest of the team had spent two days writing it, and had gone over it again and again, editing, tweaking and refining. He was confident that it was as close to perfect as it could possibly be, but deep inside he was still a bit unsure.

Thirty minutes later Chad stood up and brushed his pants. "Alright, Ish," he said. "I think we're ready."

Even though the video lights were emitting a fair amount of heat, they had the A/C turned up and the room was chilly. Ish was clad head to toe in black. He wore black leather shoes with matching black leather gloves and black jeans, socks and hoodie, with a thin black ski mask to cover his hair and ears. But the Fawkes mask was the finishing touch. They had ordered them online, paying with a money order, and had them delivered to the address of an empty warehouse in an industrial park 100 miles away. Bird went to pick it up. He waited for UPS to leave the package at the door and retrieved it after they left, making it untraceable back to them. They also airbrushed the masks to change the color from white to a bronzed brown, and wore dark wraparound shades over it to complete the look. A clip-on lavalier microphone ensured that Ish's voice would be heard loud and clear.

Ish cleared his throat and donned the masks and glasses. He looked at himself in the large mirror that adorned one of the walls. There were no identifying features that he could see. "The mic is hot," said Chad.

"Testing one, two. Testing one, two," said Ish.

"Audio is perfect," said Chad, who was wearing a pair of headphones and standing behind a video monitor. "Let's get ready for take one."

Ish looked around at the faces of his four friends. He was the leader here. He didn't want to be, but clearly, he was. These people were depending on him to lead them into battle against injustice and oppression. Even at this late stage of the game, part of him wasn't sure he was up to the task. People had often labeled him 'hero', but it was not the way he thought of himself. He may have been a natural leader, but he wasn't necessarily always a completely willing one. He closed his eyes and thought of Sumatra and Layla. He could see his daughter smiling at him, expectantly. He imagined her saying, "You can do this, Daddy," and suddenly he knew that it was true. The doubt lifted away from his heart like clouds parting for the sun. He was ready. He slowly opened his eyes. "Let's rock," he said.

It took three hours to complete the filming of the first video, which was only six minutes long. Ish was not used to speaking in public and certainly not in front of a camera. Still, he was a bit surprised by how difficult it was to remember the script and deliver the lines smoothly and naturally. He started to feel a bit embarrassed as he continually flubbed his lines and they shot take after take. But the rest of the crew seemed to have a better understanding than he did about how challenging shooting a video was. None of them appeared the least bit frustrated by how long it was taking.

Finally, shortly after midnight, Chad reported that he thought he had what he needed; that he could cut and splice during the editing process and make it all come together. Everyone except Chad went back to Chad's house to crash, leaving him with a large pot of coffee and a ton of footage to work through.

At about 7:00 the next morning, Ish's phone rang. He looked at the screen before answering. It was Chad.

"Hey, brother," said Ish.

"I think we have it!"

Ish took the phone away from his face to look at the time. "Have you been working on this all night?"

"Yeah, man, and it's amazing!" Ish couldn't understand how anyone could be as awake and excited as Chad was after working straight through the night. "I can't wait for you all to see it! When can you get here?"

"Um, I think everyone is probably still crashed, so I'll have to get them up. Plus, I don't know about them, but I could use some breakfast, and you could probably use some, too. How about you call the new place around the corner from the office and have them deliver, and we meet you there in forty-five?"

"Deal."

When Ish and the gang arrived at the office, the food was waiting and Chad was already seated. It was a spread fit for royalty. There was a huge carafe of fresh coffee on the table, along with orange juice, fresh fruit, muffins, scrambled eggs, pancakes, French toast, sausage, bacon and a stack of cinnamon rolls, one of which was sticking out of Chad's mouth. Chad was one of those guys who could consistently eat the worst, most unhealthy food imaginable and never gain an ounce. He had been sporting a six-pack since Ish met him in high school, and no amount of junk food affected it.

"Wait till you see some of the stuff I added!" said Chad before everyone had even had a chance to sit down.

"Good morning to you, too, my brother," said Bird.

"Yeah, before we start talking shop, I need to at least refuel my caffeine meter," said Jag.

"Amen to that," added Ma'am.

Everyone helped themselves. Once their plates were full and they were comfortably seated, Chad could contain himself no longer.

"I took a bunch of the videos that the software scraped and edited them into the footage we shot of you last night—which you were amazing in, by the way," he said to Ish. "I also added titles, captions and music. I wasn't sure how it was going to turn out, but I think you'll all be surprised by the results."

"You're like a kid on Christmas mornin'!" said Ma'am.

"He's easily excited," said Ish, grinning. "Alright," he said to Chad, putting his fork down. "Let's see what you've been up to all night."

Chad lowered the lights and the giant TV came to life. The screen momentarily went black and then a white title appeared: *People's Revolutionary Organization for Police Reform.* The title dissolved, replaced by the image of a Guy Fawkes mask, painted in dripping red, black and green spray paint on a bare brick wall, with the word "PROPR" beneath it. The logo faded and was replaced by the word "Introduction", which then dissolved and was replaced by the image of Ish as he walked into the frame, clad in all black, concealed behind the mask and shades and covered with the hoodie. He was a frightening and imposing figure.

"Good evening, America," he said, his baritone voice causing the walls of the room to vibrate. I represent the People's Revolutionary Organization for Police Reform: 'Proper', for short. PROPR was formed by a group of like-minded fellow Americans that have grown tired of constantly waking up in the morning to a new report of an innocent, unarmed black person gunned down by a white police officer." He took a couple of steps towards the camera and to his left, casually clasping his hands behind his back. A virtual screen appeared to his right, and displayed the video footage of the Rodney King beating.

"Since the early days of slavery when African Americans, as we've come to be called, were considered property and only 3/5ths human, we have been hunted, beaten, raped, tortured and killed, often for no other reason than the color of our skin. America likes to pat itself on the back and speak of the success of integration, affirmative action and the first black president, but we all know differently. This 1991 video of motorist Rodney King being savagely beaten by a group of Los Angeles police officers shocked many in our nation. But few of those who were shocked were black. This has been part of our experience with the police since our people came to this country. The only aspect of this that shocked black people was the fact that the video was actually allowed to be released to the public."

Newspaper headlines begin to splash across the virtual screen, detailing police attacks on blacks spanning twenty-five years.

"Some people," continued Ish, "those that were the most shocked by the King video, assumed that this was an isolated incident. But thanks to the constant march of technology and the development of the camera phone, almost everyone over the age of ten has the potential to be a video journalist, and more and more incriminating videos are seeing the light of day.

"For the last 50 years, various groups of people have organized in an attempt to shine a brighter light on these atrocities and deliver a greater amount of justice to minorities in this country. We've seen groups as disparate as the Black Panthers on one hand and the #BlackForLife movement on the other. But so far, our brothers and sisters keep dying at the hands of law enforcement. Why?" The virtual screen began streaming video clips of policemen in riot gear fighting protesters and headlines showing cases against police officers that minorities had lost in court. "Because the system is racist and weighted heavily against minorities. The reason police prey on innocent black people is the same reason hunters go to Africa and shoot lions: because they can; because they know that even if there are laws against it, the system is always on their side."

The video of headlines had begun to stream faster and faster until it became a blur. Suddenly, an explosion of white light, like the death throe of a supernova, filled the screen, accompanied by a deep, booming sound effect of a detonated atomic bomb. The screen slowly faded to black. A new video stream faded in, showing scenes from a variety of funeral services and wakes, with black family members grieving and consoling each other.

"After going to one funeral too many, my colleagues and I decided that it was time someone tried something new. We've tried taking these police perpetrators to court. We've tried introducing new legislation. We've tried marching. We've even tried kneeling. Nothing seems to have made much difference. So, we've decided to try a more direct approach. We've created a system for identifying the worst offenders. These are officers whose crimes against the innocent are beyond doubt; whose crimes have been corroborated by eyewitness reports and with accompanying direct and sometimes explicit video evidence. In other words: their guilt is undeniable. It's their punishment that has been elusive. Until now.

"We created this video to let the public know that, over the next few weeks, we will be going after three specific police officers that we have found guilty of egregious crimes against innocent black citizens: a bully, a rapist, and a murderer. We're making this public announcement for two reasons. First, we want to let the public know that someone is watching out for them; that someone is exacting justice on their behalf. The second, and perhaps most important reason, is that we want to put the police themselves on notice." The camera zoomed in until Ish's mask filled the screen, the lights creating white halos in the center of each lens of his black shades. "Your days of operating with impunity are over."

"I know what you're thinking," he said as the camera panned out again, his voice low and smooth, like thunder on a dark summer evening. "You're saying to yourself, 'This must be some kind of prank'. But I assure you, nothing could be further from the truth. In fact, at some point within the next few days, we will be uploading video footage of our first example of justice served. You will have already heard about it in the news, but the video footage will be your proof that PROPR is the group taking responsibility.

"Some of you may also be wondering, 'How is this going to change anything? There are thousands of police officers. How is delivering justice to a handful going to make any difference?' The answer to that is one word: fear. Once officers across the country begin to understand that we are serious, that we are a real threat, maybe they'll think twice the next time they raise a boot or a baton or a pistol against an unarmed suspect. Maybe they will wonder if PROPR is watching, and if they might be the next name on the list, the recipients of which will all receive a PROPR trial and a PROPR sentence so that the people can receive PROPR justice.

"Before I end this presentation, I want to make a few things perfectly clear. This is NOT an indictment of all police officers. We know that the vast majority of the men and women in uniform are doing a great job, protecting, serving and treating everyone with the same sense of respect that we're all due, regardless of the color of our skin. We are just shining a light into the shadows, bringing the bad actors into the light of day and doling out the punishment that we feel they deserve. So, if you're a 'good cop', you have nothing to fear from us." The camera slowly zoomed in again.

"But if you're a 'bad cop', start looking over your shoulder. We may be coming for you sooner than you think. Good night."

When the lights came back on, everyone looked around the room at each other, a thinly veiled look of excitement in their eyes.

"That's some pretty slick production," said Bird.

"Righteously slick!" said Jag.

"Thanks," said Chad, beaming.

"What about the voice?" asked Ma'am. "The FBI has voice analyzers that could easily connect that to Ish. Anything you can do to alter it?"

"I'm glad you mentioned that, Ma'am. I'll be applying a masking filter to the audio track before the final editing is complete. Actually, it's really more of an encoding than a mask. But the bottom line is that it would be virtually impossible for anyone to link that voice back to Ish, even if they were aware of the source of the original voice."

"You're a man of many talents," said Ma'am as she draped her arm around his shoulders. Clearly, it was done more in a 'brotherly' way than a romantic way, but Ish noticed that Bird was keeping his eye on them.

"So, what's next?" asked Jag.

"I'm going to make a couple of small changes. I'll adjust the light balance, mask the voice, etc., and then I'll post it to the website," said Chad.

"And when do we go after the first target?" asked Jag.

"After we get a bit of news coverage on this," said Ish. "It will increase the power of the message if it's already in the public consciousness before we begin. We have the emails of 50 top reporters that we'll be sending the video to directly. Once we start to see some attention in the media, we'll be ready to make our move. Shouldn't take more than a couple of days."

"And in the meantime?" asked Bird.

"We relax. Consider yourself on R&R," said Ish.

"I can work with that," said Jag, grinning widely. "As a matter of fact," he added as he stood up and stretched, "I think I'll go for a run; work off some of these flapjacks," he said, patting his stomach.

"Mind if I join you?" asked Ma'am.

"Not at all. We'll catch you guys later."

Bird looked like he wanted to say something as they left the room, but he remained quiet.

Later that day, Chad published the video on the website and emailed it to the media. He had written a programming script that continually monitored the web for any mention of PROPR. Less than twelve hours later small mentions began to show up on some of the online news sites. Most reporters were considering it some kind of 'internet prank', but not all of them were convinced.

The next morning, Ish and Chad ran into each other in the kitchen as Ish was preparing breakfast.

"This video is really starting to get some traction," said Chad. "It's snowballing by the hour."

"That's good news, because I can feel things already starting to get a little tense around here," said Ish. "Breakfast is served!" he yelled, as he placed a plate stacked with turkey sausage patties on the table.

Jag and Ma'am walked into the dining room together, laughing about something. Ish wondered if there could be something developing between the two of them. What an odd couple that would be, he thought to himself. And a hell of a distraction for the mission.

Once everyone was about done with their meal, Ish pushed his plate back and addressed the group.

"We're finally seeing some online chatter," he said. "Over the last few hours there have been several stories published. They don't seem fully convinced that we're real yet, but they're also not quite willing to write us off as a hoax. So, it's time for us to get tactical. There's a couple of minor issues Chad and I want to look into first, but let's all plan to meet back here tonight at 7:00 and we'll go over the final details of the first operation. Cool?"

Everyone nodded in agreement.

After helping clear the dishes, the individual members of the group began busying themselves with the same things they had been busying themselves with the last several days: exercise, reading, watching TV or surfing the web. Ish was in the kitchen, drying some dishes and putting them away, when Jag strolled in and casually leaned against the counter, facing Ish. For a moment he didn't say anything, and Ish looked at him expectantly.

"Mind if I ask you a question?" said Jag, keeping his voice kind of low.

"What's up?"

"What do you know about Ma'am's, uh, 'personal preferences'?"

"In regards to what?"

"Well...like, is she a carpet muncher? Is she only into the brothers? Is she—"

"Whoa, whoa, whoa," said Ish, holding up his hands. "'Carpet muncher?' Really? Dude, you need to come into the 21st century."

"What?" asked Jag, confused.

"The term 'carpet muncher' is considered offensive."

"To who?"

"Never mind," said Ish, shaking his head in astonishment. "Look, are you asking me if I think Ma'am could be interested in a foul-mouthed, politically-incorrect, blue-eyed white boy from Tennessee?"

"Yeah," said Jag, smiling somewhat awkwardly.

"I have no idea."

"Okay," said Jag resignedly.

"But why the hell are you asking me instead of her?"

"Well, you know, with the missions coming up, I didn't want there to be any unnecessary drama, especially if she's looking more for an innie than an outie. Plus, I don't think Bird would take very kindly to the idea, so no need to get him all riled up before I even know I'm in the game."

"I've seen you two flirting or whatever it is you're doing. She seems open enough. I've never asked her about her sex life, but what I can tell you is that she's a strong, straight-up, shoot-from-the-hip sister. You asking her if she's gay is not going to fluster her. If you want to ask her out, just go for it. I've seen you step to many a woman, Mr. Smooth Operator. I don't understand why this one is making you so nervous."

"Well, as you know, I've dated other sisters before," he said, grinning slyly. "But never anyone like Ma'am. But thanks for the advice. I appreciate it." Ish nodded, and they both looked up to suddenly find Ma'am standing in the doorway. It was hard to say whether the look on her face was one of anger or amusement.

"Gentlemen, let me just say, for the record, that I am, and have always been, 'strictly dickly'. Don't get it twisted and let the hard edge fool you. And as for you, 'Mr. Smooth Operator'," she said, cutting a sharp sideways glance at Jag. "We can talk about the rest of that later." She then turned around and promptly walked away, but not before Ish saw the trace of a smile playing at the corner of her mouth.

A few minutes later Ish was in his room getting dressed. He stopped in the middle of buttoning his shirt and shook his head in wonder, thinking back to that day in Afghanistan when he first met Jag. He had initially thought the man had more in common with the

KKK than MLK. Who would have ever imagined that a lily-white country boy like Jag would ever be interested in someone like Ma'am? The world was full of mysteries.

Chapter 28

Ish and the team had been following Officer Dexter Pogue for two days. They had arrived in Nashville three days earlier, all on separate flights, and spent the first 24 hours getting familiar with the city, with Jag as expert tour guide. All their gear, which included tasers, tracking devices and .380 semi-automatic pistols with silencers, had been special-delivered to an anonymous Post Office box Jag had set up several days prior using a fake ID.

They had been surveilling Pogue both visually and via Chad's constant triangulation of his cell phone. For someone so violent and heartless, Pogue led a fairly boring life; at least, that's how it appeared.

It was Ish and Ma'am's turn to man the tracking vehicle, a van with the words 'Smith & Sons Plumbing' painted on it. It was clichéd as hell but still amazingly effective. People never gave it a second look, no matter where it was parked or for how long. To the casual observer, it appeared to be a plain, well-worn commercial service vehicle. But inside, not only was it full of cutting-edge surveillance equipment, it was also completely soundproof. No matter how loud the conversation inside became, no one outside could hear the slightest trace of it.

The coffee was cold again, and Ish got up and stepped to the built-in coffee machine to start a new pot. He took the opportunity to steal a few long glances at Ma'am. She had been uncharacteristically reserved the last few days.

"What is it, Ish?" she asked. She had noticed the glances.

"Nothing really. It's just that you've been a bit quiet since we touched down. I was wondering if everything was alright with you."

"If you're asking if I have some reservations about the mission, the answer is no. Bird told me that you've been neurotically fixated on that lately."

"Maybe he has a point," said Ish. "Sometimes I just feel like I can never be sure enough. I worry about what I've gotten you all into."

Ma'am didn't answer. Ish felt grateful that she had apparently decided the line of questioning wasn't worth pursuing. For several minutes they both just watched the monitor screens and listened to the sound of the coffee machine working to produce the life-preserving liquid that had been their mainstay the last couple of days.

"Tell me something," said Ma'am as the brewer was finishing up. "What was it like to go from being normal, like the rest of us po' black folk, to having more money than you knew what to do with?"

"What?"

"Chad told me about how you two started the company, and that you were actually the one that made the breakthrough on the program. He said that you were the real genius behind the company's success."

"Well, I think Chad exaggerates a bit. We both had our roles in getting our company to where it is today. And I couldn't have done it without him."

"Okay, but that doesn't answer my question."

"The full answer really isn't quite that simple. It was a long road, and it's a long story."

Ma'am looked around them and then back at Ish and raised her eyebrows and shoulders simultaneously as if to say, *I have nothing but time.*

"I was the jock in high school," Ish began. "The neighborhood I grew up in didn't put a lot of value on scholastic excellence or anything that didn't involve chasing a ball around, so I intentionally avoided studying. It wasn't until my final year, when my mom really started to put the bug in my ear about going to college, that I started working on my grades. She got me by telling me how disappointed my father would have been to know that I let such a great opportunity pass me by." Ish paused for a moment. "My dad was shot and killed during a robbery when I was nine, right before we moved from Chicago to L.A.

"Anyway," he continued, "I was a bit of a football star, and once I got my grades up, I pretty much had my choice of scholarships. I chose USC and got a full ride."

"Is that where you met Chad?"

"No, we met in high school. We were good friends then, but it was just by luck that we both ended up at USC together. I minored in Language Studies, but we both majored in Computer Science."

"I guess it was just meant to be."

"Yeah," said Ish, smiling nostalgically, "I guess it was.

"So how did you end up interested in computers anyway, of all things? I grew up in the hood, too, and I don't remember there being a whole lot of brothas and sistas doing anything with computers, other than maybe playin' video games."

"Yeah, it isn't as common as it should be. And that was especially the case back then. But the thing is, computer code is just another language, and I was always good with languages. My mother was Brazilian and spoke English and Portuguese, and my father was from New Orleans, and that added French and Creole. So, we regularly communicated in four different languages in my house. And once I moved to South Central, I picked up Spanish, too, because it was easy and it allowed me to fit in more places. That's why language was the natural choice for a minor. That's where I started learning the Arabic languages—Kurdish, Pashto, Urdu, what have you."

"Damn," said Ma'am.

"It sounds a lot more impressive than it is," said Ish, smiling. "Once you know a second language, it's a lot easier to learn others. And that includes computer languages."

"I always wanted to get into computers," said Ma'am. "I had this probation officer once that was tryin' to get me to join one of those tech schools. IT Tech? Something like that. Anyway, I told him that I had a' interest and he was really pushin' me to enroll. Even told me he could get the tuition covered by the state. But it never happened. I couldn't stay clean long enough. I was barely able to avoid violating my probation, let alone actually making something of my life." She had a sad, faraway look in her eyes.

"It's never too late, Ma'am. Chad and I started this non-profit last year where we fund programming classes for inner-city schools. I wasn't too hands-on with it because I was still on active duty, but Chad was. He's taught a lot of kids how to write code. He could teach you, too."

"I'm not a kid anymore, Ish."

"He's taught old people, too."

"I damn sure ain't old, either!" she said, leaning back and smiling widely.

"I know, I know! I'm just saying, if you want to learn, after this is all over, we'd love to teach you."

"I just might take you up on that. But back to your story. How is that you ended up working for the government?"

"When I got to college, it was like the floodgates of knowledge opened up to me. It was as if I had spent my whole life hiding from it and suddenly it had found me and attacked my brain, like some strange virus." He laughed. "That may sound melodramatic, but that's exactly what it felt like. Again, I was an outsider. Most of the other students that were doing well had spent the majority of their lives studying and applying themselves. For me, it was all new. And I loved it! I didn't want to do anything else. I played ball, and eventually I started taking flight lessons, but I didn't party, I didn't watch TV, I didn't even date much. I felt like I was making up for lost time; like I was always under the gun."

"Your mama must have been proud."

"She was, but I think she was a little bit concerned, too. She had never seen me act like that, and I think she wondered if there might be something wrong with me. Not that I was a bad kid, but I made a life in the street, and I was much more likely to be caught fighting than cracking open a book. But I think she took some comfort in the fact that Chad and I were not only going to the same school, but had some classes together. She always liked him. She always believed he had a 'grounding' effect on me. Maybe she was right."

"She might change her mind if she knew what that boy was up to these days," said Ma'am, shaking her head. "I think that he just may be more of a revolutionary than any of us."

"Yeah. But to be honest, he always was," said Ish. "But one of his gifts is being able to fit in anywhere. He's like a chameleon but totally 100% authentic at the same time. He's a real visionary. When I first wrote the code for the program that our company was built on, it was Chad that realized how valuable it was. I was using it like a resume, showing it to different tech recruiters, hoping they'd give me a job."

"I thought your scholarship was covering all your costs?"

"Most of them, but things like the flight lessons I wanted had to come out of my own pocket. The problem was that these companies I was applying to didn't seem all that eager to offer a position to a young black kid. But then the Defense Department came calling. Someone at one of the companies I had met with tipped them off to what I was working on, and they saw the possibilities."

"I'm surprised those muthafuckas didn't have a problem working with a black man."

"Actually, they kind of did. The first time they met me, they were less than enthusiastic. They kept asking me who else I was working with to develop the program. Chad had helped me work out some of the kinks, so I gave them his name. They rescheduled the meeting and strongly suggested that I bring him with me next time. I had to talk him into it. When they met him, it was as though I didn't exist, like I was a fucking secretary. They spoke directly to him and ignored me altogether. But in the end, it was all worth it. They offered us a contract that forever changed both of our lives. It was our Cinderella story."

"So, if it was such a Cinderella story, how the hell did you ever end up in the army? Did you break your glass slipper somewhere along the way?"

Ish gazed down at his feet. "Yeah, I guess I kind of did. I thought it was the best way to help."

"Help what?" she asked, scornfully.

"Help the country. The war effort. My fellow troops."

Ma'am laughed.

"You know, when my brother first told me about you, I almost didn't believe him. A rich black man that wants to join the army? I said 'You mean the *army* army? Like where they shoot at you and shit?' He said, 'Yeah, the *army* army.' I told him you must be crazy. And when I met you that first time in Germany, I was prepared not to like you. But you turned out to be a' alright brother. But I still don't understand why you did it. How you were able to leave your wife and daughter—" She caught herself. "Sorry, Ish," she said self-consciously.

"Don't worry about it," he said, waving his hand dismissively. "You not saying it out loud doesn't change the fact that I left my girls to go off and fight a pointless war, and in return one is dead and the other is in jail and possibly headed to prison. I used to think that while no one else could understand why I did what I did, at least it made sense to me. Now I can't even say that." His face was set with hard, deep lines.

Ma'am suddenly tilted her head to the side and looked at him rather strangely. "Now that I'm thinking about it, maybe I do understand," she said.

"What do you mean?"

"Well, it's obvious that money was never what drove you. My panties get wet just thinking about how much money you have in the bank. But that's not you. If money was enough for you, you never would have left it."

"True," said Ish, not sure where she was going with this.

"See, it's the money that made what you did seem crazy. Black men join the service every day. Rich black men don't, but regular black men do. You were so disconnected from the money that you'd made that it was not even part of your equation. Which means you joined for some of the same reasons others join—not because you wanted college tuition, a VA loan or a job, but because you were a patriot. Contrary to popular belief, there are black patriots. My brother is one. And you're another," she said.

Ish took a moment to think about what she'd just said. In thirty seconds, she had been able to articulate what had eluded him since the fateful day he first walked into the recruiter's office.

"That makes a lot of sense," he said finally. "But it doesn't change anything. It doesn't change what happened to my family while I was gone."

"The truth is not a time machine, brother. It's just the truth. Knowing why something happened is not enough to change the fact that it happened. But sometimes, if you give it enough space, the truth can light you a path to peace. Or at the very least, understanding."

"Looks like our boy is on the move," said Ish, interrupting Ma'am and motioning to the monitor behind her. A black pickup truck was backing out of the driveway of the house they were watching. Ish grabbed a controller and, zooming in with the lens, confirmed that it was Pogue behind the wheel.

Ma'am slid open the panel that separated the front seat area from the rest of the van and got behind the wheel. As the truck approached the first corner, she started the engine and slowly inched away from the curb, keeping a discreet distance.

Fifteen minutes later the truck pulled into the parking lot of a bar. The sign above it said 'Sutton's Pub'. The parking lot was full, as it had been on the other two occasions that they had followed him there.

Ish checked his watch; it was 8:29pm. "Just like clockwork," he said, almost to himself.

"At least he's predictable."

Ish grunted in acknowledgment. "I think we've seen enough," he said as he typed some notes into his phone, his thumbs a blur that even a teenage gossip queen would have envied. "If he sticks to the script, he'll be here for another two to two-and-a-half hours. Let's head back to base."

"Roger that," said Ma'am as they slowly rolled past the bar.

'Base' was actually a small warehouse that they had rented on the outskirts of town. It was formerly owned by a meat packing company and had a large, walk-in freezer that was perfect for their needs. But because of how far it was from their hotels, most discussions the team had as a group took place in the van. Ish had called ahead to let everyone else know that they were coming. They picked each person up a block from their respective hotels, to reduce the chance of someone from the hotel seeing them entering the van. Once everyone was assembled, space was tight with them all jockeying for a comfortable spot. But there really was no alternative that didn't involve them either being out in the open or susceptible to eavesdropping.

"So, I think we have this guy's schedule pinned down," said Ish. "Luckily, he's a creature of habit, which helps to reduce the amount of time we have to be here for this mission. Have you had any reception problems with the triangulation receiver?" he asked, turning to Chad.

"No, everything's been fine."

"Good. In that case, I say we make our move tomorrow night. There's a stretch of road here," he said, using the mouse cursor to highlight an area on the map that was displayed on one of the monitors. "Ma'am will drive the van with Jag and me. Chad and Bird—you shadow us in the second vehicle."

"After the extraction, Chad can drive Pogue's pickup, and we all meet up at the warehouse. At that time of night, we shouldn't have any interruptions."

* * *

Twenty-six hours later, as Pogue's truck pulled out of the parking lot of Sutton's, Ma'am let two cars pass before proceeding after him. They drove in silence, everyone seemingly lost in their own thoughts or doing whatever mental preparation they normally did before going into battle. This was typical of the behavior Ish had noticed in his time in the field. There was often a spooky silence that descended upon the team right before engagement. But he wondered how Chad was holding up. As the only non-soldier in the group, there was no way to know how he was going to react to the stress of the moment. Ish began to think it might have been a mistake to assign him to the shadow car instead of the lead, where Ish could keep an eye on him. But it was too late to change it now.

The cars that were separating them had moved on, and as they approached the contact point, Ish looked around and could see that Pogue's truck and their plumbing van were the only vehicles on the street. The shadow car had stopped two blocks back and was around a corner, out of sight. They had chosen this particular street because it tended to have very light traffic this time of night, was in a retail district with all the stores long closed for the day, and was free of street cameras.

Ahead of them was a traffic light, and when the truck was half a block away, Ish hit a switch on the control board that changed the light from green to red. On cue, Ma'am, Jag and Ish all pulled black ski masks over their faces and donned black shades. The plan was a simple one: gently tap Pogue's back bumper with the van and grab him when he got out to check the damage.

"Let's do it," he said. Ma'am nodded and inched the van forward at about five miles per hour until it collided with the truck.

"What the fuck!" they heard Pogue say through the open window of his truck as he shifted it into park and began opening the driver's door.

Ish was just reaching for the door handle of the van when the walkie talkie that was sitting on the center console crackled. "You got company!" said Chad's voice.

"There's a vehicle coming up behind us," said Ma'am, looking in the side mirror. "What's the move?"

They had anticipated this as a possibility, but there was no clear best solution. They had already engaged with Pogue, so this stunt was unlikely to work a second time. Also, they couldn't afford for him to see any of their faces, hence the masks, and once he saw the masks, he would know he was being hunted and catching him off guard again would then be a hundred times more difficult. The options were: try to grab him now, hopefully before the approaching car was close enough to recognize what was going on, void the mission and try again another day, or try to delay their interaction. Pogue was walking towards them, cursing under his breath. In the glare of the overhead street lights on their windshield, he still wasn't close enough to see the masks. The approaching car was now a little over a block back and closing quickly.

"Boss?" said Ma'am, as Ish sat motionless, his mind spinning as he calculated the odds.

"Ish?" said Jag, his tone urgent.

"Turn on your hazards and slowly back up along the curb," said Ish as he hit the button on the console again, changing the light from red to green.

Ma'am hit the switch for the blinkers and put the van in reverse, angling them towards the curb.

"Jesus, what the fuck are you doing?" yelled Pogue, throwing his hands into the air in frustration. Ma'am stopped the van half a block back, and Pogue quickly began walking to meet them. They all turned their heads away as the approaching car passed, so that its occupants couldn't see the masks. Thankfully, the driver wasn't interested in them, and seeing the green light, drove through the intersection and continued on down the street. Just as it turned the corner, Pogue reached the front of the van.

"Who the fuck taught you how to drive—" he began, but his rant was cut off as Ma'am jumped out of the driver's seat and shot him with the taser. His body stiffened, and he began to fall, but before he hit the ground Ish grabbed him as Jag slapped a piece of duct tape over his mouth and a black bag over his head. Eight seconds later, he was safely in the back of the van with his wrists and ankles in cuffs.

Ish grabbed the walkie talkie, depressed the 'talk' button and used a pencil to tap out a complex seven-note rhythm against the metal door frame, which allowed him to give Chad the order to come forward without having to reveal his voice to Pogue. Moments later, the shadow car approached. Chad quickly climbed out and jumped into Pogue's truck. The three vehicles slowly drove off, safely on their way to the warehouse.

Chapter 29

Once they arrived at their destination, Ish jumped out and raised the garage door, closing and locking it again after the three vehicles had driven in and parked. As previously planned, no one spoke so as not to give the police officer any vocal characteristics that could be used later to identify any of them.

Ma'am unlocked Pogue's ankle cuffs and roughly pulled him from the van. He stumbled slightly as Ish steered him towards the cavernous walk-in fridge. He mumbled something through the tape, but Ish ignored him. Once inside, he guided the man to a chair that was stationed against the far wall and shoved him into it.

The chair had a heavy metal frame. It was tarnished but sturdy. After making sure Pogue's wrists and ankles were securely cuffed to the chair, everyone grabbed a black hooded sweatshirt, a black ski mask and one of the custom-made brown Fawkes masks and put them on. They all wore black jeans, black sneakers, black leather gloves and dark shades, and when they assembled in a semi-circle around the seated officer, the only thing distinguishing one of them from the other was height and weight.

Chad had spent the previous day setting up several photography lights and four different video cameras, so that the action could be captured from multiple angles. A small table in a corner on the other side of the room held a laptop, which was set up to control a video projector that was mounted in the ceiling overhead.

Ish walked up to Pogue, whose chest was rising and falling rapidly, and pulled the hood off his head. Sweat was streaming down his face, even though the temperature in the room was a cool sixty-eight degrees. His head was swiveling back and forth frantically as he tried to speak through the duct tape. Ish nodded at Chad, who went to the laptop and pressed a button.

"Hello, Officer Pogue," boomed a digitized voice through the speakers arranged in the room's corners. "We are about to remove your gag. We kindly ask that you refrain from talking as we explain to you why you're here."

Ish reached forward and ripped the tape off his mouth. Pogue yelped as a small patch of skin was torn off his lower lip, sticking to the tape's adhesive. Per instructions, Pogue was suddenly quiet. He leaned back in the chair, as though there was some safety to be found even in putting an additional two inches between himself and them. He looked from one to the other, his eyes wide with fear.

"What do you want with me—" he began before Ish delivered a hard slap to the left side of his face. His lips began to tremble, but he did not try to finish the question.

"You are here because of certain crimes you have committed against humanity," continued the digitized voice. "May we direct your attention to the screen." The ceiling mounted projector came to life, and a video began to play on the dingy white wall of the refrigerated room.

Displayed on the wall was the video footage of Pogue beating a black male teenager. The footage was somewhat grainy on the big screen, but the terror reflected in the eyes of the young victim was undeniable. Even with the bad audio, you could clearly hear the thud of the punches and kicks the cop was inflicting on the boy.

They all waited quietly while the entire three-minute-long video played. Pogue appeared to be a quick learner, because he wisely chose not to comment and earn further assault from Ish. His face still displayed the shock and panic that he had expressed when the bag was first removed, but underlying that was a trace of belligerence or anger or maybe both. Instead of being embarrassed or ashamed of his actions, he radiated a certain amount of defiance, even in the presence of people who clearly had an issue with it and were in a position to do him harm.

"This is one of many infractions you have committed in your role as a police officer," continued the voice after the video finished. "And yet, you have miraculously been able to avoid paying any price for it. You have been an officer of the law that believed he was above the law. A corrupt legal and political system allowed you to maintain that invincibility. But that all stops today.

"Officer Dexter Pogue, you have been charged with forty-seven counts of aggravated assault under color of law. The verdict is guilty on all charges."

"This isn't a court of law!" said Pogue, no longer able to restrain himself. Chad tapped a button on the laptop, pausing the audio playback. Pogue looked up at Ish and flinched, expecting to be slapped again, but Ish just stared at him. Emboldened, Pogue continued.

"What are you, a bunch of bleeding hearts? Are you a bunch of niggers? Is that what the browns masks are supposed to represent? This guy was a danger to the community. I was doing my fucking job! What about 'black on black' crime? I'm all that stands between these wild baboons and total anarchy! You should be getting down on your fucking knees and kissing my ass for what I do! I put my fucking life on the line every day to stop this city from turning into fucking Uganda!"

He was breathing hard again as he once more looked around at his band of captors. Ish could almost see the wheels turning in his mind as he looked for some way out of his predicament. After a few more seconds of quiet, Chad resumed the playback as Ma'am stepped around and unlocked the cuffs.

"Unlike the politically correct courts of America, this tribunal believes in a more biblical approach to punishment: the classic 'eye for an eye'. To that end you will now be assaulted in the same manner that you have assaulted so many. Please rise."

"Fuck you!" said Pogue, spittle flying from his lips. Jag walked forward, adjusting his black leather gloves. Pogue stayed seated and began kicking his legs out to keep him away, but Ish and Ma'am each grabbed an arm and lifted him out of the chair while Ish delivered a clean punch to his solar plexus. Pogue stopped kicking as all the air evacuated his lungs. He began wheezing and would have fallen if Ish and Ma'am hadn't been holding him. It took him a full minute to regain his composure enough to stand without their help, at which point they both let him go and stepped back.

Jag, who had been standing about three feet away, waiting, suddenly moved with a blinding speed, closing the distance between them and landing a sharp right cross on Pogue's chin. He landed three more punches before the police officer hit the ground. A digital timer had appeared on the wall, via the projector, and for the next three minutes Jag delivered a beating very similar to that which they had all just witnessed Pogue deliver to the teenager.

Once Jag had finished, he and Ish took Pogue's unconscious body, reapplied the gag and the black bag over his head, and put him back in the van. They drove him, along with his truck, to another vacant industrial park on the other side of town. After setting his body down in front of an office, they used his cell phone to call 911 and give the police the address before setting his truck on fire, destroying any forensic evidence that they may have inadvertently left inside. Chad was left to clean up the warehouse and pack up all the equipment.

Back in the living room of Ish's hotel suite, everyone had a drink in hand—iced tea for Ma'am—and they all looked surprisingly unruffled.

"So," said Ish, "how's everybody feeling?"

Jag raised his eyebrows and shrugged nonchalantly. "No problems. Just another mission."

"It's actually better than most missions," said Bird. "At least we didn't have to kill anyone."

"I think the muthafucka deserved to die, but at least we gave him enough to think about to perhaps alter his future behavior," said Ma'am. Ish nodded.

"How about you, Chad? How are you holding up?" asked Ish.

A big, sheepish smile spread across Chad's face. "You know, I hate to say this, but I feel like I'm high on some kind of drug right now! The adrenaline rush is serious! I think I was shaking a little bit as we were waiting to grab him, but once we started moving, it felt natural."

"Yeah," said Ish, "I think we all kind of felt that way the first time we went into the field and engaged the enemy." The others nodded in agreement.

"So, what's next?" asked Bird.

"Well, first I'll record a short intro with Ish, then I'll get it all edited," said Chad. "That'll take about eight hours. Then I'll upload the final product to the site."

"Shit's about to get real," said Ma'am solemnly.

"It's late," said Ish. "I'm going to hit the hay. Let's get together for breakfast in the morning before we head to the airport."

Everyone finished their drinks, said their goodnights and retired to their own hotels.

Ish lay in bed, a glass of scotch beside him on the nightstand, and let his mind replay what had happened that night. It was a successful mission. They say any mission that you can walk away from is a successful one, but this one was successful on several levels. It proved that they could all work together, and that they were all committed to the mission and ready to deal with the consequences.

He was particularly impressed with how composed Chad had remained. Ish had seen many a soldier freeze under the fire of their first assault. The fear of death had the power to turn even the most macho man into a coward. Here, of course, the threat was less one of death and more one of capture and imprisonment, but in some ways that could be even more terrifying. Bleeding out from a couple of AK-47 rounds was a fairly quick resolution to a negative outcome. In addition, you got to die a hero's death. Being locked up in prison for the rest of your life or sitting on death row for the next twenty years was a lot harder pill to swallow.

* * *

Back in L.A., everyone gathered in the War Room. After exchanging pleasantries and grabbing coffee and bagels, Chad powered on the plasma screen. On the laptop he scrolled down a list of files until he found the one he was looking for and hit the 'play' button. A pretty blond woman, an anchor reporter, appeared on the screen sitting behind a desk, a stack of paper before her. She began speaking.

"Our top story today centers around the vicious attack and beating of Nashville police officer Dexter Pogue. Officer Pogue, a decorated twelve-year veteran of the Nashville Police Department, was attacked at a stop light on the way home late last night by unknown assailants. Officer Pogue was reportedly blindfolded and taken to an undisclosed location, where he was handcuffed and beaten by a gang of masked men. His body was then dumped on the street and his truck set ablaze. Firefighters responding to the fire found him unconscious. The officer was taken to the hospital and is listed in critical condition.

"A few hours later, an organization calling themselves the People's Revolutionary Organization for Police Reform, or PROPR for short, posted a video on the website NowBeginsTheRevolution.com, taking credit for the attack. We have acquired a copy of the video, but I must first warn you that some of this footage is extremely graphic. Viewer discretion is highly advised."

Ish, masked and dressed exactly as he had for the first video, appeared on the screen.

"Good morning, America," he said, his voice again digitally altered but still full of bass. "Welcome back to the channel of the People's Revolutionary Organization for Police Reform. As we stated in our introductory video a week ago, our organization was born out of the frustration of seeing case after case of young, innocent, unarmed black men and women being attacked, and sometimes killed, by out of control, often racists, police officers. You've all seen the headlines. You've all read the stories. You know that very seldom are any of the officers punished. And absent the threat of said punishment, our police have become more and more brazen in their attacks against what they clearly consider to be second class citizens.

"So, we created PROPR in an effort to extract some of the justice that these victims are being denied by our courts. Again, as we said in the first video, we are NOT declaring war on all police officers. We understand that the majority of officers are doing their jobs and upholding the law equally for all citizens. It's the bad apples that we are after. To that end, we chose three initial cases to focus on—three officers guilty of three separate crimes: assault, rape and murder. As we announced, we pledged to go after these three officers and dispense our own version of justice.

"By the time you see this video, news of the success of our first mission will have already flooded the media outlets. Our target: Officer Dexter Pogue of Nashville, Tennessee.

"Officer Pogue has a long, lurid history of being, let's just say, 'less than gentle' with many of the people he has been entrusted to protect and serve. Officer Pogue has been accused of using excessive force almost 50 times, and those are just the cases that were officially reported. Undoubtedly, there are many more that have gone unreported because the victim was intimidated or simply had no confidence that the charge would be taken seriously. Let me direct your attention to this video of one of his most recent, and most brutal, assaults."

The video of Pogue beating the helpless black teen filled the screen. Amazingly, the news program played the entire three minutes of video exactly as it was posted online.

"This video is not exactly news; you've probably seen it before, when it originally occurred two years ago. And if so, then it probably comes as no surprise to you that Officer Pogue was not charged with any crime for this incident. He wasn't even reprimanded by his superiors. And that's where we come in. Last night PROPR paid Mr. Pogue a visit, reminded him of some of his indiscretions, and meted out what we felt was an appropriate punishment. Here's some video of that exchange."

The screen now showed some of the video footage shot in the warehouse. The quality was amazing—crisp, well-lit imaging, shot from fantastic angles and with crystal-clear, riveting audio. Chad had done a superb job editing it. Considering how many cameras he used and how quickly he finished it, he must have been up all night. The total time of the video was a bit over three and a half minutes, and it included Pogue's tirade before the assault.

"While I'm sure it was a painful lesson, we made sure Officer Pogue received prompt medical care and are confident he will make a full recovery. We hope this will act as a catalyst for change in Officer Pogue's worldview in regards to his job as a police officer, and that he will either decide to amend the way he dispenses his duties or decide that perhaps a different line of work might be in order.

"We present this to you, the American public, as proof that we are not helpless; that we do not have to idly sit by and accept this kind of mistreatment at the hands of those whose salaries are paid by our taxes. You may not be personally qualified to fight back the way we're doing, but if you are a person of color that feels that you have been victimized by a police officer, and you have video proof, feel free to send it to us at help@NowBeginsTheRevolution.com and we'll look into it. In the meantime, we are preparing for our next mission: a police officer guilty of rape in the line of duty. Check back here in a few days for an update. Until then, good day and stay safe."

The blond news reporter returned to the screen.

"The FBI has officially deemed PROPR a terrorist organization and is heading up the investigation to capture them. A spokesman has reported that they have several suspects and leads in the case and are vigorously pursuing all angles. They expect to have someone in custody soon. On to other news..."

Chad pressed a button on the remote, and the blond woman was replaced by a black screen. He looked around the room, and a large smile spread over his face. Everyone answered with a slow smile of their own; everyone, that is, except for Ish.

Book 2: RAGING AT THE SUN

Chapter 30

FBI Special Agent Dexter Madden was getting irritated. It was his and his wife's tenth wedding anniversary, and he had made the dinner reservations over a month ago. They had arrived on time, yet here they were, forty-five minutes later, still sitting in the lobby of Chateau Bleu waiting for a table.

Madden was a tall, dark-complexioned, forty-two-year old black man. He was of a trim, athletic build, with warm eyes, a high forehead and a wide, flat nose. Most women seemed to consider him quite attractive, but he never really understood why. His wife, Kelly, said it was because he possessed a unique combination of charm, kindness and sincerity. He felt she was biased, but he took her word for it.

Kelly, nine years Madden's junior, looked like the typical California girl-next-door beach bunny—5'8", long blond hair, sparkling blue eyes and a body that would have been picture perfect for bikini commercials. No one could have guessed by looking at her that she had never actually set foot on a beach, was born and raised in Utah and had a PhD in biology from MIT.

The door to the restaurant opened, letting in a chilly breeze. An elderly man and woman, both white, entered and approached the maître d'.

"Mr. and Mrs. Giovanni, welcome! Two for dinner?" asked the headwaiter, smiling warmly.

"Yes, if you can fit us in," said the old woman. "Victor forgot to call for reservations again!"

"Certainly. Right this way," said the headwaiter as he grabbed two menus and led the couple away.

Kelly could read her husband's mind just by the look in his eyes. "Dex, let's just get out of here," she said, hugging him. "French food is too rich anyway. I think I'd prefer a nice burger from that place you like over on King, the one with the portobello mushrooms."

Her husband bowed his head and closed his eyes. He should be used to this by now. He and Kelly dated for four years before they got married. Both his family and her family were completely accepting of their relationship. Madden's father had passed when he was still a child, but his mother treated Kelly like her own daughter, and Kelly's parents had often asked why they were taking so long to make it legal, making it clear that they were eager for some grandkids. But there were many other people, both friends and strangers, who were not so welcoming.

The maître d' returned, and Madden rose and approached him.

"Excuse me," he said. "Can you tell me how much longer it will be?"

"I'm sorry, sir, but I really can't."

Madden paused to look back at his wife, standing behind him, and gave himself a moment to gather his thoughts.

"Clearly, the couple that you just seated had no reservation, and ours was made weeks ago. So, can you tell me why they are currently ordering appetizers and we're still freezing here in the lobby?"

"Sir," said the man smugly, "that couple has a standing reservation with us. They—"

"A 'standing reservation'? This is bullshit! Let me speak to the manager, please," said Madden, fuming.

"Sir, I am the manager," said the maître d', backing away from him. "I don't think we're going to be able to serve you tonight. Please leave now, or I'll be forced to call the police."

"I am the goddamn police!" said Madden, pulling out his badge and shoving it at the man's face.

Kelly quickly darted in between the two men and put her hand on her husband's arm.

"Let's go, hon," she said. "This asshole isn't worth it."

For a moment they were all statues: Madden leaning forward as if his wife's presence was the only thing keeping him from pouncing, the maître d' leaning back with his hand covering his throat as though he felt he could be attacked at any minute and Kelly in the middle, looking like a cage fight referee.

Finally, Madden made a decision. His body relaxed as he put his wallet back in his pocket and straightened his jacket. "Yeah, let's get out of here," he said to Kelly, but his steely gaze stayed locked on the eyes of the white man until his wife's arm turned him. They headed out the door and into the parking lot.

Madden activated the remote, unlocking their black Tesla Model S and walked around to his wife's side to open the door for her before he got in behind the wheel.

"Sorry," he said. His wife grabbed his right hand in response and began to rub it between both of hers. She leaned forward and gave him a gentle kiss on the lips.

"Let's go get some portobello burgers!" she said, smiling.

On the drive to the burger stand, Madden began to calm down. The R&B singer Seal was playing on the stereo. Seal's music always relaxed him. He remembered that Seal was married to a white woman; a former model. Heidi something. Klump? He couldn't remember. Maybe they weren't even married anymore. He didn't really keep up on entertainment gossip, but everyone knew these Hollywood romances never lasted long. But he wondered if Seal ever had to deal with these kinds of experiences when out and about with his blond-haired, blue-eyed mate. Probably not. Celebrities usually seemed to get a pass.

Moments later they pulled into the lot of the Burger Ranch. Technically in 'the hood' even though it was only twelve miles from the ritzy area they had just left, it was a Washington, D.C. institution, known for having some of the best food in the city, regardless of price. The place was popular and, as always, crowded. He circled the lot a second time, looking for a spot.

"I need to go to the restroom, honey," said Kelly. "Can you just drop me here at the door while you park?"

"Sure."

Madden watched his wife walk from the car to the restaurant and felt a pang of guilt. She was a good woman; maybe the best woman he had ever met. Their love affair was pure and classic and rich, like something out of a Nicholas Sparks book. Few people believed that they could actually be as happy as they appeared. But it was true. They were. Still, it was moments like this that he wondered if it was unfair to marry her. She deserved so much better than this—to be forced to suffer the slings and arrows of ignorance and cruelty from people who were too focused on the color of their skin to realize that they were real human beings.

Madden lucked out. An SUV pulled out of a spot right next to the restaurant entrance, and he darted into it. His luck held as he entered the restaurant to find no line at the register. A pretty black girl smiled at him from the other side of the counter. She looked to be about nineteen or twenty. Her medium length hair was straight and hung just above her shoulders, and her lips were a shiny plum color. She had an hourglass figure and wore her uniform tight enough to show off all her curves.

"Welcome to Burger Ranch," she said. "May I take your order?"

Madden looked around for his wife, but she must have still been in the restroom. No matter. He knew what to order for her. They came here regularly, and she always ordered the same thing: portobello cheeseburger, sweet potato fries and a diet coke. He placed the order for both of them and paid the girl.

"It'll be just a few minutes," she said, still smiling, her eyes locked on his. "How are you tonight?" she asked as she began to playfully twirl a strand of her hair. He noticed her glance at his wedding ring.

"Good. Yourself?" he replied, returning the smile.

"I'm okay. We've been pretty busy all night, so it's nice to finally have a minute to breathe."

Madden nodded. Was this girl flirting with him? It made him smile inside. He had been with Kelly for fourteen years, and even though he used to think of himself as a bit of a ladies' man, he never missed those days—or those women. Kelly was every woman he had ever needed.

He glanced down at the receipt in his hand, and the total caught his eye.

"Excuse me," he said to the girl, "I think you forgot to add the two fries."

"Did I?" she asked, taking the receipt from him and looking it over. "No worries. I did add it to the check though, so they're working on them."

"How much extra do I owe you?" he replied, pulling his wallet from his pocket.

"For you?" she said, seductively lowering her voice. "No charge."

"Wow. Thank you. I appreciate it."

"No problem," she said. "Let me go see if it's ready yet." She walked around the heat station, the sway in her hips slow and pronounced, and disappeared into the back of the prep area.

Moments later Kelly appeared at his side. "Hey, hon," she said. "Did you order for me?"

"Yes, I did. You know I know what you like," he said smoothly.

"You do, do you?" she replied, smiling and putting her arms around him.

"Yes, I do."

At that moment, the cashier returned, a bag in each hand. As she rounded the corner and saw Kelly, her smile was instantly transformed into a cold, icy grimace. Her eyes were full of a combination of pity and disgust as she assessed Kelly from head to toe. She tossed the bags on the counter and looked accusingly at Madden.

"Um, you owe me another $6.42 for the fries," she said coolly.

Madden, feeling his anger beginning to rise all over again, took a $10 bill out of his wallet and slammed it down on the counter.

"Keep the change," he muttered, as he grabbed the bags and walked out of the restaurant, hand-in-hand with his wife.

Chapter 31

It had been several days since Madden had received the initial phone call from his boss, and he was still unsettled. Sitting in the passenger seat, he gazed out the window as Kelly drove. "What's wrong?" she asked. He had been quiet the entire ride, but his wife knew him well. Externally, he was a calm pool, but internally, he was nursing an intense, simmering tension.

"I don't know. It's just a bad time to leave town, with so much going on here. There's the remodeling, your mother coming in..." He shook his head, trailing off. She silently stared at him, waiting for him to add more. Only when the light turned green did she shift her eyes back to the road, but she continued to occasionally glance in his direction.

"This case is a potential powder keg, and there's a lot that can go wrong," he said finally. "I know that one of the major deciding factors in assigning it to me is that I just happen to be black. That means that any failure is going to be more heavily weighed than in a similar case without the racial overtones."

"But doesn't that also mean that any successes will also be more heavily weighed?"

He scoffed. "I wish that was the case, but you know it's not. That's not how the Bureau works. Things are always much more complicated than that."

"Maybe it won't be as difficult as you think. These animals created a website, for Christ's sake. They don't seem like the sharpest pencils in the drawer. And if it goes well, a case like this could make for a great swan song for you."

"Babe, let's not start talking about that again right now, okay?" he asked.

"Sorry," she whispered. After a few moments of silence, she appeared to have recovered from the chastisement.

"So," she asked, "what leads do you have so far?"

"That's what's so troubling," he said, grabbing her hand and squeezing it lovingly as he continued to stare straight ahead. "There are no leads. None. These guys are like ghosts. We've been analyzing the video footage but still haven't even been able to discern a single detail about where they filmed it."

"What about the website?"

"Tech is on it, but so far they're stumped. One of them said the signal is like a digital whack-a-mole, bouncing all over the planet and never in the place they expect it to be. They've never seen anything like it, and these guys are the best there is."

His wife was still watching him, sizing him up. He knew that she wasn't satisfied with his answers, but he forced himself to ignore her. He wasn't ready to speak out loud what was really bothering him about this case, not even to Kelly, his closest confidant.

As they pulled up to the curb of the airport, Kelly punched the trunk-release button and they both exited the car at the same time, meeting at the rear of the vehicle. As he reached for his bag, she put her hand on his back and gave it a rub. He turned to her and, taking her in his arms, kissed her deeply, keeping his eyes open and on the cop who was watching them, knowing that he would be ushering her to move along any minute now.

"Give your mother a hug for me and tell her I said I still like the bathroom tile she picked out best."

"You traitor!" she said, smiling at him for the first time since they'd left the house. He smiled back just as the cop appeared beside them.

"Let's move it out! This is not a parking lot," he snarled. Madden gave him a sideways glance, gave his wife one more quick hug, and walked into the airport.

As the plane taxied down the runway en route to Tennessee, Madden was relieved by the fact that both the seat next to him and the ones directly across the aisle were all empty, so that he could review his files without worrying about any prying eyes. After ordering a hot tea from the flight attendant, he powered up his laptop, entered his password and began digging through the case files. He was rereading information that he had already read several times, but experience had taught him that sometimes the truth is reluctant to reveal itself, even when it's right there in front of you.

Madden scrolled through the digitized copy of Pogue's employee file. His face slowly evolved into a scowl as he read. This guy was a real piece of work. He had a high arrest profile and exemplary attendance, but it was all overshadowed by the mile-long list of complaints that had been filed against him over the years. Particularly alarming was how much these complaints had in common.

Anyone reading this file could see that Pogue appeared to have an issue with race; specifically, he seemed to have a difficulty peacefully engaging with African Americans. Although employment files seldom told the whole story about any individual, Madden had a feeling that, in this case, the book was probably true to the cover: Pogue was a disgrace to his uniform.

Surely the officers serving with him were aware of his shortcomings, yet there was nothing in the file indicating that any of his peers had ever raised any concerns to management. The thin blue line. Far too many bad cops used it as a shield and a license to do whatever they pleased to whomever they pleased. Madden felt a burbling in his gut. Officers like Pogue, and the departmental environments that allowed them to thrive, literally made him sick to his stomach.

However, that didn't mean that a vigilante group was justified in kidnapping him and beating him half to death. Laws were created to instill order, and when people decided to ignore those laws, people like Madden had to step in and make things right again. But order was a fickle mistress. Sometimes it had the potential to destroy as much as it had the power to protect. Much like justice, it was seldom a black and white proposition, and it was easy enough to get lost in the shadows of the gray.

Madden took a sip of his tea and, leaning his head back against the headrest, closed his eyes and tried to slow his breathing. Maybe Kelly was right. Maybe it was time to think about retiring. He had been with the Bureau for twenty years. They hired him right out of college. In fact, he had never had any other job, other than flipping burgers after school.

But Kelly ran a thriving plant nursery. It was what she had retreated to after finally getting burned out from years working in biotechnology, researching climate change and agricultural genetics. Madden had been promising her for years that one day he would hang up his gun for good and come help her run it. But every time he started to seriously consider that the time might be at hand, a new urgent case would be thrown into his lap and his attention would be diverted elsewhere.

The truth was, gardening was the only thing that had ever really relaxed him, and it was his love for gardening that had prompted Kelly to open the nursery. They had actually met in a nursery, when they both simultaneously reached for the same potted rose bush. He agreed to let her have it if she'd have a cup of coffee with him. She accepted, and the rest was history.

Originally, Kelly said she decided to open her own nursery because plants and gardening had always been her first love, so it was a natural choice when she was looking for a new career direction outside research. But over the years she began to express to him her deeper motivation: that its lure might be strong enough to one day eventually drag him away from the FBI and closer to her.

As he walked into the hospital, Madden was met by Agent Casey Phillips. Phillips was a classically attractive, tall, dark brunette with rosy cheeks and a sleek, solid build. She walked with a pronounced limp, the result of a shotgun blast she had received while serving a warrant at the location of a suspected meth lab. She had insisted on being first through the door. The injury hadn't softened her attitude or her dedication to duty—or her eagerness to be first through the door.

"Good afternoon, Phillips."

"Sir."

"What's the sit rep?"

"Nothing new of any significance. Tech is still working on unraveling the ball of yarn that surrounds the website. We had a lead on the van which turned out to be a dead end, and we're still dark on the location of the assault. So basically, we're still at square one." Madden kept walking as she spoke, and she fell in step beside him.

"What about Pogue?"

"His condition continues to improve, but he hasn't had much to add to his original statement." They had arrived at Pogue's room. There were two uniformed police officers stationed at the door. They both stepped aside, allowing Madden and Phillips to pass. Inside, a nurse was fluffing Pogue's pillow, and a doctor was making notes on an electronic tablet.

Pogue looked like he had been hit by a bus. Madden had seen the pictures, but he had assumed that much of the facial swelling would have subsided by now. But one eye was still completely closed, and the other was little more than a tear-encrusted slit. His left leg was in traction, and a cast covered his right arm from fingertip to shoulder. As pitiful as the officer looked, Madden was unable to muster the slightest bit of sympathy for him. Phillips introduced Madden to the two caretakers, and after exchanging a few pleasantries, he kindly asked them to clear the room.

"Officer Pogue, I'm Special Agent Madden. If you don't mind, I'd like to ask you a few questions regarding your statement."

"Yeah," he mumbled. His jaws appeared to be wired shut, but he was still able to speak well enough to be understood. You could even still hear his southern accent.

"Is there anything you can tell me about the way your attackers moved that could be a clue to their identities? Maybe one cracked his knuckles or stood with a particular posture or—"

"Do you read?"

"I'm sorry?"

"I said do you fucking read? I've answered all these questions like eleven, twelve fucking times already. How many more ways can I say it? I don't remember shit about those assholes, alright?"

As an FBI agent, Madden had questioned a lot of people over the years, probably thousands, and with a fairly even mix of suspects and victims, so he was generally unfazed by these types of reactions. In fact, when someone was too compliant in answering the same questions over and over again, it was often a red flag that they were hiding something. But Pogue just rubbed him the wrong way. He was a rotten cop, probably a racist, and at least on some level deserved what he got. So, Madden wasn't feeling particularly patient.

"Listen to me," he said calmly. "You've been on the beat for over ten years. You know the drill. I don't have time to hold your hand and pat you on the ass. I need as much information as I can get, and I need it as quickly as possible. So, you can either cooperate fully or I can put a call in to your commander and see what he can do to loosen your lips and dial back your attitude."

Pogue seemed to take a moment to consider his options, staring at Madden with as much hate as his one, partially opened, eye could exude.

"There was nothing," he said finally. "They were all dressed the same, all in black, none of them spoke, and movement was kept to a minimum. The only thing I remember thinking was that I had been kidnapped by ghosts."

"Ghosts?"

"Yeah. Black ghosts."

It was going to be a long day.

After leaving the hospital with exactly the same information he had walked in with, Madden followed Phillips to the offices of the nearby FBI Nashville resident agency. An FBI resident agency is basically a smaller field office. It wasn't nearly as well-staffed as the larger field offices in the adjacent cities of Memphis, Knoxville or Louisville, but those were all 175-200 miles away, and they needed to stay as close to the scene of the crime as possible.

The six other agents assigned to the case were already seated in the tiny FBI Nashville conference room by the time Madden and Phillips arrived. He had previously worked cases with a couple of the agents before, but the rest were unfamiliar to him. After introductions and the customary hand-pumping all around, Madden leaned forward in his seat at the head of the table, fingers intertwined in front of him.

"I'm sure I don't have to tell anyone here that the pressure is on. The media blitz on this is building as more and more people realize the implications of what's happened and what potentially might still be yet to happen. So, what do we have?"

A burly man in a rumpled brown suit that matched his hair opened a notebook that was on the desk before him and began flipping through pages. His name was Bill Derry, and he was one of Madden's most trusted agents. He had absolutely no fashion sense, but he more than made up for it in loyalty, efficiency and uncanny investigative abilities.

"There has been some progress," said Derry. "We discovered the location of the warehouse in which the engagement took place. Our people already did an initial sweep through it. All they found were some trace amounts of the cop's blood, confirmed through DNA. They're still digging, but I wouldn't hold my breath."

"And the owner of the warehouse?" asked Madden.

"That's where things get interesting. The owner leased out the space two weeks ago. Never met the new tenants. All transactions handled by mail. Mailed the keys to a P.O. box in Memphis. The name on the box, and the name used by the person that leased the warehouse, is one 'Josh Carlyle'. By all accounts, Mr. Carlyle has been deceased for almost a year. The box rental had been paid in advance before he passed. Apparently the 'real' Carlyle had used the same box for years, so it was still active after he died and easy for our suspects to access, though God only knows how they were aware that he had the box in the first place."

"Do any of the employees at the mail receiving location remember anyone coming in to pick up the mail over the last few weeks?"

"Negative. They offer 24-hour access, and it's presumed that our perp or perps came in after hours. They have security cameras, but they only keep the footage for a week, and no one accessed that box on camera in the last seven days."

Madden's mood had perked up a bit at the beginning of this conversation, but now it was turning grim and dejected again.

"What was their method of payment for the warehouse lease?"

"Business check drawn on a Memphis branch of B of A. Funds have already cleared the account. And that's where these guys are really showing their pedigree."

"What do you mean?" asked Madden.

"B of A has no record of the checking account. Someone created the account out of thin air, and then populated the account with enough of a balance to cover the check."

"Inside job?"

"They don't think so. Their data security team doesn't think it could have been initiated from inside the bank."

"Meaning what?"

"Someone hacked them from the outside."

Madden took a moment to stroke his goatee, an unconscious twitch reserved for when he was deep in thought. "So, it looks like we can add bank robbery to the charges."

"Not exactly. The bank president reported that he received an anonymous envelope full of cash in the mail yesterday. The amount is the exact amount of the balance uploaded to the account. Looks like the perps have covered the bank's loss."

"Jesus Christ," muttered Madden. "Who the hell are these guys?"

Chapter 32

Ish awoke with a start. He thought he heard a noise at the door. His head swiveled slowly, his ears straining to confirm or deny his suspicions. But there was only silence. He got up from the bed and quietly crept into the living room. The blinds were drawn, but he could see that it was dark outside, and there was only one small table lamp illuminating the room. Again, he listened, but there was nothing. Then he saw it. The doorknob was slowly rotating. He couldn't remember if he had locked it. He looked around the room for something he could use as a weapon, but there was nothing.

He quickly started walking backwards, moving towards the rear of the house. As the door began to open, he stepped behind a wall and darted down a hallway, ducking into a doorway that led to another bedroom. He again looked around the room for something that he could use to defend himself and again found nothing. His pulse was beginning to rise, and he could feel the heat creeping up his neck and around the back of his head. He took a deep breath, held it, and slowly let it out through his nose, willing himself to calm down and relax. A cool sensation began to wash over him, almost as though he were standing under an air-conditioned vent. He was trying to decide his next move when the intruder spoke:

"Carter, this is the police. I know you're in here." The voice echoed off the walls of the hallway, making it difficult to pinpoint exactly where it was coming from, but it was clear that the cop was close. "Listen, this doesn't have to end badly for you. We just want to ask you some questions. Come out with your hands up, and you won't be harmed."

Somehow Ish had known the intruder was a cop. He didn't immediately respond. He was weighing his options. But giving up was not on the list.

"Or," said the voice, "we can do it the hard way, and take you out in a body bag."

"Come and get me!"

"As you wish, asshole."

Again, Ish's ears strained to detect some sound in the suffocating silence.

Suddenly, he heard a board creak directly outside the door of the room he was in and he sprang into action. He stepped into the hallway and pivoted on his left heel, slamming an elbow into the area where he thought the cop's face would be. But instead of connecting with a jaw, his elbow smashed into the sternum of one of the largest cops he had ever seen. The man had to be 6'8", maybe 6'9". He had pale, pasty skin, with hair so blond it was almost white, and was built like a linebacker, with muscle atop muscle, so much so that his uniform barely fit him. The sternum shot was hard enough that it would have immediately dropped most men. This man simply bent forward a bit, more in surprise than pain, and smiled at Ish, an evil kind of smile that was all darkness and no light.

The giant cop took a step forward and threw a straight right with lightning speed. Ish slipped his head to the side and felt the breeze as it floated past his left cheek and slammed into the wall like a sledgehammer. The hole it created and the tremor that it caused to vibrate through the frame of the house told him how close he had come to disaster. Ish immediately countered with a downward kick to the cop's knee. He put all his weight behind the kick, and he thought he heard a crunch as the cop stumbled and leaned back into the wall.

Ish quickly looked up and down the hallway, desperately searching for some tool that might give him an advantage, but the only weapon available was the gun that was in the cop's holster. Obviously, the cop didn't feel he needed to resort to bullets to stop Ish, and if the last punch was any indication, he was probably right. Ish knew his only chance of getting out of the house alive was to get ahold of that gun. He tried to spin around the officer, but the man bounced off the wall and threw a left hook. Again, Ish moved his head out of harm's way, but the punch still caught him on the shoulder. The left side of his body exploded in pain, and he could no longer will his feet to move.

The cop grinned his evil grin again and reached both arms out to grab Ish. Ish bent forward at the waist, leaving the cop clutching air, but before he could rise back up, the cop had him in a headlock. The powerful arms began cranking on his neck. He felt the muscles of the cop's arms begin to constrict, tighter and tighter, like the coils of some monstrous python snake. He pulled at the arms that were holding him, but it was like trying to bend steel. His heart was pounding in his ears, and he could faintly hear the cop laughing. A black spot appeared in front of his eyes and began to slowly increase in size, blocking out the light; he was losing consciousness. Realizing that it was futile to continue to struggle, he let his hands drop and welcomed the darkness. But one hand brushed against something hard and cold as it fell—the gun.

With his last ounce of strength, Ish reached for the pistol, and in one smooth movement, he had unsnapped the safety strap and pulled it from the holster. Either the cop didn't realize he had the gun or he didn't care, because he simply continued squeezing Ish's neck. Knowing that he was mere moments from passing out, Ish pointed the gun toward the floor, as close to the cop's body as possible, and started pulling the trigger. Three bullets fired before he heard a yelp and the cop let go of his neck, allowing Ish to fall to the floor gasping for air. When he looked up moments later, he was alone in the hallway, but there was a trail of blood leading further toward the back of the house.

Ish wiped the sweat from his forehead with the back of his hand and proceeded to tiptoe down the hallway. He had the man's service weapon, but he knew cops often kept a backup weapon in a leg holster or hidden somewhere else on their person, so he couldn't be too careful. Based on the minimal amount of blood he was seeing and how fast the cop had moved, he guessed he had probably hit him in the foot. An ankle shot should have hobbled him more, and a thigh wound would probably have produced more blood, especially if the artery was damaged. That meant that even if the officer was weapon-less he was still dangerous.

Ish inched up to the doorway and waited to see if he could hear any indication of movement inside, but all was silent. He began to peak his head around the door frame and pulled it back just as three slugs slammed into the wall behind him. His split-second glimpse of the room had revealed important information; the cop was hunkered down on the other side of a queen-sized bed beneath a window. There wasn't much else in the room to use for cover, other than a bulky nightstand.

Improvising, Ish reached into his pocket and pulled out a handful of coins. Then he waited. One minute passed. Then two minutes. Then three minutes. As expected, he heard no sound of movement from the room. When his clock told him that six minutes had elapsed, it was time for him to make his move. Whipping his arm like an MLB pitcher trying to throw a slider, he flung the coins into the room, causing them to clatter off the back wall to the right of the window. As the cop turned his head toward the noise, Ish dived into the room onto his belly. He fired four shots under the bed, and heard the officer yell in pain as Ish scrambled to the wall and the safety of the nightstand.

There was an empty soda bottle on the nightstand, and Ish grabbed it and tossed it overhead into the cop's direction, bouncing it off the far wall. Two more shots pierced the air, and Ish front-rolled from behind the nightstand, landing in a kneeled position and fired three more shots in the general vicinity of where he had seen the muzzle flash. He heard a loud groan, then the sound of a something heavy hitting the floor. He quickly crab-walked back to the cover of the nightstand. For a moment there was silence, then he heard something. It sounded like a wheezy breath followed by a click and another breath, rhythmically repeating over and over. *'Houuu…click…houuu. Houuu…click…houuu. Houuu…click…houuu'.*

Holding the gun tightly, Ish rose to a low crouch and made his way around the bed. What he saw made his blood freeze as he dropped the gun and raised clinched fists in agony. The cop was dead, lying on his back with his eyes staring blankly at the ceiling. Behind him, leaning against the wall and feebly stretching one arm out towards him was his daughter, Sumatra. The left side of her head was blown away, her brain splatter creating a Rorschach pattern. The wheezing sound was the air she was desperately trying to pull through lungs that no longer worked right, and the clicking was her attempting to speak.

"Sumatra!" he screamed, dropping to his knees in grief.

"Ish! Ish!"

Ish felt his body jerk upwards toward the sky, like a puppet on strings from heaven. He quickly realized that his eyes were closed.

When he opened them, Ma'am was sitting on the bed beside him, and Chad, Bird and Jag were standing in the doorway to his bedroom.

"It's alright," he heard her say. "It's just a dream."

Sweat dripped down his back, and he realized that she was right. He was sitting up in his bed, his sheets soaked with perspiration. He tried to wipe his tears away before anyone could see, but he could tell by the way Ma'am patted his back that she knew. Once they all confirmed that he was okay, they left him to try to return to sleep.

On the one hand, he was embarrassed by his display of what he considered a kind of weakness. On the other hand, it felt good to have such true friends in his corner. But even he had no idea how much he would come to rely on them in the days and weeks to come.

Chapter 33

The team was scheduled to meet in the War Room at 8:00am the next morning. Ish slept fitfully the rest of the night and was up at 4:00am. He had worked out, showered and left before anyone else in the house was even awake. He drove down to the Santa Monica Pier, parked and walked along the edge of the shore. The gritty sand beneath his feet felt comforting, and the cold water of the incoming tide was stimulating and bracing. Just as he was never one to put much belief in religion, he also wasn't too open to the ideas of the metaphysical. Still, he couldn't help but wonder if the dream was some type of message.

It wasn't uncommon for him to have nightmares. In fact, it was a fairly regular occurrence, but seldom did they stick with him the way this one did. What did it all mean? Did he believe, somewhere deep inside, that he was responsible for Sumatra's death? Surely, he felt guilt over not being there to support Layla through the tragedy, but he had overall felt pretty sure that what happened to Sumatra would have happened had he been there or not. Now he wasn't so sure.

Wheels were turning in his head. It felt like there was an assortment of loose puzzle pieces tumbling around in his brain and that if he could just figure out how they all fit together, a picture would reveal itself and a mystery would be solved. But he'd have to figure it out later. It was time to face the day.

Ish had been sitting in the conference room drinking coffee and nibbling on biscotti for an hour before the rest of the crew showed up. They looked tired, and he hoped it was only because their sleep had been disturbed by his nocturnal ranting and not by some other, more insidious, cause.

After everyone had gotten a pastry and something hot to drink, he stood up and addressed the room.

"First, before we get into all this other stuff, I want to apologize for last night. I—"

"Hey, brother, there's no need for any apologies," said Bird, cutting him off. Everyone else voiced some version of agreement to that. Ish pursed his lips and took a deep breath, bowing his head momentarily.

"Thank you for that. All of you. Your support means a lot to me. On to the business at hand," he said, clearing his throat. "Needless to say, mission one was a major success. We worked great as a team, were able to think on our feet and were able to avoid any major mistakes. You all deserve a round of applause." Everyone began clapping, and Chad and Jag began whistling.

"So," continued Ish, "the next mission is ready. Who's with me?"

Everyone raised their hands, but Ish noticed that Bird's hand was the last one up.

"Ish," said Bird. "Before we dive in the next mission, I think it might be helpful to talk a bit about the reaction we're seeing from the Pogue assault."

"Okay," said Ish. "The floor is yours." Bird didn't stand, but everyone turned their attention to him.

"I'm sure I'm not the only one that's been following the news on this. I can't imagine that any of you missed the rash of marchings and riots that have been happening all over the country."

"I think the word 'rash' might be overstating it a bit," said Chad. "But I get your point. There has been some reaction from the public."

"I think the words 'some reaction' is understating it a bit," answered Bird. "Several businesses were burned and looted. Cars were destroyed. Almost fifty people have been arrested in the last forty-eight hours alone."

"Isn't that one of the reasons that we all decided to do this in the first place? To get America to wake up and demand justice? To show them that justice is possible?" replied Chad.

"Yeah," said Bird, a tinge of frustration in his voice, "but I somehow feel responsible for the trouble these people are getting themselves into."

Jag laughed, a heavy, belly-deep guffaw. "You're fuckin' jokin', right? You've got to be jokin'. You can't poke the virgin without expecting a little blood, a little pain, maybe even a little indignation after the fact. If you got involved with this little project thinking you'd just get away with a hand job, I think you miscalculated, brother." Bird leaned back and looked at him with even more scorn than usual.

"Jag—" said Ish.

"No, I'm not trying to be disrespectful, I'm just trying to keep it real, Ice-Man. I saw too much of this over in Afghanistan. I encountered too many situations where some vegetarian-minded, bleeding-heart liberal masquerading as a jar-head is afraid to pull the trigger because he might kill something. Don't tell me you haven't experienced the same," he said, turning to Bird.

"Of course, but that was war, and those men enlisted and knew what they were getting into."

"This is war, too, baby brother," said Ma'am, "and what the man—and woman—on the street might not realize is that they enlisted the day they were born. We're not telling them what to do. We're just showing them what can be done." Her voice was calm, and there was caring and love in her eyes, along with a certain amount of sympathy.

"I know that!" said Bird. "You're all right. I just hate to see our communities imploding like this over something that we did."

"This is how it's always been," said Ish. "Every advancement in civil rights that has ever been made in this country was born out of chaos and turmoil. Unfortunately, we as a people don't always express the greatest amount of tact and control when we're trying to push these agendas forward. All that matters now is that we move the needle, even if it's only a fraction of an inch."

Jag patted Bird heartily on the back. "Shit is fucked up. And sometimes when shit is this fucked up, you have no choice but to burn it all down and start over. Relax your asshole, son. Everything is gonna be alright."

Bird paused for a moment, just long enough to lock eyes with Jag, and then he sprang. His chair toppled over behind him as he locked one arm around the one Jag had on his back and threw a punch with the other. Jag blocked it easily and smiled in return. He stood and shifted his weight in preparation to throw a counter, but before he could, Ma'am had stepped between them.

"I'll show you a fucking son! Get out of the way, sis!" said Bird. "This dude has been asking for an ass-kicking for a long time!"

"You think you're ready to be a cowboy? Hop on, then!" said Jag. He was still smiling, but there was a glint of menace in his eyes. Ish had known him long enough to know that look; it meant trouble was brewing.

"Stand down!" he yelled. Jag and Bird both relaxed and took a half-step back, but Ma'am continued to stand between them. "What is wrong with you two? We can't afford this kind of foolishness. We have too much to do."

"Jag's been trying to press my buttons ever since—"

"You know he doesn't mean any harm. Jag is just being Jag. He's nothing if not consistent."

Bird looked away in resignation.

"And you," continued Ish, shifting his gaze to Jag. "You know the man has thin skin. Why do you keep prodding him?"

"Because it's fun?" said Jag.

"No man, it's not. Not when it threatens the operation. Come on. For me. Please just tone it down a bit. Give the man a break."

"I hear you, boss," said Jag. "I didn't mean to cause such a rag. I'm sorry, brother," he said to Bird, and then held up his hand. "Friends?"

Bird hesitated for a moment, as if he were debating, then reached up to accept Jag's hand. But Jag quickly stepped forward and embraced him.

"Let's hug it out, bitch; come on!" he said.

"Get the fuck off me!" said Bird, pushing him away as Jag laughed and tried to kiss him on the cheek, but you could see that he was beginning to relax.

"Alright, alright," said Ish. "Before we get into the nitty gritty of this next plan, maybe we should all take a few moments to breathe."

"Actually, I'm kind of hungry," said Chad. "That danish didn't really do it for me. Anybody else up for some real breakfast?"

"That's not a bad idea," said Ish, checking his watch. "Danny's is open. We could put in an order for delivery."

"I'm burnin' out on their stuff," said Ma'am. "What about that Jewish place down the way? Feinstein's? I grabbed a muffin there the other day, and it was so good I think I got a little moist."

"Shit, sounds like the kind of muffin I need," said Jag.

“You’re a fool,” said Ma’am, grinning.

“They’re good, but they don’t deliver,” said Chad.

“You muthafuckas is so spoiled!” said Ma’am. “There are other ways to eat than to wait for people to deliver it to you! But you sit here and relax. Tell me what you want, and I’ll go pick it up.”

Everyone shouted out their order, and Ma’am jotted it all down on a notepad.

“Damn,” said Jag, staring at the list. “That’s a lot of food. And I need some fresh air anyway. I’ll come help you carry it.”

“Okay,” she replied, smiling. “Let’s go.”

As Jag and Ma’am walked out of the room, Bird looked like he wanted to invite himself to join them, but he stayed silent.

A few minutes after Jag and Ma’am left, Bird stood up and stretched.

“I need to get out of here for a minute, too. I’m gonna go grab a smoke.”

Chad watched him walk out and waited till the door was closed securely behind him, then turned to Ish.

“Now that we’re alone, this might be a good time to have a quick chat,” he said.

“Sure. What’s up?”

“Bird seems to already be feeling the heat from the public reaction to this, but I think what he’s seen is only the tip of the iceberg. I’ve had a script crawling the net, gathering all relevant stories related to this, and this thing is like a storm that’s slowly gathering mass and power.”

“What are your thoughts?”

“I’m sure Bird has only seen a fraction of the reports I’ve seen. And that number is growing as we speak. And all of this just off the first mission. How do you think he’s going to hold up as the weight increases?”

Ish stroked his chin with one hand. “I don’t know. I served with Bird. I know he’s a good man. And a great soldier. We’ve rubbed shoulders on some really hairy missions, and he’s always been solid as a rock. But this is different. Overseas our actions were co-signed by the United States government. This is something else entirely.”

Chad nodded his head.

“I guess the bottom line,” said Ish, “is that we probably didn’t spend enough time working through all the possible outcome scenarios." He paused, his eyes far away as his mind searched for what he wanted to say next. "The worst case is that he walks."

"Is that the worst case?" asked Chad, skeptically.

"If you're concerned about him betraying us, don't be. He may decide that he doesn't have the stomach for what we're trying to do, but he'd never turn on us. Not the Bird that I know."

"I hope you're right."

"So, you said you've been monitoring all this chatter," said Ish. "Is there anything in particular that we should know about?"

"Most of it is pretty much in line with what we expected: protests, marches, denouncements. But there was a small blurb about a woman that died at a march in Philadelphia. Her family's side of the story is that she had a water bottle in her hand, raised it to take a drink, a cop overreacted and hit her on the top of the head with a baton. She died instantly. Of course, the cops say she was about to throw the bottle at them."

"How's the story trending?"

"I think it's still fairly local. For now."

"Then there's no reason to report that back to the crew right now. If one of them finds it on their own, okay. But let's not willingly throw fuel on a fire that's already burning hot."

"Got it. Speaking of women, any word from Layla?"

"No, but I need to try to reach out to her; maybe through the attorney. I worry about her constantly. I've got to figure out some way to let her know what we're up to. It could be the hope she needs to hold on long enough to make it out of there."

"Yeah, that's going to be tricky," said Chad. "Everything is monitored—letters, phone calls, visits."

"True. But I think I might have an idea," he said, his voice trailing off.

As Chad went to start another batch of the ever-present coffee, Ish gazed out the window and thought back to a happier time, back before life was so complicated. He and Layla had only been dating for a few months, and were still in the process of getting to know each other. One particular day, they had decided to meet for a picnic at one of the local parks. There was a lake in the center of the park and people from miles around liked to spend time relaxing there and feeding handfuls of bird food to the local ducks at twenty-five cents a pop.

"What are you thinking about?" asked Layla. He was watching a couple of uniformed officers interacting with a couple and their young child. He could hear the cops cursing at the man, who's apparent offense was that he had an open container of beer.

"I'm just wondering why it is that the police are not better trained than that," he said, nodding his head in the direction of the skirmish. "I remember my grandfather telling me about the neighborhood he grew up in. The cops that patrolled those neighborhoods were members of the community. They lived in the neighborhoods they worked in. They knew the people and the people knew them. It created a different level of respect, even in light of the more widespread racism of the time."

"I heard those same kinds of stories from my grandmother. But baby, those days are gone. That was back when cops were like German shepherds. Now they're like pit bulls."

Ish chuckled. "I've never heard it described quite like that before."

"No, think about it," she said, smiling that beautiful smile of hers. "What comes to mind when you hear the word 'German shepherd'? You think regal, fierce, controlled. You think deadly but disciplined."

"Okay, I guess that sounds right. But I think I know what you're about to say next, and I think you may be maligning the reputation of the pit bull."

"Oh please! You grew up in the hood. Don't act like you never heard stories of 'pit bulls gone bad'; dogs that were mean, vicious, unpredictable and completely out of control!"

"My aunt had a pit bull that was as gentle as a lamb. Wouldn't hurt a flea. I think you might be stereotyping a little," said Ish.

"The only reason stereotypes exist is because some pattern repeats itself often enough that people start to be able to predict it. I'm not saying all pit bulls are bad. Nor am I saying that all cops are bad. I'm just saying that there are enough of the bad ones out there that everyone should be especially careful around them. Cops are like pit bulls in the sense that when you run up on one you never know what you're going to get."

Ish leaned over and kissed her. "I guess I can't argue with that," he said.

"So, promise me one thing," she said.

"What's that?"

"That you'll stay as far away from the pit bulls as possible."

"I promise," he said as they embraced and kissed again, and he tried to block out the sounds of the cops verbally abusing the man on the other side of the park.

* * *

Jag, Ma'am and Bird returned to the office at the same time. Ish was relieved to see that they were all smiling—even Bird. It was nice to have at least a little bit of reprieve from the bickering. And good food always helped make everything better. They cleared the conference table and dug in. It was amazing how relaxed everyone was. They were all cracking jokes and telling stories and just having a good time. There was no trace of the stress that had been so constant since they began this whole ordeal. He wondered what the source of this sudden camaraderie was, and whether it was just the calm before the storm.

Everyone had their fill of food and took their time sipping their coffee. Feinstein's coffee was like something from another planet. They roasted their own beans, which they had flown in fresh on a weekly basis. Delicious didn't even begin to describe it. No one had mentioned the mission or its aftermath during the entire meal, and Ish hated to be the one to spoil the mood, but their coffee cups were almost empty and it was time to get back to business.

"If I could have your attention, please," said Ish as he stood up and made his way to the head of the table. "Now that we've all had a chance to get our grub on and to decompress a little, I'd like to pick up where we left off and get back into the details of the next mission." He took a moment to search for a file on the laptop in front of him, giving everyone a minute to switch gears and get their minds focused on what he was about to present to them.

"As I said before, you all did a great job, and I'm proud of you and of the work we did. I think this next job will be even smoother than the first one. Chad, do you mind—"

Bird raised his hand, cutting him off. "I hate be the one that keeps interrupting, but I have another question, if you don't mind."

"It's your job to interrupt, if you have something to say," said Ish. "What's on your mind?"

"I know we have these next two jobs in the pipeline, but then what?"

"What do you mean, specifically?"

"I mean what's next after that? Are there more jobs waiting? Do we simply walk away? Do we continue here on the payroll as 'security experts'?"

"I thought that we initially agreed that we would kind of play it by ear and cross that bridge when we came to it."

"We're coming up on the bridge. I just want to make sure that I'm not scrambling to change lanes at the last minute."

"I understand your concern," said Ish. "I don't really have an answer for the first part of your question. Once we get through these next two missions, I think we have to vote on what our next move will be, if any. As far as your employment with Macrolox goes, you'll always have a job here, either in security or some other capacity, for as long as you want one." He looked over at Chad, who nodded his head in agreement.

"Any other questions?"

"No, I guess I'm good for now," said Bird.

"So, back to what I was saying. I—" Ish felt his pocket vibrate. His phone was ringing. Usually he ignored calls when he was in a meeting, but something told him to get this one. He didn't even look at the phone first to check the caller ID.

"Yes," he said after pushing the 'answer' button.

"This is a Global Tel-Link prepaid call from Layla Carter, an inmate at a California Correctional Facility. This call will be recorded and monitored."

"I'm sorry, but I have to take this," said Ish to everyone in the room but to no one in particular, and he quickly left to find someplace where he could speak in private.

Chapter 34

One of the outer conference rooms was empty and Ish darted into it, locking the door behind him.

"Hey, you," said the smoky, honey-caramel voice that he had so grown to love.

"Hey, baby, how are you?"

"I'm good. How are you?"

"I've been going crazy worrying about you, but other than that, I'm okay. Where are you?"

"They sent me up to OCJ—Orange County Jail. They told me I was going further upstate, but I guess they changed their minds. But you know how the system works. They could change it again tomorrow."

"How is it there?"

"It's jail. Same ol' shit, I guess."

"How long have you been there?"

"About a week."

"And you're just now calling me?"

"They gave me a bit of a 'time out' when I first arrived."

"You were in the hole already?"

"It wasn't my fault, Ish. Some bitch was trying to fish and I had to show her what time it was."

"What the hell does that mean?"

"She was trying to square off against me and a couple of the other new fish. So, I beat her ass down."

Hearing these words made Ish's heart hurt. He couldn't even picture that scene in his mind's eye. He always knew Layla had a 'street' side to her. Hell, she grew up in the same streets that he did. But he'd never really seen it. She was always the epitome of poise and grace. There were times that they'd been together in clubs and other women would totally disrespect her, trying to get to him, and she never batted an eye. He used to call her 'Zen Mama' because she was so consistently and utterly unflappable. But apparently the death of Sumatra had changed all that; it broke something inside of her, and he wasn't sure it could ever totally be repaired.

"Layla, you've got to—"

"Yeah, I know, Ish. You don't have to say it again. We've already had this discussion before, remember?"

"Yes, I do. And do you remember my promise?"

"You shouldn't make promises that you can't deliver on."

"Have I ever not been able to deliver on a promise?"

"You've never made a promise that big before."

"Yeah, but—"

"My time is almost up, Ish. I'm not even supposed to be on the phone. I just called to hear your voice, and to let you know that I'm still surviving."

"Listen, I don't want to end this on a bad note. Let me tell you about something crazy that happened to me the other day. Do you remember that time we had that picnic in the park? The one with the lake? It was probably our third or fourth date."

"Lake? You mean that time you tried to make tuna sandwiches and used too much mayo and our fingers were leaving prints in the bread?"

"Uh, yeah."

"Yes," she said, laughing, a sound he hadn't heard in such a long time. "How could I forget that wonderful day!"

"Well, I was hanging out with a couple of buddies the other night and we got attacked by a pit bull. It was the same kind of pit bull that you saw in the park that day."

"A pit bull? Are you alright?" she said, alarm in her voice.

"Yeah, we're fine. The pit bull was not so lucky. We beat the shit out of it. Someone shot a video of it. If you search online, you might find it."

"Wait a minute. Pit bull? What kind of pit bull are you..." Ish could hear her breath catch as she slowly began to realize what he was trying to tell her. When she spoke again, her voice was strained as though she was working hard to keep it steady.

"I think I did see something on the news about that," she said, her voice just above a whisper. "I didn't know that was you."

"Don't worry; it all turned out alright."

"You need to watch your back. I've been hearing a lot about dog attacks lately."

"Yeah, for some reason they seem to be running wild in my neighborhood. Attacking innocent people for no reason. I wouldn't be surprised if I have to deal with another one before too long."

"Ummm," she began and then paused, apparently struggling to decide what to say next.

"Listen, I know they're about to cut you off any minute. Just know that I'm making good on my promise, and I hope to get you news of my progress real soon. Just hold on. I love you."

"I love you, too," she said. Then she was gone.

Ish was sitting on the edge of a table, staring at the floor, deep in thought, when he heard the knock.

"Hold on," he said, walking over to unlock and open the door.

"Are you alright?" asked Chad. Ish looked at his watch and realized he had lost track of time. It had been twenty minutes since the call ended.

"Yeah, I'm okay. Sorry for keeping you all waiting."

"No, it's no big deal," he said. "Um, is there anything I can do?"

"That was Layla," said Ish, collapsing into a chair and running a hand through his hair.

"I kind of figured," said Chad, taking the seat beside him. "Is she okay?"

"Layla hasn't been okay since Sumatra died. But she's safe. And she seems well. They moved her to OCJ, in Orange County."

"Well, that's something to be thankful for. At least now you know where she is. OCJ is supposed to be pretty easy time. I had a buddy up there once. He said it was pretty low key as long as you stay on good behavior."

Ish actually laughed. "Good behavior? She just got out of the hole. Again. I don't see 'good behavior' in her immediate future. I'm worried about her," he said.

"Layla's strong. She's a fighter."

"I know. But that's part of the problem. She doesn't know when to stop fighting."

"I never told you this," said Chad, "but when Layla called and told me what had happened to Sumatra, I called the attorney and I raced to the jail to wait for her to be released on bail. When she walked out into the lobby area, she was a mess. I don't mean just physically. She was bruised and battered, and her clothes were all tattered, but there was something else."

Ish was watching Chad intensely, hanging on his every word.

"She ran and hugged me and started sobbing. We were just standing there, frozen, right in the middle of the crowded waiting room. I wanted to get her out of there, away from all the stares and the whispers, all the people embarrassed by her grief. But she was holding on so tight, I knew that she wasn't going to move until she was ready. Fifteen minutes. We stood like that for fifteen minutes. I thought for sure that the desk cop was going to kick us out, but he just let her go on."

"Wow," whispered Ish.

"Once we got outside the station, I asked her if she was alright. Looking in her eyes, I could tell that she wasn't. There was a softness there; a vulnerability. It was like looking into the eyes of a wounded bunny or something. But right there in front of me, she began to change. Whatever that softness was in her eyes began to harden. They went from the eyes of a bunny to the eyes of a wolf. For a moment I actually thought she was going to attack me. Then she leaned over, kissed me softly on the cheek and said 'Let's go.' From that moment forward, I knew she was going to be alright. Don't give up on her, Ish. She'll find her way home."

When Ish and Chad re-entered the main conference room, everyone looked up expectantly. It was Ma'am who voiced what was on everyone's lips.

"Is everything alright?"

"Yeah. Sorry for the holdup. That was a call from Layla."

"Is she okay?" asked Jag.

"She's fine. Just checking in, is all." Jag had never actually met Layla, but he had heard so much about her from Ish that he probably felt like he knew her. They had spent many a night hunkered down in some bunker or other, whispering about their stateside lives and the people who were waiting for them back home.

"So, let's get back to it," said Ish as he grabbed a stack of papers and began flipping through them. "Chad, can you bring up the video, please?" Chad began manipulating a small remote, powering up electronics and searching menus. Moments later he was set.

"Detective John Ratcliff," said Ish by way of reintroduction, just as the officer's face appeared on the screen. "As we laid out for you before, he's guilty of, among other things, rape. He works out of a New York City precinct, but he lives in Jersey. You two have spent some time in Jersey, haven't you?" he asked, looking at Ma'am and Bird.

"I've spent way too much time in Jersey," Bird scoffed.

Ish picked up on a look that passed between Bird and his sister. It was subtle, but unmistakable. "Is there something about Jersey that we need to know?" he asked. Bird and Ma'am traded glances again. Ish waited patiently for one of them to speak.

"I had a little trouble there once," said Ma'am. She unconsciously began scratching the back of one hand with the other. "This was years ago. I was deep into my addiction then. I was walking my usual tract in New York City and this dude picked me up. White boy. Seemed nice enough. Young, but driving a sweet ride. A white BMW."

"Ma'am, you don't have to go into all this for us—" Ish began.

"Nah, it's okay. We family here. There ain't no need to keep any secrets from family," she said, looking around the room. Her gaze momentarily paused on Jag before she continued.

"Anyway, we was supposed to be going to a hotel right down the street, but he said he wasn't really comfortable with that. He wanted to know if I'd go to his house, out in Jersey. I said 'hell no', and he threatened to throw me out. It was cold as shit that night, the car was cozy and I was broke and in need of a fix, so next thing I know we're on the way to Jersey.

"I wasn't in this dude's house for a good fifteen minutes before he hit me in the back of the head with something and threw me down into the basement. I woke up chained to the wall. He beat me and basically had his way with me for maybe four or five days. I don't really remember exactly. I think I had a concussion.

"I don't believe he ever planned to let me leave there. But a few days later, I found his cell phone. It had dropped out of his pocket. The only person I knew to call, whose number I knew by heart, was Bird, who was still in New York at the time. The problem is, I didn't know where the fuck I was! I knew I was in Jersey, but I had no idea of the address."

"I was in panic mode," said Bird. "I wanted to call the police, but I knew they weren't going to be of much help. So, I just drove to Jersey and started driving up and down the streets, looking for a white BMW in someone's driveway, hoping I might get lucky."

"How were you going to know it was the right BMW?" asked Chad.

"I didn't think that far ahead," he said. He and Ma'am again exchanged nervous glances.

"So, what happened?" asked Jag.

"The dude realized that he had dropped his phone, and he came back downstairs. I put it by my feet and acted like I was unconscious. When he bent down to grab it, I made my move. He and I went toe to toe. I was still chained up, but there was enough slack in the chains for me to move my arms just enough.

"It was a good fight, and he almost had me, but he had this long hair, and once I got a handful of that, I just I started slamming his head against the concrete wall until he stopped moving. When he was out, I got the key off him, unlocked myself and ran out of the house. It was night when I got outside, and I just remember running as fast as I could, trying to put as much distance between me and him as possible. I must have run for an hour before I found a payphone and called Bird again. He was there in fifteen minutes."

"Damn," said Jag. "Talk about luck!"

"Yeah, we were lucky," said Bird, but there was a sadness in his voice.

"So, what happened to the guy?" asked Chad.

"Nothing. Or maybe everything," replied Ma'am. "I couldn't remember where the house was, because I was just running blind, zig-zagging through the streets, hoping he wouldn't catch me again. But also, I really didn't know if the dude was dead or alive. I hit him pretty hard, and I didn't stick around to find out what his condition was. In the end, we decided to just get the hell out of the neighborhood as fast as we could and forget that shit ever happened."

"Speak for yourself," said Bird, frowning. "That's something I'll never forget."

"This sounds like a sensitive subject," said Ish, addressing Bird and Ma'am. "Is this going to be a problem for either of you?"

"Shit, if I let places I had a bad experience with stop me from going back there, I would have to cross half of the eastern seaboard off the list," said Ma'am, a glint of humor in her eyes. "I don't live in the past," she added, her tone a bit more serious.

"I'm cool," replied Bird.

"Okay, good. So, here's the plan," continued Ish. "Contrary to the comment he made about telling the rape victim in our video that he was married, Ratcliff is a bachelor; no wife or kids at home. So rather than expose ourselves in the street again, we can take care of our business inside his house, assuming he doesn't have any 'guests' at that particular time."

"Have you seen the house?" asked Jag.

"Yeah, here's a picture of it," said Chad as he clicked the buttons on his remote and brought to the screen several still photos and some video of Ratcliff's house and the surrounding neighborhood.

"Looks like the kind of sleepy town I grew up in," said Jag.

"I wouldn't exactly call Newark 'sleepy'," said Ma'am. "There's a lot going on there."

"Correct," said Ish. "Which is to our favor. The more activity, the less strangers like us will stick out. We have a couple of ideas of how we can get into the house without arousing any suspicion from the neighbors."

"Who all is going in?" asked Bird.

"We want to keep it to a minimum," said Ish. "So, it'll be me, you and Ma'am. Jag and Chad will be in separate vehicles a couple of blocks away, monitoring the police channels and ready to assist if there are any unforeseen complications."

"Ma'am," said Ish, resting his hands on the table and looking directly at her, "I feel obligated to ask you this, even though I think I already know the answer: are you sure you're up for this?"

She smiled grimly. "I've been fucked over by police officers for more than half my life. It's about time I fucked back."

"That's pretty much what I thought you would say." Ish spent the next thirty minutes going over the details of the assault, making sure everyone was clear on their role in the mission.

"And that's pretty much it," he said in conclusion. "We're all geared up; everything is waiting for us at a luggage storage facility near Grand Central Station. We've got 48 hours to get our heads right, then we all take individual non-stop flights sometime between Thursday morning and Friday afternoon. We all meet at Chad's hotel room Saturday morning to go over the plans one final time, then begin our surveillance. Any questions?"

Everyone shook their heads 'no'. Mission two was officially on.

The flights were uneventful and everyone arrived safely in New York. Before they left Nashville, Jag had driven the van to West Virginia, rented a paint booth and repainted it, re-purposing it as a vehicle from a heating and A/C company, before driving it on to New York and leaving it in a rented garage. It was waiting for them when they arrived.

The plan for the first few days was the same as the previous mission: follow the target to become accustomed to his daily routine in preparation for the actual assault. It was Jag and Ish's turn to run the van. They were sitting at the curb, half a block from Ratcliff's precinct, waiting for him to emerge and head back home.

Ish and Jag had spent a lot of time together in Afghanistan, waiting for things to happen. They'd had many lengthy conversations about their lives, which was nice. But Ish also appreciated the fact that they were equally comfortable not saying anything at all to each other for long stretches of time. Today they had already been in the van for four hours with hardly a word spoken between them. It was Jag who broke the silence.

"There's something I kind of wanted to discuss with you," he said cautiously. "About Ma'am."

"Yeah?"

"You know, I've been kind of digging her, and I think she's been kind of digging me a little, too."

"Jag, unless it concerns the mission, I really don't need to know the details of your romantic escapades. You're both adults."

"Dude, I'm not asking your permission," said Jag, irritation rising in his voice. "We're buddies and I thought we could talk about shit together, and that that included women."

"You're right, man. I'm sorry. I guess because of the fact that I know her and care for her so much, I'm somewhat protective of her.

Kind of like a little sister. A 'big' little sister," he said, smiling. "At the same time, like I said, you're both adults so I have no right to interfere with whatever it is you're doing. I guess that's what made me want to try to separate myself from the entire situation. But you're right, we are buddies, and we should be able to talk about anything, even if it's concerning someone else that I care about. So, talk to me. What's up?"

"Well, as I was saying, we've been kind of digging on each other and—"

"Wait a minute. I want to make sure I'm following you. What exactly does 'digging on each other' mean? Are you dating? Are you flirting? What are we talking about here?"

"I don't know if I could actually call it dating," said Jag. "We've been pretty tied down by these missions." Ish raised his eyebrows, urging him to continue. "I guess maybe you could call it flirting. But we shared a kiss on the way back with the breakfast the other morning." Ish looked surprised.

"Really? So, then things are...progressing?"

"I guess you could say that. I really like her, man. She turns me on in a way I've never really been turned on before. I can't explain it. But I have a problem."

"What's that?"

"I don't know if I can get over the fact that she used to be a prostitute."

Ish nodded slowly. "Tell me, how many addicts have you known?"

"I guess I've known a few guys that have had some issues," said Jag.

"Some issues? Like what? Alcohol?

"Yeah. Maybe a little smack."

"Ma'am's battle was with crack. Have you ever known a person hooked on crack? A woman hooked on crack?"

"Cain't say that I have."

"I spent most of my childhood in South Central L.A. which, during those years, was 'crack central'. I saw how it ravaged neighborhoods and destroyed not just families, but generations of families. I saw 50-year-old straight men that would suck your dick for a $5 rock. I think it was even worse for women. I'm not a scientist, but based on what I observed, females have always had a harder struggle with the drug than men. I've seen women offer to sell their babies for a rock. Their fucking babies, man! Compared to that, sex ain't shit."

"I guess I understand that. But..." said Jag, shaking his head.

"I don't know if you're ever going to be able to understand what an addiction to crack cocaine is like. I don't know how much I understand it myself, because I've never used drugs. But there was this dude in the neighborhood that they called Slim Willy. Total crackhead. Anytime you saw this dude he was either begging for money or trying to sell you some shitty car stereo or what not that he'd just stolen. One day I asked him what it was like to be hooked on crack. He said it was like not having eaten for three months and knowing that $5 could get you a full meal at the nicest restaurant in Beverly Hills. Times one thousand."

"That's some serious shit."

"No doubt." Ish stared at Jag, who still looked unconvinced.

"Look, I can't tell you what to feel. But my position, having hung around so many crackheads, is to not trust them as far as you can throw them while they're using. But once they're clean, I forgive anything they might have done while they were using."

"Kind of like a ghetto Catholic priest?"

Ish laughed. "Yeah, kind of. But without the whole kid-fucking thing."

"Yeah, there's that." Jag chuckled. "So, you think I should just forget about her past and accept her for who she is now?"

"Dude, like I said, I can't tell you what to feel. We all have our own demons to deal with. It's a personal battle, and we have to face it head up, one-on-one."

"I guess I've got to give it some more thought. I can ignore it now, but I don't know if I can ever really get it out of the back of my mind. I mean, I'm trying to think about the future. For example, what my mother's reaction will be. I've dated black women before, but I've never dared bring one home. But Ma'am is different."

"Sounds to me like you have more issues than just whether or not she used to sell herself for drugs. I think you might be doing both her and yourself a service to spend some significant time soul searching and trying to decide whether this is a journey you're ready to embark on."

Jag nodded knowingly and turned to silently stare blankly at one of the video monitors.

"Tell me something," said Ish, after a few more minutes of peaceful silence between them. "What was it like for you, growing up in that little Podunk town of yours? What was the diversity situation?"

"Diversity? I guess you can say diversity was sometimes a bit of a challenge for us."

"Yeah, from what you've told me so far, it doesn't sound like it was a very popular place with the brothers."

"Dude, when I was growing up there was only one black family that lived in my town. They had a son about my age, but he didn't go to my school, so I hardly ever saw him. The only black people I saw were on TV. *Fresh Prince of Bel-Air, The Jamie Fox Show*, reruns of *Good Times* and *The Jeffersons*." Ish chuckled and shook his head.

"Did you ever watch anything besides comedies?"

"I like to laugh. Sue me. The shit was funny."

"I'm just fuckin' with you. I watched the same shows. The problem is that people that lived in cities like the one you grew up in, without many local blacks to interact with on a personal level, inevitably believed that all black people were like the ones they saw on those TV shows; that they were basically buffoons."

"I don't believe I ever really thought like that. I don't think I really had much of an opinion on black folk before I left home and went to college. My daddy? Well, he didn't have many kind words to say about the Negro. And that's being generous. But I always had a hard head. I always felt that before I could make up my mind about something, I needed to experience it for myself, not hear it second-hand from someone else."

"I imagine that made you stand out a bit from your peers."

"I guess. And my daddy wasn't too happy about it, neither. I just couldn't understand hating someone for the color of their skin. But I loved my daddy like a fat woman loves cheesecake, so I struggled, because if he hated them, there must be something wrong with them. I just couldn't figure out what it was."

Ish had a faraway look in his eyes.

"That's how racism perpetuates itself," he said. "It's spoon-fed to children by those they love, and logic dictates that there has to be a reason for the hatred, even if the kid doesn't understand what it is. So, they just blindly follow suit. Kind of like religion."

"Don't even get me started on religion again," said Jag. "You and I have been down that road far too many times."

"Granted. I'll let that one slide," said Ish. "What about your mother? Did she share your father's views on race?"

"My momma was a church-going woman that read the Bible on a daily basis. I don't know if it was because of her religion, or in spite of it, but she pretty much accepted whatever my daddy told her."

"I thought you were trying to avoid speaking of religion?"

"Man, you can't talk about my momma without talking about religion. They were one and the same. It would be like trying to talk about titties and not talk about women. I think both my folks used the Bible to justify their racism."

"I know a little bit about the Bible, and I don't really remember ever seeing the word 'nigga' in there."

"I guess that's both the blessing and the curse of religion," said Jag solemnly. "People can see in it whatever it is they want to see."

"Amen," said Ish.

Chapter 35

The next two days were spent either trailing Ratcliff as he executed the duties of his job or following him on errands. Bird and Chad were on surveillance detail when Ish called for a meeting and patched them in via a conference call.

"I think we've seen enough. We should make our move tomorrow night."

"Friday night isn't necessarily the best night of the week to do something like this," said Jag. "Tactically speaking, there are too many unknowns that could appear and spoil all the fun. What if he has a date?"

"I agree," said Ish. "But the longer we run this operation, the greater the chance that our cover gets blown—he recognizes that he's being followed, someone notices our van one too many times, etc. If things turn sideways, we can always retreat and regroup for a later date. Everyone in?"

They each issued some form of verbal affirmation.

"Speaking of getting in, have you decided exactly how we're going to get inside the home without being noticed?" asked Bird.

"I've been thinking about that ever since we picked Ratcliff out of the hat, and I already have some things in storage that might make it easier. I think the best bet is to go in during the day and make ourselves comfortable until he gets home. Chad hacked his computer, and we know his pool guy comes one Friday a month, which just happens to be this Friday."

"Fortune smiles," said Jag.

"Right," said Ish. "We know that he communicates with the pool guy via text. Chad can send a text that appears to come from Ratcliff's phone and reschedules the appointment for the following week. I have pool cleaning supplies and clean license plates in storage. We steal a truck that's the same make, model and color that the pool guy drives, slap a magnetic sign on the side, throw on some light disguises and we're in the backyard. Four go in, one leaves to drive the truck away. We monitor the police band to make sure that no nosy neighbor has become suspicious and called the cops, and we simply wait for loverboy to get home from work."

"And if he doesn't come home alone?" asked Bird.

"We'll have to cross that bridge when we come to it. But no plan is perfect. It's like jazz. The coolest cats are always those that improvise the best, right?" replied Ish, smiling.

"I suppose," answered Bird. Ish could tell he wanted to make some kind of smart remark about how you don't go to jail for playing a bad solo or something similarly sarcastic, but he managed to keep his thoughts to himself.

"You gotta lighten up, baby brother," said Ma'am. "Relax. We're doing the Lord's work!"

* * *

Chad's hotel room had become the de facto command center for the New York operation, and everyone tended to congregate there when they weren't sleeping or taking advantage of some alone time. Bird had been back from surveillance duty for a couple of hours and had been stomping around the suite, looking pissed off at everyone. Ish wasn't sure how to handle the situation.

Ish knew that Bird already felt that Ish had some doubts about his fitness for this job. While there was certainly some truth in that, if Ish really felt that Bird was a threat to the mission, he would have sent him home. He had been contemplating what to do all evening and had finally decided to wait for Bird to come to him. Ish was in the suite's kitchen making himself a sandwich when Bird walked in.

Bird opened the fridge and grabbed himself a beer. He flicked the bottle cap into the trashcan and then turned to lean back against the counter.

"Any more of that black forest ham left?" he asked, gesturing towards the box of sliced deli meat.

"No, I think that's all gone," said Ish, leaning over for a quick peek into the top of the box. "But there's still plenty of turkey left."

"I can't stand turkey. Too damn dry."

"Sorry, brother. If I had known, I'd have ordered more ham."

"No, that's alright, I'm cool," said Bird, but his face was engraved with a deep frown.

"We can make a call and have something delivered, if you like."

"No, I'll find something in the fridge. Thanks."

"You know, you've seemed kind of tight lately. If it's the cold cuts that have been pissing you off all week, I'll throw all this shit in the trash and we can go get some burgers or something," said Ish, smiling.

"No, it's cool," said Bird, trying to return the smile. "I think I'll survive."

"Okay," said Ish, nodding his head. He returned to the work of constructing his sandwich. Bird had not moved from his position against the counter. Ish let the quiet settle into the room and waited.

"You know, I was arrested for rape once," said Bird, staring at the wall, his eyes unfocused.

"Is that right?"

"Yeah. I was jogging in a park one night, and these cops swooped in and snatched me up. Said I fit the description. Some white woman had been raped, and they were trying to put me on the hook for it. At the time, I didn't know what the fuck was going on. After the lineup, they threw me back in the cell, and I overheard two of the cops arguing. One was saying that the woman clearly said I wasn't the one that attacked her, but the other one said he didn't care whether I did it or not. He said when it came to crime, there was no such thing as the 'wrong nigger'. I was only twenty-two at the time. I've never been so scared in my life."

"I guess I've been lucky," said Ish. "I somehow was able to avoid any bad situations like that. In fact, all the cops I ever had dealings with were cool; treated me with respect and sometimes gave me a break. But if I had a nickel for every time I've heard a story like yours—"

"Don't tell me you were about to say 'I'd be a rich man,'" said Bird, grinning slightly.

"Nah," said Ish, shaking his head ruefully. For reasons he couldn't explain, he was often embarrassed by the amount of wealth he had managed to accumulate at such a young age. Very seldom had anyone overtly treated him in a negative fashion because of it, but he could imagine what some people might be thinking. Some people already assumed he was arrogant when they first met him. Being both somewhat of an introvert and physically intimidating tended to often have that effect on people. Thankfully, most people were able to reassess after knowing him for a while and accepted him for the down-to-earth person that he was. But even with his closest friends, there were often those awkward moments where they'd make a comment that seemed to contain just a bit of either envy or contempt.

"So, what happened?" he asked, changing the subject. "What finally convinced them to let you go?"

"Believe it or not, it was the woman—the victim. I was there for two days, man. Two fucking days. I had no idea if I was going to be indicted or what."

"You didn't have a lawyer?"

"They were supposed to be arranging for a public defender, but I never saw one. So, I sat there, seething; hatred of white people building up in my soul. Then they just let me go. No explanation. But when I walked out into the lobby of the station, there was this woman. She was blond, beautiful, probably about thirty-five. You could tell by what she was wearing and the way she carried herself that she came from money. She introduced herself. Charlotte Maple. I'll never forget that name. She asked if I would join her for coffee."

"That must have been as big a shock as the arrest."

"It was. I didn't know what to think, but I accepted. We walked to this cool little coffeehouse a few blocks away, and she explained to me what had happened. She told me about how this guy had dragged her into the bushes. And then at the station the cops tried to convince her that I was the one that did it, even though she kept telling them I wasn't. It was her that got me released. She got her lawyer to pester them until they finally let me go. Sitting there, sharing a cup of cappuccino, she wept, and the anguish in her voice was like nothing I had ever heard before. I think she was mourning as much for the fact that she was violated as she was for the fact that I was violated."

"Wow, that's deep."

"Yeah. It changed my life, man. It changed my view of white people. It also changed my view of rape. I used to be one of those typical guys that thought that when a woman said 'no' it was just a coy way of saying 'yes'. All that changed that day. I developed a real hatred for anyone that would violate a woman like that. I've had to step in on more than one occasion to stop some fool from taking advantage of a woman."

"I'm with you on that. My mother raised me to be a gentleman at all times. I guess we've all had some version of our own run-ins with rapists." Ish knew they were both thinking back on the Stanwick incident.

"Still, I couldn't save Ma'am that day in Jersey," said Bird.

"What?"

"That time she was kidnapped. I wasn't able to rescue her. It still weighs on me."

"I thought that by the time she called you, she had already been gone for a couple of days?"

"True. But I should have been there for her long before that, man. I should have prevented her from ever getting into that position."

Before Ish could reply, his phone buzzed. He looked at the text.

"Shit. I think we have trouble," he said.

Ish pressed a button, and the phone was picked up on the other end on the first ring.

"Ma'am, it's me and Bird. You're on speaker. What's going on?"

"We tracked him to a bar where he must have hooked up with this woman, because they came out together and got in his car. We followed him to this park. Ten minutes later and this muthafucka is attackin' this woman!"

"What do you mean?" asked Ish.

"I mean the woman started screaming and tried to get out the car, but he pulled her back in. I say we snatch his ass up right now!"

"Shit!" said Ish, looking over at Bird, whose face was grave and intense. "So, what are they doing now?"

"I don't know. He's probably raping this poor lady. But we can't tell from here. We're about 300 yards out, and the windows are dark. Do we have permission to engage?"

"Ma'am, it's too risky. We don't know what cameras are around there, we don't know what patrols might be in the area. This is not part of our plan."

"So, what the fuck am I supposed to do? Just sit back while this asshole rapes another innocent woman?"

"Let me talk to Jag."

"I'm here."

"What's your take on this?"

"I'm seeing the same thing she is, boss. Looks like this dude is behaving badly again. I think we can sneak up on him without too much trouble. Especially since he's kind of, um, preoccupied right now."

"OK. Put Ma'am back on."

"I'm here," she said. "What's the move?"

Ish could feel his blood pressure rising as his mind raced to come up with an answer for her. This woman, whoever she was, wasn't their mission. They were there for him, and horrible as whatever was happening to her was, was it worth jeopardizing everything, including their freedom, to rescue her?

"Ish! Tell me something!"

Ish looked at Bird again.

"Ish, we can't sit here and let this woman get violated like this," said Bird.

"Fuck!" said Ish in frustration. "Alright. Mask up and grab him. Don't speak to him. We don't need the witness being able to recognize your voices. Leave the channel open and let me know as soon as you have him subdued and unconscious."

"On it!" said Ma'am.

Ish could hear the sounds of them moving around inside the van, probably in the process of donning masks and gloves. Moments later he heard the door open and close quietly. He looked at the clock on the wall as the seconds ticked by in slow motion. At that moment Chad walked into the kitchen. He saw the way Ish and Bird were both staring at the phone and knew something was wrong.

"What's going on?" he asked.

Ish filled him in, glad to have something to do other than count seconds as they waited. The phone's speaker had been silent for almost two minutes already. For two more minutes Ish, Chad and Bird gazed intently at the clock, the phone or each other. Neither spoke.

Suddenly the silence was broken by the sound of the van door opening. There were a couple of muffled moans and then a commotion that sounded like a struggle. Seconds later an engine turned over and began to rev. The van was on the move. Ish held a hand up, indicating to Chad and Bird to maintain 'radio silence' until Ma'am or Jag confirmed that the target was secured. Seconds continued to tick by. And then she was back.

"He's bagged, tagged and out cold," she said, her breathing a bit heavier than before. "Where to? His place?"

"No, I think that's too risky now," said Ish. "Give me a minute to think this over."

Since the plan to grab Ratcliff in his house was now off the table, they didn't have a lot of options of where to take him. They needed a place that was private, fairly soundproof and easy to get in and out of undetected. When they were setting up the New York operation, they had considered renting another warehouse, something that they could use in emergencies just such as this one. But it was too risky. No doubt the FBI was already investigating how they had rented the warehouse in Nashville, and while it was a big country, there was no need to roll the dice unnecessarily.

What they had done instead was scouted the outskirts of the city, and they had been able to find several areas where for entire blocks the buildings were either condemned or all for lease. This meant no neighbors, and it gave them several choices of places that they could break into. It wasn't perfect. There was always the chance they'd get interrupted by a real estate agent or a homeless person, but it was something.

"Head towards sector one," said Ish. "We'll pinpoint an address and text it to you, then meet you there."

"Roger that," said Ma'am.

Ish wondered how the engagement had gone, but now was not the time to ask questions. He had hoped that both Ratcliff and the woman he was accosting hadn't sustained too much damage. Rendering

Ratcliff unconscious was the only way to ensure that he didn't hear their voices.

But unlike what is shown on TV and in the movies, knocking someone out was not always as simple as it might seem. Sometimes people suffered from severe concussions that had lasting effects. It was even possible to fracture someone's skull from such a blow to the head, leading to permanent brain damage or even death. Some people would say that a rapist deserved worse, and he couldn't argue with that. But that wasn't in the scope of their plan. They had decided to teach Ratcliff a lesson, not to kill him. Hopefully, he was alright.

"Chad, what do you think is the best location for us to finish this?"

Chad had gone to the other room and grabbed a laptop. He brought up a map that displayed several red dots, the locations of places they'd scouted.

"It's Friday night," he replied, "so I think one is as good as any other. It would be unusual for an agent to be showing any of these properties at this time of the evening. But with vagrants and other trespassers, they're never on a schedule so that's always going to be a black hole as far as calculations go. So, if I had to choose, I think I'd go with this one here," he said, tapping one of the red dots so that it brought the building's details up on the screen. "It's the closest to where they are now, and it's probably one of the easier ones to get into."

"Great," said Ish. "I'll text Ma'am. Unless either of you has any questions, let's grab the gear and be ready to roll in ten."

Ish, Bird and Chad quickly loaded their gear into a second van, one without the customized computer and surveillance equipment. It had been rented locally and they had kept it parked in the hotel's underground parking. There were two dollies worth of equipment that they needed to rapidly pack into it, including photo lights, cameras, computers and a gasoline-free generator just in case they found themselves in a building without electricity, which just so happened to be the case at the address they were on their way to.

Ish was sending Ma'am a text to let her know they were ten minutes away when he heard Bird, who was behind the wheel, mutter something under his breath.

"What is it?" asked Ish.

"There's a black and white that's been behind us for six blocks now."

Ish glanced at the van's instrument panel. "What's your speed been like?"

"Five miles under the entire way."

"Maybe it's nothing," said Ish. "But let's take a left up here at the next main street and lead them away from—"

He was interrupted by a chirp from the police car's siren as the red and blue rooftop lights began to twinkle ominously in the van's side mirrors.

Chapter 36

"Shit!" said Chad as Bird pulled the van over to the curb and brought it to a stop.

"Relax," replied Ish. "This is something we've planned for. Everything's cool."

They waited calmly for the police officers to approach them, but five minutes passed and the cops were still sitting in their car. Ish glanced at his watch.

"What the hell are they waiting for?" asked Chad, speaking to no one in particular. His voice had a nervous edge to it.

"It's a mind game," replied Bird. "S.O.P."

"S.O.P.?"

"Standard operating procedure."

Chad nodded, then leaned back in his seated position behind Ish and tried to get comfortable. Finally, they heard the doors of the cruiser open, and two white police officers got out and approached them, one on each side of the van. Ish noticed that the one on the passenger side was standing with his hand on the butt of his gun. The other officer walked up to the driver's side window as Bird rolled it down.

"How are you boys doing tonight?" he asked. He spoke slow and casually, but his voice was full of contempt and sarcasm.

"Fine," said Bird. "We're just doing some sightseeing while we try to decide where to go for dinner," he answered.

"Oh, you're from out of town?"

"Yeah."

"OK. I guess that would explain the rental van. License and registration please."

Bird produced a license that matched the name that the van's rental contract was registered in. It was counterfeit, but Chad had hacked the DMV database and added the necessary records, so if a police officer ever ran it, it would come up as valid.

"Wait right here," said the officer before walking back to his patrol car with the license and rental documents in hand. The second cop maintained his position near the passenger rear bumper.

A few minutes later, the other officer returned.

"Alright," he said, "everyone exit the vehicle."

"What for?" asked Chad, not bothering to mask his irritation.

"Because I said so. And because we need to search this van."

"For what? Why did you stop us? What's your probable cause?"

"My 'probable cause'?" he asked and chuckled. "It's 'cause' I think it's very 'probable' that you boys are transporting some type of illegal contraband. Now shut the fuck up and get your asses out here."

Ish chose to keep quiet, but before he moved to exit the van, he gave both Chad and Bird a look that he hoped conveyed to them the message that he wanted to send: Ma'am and Jag are waiting—relax and cooperate so we can get on with our business.

The three men were directed by the officers to the passenger side of the van, where they were instructed to place their hands on the vehicle while they were each frisked. The look of twisted anger on Chad's face concerned Ish. It was the look he'd sometime seen in old photographs of white people who were being harassed by the police while participating in some civil rights march or protest rally in support of equal rights. It was a look of indignation and shock, as though they couldn't believe that what was happening to them, which they knew happened to black people on a regular basis, was *actually happening to them.* Seeing the degradation and experiencing it firsthand were two entirely different things.

The reality was that, for most non-blacks, regardless of how dedicated they were to the freedom movement, mentally and emotionally they were still coming from a place of privilege. It was a privilege that had nothing to do with money but was more rooted in their place in the caste system that America had unconsciously established to separate the different minorities from the majority, because contrary to popular belief, all minorities were not created, nor discriminated against, equally.

That was a hard pill for some to swallow. A lot of people liked to paint racists with a broad brush, as though the typical white American racist hated blacks, Hispanics and Asians equally. But you had to look no further than TV to see that wasn't true. Hell, one of the most popular and beloved shows of all time, the *I Love Lucy* show, presented a mixed-race couple, white and Latino, and no one seemed to bat an eye. And that was in 1951! Lucille Ball's life and career would have been drastically different had the show depicted her married to a black man.

The cops opened the back of the van, and the one who had been doing all the talking so far, whom Ish assumed was the senior officer, began pawing through their belongings while the other one kept an eye on them.

"What the hell do you have a generator in here for?" he asked as he stepped back out of the van.

"We work for a production company," said Ish calmly. "We're doing some location scouting while we're here. We brought a few lights with us in case we wanted to take some test shots."

"Do you have a permit for that?"

"No," said Ish "We—"

"You do realize that you need a permit for that, right?" said the cop, interrupting him.

"Actually, sir, any test shots we did would be with a handheld camera, so I don't believe we'd need a permit for that," said Ish. He mentally said a prayer of thanks that they had done the proper research to make sure they were prepared for this type of confrontation. The cop looked irritated and climbed back into the van without any further questions. Ish could hear him throwing things around, and hoped that he wouldn't break anything. Or find Ma'am's so-called 'love kit', which would take a different kind of explanation and potentially link them to the pending mission.

The cop that was standing guard stared at them with a slightly nervous look on his face. He appeared to be young; probably no older than twenty-five or so. He was clean shaven, with blue eyes and blond hair that peaked out from the edges of his cap. Ish felt sorry for him. Clearly, the cop he was training under was not exactly setting a shining example of how to interact with those he was sworn to serve and protect. This young cop would likely follow in his footsteps.

The senior cop was still inside the van riffling through stuff when the radio crackled. When he answered, the dispatcher rattled off some codes regarding a nearby crime in progress. Ish wasn't familiar enough with the municipal codes to understand what they referred to, but it was obviously important, as the cop immediately jumped out of vehicle.

"Alright," he said, his face a bit red from the exertion of the search. "We're going to give you the benefit of the doubt this time. But if I see you around here filming illegally, I'll throw your fucking asses in jail, understand?"

Ish simply nodded, and moments later the two officers were back in their cruiser, screeching down the street with sirens blaring. "Let's get out of here," he said, and they all piled back into the van.

"That shit could be problematic," said Bird as he drove to the corner and made a legal U-turn. "These cops might remember us and put two and two together once Ratcliff is discovered."

"I know, but it was unavoidable. We always knew that getting stopped on a DWB was always a possibility. I just hoped that we'd be lucky enough to avoid it," said Ish.

"Actually, it's a DWBY," said Chad.

"DWBY?"

"Driving While Black 'and Yellow'," he said. He smiled at his own attempt at humor, but the smile didn't reach his eyes.

"Unfortunately, this is par for the course," said Ish as he checked his phone. There were four text messages from Ma'am:

7:42—We've arrived.

7:49—ETA?

7:58—We're wearing the emperor's new clothes and freezing our asses off.

8:08—If we haven't heard from you in 10, we'll abort and proceed to the love shack.

Ma'am and Jag had tools that they could have used to enter the abandoned building, but without someone to stand guard outside they would have increased their risk of discovery. Her last message was letting Ish know that if she didn't hear from him within ten minutes, they'd take Ratcliff to the only other place that made sense—his house. He immediately sent a reply.

8:13—Got delayed by traffic stop. En route. ETA 12 min. Hold position if possible.

She instantly responded.

8:13—Roger that. Maintaining.

It looked like this was going to be a long night.

After making sure there were no other vehicles within their field of vision, Bird turned into the industrial park that housed the address of their destination. He began weaving the van through the streets towards a building that was a considerable distance from the main drag.

"Remember," Ish advised, "we don't need to give this guy voices that he can later identify. If we need to communicate, we can do so by text." Bird and Chad nodded in agreement.

As they rounded the last corner, Ish spotted the surveillance van parked next to a brown brick building. Jag was leaning against the side of it, looking casual and without a care in the world. He smiled and greeted them with a tilt of his head.

Jag was a natural lock picker, so while he grabbed the lock pick set out of the second van and began working on the door, Ish stepped into the surveillance van to evaluate the situation. Ma'am was sitting, carefully watching Ratcliff, who was lying still on the floor with his hands zip-locked behind his back and a black bag over his head. It was impossible to tell whether he was conscious or not. Ish motioned for Ma'am to join him, and they stepped out of the van together and walked a couple of hundred feet down the street, far enough to be out of earshot of Ratcliff, just in case.

"What the hell happened?" asked Ma'am before Ish could speak. "I been sweatin' like a nigga at a white woman's funeral out here!"

"I know. We got stopped."

"I assume there were no complications?"

"Luckily, they got another call; otherwise, who knows how many questions they may have started asking. How's Ratcliff?"

"Seems unharmed. I checked his vitals fifteen minutes ago, and he's resting comfortably," she said.

"Are you ready for this?" he asked, gazing intently into her eyes.

"Absolutely. I'd feel better if we didn't all have our asses hangin' in the wind, but after what that muthafucka just did, I can't wait for a chance at payback."

"Speaking of which, what happened with the woman?"

"I think we got to them before he could seal the deal. He slapped her around a little, but she didn't appear to be any worse for wear."

"How did she react to the cavalry?"

"How the fuck was she supposed to react? She looked like she was witnessing a fuckin' alien invasion. But I think she was ultimately grateful."

"Good," said Ish. "It's going to take a good twenty minutes for Chad to get set up, even with me, Bird and Jag assisting, so you'll need to babysit Casanova out here."

"Not a problem," said Ma'am.

Inside the office building, Ish and the other guys worked quickly and efficiently, following Chad's instructions on where to place lights or in which direction certain cables needed to be strung. As they worked, Ish was trying to get himself mentally prepared for what was about to happen. He had no problem with the violence or the brutality, but the intimacy of it was something completely foreign to him. His previous experience with rape had been from the position of trying to save the victim, not perpetrate the act. He mentally shook his head to clear it, reminding himself that what they were about to do was as much an act of preventing future sexual victimization as the justice they'd meted out to Stanwick.

At that moment, Chad walked up close to him. "We're ready," he said in a quiet voice. Ish could tell that even Chad was more tense now than during the first mission. Of course, some of that was probably attributed to the fact that this was all rushed at the last minute and that their location was not particularly secure. Ish nodded and took out his phone to text Ma'am.

8:48—We're ready to go in here. How's sleeping beauty?

8:48—Slowly becoming aware that a midlife crisis may be at hand.

8:49—On my way to pick up the package. Your satchel is in the other vehicle.

8:49—Roger that.

Jag exited the building with Ish. He would be their lookout while they conducted their business inside. They exchanged glances, and Ish could see the humor in his eyes and how the fact that Ratcliff was now fully awake and within earshot was the only thing stopping him from making some crude remark.

Ish pulled the surveillance van's door open and found Ratcliff sitting upright on the floor. His head was still covered with the black cloth bag. Ma'am was still seated across from him. Ish nodded at her, and she went off to retrieve her supplies from the other van as Ish grabbed Ratcliff by the back of his collar and half-pulled, half-dragged him out of the van. He mumbled something from inside the bag, and when he started struggling Ish simply let him go. He hit the asphalt hard and began rolling back and forth in pain. Ish yanked him to his feet and pushed him towards the building. This time he didn't try to resist.

Once inside the building, Ish guided Ratcliff to a folding chair that had been placed against the wall and pushed him into it. Since this was all supposed to have taken place in Ratcliff's house, extra tables and chairs was not something they had planned for. That was the kind of thing you picked up at the last minute, if needed. But this had gone from a 'last minute' operation to a 'last second' operation, so there was no time to make an Office Depot run.

Fortunately, they had a couple of small folding chairs and a small folding table on hand that were easy to transport, and this building had a large rectangular table that they were able to make use of. It was one of those old, heavy-duty, brown, laminated tables that Ish sometimes saw in schools and at picnics when he was a kid. It was beat up and covered with all manner of gouges, stains and cigarette burns, but it was sturdy enough for their purposes. Ish imagined it probably didn't make a particularly good impression on potential lessees. The agent's loss was their gain.

Ish, Bird, Ma'am and Chad all donned their masks, gloves, shades and hoodies. Once situated, everyone gave a 'thumbs up', and Ish removed the bag from the prisoner's head. He had two long strips of wide black tape plastered to his face; one over his mouth and one over his eyes.

Ish grabbed a handful of the man's hair to steady his head, and then ripped them both off. Ratcliff winced in pain as he blinked at the lights, waiting for his eyes to adjust. Once his eyes were able to focus and he saw Ish staring at him through the mask, he jerked back in his seat so violently that he would have toppled over if the wall hadn't been behind him. The look on his face was one of sheer terror, as though he was facing a legion of demons from Hell itself.

Ish leaned forward towards Ratcliff, and slowly raised a single finger to the lips of his mask in the universal sign for 'stay quiet'. This raised the cop's level of horror another notch, and his face reflected it, his eyes bulging even further out of his head as his mouth fell open, but no sound escaped. Ish nodded at Chad, who hit a button on his laptop. The status lights on the three cameras all changed from green to red as they each began filming from their respective positions in the room.

"Good evening, America. Welcome back to the official website for PROPR—the People's Revolutionary Organization for Police Reform," said the voice coming from the speakers.

"As previously promised, we are back with the next in our series of exposés. If you're joining us for the first time, allow me to offer an introduction. PROPR is a group of citizens formed out of necessity, self-tasked with the mission of stopping the systematic abuse of innocent black Americans at the hands of corrupt police officers. Our first example was an officer whose specialty was assault and battery. If you'd like more details on that, please refer to our archive page.

"Today, however, we are dealing with an officer who prefers a bit more intimacy in his relationship with those he's sworn to serve and protect. I present to you Detective John Ratcliff: serial rapist."

Ratcliff was frozen in place, with the exception of his eyes, which kept blinking rapidly and looking from one side of the room to the other. It wasn't what Ish expected and he began to wonder if the man was in neurogenic shock from the blow to the head. But this was no time for a medical evaluation. The voice recording continued.

"Detective Ratcliff has repeatedly abused his authority. Here is a listing of dates and descriptions of some of his documented crimes." Here the voice paused. Per the plan, once they were done and in post-production, Chad would splice in a video showing a scrolling list of the officer's offenses.

"Though this officer has a long history of what we consider to be substantiated sexual assault allegations, today we are only focused on punishing him for one particular incident."

The voice continued, describing what happened the day Ratcliff went to question the lady who was the wife of the robbery suspect and introducing the video footage, which would also be spliced in later.

As the voice droned on, Ish glanced at Ratcliff. Tears were streaming down his face, and he was making some kind of high-pitched mewling sound deep in the back of his throat.

"Based on the footage that you have just seen, we charge Detective Ratcliff with the crime of aggravated sexual assault and hereby find him guilty as charged."

A sharp whimper escaped Ratcliff's mouth.

"If you saw our previous broadcasts, then you know that while PROPR is not a religious organization, we do very much believe in the biblical concept of an-eye-for-an-eye. Detective Ratcliff has made a habit of sexually abusing women. It is now time for him to experience some of the same shame, pain and humiliation that he's been callously dispensing for years. Please be warned that what we are about to show you is going to be extremely graphic. Viewer discretion is advised."

Ish watched with great respect as Ma'am walked over to the table and picked up the black bundle that was lying on the floor beneath it. She ceremonially reached inside and removed its contents: three brand new dildos—sizes 'normal', 'large' and 'holy shit!'.

When they had discussed the details of this operation, things had gotten somewhat touchy as they began to get into the specifics of exactly how it was going to go down. Agreeing to sexually violate someone was one thing. Working out the logistics of it was something else altogether. But Ma'am had a pretty solid plan.

"So, what are we going to actually use to do this?" Jag had asked.

"We're going to use the same thing he used," she had answered. "A dick. Only this one will be artificial. Don't worry, I'll take care of the shopping."

When she returned from the adult store and poured her bag out onto the table, the guys only had two questions for her: "Why did you need three?" and "Don't you need some lube?" To which she replied, "Assholes come in all shapes and sizes. And rapists don't use lube." Those two answers were good enough for all in attendance.

When Ratcliff spotted the dildos, his panic level hit critical. He immediately tried to get up from the chair and run, but Bird, who had moved to the position on the other side of him, grabbed him by the shoulder and swung an elbow into the side of his face. Ratcliff stumbled back to his seated position as his eyes began to swim around wildly in his head. Ish thought that maybe Bird had hit him a bit harder than necessary, but it was difficult to feel much sympathy for someone who had ruined so many lives.

"Detective Ratcliff," resumed the voice from the speakers. "It is now time for you to accept your punishment. Please stand."

Chapter 37

Hearing that booming voice command him to rise was the breaking point for the cop. He began shaking his head back and forth, his pleading and begging interspersed with gibberish and fragments of prayers. He refused to stand, so Ish and Bird each grabbed an arm and stood him up. Saliva began drooling from his mouth, and Ish thought he smelled urine. They half-dragged, half-guided him over to the table. Bird produced a wicked looking knife, its blade glinting in the glow of the studio light. When Ratcliff saw it, his eyes got even larger, if that was possible, his imagination no doubt running wild again with how it was going to factor into his punishment. But in one swift movement Bird used the knife to cut the zip tie that bound Ratcliff's wrists.

Bird and Ish each took an arm and, pulling a two-foot length of thick, pre-looped rope from their back pockets, wrapped one around each of the cop's wrists. Bird body-checked him up against the edge of the table while Ish used fresh zip ties to bind his ankles to the table's legs. Bird then grabbed him in a half-nelson from behind, leaning him back while Ma'am undid his belt and roughly pulled him pants and underwear down. Ish was right. His boxers were soaked with piss.

Ish and Bird grabbed the end of the rope attached to each of the man's arms and pulled them forward, forcing him to lay his torso flat against the table. With his ankles tied to the legs of the table, he was left with very little room to move.

Ma'am grabbed the smallest of the three dildos and, turning to look at the officer, paused. Since her face was obscured behind the mask, Ish had no idea what emotion she might be feeling right now. Disgust?

Sympathy? Bloodlust? It was impossible to tell. Knowing her the way that he did, and knowing some of the things she'd had to suffer in her own life, he had to imagine that this was something she had been looking forward to for quite some time.

He wondered how she would emotionally deal with this. One didn't spend as much time living in the street as she had without being psychologically damaged. Sometimes the damage was reversible, and sometimes it was fatal. He had witnessed the effects on many occasions in his South-Central neighborhood. He had met some men, but mostly women, who had completely disconnected from life due to the atrocities they had endured.

Sometimes they appeared normal for the most part. They laughed and joked and loved, like anyone else. But there was always something in their eyes that was different; it was as though they were looking out into the world from someplace else as opposed to being an actual part of it. And eventually, they broke. And when they broke, they often did something tragic—overdose, assault, murder, suicide. It took many forms, but the message was the same. They no longer belonged in this world, and this was their way of proving it to themselves and everyone else.

But unlike some women, Ma'am had gone into the army after she got clean, and the army was a vehicle that many were able to use to exorcise themselves of their demons. And as inexplicable as it was to him, she had also had her religion to help prop her up. As a nonbeliever, it was hard for him to understand the power of faith as a vehicle for healing, but he didn't need to understand it to realize that it often worked wonders. So maybe she was okay and not as afflicted as he thought she might be. But if that was the case, why did she seem so eager to be the one to execute this particular aspect of the mission? He could only speculate.

And what of Jag and this 'thing', whatever it was, that was developing between the two of them? Would this incident affect that? It wasn't just by chance that Jag wasn't present for this. He already had issues with things that she had been involved with in her past. This would not help the situation.

Ish's focus was brought back into the moment by Ratcliff's scream. Ma'am, who had just approached the man from behind, hadn't even touched him yet, but for the cop it must have been like waiting in the dentist's chair after being told that they had just run out of Novocain. He knew that pain was imminent, and the waiting was almost unbearable in and of itself.

As Ma'am moved closer to the cop, both his screaming and his struggling increased. At this point, Ish had no desire to shut him up. The expression of his suffering was part of why they were presenting this to the public in the first place. And due to the way he was draped over the table, with the ends of the arm ropes tied to the far legs, his fighting was pretty futile. Ish and Bird both took a half step back and waited for the show to begin.

As Ma'am inserted the first of the three artificial appendages, Ratcliff's screams instantly raised an octave. His pleading gaze darted from Ish to Bird and back again, begging for help that he knew would never come. Ish had a limited view from his angle in front of the man, but he could tell from what he could see of Ma'am's arm that she was using a rhythmic in-and-out motion to slowly, but not too slowly, breach his body. After about five minutes, she withdrew the dildo, slick with a mixture of blood and fecal matter, and threw it into an empty bag. Ratcliff breathed a sigh of relief and his body relaxed and fully collapsed onto the table. Obviously, he thought that the worst was over.

When Ma'am returned for round two, using the middle-sized of the three plastic appendages, she was less gentle. Ratcliff resumed his screaming and begging, shaking his head back forth, slinging saliva and mucous from his nose and mouth. After five or six minutes with the second implement, Ma'am retreated and Ish saw her chest heave as she took a deep breath. He hoped it was the result of the physical exertion of fighting against the man's sphincter muscles and not because she was distressed in some way. But he did notice a slowness to her actions as she bent down to reach for the third device. It could have been fatigue or just her relishing the moment.

The next five minutes was the most horrific yet. It could have been his imagination, but Ish would have sworn he could hear Bird's breathing. It sounded harsh and heavy, like maybe the mask was causing an obstruction. Ish had no idea how Bird, Ma'am or Chad felt, but personally, he was glad it was almost over. During the entire event, Chad had remained still as a statue, and completely unreadable. As Ma'am began putting her supplies away and Ratcliff lay sobbing on the table, Chad activated the final segment of Ish's pre-recorded speech. Once that was done, Ma'am cut the straps off of Ratcliff's legs while Ish and Bird untied the ropes that bound his arms. Ish threw Ratcliff a rag so he could wipe his face.

Chad turned off the studio lights and began putting the cameras away while Ish and Bird kept a close eye on Ratcliff. They hadn't heard any word from Jag, which meant they were still safe, but no one wanted to push their luck, so the sooner they got out of there, the better.

Once Ratcliff had cleaned up his face and pulled his pants up, everyone relaxed a bit. The covering of his nakedness seemed to lower the level of tension in the room. Ish watched as Bird pulled the cop's arms behind him and zip-tied them.

The team had originally discussed the possibility of kicking the cop out of the van completely nude to add even more humility to the experience. But in the end, they voted that while it was a fitting final stroke to his punishment, considering all the embarrassment he had caused so many others, it would increase their risk of detection; someone could witness the event and have a description of the van and the driver. Instead, they decided to simply secure him here in the office and call 911 with an anonymous tip and the address of his location.

As Bird finished with Ratcliff's hands and returned him to his seat, Ish noticed a transformation begin to take form in the cop's face. Pain and fear began to give way to defiance. With the tears and the snot cleaned off his face, a twinkle had returned to his eyes, and as he watched Ma'am, a smile began to play at the corners of his mouth.

"You're a chick, aren't you?" he asked. Ma'am ignored him and continued helping Chad pack. "I could tell. There was a lovingness to the way you handled me. Kind of sexy, really. I almost enjoyed it." Ma'am paused for a moment to stare at him before resuming the packaging of lights, cameras and cables.

"You're kind of big for a chick. What are you, black? Latino? Probably black, huh? I love black chicks. We tend to have a lot of fun together."

Ish could hardly believe the hubris this guy was exhibiting. He wanted to tell him to shut the fuck up, but couldn't without compromising his vocal identity. Ish could tell by the way Bird's shoulders were flexing that the comments were getting to him.

"Yeah, you and I—" began Ratcliff before Bird slapped him on the side of the head. He struck him open-handed, but it was a hard shot. Ratcliff bowed his head in pain, but when he looked up, he began laughing, blood staining his teeth.

"Is that your lady or something?" he asked, a stupid grin plastered on his face. "I don't mean to be disrespectful or anything, but you have to admit, she and I kind of have a history now." Bird quickly moved around to face Ratcliff and raised his hand to punch, but Ish stepped forward and shook his head 'no'. Bird slowly lowered his fist.

Ratcliff began laughing again. "Baby," he said, looking over at Ma'am, "looks like you got this dude pussy-whipped. If it's that good, I'd like to get a taste of that myself one of these days. I don't know how he's treating you, but I'd fuck the shit out of—" A muffled scream erupted from inside Bird's mask as he threw a vicious right hook that knocked Ratcliff out of the chair and sent him slamming into Ish, sending them both to the floor.

Before Ish could get to his feet, Bird had descended upon the cop, towering over him as he delivered thundering kicks to the man's face and body. Ratcliff screamed and tried to cover up with his shoulders, but with his hands still strapped behind his back, he was completely helpless. By the time Ish reached them and grabbed Bird in a bear-hug embrace, a small pool of blood was already gathering around the cop's head.

"Get the fuck off me, Ish!" yelled Bird. Ish immediately released him, and Bird took a swing at him, which Ish easily ducked under. As they stood facing each other, Ish raised his hands, showing his empty palms, and shrugged as if to say "Hey, no harm done". That caused Bird to momentarily relax, and that split second was all Ish needed. With lightning speed, he lifted his right leg and planted a front kick directly into the center of Bird's solar plexus. The effect was dramatic, leaving Bird on his back, gasping for air like a man that had just been saved from drowning. Ish nodded at Chad and Ma'am, who each grabbed an arm and dragged Bird out of the building.

After quickly checking a dazed Ratcliff to make sure his injuries weren't immediately life threatening, Ish zip-tied his ankles to the table and helped Chad finish loading the gear. Within seconds he was in the back of the surveillance van with Ma'am and Bird, with Chad driving as they followed Jag in the second vehicle back to the hotel. Bird was lying back on the padded bench, rubbing his chest and coughing.

Ish closed his eyes and slowed his breathing, willing his blood pressure back to normal levels. He could still hear Bird's wheezing and sporadic coughing, but no one said a word, and for several minutes they rode in silence. Once they were about fifteen miles out from the office building Ish made the 911 call, via the secured line, reporting the cop's location. They drove another ten minutes before anyone tried to speak.

"Ish, I'm sorry—" began Bird.

"Shut the fuck up, Bird," said Ish. "Now is not the time."

That was their first and only attempt at conversation for the rest of the drive. Ish again closed his eyes and let more of the tension ease out of his body. He focused all of his attention on the stream of air cycling in and out of his lungs. The noisy static in his head began to subside, and by the time they pulled into the hotel parking lot, he felt he had regained his composure.

They all rode the elevator together, still maintaining the same silence they had adopted en route, but Ish could see the questions and concern in everyone's eyes. Once they were back in the room, with the door firmly locked behind them, Ish took a seat at the conference table and waved his hand for the rest of the team to join him.

"The silence is killing me," said Jag. "What the fuck happened in there?"

Everyone, including Bird, was looking at Ish for the answer, but it was Chad who supplied it.

"Bird compromised us," he spat. "Completely lost his shit."

Everyone turned their attention to Bird, who silently opened and closed his mouth, as though he were stuttering without actually saying any words.

"What happened to you, man?" asked Ish, his voice kind and even.

"I'm sorry, Ish," he said, his eyes issuing their own plea of forgiveness. "When he started talking about Ma'am, well, I guess something inside of me just snapped."

"How bad are we burned?" asked Jag.

"He spoke Ish's name," said Ma'am. "If Ish hadn't dropped him, who knows what else he might have said."

"It's possible Ratcliff didn't even hear it," said Ish. "There was a lot going on."

"Yeah, but if he did, it could be enough to make a connection," said Chad.

"As my granddaddy used to say, you can't put shit back into an ass," said Jag. "So, the only question that matters now is, how do we move forward from here?"

Ish began drumming his fingers on the table, thinking as he looked around the room at his team.

"I don't believe that anything has changed," he said finally. "Worst case scenario is that they can tie this back to me. None of you were implicated."

"And how long do you think it would take investigators to figure out who the rest of your cohorts were?" asked Jag. "Not only has everyone and their mother seen us together, but we're on your goddamn payroll." His words were pointedly serious, but he still had that ever-present humorous twinkle in his eyes.

"This is still America," answered Ish. "It's not about what they know, it's about what they can prove in court."

Jag nodded his head in agreement.

"Besides, the third mission is largely a solo mission for me. That was always the plan." He looked around the room again, letting his gaze momentarily linger on each of them. "And more importantly, you all know that you're not under contract here. You have no obligation to me or these missions. You've always been free to leave at any time, with no notice. If you like, you can go back to L.A. and continue to work for Macrolox. We can always find you something legitimate to do there."

"Shit, Ice-Man," said Jag, breaking out in one of his trademark grins, "why the hell would I do that when I'm having so much fun here?"

Ish nodded in reply. "What about the rest of you?"

"I'm still in for the long haul," said Chad, his voice resolute.

"Same here, boss," said Ma'am. Everyone turned in unison to look at Bird.

Bird was looking down at the table, as though he were too ashamed to face any of them directly.

"I...uhhh..." he started, still without looking up. "I think I need a little time to think about it."

Ish reached over and gently patted his shoulder. "Take all the time you need," he said before getting up and pouring himself a glass of water. "So. What are we doing for dinner?"

As they all discussed the pros and cons of pizza versus Thai versus Mexican, Ish observed Bird from across the room. He was making an effort to engage with the rest of the team, which likely helped him feel less disconnected and alienated. From what Ish could detect, none of them seemed to be treating him any differently because of what had transpired earlier, but he knew that in the back of their minds, each of them was making their own decision about whether or not they were willing to continue to work with someone who didn't have complete control of his emotions.

Ish had seen so many soldiers break down under the stress of combat that it wasn't surprising to him that someone might crack during the mission. But he thought it would more likely be Chad. Or maybe even Ma'am, as tough as she was. The fact that it was Bird was a complete shock. He needed to find out the source of the breakdown and get an assessment of exactly where Bird's head was at, and he needed to do it soon.

Food and drink had been delivered, and everyone began to act a bit more relaxed. They had all booked afternoon flights for the next day, which meant freedom to drink as much as they liked and sleep in if they wanted.

Ish noticed Bird and Ma'am standing out on the balcony, heads together in some kind of deep discussion, but they had chosen to leave the door wide open. Ish interpreted that to mean that the conversation wasn't particularly private, so he stepped out to join them.

"How are you two?" he asked as he approached.

"We're hanging tough," said Ma'am.

Bird still seemed to be doing his best to avoid Ish's gaze, instead focusing on some point off in the distance, above the twinkling lights of the city. An uncomfortable silence settled around them.

"Um. I think you two probably want to chat," said Ma'am. "I'ma catch you later, bro." She closed the door on her way back into the suite, leaving the two men alone. Ish stared at Bird and held his tongue until Bird finally gave in and met his gaze.

"I'm not here to get on your shit about what happened," he said. "Like Jag said, the past is the past. I'm just trying to at least come to terms with why it happened."

"I'm not sure I really know," said Bird. "I guess I've been carrying some baggage around with me for quite some time, and just chose the most inopportune time to drop it."

"Is this about Ma'am?"

Bird nodded. "I've never really been there for her, man. When she started using, the family basically turned their back on her. I mean, my mother tried to help her out for a while, but by the time she had gotten so far gone that she stole mama's wedding ring, that was pretty much the last straw."

"I've had some conversations with Ma'am about this. I've always gotten the impression that she believed that she was 100% to blame for her problems."

"Yeah, that's what she says," said Bird, frowning, "but I know better. I was there. I was ashamed of what she had become, and I didn't want to have anything to do with her. I remember the last time I saw her before I went off to college. She showed up at the door, asking me for $20. I slammed the door in her face. When I looked out the peephole, I saw her staring back at me. I'll never forget that look in her eyes. That look of pain and betrayal. It's haunted me ever since."

"I feel you. But you can't hang onto the past forever. Life is for the living, and people live in the present."

"You sound like one of my philosophy professors," said Bird, smiling weakly. "If only life was that simple."

"You also have to remember that you were young then. A lot has changed. You've matured; become a man. You're there for her now like you've never been before. Focus on that."

"I try. But I keep coming back to that incident that happened in Jersey, with the kidnapping." Ish nodded. "I had a chance to make it all up to her that night. To be the proverbial 'knight in shining armor' and save the day. But I couldn't make it happen. And I can never forgive myself for that."

"You're a soldier," said Ish. "You know as well as anyone that sometimes being the hero is not about being there before the bombs fall, but about offering protection and assistance to the fallen. Don't make yourself into a martyr. It's not a good look for you." Ish smiled at him, and he smiled back before reaching across and embracing him. He clapped Ish on the back as they released.

"I think I need a drink," said Bird.

"Lead the way, brother," said Ish. As they went in to join the others, he looked back at the setting sun. It should have looked comforting, but instead it just looked angry, like it was hinting of bad things to come.

Chapter 38

Madden was back in D.C., and his boss wanted to see him. His 'boss', in this case, was Associate Director Wesley Bainbridge. Bainbridge was only in his late forties, but had always been an overachiever. He tended to lord his accomplishments over people, expressing a sense of elitism that was often subtle but still visible enough to be regularly noticed. He had risen quickly in the ranks of the Bureau, but the fact that something about him rubbed people the wrong way had created a glass ceiling that had kept him stalled and static for the last six years.

A.D. Bainbridge was rather short for an FBI agent. Maybe that was the source of his apparent contempt for his colleagues; a classic Napoleon complex. He was a handsome man with a strong jaw, an elegant, angular nose and sharp blue eyes. His hair, which had been jet-black when he was younger, was starting to show its silver, but it looked distinguished on him. He was somewhat stocky for his height, but he worked hard to keep himself in top physical shape.

Madden had enjoyed his years of being an agent for the Federal Bureau of Investigation, but every job had its downside; Bainbridge was his. Bainbridge had replaced Madden's previous manager a couple of years back. Madden never knew the complete story of exactly why his prior supervisor had transferred out of the position, but rumors were that it wasn't anything good.

Bainbridge's reputation preceded him, but Madden was the kind of man who believed that everyone deserved a fresh start. He was never much concerned about what his new boss had done in the past, only what he was going to do in the present. Unfortunately, it appeared the reputation was well-earned and that the past would be repeating itself. From the moment they met, there was immediate friction. And to make matters worse, it was extremely clear to Madden that the man had a problem with agents of color.

In the case of someone like Bainbridge, racial discrimination was a difficult thing to confidently assert, because while it appeared that he didn't like blacks, he also didn't seem to like anyone else, either. Madden had once explained to Kelly that his new boss was an 'equal opportunity asshole', but Madden believed he was a little more 'equal' when it came to the brothers.

The office in which Madden worked was fairly diverse. In addition to Caucasians, it was also host to African-Americans, Asians, Latinos, a gay man, two lesbians and a Native American. So, there was a lot of opportunity for Madden, and anyone else with an interest, to observe how Bainbridge interacted with the various minorities he supervised.

From where Madden sat, it seemed that Bainbridge was always a little harder on the blacks—a little more critical, a little more condescending, a little more disrespectful. It was something that Madden had spent a lot of his career trying to overlook. Bainbridge wasn't the first government executive that he'd overheard using racial epithets or favoring a white agent over one of color, and he was sure he wouldn't be the last. But Bainbridge did it with a certain viciousness, a certain pleasure that sometimes made Madden's blood boil in spite of his best attempts to ignore it.

Bainbridge's secretary told Madden to go on in, but he still knocked before he entered, out of courtesy and because that's how he was raised. Bainbridge didn't speak a word to him until after he was seated in one of the two guest chairs. The chairs were slightly lower than normal. Madden had particularly long legs, so he probably noticed it more than others might have. But no one could have missed the fact that Bainbridge's desk was stationed on a small platform. It was only about five inches off the ground, but that, along with the inch and a half or so drop on the chairs, meant that Bainbridge was always looking down on the people he was conferring with.

Madden couldn't imagine that he subjected the upper level executives to this type of disadvantage. He always saw two normal chairs sitting against a far wall and had always assumed that the A.D. swapped them out before more respected guests showed up.

For three- or four-minutes Bainbridge shuffled and read through various papers on his desk. He hadn't yet even bothered to glance in Madden's direction. It was yet one more aspect of his mind game, one more way for him to show his superiority over those under his control. Unfortunately, Madden had been privy to many meetings in this office, with a host of other agents, and he knew for a fact that people of color suffered this lack of respect much more often than did the individuals with white skin.

Finally, Bainbridge decided that he had done enough to make his point. With one final shuffle, he laid the stack down, straightened the pen lying next to it so they were all properly aligned, and looked up to acknowledge his visitor.

"So, Madden, have you solved the case yet?" he asked. He was smiling, but the sarcasm was heavy in his voice. It was how he always greeted Madden, no matter whether they were at the very preliminary stages of an investigation or wrapping up the final details.

"No, not quite yet, sir," answered Madden, his tone clear and business-like.

Madden had always been an FBI all-star. If this were high school sports, he would have been the quarterback, the pitcher and the point guard, all in one. His record for solving cases had been in the top three for the last five years running. Bainbridge had always made it clear that he resented that.

It went against all logic. As on any sport team, when the individual players did well, the coach got to take at least half the credit, if not more. But Bainbridge was one of those coaches that had a permanent chip on his shoulder. He never felt that his own shine got recognized enough, so he couldn't stand to see anyone else shining around him, even if they increased his own luster.

"I see," said Bainbridge, his expression souring a little. "So, what exactly do we know about these fucking monkeys?"

"Monkeys, sir?" asked Madden, his head tilting forward ever so slightly. This was new.

"It's just a figure of speech," said Bainbridge, waving his hand dismissively. "I want to know where we are on this thing."

"Well, sir, our progress has been minimal. We found the warehouse in which the video was filmed, and we have a preliminary psych profile, but that's about it."

"I see," he said again, looking up from tented hands. "What did BAU have to say?" BAU was the Behavioral Analysis Unit, the division of the Bureau responsible for trying to create psychological profiles of criminal suspects.

"Based on several factors, including the way the suspects physically moved in the video and how well-organized their operation was, they're almost certain that they have a military background. Or perhaps law enforcement."

"Cops did this? I'm not buying that shit for a second."

"It's just a theory. I think they're just covering all their bases. They're pretty confident that these guys are ex-military. Maybe Spec-Ops. Maybe Seals. It's impossible to say at this early point in the investigation."

Bainbridge nodded slowly, but he was frowning. "What else?"

This was the part that Madden was dreading having to say, even though he knew that Bainbridge was already aware of everything that was in his report. Bainbridge had been a lawyer before he joined the Bureau, and if there was one thing that Madden knew about lawyers, it was that no lawyer worth his salt ever asked a question he didn't already know the answer to.

"Based on some visual cues reported by the victim, we think it's possible one of the perps is a woman. BAU estimates they are probably all between the ages of twenty-eight and forty-two. It's unlikely that they live in the area. And there's a high probability that some, if not all of them, are African-American."

That was it. That's what Bainbridge had been waiting for him to verbally admit. A smirk played at the corner of his mouth. It would have been too blatant for him to have made the 'monkey' comment now, but it was still hanging in the air from when he volleyed it at the beginning of the conversation. Madden knew exactly what Bainbridge was trying to infer, and Bainbridge knew that he knew.

"What about tracing the source of the video broadcast?"

"Zero, so far. The signal is encrypted with some type of code our guys have never seen before. And it's also bouncing in and out of servers all over the world. It's some ultra-sophisticated tech. They're bringing in some extra bodies to throw some more brain-width at it, and we hope to have something soon."

"Is that it?"

"Yes, sir, that's it in a nutshell. We're still combing the area, looking for possible witnesses, but I wouldn't hold my breath."

"No, we wouldn't want you turning blue on us, Agent Madden," said his boss, smiling coldly. "So, basically, we have a group of black guys, maybe along with one of their sisters, running around kidnapping and torturing innocent police officers, and we're standing around with our dicks in our hands, whistling at the moon."

Madden wasn't exactly sure if that was a question or a statement. He hoped it wasn't a question, because if it was and he was pressured to be honest he might be forced to point out that the cop wasn't exactly innocent, that he wasn't quite tortured and that nobody was just standing around. His team was working around the clock to make some kind of dent in this case, and to suggest anything less was disrespectful.

Instead of asking for clarification, Madden assumed it was a statement, and patiently waited silently for Bainbridge to follow it up.

"When did they say we should expect the next broadcast?"

"Should be any day now. Assuming they actually follow through."

Bainbridge stared off into the distance for a few moments, contemplating something, before grabbing his stack of papers and resuming shuffling through them. "Thank you, Agent Madden," he said, without looking up.

Recognizing that he had just been dismissed, Madden rose and quietly exited the office.

As Madden was getting into his car, this phone buzzed. When he glanced at the screen it read 'Phillips, Casey: FBI'.

"Madden," he said into the handset.

"Chief, they've hit again," said the agent. There was an urgency to her voice, added to by the fact that she sounded slightly out of breath. She had probably been racing up and down the stairs at the office, rallying the troops. Her chronic limp didn't make it any easier, but she never let it stop her from going all out.

"I'm across campus. Grab the principals and meet me in Room 3 in fifteen."

"You got it," she replied, and the line went dead. Phillips was a classic 'type A' personality, but Madden often joked to Kelly that his Number One was really more like a 'type A+'. She was always pleasant enough, but her intense drive kept her laser-focused. She was an ex-marine, and to many she acted like she was still in the Corps. But she and Madden had gotten to know each other well over the years, after working together on so many intense and challenging cases, and he considered her a true friend.

Madden rushed into the building and through security. As he entered the meeting room, he found Phillips and five other agents waiting for him.

"What do we have?" he asked as he set his briefcase down and took off his jacket.

"They grabbed another cop last night, in New York City. A Detective John Ratcliff. Worked him over in an abandoned office building and dropped an anonymous 911 call," said Phillips.

"Is he alive?"

"Yes, but he may wish that he wasn't."

Madden cocked an eyebrow in question.

"You may recall from the first video that the perps declared that their next target would be a rapist. Ratcliff is that guy."

"Let me guess. They raped him and broadcast it for all the world to see?"

"Yes, but in a twist of real poetic justice, when they snatched him, he was allegedly in the process of raping someone himself."

"What?"

"A woman reported last night that she met a guy for drinks that she was introduced to through an online dating site. The name is different, but the description matches Ratcliff perfectly. She was also found in an abandoned vehicle registered to him. Her story is that she accepted an invitation from Ratcliff to go for a ride and that he drove her to an abandoned parking lot and began to force himself on her. She tried to fight him off and got a couple of stiff shots for her trouble. But before he could finish, two figures in masks snatched the doors open, dragged him out and disappeared with him into the night."

Madden was shocked, but at the same time the whole thing was so comically absurd that he almost wanted to laugh.

"And what did they say?"

"According to the woman, not a single word."

Madden rubbed the back of his neck and walked across the room, deep in thought. His team watched him, giving him time to process it. After a moment, he looked up.

"I don't suppose she got a license plate?"

Phillips smiled. "Chief, if it were that easy, we wouldn't be getting paid the big bucks."

"Alright," said Madden. "Let's go ahead and take a look at this video, so we can get it out of the way."

Moments later the footage was playing on the room's wide-screen monitor. When the screaming began, Madden noticed that a couple of the agents began to squirm a bit in their seats. Even though they were experienced investigators who had witnessed a lot of violence, he couldn't really blame them. It was kind of like whenever men saw video of another man taking a hard shot to the groin—getting kicked, hit with a ball, falling on a bike, whatever. Most men cringed at the sight, because they knew how painful it must be, and they had true sympathy for the victim. This was kind of the same thing, notwithstanding the fact that this asshole was more than likely 100% guilty of rape. Only Phillips seemed completely unmoved.

As the act reached its conclusion and the yelling was reduced to a whimper, the image on the screen of the naked cop, with only his genitals blurred out, dissolved, replaced with that of one of the perps, clad in the now trademark mask, shades and black hoodie.

A slightly mechanized voice emerged from the speakers.

"America, what you have just witnessed is what we consider to be justice that was long overdue. Again, we apologize for the graphic nature of the footage but felt it necessary for you to at least have the opportunity to witness the carrying out of this sentence in its full, mostly uncensored form. As before, we immediately contacted the proper authorities and ensured that Detective Ratcliff received prompt medical attention, and we are able to report that he is recovering and resting comfortably. However, we believe that we have made an impression on him that will, hopefully, forever affect his future behavior.

"As we stated before," the voice continued, "we are doing this not just for us but for all minorities, to empower us as a nation and give evidence to the fact that we have the ability to take back our streets from corrupt cops. We hope that this will give you the courage and resolve to stand up to the injustices you see in your own neighborhoods. But we must emphasize yet again that this is *not* a declaration of war on all police officers! It is simply a clarion call to those that are tired of being preyed upon to stand up against injustice and make a difference.

"Our next target is an officer guilty of, arguably, the most serious of all crimes: coldblooded murder. Please check back in the next week or two for updates on that operation. In the meantime, if you need to contact us, please feel free to do so at help@NowBeginsTheRevolution.com. Until then, good day and stay safe."

The screen faded to black, and the mood in the room seemed to follow suit.

"Before we get too far into this, just so I can cross it off the list," said Madden, "did we get any traction on the email?"

"No, sir," said Phillips. "We've sent ten separate emails to the address stated in the video, each requesting an open dialog with whoever is the leader of the group. So far they have yet to respond."

"Well, we're in the early innings, so who's to say that tree might not bear fruit at some point?" he said, mixing metaphors. "Make sure someone is monitoring our in-box every hour on the hour until we wrap this up."

Phillips nodded her acknowledgment.

"So, what do we have from the cop?"

Phillips took a deep breath. "Not a lot. According to him, he was indeed with the woman that filed the assault complaint, in his car, in the parking lot, but they were in the midst of a—" she began, then paused to glance at her notes, "a 'consensual romantic interlude'—his words—when he was dragged out of the car by two masked figures, accosted and knocked unconscious."

"Have the locals already canvassed the area for witnesses and security video?"

"Affirmative," said Phillips. "Negative on both."

"Figures. Did Ratcliff have any other details to offer?"

"Not according to the investigating officers."

"Okay," said Madden. "No need to keep slogging through this crap second-hand. Let's get our boots on the ground and see what we can see."

"I already have us all booked standby on the 6:10am flight," said Phillips.

"Great. Thank you. I'll take these files with me and get more familiar with them between now and then. See you all in the morning."

As the members of his team filed out of the room, Madden quick-dialed his wife.

"Honey!" she said, picking up on the second ring.

"Hey, babe. How are you?"

"I'm good, you?" she replied, a bit tentatively. They had been together long enough that she knew if he was calling her in the middle of the day it was because something had come up.

"I'm fine. But I have to fly out to New York in the morning."

"Shoot. How long?"

"Hard to say. Probably not more than a day or two. What are your dinner plans?"

"I just bought a bunch of stuff. I was planning on cooking."

"That sounds great. I'll see you at 5:00?"

"I'll be here," she said. "I love you. Drive safely."

"I love you, too," said Madden, and he hung up.

It always struck him as a little funny that even though he investigated some of the most horrific crimes in the nation and had served warrants on armed suspects too many times to mention, his wife always reminded him to drive safely. It was sweet, but he suspected that it was also a coping mechanism for her; a way of exerting a little bit of control or influence over a situation in which she knew she was, in reality, entirely powerless.

She had known what she was getting herself into when they married, and he felt she had done a pretty good job of dealing with the stress of it all, but of course he knew that she worried. She was actually a lot stronger than he was in that regard. He knew that there was absolutely no way he could have sat home every night knowing that she was out doing the things that his job required him to do. Thank God for strong women.

Chapter 39

Back in L.A. the crew spent most of the first twelve hours sleeping. No one realized how stressful the entire trip had been until they were back in town and away from the drama of it all. Not much more had been said, at least not to Ish, regarding what had happened in the office building between Ish and Bird. Ish was thankful to be able to have a little bit of a buffer; a respite that he could use to just process exactly what had happened and how it might change the future.

As he came back in from a six-mile jog, Ish could smell bacon cooking. He walked into the kitchen, toweling the sweat from his brow and found Ma'am leaning over the stove. She was alone, but there were two half-empty cups of coffee on the table.

"How was your run?" she asked as she began moving the bacon strips from the skillet to a stack of folded paper towels to drain.

"It was good. I don't get to work out nearly as much now as I did when we were deployed. You know how it is. Sometimes I forget how helpful it is for managing stress. How long have you been up?"

"Not long. I think I'm still on New York time, and my stomach was starting to complain."

"I'm with you. Is everyone else still asleep?" he asked, glancing again at the pair of coffee cups.

"Jag's up," she said. "I think our stomachs are both on the same timer."

Ish nodded in understanding. At that moment, Chad walked into the kitchen, looking his normal, eager self.

"Morning!" he said, sniffing in the direction of the bacon. "Is there enough of that to go around?"

"Of course," said Ma'am. "Help yourself. I'll have some eggs and flapjacks ready in a few."

"Thanks, Ma'am," he said, grabbing himself a slice of bacon.

"Your stomach wake you up, too?" asked Ish.

"Actually, no. I've been up for hours, reading stories about what's going on in the streets." There was a sparkle in his eyes. "There's lots to talk about."

"I can imagine," replied Ish. "But let's save it for after I've had breakfast and a shower if you don't mind."

"No problem. But the sooner the better. There are some things going on that we need to get on top of ASAP."

Ish nodded and headed upstairs. As he got undressed, he glanced at his phone and checked his email account.

Very few people actually had his personal email address, but there were still almost fifty unread emails in his inbox. Several were from Virginia and the law firm in Baltimore. There were also a couple from Khadija of #BlackForLife. They had also tried calling at some point in the last few days, but he hadn't called any of them back. The rest of the emails were business—the realtor, their corporate lawyer with some papers to sign, his insurance agent. But then he saw one email that stopped him in his tracks. It was from one of Layla's attorneys.

Ish stood still for a moment, staring at the message on his phone, almost afraid to open it. He didn't remember seeing any missed calls from them, and he had to assume that if they needed to contact him about anything important, they would have tried to reach him by phone first. On the other hand, he'd had a ton of missed calls over the last two weeks, and it might have just slipped by him. Taking a deep breath, he tapped the button to open the email.

Dear Mr. Carter,

We trust this finds you well. We have been trying to reach you via the phone number we have on file but were unsuccessful. There have been some new developments in Layla's case that we would like to discuss with you. Please give us a call at your earliest convenience at...

It was signed 'Manuel Aquila, Atty at Law'. He stopped reading and sat down on the edge of the bed. He should have known that they wouldn't put anything of real importance in an email if they could avoid it. He looked at the clock. 7:15am. The law office probably wouldn't be up and humming for another hour or two, so he'd have to wait to find out what was going on.

After a quick shower, Ish joined the rest of the gang for breakfast. Everyone appeared to be in a fairly good mood, considering the events of the last 24 hours. No one mentioned the mission, but he noticed that Chad kept glancing in his direction. There was something in his eyes, something that hinted that there was something urgent that he needed to discuss with Ish in private. After breakfast he walked into the back yard and Chad followed.

"You know when I set up the website, I also created an email account for it, right?"

"Yeah," said Ish. "The one we reference in the videos, right?"

"Exactly. Well, in the excitement of the last couple of weeks, I haven't been checking it very regularly. In fact, I haven't checked it for the last seven or eight days. Until this morning."

"And?" asked Ish.

"We've received over 3,000 emails. Half of them in the last 24 hours."

"That's not really surprising, is it?" he asked. "What we're doing is rather unique."

"It's not the number of emails that is so surprising. It's what they contain. And who they're from. Let's start with the FBI."

"Really?" said Ish in a tone suggesting that he wasn't actually all that surprised.

"Yeah. They've emailed us at least ten times already. They want to open a dialog; want to know what it is they can do to convince us to stop this."

Ish chuckled. "Nothing ventured, nothing gained. You've got to give them credit for thinking outside the box. I'm sure that's not in the manual. Did you respond?"

"Of course not. And I'm not sure that we should."

"Why not? We're still fully encrypted, right?"

"Absolutely. But you don't want to give these guys anything. They've got some good people working for them. Some really smart people. They could latch onto a phrase and turn it into some evidence that could later work against us. Besides, they have nothing to offer that we want, so responding would serve no purpose other than simply to fuck with them."

"Yeah," admitted Ish, "there's that. What else?"

"Well, of course there are emails from reporters all over the world asking for interviews; at least two or three hundred and growing. I know it's not something we've ever discussed, but it's something we may want to consider at some point," said Chad.

"Do we? You just said we shouldn't give any response to the FBI for fear of leaving them clues, but now you're advocating speaking to the entire world?"

"I know. It's complicated. But the press is interested in spreading our message, while Freddy Pig is only interested in locking us up and/or killing us. And isn't that why we started this campaign in the first place—to get a message out to the world?"

"Point taken," said Ish. His mind spun as he considered the pros and cons. "Who are the other emails from?"

"That's the exciting part!" said Chad, his face lighting up. "People from all over the world are sending us messages of love and support. It's amazing!"

"They can't all be supportive," said Ish.

"Well, no. There are a few haters."

"*Just* haters?"

"There are a few death threats mixed in with it," he admitted sheepishly. "But fuck those people! We're in this to help the downtrodden, and the people that can't get behind that are not on our team."

Ish nodded in agreement.

"But what's great is all the people writing in to ask for our help! I don't even have to search the databases anymore. The cases are coming to us, now. We just need to pick and choose which ones we want to go after next."

"Chad, that's something that we all need to sit down and—" began Ish, when Jag slid the glass door open.

"Hey, pardon the interruption, but I think you two need to get in here and see this."

The rest of the team was situated around the television in the living room, watching a news story that showed a large group of people, mostly African American, marching down a street.

"This has been going on all morning, in cities all around the country," said Ma'am, smiling. "After last night's video hit the airwaves, people starting organizing this morning and marching on police stations and capitol buildings. Check this out." She starting flipping through various news channels, each one showing a different group of marchers in a different city.

Something caught Ish's eye. "Wait! Go back one."

Ma'am hit the remote to return to the previous channel, and on the screen was Khadija and Marquita from #BlackForLife, being interviewed by a reporter.

"But isn't this somewhat in line with what #BlackForLife has been campaigning for all along?" asked the reporter.

"Absolutely not!" said Khadija. "#BlackForLife is, and always has been, an organization guided by the principles of nonviolent protest. We do not, cannot, and never will, support what PROPR is doing: physically attacking police officers. That is not the way to create positive change in this country. Fighting violence with violence makes us no better than the crooked cops that we're trying to eradicate."

"But aren't you—" The reporter was interrupting by yelling and people running in the background. The camera began tracking the action, and after a few moments the reporter's face filled the screen. "It appears that an altercation has broken out between people marching to support PROPR and members of #BlackForLife..."

Chad looked over at Ish, grinning, his eyes shining with something akin to bloodlust. "Let the games begin!"

"You look a bit shocked," said Jag, speaking to Ish.

"Well, I guess maybe I am, just a bit."

"Dude," said Chad. "This is what we hoped for all along. You had to know this was a possibility."

"Of course. I just didn't think it was all going to happen so quickly. I guess I figured it would build a bit more slowly."

"This is the age of social media," Chad responded. "Everything moves at the speed of light."

"Not to change the subject, but now that we're all together and have had some time to reflect," said Jag, turning to face Bird, "let's address the elephant in the room. Namely, what the fuck happened yesterday?"

Bird gazed down at the floor and shook his head. "I don't know. Ratcliff started taunting Ma'am, and I let it get up under my skin."

"That doesn't sound like you, man," said Jag. "I've been in some crazy combat situations with you, and I've never seen you show any sign of being rattled."

"All I can say is that I was never in a combat situation with my sister. It's different. I feel protective over her."

"I guess that makes sense," said Jag. "But you know Ma'am can take care of herself, right?"

Anger flashed on Bird's face. "Who the hell are you to tell me about my sister? Just because you're hot to fuck her doesn't mean you know more about her than I do!"

"What!?" exclaimed Ma'am.

"Whoa! Everyone relax!" said Ish. "I'm getting tired of being the playground monitor between you all. If any of you have personal shit that you need to deal with, take it outside. Fight, kiss, hug or whatever it is you need to do to squash it, and come back when you're clear. We don't have time to deal with this petty nonsense." He looked around the room at each face.

"Alright," said Bird, staring at Jag, "let's deal with it. What the hell is going on between you and my sister?"

"I think you're way out of line, but I'll answer your fuckin' question," said Jag. "Yes, I dig your sister. I've been diggin' her for a while now. And if she's open to it, I hope that it develops into something. I didn't ask your permission because I'm a grown fuckin' man and she's a grown fuckin' woman. I can understand if you've got 'baby brother' syndrome or whatever the fuck it is you're strugglin' with, but if you didn't think you could handle runnin' a mission with your sister, you should have declined it. End of story. But now you're here, so you need to either man up or step off before you get us all killed or thrown in prison."

Bird sat stone-faced and completely unreadable. He seemed to be trying to decide how to respond. The look on Ma'am's face was a mixture of hurt and anger. She could have been directing that to anyone, but she was looking at Bird. Ish assumed she was angry that Bird had put her in that position, but hurt by the sting the words must have caused her brother.

"Okay," said Bird finally, bowing his head. "You're right. It's none of business what may or may not be going on with you and Ma'am. She is a grown woman. And I know you're a good guy. I apologize."

Jag nodded his acceptance.

"Good enough," said Ish. "Let's get back to the business at hand."

"You've had a bit of time to think about things," said Ish to Bird. "What's the verdict? Are you going to stick with us or do you need to bow out?"

"I—" began Bird.

"Wait," said Ish. "Before you answer, I just want to say that I won't hold it against you if you decide that you've had enough of this. I think I speak for all of us when I say that we love and respect you as a brother, and appreciate what you've contributed thus far. Ultimately, we all have to do what feels right for us as individuals."

"Thanks, Ish. I appreciate that," said Bird as he leaned back and slowly rubbed his palms along his thighs. "You all know that having my sister with me on this has been a challenge. Even though she's technically my big sister, I've always felt a responsibility to protect her." He glanced in Jag's direction.

"And the truth," he continued, "is that I always felt I let her down; that I was never there for her when she needed me most. My sister has had a hard life, but she's one of the strongest, most special people I've ever met. She's come back from rock bottom, from a life that would have emotionally crippled most of us, and she rose like a phoenix from the ashes. I would gladly give my life to protect her." Ma'am was slowly shaking her head back and forth, and tears were forming in the corners of her eyes.

"So please accept my apology for losing control yesterday. I dishonored the trust that Ish, and all the rest of you, have had in me. I can only hope and pray that I haven't fucked us all by what I did. Having said all that, there is no way that I can voluntarily walk away from this now and leave you all to deal with it alone. I now understand my weakness and if you'll still have me, I vow to never again let it get the better of me."

Bird paused and looked around the room. Tears were streaming down Ma'am's face, and everyone was clearly waiting for Ish to be the first to respond.

"It's always been an honor to serve with you," said Ish, "and now is no different. Everyone makes mistakes sometimes. We learn from them and we grow." He looked around at the group. "Let's get a show of hands. Those in favor of keeping Bird on the team?" All hands immediately went up. "It's unanimous. Welcome back."

Before anyone else could make a move, Ma'am was out of her chair and embracing her brother. Tears continued to stream down her face as she and Bird rocked each other back and forth. Bird was mumbling apologies into her ear.

"Um, I'm going to go grab a glass of orange juice," said Chad. "Anyone else want anything?"

"I'll join you," said Jag, rising from his seat.

"Actually, I need to go make a couple of quick phone calls," said Ish. "Let's meet back here in thirty."

"Cool," said Jag and Chad in unison. Bird and Ma'am were still wrapped in each other's arms as the rest of the team left the room to give them some privacy.

Chapter 40

Behind the closed door of his bedroom, Ish dialed the number to the office of Layla's attorney.

"Manuel Aquila, please," he said to the woman who answered the phone.

"One moment, please."

Muzak played in his ear. It was a smooth jazz version of some Metallica song. After five minutes, Ish was starting to get impatient.

"This is Manuel!" said a voice with much more cheerfulness than you'd usually associate with criminal lawyers.

"Good morning, Mr. Aquila. This is Ishmael Carter, returning your call."

"Good morning, Mr. Carter! Thank you for calling me back. We've been trying to get in touch with you for several days now."

"I'm sorry, I've been out of town, and my reception has been a bit spotty."

"No worries. I was calling because I had some new developments to report regarding your wife's case. I have both good news and bad news." Ish could hear him riffling through some papers.

"Here it is," he said. "So, the good news is that, considering the circumstances surrounding the incident, we were able to find a precedent for petitioning the court to drop all charges, or at the very least have it reduced to simple assault and time served. There are no guarantees, of course, but it's something to shoot for."

"Does that include the assault on the guard as well?"

"Yes, it does," said Aquila. "We maintained that Layla's actions were simple self-defense and promised a lawsuit if the guard didn't play ball. Considering the fact that there were several witnesses there who saw him use excessive force against her, he really didn't have a choice. Besides, he suffered no permanent damage to his ear, so he didn't have a strong position to begin with."

"That's great news," said Ish. "And the bad news?"

"The bad news is that she had another fight last week, and the other inmate suffered some pretty severe injuries. The jail is threatening to file additional charges of felony assault—maybe even attempted murder."

"Fuck," said Ish as he ran in hand through his hair. "Is Layla alright?"

"She's fine. I actually visited her three days ago. She had an abrasion above one eye and a loose tooth, but that was the extent of it. Right now, we're more concerned with the effect this latest incident could have on our dismissal motion."

"I understand," said Ish. "When do you expect to know more?"

"Hard to say right now. The wheels of justice turn slowly, as they say. But we wanted to let you know what was going on and that we're on top of it. Of course, we'll keep you updated every step of the way."

"Thank you very much," said Ish. "I appreciate it. And as I've said before, spare no expense in respect to Layla's case."

"She's in good hands."

They said their goodbyes and Ish hung up. He sat on the edge of the bed for a few moments, deep in thought, before walking back downstairs.

In the kitchen, he was looking in the refrigerator for something cold to drink when Chad walked by. Chad caught the look on his face and knew.

"Layla?" he asked with concern.

"Yeah," said Ish with a sigh. It always amazed him how well Chad was able to read his mood. They really were like brothers; maybe even closer than most brothers. "I just got off the phone with her lawyer. There's a possibility of getting the original charges dismissed, but she had another fight, and this time they're thinking about filing new charges."

"Fuck," said Chad.

Great minds think alike.

"Are you going to go see her?" asked Chad.

"I've been thinking about it," said Ish, frowning. "But I really need to stay focused on what we're doing here."

"Dude, this will wait. You need to take care of your family. Wasn't that one of the reasons you started this to begin with?"

"True," said Ish. "But in case you haven't noticed, things aren't exactly rock solid here. Regardless of what he said, Bird is on shaky ground. I don't doubt his resolve, but he's been compromised. If I leave him to sit around here with nothing to do, there's no telling how his mindset might shift."

"I feel you on that, but you can't control everything. You have to sometimes be able to step back and hope that things will retain their shape without any help. And I'm sure I can find something to keep the team busy till you get back."

"Yeah? Like what?"

"We have an email box full of requests for help. We could do a mini-mission while you're gone," said Chad.

"No, no, no," said Ish, shaking his head. "That's the last thing we need to do. Too much can go wrong, especially if we try something without the proper planning. I can leave for OCJ tomorrow morning and be back by mid-afternoon. Why don't you take everyone down to the office tomorrow and talk to them about possible roles within the company? Maybe having a more solid endgame in sight will allow them all to settle down a bit."

"That's a good idea," said Chad. "Stacy from H.R. has been calling me daily asking for details on the three new hires. If I don't tell her something soon, she's going to start getting suspicious. This will be a nice formal introduction for everyone."

"Perfect. I'm sure everyone has errands they need to catch up on—bills to pay, checks to deposit, etc., so let's make this a free day. Tomorrow you all will be at the office and I'll be with Layla. The next day we'll all be back on track for the next mission. Assuming nothing has changed by then."

With that settled, Ish walked into the office at the back of the house and settled down to return a few more phone calls. The first was to Khadija at #BlackForLife. He expected to have to navigate past an assistant or receptionist, but Khadija herself picked up on the first ring.

"Good morning, Ishmael," she said after he identified himself. "It's good to hear from you."

"Thank you. It's good to be heard. How goes the movement?"

"It's been insanity these last few days. This PROPR organization has set everything in flux, threatening to destroy all the progress we've made the last eighteen months."

"Yeah, I saw you with them on CNN this morning. I can see things are heating up."

"That's a massive understatement. Anyway, I know you must be busy. I just wanted to let you know that we haven't forgotten about you or Nathaniel. He's still a part of our campaign, and he and his family are always in our prayers. As a matter of fact, we're having a candlelight vigil in his honor next Saturday, and we'd love you to join us if you're available."

"Thanks, Khadija. I appreciate that. I really do. Unfortunately, I'm totally swamped at work right now, so I'll have to pass on this one. But please let me know if there's anything else I can do to be of assistance."

"Well, it would be nice if you could make PROPR disappear," she said and chuckled.

"Do you really think they're that bad?"

"Without question! We can't tell the establishment that we come in peace, unarmed and open-handed while behind their backs this other organization is snatching police officers off the street! That's no way to develop the kind of trust we need for what we're trying to accomplish."

"Many would disagree. There are those that believe that this is the only way to achieve real change."

"Is that what you believe?" asked Khadija, challenging him.

"I try to stay out of politics whenever possible," said Ish, a smile in his voice.

"Smart man," said Khadija, her voice returning the smile. "Let's stay in touch. Please let me know if there are any developments in Nathaniel's case."

"I will," he said. As he hung up, he wondered to himself if he could be wrong. Was it possible that this movement wasn't big enough for both organizations? Perhaps only time would tell.

* * *

Ish sat down on the plastic chair in front of the glass barrier and waited. When the door opened and he saw Layla enter the visiting room and start walking towards him, his breath caught.

In the heat of battle, with other lives to protect and unforeseen circumstances to contend with, it was sometimes easy to forget exactly how much he loved this woman and how much his heart was completely hers. Maybe sometimes he didn't want to remember it. He was told once in boot camp that holding on too closely to your life at home can get you killed; that if you're focused on what you're trying to one day get back to you can't fully focus on the task at hand, which was staying alive, protecting your fellow soldiers and successfully completing your mission. At the time, he didn't think he really believed that. But maybe, somewhere deep inside, he actually did.

He watched her body as she glided towards him, lithe and athletic, her eyes scanning the room with a confidence born of grace and power. Some of the female prisoners she passed, already in the midst of their own visiting sessions, caught sight of her in their peripheral vision, and the way their bodies tensed signaled that they were wary of her, that they knew her as a force to be reckoned with. On the one hand, this made Ish proud, knowing that she was able to handle herself in here, in the so-called 'belly of the beast'. On the other hand, it made him nervous. The king—or queen—of the hill is always a target, because there's always someone who wants that spot and will do anything to get it.

Layla sat down in the seat opposite Ish. Before she picked up the phone, she conspicuously looked at the rows of women seated on each side of her, her face fixed in a hard scowl, as though to say, 'I'm here. Does anyone have a problem?' They all immediately turned away and back to their conversations. Finally, she lifted the receiver, and her face instantly transformed. She changed from a lion to a gazelle right before his eyes.

"Hey, boo," she cooed, a bashful smile slowly revealing itself. As her lawyer had reported, her face showed a couple of light abrasions, but it was as beautiful as ever.

"Hey, love. How are you?"

"I'm good. Just trying to keep my head down," she said.

"Really?" he asked, smiling and staring more closely at her bruises. "Maybe you should have ducked a little lower."

"You're probably right. But I was never much good at ducking. I'm an offensive fighter."

Ish chuckled. "Yeah, I can't argue with that. Listen, I know we don't have much time. I had a conversation with your lawyer yesterday. Aquila. He updated me on the situation."

"Yeah, I figured he would. Are you here to tell me I've been a bad girl?"

"Is it against the rules for me to care about you now?"

"Ish—" Layla began, but he cut her off.

"Okay," he said, waving his hand dismissively, "I didn't come here to fight with you. But I can't help worrying about you."

Layla sighed deeply and fell silent.

"So," said Ish. "You didn't seem surprised to see me."

"I wasn't. Sumatra told me last night that you were coming."

"What?"

"Yeah. We were talking and laughing together about something, I can't even remember what now, and suddenly she stopped and said 'Daddy's coming to see you tomorrow.' I said, 'Is anything wrong?' And she said, 'No, all good,' and gave me that sweet little smile, tilting her head to the side like she always used to do when she was trying to keep from revealing a secret."

Ish smiled sadly as he pictured his daughter's face in his mind's eye.

"So, she's still...in contact?" he asked, not sure what to say that wouldn't sound patronizing.

"Of course! We talk all the time. I don't think I would make it in here if it wasn't for her."

"What kinds of things do you talk about?"

"All kinds of stuff. Mother/daughter stuff. Life stuff. Daddy stuff."

"What kind of 'daddy stuff'?"

"Well, she told me that you recently had another incident with a stray pit bull. She said you took him in and was trying to get him to heel, and things got a little out of hand."

Ish tensed, his eyes narrowing. He leaned forward to get his face closer to hers.

"What?" he asked, his voice reduced to a whisper.

"She was worried. She said the dog catcher might be coming for you. I told her you're too smart for any old dog catcher."

Ish paused and stared deep into her eyes, trying to evaluate her state of mind. Was she coherent? Was she speaking in code? Maybe she had caught the news, but no report he had seen had yet hinted that there had been any problems with the mission. Was it possible that she really was speaking to Sumatra? All these questions flashed through his mind in a fraction of a second, leaving him in doubt and wishing that he hadn't made this trip. The only thing he could do was play along and assume that she was cognizant enough to realize how dangerous what she was saying actually was were it to get into the wrong ear.

"She's right," he said quietly. "Things did get a bit hectic. You know pit bulls. They have a bad reputation for a reason, and this one was no different. Sometimes you think you have everything under control, and before you know it, they've got their teeth in you. I got nipped, but I'll live."

"Alright, Carter, let's wrap it up!" yelled a guard at the other end of the room as he slowly started making his way towards Layla.

The smile that had been on her face for the last few minutes slowly faded, and this time she was the one who leaned in towards the glass.

"Knowing that you're out there, helping to take these wild animals off the street, definitely makes me feel safer. It makes me think that coming home one day might actually be a possibility."

"I'm so glad to hear that," said Ish. "Just know that I'm working with a great group of 'dog whisperers', and we're going to make this happen. Change is in the wind. Just hold on."

With the guard now standing behind her, Layla hung up the phone without another word, then stood up and placed her open palm against the glass. Ish did the same in return, and then she was gone.

Chapter 41

While Kelly finished setting the table, Madden pulled out one of his pristine LPs, Marvin Gaye's *Trouble Man,* and set it spinning on the turntable. They had always enjoyed eating dinner to music, and he loved the warmth of sound that vinyl offered, especially when played on a high-end turntable. Over the years he had amassed a collection of almost 700 discs. His taste was eclectic, with everything from R&B to rap to classical to country and beyond.

"I saw the story online: 'Rapist Cop Attacked By PROPR'," said Kelly between mouthfuls of salad. "This thing sounds like it's getting serious."

"That's putting it lightly. Bainbridge is all over me to get it solved yesterday. But I can't blame him. This is a potential powder keg the likes of which we've never seen before."

Kelly's face clouded with concern. "Is it true that the cop was in the middle of raping some woman when these people grabbed him?"

Madden set his fork down and considered the question for a moment while he finished chewing the food in his mouth.

"That is the allegation. Of course, he denies it. Says it was consensual."

"When was the last time you actually had a rapist openly admit that he committed rape?" she asked.

"Point taken."

"You know there have already been a couple of women's rights activists that have been interviewed and have stopped just short of calling this group 'heroes'."

"Yeah, I was following some of that on the drive in. I'm more concerned about the demonstrations. They're springing up all over the country. It's like a wave of poison is sweeping over the nation."

"Poison? They're just people marching to support their rights."

"Okay, maybe poison is too strong a word. But we can't underestimate the power for destruction that a movement like this is liable to manifest. I once knew a cop that was in L.A. during the '92 riots. He said everyone on the force was scared shitless. He said they may not have admitted it out loud, but that you could see it in their eyes. This has the potential to be a hundred times worse than that."

Kelly reached across the table and gave his hand a squeeze. "I'm sorry, hon. I know how hard this must be for you. And the fact that they've only gone after bad cops has to make it even worse; forcing you to fight for the bad apples."

Madden nodded and cut into his steak. The food was delicious as always, but the discussion was creating a bit of acid in his gut, and Kelly was looking at him with that 'concerned' face that she only used when something was really bothering her.

"Have you thought about asking to transfer this case to someone else?"

He stopped chewing and swallowed. "Why would I do that?"

"Well, for starters, because it appears that there may be a black militant group behind it, and they're going after dirty cops that have histories of abusing blacks."

"And I'm black?"

"That goes without saying. I just wondered how you're dealing with the conflict."

Madden nodded his head and shrugged. "There's really no conflict. My job isn't to bring the cops to justice. It's to stop a group of kidnappers and torturers. Their skin color doesn't factor in."

"Alright. I just thought I'd ask," she said.

But as they sat in silence and finished their dinner, they both knew that he wasn't being entirely honest.

* * *

When Madden and Phillips walked into Ratcliff's hospital room, he was sitting up in bed, eating ice cream and watching 'The Bachelor'. His face dropped when he saw them, and he looked embarrassed, though Madden wasn't quite sure what he was embarrassed about. It could have been the fact that he was eating ice cream like he had just had his tonsils out, the fact that he had been publicly raped or the fact that he had been caught watching a mindless reality show about women competing for Mr. Wonderful.

Madden had stopped on the way in and chatted with Ratcliff's doctor. The damage done from the anal violation was minimal. But he had some bruised ribs and had complained about back pain, so against the doctor's better judgment, he had agreed to give him one more day of bed rest and a final round of testing before kicking him out. It was clear that Ratcliff wasn't looking forward to facing what was on the other side of the hospital's front doors: rabid reporters and rape charges.

"Good morning, Detective Ratcliff. I'm Special Agent Madden, and this is Agent Phillips. We're from the FBI. We'd like to ask you a few questions." Madden declined to offer his hand, and Ratcliff, perhaps sensing that the slight was intentional, did likewise. The truth was, Kelly was right. He despised this man who represented everything that was wrong with law enforcement.

Of course, it was bad enough that he was a sexual predator who preyed on the innocent. What made it worse was that he did it under the color of law, and that reflected poorly on everyone involved in law enforcement, from meter-maids all the way up to the FBI. The only thing Madden felt thankful for was the fact that at least Ratcliff wasn't black, because that would have been the double whammy.

Madden couldn't count the number of times he had heard the first reports of some heinous crime and silently prayed that the perpetrator was not black. Because he knew, as every black person with any sense of social awareness knew, that whenever a black face was plastered under national headlines for doing something awful, it lowered the stock of every black person in the country. For many, it was all the proof they needed to justify their distrust and fear of blacks, and their belief that black people were simply 'lesser than'.

Madden looked around the room for a suitable chair that he could use but then decided he wasn't going to be there long enough for that.

"I've read your statement, so I'm familiar with the basics of what happened to you. But you're a detective that has been on the job for some time, so you know the drill. We're here to see if maybe some memory might be jogged loose as we dig into it a bit." Ratcliff nodded and put his ice cream down to give Madden his full attention.

Madden had seen his pictures in the file, but seeing him in the flesh, he marveled at the fact that he was even more handsome in person. Even though his face was lacerated, swollen and discolored, he still looked like he could easily leave the force tomorrow and start a new career as a model next week. It was no wonder the woman from the bar had left with him so readily. But that made him even more dangerous than your typical predatory rapist, because most people would never believe that a person who looked the way he did would need to take it by force when there were so many women throwing it at him. Of course, those people confused rape as a crime of passion instead of what it really was: a crime of power.

"So, let's start at the beginning," Madden said as he took a small notepad out of his breast pocket and flipped it open. "You got off work between 6:00 and 6:30, and you had a date with a young lady you met on the internet. A Miss Maurine Danvers, correct?"

"Yeah," said Ratcliff. "She had been blowing my phone up all day, hoping we could get together. Feel free to verify that with the phone company."

"Sure," replied Madden, his voice hinting at sarcasm. "So, you and Miss Danvers meet at a bar. How did you two get on?"

"She was a nice girl," he said, nodding his head. "Sweet face, nice figure." He glanced at Phillips and shifted uncomfortably in his bed. "But I was tired. I'd had a long day, I was tired and I hadn't eaten. And I didn't really feel like springing for dinner for this chick, if you know what I mean. So, I tried to excuse myself so I could get home and tuck myself into a pizza and the last half of the game. But she kept whining about how she was new in town and was dying to see some of the sights, so I agreed to drive her around a bit."

"Right. And that's how you ended up in the park?"

"Yeah. I think she was hoping for a little 'Inspiration Point' scenario, and that was the best I could find on short notice."

"I understand," said Madden. He paused to flip through his notepad a bit. "Now, I've also read Miss Danvers' statement, and while there are certainly differences from the beginning in your individual recollections of the evening, up to this point the variances are fairly minor. What happened between the time you parked and right before you were approached by the suspects?"

"Well, we started chatting, just shooting the shit, and the next thing I know she's in my lap with her tongue halfway down my throat. Not that I was really trying to push her off too hard, you know..." said Ratcliff, tilting his head and raising his eyebrows in a knowing way.

"Right. Sweet face, nice figure. I remember," said Madden. "What happened next?"

"Out of the blue, my door is snatched open and I'm staring at two fuckers in those freaky-ass masks! I only get a moment to look at them before they drag me out and hit me over the head with something. And the next thing I know, I wake up in the back of a van. I don't know how long I was out."

"And did your attackers say anything to you during that initial altercation?"

"Not a word."

"So, when you woke up in the van—" began Madden when he was interrupted by Phillips, exactly the way they had planned it.

"Before we move on," she said, taking a step forward, "if I could just ask a couple other quick questions. This is the point at which your story and Miss Danvers' story are in greatest contrast. You stated that she 'threw herself' at you, while she remembers it quite differently. She says you attacked her."

"That's total bullshit. Look, we both had a couple drinks, so maybe that clouded her memory. Besides, I got the impression that she was one of those women with a really fragile ego. Maybe she thought I had some friends yank me out of the car just to end the date. Who knows? Maybe she's just psycho. I've known lots of women that were."

"That's possible. But how do you explain the bruises on her face? The black eye?" asked Phillips, staring at him.

Ratcliff shrugged his shoulders. "Maybe my elbow hit her as I was struggling to fight these guys off. Or maybe they touched her up a little bit to scare her into not saying anything."

"I suppose that's possible," said Phillips, "but if that were the case, why did she call 911 immediately after they drove away to report that you were the one that assaulted her?"

Ratcliff shrugged again. “Maybe she was afraid they’d come back.”

As Phillips and Ratcliff silently stared at each other, each waiting for the other to say something provocative, Madden took the opportunity to jump in.

“We can examine that in more detail at a later date,” he said, “but right now, I’d like to get back to establishing the timeline.” Ratcliff rolled his eyes as he shifted his gaze from Phillips back to Madden. “What was the first thing you noticed when you regained consciousness?”

“Darkness. I had some kind of bag over my head.”

“And what did you hear?”

“Nothing.”

“Then how do you know you were in a vehicle?”

“Well, for one thing, I could hear the engine. And I could feel the vehicle swaying.”

“And they didn’t say anything to you?”

“No. And I didn’t move right away. I laid there for a while, hoping they would think I was still out. But I still didn’t hear anything.”

“Okay, think back for a second. Close your eyes.”

“Fuck, I already told you I didn’t—”

“I know, I know. But just humor me for a minute, and we’ll get out of here and let you get back to your, uh, ice cream.”

Ratcliff huffed in frustration, but closed his eyes as directed.

“You’ve just woken up. You hear the van’s engine, rising and falling as it accelerates and slows. You feel it lurch as it turns corners and brakes are applied. Any brake squealing?”

“No.”

“Anything unusual about the engine? Any ticks? Knocks?”

“No.”

“You said you didn’t hear any voices. What about other noises inside the cabin? Any heels clicking on the floor?”

“No.”

“What about phones? Did you hear any phones ring?”

“No. Wait. Now that you mention it, I did hear a slight vibration repeat a few times.”

Madden looked at Phillips. “Could be incoming texts. Anything else?”

“I don’t think so.”

"Okay, go ahead and open your eyes."

Ratcliff did as he was told.

"We're making some progress," said Madden. "So, you drive along for a while..."

"Maybe another twenty minutes or so. It's kind of hard to say, because I had a headache and my muscles were cramping. So, it's possible it only seemed that long."

"Then they stopped the van and—"

"Let's move this along," Ratcliff interrupted, glancing at his bowl of melting rocky road. "I lay in the back until they picked me up and hauled me into the office building. I heard people going in and out of the building, but no voices or anything else. And I suppose you've seen the video, so I think you know as much as I do about that," he said sourly.

"We saw what the video showed. But you had a view of the entire room—"

"I didn't see anything else that I thought would be helpful in this case."

"Okay, okay," said Madden, attempting to deescalate the tension. "Let's move on to what happened after they turned the camera off. One of the guys attacked you?"

"Yeah. Real tough guy. Kicking a man with his hands cuffed behind his back."

"What brought that on?"

"I made a few comments about the chick that had just...attacked me."

"How did you know it was a chick?"

Ratcliff smiled slightly. "If there's one thing I know, it's chicks."

Phillips scoffed and shook her head.

"And during all this, no one said a single word to you?" asked Madden.

"The only thing that was said was when the one guy stopped the other guy from kicking me. The tough guy said something like 'get off me'. No. 'Get the fuck off me.'"

"Why don't you try closing your eyes again?" Ratcliff stared at him defiantly. "Come on Detective, we both want to get this over with." Ratcliff shook his head with irritation, but complied.

"Okay. The one guy is kicking and punching you. But he didn't say anything before that?"

"No."

"How long was he beating you?"

"Seemed like forever, but it couldn't have been more than a few seconds."

"And then, the one guy pulls him off—"

"No, grabs him. Like in a bear hug."

"And he says?"

"'Get the fuck off me'. Wait. There was something else." Ratcliff squeezes his eyes tighter as he concentrates on recalling the memory. "There was another word. It sounded like 'get the fuck off me, itch.' Or maybe 'get the fuck off me, ash.'" Madden and Phillips both began scribbling in their note books. Ratcliff opened his eyes.

"That's it," he said. "That's all I can remember. Are we done here?"

"For now," said Madden as he reached into his pocket for a business card. "But if you remember anything else, please—"

"Yeah, yeah, leave it on the table," said Ratcliff as he reached for his dessert.

As Madden turned to leave, he wondered what kind of ice cream they served in the state penitentiary.

Chapter 42

The hallways outside Ratcliff's hospital room were crowded, and several people entered the elevator with Madden and Phillips, so they waited until they were back in the car before either of them spoke.

"What do you think?" asked Phillips as she adjusted her seat belt.

"Could be something, could be nothing at all. 'Itch'? 'Ash'? The word he heard could have been 'bitch' or something else entirely. Witnesses under that degree of stress are hardly what one would consider reliable."

"But if it's a name, then at least we have something to start digging into."

"Right, but what kind of name? First name? Last name? Nickname? The possibilities are endless."

Madden started the engine, but they both sat quiet for a few moments, staring out the window.

"Let's back up for a second," said Madden. "Let's go over what we know. First, we know that these guys—and possibly girls—are willing to travel, so there's no telling where they're headquartered. Could be New York, could be Nashville, could be anywhere, so that doesn't help us. But we suspect that they have military backgrounds."

"And if they served in the military, we can eliminate the rest of the public as suspects, and start our search in the VA databases."

"Exactly," said Madden.

"So that narrows it down to about 20 million people," said Phillips.

"Not exactly," said Madden. "Something tells me these guys are more highly trained than a typical soldier. That may be a stretch, but at least it gives us a much smaller pool to play in, and we can widen the circle from there. So, we should start looking at Special Ops, Seals, Rangers, etc. Also, as Bainbridge likes to keep explicitly pointing out, the suspects are more than likely African American."

"Black Seals," said Phillips, nodding her head. "Can't be a ton of them, right?"

"Exactly."

"Anything else?" asked Phillips as she began jotting more notes in her notepad.

"Yeah. I keep going back to motive. It's unlikely that these people just woke up one day and decided that they had nothing better to do than to make the world a better place by attacking dirty cops. Something had to have sparked it. Something happened that set at least one of them off. The most obvious event would be that they had a close family member fall victim to some unprovoked police attack. Just for the hell of it, let's start with all the recent black victims of police brutality that have been in the headlines. Check all their family histories for relatives connected to the military, between the ages of twenty-five and fifty."

"Wouldn't it be something if it were that simple?"

"It would," said Madden. "But you never can tell. Somebody has got to win the lotto, right?"

"I guess," said Phillips as she continued to scribble in her book. "And exactly what name, or names, should we be concentrating on?"

Madden sighed. "That's the tricky part. Let's start with any name that contains the words 'itch' or 'ash', including nicknames. 'Ash' could be short for 'Ashford', or it could be a nickname of someone that smokes a lot. Who the hell knows?"

"Got it," said Phillips. "I hope the geek squad likes coffee, 'cause they're not going to be sleeping for a while."

Madden nodded, put the car in gear and headed back to the hotel.

After dropping Phillips off, Madden drove to the office building that Ratcliff had been found in. The area was abandoned but covered in yellow police tape. The crime scene team had already spent two days there collecting prints and fibers, all of which were already back at the labs in D.C. being analyzed. But Madden knew in his bones that it was probably all pointless. These guys were too good to leave prints or any kind of fibers that could be traced in any way.

However, they did make a mistake, didn't they? He ducked under a strip of caution tape that was draped across the front door and tried the handle. It was locked, as he expected. He began walking the perimeter of the building, peering through the windows as he let his mind wander.

Something happened in here. One of these guys came unhinged. Ratcliff thought it was because he made comments about the female. Correction, alleged female. So, what were they? Husband and wife? Girlfriend and boyfriend? Or were they just friends? Maybe fellow soldiers who served together? While it was true that the ban on women serving in combat roles had been lifted in 2013, only a trickle had actually been integrated. But even though they weren't actually performing in combat, there were still many women who trained for it just like men and were every bit as tough as their male counterparts.

What would prompt a woman to join this group? More than likely, one of two things: either she had lost someone to police violence, or she had joined to be with her man. And why would a group like this invite a woman to join? Probably one or the other of the same two reasons. Of course, thought Madden, this was all just a guess, but at least it gave the researchers one more thing to look for—a male and female with some type of relationship. Husband and wife would be obvious, boyfriend and girlfriend much less so, but beggars couldn't be choosers.

He came around the far side of the building and walked back to his car. Standing beside the driver's door, he scanned the area. Why here? It was abandoned, and obviously they made it work for them, but it was far from ideal. The building wasn't soundproof, and anyone could have drifted by and noticed what was going on. PROPR may have identified this place ahead of time, but it couldn't have been anything other than an emergency backup location. They must have originally planned to carry this out someplace more secure. Maybe they had rented another warehouse, like they had used with the first cop. Or maybe even Ratcliff's house.

The standing theory was that it was just a lucky coincidence that the group had grabbed Ratcliff when he was parked with the woman. But now Madden was starting to realize that it likely wasn't coincidence at all. The woman was lucky alright, but it wasn't that she happened to be in the right place at the right time, it was that PROPR happened to be in the right place at the right time. This was a rescue. They were probably surveilling Ratcliff, saw what he was doing and were compelled to act. That was a bold move, them putting the entire operation on the line to save some random woman that they knew absolutely nothing about.

Terrorists with heart, thought Madden, smiling grimly as he climbed into the car and started the engine. He didn't know whether this would make them easier to catch or not, but he knew that once the press started working this angle, things on the street were going to get hotter. And he was feeling more than enough heat already.

Madden and his team were scheduled to fly out early the next morning, but they missed their flight and had to catch the afternoon connection. They had left the hotel in plenty of time, but it took them twice as long as normal to get to the airport because the streets were clogged with marchers. There was a throbbing mass of people carrying signs and chanting their support of black rights and protection from dirty cops. Only a couple of the signs being carried actually contained the word "PROPR", but it was clear that it was the actions of the terrorist group that had drawn these people into the streets.

Back in D.C., things were even more hectic. Again, they fought traffic every inch of the way from the airport to their offices, dodging protesters and trying to find lesser used shortcuts around the main crowds.

"This is starting to get scary," said Ken Tassel, one of the younger agents, smiling slightly. He was seated in the back of the black SUV with Madden. He obviously meant to be flippant, but there was an edge of real fear in his voice. Madden looked at him, stone-faced, and nodded once in response. Tassel had only said what everyone else was thinking.

You would seldom get any to openly admit it, but the only thing that truly scared the average law enforcement officer was the mob. Single suspects, pairs, even small groups, were hardly any challenge at all. No matter how many guns they had, the cops had more. And no matter how fast they ran, the cops could follow, especially once they had eyes in the sky.

But mobs were an entirely different ball game. Not only were they completely unpredictable, but you couldn't open fire on a mob the way you could open fire on an individual. The protocol was completely different. It was one of the few situations in which the cops were completely at the disadvantage.

You never knew when a peaceful group was going to turn violent, or when a single member of the crowd might pull a gun and fire at the cops. And the cops were handicapped, forced to resort to batons, rubber bullets, tear gas and pepper spray to try to keep the powder keg from exploding. Even when they made arrests, many of the people were never actually charged. And mobs were fully aware of their advantages, knowledge that made them all the more dangerous. If this was what the rest of the country looked like, which was what the news reports were beginning to show, things were going to get scary, indeed.

When they finally arrived back at HQ, the first thing Madden did was go to his office and call Kelly.

"Hey, hon," she said. Her voice sounded different. Not quite as energetic and carefree as usual.

"Hey."

"Are you alright?" she asked.

"I'm fine. You?"

"I'm okay, but I'm starting to get worried," said his wife. "What the hell is going on out there?"

Madden wasn't sure how much he should tell her. To be honest, he wasn't sure exactly how much he himself knew about what was going on out there. Things had been moving fast in the last 24 hours, and much of that time they had been in the field and therefore not monitoring the news channels. What he did know he had picked up from news broadcasts, tweets and a few emailed reports viewed on his laptop in transit to and from the airports.

"I still haven't had a full briefing," he said, "but it appears that this group PROPR, that abducted the two cops, is getting a lot of the citizenry riled up. People were already pissed off and frustrated. It doesn't take much to set them off."

"It seems like it's getting scary out there," she said.

Madden chuckled. "That's the second time I've heard that today. Don't worry, babe, we're on the case. We already have some significant clues, and we're a lot closer to making some real progress on this than we were just a couple of days ago. With a bit of luck, we might even get this closed in the next few days." He hoped that he sounded more optimistic than he felt.

"Okay," said Kelly. "Just be careful."

"I will," he said. "I'll try to be home in time for dinner."

After they hung up, Madden checked his messages. As expected, there was one from Bainbridge. He wanted a meeting immediately upon his return. Figured.

This time, when Madden entered the office, his boss didn't waste time playing the game of ignoring him for the first few minutes as he normally did. He was agitated and ready to engage immediately.

"What do you have for me?" he spat before Madden even had a chance to get properly seated.

"The last victim thinks that he might have heard a name or a snippet of a name. We've got the researchers working on it. But it may take a while."

"Do you know what's going on in the streets?" asked Bainbridge. Madden wasn't sure if the question was rhetorical or not, but he decided it was probably best to answer.

"I read some reports on the way in, but I'm still working my way through them."

"You're still working your way through them?" mimicked Bainbridge. "There's a storm brewing, and it's threatening to drown this country in a sea of red if we don't stop it!"

"Sir, I understand that people are starting to get tense, but I don't see how we could be doing any more than what we've done so far. Even if we had more money and manpower, I'm not sure how much more we could accomplish right now."

Bainbridge leaned back in his chair and sighed. His hands formed a steeple beneath his nose as he took a few moments to think.

"These are your people, Madden. What do you think it is that this group ultimately wants?" he asked.

Madden ignored the inferred racial connection. "I'm not sure, sir. My opinion is that they simply want what they've been saying they've wanted from the very beginning: protection for black people from cops that are predisposed to abuse."

"And what do you think they expect to see as proof that they've achieved their objective?"

Madden had actually been thinking about that a lot lately, and he didn't think Bainbridge would like his answer.

"To be honest, sir, I'm not sure that they're looking for anything specific to happen. It seems to me that they've decided that their mission is to create awareness; to shine a spotlight on not only the problem, but on what they propose as the solution."

Bainbridge tilted his head and began to gaze at some point on the far wall. Madden thought he could see a slight twitch under the man's right eye. "That will be all," Bainbridge said, never taking his eyes from whatever it is he saw. Madden let himself out.

Back at his office, Madden finally had a chance to get comfortable and read through the remainder of the reports he had received.

What he read in these briefs made his blood run cold. He now understood why both Kelly and Bainbridge had reacted the way they did. Kelly couldn't know a fraction of what Bainbridge knew from the various intel that he had received. If she had, he had no doubt that she would be ten times more freaked out than she actually was.

In one of the reports was a map showing pinpoints of what the analysts called 'hot spots', which were places where the protests and demonstrations had a high potential for developing into something a lot more dangerous. That was the frightening part. These pinpoints were all over the country, mostly in the larger cities, but there were many small towns that were also joining the ranks of what many had dubbed the 'PROPR Revolution'. And they weren't just comprised of blacks. People of all races and nationalities were joining the effort.

Madden's eyes glazed over, and he started contemplating what their other options were for containing this, or at least slowing it down. But he also had to admit that he was conflicted. What these people wanted was simply the same rights and considerations for blacks that already existed for whites. Who, other than actual racists, could be against that? And as a black man, he was as aware of the longing for justice as anyone. Needless to say, being a government official had only given him limited protections. So, he felt no malice towards these demonstrators. Quite the opposite. The difference between the demonstrators and the terrorist group was that the demonstrators had not resorted to violence. At least, not yet.

And that was the issue. They needed to find a way to nip this in the bud as quickly as possible before people who were otherwise law-abiding citizens got swept up in the frenzy of the moment and started doing things that would change, and possibly even destroy, their lives.

Madden had studied 'mob mentality' in college in some of the psychology classes he had taken. He had also had some training on it when he joined the bureau. Some of his colleagues didn't have a lot of sympathy for people who succumbed to 'mob rage'. They believed that each individual was responsible for their actions at all times and that they needed to own the consequences of those actions.

But Madden knew it wasn't quite as simple as that. There was a shift that happened in some people's brains once they were part of a group of riled up, emotional people. There was a 'group think' that took place, that had the potential to override the minds of some people and make them susceptible to doing things they would have otherwise never considered doing. He had seen it in person many times, and he knew that it was a powerful force that only fools took lightly.

There was a knock at Madden's office door. Somehow, he knew by the sound of it that it was Phillips.

"Enter," he said.

"Hey, Chief," said Phillips as she walked into the office, her hobble almost unnoticeable.

"Hey," said Madden as he attempted to rub the fatigue from his eyes. "Have you seen these reports?"

"Yes, I have. My guess is that Bainbridge is grumpy."

"To say the least. If we don't get a handle on this soon, there are a lot of other government officials that are going to get even grumpier. Tell me you've been to research and you have some good news for me."

"I have spoken to them and I do have news, but I'm not sure how good it is. They're putting together a list that is already 257 names long and growing. But field agents have already run down a third of those names and more or less eliminated most of them as possibilities. We're looking deeper into a couple, but I'm not super optimistic. It might be time to widen the net."

"What do you suggest?" asked Madden.

"Right now, we're searching for iterations of 'itch' and 'ash'. Maybe we should switch out the first letters; add words like 'otch' and 'etch, 'osh' and 'ish'."

"It can't hurt," said Madden. "Right now, I'll take whatever I can get."

"You look tired," she said.

"Me? That's the pot calling the kettle black. At least promise me you're not going to be sleeping on your office sofa tonight."

"It saves me the commute time, and the savings in gas is my contribution to the fight against global warming," she said, smiling. "Besides, it's not like I have anything in particular to go home to. Speaking of which, how is Kelly dealing with all this?"

Kelly and Phillips knew each other from numerous parties and backyard BBQs that they had attended together, and more or less considered themselves to be friends. Kelly had always said she'd like to get to know the agent better, but Phillips kept most people at arm's length. She wasn't exactly antisocial, but neither was she a social butterfly. She often described herself as 'nonsocial', which, apparently, was a real word.

"She's concerned," said Madden. "And now that I've read these reports, I don't blame her. And living in D.C. just makes it all the more tenuous."

Phillips nodded her head. "So, let's get out there and put an end to this circus show, before all the freaks get warmed up and into the game."

"I'm all for it, but can I at least go home and have a last supper with my wife?"

"Leave granted. Sir," said Phillips, smiling again as she strolled towards the door.

Chapter 43

On the drive back to L.A., Ish turned on the radio, and while flipping through stations came across a talk show. It was some type of NPR public radio station that was in the middle of a pledge drive. Ish was about to keep moving down the dial until he heard the topic. The host was a woman, Rhonda Keyes, and her guest was a professor of sociology from some university that Ish had never heard of. His name was Professor Naidu. They both sounded black, but Keyes was obviously born and raised in the U.S., her slight Brooklyn accent being a dead giveaway, while Naidu sounded South African.

"Thank you so much for the donations we've received so far this hour," Rhonda was saying. "We'll get back to our guest and the discussion of the PROPR Revolution in just a moment. But first, I wanted to let everyone know that we are only $600 shy of our goal for the hour. So, if you are one of the people that listens to this show every day and derives value from it, please call in. A small donation of just $25 a month..."

Ish tuned out. There were few things he found more annoying than public radio stations begging for handouts. But it was one of Layla's great loves, so when they had started dating, he had been forced to listen to it from time to time when they were in the car. Layla felt that there was a lack of both culture and unbiased news in the media, and that the nation's public radio stations helped to bridge that gap. Not only was she a member of several stations, donating to their pledge drives several times a year, she even volunteered her time on a regular basis, answering phones for them or doing other minor chores around the office. She felt it was her way of giving back.

Personally, Ish wasn't convinced. He couldn't understand why these stations didn't just sell advertising like everyone else. He was all for restricting the monopoly that the corrupt, money-grubbing big corporations had on the media, but to refuse all advertising was to assume that there were no good companies out there with ad dollars to spend. That seemed like an overly pessimistic view for organizations that came off as being pretty 'airy fairy', as one of his aunties used to say.

But he was young and in love, so he listened to the stations, sent in a few dollars every now and then, and even spent some time volunteering with Layla. He would have done anything to be able to spend more time with the woman he loved. And the cool thing was that Layla knew how much of an effort it was for him to do these things and often told him that it made her love him even more. So, of course, he gave it even more effort.

But that was a long time ago; at least two lifetimes in the past. Layla wasn't around, and he had had no other reason to listen to any of these stations. Until now.

Ish turned his attention back to the radio show, just as the host was profusely thanking some especially charitable person who had just called in and donated $5,000.

"That really made my hour!" she said. "Not only did we knock this hour's goal out of the park, but we got a big leap on next hour's goal! Thank you again. So now I would like to get back to our interview with Professor Naidu. If you missed the beginning of this segment, we've been speaking with the professor regarding the societal impact of the terrorist organization PROPR and how it's changing the thinking of the ordinary citizen on the street."

"Professor," she continued, "before the break you were saying that you believe that PROPR is actually the natural evolution of the civil rights movement in this country. Can you please expand on that?"

"Well, Rhonda," he began, his accent thick and melodious, "it's perfectly clear when you trace the history of civil rights in America back to the inception of slavery and map the progression of where African Americans were to where they are now. African Americans have always opted for non-violence methods to achieve liberation before resorting to more radical means."

"I understand, but I'm sure there are people that will point to certain black civil rights figures and organizations, particularly Malcolm X and the Black Panthers, as examples of periods in our history where blacks were more prone to advocating violence to effect change."

"Neither Malcolm X nor the Black Panthers were created in a vacuum. Each was a response to the frustrations experienced by Black America in its attempt to convince the white establishment to accept and treat them as equals. Only then did you have people like Malcolm X preaching the 'any means necessary' doctrine. You have to keep in mind that African Americans striking out violently in their demands for civil rights was a last-ditch effort; an act of desperation. Black people in America are labeled a 'minority' for a reason. The fact that they only account for perhaps 12%-16% of the population makes it clear that they could never win a 'race war', so any violence they might express is really only symbolic or simply an emotional expression of their anger. Fortunately for the blacks in this country, these isolated outbursts have been enough to slowly change minds and sometimes hearts. The result has been some real progress."

"So that brings us to the present," said the host, "and I have to ask you the most obvious question: is PROPR good or bad for Black America?"

Naidu chuckled. "Rhonda, I wish it were as simple as a yes or no answer, but it is much more complex than that. First, you must separate the actions of this group from the reactions to them. I think only the truest of radicals in this country would ever publicly endorse the idea of ordinary citizens taking the law into their own hands, especially in a manner as violent as what we have seen from PROPR in the last couple of weeks. However, one only need look out their window to see the effect, much of which I would argue could ultimately prove to be positive."

"You're right, this is confusing. It sounds like you're simultaneously both praising them and condemning them in the same breath," said Rhonda.

"Let me clarify," said Naidu. "I am a civilized man and a scholar, and as such I agree with most civilized, scholarly people that violence is something that we should always strive to avoid. However, one cannot deny the fact that violence is often effective. In fact, while many would like to believe that violence is never the answer, the reality is that violence is sometimes the only answer. If a man breaks into your home with bloodlust in his eyes, intent upon doing harm to your family, the option for diplomacy is probably nonexistent. Many black people feel that White America has been breaking into their homes and harming their families for generations. For many, violence is a very viable option." He took a moment to clear his throat.

"Am I conflicted in regards to my position on the use of violence to effect change in civil rights policies? Absolutely. But this is the situation that the government has created, or at the very least allowed to develop. As my father used to say, you can close the door and douse the lights, but it will not prevent your chickens from coming home to roost."

"I read a piece you wrote in *The Atlantic*," said Rhonda, "in which you stated that you believed that America was on the precipice of a civil rights upheaval; that the racial imbalance had existed for such a long time without any significant progress that a shakeup was imminent. You wrote this several months ago, long before anyone knew of the existence of PROPR. Do you see the emergence of this group as a validation of your prediction?"

"Yes, in many ways I do. But even I could not have imagined that the movement would be so organized or would come together so quickly. The way that this organization has galvanized the nation is fascinating to me as someone who has spent his life studying social evolution."

"A lot of people have expressed concern about how this 'movement', if you will, is taking form. People are beginning to fear for their safety in the streets. Do you have any predictions about how this may ultimately play out?"

"That is very difficult to say. It depends on how long PROPR can continue to act with impunity. They are like a social snowball. The longer they continue rolling down the hill, the larger and more powerful they will become. And the harder they will be to stop."

"Let me switch gears for a moment," said Rhonda. "Some public officials have suggested that once this group is finally brought to justice, in addition to the other charges, they also be charged with hate crimes for their actions. What is your response to that?"

"Hate crimes?" replied Naidu. "I think that would be difficult to secure a conviction on in a court of law. And it's not like the prosecutors need any additional charges. The crimes they have indisputably committed are already enough to get them life in prison. Neither police officers nor white people are a protected group, unlike minorities, gays and the like. To try to charge these individuals with hate crimes would be seen by many as a complete lack of regard for what inspired the actions to begin with; namely, police abuse in the minority communities."

"Professor Naidu," said Rhonda after a brief pause, "normally we don't allow listeners to call into the show. However, my producer has just informed me that our Twitter feed has been literally blowing up for the last fifteen minutes. There are so many people with comments and questions that we thought it might be interesting to break tradition and open the lines up to a few callers, if you're okay with that."

"Certainly," said Naidu.

"Fantastic! Hello, caller, you're on the air. What is your name, and where are you calling from?"

"This is Juan," said the caller, "and I'm calling from Houston, Texas." The man was clearly of Hispanic descent. Ish was fairly sure the accent was Peruvian.

"Welcome. Did you have a question for the professor?"

"Yes. There's been all this talk going back and forth about black and white, but what about us Latinos? We get beat up by the police, we get shot by the police, we get arrested by the police for no good reason. How come no one is talking about our communities?"

"You make a very valid point, Juan," said Naidu. "The people in the media—no offense, Rhonda—are often like a mule with blinders that only sees what is right in front of it. And like a mule eating apples from a shady tree, they are usually only concerned with the low-hanging fruit. This organization, PROPR, has made it a point to focus on officers that have violated the rights of African Americans, so that is what the media focuses on. So, I can understand your frustration. However, a rising tide lifts all boats, so it's very likely that any positive change that is derived from this situation will benefit all minorities, not just blacks."

"Thank you, caller. Let's try line eight. Hi. What's your name and where are you calling from?"

"This is Cathy and I'm calling from eastern Mississippi, and I got a couple of questions for your professor there."

"Great," said Rhonda. "What would you like to ask him?"

"Why aren't the police doing more to stop these people?"

"Well," said Naidu, "I am not privy to any particulars of the investigation, but I would imagine that the authorities are doing everything in their power to track down the members of the organization and bring them into custody."

"I'm not just talking about this organization, PROPR or whatever it's called. I'm talking about the people that are marching in the street. These people are trespassing, looting, attacking innocent bystanders—"

"I, personally, am not aware of any such actions," said Naidu.

"Are you calling me a liar?"

"Certainly not. I simply have not heard of any such reports myself. Of course, there have been minor incidents of vandalism, but that's always associated with these kinds of events. Rhonda, are you familiar with that of which Cathy speaks?"

"Actually, no I'm not, and I've been following this story all over the country for the last two weeks. The only incident that I'm aware of that might possibly fit that bill is an altercation between pro-PROPR demonstrators and members of the African American civil rights group #BlackForLife, and that was very mild. Cathy, if you tell me where these reports you heard originated, I'll promise to look into it for you."

"They're everywhere!" said Cathy, her voice rising. "This is a war on America! This is a war on white people! We're becoming minorities in our own damn country! It's time for us to take it back! It's time we kill all the nig—"

The call was cut off.

"I'm sorry," said Rhonda, "but this show does not allow hate speech. We are here to create a civilized dialog about important topics, not spew vitriol and racial slurs. I apologize for everyone that had to hear that. Professor, do you have time for a couple more calls?"

"Of course, Rhonda. I am here as long as you need me," said Naidu.

"Hi, caller," said Rhonda. "What's your name and where are you calling from?"

"Hello. My name is Theo and I'm calling from the city of Chicago." The man had a heavy British accent. "First, I'd like to thank you, Rhonda, and Professor Naidu, for presenting this show. I've found it very interesting. You've probably already guessed that I'm not a native of Illinois, and as an outsider I find it particularly interesting to be able to observe American social change in action. But while I agree with much of what the professor has said, I find it curious that he has only spoken positively regarding how this situation may affect the common citizen. What about the issue of how this could inspire copycat vigilantes and endanger the lives of innocent police officers?"

"Theo, you are correct," said Naidu. "In situations like this there is always the danger of people taking things too far. It's always been like that with the civil rights movement in this country. Even with Dr. Martin Luther King, Jr., who unwaveringly preached a non-violent path to change, there were followers who supposedly supported him but still chose to strike out in violence. Should Dr. King have abandoned his efforts simply because of a handful of upstarts that were beyond his control? Of course not. If I could expand on my previous chicken analogy, you cannot make an omelet without breaking a few eggs."

"With all due respect," said Theo, "I think it's very callous of you to refer to the possible attack, maybe even the murder, of innocent police officers as 'breaking a few eggs'. These men and women have one of the toughest jobs in the world, putting their lives on the line day in and day out, week after week, month after month, year after year. I don't think they deserve to become targets simply because there are a few bad apples amongst their ranks."

"That is very well stated, Theo," said Naidu. "And I can find no fault with what you have just said. However, you began your comments by stating that you also agreed with most of what I have been saying during this show. So, what is your opinion of PROPR? Do you consider their actions constructive or destructive?"

Theo paused, but you could hear him sigh over the phone. "Much like yourself, I too am conflicted. I have plenty of black friends, several of which have confided in me stories of the mistreatment they have suffered at the hands of unscrupulous members of the police force. But my father was a police officer in London for fourteen years before moving here to Chicago where he's served on the force for the last ten. He is as straight and honest as the day is long, as are most of the officers that serve with him, so I know firsthand that not every cop is bad." He sighed again. "But there are bad ones. Here in Chicago and many other places. Nothing else has seemed to work, and the problem is only getting worse. Maybe PROPR is the only answer. But what do we say to the family of some innocent cop that gets caught up in this firestorm?"

Now it was Naidu's turn to sigh. "That, sir," he said, "is unfortunately a question I must confess I do not have the answer to."

"Thank you, Theo," said Rhonda. "I think we have time for one more call. Hello, caller. Please state your name and where you're calling from."

"Hi, Rhonda, I love your show! This is Jasmine from Oakland, California. I'm an undergrad at Mills College, and we've been discussing this topic quite a bit on campus. A lot of us at Mills believe that this represents a historic moment in the struggle for civil rights in this country, unlike anything seen since the sixties. While some of the students denounce the violent tactics that PROPR is using, most agree with their ultimate objective. What I would like to ask the professor is, what can we as young people do to support this movement in a legal, positive manner?"

"That is an excellent question, Jasmine, and thank you for posing it! I am always delighted to see young adults like yourself showing an interest in social politics. It seems that so many people fail to stay cognizant of the fact that the children of today will definitely be the leaders of tomorrow, and that the sooner we can get them thinking like leaders, the sooner we can get them to open their minds to new possibilities and options. But on to your question—I believe you must think in terms of both long term and short-term strategies.

"In the long term, it all comes down to legislation. There will always be discrimination. There will always be racism and bigotry and xenophobia, and try as we might, we cannot force people to change their beliefs or the way they feel. However, we are a country governed by laws, and while we cannot govern how people feel, we can, to a large degree, govern how they act. So, in the long term, I would encourage you and your friends to get as involved in the political system as your time and interests allow. Sometimes the easiest way to help create new policy is to become one of the policy makers."

"That's great advice," said Rhonda. "Many years ago, right after receiving my undergraduate degree, I ran for and won a seat on the city council of my home town. It was an invaluable experience that has served me well in everything I've done since. What advice would you give Jasmine for the short term?"

"For the short term," said Naidu, "I think we have to rely on the tried and true techniques that have worked to create social change the world over: demonstrations, protests, marching, signing petitions and so on. Some people believe that these methods are no longer effective, but they are wrong. In this fast spinning world of Twitter and Instagram and Facebook, people have shorter attention spans than they have ever had since the beginning of time. When it comes to news, they tend to focus on the big headlines, blocking everything else out, and they don't even focus on that for long. So, the trick is to make sure that these important topics appear on their radar, as big and as frequently as possible. If you hammer a nail long enough, even with the smallest hammer, eventually it will find a home in the wood."

"Thank you, Professor," said Rhonda. "I think that's all we have time for today—wait!" There was a brief pause. "My producer has just informed me that we have breaking news. Moments ago, a member of the group PROPR allegedly tried to assault a police officer in Hollywood, and was captured and is now in custody!"

Chapter 44

Ish couldn't believe what he had just heard. He could feel his blood pressure skyrocketing, his hands gripping the steering wheel so tightly that his knuckles were turning white. He forced himself to take some deep breaths, willing his heart rate to slow. No one observing him would have even noticed the change. His face was blank and stony, but inside he was reeling. He turned his focus back to the radio program, but he must have hit a bad reception area, because the broadcast was cutting in and out, a jumble of static and word fragments. By the time the static cleared, Rhonda was back to rallying for the pledge drive. He turned the radio off.

How the fuck did this happen? And who was it that they had captured? It had to be a mistake. He just couldn't believe that anyone on the team would be reckless enough to try something alone and unplanned. Then again, maybe he could believe it. He thought back to his conversation with Chad about how unstable he thought Bird was becoming. But was he unstable enough to go off on his own and do something rash? And what the hell would he even be doing in Hollywood? He was supposed to be in Santa Monica touring the offices.

After checking that the path was clear, Ish maneuvered his car over to the far-right lane and took the first offramp. He needed to sit for a minute and try to get his head around this. As he came off the freeway, he spotted a supermarket and parked at the edge of the lot. He tried Chad's cell but got no answer. His stress levels were continuing to rise. Calling anyone else was risky. What if the police had the phone and were just waiting for his call? If someone was compromised, Bird was the most obvious choice, but it also could have just as easily been Jag, Ma'am or even Chad himself. He needed more info. He turned the radio back on and began station surfing, looking for the news.

He was surprised how many of the radio stations were now in Spanish, especially those with the stronger signals. Fortunately, he spoke the language fluidly, but none of the stations he paused on, Spanish or English, had anything to say about the PROPR story. He leaned his head back against the headrest and took another deep breath, forcing his heart rate to slow even more. He again focused on the idea that this had to be a mistake. He leaned forward and once more began spinning the knob, cycling through the stations that he was able to receive. Finally, after another fifteen minutes of fiddling, he had a hit.

"And the top news of the hour," said the announcer, "is the story coming out of Hollywood, Florida that a member of the alleged terrorist group PROPR attacked a police officer and was captured after an extended vehicle and foot pursuit. We have a reporter on the scene, Amy Geller. Amy, what can you tell us?"

"Hello, Ted. Details are currently sketchy. All we know right now is that an unidentified man was approached by a police officer about an hour ago here in Hollywood, Florida. Apparently, some type of altercation took place, and the officer was rendered helpless and his service revolver taken by the suspect, who then fled the scene on foot. He was apprehended after a brief pursuit and is reported as being unharmed and in custody."

"Amy, have the authorities given any clues to the man's identity?"

"No, Ted, they have not. All they have released to the press is that the man identified himself as a member of the group PROPR. But we will stay on the story and give you updates as we receive them."

"Thank you, Amy. In other news..."

Ish turned the radio off and leaned his head back against the headrest. *Fuck.* The copycats had started already.

Ish was relieved, but he knew that it wasn't a time for celebration. Even though the person who had been captured wasn't one of his people, it could still cause them some problems. For one thing, their objective had always been to win the hearts and minds of the people which, ironically, was pretty much exactly what the military had trained and hired him to do in the Middle East. If this impostor came off as a loon, it would hurt their credibility, and as a result it could sabotage their efforts in rallying people towards their common cause. Even as it became common knowledge that the guy was a copycat completely unaffiliated with PROPR, many people would still associate his actions with theirs and paint them both by the same brush.

As he drove towards Chad's house, he pondered their options for damage control. They would have to address it in the next video; that was a given. People needed to hear from them directly that this man was not associated with their organization. But maybe they could make this work for them. Maybe they could flip it around and use this guy as an example of what not to do in support of the cause. He'd have to discuss it with the group, but that was a real possibility.

Ish tapped a button to access his hands-free speaker. "Call Chad," he said.

"Calling Chad Yang, cell," replied the robotic, female voice. The phone rang for a few moments and then went to voicemail. Once the greeting finished playing and Ish heard the beep, he left a message for Chad to call him immediately. He made similar calls to Bird, Jag and Ma'am but didn't leave any messages.

He was in the process of parking his car in front of the house when his phone began to vibrate and the same female voice announced over the car speakers, "Call from Chad Yang".

"Hey, Chad," he said in greeting.

"Sorry I missed your calls. Stacy was giving us the royal tour. What's up?"

"I guess you haven't heard then," said Ish. "They captured a member of PROPR after he tangled with a cop."

"What?!" exclaimed Chad, his voice sharp with equal amounts of concern and confusion.

"Yeah, that was pretty much my reaction, too. A poser in Hollywood, Florida got into it with one of their city's finest. When he was nabbed, he said he was a member of the group."

"Shit," said Chad. Then after a moment, he added: "I don't know why I'm shocked. We always knew this was probably going to happen at some point. I guess I'm just surprised that it happened so soon."

"Same here," said Ish. "You've spent some time analyzing situational outcomes on this. What's your gut telling you about how we should react?"

"I think we have two basic options," said Chad. "We can ignore it altogether or we can publicly address it, either through video or through a press release. A video will have the most impact."

"Those were my thoughts exactly," said Ish. "Where are you now?"

"We're leaving the office. Be there in twenty."

"Cool. I'll start working on a script. See you when I see you."

By the time Chad and the rest of the crew arrived back at the house, Ish had already sketched out a rough draft of what he felt needed to be communicated in the video. It was short and to the point, which he believed was better than a long drawn out speech.

Jag and Ma'am volunteered to whip up a late lunch of fish tacos and coleslaw while Bird, Ish and Chad did some basic cleaning. Once the food was ready, they all gathered in the living room to eat and watch TV, scanning the news feeds for reports on the Florida arrest.

A head-shot was flashed briefly on the screen. It showed a black man in his mid-twenties with a mustache and light beard. He had a youthful face and was well-groomed, with his beard and hairline neatly lined and edged. The name beneath the picture read 'Delvin King'. They had tuned into a segment of a news show that was already in progress. The reporter, Chuck Singer, was seated at a desk. He was a dark-haired white man, wearing an expensive-looking suit and tie. He was interviewing a man from a remote location that was identified at the bottom of the screen as the Chief of Police of Hollywood, Florida.

"...And so, we immediately gave chase and were able to locate and detain him fairly quickly and without further incident," said the Chief.

"According to the reports we have," said the reporter, "the suspect was stopped by the officer because he had reason to believe the suspect was in possession of illegal drugs. Can you provide any more details?"

"Yes. The police officer was on routine patrol when he drove by the suspect, who was traveling on foot, and smelled what he believed to be marijuana, so he pulled over to investigate."

"So, the officer smelled the marijuana from inside his patrol car?"

"That is correct," said the Chief.

"And was any marijuana actually found on the suspect?"

"We're still investigating that," said the Chief. "What I can tell you now is that at some point the suspect became uncooperative and combative. A struggle ensued in which the officer lost control of his service weapon, which the suspect then retrieved as he ran from the scene."

"Thank you for that, sir. We appreciate your time."

"My pleasure," said the Chief.

"Next, we have one of the actual witnesses of the event joining us. Mr. Reginald Parras is a longtime resident of Hollywood, Florida, who was coming out of a grocery store across the street from where the police officer encountered Mr. King. Welcome, Mr. Parras."

"Thank you, Chuck," said Parras. He was a middle-aged white male with medium-length blond hair streaked with gray. He had blue eyes and a thick, bushy mustache that matched his eyebrows.

"Our reports suggest that you witnessed the entire encounter; is that correct?"

"That is correct," said Parras. "I come out of the store just as the patrol car came to a stop, and I saw the whole thing."

"Was there anything that initially drew your attention to the scene?" asked the reporter.

"I guess it was the speed of the police car," said Parras. "It was moving really, really slowly, kind of just creeping along. And the black guy—ummm, is it okay to say 'black guy'?"

"Uhhh...yes, I think that's fine," said Chuck, looking slightly uncomfortable.

"Okay," continued Parras. "So, the cop was creeping along, following the black guy who was walking and kept looking over his shoulder. After a few moments, the cop turned on his flashing lights and whooped the siren. That caused the black guy to stop and turn around. By this time, I had reached my car, but I wanted to see what was gonna happen, so I just sat there in the driver seat and watched it all play out."

"Could you hear their conversation from where you were?"

"Not at first; not until the yelling started."

"So, what happened after the police officer stopped his car?" asked Chuck.

"He got out, and it looked like he said something to the guy, because the guy held out his hands, either like he didn't know what the police officer was talking about or maybe to say that he wasn't doing anything. Next thing you know, the black guy was turning around and putting his hands against the building and the officer was frisking him."

"Did you notice the suspect smoking anything as he was approached by the officer?"

"Nope."

"Not even a cigarette?"

"I did not see anything in his hands or his mouth," said Parras.

"And did you see the officer take anything off of the suspect?"

"I saw him pull out keys, a cell phone and what looked like a wallet."

"And did you see what the officer did with those items?"

"Yeah. He gave them back to the guy, who put them back in his pockets."

"So, you didn't see the officer retrieve anything that looked like it might have been marijuana or any other drug?"

"No, I didn't. And if he did, he would have given it back to the man, because everything he pulled out, he gave back and the guy put it all back in his pants."

"And then what happened?" asked Chuck.

"The black guy was still leaning with his hands on the wall, his back to the cop. The cop got close to him, like he was whispering something in the black guy's ear. The black guy turned his head, I guess to respond to whatever it was the cop had said, and the cop punched him in the back of the head."

"And you saw no threatening action from the suspect that might have justified what the officer did?"

"None at all. The guy was leaning against the wall with his legs spread. How much of a threat could he have been? Anyway, next I saw the cop look around him, like he was looking to see if anyone was watching. I guess he didn't see me sitting in my car, because the next thing he did was pull out his baton and whack the guy across the ass with it. Sorry—can I say ass?"

"I think so," said Chuck.

"That was when the guy—the black guy—screamed. It looked like he was about to collapse from the pain. The cop appeared to say something else into his ear, and then hit him again with the baton, this time in the back of the legs. This time the guy did collapse, but he fell backwards, into the cop. I think the cop tried to hold him up, but maybe he was at the wrong angle. Next thing you know, they're both on the ground, wrestling. The cop still had the baton for a minute, and he smacked the guy in the head with it once. But on the second swing the black guy was able to pull it out of his hand and began to hit the cop with it."

"How many times did he strike the officer?" asked Chuck.

"I think probably five or six times. Then I saw the cop reach for his gun. He got it out of his holster and pointed it at the guy, but before he could pull the trigger, the guy knocked it out of his hands and it slid across the sidewalk. Then they both froze. I guess the black guy was trying to think of what to do next. After a moment, he jumped up and took off, picking up the gun as he ran and tossing the baton into some bushes. He disappeared around the corner, and seconds later the cop screeched off in his car in the same direction. That was the last I saw of either of them."

"Thank you very much for your time, Mr. Parras."

Chad turned the sound down and faced Ish.

"Same old, same old," he said.

"Actually, it's not the same at all," said Bird. "This guy is claiming to be one of us."

"Yeah, that is somewhat of an inconvenience," said Chad.

"I think it's more than an inconvenience," replied Bird. "What are we going to do when we start getting the blame for foolishness other idiots are engaged in?"

"As we discussed before," said Ish, "that's going to be an ongoing occupational hazard with this job. However, I think we can control the damage to a large degree by taking our story directly to the people, the same as we've been doing all along. As a matter of fact, I already have a rough idea of the video I'd like to record. I was working on it before you guys arrived."

"Okay," said Bird. "I just hope that's enough."

"I think it'll be totally fine," said Chad. "Unless we end up in a court of law facing charges for what someone else did."

"And I doubt that any of us would ever do anything that might cause that to happen," said Jag, his voice tinted with sarcasm as he looked sideways at Bird. Bird returned the gaze but didn't answer.

"This is gonna be the top story for a while," said Ma'am, attempting to change the subject. "Maybe we should delay the next mission; give things a chance to cool down."

"No," said Ish, "I think that would be a mistake. We always knew there were going to be copycats. We need to make sure that we maintain a presence in the social consciousness of the people, so that it's clear to them what actions we are and are not responsible for. Otherwise, it would be like we were turning the reins over to the public at large, giving anyone and everyone a free license to operate as representatives of PROPR."

"Ish is absolutely right," said Chad. "We always planned for this to be the spark that sets off a grassroots revolution, but it's important that people be able to easily recognize what is the grass and what is the root."

"That makes sense," said Ma'am. "So, when do we begin prepping for the next mission?"

"As soon as possible," said Ish. "Chad and I are going to be spending some time tonight analyzing the online chatter, to kind of take the temperature of the situation overall. Then I'll strategize something, and we can get together and go over it. How about tomorrow afternoon?"

"Sounds good," said Ma'am, and the rest of the group nodded in agreement.

Everyone took that as a signal to go back to finishing the last of their lunch and begin clearing the table and retiring to their respective room to do whatever it was they did during down time. Ish found himself in the living room alone with Chad.

"How's Layla?"

"She's good," said Ish. "Still as feisty as ever and trying to stay out of trouble. Though maybe not trying hard enough," he said, smiling.

"Were you able to give her any hints as to what we've been up to?"

"I was. I think she understands."

"That's good," said Chad. "Maybe she'll start to believe that there really is some light at the end of her tunnel."

"Yeah," said Ish. "But showing her the light and getting her to walk towards it are two completely different things."

Chapter 45

Madden had trouble sleeping that night. He tossed and turned until he saw that Kelly was beginning to toss and turn with him, so he gave her a reprieve by getting up and going into the den. He turned on the TV and began flipping through his favorite news stations.

Before he joined the Bureau, Madden had usually found the news depressing. All the doom and gloom bothered him, even as a kid. But all that changed once he joined the FBI. The news became a prism that reflected not only the world he lived in, but the world he worked in. Sometimes it was like a living 'table of contents' of issues that he knew someone in the Bureau was looking into, even if it wasn't something that was assigned to his team. Tonight, far too many of the stories he saw had a place in the table of contents of his team's book. Madden eventually fell asleep in front of the TV, watching a CNN story that featured a talking head who believed that the country was on the brink of anarchistic collapse due to the 'example of social disobedience' being promoted by the terrorist group PROPR.

He had a 7:30am meeting scheduled with the rest of the task force, so he wasn't dozing long before his watch began to beep, rousing him from a fitful sleep. After a quick shower and an even quicker kiss on the cheek of his still-sleeping wife, he was on the road. He stopped at Starbucks for coffee and a breakfast sandwich. He knew someone at the office was sure to show up with donuts, but he was trying to reduce his sugar consumption.

He walked into the building at 6:54am and headed straight for Phillips' office. As expected, she was already there, her nose deep into a thick manila folder that Madden knew had to be some kind of report on the current case.

"Hey, Chief," she said, looking up and smiling at him as he approached her desk.

"Hey, Phillips," he said. "As usual, looks like the worm of the day belongs to you."

"Somebody has to get it," she answered.

"True. What are you working on?" he asked, nodding at the folder she had open in front of her.

"Psychology report on PROPR. There's nothing in it that's surprising. Anger issues, anti-government, feelings of persecution, yada, yada, yada. Based on this, half the black people I know are suspects."

"And almost all the black people I know," said Madden, smiling sadly. "I hope you have something for me that's a bit more promising than what's in that report."

"Actually, sir," said Phillips, "I think I do."

Madden headed towards his office and Phillips grabbed her laptop and followed, briefing him along the way.

"We've come up with several names that are green for many, if not all, of our search terms. The current list is 117 long," she said.

Upon entering his office, Madden took his jacket off and hung it over the back of his chair. Phillips took a seat in the chair opposite him.

"So, who are the stars so far?" he asked as he began rolling up his sleeves.

Phillips turned her attention to the laptop, her fingers flying over the keyboard. Seconds later she turned it around so Madden could see the screen.

"We have fourteen that look particularly promising," she said.

Madden looked at the list and began reading the brief descriptions.

1. Michael Ashland, 34, Miami, Florida, bi-racial: African American/Caucasian, ex-Marine, has filed several complaints of police brutality.

2. Luther Ashe, 27, Dallas, Texas, African American, ex-police officer, terminated due to charges related to drug possession and distribution, which were later dropped.

3. Billy Ishmael, 32, Dayton, Ohio, African American, no military record, martial arts expert and self-proclaimed survivalist, was convicted 6 years ago of assaulting an off-duty cop, claimed self-defense, served 18 months in state prison.

4. Francis Itchon, 42, New York, New York, Pacific Islander/Samoan, ex-Army Special Forces, nephew died while in police custody, ruled accidental overdose via consumption of cocaine to avoid discovery.

5. Daniel Ishimoto, 40, La Mirada, California, Japanese American, ex-Navy, police performed a drug raid on his house by accident, due to transposition of his house number. He resisted arrest and was injured in the struggle, losing vision in his left eye. His lawsuit was eventually dismissed.

6. Tina Fishburne, 31, Concord, New Hampshire, African American, ex-Marine. Her seventeen-year-old son died after being repeatedly tasered by a police officer during a routine stop-and-frisk. She won a $2million lawsuit but the ruling was later overturned.

Madden stopped reading and looked up at Phillips. “A woman?” he asked.

Phillips shrugged. “Maybe. Beggars can’t be choosers.”

“Even the name is a stretch,” said Madden. “‘Ish’ doesn’t strike me as a common nickname for ‘Fishburne’.”

“You’re probably right,” said Phillips, “but we agreed that the name Ratcliff heard could also have been ‘bitch’. I’ve suffered through my fair share of rap music. If this guy in the video really is black, maybe he wasn’t calling her by name. Maybe he was just using his common term for female.”

Madden had to grin and shake his head. If this comment had come out of the mouth of just about any one of his other white co-workers, he would have taken instant offense. But he knew in his heart that Phillips was as far from racist as any white person could be. She was simply stating a basic fact, and it was one that Madden really couldn’t refute.

“Okay, let’s check her out,” he said as he scanned the other names on the list. Phillips was right; some of them looked especially promising.

“Would you like me to grab some of the guys and start running these down today?”

"No, I need you here. I need all of you guys here, just in case something else breaks. Please contact the appropriate field offices and have the local agents get on this ASAP. And let's keep our fingers crossed."

A couple of hours later Madden was walking out of his office, file in hand, on the way to speak to Phillips when he nearly collided with Bainbridge.

"Excuse me," he said, almost dropping the file. Madden could count on one hand the times his boss had actually traveled to his office for a meeting. Generally speaking, Bainbridge had the reputation of only leaving his office to travel 'upstairs', as they say, not 'downstairs'. The fact that he had shown up unannounced without even confirming whether or not Madden was in was particularly troubling.

As Madden recovered, Bainbridge stood watching him, hands behind his back, a look of slight amusement on his face.

"You look busy," he said. "I hope that means you have some positive news for me."

"Uhhh," said Madden, feeling annoyed but trying not to show it. "We do have news. I'm not sure, quite yet, how positive it is, but at this point any progress is good progress."

Bainbridge continued to stare, as though he were waiting for something.

"Am I interrupting?" he finally asked, a hint of sarcasm in his voice.

"Not at all," said Madden as he turned and led Bainbridge back into his office. As Bainbridge entered, he closed the door behind him. His suit jacket was buttoned, and he made a show of taking his time to slowly unbutton it before taking a seat.

"Do you know where I've just been?" he asked as he crossed his legs and folded his hands in his lap.

"Sir?" asked Madden, shaking his head slightly.

"Having my ass handed to me by Director Roberts, that's where." He spoke the words quietly, with an even tone, but there was an unmistakable menace in his voice. "Can you guess why he was in such a disagreeable state?"

Madden didn't answer but nodded his head in acknowledgment.

"That's right. He wants to know why the hell we don't have any stronger leads on this case. There's anarchy spreading in the streets, and we've got nothing. How does that happen?"

"Sir, as I said before, we're devoting all available assets to this. Some things are opening up, but we need more time."

"Time, Madden, is the one thing we do not have. This goes all the way up to the President. My political career is on the line. I have aspirations beyond this office, and you're fucking it up for me. It's become a pissing contest. The President pisses on the Director, the Director pisses on me, and guess who I piss on?"

"I understand," said Madden.

"No, I don't think you do. If you want to keep your job, you need to stop these motherfuckers and bring them to justice. And I don't care if justice is in the form of a jail cell or a bullet. Do I make myself clear?"

"Crystal," said Madden solemnly.

With that, Bainbridge stood, made a ceremony of re-buttoning his coat, and strode out of the office.

Five minutes later Madden was still sitting quietly at his desk, deep in thought over the interaction that had just taken place, when he heard a knock against his open office door and looked up to see Phillips.

"Hey," she said, "I just passed His Royal Dictator in the hall. Is everything okay?"

"Yeah," said Madden. "Why wouldn't it be?"

"Well, because I hardly ever see him slumming down here with the regular folks, and I doubt that he would have subjected himself to the indignity of it if there wasn't something important afoot."

"He just came to tell me that I may be up for a long vacation soon. The permanent kind. The kind that doesn't come with health-care."

Phillips nodded. "Yeah, I just caught the President's press conference. He swore that we would get to the bottom of this and 'get our country back', and that we were 'on the brink of making a series of arrests'." Madden's face showed momentary confusion. "I was as surprised as you are," she said.

Madden smiled wanly. "So, I guess that means you aren't coming to tell me that you've got something and that we're 'on the brink of making a series of arrests'?"

"Not exactly. But I didn't come empty-handed, either," she said, holding up a green manila folder. "We've added more names to the list. But our agents all over the country have been running them down and more or less eliminating them almost as fast as we can add them."

Madden sighed. “Any that especially pop out at you?”

“There was a guy in Baton Rouge that I liked a lot. African-American. Ex-Seal. Thirty years old. His twin brother was shot to death by cops two years ago. Police answered a domestic dispute call. He answered the door with a screwdriver in his hand and when he refused to drop it, they opened fire. The thing is, the Seal was serving a week in county jail for traffic tickets during the Ratcliff attack. That doesn’t mean that he’s couldn’t be part of PROPR, but it definitely means he wasn’t with them that day. We’ve moved his name to the ‘Person of Interest’ list, but I doubt there’s anything there.”

“Damn,” said Madden. “What about the geek squad? Any progress on tracing the website?”

“None,” said Phillips, shaking her head solemnly. “They can see the signal, and they can follow it fairly easily, up to a point. Then it just hits a dead end. It’s like they find the castle and follow the maze to the dungeon door, but they can’t get it open. And while they’re working on trying to pick the lock, the castle starts moving again and they’re back to chasing after it. But they’re not giving up. You know how these guys like a challenge, and they’ve never seen a challenge quite like this.”

“I’m feeling worthless, just sitting here waiting for my walking papers,” said Madden. “Maybe I’ll run down some of these names myself. At least it’ll give me some distance from Bainbridge.”

“He can’t fire you if you aren’t here.”

“Exactly. Any other names on the list that your gut tells you might have promise?”

“Now that you mention it, there is a name that just popped up today, a few minutes ago. A guy out of L.A. That’s about as far from Bainbridge as you can get without actually leaving the continent.”

“Sounds like a winner. I’ll take it,” said Madden. “What’s the name?”

“Carter,” said Phillips. “Ishmael Carter.”

Chapter 46

The video opened with a slow fade showing Ish, masked and dressed as usual, standing with his arms by his side, feet spread apart, looking directly into the camera.

"Good evening, America. By now, many of you have heard about the incident involving Delvin King. Mr. King was the victim of an unprovoked attack in Hollywood, Florida, by a police officer by the name of Andrew Weaver. Mr. King was innocently walking down the street, minding his own business, when Officer Weaver decided to stop and harass him. The officer later stated in his report that he stopped Mr. King because he smelled marijuana smoke as he drove by him, even though no marijuana was found on Mr. King's person when he was stopped and searched by Officer Weaver, nor was any marijuana or any other drugs found anywhere in the immediate area.

"Per statements given by several first-hand witnesses of the incident, Officer Weaver physically attacked Mr. King for no reason, striking him with his fists and baton. In an act of pure self-defense, Mr. King fought back, managing to take both the officer's baton and his service weapon. Fortunately for Officer Weaver, Mr. King opted not to fire, which is quite the opposite of what surely would have happened had the situation been reversed. Instead, Mr. King ran for safety and was later apprehended. He now sits in a Hollywood, Florida, jail cell, awaiting trial for assault on a police officer, among other charges.

"All this, in and of itself, isn't really news in this day and age. The reason we are addressing it in this special announcement is that Mr. King indicated at the time of his arrest that he was associated with

PROPR. He is not. Until the news of his arrest was broadcast by the media, we had no knowledge of Delvin King whatsoever. He is not, and has never been, associated with our organization in any capacity.

"We are honored that Mr. King feels a kinship with PROPR and the change we are attempting to institute. That aligns with why we originally formed PROPR in the first place, which was to inspire the people to take back the streets from dirty cops. However, we would be doing the public a disservice if we were to allow you to believe that certain self-proclaimed people were acting on our behalf when they are not. That being said, we wholeheartedly support the actions that Mr. King took to protect himself, and if there is anything we can do to help him, we will do so.

"We hope that you all can derive some lessons from this event. First and foremost, we hope that you now understand that it is possible for you to fight back and protect yourself. Your own actions may be all that stands between you and death at the hands of a rogue police officer. And second, we would ask that you please not insinuate that you are associated with our organization when you are not. Not only does it cause confusion, but it could ultimately cause you to be charged with crimes for things that we've done, which of course you had nothing to do with. If you want to strike a blow for justice in our name, that's fine, but you don't need to put yourself at risk of being made to pay the price for actions that we've committed.

"We hope this has helped to clear up some of the confusion that has been generated over the last 48 hours. Please stay turned for our next broadcast, which will be very soon. Until then, good day and stay safe."

* * *

As promised, Ish and Chad spent the evening looking over news reports, blog posts and social media feeds to get a feel for how the group's actions to date were affecting the country. They knew that there would be a lot of movement, but they were still a bit shocked by exactly how much movement there was. As Ish had already learned from the radio show the previous day, there were demonstrations breaking out all over the country, and for the most part they had been peaceful.

But the arrest of Delvin King had started to create a shift in that reality. Within the last 24 hours there had already been two skirmishes between demonstrators and police, one on the East Coast and one on the West. The chatter on social media was starting to indicate that more violence was on the way, and that it was going to escalate in intensity. Some people were even calling for every able-bodied black man and woman over the age of eighteen to take up arms and get ready to mount an offensive against the government forces thought to be behind the oppression. In other words, the police.

Of course, Ish and Chad were both savvy enough to know that what people say behind the anonymity of a keyboard and what they are willing to do, or even say, face-to-face in the real world were often light-years apart. But still, at the very least, it was clear that people's level of frustration was rising. What they had started was truly beginning to take hold in a real, tangible way.

Ish was up early the next morning, his phone alarm vibrating at 5:00am to wake him. He threw on some sweats and a pair of jogging shoes, eager for the peace and tranquility derived from a pre-dawn run. As he opened the door to his bedroom, he almost collided with Jag, who was in the process of tiptoeing out of Ma'am's room.

"Hey, Ice-Man..." he whispered, seeming somewhat unsure of what to say.

"Hey, Jag," said Ish. "Everything alright?"

"Oh yeah, yeah, everything is peaches. Uhhh..." He turned around towards Ma'am's door before turning back to face Ish. "Just spending a little quality time with Ma'am."

"Nothing wrong with that," said Ish, smiling.

"You off for a run?"

"Yeah. You wanna join me?"

"Nah, thanks. I think I need to get a few more winks in before breakfast."

Ish smiled again. "No problem. If you oversleep, I'll save you a pancake."

Jag returned the smile and shuffled off towards his own room.

The jog did what it was supposed to do. It gave Ish a chance to clear his head, to filter and distill everything that had been stewing in there the last few days down to the pure essentials required for the task at hand: the next mission. Part of the preparation was looking ahead towards what would happen after Mission Three.

Ish and Chad had touched on it briefly the night before while working together analyzing news feeds. He and Chad had slightly different ideas of what the next step in the grand scheme was. But focusing on their differences right now probably wasn't the best use of his time or energy. What was most important were the points in which they were in agreement, and that's what Ish directed his current thoughts to. They both believed that, regardless of how crude their methods might seem at the present time, they were at the helm of a movement that had the potential to change history.

But he couldn't forget that he also had a more personal stake in this: Layla. He wasn't actually sure how yet, but he had high hopes that somehow this would reunite him with the love of his life. All of this was meant to save lives, as many lives as possible, but the one life he held above all others, including his own, was Layla's. He had never discussed this topic much with Jag, Bird or Ma'am, but he had no doubt that they would understand. They were all combat-savvy soldiers who believed in the 'no man left behind' edict. And they all knew enough about his life to know that he considered Layla to be a POW trapped behind enemy lines.

When he finally walked back into the house, breathing heavily and covered in sweat, he was a little surprised to be greeted with complete silence. Normally at least one other person was up early. *That's okay,* he thought. *Let them sleep.* They deserved it.

Ish walked into the kitchen as he toweled sweat off his face and arms and grabbed a glass of almond milk from the fridge. As he stood looking out the window, marveling as more and more of the horizon turned from gray to orange, he felt enormous gratitude for his life and the opportunities he had been given, not the least of which was the chance to be part of something so great with such an amazing group of people. There was a lot of love in this house. They were, for all intents and purposes, a family. And there was nothing quite like family.

A couple of hours later, while they were in the middle of cooking breakfast, it began to storm. Anyone who has ever driven in L.A. during a heavy rain knows what havoc it wreaks with what is already typically horrid traffic. So rather than subject themselves to the agony of navigating through such chaos, Ish decided to have their team meeting in the house. The Macrolox office was much more secure, with its soundproofing and anti-eavesdropping technology. However, they felt safe enough in Chad's home.

"So, let's begin," said Ish once everyone had poured themselves a cup of hot coffee or tea and settled in. "I think you all know what the conditions are on the street right now. Things are heating up. Our first two missions have ignited the kind of change we had hoped that they would, and I don't want to lose the momentum by delaying the launch of the next mission."

Bird raised his hand. "I know that we've touched on this already, at least to some degree, but I assume you and Chad have been discussing what comes next. I mean, next after this third mission. What have you come up with?"

Ish glanced at Chad. "You're right, Bird, we have discussed it a bit, but we haven't come up with a definite plan yet. At least, not one that we both are completely onboard with."

"What exactly does that mean?" asked Bird.

"Well," said Ish, "Chad feels that we should keep the train running; that we should immediately plan additional missions, maybe responding to some of the emails we've been receiving from people in various communities that are asking for our help."

"Sounds like the logical next step," said Jag.

"Maybe," said Ish. "But this next mission will take us to an entirely new level of threat in the eyes of the government. I'm sure the FBI is working around the clock to try to catch us now, but once we actually make the transition from kidnappers to killers, they will pour every ounce of their considerable resources into tracking us down. It will be an all-out offensive. And every additional mission we run after that will give them an additional opportunity to take advantage of any mistakes we might make. It raises the stakes for everyone involved."

"So, what are you saying?" asked Jag. "That we should just stop after this mission and retire?"

"It's an idea," said Ish.

"You just spoke about maintaining momentum," said Jag. "This is only our third mission. Ain't that kind of like ringing the bell to the whore house and walking away before anybody comes to the door?"

"I don't think so," said Ish. "Look, we've only completed two missions, and already we're seeing a massive change. This next mission is going to blow the lid off. Maybe what we've already done has sufficiently set fire to the kindling. Once you get the fire going, you don't have to keep feeding it sparks. It begins to feed itself."

"Anyway," continued Ish, "I don't want to get too bogged down debating the future right now. Let's stay focused on the task at hand and wait till we get a little closer to that bridge before we start devoting a lot of energy figuring out how to cross it."

Bird didn't respond at all, but Jag and Ma'am both nodded in unison.

"Chad?" said Ish, signaling for his friend to start the PowerPoint presentation he had created specifically for the occasion. The living room TV sprang to life, showing a well-lit, head-and-shoulders portrait of a smiling Caucasian man. The label below the picture read 'Officer Thaddeus Janssen'.

He had a large, thick, misshaped head. His black hair was oily looking, in addition to being scarce enough on top that the crown of his scalp was clearly visible. His face displayed a mass of old acne scars and, coupled with his sharp, pointed nose, gave him an appearance of meanness, in spite of the fact that he was smiling.

"I know we already gave you a rundown on Janssen in the initial briefing, but let's go over the numbers again. Forty-three complaints of police brutality. He's shot eight unarmed people dead in the line of duty. Seven of those eight were African-Americans. One of the most egregious of those eight incidents is also the most recent. This is the video, which you also viewed before, but I think it's worth viewing again."

Ish nodded at Chad, who activated the playback. It looked like the video was shot from perhaps 30 to 60 feet away, but whoever was operating the camera had used the zoom feature. Chad had confirmed that it was shot on an iPhone, and Ish was again amazed at the clarity produced by a camera inside a tiny cellphone. One thing he noticed this time that he hadn't really noted in his previous viewings of the footage was the little girl in the backseat occasionally coming into the frame and glancing repeatedly at the camera.

There was terror in her eyes. But there was also pleading. She was only five years old, yet somehow, she must have sensed that something was horribly wrong even before the traffic stop turned confrontational. She was a beautiful little girl with dark chocolate skin that glistened in the sunlight that was streaming into the car. Her eyes were large and expressive, and there was a hint of dimples in her slightly chubby cheeks. Her hair was a draping of curls falling down around her face.

Ish wondered if the person who shot the video felt any guilt when looking back at the footage and seeing the girl's silent cry for help. He wondered if that person tossed and turned at night, wondering if there was anything he might have done that could have saved her father's life. Of course, the facts were that nothing any civilian did would have likely changed the outcome of the events of that day. But Ish wouldn't have been surprised to learn that the man felt guilty anyway. He felt guilty himself, and he wasn't even there. It was impossible to watch this little girl suffer the way she had and not wish that there was something you might have done to help prevent it.

After the video finished, Jag was the first one to speak.

"Anybody know what happened to the little girl?"

Ish looked to Chad.

"She was unharmed," he said. "According to the reports I read, she was with Child Protective Services for about 48 hours before she was released to the mother. Of course," he continued, shaking his head, "while she was physically unharmed, there's no telling what kind of lasting emotional damage this all may have caused."

"That baby is gonna to be fucked up for life," said Ma'am grimly. "You don't see shit like that at her age and come out the other side in one piece. I've seen a lot of shit in my time, and that would even fuck me up."

"It's a sad situation all the way around," said Ish. "But maybe what we're about to do will one day give her some degree of peace. It may be years before she can understand it, but hopefully it will make it just a little bit easier for her to cope." Everyone nodded.

"So, back to the task at hand. This guy lives in West L.A., so he's local. A few days ago, Chad attached a tracker to his car. We've been tracking his travel patterns to make it a little easier to predict when and where he's likely to be at any time, on any given day. As I mentioned before, I think a sniper attack is the best way to deal with this, and since I'm the best shot in the group, I'll take the lead."

"Then this should be a piece of cake," said Jag. "You can shoot the asshole off a hummingbird at a thousand yards. You can post up nine or ten blocks away and send him a long-distance love letter. No muss, no fuss."

"It's not quite that easy," said Ish. "The one thing I need to be concerned with here that I didn't have to deal with in Afghanistan is collateral damage. I have to be careful that the round I fire isn't going to pass through his body and potentially hit anyone else. And this will probably all take place in a public area, so it's going to be tricky."

"Yeah, you're right," said Jag, rubbing his chin as he began to think about the possibilities.

"So, what are the options?" asked Ma'am.

"The most obvious answer is to get closer and use a smaller caliber round traveling at a slower speed. Of course, the closer I get, the lower the chance of getting away unnoticed. I'm going to go out later today and scout the areas along his travel pattern. There's a coffee shop he stops at most mornings that may be a possible engagement point, but finding a good elevated attack point might be a challenge."

"And what is our role going to be in this operation?" asked Bird.

"Mainly surveillance and extraction. We'll need him trailed, and we'll also need the police bands monitored so we're aware of any other police activity in the area. I'll also need someone with me to operate as my spotter. Jag, are you up for that?"

"Put me in, coach," he said, smiling.

"Cool. After the deed is done, we'll need to be scooped up and, hopefully, we'll all drive off merrily into the sunset."

"Hopefully," said Bird. Everyone turned to look at him. Ish wasn't sure what they were all thinking, but he had an idea.

Chapter 47

Later that afternoon, Ish was ready to take a drive and do some recon. He was surprised that Bird asked to tag along. They drove in silence for a while, with Bird alternating between staring at his feet, staring at his hands and staring out the window.

"You know," he said finally, "I was never really that great of a soldier."

"What are you talking about?" asked Ish. "You're one of the best soldiers I've ever served with."

"What do you base that on?" asked Bird. "The fact that I was able to shoot people and take orders?"

Ish smiled and shook his head. "Well, that is kind of what soldiers do. But it's more than that. Come on, Bird, you know this. It takes more than just being able to shoot a gun and follow directions. It takes nerve. It takes courage. It takes—"

"It also takes control," said Bird, turning to stare across the seat at Ish. "A certain mindset. I've never really had that mindset. I've always had a problem with control. My temper has often tended to get the better of me. I have more insubordination reports in my file than I can even remember. So, it's no wonder I lost it back in that room with Ratcliff."

"Do you think you're that much different than the rest of us?" asked Ish. "Most of us won't admit it, but we all have varying degrees of issues with authority, which is just another form of a lack of control. And most of us have done reckless shit at some point in our lives, both inside and outside the military. As a matter of fact, sometimes those reckless actions were the only things that kept us alive."

Bird chose not to respond and returned to staring out the window.

Ish was starting to feel a bit irritated. He'd had conversations like this with other soldiers over the years, but most of the time they were kids fresh out of boot camp. He would have thought that by now Bird would have a better understanding of the reality of combat. Or maybe Ish was just being too hard on him?

"What is it you're trying to tell me?" he asked. "I mean, I get the impression that you're not here simply to enjoy the fresh air and my delightful company."

"I'm not really sure," said Bird.

"Are you still having doubts about whether you want to be part of this project?"

"It's not that I have doubts about wanting to be a part of it," he answered, frowning. "It's more like I don't know if I have anything to offer. I'm starting to feel more like a liability than an asset."

"Bird," said Ish, sighing deeply, "I just don't get you, man. I've stood shoulder to shoulder with you in the heat of battle so many times, and I never once doubted that you had my back. Where is all this coming from? Just because things got a little heated with that asshole Ratcliff?"

"I don't know. Maybe what happened in New York was a sign. Maybe all those years in the field I was just lucky, and maybe me going off on Ratcliff was a sign that my luck is running out. What I did was unforgivable. And it could have been a lot worse. It scares me when I think about exactly how much worse."

"Let me ask you this," said Ish. "Who exactly are you afraid for—us or yourself?"

Bird stared down at his hands again for a few moments before turning again to meet Ish's gaze. "I think I'm still trying to figure that out."

They arrived at the intersection directly adjacent to the targeted coffee shop, and Ish pulled over to the curb to have a look around. The name of the shop was *Well Grounded.* It was one of those new, modern places, with Italian-inspired furniture and walls covered with an eclectic array of artwork. The times that Chad had seen Janssen there, he had always gone in and drank his coffee at a table as opposed to using the drive-thru.

Ish scanned the surrounding buildings. Directly across the street was a large supermarket. On the other side of the street was a six-story office building. Littered among these were smaller businesses. There was a 7-11, a laundromat, a Mexican restaurant and a three-story condo building. There were a variety of options here, but none of them was ideal. He also noticed that there was a traffic camera high on a pole on the northwest corner. He would need to make sure to disable it the day of.

"What do you think?" he said to Bird, who was also examining the area.

"Of course, the most obvious place to post-up is the office building."

"We already looked into that. None of the offices that would give us the right positioning are vacant. Same with the condos."

"Maybe you could get creative and figure out a way to temporarily empty one of the units?"

"Chad's looking into that," said Ish, "but nothing is looking too promising yet."

"If that doesn't work, then you're left with the roofs."

"Right," said Ish. "And all the exposure that comes with it."

"There's no law that says you have to engage him here," said Bird.

"True," said Ish. "But based on what we know so far, this is the location with both the highest probability of success and the lowest probability of collateral damage." They both went back to perusing the area, looking for weaknesses and opportunities.

"I know you and Chad put a lot of emphasis on avoiding getting any innocents caught in the crossfire on these operations, but with all due respect, I don't know how realistic that is. Eventually, especially if we keep this up, someone is going to get hurt. After all, you said it yourself once before: this is war. And as you and I both know from personal experience, it's real hard to wage a war without a certain amount of collateral damage. Trying to do so is one of the reasons so many of our fellow soldiers ended their tours in coffins."

"This isn't Afghanistan," said Ish. "This is America. And we're not the government. We're a team of elite fighters that answer to no one. We're more agile and adaptable than anything the armed forces has at their command. We should be able to make this work without impacting the lives of any innocent people."

"You seem to be forgetting that these officers that we're going after are all connected to other people," said Bird. "Even if they don't have wives and kids, they have mothers and fathers, sisters, brothers, cousins and nephews. I read a story yesterday about how Ratcliff's sister has gone into seclusion. She's a college student somewhere in upstate New York. After the video went public, she tweeted something in defense of her brother, and was deluged with negative comments in reaction. She received several death threats, a couple of which were serious enough that the FBI is apparently looking into them. So, so much for protecting the innocents."

"Yeah, I read something about that myself," said Ish. "Who was it, Sherman, that said 'war is hell'? Whoever it was, they were right. We can only do so much, man. The alternative is to do nothing at all, and if that were really an option, you and I wouldn't be having this conversation right now."

Bird shrugged and nodded his head in acknowledgment, then went back to reconning the area.

"Let's take a walk," said Ish.

They both grabbed baseball caps from the back seat and donned dark shades before leaving the car. They walked down the block at a comfortable pace. They were coming up on the office building. Ish knew there was an alley behind the building, which he wanted to get a closer look at, but he also knew that in this neighborhood, two black men walking through the alley in the middle of the day had the potential to garner far too much attention. They would drive through it on their way out.

They crossed the street and walked back toward the car on the other side, passing by the coffee shop. The glass of the front windows was plate-thick. There was no way a slow-velocity round was going to penetrate something this thick and hit its target with any degree of accuracy. This was going to be more complicated that he'd first imagined. Just then, an 18-wheeler pulled up to the curb in front of them, which was a 'no parking' zone. A man jumped out of the passenger seat, ran into the coffee shop and moments later ran out with two cups of some unknown liquid. He quickly climbed back into the cab of the truck and seconds later they were pulling back into traffic. This gave Ish an idea.

"I think I've seen enough," he said. "Let's head back."

Once they made it back to the car, he immediately called Chad and asked him to start looking into the logistics of getting an untraceable high-sided transport truck.

"Are you thinking about posting up inside a moving vehicle?" asked Bird as Ish hung up and put his phone back into his pocket.

"Worked for the Beltway dudes," said Ish as he started the engine and put the car into gear.

When they arrived back at the house, Jag and Ma'am were sitting on the couch, laughing hysterically about something. A platter of sliced cheese and meat was on the table before them, and they were each holding what appeared to be a glass of red wine. Bird froze and did a double-take, looking first at Ma'am and then at Jag. His face scrunched into a frown and one corner of his mouth began to twitch. He was about to speak when Ma'am cut him off.

"Don't trip, baby brother. Mine is only Concord grape juice," she said, smiling as she took a sip.

Bird's face deflated, as though he had just lost ten pounds of air. He looked relieved but still a bit irritated.

"Jag, I didn't know you were into the whole 'wine and cheese' thing," said Ish, trying to lighten some of the tension.

"You're right. Most of my experience with cheese has been on a burger or on top of a buffalo chicken pizza. But Ma'am's opening me up to all kinds of new experiences," he responded, smiling slyly.

Jesus, thought Ish. Was Jag, once again, purposely trying to push Bird's buttons? Or was it just him being his typical thick-headed, insensitive self? Ish thought he had made it clear to everyone that Bird was having some coping issues right now and that they needed to give him some space. Obviously, Jag didn't get the message. Ish made a mental note to have a private chat with him later.

"Hey, what's up?" asked Chad as he entered the room. His hair was wet, and he had a towel draped over his shoulders. "How did your recon go?"

"Not bad," said Ish. "We weren't able to find any spots in the surrounding buildings, but we did come up with a new idea that might work."

"I'm all ears," said Chad.

"You remember the Beltway snipers, right?"

Chad tilted his head, his face blank for a moment. "Wait...was that the two black dudes from D.C. that were shooting people out of the back of a station wagon?"

"More or less. As we were looking around, trying to figure out a good vantage point, a passing truck made me think about those guys. All we need is a tall moving truck. We can build a platform inside for me the rest on near the ceiling. Then we cut a hole and cover it with a plastic screen, then camouflage the entire area with a well-placed logo painting. From the outside, it should be all but invisible, and I should be able to get my shot off without anyone even noticing where it came from."

"That's some clever shit," said Jag, nodding his head in appreciation.

"For real," said Chad.

"Are you going to park the truck or try to take the shot moving?" asked Ma'am.

"We'll have to stop, at least momentarily. But if we can time it right, we'll be like ghosts. Even the people that see us won't see us."

Sixteen hours later Chad had acquired the truck. He found someone who was selling a 6-year old 16-foot box truck with a recently rebuilt engine for $29,000. He told the seller that he was out of the country but needed the truck right away. He wired the money into the seller's bank account. The seller was instructed to leave the paperwork and keys under the driver's seat of the unlocked vehicle, and someone would be by later to pick it up.

It was an unorthodox way of doing business, requiring mutual trust. He made the offer to eight different sellers before he found one willing to accept the terms. He and Jag staked out the truck for four hours after it was dropped off to make sure no one was around to see who came to pick it up. When they did finally pick it up, they wore shades, wigs and baseball caps as disguises, just to be especially careful.

They could have simply stolen a truck and made a duplicate of a clean license plate for it, since hacking the DMV database and finding an adequate plate would have been a piece of cake. But they were all against the idea of cheating someone out of their hard-earned money.

In addition, most people used these trucks for work, so they would also potentially be affecting the owner's ability to earn a living. Buying the truck increased their risk potential, but it allowed everyone to sleep better at night.

Chad drove the truck to a small warehouse that Macrolox had a twelve-month lease on. Jag and Ish immediately began the work of modifying it for the mission. Ish was constantly impressed by how resourceful Chad was. He had the mind of an engineer, and seldom was he not able to figure out a solution to any problem. Ish once again counted his blessings for having been able to put together such a strong team. And he still included Bird in that blessing.

Ish and Jag built a metal platform inside the truck and hand-painted a banner on the outside along the top of the truck where the sniper hole would be concealed. As they were waiting for the paint to dry, they munched on meatball sandwiches and Gatorade that they had brought with them.

"Let me ask you something," said Ish through a mouthful of bread and meat. "These things that you say about Ma'am when Bird is present—are you *trying* to fuck with him, or are you just clueless to what's going on?"

Jag smiled and took a long swallow of his sports drink before he answered. "Sometimes I can't help myself. I love him, but he's so easy to fuck with!"

"Jag, I thought I made it clear. We're in the middle of an operation here, and you're not making it any easier. I'm not trying to step on your toes with Ma'am, but maybe you need to think about putting your love life on hold for a minute. I know you're digging her, but that's not worth putting us all at risk."

Jag's smile faded a bit, and he paused to take another long drink. "You're right, Ice-Man. Maybe it's time for me to give my curtain call on this; to bow out gracefully while the bowing is good."

"What?" asked Ish.

"I don't just dig her, man. I think I'm in love with her. I think she might be the one. I think we might have a real future together. I mean *together* together."

Ish froze and realized that his mouth was hanging open.

"Wait. Are you talking about marriage?"

"Yep, I think I am," said Jag, smiling sheepishly. "Who would have thought this old hound dog would ever get hitched, huh?"

Ish was momentarily stunned into speechlessness.

"Wow...I...ummm...," said Ish, struggling to find the words. "I...wow. Ummm..."

Jag began chuckling. "It's okay," he said. "I know it's a bit of a shock. Take your time."

Ish followed the advice, taking a long swig of his drink while he let the idea of Jag getting married roll around in his head. Ish and Jag were the same age, but sometimes Ish felt like his older, more mature, brother.

As long as Ish had known him, Jag had always displayed the impetuousness of a bratty kid. Some of the soldiers they served with couldn't stand him. Some labeled him as a racist. Some as an idiot. Some just thought he was your garden variety, run-of-the-mill asshole. But in reality, Jag was none of those things. He was a good, intelligent man, with a strong lust for life and a lack of filter between what was on his mind and what came out of his mouth.

"I've known you for a while, Jag," said Ish once he was finally able to speak again, "and I know you have a reputation for living in the moment, but this is wild even for you."

"What's so wild about it?"

"Well," said Ish, his eyebrows arching in response, "for one thing, most of your family wasn't crazy about the fact that you were even dating blacks. Now you want to not only bring one home but give her the family name as well?"

"To be honest, I'm as surprised as you are. I never expected to fall in love with Ma'am. Initially, I was attracted to her strength and thought she might make for a good roll in the hay to kill some time. You know, just to keep the joints lubricated. But man, somehow, we just clicked. Really clicked. It's not something I can really explain. All I can say is that it just feels right."

"If I were your father," said Ish, taking his time to gather his thoughts, "I would tell you that you're being rash. That you don't decide you want to marry a girl you have been dating for less than a month."

"No," said Jag. "If you were my father, you would say something like, 'It's okay to fuck one of these nigger bitches behind closed doors, but you don't bring a monkey to the family reunion'. I'm paraphrasing."

Ish took a deep breath and sighed. "So, I assume that Ma'am knows how you feel about her?"

"Pretty much," said Jag. "And she says she feels the same about me."

"I think you two have the potential to be great together," said Ish, "but it sounds like this is going to be a hard pill for your family to swallow."

"You're absolutely right, but it's worth a try. Besides, you can't fight love, man, remember?"

"What?" said Ish.

"'You can't fight love'. That's what you told me once when I asked you why you hadn't been with anyone but Layla since college."

Ish did remember. They were on patrol in Kandahar Province one day when they were ambushed by a group of Taliban. They were pinned down for more than five hours before someone was able to flank the shooters and take them out. They did a lot of talking in times like that.

Ish took another big bite of his sandwich and used the time spent chewing to compose himself for his next question.

"So," he said once he had swallowed and cleared his palate again with another mouthful of Gatorade, "you're ready to hang up your 9mms?"

Jag paused as though he was trying to compose himself before he responded. "I was never a guy that had to be begged to join a good fight. And it's been a helluva lot of fun, both overseas as well as what we've been doing here. But now I have other things to think about. I have a woman that's also a soldier, but she's been a soldier long enough. It's time for her to relax and let someone else do the heavy lifting for a while. Now that she and I are going to be one I feel the need to protect her. It's hard to do that out in the field, shaking my dick at bad guys."

"I can understand your position," said Ish. "Was it difficult to get Ma'am onboard with it?"

"I, uh, haven't exactly told her that part yet."

"You haven't?"

"I hadn't really made the decision until right here, tonight, when you opened the discussion."

Ish raised his eyebrows again. "I'm not trying to tell you how to handle your business, but this might not go over so well with her. I think you might want to approach her delicately when you discuss it. If there's one thing I know about Ma'am, it's that she loves her independence. That's why she was so attracted to the Marines in the first place. It gave her the opportunity to showcase her strength and prove to herself that she could handle anything life threw at her."

"I get that," said Jag. "But there's no need for her to fight anymore. It's my job to take care of her. That's how we do things in Tennessee. We protect our women."

Ish grinned. "The next thing you're going to tell me is that you want her barefoot and... Wait. She's not pregnant, is she?"

Jag scoffed. "Let's not get ridiculous. I've been a poon wrangler for a long time, and I ain't never let the shark swim outside the net. Give me at least some credit."

"Alright, alright. I was just asking. I still think you're going to have a tough job on your hands, trying to turn Ma'am into one of the Housewives of Tennessee."

"Maybe. We'll see," said Jag.

"Have you thought about how you're going to support this new life of yours?"

Jag tilted his head to the side. "You know, I have. First, I want to take this opportunity to thank you again for the job offer at your company. That was super fuckin' generous. But I think I'd like to move on back to the home town. I have some money stashed away and a buddy down there that's looking for a partner in his hardware store. He's doin' real well. Ma'am and I could have a good life there."

"I'm happy for you. Any idea when you might want to make this transition?"

"Well, I definitely don't want to leave you and the rest of the guys hanging without at least some notice, so I'll definitely be here for this mission. Then maybe after that Ma'am and I can step away and start the next chapter."

Ish raised his bottle to toast. "Congratulations, brother," he said as they tapped their bottles together before taking a drink. "I don't think Ma'am could have picked a better guy. Of course, Bird might not exactly agree with that." They looked at each other and both started chuckling. Truer words were never spoken.

Chapter 48

The next morning the car to the airport arrived at the office early and, as usual, Phillips was already waiting. Madden had spent another restless night tossing and turning. This time when he got up, he went out to their backyard and began doing some gardening by moonlight. The moon was full, and along with the security floods that were installed in the back of the house, there was plenty of light for him to do his work.

Actually, it wasn't even fair to call it work. His interest in plant-life had begun in high school when, one day after one of his many infractions and run-ins with the principal, he was ordered to spend two weeks after school helping the horticulture class work on their garden. He had never been able to explain why he took to it the way he did, but after the first week he was hooked.

There was just something about growing things that called to him. Helping the other kids pull carrots and potatoes out of the ground that they had planted just a few months earlier, and then actually eating them, seemed magical to a city boy like Madden. After his two weeks were up, he continued working in the garden whenever he didn't have after-school practice.

Madden was a bit of a jock so, not unexpectedly, he did experience some teasing from some of his teammates. Everyone else in the horticulture club was either a female or a serious nerd. But he rode it out with as much dignity as he could, and after a few nearly physical altercations, the rest of the guys eventually gave up hassling him about it.

However, as much as he enjoyed working in that garden, he knew he didn't want to make a career out of it. At least, not right away. He wanted something more exciting; something more adventurous. His mother had forever been trying to steer him towards pursuing a law degree. Her uncle had been a lawyer and had done very well for himself and his family. His mother thought it might be something that Madden could also excel in.

Movies like *To Kill A Mockingbird* and *Twelve Angry Men* made him think that maybe he could be satisfied working a courtroom the rest of his life. So, he went for the degree. But by the time he was ready to take the bar, he knew it wasn't going to be enough. That's when the idea of a career in law enforcement began to take shape in his mind.

But he never stopped gardening. Even when he lived in a small one-room apartment in college, he maintained a window garden. And when he met Kelly and found out that they had this shared interest, it was an instant love connection. In fact, many of their early dates were spent on their knees, spades in hand, digging, planting and replanting various plants and flowers. It was more fun than they would have ever had going to a movie or an expensive restaurant. He missed those times more than he was sometimes willing to admit.

Maybe it was his sense of irony, but it often occurred to Madden that being in the FBI and tracking down criminals was a lot like weeding a garden. Weeds were an inevitable element of just about any garden, and keeping them at bay was a constant battle. Society was no different. As long as there were people, there would be greed, jealousy, anger and insanity, all motivations for people to break the laws and treat each other poorly. And just as a garden needs a gardener to remove the intruding growths, civilization would always need people like Madden to help maintain its balance and order. Maybe that was why he always felt an equal attraction to the two of them: gardening and law enforcement.

As Madden rushed down the stairs towards the waiting SUV, Phillips opened the door and handed him a steaming cup of Starbucks. He knew what it contained without asking: venti dark roast with heavy whipping cream and two Splenda.

"Thanks, Phillips," he said gratefully. He never took for granted the blessing of working with someone that knew him so well. As the driver pulled away from the curb and merged into the early rush hour traffic, Madden leaned back and took a sip of his drink.

He glanced across the seat and caught Phillips' profile against the tinted window. She was, as his grandfather used to say, a 'handsome woman', even with the limp. She had a strong chin and an angular, graceful nose. Her long jet-black hair was pulled back into a ponytail, which is how she usually wore it when they were out in the field. She was fit and curvy in a way that some white women were self-consciousness about, but that many black and Latino women considered ideal.

However, he had to admit that, as attractive as she was, he was more or less blind to it. He had grown to see her as more of a sister than as any kind of a sexual object, but he was well aware that some men in the department did not at all share his platonic perspective.

Like any attractive woman in an industry dominated by men, Phillips dealt with her fair share of harassment, unwelcome advances and blatant disrespect. But she had an inner strength and sense of dignity that allowed her to float above it all, as though she barely even noticed it was there. Even when she struggled with her bad leg, she still moved with an undeniable air of grace.

As close as she and Madden were, he was sometimes surprised that he didn't know more about her love life. They spoke about everything else, including her father's recent stroke, her sister's bankruptcy, her gay brother finally coming out of the closet and so many other personal things. But very seldom had he ever heard her even mention a date. Kelly had once asked him if he thought that Phillips might herself be gay, but he didn't think so. He felt that if that had actually been the case, she would have probably mentioned it, especially during some of the conversations they had had regarding her brother and his trials and tribulations as a gay man coming out to the family.

Maybe it was good that Kelly thought Phillips might not be attracted to men. His wife had never proved to be the kind of woman who was particularly jealous of other women, but Madden had never been as close to another woman since he and Kelly met as he was to Phillips. The fact that his partner was so physically attractive would probably not have helped the situation if Kelly were the kind of woman who harbored any kind of relationship insecurities.

Phillips caught him staring at her and smiled. "You okay, Chief?"

"Yeah," said Madden. "Just thinking about Kelly."

"Is she pissed about you leaving town again so soon?"

"I don't really think that's it," said Madden. "But I've been thinking that maybe I've done as much as I can here. Maybe it's time to pass the torch to the next overworked, unappreciated civil servant."

"Retirement? Seriously?"

"It's a thought. The nursery is doing quite well. So well, in fact, that Kelly is having a hard time running it by herself. She's even talked about opening a second location. But at this point, she can't do much more without bringing in some high-level help or maybe even a partner. But she's been holding off, hoping that she could convince me to fill that role."

"You've always said that you trust plants more than you trust people," said Phillips. "And that was your first love, even though it had to take a backseat to this."

Madden wasn't sure whether she was referring to gardening or Kelly, but in his mind, they were kind of one and the same.

She stared off into the distance for a moment before bringing her attention back to him. "So, what's holding you back? Are you trying to wait until you have enough years to qualify for a full pension?"

Madden sighed. "It's not the money," he said, running his thumb along the crease of his slacks. "I made some good investments early on. Some extremely good investments. Dumb luck, really, but it set me up nicely. We'd be pretty comfortable without the pension. Even without the income from the nursery, to be honest. But something about this job has always had a hold on me. Maybe it's the excitement of the chase. You don't exactly get that from growing roses."

Phillips didn't answer. She just watched her boss, her face indecipherable.

"Why exactly do you do it?" asked Madden.

"Me? I like being able to make a difference. On a national level, whatever that means."

"What are you, thirteen years in now?" asked Madden.

"Thirteen years next month," said Phillips.

"And you've never thought about doing something else? Not even after the incident?" asked Madden, nodding at her leg.

"Never," said Phillips. "When I was lying in that hospital bed, waiting for the next operation and not knowing whether I'd ever walk again, all I could think about was getting back out into the field and running after bad guys."

"And what if things had turned out differently, and you had ended up bound to a wheelchair. What would you have done then?"

"I guess I would have had to limit my warrant assaults to locations with handicap ramps."

* * *

The weather they experienced when they touched down at LAX was the kind of weather that made some people from harsher climates return home and immediately tell their family members to start packing, they were moving to the West Coast. Madden and Phillips both stopped as soon as they walked out of the terminal and took a moment to bask in the warm caress of the fresh, slightly salty breeze.

After dropping their bags off at their hotel and checking in with the local office, they wasted no time getting to work. They headed straight for Newport Beach and the last known address for one Ishmael Carter. On the drive there, Madden read through the file one more time. Ex-Special Forces, computer whiz, lost a young daughter to an accidental police shooting. And the icing on the cake was that his wife, the girl's mother, was currently in jail awaiting trial for attacking that same officer. He fit the profile so perfectly that it was almost too good to be true. But Madden had little doubt that it was.

As they pulled up to the address, they saw a woman pulling a bag of groceries out of the rear of a Porsche Cayenne. She looked to be about thirty-five, slim and athletic, with long blond hair. She was wearing a bikini top and a sarong wrap. There was a young boy waiting for her at the door of the house. Madden would have guessed him to be five or six. He had dark hair and eyes, but Madden could still see the boy's mother in his face.

When Madden and Phillips slammed their car doors, the sound caused the woman to turn to face them. Her face grew dark with suspicion, and she instinctively took a step that placed her more directly in the path between the two strangers and her son.

“May I help you?” she asked.

Madden and Phillips both drew their badges.

“I’m FBI Special Agent Madden and this is Agent Phillips. We’re looking for Ishmael Carter.”

“I’m sorry, but there’s no one here by that name. Maybe you have the wrong address.”

Madden and Phillips both looked at each other.

“According to our records,” said Madden, “this house is owned by Ishmael Carter and,” he quickly pulled a small notebook from his pocket and flipped it open, “a Layla-Rose Carter.”

“I’m afraid you’re mistaken,” said the woman, shifting her grocery bag from one arm to the other. “I’ve owned this house for the last two months. Maybe you’re referring to the previous owners.”

“Do you have some ID?” asked Madden.

After confirming the woman’s identity, they thanked her for her help and returned to their car.

“How the hell did we miss that?” asked Phillips as Madden started the engine and began navigating his way back to the office.

“No one’s perfect,” said Madden. “Sometimes things just fall through the cracks. Get on the phone to the local Director and see if we can get an address for any of this guy’s local relatives. There has to be someone in the immediate area that has some connection to him.”

Forty-five minutes later, Madden and Phillips were seated in the living room of the home of Adriana Carter, waiting for her to return with glasses of iced tea. They had both kindly refused the offer, not wanting to impose, but she had insisted.

“Here we are,” said Adriana as she walked into the room carry a silver tray containing three glasses filled with ice and an amber liquid. She was a tall, stately woman, with short, gray hair but supple, caramel-colored skin. She moved with a grace and confidence that belied her age.

They all simultaneously took a sip of their drinks.

“That’s delicious,” said Phillips. “The mint gives it just the right kick.”

“It’s an old recipe passed down from my great-grandmother,” said Adriana. “The secret ingredient is baking soda, but don’t tell anyone I’m the one that told you.”

“Your secret is safe with us,” said Phillips, smiling warmly.

"Mrs. Carter," said Madden, placing his glass down on the provided coaster, "as we stated earlier, we are in the midst of an investigation that we think your son may be able to help us with. Do you know where we might find him?"

"I assume you tried his home?"

"It appears he no longer lives there. He apparently sold the property a couple of months ago."

Adriana responded by simply taking another sip of her tea.

"What exactly is this about?" she asked.

"We're not really at liberty to say."

"You're here asking for my help in finding my son, yet you won't tell me why it is that you're looking for him?"

Madden and Phillips glanced at each other.

"Are you familiar with the..." Madden paused, searching for a substitute for the word 'terrorist', "vigilante group PROPR? The one that has been attacking police officers in the name of justice?"

"Yes, I do believe I saw something on the news about that. Are you saying that you think my son might be involved with this group?"

"We don't know, ma'am," said Phillips. "We're just contacting anyone that we believe could possibly have any information. It's standard procedure. We believe that group might have connections to the military, and since your son was only recently discharged, it's possible that he may be in possession of some information that might help us in our investigation."

"I see," said Adriana. "I haven't seen Ishmael in several weeks. I've only seen him a couple of times since he arrived back in the States."

"Do you know where we might find him?" asked Madden.

"I can't say that I do. Ishmael always had a restless soul. The only thing that ever really settled him was his wife and his daughter. But his daughter recently passed and his wife...well, I suppose you're well aware of that situation. So, I'm sorry that I can't help you, but I honestly have no idea where he might be."

Madden nodded his head before taking another sip of his tea. "Well, thank you very much for your time, ma'am, and your hospitality. Here's my card. If you hear from your son, I would very much appreciate it if you would ask him to get in contact with us. It's very important."

"Certainly," said Adriana as she rose and walked them to the door.

"Do you believe her?" asked Phillips as they approached the car.

"I don't know. Anything is possible. I've been on the job quite a while now, and in my experience, mothers hardly ever give up their sons. Their daughters? Sometimes. But never their sons."

Moments later Madden and Phillips were on the road heading to their next stop: Macrolox.

Chapter 49

With the modifications on the truck finally complete, Ish and Jag returned to the house. Ish was in the workshop that adjoined the garage, cleaning the rifle that he would be using the next day, when Ma'am stuck her head in the door.

"Hey," she said.

"Hey, yourself," said Ish, smiling.

"That doesn't look like the typical SOF-issued sniper setup," she said, eyeing the pieces of rifle disassembled on the bench before him.

"To say the least," he said. "Those rifles would be far too loud for our purposes tomorrow. And far too powerful. This unit is specially modified, built from a CCI .22lr but with an even more effective suppressor than the CCI normally comes with. And, of course, the rounds are subsonic. With the thick insulation we've added to the walls, floor and ceiling of the truck, this should be about as loud as an old lady's sniffle. And just powerful enough to pierce the glass before being stopped by the target. Percentage of probability of collateral damage: practically zero."

"That's a bad muthafucka," she said almost lovingly. "How'd you get it?"

"Arms dealer out of Asia somewhere, believe it or not. He runs his business on the dark web. You know, underground, completely off the grid. You send him bitcoin and tell him the address you want it delivered to. Clean, easy and virtually untraceable."

Ma'am nodded. "You need any help? I feel kind of bad, you doing all the work out here by yourself."

"No, but thanks for the offer. Actually, I've always found cleaning firearms relaxing. After a while, it becomes like a form of meditation. It kind of reminds me of writing code in a way. It's all logic-based. If your code is right, you'll get the result you expect. Every single time. Same with guns. If your parts are clean, well-machined and correctly assembled, it will fire reliably every single time."

"Solid," said Ma'am. "Are you okay with a little conversation while you work?"

"Sure," said Ish. "What's on your mind?"

"I wanted to get your advice on something."

"Sure, but I'm starting to feel like Dr. Phil up in here," said Ish. "Not that I mind helping in any way I can, but it seems like you all think I have all the answers, and let me tell you, I absolutely do not."

"I know what you're trying to say," said Ma'am, "but you've always had a way of cutting through all the bullshit and gettin' right down to the heart of the matter."

"I don't know about all that, but I'm here for you. What's going on?"

"It's about Jag."

"Yeah, somehow I kind of figured it would be."

"So then I guess you know things are getting kind of 'serious' between us."

"So I gather."

"Today, he asked me if I would marry him."

Ish stopped what he was doing and put his rag down. "Normally, I would say congratulations, but from the look on your face I'm not sure that's what you're feeling."

Ma'am frowned, struggling to find the words to respond.

"I do think I love Jag, and I should be happy. But there's something my mother told me once that I can't seem to get out of my head."

"Yeah? What's that?"

"That you can't turn a ho into a housewife."

"Ma'am," said Ish. "You're a Christian, through and through. You've preached to me several times about God's forgiveness. Why do you think your past matters now?"

"I said God forgives. People? That's a whole 'nuther story. My past matters because I don't want my past sins fuckin' up someone else's life. God's forgiven me, and I've forgiven myself. I did what I had to do to survive, with what I was dealing with at the time. But just because me and God accept it don't mean everyone does."

"I think you're underestimating Jag. He knows about your past, and yet he still wants to be with you. That has to mean something."

"It does. It means *something.* I'm just not sure if it's enough. There are so many things I'm battling with over this. First of all, he's white."

"You know, I knew there was something different about him," said Ish, smiling.

Ma'am smiled back. "You don't understand. He's the first white man I've ever been with. That is, that wasn't paying me."

"Oh, I see," said Ish, nodding his head slowly.

"Every other white guy I've ever been with, I met on the stroll. And nine times out of ten I was high as fuck when I was with them. So, this is all new to me."

"I understand," said Ish. "But it shouldn't make a difference unless you allow it to. People are people. Skin color is just a paint job."

"Intellectually, I know that," said Ma'am. "But emotionally, it's not that easy. Not for someone like me."

"Have you expressed all this to Jag?"

"Of course, but he said something about how skillets don't know the difference between brown eggs and white eggs, 'cause they all sizzle the same, or some crazy shit."

Ish chuckled. "Yeah, that sounds like Jag. So, he's clearly not too worried about it. And that's saying a lot for a white boy from a deeply racist southern family like his."

"I suppose. But it's more than just that. Everyone seems to forget that for all intents and purposes, I'm just on a leave. My plan was to re-enlist when this whole PROPR thing was over. Or at least under control. He's already talking about this house he has back in Tennessee that his family owns that we can move into whenever we're ready. Tenne-fuckin'-ssee? Can you see my black ass anywhere 'round there?"

Ish smiled again. "I'm sure you wouldn't be the only one, Ma'am. I don't think it's anywhere near as bad as you think it is."

"Maybe. I just can't see myself being a housewife. What the hell would I do? All I really know is the service. I was nothing before I joined the Marines. Nothing but a fuckin' junkie. And the worst kind of junkie, at that. Being a soldier gave me something to live for. It gave me a sense of self-worth and acceptance in something larger than myself."

"Um, don't take this the wrong way, but I thought that religion was supposed to do that, too?"

Ma'am sighed. "It's not that simple, Ish."

"Okay," said Ish. "Explain it to me."

Ma'am grabbed a nearby stool, pulled it over to where Ish was working and sat down.

"Being a Christian isn't as cut and dry as some of you, uh, 'non-believers' may think it is."

"You were about to call me a heathen, weren't you?" asked Ish, smiling.

"No, my brother, I was not going to call you a heathen. A lost soul, maybe," she said, returning the smile, "but never a heathen."

Ish nodded. "I'm sorry," he said, "I didn't mean to interrupt. Please continue."

Ma'am cleared her throat. "The Christian church welcomes all types of people from all walks of life. No matter what the rest of their lives may look like, all are welcome in the house of the Lord. But the thing is, while God walks with everyone that calls themselves a Christian, not everyone that calls themselves a Christian walks with God."

"What the hell does— Sorry. I mean, what exactly does that mean?"

"Well, when it comes to a person like myself, it means that, as a child of God, the Lord always has love for me, but the same can't be said for all the people in the church. I don't come into church wearing fancy dresses with my hair all straightened and my face covered in makeup. I ain't all siddity and stuck-up like a lot of the women in these congregations. I don't even talk the way they do. You know I've always been a little rough around the edges. But God don't mind rough edges. Even Jesus had his rough edges."

"Yeah, I've seen the pictures," said Ish.

Ma'am smiled, ignoring him.

"So, in every church I've ever been a member of, I've always been a little bit of a' outsider. But the Marines was never like that. I mean, yeah, there was some sexism in the beginning, I'll admit it. But once you've proven yourself, most guys will accept you."

"Ma'am, I'm not exactly sure what Marine Corp you were in, but that certainly wasn't my experience. I saw sexism, racism and a whole bunch of other 'isms among the people I served with."

"No situation is perfect, Ish. I guess what I'm saying is that in spite of all the discrimination, I always felt more welcome in the military than I did in church."

"Wow," said Ish. "That's some serious shit; to say, as a child of God, that you felt more at home in the military with all its killing than in Sunday service worshiping with other Christians."

Ma'am bowed her head and when she looked up again there was a sadness in her eyes.

"Yeah, I guess that is some serious shit, at that. My point is, the Marines is the only place that I've ever felt completely at home. Clean, and at home. And now Jag wants me to walk away from all that. I don't know that I can do it."

"What I don't understand is what all the rush is about anyway? This whole thing is brand new. Why don't you both just take a breath and relax? Maybe give it a little time to simmer?"

"I don't know," said Ma'am. "Jag has this sense of urgency when it comes to he and I, and I'm not sure what's behind it. It seems like he takes everything else in his life in stride, but when it comes to our relationship, he's running for water with his head on fire."

"Maybe you just put it on him too good," said Ish, smiling again.

"No, it's not that. I've seen enough pussy-whipped muthafuckas to know one when I see one. This ain't that."

"Well," said Ish, "I don't know that I have any answers for you. You're a good woman, and Jag is a good man, and I think you two make a great couple. Forget what the rest of the world may say about it. All I can tell you is that when it comes to love, there are no guarantees. So, you can't live for love tomorrow; you have to live for love today. Let tomorrow take care of itself."

"What the hell does that mean?" asked Ma'am.

"It means listen to your heart, lady. Bask in the moment, and listen to your heart."

* * *

Everyone was up early the next morning. Chad left the house first, his job being to tail Janssen and make sure that there were no surprises and that the target was following his normal routine and would be where they expected him to be. But before he left, he double-checked the video camera they had mounted on the truck. As with the port for the rifle barrel, the lens for the video camera was camouflaged, mounted inside what looked to the casual observer to be a rooftop 'clearance' light. It featured a high-quality wide-angle lens that would record the entire scene in marvelous HD.

When Ish walked into the dining room on his way to the kitchen to scrounge up some breakfast, Bird was chewing on a glazed donut and reading a newspaper.

"Good morning," said Ish. "I didn't know Chad received the paper."

"He doesn't," answered Bird. "I went out earlier. Couldn't sleep. There are more donuts on the counter," he added, nodding toward a large, pink box.

"Thanks," said Ish as he grabbed a bear claw and poured himself a cup of coffee before taking the seat across from Bird. "Anything interesting?" he asked, referring to the paper.

"I guess that depends on what interests you. But some of this stuff they're writing about us and what we've been stirring up is kind of tripping me out. It's like a fungus that started as a small speck and is exponentially replicating itself, growing larger and larger every day."

"Some people might have used the term 'snowball' instead of fungus, but I get what you're saying," said Ish, smiling.

"I'm actually kind of surprised that the L.A. Times is so vocally against us. They're about as liberal as a newspaper can get, so I would have expected a little more sympathy. Or, at the very least, some understanding."

"Then you expect too much," said Ish. "Very few people in the mainstream establishment are going to come out in support of a group considered by most to be a 'public enemy'."

"Look at this article here," said Bird, folding the paper and turning it around so Ish could read it. "They're actually comparing us to the KKK! The fucking KKK?"

"Shit!" said Ish, leaning over and scanning the article. "You're right. That's going above and beyond. But did Chad tell you about the website? The last video has gotten over 14 million views, and he said there are at least five thousand comments, and almost 80% of them are supportive. That's a lot of people, man, and a lot of power."

"Yeah, I guess it is," said Bird before turning back to his paper.

"I'm going to go finish getting dressed and then we'll all hit the road. You ready?"

"As ready as I'll ever be," said Bird without looking up.

Jag drove the truck with Ish in the back, and Bird and Ma'am followed in a rented car, a Dodge Charger. The car Chad was driving, a Mustang, was also rented. All three vehicles sported fabricated license plates, each plate number having been created by Chad and inserted into the DMV database, therefore guaranteeing them to come up clean should anyone from law enforcement run the numbers. As before, everyone on the team likewise carried a phony driver's license that would also come up clean.

Chad had set up an intricate wireless communication system for everyone, similar to an open conference call, so that not only could Ish and Jag easily communicate and stay aware of what was going on in their respective areas, but all parties could hear and speak to each other the entire time. Once they were on the road, Ish called out to Chad from his headset.

"Hey, dude," said Chad when he answered.

"How's everything?"

"Chilly like a polar bear wearing a fur coat in an igloo," chirped Chad.

"Our boy still in character?"

"No surprises," said Chad. "Hey, by the way, have you spoken to anyone at the office? Stacy was blowing my phone up last night, but I was working on the plates and getting the truck rigged."

"No, I haven't," said Ish, "but she left me several messages, too. She didn't say what it was she wanted, only that it was important. One of the programmers probably had a meltdown or something. I'll call her when we get back to the house. We're on the road now. ETA: about thirty-five."

"I'll be here," said Chad.

"Hey, Jag, did you get that?" asked Ish.

"Loud and clear," said Jag.

Ish confirmed that Ma'am and Bird were also receiving the signals without issue, then he sat down on the floor to relax and get his head right for what he was about to do. A lot of the guys he met in the service thought that being a sniper was all about having good eyesight and a steady hand. But the greatest challenge was actually mental. Not only did you need nerves of steel, you also had to be a virtual math whiz, able to do complex distance and trajectory calculations not only on a ballistics computer but also in your head while out in the field, sometimes under torturous conditions.

Math had always been Ish's favorite subject, and one that he had always excelled in, which of course was one reason he ended up creating a software company. But he never knew what an excellent shot he was before he joined the service. Growing up in the hood, he was around guns on a daily basis. Most of the people he interacted with in the street were 'strapped' on a regular basis. But he never dealt with firearms himself. He saw too many people get shipped off to prison for years over firearm violations.

His buddies used to try to get him to carry a piece for his own safety if nothing else. They often told him he was like a sitting duck, walking around unarmed. But he always declined. He developed a reputation for letting his fists do his talking, and most people respected that. There were a couple of close run-ins, but ultimately, he had graduated high school without having to duck too much gunfire. And then he went and joined the military, where his fists didn't have much value. It turned out Uncle Sam didn't really care how great your right hook was.

"We're three blocks out," came Jag's voice over Ish's ear-piece.

"Thanks. Find a spot to pull over," said Ish. "Chad, are you ready?"

"Yes, sir. Me and the target are right on schedule. We're about six minutes away. I'll buzz if there's any change in plans."

"Roger that," said Ish.

They needed to stay put until Janssen was comfortably seated. The spot they were going to stop at for the shot was a red 'no parking' zone, so stationing themselves there to wait was not an option. But as Ish had observed during the recon, since drivers sometimes did stop at that curb to run in and grab their orders, they wouldn't be at all conspicuous for the amount of time they'd need to be there, which would likely be less than thirty seconds.

Ish stood up and stretched his legs. As a sniper, he was used to sitting in cramped positions for hours upon hours at a time. But there was no need to make things any more difficult than they needed to be. He was also used to operating in stifling heat, but the truck they had featured a refrigerated storage area, so the temperature was a very comfortable 72 degrees. He leaned back against the cool metal wall and willed his already slow breath to slow even more.

After a moment, he stepped up onto the sixteen-inch platform he and Jag had built and looked out of the camouflaged rifle hole. Most sniper positions had the shooter on the ground in a prone position or perhaps kneeling behind a rock or other solid structure. But after considering the dimensions of the truck and the fact that his location was mobile, Ish had decided that he would fire from a standing position. They had built two platforms. There was the one that he was standing on, which raised him closer to the roof of the truck so that he was at eye-level with the hole, and a second one that was a mounting station for the rifle.

The amount of foot traffic that he was currently able to view from his position was about normal for a Los Angeles street during the weekday commuting hours. There were people jogging, bike riding and walking in and out of various buildings. Several people passed by walking their dogs. Two actually stopped inches from the truck. One woman was so close that he could actually smell her perfume. But no one took any notice whatsoever of the truck or even thought to look up anywhere near the camouflaged hole. He and Jag had done their job well.

"Start camera," he said into the mic.

"Roger," replied Jag.

There was no need to wait till the last minute to get the video camera recording. Any extra footage would easily be cut out during the editing process. Besides, the feed was live to a laptop that Chad was monitoring in his car, so that they would know right away if there was any kind of camera malfunction. Moments later his friend's voice interrupted the silence.

"Touchdown," said Chad. "The chicken is in the roost."

"Beautiful," replied Ish. "Are you getting the video feed alright?"

"Yep. Clear and in perfect focus."

"Roger. On our way."

Jag, having heard the conversation, immediately started the truck and pulled away from the curb. It was time for action.

Chapter 50

Ish put his eye to the scope of the rifle and began focusing on various targets. At his position, he was above the roofs of the cars they passed and was at the perfect height for the shot he was about to take. There was a light plastic mesh over the hole that he would be shooting from, but when he focused on a distant object, the mesh all but disappeared from the viewfinder. The material the mesh was made from was so thin that not only would it not affect the trajectory of the round, but it would only separate enough to let the bullet pass, as opposed to having the round blow the entire screen out as it might if it were thicker.

"Three hundred feet," said Jag, but Ish already knew. Even though his field of vision was very narrow, he had memorized all the surrounding buildings, so he knew they were almost there. He began to count it down. Two hundred fifty feet. Two hundred feet. One hundred fifty feet. One hundred feet. Seventy-five feet.

"Fuck!" said Jag.

"What is it?"

"Another truck just pulled into our spot. Hold tight, I'll circle the block."

"Roger that," said Ish. Someone cleared their throat. It was Bird.

"We saw what happened," he said. "We should have driven in front of you and tried to save the spot."

"No," said Ish. "You're where you're supposed to be. Even if you had gotten there first, there's no guarantee that you'd have been able to keep that spot for us without taking the risk of drawing undue attention. We're cool with circling around."

"Roger that," said Bird.

It felt like it took forever for them to navigate around the block. It would have been much faster if they were driving a little sports car or even the Mustang. But the truck was slow and unwieldy. Finally, they were back at their starting position.

"Three hundred feet, and it looks like we're clear," said Jag.

Ish returned to his position behind the rifle and began to mentally block out all sound except for that of his own breathing. As he tightened his hands around the weapon, the sound of the air slowly entering and exiting his nostrils filled his ears. The truck was inching along: one hundred fifty feet. One hundred feet. Fifty feet. Twenty feet. He felt the truck sway as Jag spun the wheel and stopped the vehicle at the curb.

Directly before him sat Officer Janssen, a cup of coffee in one hand and a croissant in the other. He was wearing his blue uniform, and Ish could see the morning sun glinting off his silver name tag. He was gazing out the window, watching the passersby. He turned away momentarily to frown and say something to a nearby waitress before returning to his people watching.

Janssen was sitting in the perfect position, just where they predicted he would be. There was no one seated either in front of or behind him, so there was no one at risk of fouling the shot. But there were still people on the street, walking in and out of Ish's line of fire. It was impossible for him to look through the scope while at the same time keeping an eye on the civilians. That's why snipers used spotters, and today that was Jag's job.

"You're almost clear," said Jag, his voice loud in Ish's ear. "A man and a woman walking together are coming up, then a lady with a poodle is moving in the other direction. Hold tight."

Ish saw the three people pass in front of his scope, momentarily obscuring his view of Janssen.

"Clear!" said Jag.

Ish refocused the cross-hairs on the center of the officer's head and began to slowly squeeze the trigger. Just as he felt the faint kick of the round leaving the rifle, something crashed into the rear of the truck. The impact knocked him from his perch, and he slid across the floor of the truck on his shoulder.

"Shit!" yelled Jag.

Ish leaped up and ran back to the sight hole. He saw Janssen crouched down, his head barely visible from behind the wall of the coffee shop, his face looking stricken. He had his gun in hand and his eyes were wildly probing the area, looking for the shooter. Some of the people around him were also crouching down, but a couple were still standing, looking confused. Ish could see the bullet hole in the glass, very close to where Janssen had previously been sitting, but he didn't see any indication that anyone had been hit.

"What the hell happened?" he asked, speaking into the mic.

"We were rear-ended!" said Jag. "It was a guy in an SUV. He's struggling to get the driver's door open. What do I do?"

Before Ish could answer, Chad interrupted.

"We've got trouble!" he said. "There's a patrol car half a block back that saw the accident and is making its way to you right now!"

"Damn," said Ish. "Jag, looks like we're compromised. Mask up and get us out of here."

"I'm on it!" said Jag as he punched the accelerator and the truck lurched back into traffic, rocking from side to side from the exertion. They had each brought a mask set with them so that in the case of a chase like this one no one would be able to get a look at their faces.

"Let's take route B!" said Ish. Route B was a route they had previously decided on in case of emergencies. It was chosen partially because it offered opportunities to evade helicopters if they were being employed by the police, but also because there were no traffic cameras along the way that might snap a photo of any of them before they had their masks in place. "Chad, wait for us at rendezvous point D."

"On my way," said Chad.

"Bird?" said Ish.

"We're here," said Bird. "What's the plan?" His voice was calm and controlled.

"We need to shake this cop," said Ish. "Do you have eyes on him?"

"He's about three cars ahead of us," said Bird. "And we just heard on the police channel that another unit is going to be joining the chase in about two minutes."

"Hold on!" he heard Jag yell seconds before the truck swung violently to the left.

"The cops are going to soon realize that you're part of the chase, so you'd better get your masks on," said Ish to Bird.

"Already ahead of you," answered Ma'am.

"Ish, we're approaching a bottle-neck!" said Jag. "Should I punch through it?"

"No, someone might get hurt! How close is the cop?"

"Right on our tail!"

"Alright, slam the brakes!" he said.

Moments later Ish could hear the tires screeching even through the sound-reducing padding. He grabbed onto the frame of the sniper platform just before impact. The truck shuddered as if it were trying to shake loose of some ensnarement before the engine groaned and it lurched forward once more.

"That did it!" said Jag. "I think he's out of commission!"

"Bird, how's it look from your end?" asked Ish.

"A new bogey replaced the one you just smashed, and the radio says two more are on the way," said Bird. "It may be time for you to reach into your little bag of tricks."

"Roger that," said Ish. He had brought along a large duffel bag full of supplies and tools that he hoped he wouldn't have to use, but they were quickly running out of both time and options. He unzipped the bag. On top was his masks and shades, which he immediately put on. Next, he grabbed a green metal box and set it on the floor before him. Inside were a few hundred caltrops. Caltrops were antipersonnel weapons. They were small objects made of black metal, consisting of four sharp points configured into a tetrahedron shape, so that when thrown onto the ground one spike would always be pointed upwards. They were used the same way police departments sometimes used spike strips to stop suspect vehicles during car chases. He would have rather not had to use them, because he was concerned about bystanders possibly getting injured, but at this point he had no choice.

"Listen, everyone," said Ish. "I'm about to drop some steel. Ma'am, you peel off and catch up with us a few blocks ahead. Chad, get onto the city system and see if you can figure out where the other cars are approaching from and how we might avoid them."

"Roger," said Ma'am and Chad in unison. With orders given and acknowledged, Ish went back to work. He slid the green box against the rear doors and unlatched them. He and Jag had modified the doors of the truck so that they could be locked and opened from either inside or outside. They had also attached cables to each door, so that after they swung open, they could be pulled shut again from inside.

"Jag, let me know when you have a clear straight-away."

"Coming up," answered Jag as Ish felt the brakes grab momentarily before the truck accelerated forward again. He wanted to wait till they had a clear road ahead of them before he deployed the caltrops. If the cop car was too close, it would be difficult to drop them at the right spot in the car's path. If they were too far away or moving at too slow a speed, it would be easier for the cops to possibly maneuver around them. With a clear stretch of road in front of them, they could speed up, putting a little distance between them and the cops and forcing the cops to also increase their speed accordingly. Ish took a deep breath and waited for the signal.

"Fire!" said Jag.

Ish leaned back and kicked the spot where the two doors came together, and they both flew open. The patrol car was about two and half car lengths back, but Ish could clearly see the faces of both officers. They both look terrified at the sight of him all dressed in black. They were probably afraid he was going to begin shooting.

But instead, in one fluid motion, he knelt down and grabbed one side of the box, tipping it over and moving it from one side of the truck to the other. The caltrops tumbled out onto the roadway. The cops never knew what hit them. Both front tires immediately blew, and the car spun, mashing into a parked mini-van. Instantly, a second cruiser careened around the corner, lights and sirens at full alert. It cleanly avoided the wreck, steering deftly around it, but also didn't anticipate the caltrops. It suffered a similar fate—blown tires and a head-on collision with a telephone pole. Ish grabbed the cables and pulled the doors shut.

"We're free!" he said.

"Not quite!" said Chad. "I just tapped into the city's traffic cam system. There are two more units in the area that are responding. Where are you now?"

"Coming up on the hospital!" said Jag from behind the wheel.

"These two units are converging," said Chad. "One is behind you and the other is about two miles ahead. Make a left at the hospital!"

"Roger that!" said Jag, and moments later Ish felt the truck sway as Jag swung it into the turn.

"Ma'am!" said Chad. "I just saw you on camera. You're about to run right into one of the units coming from the south. Pull over now and park! It'll probably speed right past you!"

"Roger!" said Ma'am, and Ish could hear the tires squealing over the phone at the same time that he began to hear the police siren. The sound of the siren was rapidly increasing as it got closer and closer to Ma'am's location. Ish held his breath in anticipation. The sound reached its zenith and then began to fade.

"You were right," said Ma'am. "They just flew by us. Which way now?"

"Swing a right at the next street, and you'll be in line to intercept Ish."

"Roger!" said Ma'am, followed by the sound of tires peeling out as she and Bird rocketed back into traffic.

"Jag!" said Chad. "There's a bird in the air! It's probably still about fifteen minutes from you, but if you don't get here soon, things are going to get complicated!"

"I'm doing my best!" said Jag. "But this traffic is tighter than a duck's ass on Christmas. We can only go so fast without doing a demolition derby with these commuters!"

"We just pulled up behind you, lover-boy!" said Ma'am. "We're breaking out the siren. Maybe we can clear a path!"

Ish could hear a police siren passing by outside the truck. One of the other emergency tools that they had brought with them was a magnetic police light and siren, the kind often used by plainclothes detectives, that they were able to slap onto the roof. It was doubtful that it would ever fool a real cop, but it would get civilians to move over so they could pass.

"Yeehaw!" said Jag. "Now we're cooking with gas, pretty mama!"

Ish could feel the truck gaining speed. They just might make it.

"Shit!" said Chad. "I see you, but there's a third unit coming that's right in your path! Take the next right!"

Ish was slammed against the wall as the truck abruptly changed direction. There were a few moments where no one spoke, and the only sound was the siren up ahead in Bird and Ma'am's car.

"Did we lose them?" he asked.

"Almost," said Chad. "They drove by you, but now they're busting a U-turn!"

"Jag, how far are we from point D?"

"At this speed," said Jag, "about six minutes."

"How far is the chopper?" asked Ish.

"I've lost track of it," said Chad. "It could literally be anywhere now, but if it finds you before you get here, we're going to have to change our dinner plans!"

"I see that cruiser in my side mirror," said Jag. "It's gaining fast."

"We need to shake it before we get to the rendezvous," said Ish.

"I'm well aware," said Jag, his tone indicating slight irritation.

"I'm not trying to be a party pooper," chimed Chad, "but the annoying neighbor next door is about to knock."

Ish listened closely and could faintly hear the sound he had been hoping they could avoid. It was the sound of a helicopter, and it was growing louder by the second as it gained on them.

"You have any more caltrops left?" asked Jag.

"A few," said Ish. "But they are aware of that trick now, so they probably won't fall for it again."

"Yeah," said Jag, "and this cruiser is staying close, but not close enough to rear-end us. Come on, Felix. I think it's time you reached back into that black bag of yours and pulled out something magical!"

Ish had brought firepower with him that could easily have stopped the car that was chasing them, but using it was a last resort. He was adamant that they not unnecessarily put in danger the lives of any cops that might simply be innocent individuals doing the job they were paid to do. But there was another option he had up his sleeve that might work.

Ish checked the box again. There were only about twenty caltrops left. Assuming the cops currently following them were aware of what had happened to the first two cars, if he dropped these now there was a very good chance that they could avoid them. What he needed was a distraction.

"The chopper is right on top of us!" yelled Jag, but Ish could clearly hear it for himself.

"I'm working on it," he replied.

Going back to the duffel bag, he pulled out another small box. This one contained flash bangs and smoke bombs. Flash bangs were grenades that didn't emit any shrapnel; they simply made a loud noise and a bright flash of light along with a trace amount of smoke. They were generally used by law enforcement and military to disorient a suspect that was barricaded inside a structure.

Ish went back to the doors and unlocked them, then grabbed five flash bangs and clipped a smoke bomb to his belt. He tucked four of the flash bangs into the crook of his left arm, so he could easily keep the levers depressed, and pulled all their pins. With the fifth grenade in his left hand, he carefully kicked the doors open again.

The police car was about seven or eight car lengths back, its lights flashing and siren blaring. Ish visually calculated the best distance at which to drop the grenade. Satisfied that the officers in the car were watching him, he made an exaggerated show of removing the pin from the grenade that was in his left hand. He then released the lever, waved the grenade slowly above his head like a trophy, and tossed it in the direction of the car.

The explosion startled the cops, who had no idea it was not a normal grenade. They overcompensated, trying to steer around the explosion, side-swiping several parked cars but not slowing their pursuit. While they were doing that, Ish dropped the other grenades off the back of the truck, tossed the smoke bomb and kicked over the box holding the remaining caltrops.

The flash bangs began exploding, setting off several car alarms to add to the confusion. As the cops continued to struggle with their evasive maneuvers, trying to figure out exactly what was happening, the smoke bomb exploded, blinding them to the caltrops. Their car disappeared behind the gray cloud, but moments later Ish heard the tell-tale tire explosion as they hit a caltrop, followed by the sound of impact as they smashed into something large.

"One down, one to go!" yelled Ish.

"There are four more units converging on your location!" said Chad.

"Can you steer us past them?" asked Jag.

"I can try," said Chad. "But the eye in the sky is going to keep us all honest. Ma'am, traffic is pretty open in front of you. You should turn your siren off."

"Roger," said Ma'am, and the sound of the siren abruptly stopped.

"You're only two minutes away," said Chad. "If I can get you zig-zagging right, you may be able to stay clear of the patrol cars until we can shake the copter. Take the next right!"

Ish held on as the centrifugal force of the turning truck pulled against his body.

"Cool," said Chad. "We have two of them back tracking. Make a left at the next street!" After a moment, Chad continued. "We need to make the call, and I'm a little tied up right now. Bird, can you make it?"

"Consider it done," said Bird.

'The call' was a call to the security office of the building that was their rendezvous point, aka point D. The building was a twelve-story insurance company located in an office plaza. The original plan was that when the time was right, Chad, who was stationed in the underground parking structure below the building, was to call in a bomb threat to the security office, posing as someone from the police department. He would then remotely trigger the fire alarm via computer. But since he was busy navigating them around their pursuers, it was now up to Ma'am and Bird. Thirty seconds and Bird was back on the line.

"Call made!" he said. "Better hit that alarm!"

"Alarm tripped," said Chad. "Take a left at the next street, go up two blocks and then hang another right. You should be able to skate by them and swing into the underground lot by the skin of your teeth."

"Roger that," said Ma'am.

It was now silent inside the truck except for the faint beat of the helicopter overhead, the squeal of the brakes and the grind of the engine as Jag followed Chad's directions.

"Destination in sight!" said Jag. "Get ready!"

Ish removed his mask and pulled off his black hoodie and sweat pants to reveal the white shirt, tie and gray slacks underneath. He then went back to his bag and grabbed the last two things he would need out of it. The first was a black leather briefcase and the second was a low-level explosive device with a timer already set for 75 seconds. Moments later he felt the truck come to a stop.

"Touchdown!" said Jag.

Ish immediately activated the bomb's timer and partially pushed open one of the doors. After pulling off and tossing his rubber gloves, he deftly slid down out of the truck with nothing but the empty briefcase in hand. Jag was just crawling down out the of the truck cab and was also now wearing a dress shirt, tie and slacks. Ish had never seen him dressed up before. He looked like a different man.

There were no other people in sight as they both slowly started walking towards the doors that led from the parking garage to the building lobby. They could see people already moving towards the front exit in response to the fire alarm that Chad had triggered. Ish and Jag were halfway to the doors when they heard a distant explosion, which sounded like it was somewhere below them. That would have been the car Bird and Ma'am were in. They were probably already clear of the building, and if everything had gone according to plan, Chad had driven out of the garage before either of the other two vehicles had arrived.

Within seconds of them stepping through the garage doors and into the lobby, the explosion in the truck detonated. The explosives in both vehicles were small. They were just large enough to obliterate any forensic evidence, but not enough to harm anyone who might be walking nearby.

The explosions set the mass of people in the lobby into a frenzy. They were pushing and shoving each other, barely containing their panic, probably afraid the building was about to come down on top of them. Jag and Ish separated and blended in with the rest of the crowd. Ish thought he caught a glimpse of Ma'am leaving through one of the far exits, but he wasn't sure. Moments later, as he himself exited, he could hear the helicopter flying around above the building, obviously waiting for the truck or the Charger to exit.

Six minutes later Jag and Ish both arrived at another vehicle, a Honda Accord, that was parked in a nearby supermarket parking lot. Once they pulled out into traffic, with Jag once more behind the wheel, Ish spoke into the mic.

"Everyone alright?" he asked.

"A-OK and safely on the road," said Ma'am.

"Same here," said Chad.

"Beautiful. Meet you back at base," said Ish as he pulled the ear-piece out and dropped it into this breast pocket.

Now that the excitement was over, he had some time to sit back and start mulling over what had just happened: PROPR had just experienced its first complete and utter failure.

Book 3: BEYOND THE MIDNIGHT SKY

Chapter 51

Madden and Phillips had agreed to meet for an early breakfast the next morning in the hotel's restaurant. Madden wasn't surprised to arrive and see that Phillips already had two empty glasses of orange juice on the table in front of her.

"You could have ordered," said Madden. "You didn't need to wait for me."

"No, I just needed something to drink," replied Phillips. "High levels of frustration make me thirsty."

"What are you so frustrated about?" asked Madden as he took a seat across from her and began to peruse the menu.

"I just figured we would have gotten more out of the Macrolox woman. She didn't even seem all that surprised to see us. It's almost like she was expecting us."

"The company she works for does business with the Pentagon," said Madden. "She's used to keeping secrets, and with a job like that, there's probably few things that will actually rattle her. She reacted pretty much the way I figured she would."

A waitress appeared at their table. She was young, probably early twenties, with long red hair, porcelain skin, large green eyes and a Marilyn Monroe figure.

"Good morning," she said, smiling brightly. "My name is Tara, and I'll be your server. Can I start you with something to drink, sir?"

"Sure," said Madden. "How's your coffee?"

"It's delicious. We have a medium roast that many people enjoy, but personally, I prefer the dark roast. I like my coffee strong and black—no cream, no sugar. The blacker, the better," she said, smiling coyly and looking deep into Madden's eyes.

"That sounds good," said Madden. "I'll try the dark roast."

"Very good," said the waitress. "And you, ma'am, would you like another refill on the orange juice?"

"Sure, if it's not too much trouble," said Phillips.

"No problem at all," said Tara. "Are you ready to order, or do you need a few minutes?" she asked, turning back to Madden.

"I think I'm ready," he said. He and Phillips both ordered the same thing, and moments later the waitress was gone.

"How is it that you always handle that with such grace?" asked Phillips.

"Handle what?"

"You know. The flirting. The batting eyelashes. The come-hither stares. And sometimes even phone numbers on the back of the receipts. It happens everywhere we go, but you never react to it. You're too good an FBI agent not to notice it. Has your resolve always been that strong?"

"What can I say?" replied Madden. "I love my wife."

Phillips nodded, but there was something about the way she did it.

"What is it?" he asked.

"Nothing. I guess it's just that whenever I think about you and Kelly together you come across as such an unlikely couple."

"Why, because she's white and I'm black?"

Phillips slumped her shoulders and gave him a look of exasperation. "No, not because she's white and you're black. It's because she's always seemed so unprepared for life as the wife of someone in law enforcement. No offense, but she's always struck me as just a tiny bit 'fragile'."

"No offense taken," said Madden. "Personally, I've always thought of her as one of the strongest women I've ever known."

"Really?" said Phillips. There was a hint of challenge in her voice.

"Absolutely," said Madden. "Though I suppose strength is relative. For example, there are certain things that you deal with that I think might prove challenging for my wife. And vice versa."

"Is that right?" asked Phillips. "What exactly—" she began before the waitress appeared back at the table with their drinks, interrupting her.

After the waitress once again left them alone, Phillips took a long sip of her juice, seeming to abandoned whatever it was she was about to ask before they were last interrupted.

"Tell me," said Phillips, "have you always dated Caucasian women?"

Madden was taken aback. Phillips had never asked him that question before. He wondered where it was coming from, and if perhaps something he had recently said or done had rubbed her the wrong way.

"Yes and no," he replied as he poured some half-and-half into his coffee. "Yes, I've more or less dated white women from the time I started dating, but I never dated white women exclusively. In addition to Caucasians, I've also dated Asian women, Latino women, Indian women and, yes, Black women."

"How did your family react to that? You dating non-blacks, I mean."

"My father was totally cool with it right from the start. My mother? She took a bit longer to come around."

"So, your mother had an issue with white people?"

"You might say that, but that would be oversimplifying things. My mother was from the south. Born and raised in Arkansas. She experienced a lot of racism when she was growing up. And I'm not talking about 2016 D.C. racism, I'm talking about 1950 Jim Crow racism. Most people don't walk away from that without some emotional scars, and my mother was no exception."

"So, did you ever think of her as a racist?" asked Phillips.

Madden was again somewhat shocked at this line of questioning. *Where was this coming from?*

"With black people, especially those that have suffered a lot of discrimination, the term 'racist' can be somewhat ambiguous. There are some people, including some prominent sociologists and philosophers, that believe that minorities can't be racist. Their position is that being racist means having the power to oppress, and since minorities don't have any real power over their majority counterparts, they can't possibly qualify as racists."

"And do you believe that?"

"No, that's absolute bullshit. Anyone can be a racist. Racism is all about treating someone as less simply because of their race. Power need not factor into it. Why the sudden fascination with the racial aspects of my upbringing?"

"It's been on my mind the last few days. I've been wondering if it could have some bearing on how you approach this case," said Phillips.

Madden didn't immediately respond. He took a slow sip of his coffee as he stared across the table at his partner, trying to evaluate what she had just said. Phillips must have suddenly picked up on the tension, because her face changed. But before she could say anything, Madden spoke.

"Are you asking if this case is testing my loyalties?"

"No, Dexter, that's not at all what I'm saying," she said. "I'm just wondering how you're holding up. It has to be hard, being a man of color and seeing what's happening in this country right now between minorities and the police."

Madden took another sip of his coffee and then dabbed at his mouth with his napkin.

"Do you remember that case we had a couple of years ago with the woman that killed her abusive husband by pouring hot grease on his face while he slept and then fled with the kids?"

"Yes, how could I forget?" she said.

"Even though this guy was someone that some would say absolutely deserved it, someone that had already served time for filleting the skin off this woman's breasts and threatening to kill her and the kids if she ever left him, I still never saw you once falter in your efforts to capture her and bring her to justice."

Phillips' face clouded momentarily.

"That's true, but in those types of situations, there really is no other choice. Any other option is a path to anarchism. It's our job to help keep this society ordered and to make sure that people understand that we are a nation governed by laws and that there are penalties for breaking those laws," she said.

"And how is what she did any different than what the group PROPR is doing?" asked Madden.

"For one thing," challenged Phillips, "the abuse that happened to this woman wasn't the result of a systematic pattern of discrimination and injustice. No, she didn't deserve what that man did to her, but at the same time, she wasn't fighting a system that was trying to tell her that the black eye or broken arm she was reporting never really happened."

Madden chuckled.

"What's funny?" asked Phillips.

"You," he said. "I never thought you and I would be having a conversation where you took up the position of defending a criminal against the government. Actually, I'm surprised by this entire discussion."

"Why would you be surprised?" replied Phillips. "Don't you believe that I care about the rights of black people?"

"Well, I would assume that you care about the rights of all people, but I've just never heard you speaking in a manner that is so race-specific. One might think you have a special affection for blacks. So again, why the sudden interest?"

A flash of pink blush appeared on Phillips' cheeks as she shook her head in either embarrassment or dismay.

"Do I have to have a reason to care about people?"

"No, but when you act out of character, I can't help but wonder what's going on," said Madden.

Phillips took another deliberate sip of her orange juice. He could tell she was buying time, trying to decide either how to say something or whether or not she should say it at all.

"Well," she said as she returned her glass to the table, "the truth of the matter is, I've been seeing a counselor. We've been working on my...'icy' disposition."

Madden couldn't help but smile.

"Your icy disposition?" he said. "I've never thought of you as 'icy'. I think 'cool and unflappable' would be a better description. And I always considered that one of your assets and one of the many things that made you so suited for this job."

"Yes, I suppose that's right, but it's not an asset in the job of finding a man." She looked away, her face poorly masking her uneasiness. "I'm not getting any younger, Chief. My clock is ticking so loud that it's keeping me up at night."

"Okay," said Madden. "And what is your therapist's solution for solving this dilemma?"

"That I be more open; more accessible. The phrase she's used several times is 'emotionally available.' Part of that is learning to connect with others, something that has always been a challenge for me. As she says, 'it's all about being vulnerable and taking chances'."

Madden nodded with understanding.

"I see. Well, I have to applaud you, Phillips. It's admirable that you're being so proactive in trying to create the life you desire. Whomever you end up with should consider himself very lucky."

"Well, uh, that brings up the other thing that I kind of wanted to speak to you about," she said. She faltered, took a moment to take a big breath, and then continued. "You see, I—" she started but was cut off when both of their phones began ringing simultaneously. They locked eyes, both raising their eyebrows with concern. Something had happened. Madden reached for his jacket to retrieve his, but Phillips was already pulling hers out of her purse.

"I've got it," she said as she put the phone to her ear. "Phillips." She listened for a moment.

"He's right here," she said. She listened for a few more seconds before hanging up and raising her hand to summon their waitress.

"We'd better get this to go. A sniper just tried to kill an L.A.P.D. cop. They think it might be our gang."

When Madden and Phillips arrived at the scene of the crime, there was a mass of police cars parked around the coffee shop. After showing their badges, they were directed to the officer in charge, a Detective Dawkins. He was a large black man, about 6'3", with a short salt-and-pepper afro and matching mustache and sideburns. He had the air of someone slightly outside his element, which didn't surprise Madden. High publicity cases tended to overwhelm most cops. The media attention and public scrutiny made people nervous about making mistakes that might cost them their careers—and that sometimes actually did.

"What can you tell us?" asked Madden once they had all been introduced.

"The Reader's Digest version is that Officer Janssen," he began, "was having his regular morning coffee and donut here at this coffee shop when he was fired upon. The shooter was apparently stationed in the back of a delivery truck that had stopped at the curb. Another vehicle rear-ended the truck, which is probably the only reason my man is still alive.

"We had a cruiser that just happened to witness the accident and gave chase as the truck drove off. The officers in the cruiser didn't even realize anything had happened in the coffee shop. They initially thought it was a simple hit and run until they got the radio call while in pursuit.

"There was a second suspect vehicle that was also involved. Air traffic control joined the chase, but the suspects eventually ditched their vehicles and fled the scene, torching them as they left. We're still searching the area but so far have found no signs of them."

Madden nodded as he quickly scribbled down notes.

"So, you believe this is related to the PROPR case?" asked Dawkins.

"I don't know; it could be. Do you have an opinion one way or the other?"

"Not particularly. It's just that I know that's going to be the number one question asked at the press conference."

"I think the safe bet is to stick to 'no comment' at this time," said Madden.

"Right," replied Dawkins, but there was some tension in his body language. Madden figured he probably also wasn't crazy about the Bureau stomping around in his sandbox.

"Is this Janssen?" he asked, pointing his pen in the direction of an officer who was seated at the back of a paramedic vehicle, having something done to his eyes.

"That's him," said Dawkins.

"Okay, give us a minute," said Madden. Once Dawkins walked away, he turned to Phillips.

"Get on the horn, please, and get the rest of the team here," he said.

"Done," she said as she pulled out her phone and began dialing.

Madden walked over to where the cop was sitting. His head was tilted back, his face angled towards the ceiling while some kind of liquid was being sprayed into his eyes.

"Hi, I'm Special Agent Madden, FBI. What happened to him?" he asked, directing his question to the medical technician, a nerdy-looking young African American man who wore black, thick-framed glasses and a small, silver nose ring.

"He—" began the technician before Janssen interrupted.

"Got some fucking glass in my eye," he said. "That's how close the shot was! Shattered the cup I was holding just as I was about to take a drink!"

"Any serious damage?" asked Madden, once again directing his question to the technician.

"He'll live," said the man as he handed Janssen a napkin to dry his eyes and then began putting his supplies away.

Madden watched the young man for a few moments without speaking until he finally got the hint.

"Uh," said the tech, "I can finish this later. I'll go grab a coffee." Madden nodded his thanks as the man walked away.

"I spoke to your commander and he gave me the basics," he said to Janssen once they were alone. "You were having your morning coffee, someone in a truck took a shot at you and the chase began. What else can you tell me about what happened?"

"There's not much more to tell, Agent," he said. "Some asshole took a shot, he missed, he got away. That's pretty much all I know about it at this point."

"Could you identify any of the suspects?"

"I didn't see shit! I didn't even know where the shot came from until fifteen minutes later when I heard about the chase."

"So, you didn't see who was driving the truck?"

"No, I didn't. The guy in the truck was probably ten miles down the road before I even knew there was a truck!"

"Understood," said Madden. "What about enemies? Could there be anyone you've had a problem with lately that might be looking for revenge?"

"I'm a cop. As you know, there are lots of people that don't like what I have to do to them. Do I have enemies? What cop worth a shit doesn't? Have I been looking over my shoulder lately for anyone in particular? I have not."

"There's no tactful way to put this," said Madden, looking around to make sure their conversation was still fairly private, "but there's a question I need to ask you that can't be avoided: Do you believe anyone would ever accuse you of having a problem with black people?"

Janssen's face was expressionless.

"What do you mean by 'problem'?"

"Allow me to be more specific," said Madden. "Would you say that, in the execution of your duties as a police officer, you have acted in a way that might give anyone the idea that you have been systematically biased or unjust in your treatment of people of color?"

"People can say anything they want, but I treat everyone the same. It may be that I arrest more blacks than I do whites, I don't know; I haven't looked at the numbers. But if so, it's because I encounter a lot of black people, and they're the ones committing most of the crimes," said Janssen, a strained smile plastered on his face.

"Well, if that's true, you are part of a unique beat, because according to research done by the FBI, blacks do not commit a disproportionate percentage of crimes."

Janssen stood up, showing himself to be a good three inches taller than Madden, and took a step towards him, so that he had to look down at him for their eyes to meet.

"Look," he said, "I've been a cop for over twenty years. I really don't care what FBI statistics may have to say. I know who's out here, snatching purses, stealing cars, knocking their girlfriends around and selling dope, and more often than not, they look a lot more like you than they do like me."

Madden took a moment to close his notebook and put it back in his breast pocket. "Thanks for your time," he said, staring calmly into the man's eyes. "I'm sure we'll be speaking again soon."

Madden strolled over to where Phillips was leaning against a building, talking on her cell phone. She put the phone away as he approached.

"The team's on the way. They'll be here by 6:00," she said. "What's the word on the victim?"

"He didn't have much to say," said Madden. "Didn't see shit, doesn't know shit, and doesn't really give a shit."

"I was watching you two. I sensed some interactional friction."

Madden smiled. "'Interactional friction'? That's a sweet way to put it. Yes, I think we can safely say there was a tiny bit of 'friction' in our 'interaction', but nothing unusual."

"What does that mean?"

"You know, the typical 'white guy with a superiority complex that doesn't like having to answer to black folk' situation."

Phillips' face momentarily showed something that Madden couldn't quite figure out, but then it was gone.

"So, what do we have?" she asked. "Any reason to think this may be anything other than another PROPR attack?"

"Not really. For one, he definitely seems to have an issue with black people," said Madden.

"There are lots of cops that have problems with black people."

"True, but only a few of them are the target of vigilante terrorist groups. Once we get a look at this guy's personnel records we'll know more, but this quacks like a duck and walks like a duck."

"Okay," said Phillips. "What's our next move?"

"I'd like to take a look at the getaway vehicles," he said.

Twenty minutes later they were standing in the parking garage of the building where the truck and the Charger were abandoned. The area was roped off and being guarded by a large contingent of police officers. Crime scene investigators were sifting through the wreckage, collecting evidence. They were introduced to the lead investigator, a woman named Barrows.

"What can you tell us?" asked Madden.

"That these guys, whoever they are, are good," she said. "It's early yet, but so far I haven't found anything juicy. They torched each vehicle when they ditched them. Some kind of small incendiary devices just strong enough to burn away any kind of fibers, prints or other forensic evidence we might use for I.D."

"Were both of the vehicles empty?" asked Phillips.

"Surprisingly, no. Each one had a couple of weapons, some tools, remnants of burned clothing and the like. But again, probably nothing we can hang a name on."

"No serial numbers on the weapons?" asked Madden.

"None. Filed clean away," said Barrows. "We already ran the VINs. The truck was recently sold, but the new owner is a dead end at DMV. We're trying to track down the previous owner now."

"And the Charger?" asked Madden.

"Rental car. Again, it appears to have been rented with a fake I.D. The rental agent that took the order is already on the way to the station. We're hoping he can remember something about the person that rented it. Sorry. I wish I had more to tell you."

"Thanks," said Madden. He and Phillips began walking back towards their car.

"Let's get down to the station," he said. "I'd like to be there when the rental agent arrives, and I have a few more questions for Janssen."

Madden drove, and though Phillips was quiet, she appeared fidgety and distracted. Finally, she turned in her seat to face him.

"There was something I wanted to say to you back at the restaurant," she said nervously. "I wanted you to know that—" she began before Madden raised his hand, cutting her off.

"Let me stop you for a minute," he said. "If this is anything personal, anything that would possibly interfere with this case, I would rather you hold off on it, if at all possible. At least until we're back in D.C. After that, I promise to give you my undivided attention."

Phillips froze for a second, then simply nodded her head in agreement and went back to gazing out the window. Something told Madden he had just dodged a bullet. Or, at the very least, delayed one.

Chapter 52

As soon as they all arrived back at the house, everyone gathered in the living room. Chad grabbed the remote and was about to turn on the television before Ish stopped him.

"Hold up a minute," he said. "Before we start bombarding ourselves with all the things the media is going to be saying about what just happened, let's have a quick chat. First things first: is everyone alright?"

Ish was addressing everyone in the room, but he was looking at Chad. Chad was the only one who wasn't a seasoned soldier. Everyone else had been in much more dire situations than what they experienced today. Yeah, they were at risk of being captured and thrown in jail, but that was nothing compared to being shot or blown up—or captured and tortured.

No one spoke. They were all looking at Chad, waiting to hear what he had to say. His face was blank as he stared back at them, unreadable. Finally, he broke into a wide grin.

"That was fucking amazing!" he exclaimed. "It was like being in an old Clint Eastwood movie. You know, one of those old WWII joints!"

Jag returned the smile.

"I guess it's easy for you to say that," he said. "You weren't the one sweating in a multi-ton metal box, trying to outrun helicopters."

"Yeah, you got a point. But it was still a hella rush!" said Chad.

"I'm glad you enjoyed it so much," said Ish. "But let's not forget that I missed the fucking shot. The mission was a failure. Not only is that asshole still out there, but now he knows that someone is after him."

"Missions don't always go as planned," said Bird. "You know that as well as any of us. I mean, who could have possibly anticipated a car accident happening at the exact moment you took the shot? Crazy!"

"Yeah, that muthafucka must have had a' angel on his shoulder," said Ma'am.

"Apparently," said Ish, scowling.

"So, what's the next move?" asked Chad. "Do we go after him again right away?"

"Slow your roll, sparky," said Jag. "We barely got away with our asses in one piece. Now's the time for re-evaluating the situation and taking a moment to breathe before we just blindly leap back in."

"That's exactly right," said Ish. "Let's all take a moment to decompress and get a line on all the available intel out there. We need to try to find out exactly what they know about us. Then we can decide on what moves make sense from here on out."

"Cool," said Bird. "I'm starving. Anyone want to go on a taco run with me?"

"We all need to stay inside until we get a sit-rep on all this," said Ish. "We can have something delivered. Menus are in the kitchen."

Bird shrugged. "Okay. I'll be right back," he said as he rose from the couch.

Ish felt his phone vibrate and took it out of his pocket to examine it. He shook his head.

"Chad, it's Stacy again. Do you mind giving her a call? My mother has also been calling. She's left me four messages since last night."

"No problem," said Chad as he pulled his phone from his pocket and then frowned.

"That's odd," he said. "Your mother left two messages for me, too."

Ish walked into the back yard and dialed his mom's number.

"Hi, Mama," he said.

"Ishmael! How are you, son?"

"I'm good. How are you?"

"Fair to middling."

"Good. What's up?"

"The FBI came to see me yesterday."

"What?!" exclaimed Ish. "What exactly did they say to you?"

"Not much of anything. They wanted to know if I knew where they could find you. They went out to the house and found out that you had sold it. They were looking for a forwarding address. I told them that I hadn't seen you in a few months."

"Did they leave a card?"

"Yes," she said. Ish could hear her rummaging around in the background. "There were two. There was a Special Agent Madden and a young woman, Agent Phillips." She read Ish the numbers, and he copied them into his phone.

"Ishmael, what are you involved in?"

Ish took a moment to slow his breathing. "Mama, it's complicated. But it's nothing you need to worry about."

"I'm your mother. Anything that might cause you trouble is something that I'm going to worry about."

"I know, Mama, but it's not something I can talk about right now."

"Why not?"

"Because I can't be sure who's listening," he said. "I really need to talk to you about this in person."

"It doesn't look like that's possible right now, but I think I still deserve to know what's going on."

Ish didn't speak.

"Ishmael Octavius Carter, I'm going to ask you one more time. Who are these people, and what do they want with you?"

"I'm not absolutely sure, but I think they may be after me. I think they suspect that I'm one of the guys that has been attacking the cops."

"You're part of that PROPR group?"

"Mama..."

"Oh, lord Jesus," she said. Ish could hear her trying to catch her breath, and his heart ached for her. After taking a few moments to regain her composure, she continued. "How did this happen?"

He could hear tears in her voice, but she was clearly trying to hold them back.

"Mama, all I can say about this group right now is that I agree with what they're doing. Black men and women have been dying for years and years in America at the hands of the very people that swore to protect and serve them, and no one has been doing anything about it. We're living as doctors, lawyers and politicians, as entertainers, sports stars and business owners. And yet, some people still treat us as though we were runaway slaves, wild creatures that they can run down and murder in cold blood. Someone has to try to put a stop to that."

"I understand that, son," said his mother, still trying to choke back her tears. "But this is not something a person like you needs to be involved in. You have so much to live for!"

"Why, because I have money? Mama, that's the whole point. Money doesn't mean anything to these people. Money protects white people, but it doesn't do the same for blacks. No one was doing anything before PROPR came along. This is something that's needed doing for years. Do you know Layla refuses to leave jail because she thinks she's safer there than out here in so-called 'free society'? I couldn't protect her. I couldn't even protect my own daughter! At least this group is trying to make a difference, even if it's nothing more than taking two or three bad cops off the street out of the thousands that are out there!"

"Ishmael, I...I..." she said. She paused, her words faltering, as though she didn't know where to begin. She took a deep breath.

"Ishmael," she said again, her voice now full of confidence and resolve. "Did I ever tell you how you were named?"

"No," he said, knowing that the question was rhetorical. His mother had an extremely sharp mind. She never forgot anything. She knew perfectly well that she had never had this conversation with him before.

"You were a late baby. We were already two weeks overdue, and your father was getting nervous. There were some complications that made the doctor hesitant to induce labor. He had doubts that you'd survive the induction. As the hours came and went with no change, your father became convinced that you were lost to us. I tried to get him to relax, but once your father made up his mind, not even the devil could convince him otherwise. We hadn't even named you. I had already had two miscarriages, and your father refused to even consider giving you a name until you breathed your first breathe. He felt that it would lessen the pain just a little if he couldn't put a name to the loss." She paused again momentarily, apparently lost in the memory.

"Anyway," she continued, "the night before you were born, I was sitting in front of the fire, reading my Bible. I did a lot more reading of scripture in those days, especially before your father passed. I fell asleep with the book in my lap, and I woke to find it had fallen on the floor. The book was open, and in the dark of the room there appeared to be a dull glow coming from the page on one side.

"As I bent to pick it up, I saw that it was the book of Genesis, and the word that my eyes focused on was 'Ishmael'. I was half sleep and figured it was all just my imagination. I put the Bible away and went to bed, but I tossed and turned all night. I had dreams of a great man, a black man, standing before a mass of followers, and they all called him 'Ishmael'. The next morning, I went to the library and researched that name. Ishmael. It was of Hebrew origins. It literally translated as 'God has hearkened', and suggested that a child so named was to be regarded as the fulfillment of a divine promise.

"I hurried home as fast as I could and told your father that you were going to be fine, and that your name was Ishmael. At first, he wouldn't accept it, stubborn as he always was, but eventually he gave in. I think more to shut me up than anything else. But the strangest thing happened. As soon as he gave the name his blessing, my contractions started. He ran several red lights getting us to the hospital, and I was sure we were all going to die before we ever got there," she said, chuckling quietly.

"But once we arrived, I was immediately taken to a delivery room, and fifteen minutes later you were born. I never felt one bit of pain. You came out as though it was something you had done a thousand times before," she said, chuckling again. "You didn't even cry. Just opened your eyes and looked around the room at everyone, as though to say, 'Who are all these fool people?'

"The point that I'm trying to make to you, son, is that you've always been destined for something great. Something more. Something in service of others. Even as a child, you often stopped the bigger kids from bullying the smaller kids. Starting your own company and being as successful as you are is fantastic. I am so very proud of you. But I always knew that the greatness you were truly destined for had nothing to do with money. I knew that your true journey still had not yet begun."

"How did you know all this, Mama?" he asked.

"How does a mother know anything about her children, Ishmael? We just know. And sometimes we know even when we don't want to know. When you told me that you were joining the army, I cried. But my tears were not for fear of your safety. My tears were for the lives that I knew you would be forced to take, and the toll that I knew it would take on your soul."

"Joining the military was one of the most frightening things I've ever done," said Ish. "I wasn't afraid of dying or being injured. I was afraid of disappointing you. Macrolox was growing like wildfire, I had more money than I could spend in a lifetime, and I had finally convinced you to let me move you out of the hood. Leaving you to go fight in someone else's war felt kind of like a betrayal."

"No, baby," she said. "It was never like that. I was well aware of the reasons you felt you had to do what you did. And like I said, I was never worried that you wouldn't make it home, because I knew your true destiny still had yet to reveal itself and that when it did it would happen here, not in some foreign country." He heard her voice catch. "Now, is this thing with this group the 'greatness' that I foresaw for you when I named you? Is this what God ultimately brought you onto this earth to do? That I don't know. But I suppose you'll never know what's on the other side of this door until you go through it."

"So," said Ish, "are you telling me, were I ever to be involved in something like this, that I would have your blessing?"

"My blessing? You want my blessing to run around the country assaulting, maybe even killing, police officers? You want my blessing to deprive their families of their husbands, sons and brothers? You want my blessing to become a fugitive, to be hunted like an animal?" She sighed. "I don't know if I can give you that, Ishmael. You're a man, but you're still my baby—my only child! I'm a Christian woman. Taking life goes against everything I believe in. But I also know that you're on the side of the righteous in any fight you choose to get involved in. Just try to be careful, hear?"

"Of course, Mama," said Ish. "Listen, I need to get moving. My contact with you will need to be limited for a while, but if you need anything, Chad is only a phone call away. I'll touch base as soon as I can." They both said nothing, and neither hung up. Part of him felt like this might be the last time he ever heard her voice. He was about to say goodbye when she spoke again.

"When I was a young girl," she said, "during the late 50s, early 60s, it was the height of the civil rights movement. It was an exciting but terrifying time to be a person of color. We were Brazilian, but White America still treated us like we were black, so we considered ourselves part of that group. Folks used to sit around at night, sometimes around the radio or TV, or just around a fire, and speculate on how it would all turn out. And sometimes, there would be arguments. Of course, all people of color were for equal rights, but some disagreed on what path we should take to get there.

"Basically, we were split into two camps. There were those that believed in the non-violent position of Dr. Martin Luther King, Jr. and those that believed in Malcolm X's 'Any Means Necessary' approach. My daddy was a wise man, but he never had much to say during these discussions. One day I asked him, 'Who do you think is right, Dr. King or Malcolm X?'"

"He said both were. He said Dr. King preached hope, while Malcolm X created fear, and that white people were never going to be convinced to do anything just because they were hopeful *or* just because they were afraid. He said it would take a union of the two to bring about any real change in the minds and hearts of white America. And he was right. Hope and fear are two sides of the same coin, like light and darkness. You can't have one without the other. So, while you're out there spreading the darkness, don't forget to also spread some light."

"I will, Mama," he said.

"Thank you. I love you, son," she said, then the line disconnected and she was gone.

As Ish walked back into the house, he met Chad. The look on his partner's face was heavy with concern. Chad nodded his head, motioning for Ish to follow him back outside.

Once they had closed the sliding glass door behind them, Chad turned to face his friend.

"I spoke to Stacy. The FBI paid her a visit yesterday," he said.

"They're getting around. They interviewed my mother as well."

"Shit," said Chad. "That means it's only a matter of time before they show up here. As in, they could be here any minute!"

"Hold on; let's not panic. Let me think for a second," said Ish as he bowed his head and paced back and forth for a moment.

"How much danger we're in right now depends on how much information they have," he said. "If they have positively ID'd any of us at the scene of any of the missions, they'll be here with warrants and a full-on assault. But my guess is that's not the case, or they probably would have served Stacy and my mom with warrants."

"How did they get your name in the first place? How were they able to connect you to any of this?"

"That's the million-dollar question," said Ish. "But my best guess is that it has to do with what Ratcliff overheard when Bird and I went at it."

"Beautiful," said Chad sourly.

"Yeah," said Ish. "But it is what it is. Let's go break the news to the rest of the team and plan the next move." Ish walked back into the house, and after a few seconds Chad followed him.

Ish and Chad found the rest of the team in the living room, their eyes glued to the television screen. They were watching a press conference. The man speaking was a black man, wearing a blue policeman's uniform. The title at the bottom of the screen read "Detective Terrence Dawkins".

"...still in progress," said Dawkins. "Right now, we're asking anyone with any information on this matter to contact us immediately."

A reporter raised his hand.

"Detective, is it true that this appears to be related to the recent attacks on policemen by the terrorist group PROPR?"

"We have no evidence that those attacks are at all related," replied Dawkins.

"Is it true that the FBI has taken over the case?"

"No, it is not. We are sharing information with the FBI, who are looking into another case that may or may not have some relation to this one, but this is still an LAPD investigation."

Another reporter, a woman, raised her hand.

"Is it true that the suspects in this case wore masks like the ones worn in the PROPR videos?"

"It is true the suspects were observed wearing masks, but I cannot confirm nor deny that they were at all similar to the masks worn by PROPR," said Dawkins.

"Could it be that these suspects are copycats, following the example of the PROPR group?"

Dawkins bristled. "We have no information of any such connection," he said.

"What is the condition of the police officers that were injured while in pursuit of the suspects?" asked another reporter.

"None of the police personnel involved in the chase suffered any serious injuries. There were some bumps and bruises, and a couple of them were transported to a local hospital for observation, but all have been released and are back on active duty."

"And the officer who was the target of the attack?"

"He also suffered very minor injuries, but will be on paid leave until we feel it safe for him to return to work. I'm sorry, but that's all the questions we have time for right now," said Dawkins as he stepped away from the podium. Several additional questions were shouted after him as he retreated amid the pop and sparkle of camera flashes.

Bird grabbed the remote and lowered the sound.

"We're the hot topic of the day," he said. "This is on just about every channel."

"Did any of the reports have any more info than what we just heard?" asked Chad.

"Not really," said Bird. "Their official statement is that we got away, they don't have any current leads, the officer that was the subject of the attack survived and they're trying to identify the owners of the abandoned vehicles. Speaking of which, are there going to be any issues with the rental car?"

"No chance," said Chad. "I manipulated the rental car company computer records to make it look like I was a very regular corporate client and requested an 'after hours' pickup. Once they confirmed the identity, they were more than happy to leave the car unlocked with the keys under the mat. I picked it up wearing shades and a hoodie, so not even the lot cameras could have picked up anything they could use."

"Sweet," said Bird. "We missed the target, but at least we got away clean."

"Not exactly," said Ish.

"What are you talking about?" asked Bird.

"The FBI," said Ish. "They've been down at the office and they've been to see my mother. It's only a matter of time before they turn up here."

"How the fuck did they find us?" asked Jag.

No one answered, but it was clear what everyone was thinking.

Chapter 53

"I don't know how they found us," said Ish, "but I'm assuming that, for now, they're only looking for me, because they also showed up at my old house. But how they were led to me is really moot at this point. We have to play the cards we're dealt."

"Why the hell are we sittin' around here, waitin' for them to grab us? Why ain't we jettin' out already?" asked Ma'am.

"We just found out moments ago," said Ish. "Besides, rushing around without some kind of plan might make us more vulnerable than just waiting here."

"That makes sense," said Ma'am. "So, what do you suggest?"

"We need information," said Ish. "We need to know as much as possible about what exactly they know."

"I don't think we're going to find much about that on CNN," said Bird. "Can you hack into the FBI computer system?"

Chad shook his head slowly back and forth. "There is no system that can't be hacked, and together Ish and I can defeat just about any security protocol. But hacking the FBI is not exactly the same as hacking a local police system. It takes time. Maybe a lot of time, which is probably more time than we have. And then once we're in, we have to know where to look to find what we need. It's not like Disneyland, where they give you a map when you enter."

"So, you're saying you can't do it," said Bird.

Ish could see the lines on Chad's forehead begin to bunch together as he gathered himself to respond, so he interrupted before his friend could say anything that might make an already tense situation even worse.

"Listen," said Ish. "We have a few other options that don't necessarily involve a hard hack into the Bureau's system. If we can find out what hotel the agents are stationed at, we may be able to bug their rooms and possibly even hack into their phones. I have the phone numbers of the two agents that visited my mother, so we at least have a place to start."

"Okay," said Bird. "So, let's say you can find out what they know. What then?"

"That depends on who they have in their cross-hairs," said Ish. "My guess is that it's only me, and if that's the case, I break ties with the rest of you and go solo."

"Fuck no, that's not going to happen!" said Chad.

"Fuck no is right!" said Ma'am.

"I appreciate the thought," said Ish. "And no disrespect to the whole 'no man left behind' thing, but in this war, sentimentality eventually has to take a backseat to practicality." This silenced everyone.

"So, here's what I propose," he said, continuing. "Let's all split up, and we'll all check into hotels close by until Chad and I can get a handle on this."

"I guess I can live with that for the short-term," said Ma'am, "but what are we gonna do about Janssen?"

"Janssen..." said Ish, letting the name roll around in his mouth as he contemplated how he wanted to phrase his answer. "The reason we originally chose Janssen hasn't changed. As far as I'm concerned, he remains the current objective. Of course, everything else has changed now, so I won't blame you all if you decide it's time to walk away. I take full blame for the failure of the mission, but it's a mission I feel compelled to complete."

"You're full of shit," said Ma'am. "How are you gonna take the blame for a car accident? You weren't even the fuckin' one driving!"

"Hey!" said Jag, raising his hands in a questioning manner.

"I'm not blaming you either, baby," said Ma'am.

Ish saw Bird's eyes slightly narrow at the word 'baby'.

"Look," said Ish. "It was my responsibility to make the shot. I was the one holding the rifle, and regardless of why the shot missed its mark, the bottom line is that I didn't successfully complete my part of the mission. Period, end of story."

"Shit ain't never really that easy or straight-forward, Ice-Man," said Jag.

"We could sit here and discuss the finer points of fate, destiny and providence all day long, but it's not going to change anything. I'm still going after Janssen. If any of you want to join me, that's fine. I welcome the company. If not, that's fine, too. Chad and I will make sure you're well taken care of."

"If we're taking a vote, I'm in," said Ma'am, raising her hand.

"Aye, aye," said Jag, also raising a hand.

"In for a penny, in for a pound," said Bird.

Everyone looked at Chad.

"Yo, do you really have to ask?" he said in response.

"Alright then," said Ish. "Everyone start packing and get ready to move out. I think you all still have credit cards that work with your current IDs. If not, Chad will hook you up. Just let me and Chad know what hotel you're going to be staying at. I'm sure I don't have to tell you, but I will anyway: if the FBI comes knocking while you're here, remain calm, and stay out of sight as much as possible. Unless they have a warrant, which is unlikely at this point, the worst they can do is ask Chad a bunch of questions." Ish stood up to let everyone know the meeting was adjourned.

He walked into the kitchen, grabbed a bottle of vodka out of the freezer and poured himself a drink. It was his second of the day.

"Can I have a bit of that?" asked Bird, who suddenly appeared in the doorway.

"Sure," said Ish as he passed the bottle.

Bird grabbed some ice out of the refrigerator's door dispenser and began making himself a drink.

"So, tell me," he said. "Do you think the FBI could have gotten onto you because of what happened back in New York?"

"What do you think?" replied Ish, a slight edge in his voice. "I'm sorry," he added quickly before Bird could answer. "Forget I said that. New York is all water under the bridge. Don't worry about it."

"No," said Bird. "You said what I know everyone is already thinking, so let's get into it. The truth of the matter is that if you hadn't interfered, you and I would never have bumped heads and I never would have uttered a word."

"Wait," said Ish, scoffing in disbelief. "Are you trying to say that what happened in New York was my fault?"

"I'm just saying, if you had let me handle the situation the way I wanted to, none of this would have happened."

"And by 'handle the situation the way you wanted to' you mean beat the man to death?" asked Ish.

"If that's what it came to," said Bird.

"Dude, you must be outside your mind! That was never the plan. We went in with a very distinct objective, and it wasn't to kill the guy. We had already decided what the punishment for his crimes would be, and it wasn't death."

"Since when did you start acting all high and mighty? You almost killed a cop today! If it wasn't for that little unexpected fender bender, that officer would be laying in a steel drawer in the morgue right about now."

"Yeah, because that was the punishment that we decided was just!" said Ish.

"You mean like we did with Stanwick?" replied Bird icily.

"Listen, that—" began Ish.

"What's going on here?" asked Ma'am as she stepped quickly into the room.

"It's just a minor difference of opinion," said Ish, waving his hand dismissively.

"No, it's a lot more than that," said Bird. "Ish is trying to blame me for the FBI being on his tail."

Ma'am slowly folded her arms. "Well, you are the one that said his name so the cop could hear it."

"I understand that. But if he hadn't tried to stop me from giving that asshole the beating he deserved, it would have never happened."

"I guess you do kind of have a point," said Ma'am.

Ish could feel his blood starting to boil. His face was placid, but behind his eyes a storm was brewing that he was struggling to get under control.

"So, let me get this straight," he said, after taking a deep breath and closing his eyes for a moment. "You both are saying that I should have just stood back and let Bird pummel the life out of that man, even though that wasn't what we had agreed to do?"

"Just because he didn't kill anyone doesn't necessarily mean he didn't deserve to die," said Ma'am. "Do you know what rape does to some women? It destroys their fuckin' lives. Destroys them! Just because he didn't technically take the life of any of his victims don't mean that he didn't ruin their lives."

"I don't even believe this," said Ish, shaking his head in awe. "You're both soldiers. Experienced soldiers! When you get an order to go into a village and interrogate the elders, you don't take it upon yourself to start executing people. You follow the fucking orders! Or do you disagree with that as well?"

Bird hung his head in silence, but Ma'am returned his gaze, her eyes burning into his.

"Look," she said, "I understand where you're coming from. But I also understand where my brother is coming from. You both have valid points. And the bottom line is that while I love you, Ish, and I consider you family, my brother is *family* family. If a coin is being tossed, I'm always gonna have to side with him."

Jag walked into the kitchen, followed closely by Chad.

"What's all the piss and vinegar for?" asked Jag, his ever-present half-smile playing at the corner of his mouth.

Ish slowly shook his head in response and turned to take a large sip of his drink.

"We're just having a friendly discussion," said Ma'am.

"Actually, it's really more a family thing," said Bird.

Jag and Chad both looked confused and turned to Ish.

"We were just debating the morality of capital punishment," said Ish.

Jag laughed. "It's a little late for that, ain't it? That dog done already joined the hunt."

"We're not talking about Janssen," said Ish. "We're talking about Ratcliff."

"Wait, what?" said Chad.

"Bird feels that it would have been better to just kill Ratcliff instead of merely violating him."

"Based on what?" asked Chad.

"Based on the fact that rapists don't really deserve to live."

"Well," said Jag, running a hand through his hair. "There's definitely some logic to that."

"Not you too?"

"Hey, I'm just saying that one could definitely make a case that rapists don't deserve to remain a part of a civilized society. And if that's the case, why use taxpayer money to warehouse them for ten years, twenty years, maybe even the rest of their lives? Makes more sense to just erase them off the balance sheet and be done with it," said Jag.

"I have to say that does make some sense," said Chad, shrugging.

"Look, I'm not going to get into a big debate over the various philosophies of crime and punishment," said Ish. "The only thing that matters today is that before we left for New York we made a decision as a group, and it was my duty to make sure that we stood by that decision."

"What started all this in the first place?" asked Chad.

"Well," said Ish, "Bird thinks that I'm to blame for the FBI being on my trail; that we would have never been in this predicament if I hadn't gotten between him and Ratcliff."

"Whoa, hold up!" said Chad. "I didn't know that's what we were talking about! That's complete bullshit! You need to own your shit, Bird!"

"Who do you think you're talking to—" began Bird.

"Calm down, everybody," said Jag, stepping in between the two of them. "I don't know what got all of your asses so full of fire, but we need to ratchet this down. We're supposed to be packing up and getting the fuck out of here, not standing around the kitchen sink arguing about shit that happened in the past."

"You're right," said Ish as he finished his drink in one gulp and put the empty glass in the dishwasher. "You guys had better head out. We can discuss all this some other time if you feel so inclined."

"I don't think that's really necessary," said Jag, "but I will say this. Bird, you're about as wrong as a hen's egg full of pig shit."

Neither Bird nor Ma'am spoke, but they both had a scowl on their face that hinted that this was nowhere near over. Bird actually looked like he wanted to lunge at Jag, but something seemed to hold him back. Ish wondered if maybe it was a twinge of guilt.

Jag, Bird and Ma'am all left the kitchen, but Chad stayed behind.

"You okay?" he asked.

"I don't know. I'm starting to feel that I made a big mistake getting you all involved in this," said Ish.

"You have a short memory. I'm the one that set this up while you were laying on your ass in a hospital bed watching *Dancing With The Stars* and eating Jell-O," he said, smiling.

"Don't start telling lies on me," said Ish, returning the smile. "I never ate that fucking Jell-O."

They both laughed.

"Listen, man," said Chad, his face becoming more serious. "I know there have been some hiccups along the way, but this was a good idea. We're making a difference! We're changing people's lives, even if the only change is giving them a sense of hope. The views of the videos are growing by the hundreds of thousands every day. You should see some of the discussions jumping off in the comment threads!"

"Speaking of which, how do you think today's debacle is going to read in all this? How do we even spin this to make it look like anything less than the failure it was?" asked Ish.

"Well, right now no one has confirmed it was us," said Chad.

"True, but that can't last more than a few more hours," said Ish. "It's possible that this could start a major backlash against the movement and all the progress we've made so far."

Chad bowed his head in thought.

"I don't know, man. What little I know about psychology leads me to believe that our public isn't going to bail on us just because we had one misstep," he said. "And if we can eventually get him, it'll show that no crooked cop is safe from us, even if they know we're coming."

Ish nodded his head slowly as he pondered this.

"You may have a point. But getting to Janssen is not going to be easy with him now fully aware that he's a target. They'll be keeping him under wraps."

"One thing I know about white racists," said Chad, "is that arrogance is pretty much a prerequisite. He'll be afraid, but he'll probably think there's no way we'd come after him again. I predict he's going to get careless pretty quickly."

"Yeah, you're probably right. How do you think we should handle what happened today? I'm sure our audience is expecting a new video soon, and the internet is going to be buzzing about whether or not this was us or just some posers."

"We could go full disclosure and let the world know that he has a bullseye on his back."

"If we do that," said Ish, "it'll probably prompt other people to start hunting him."

Chad gave him a look that said '*And?*'

"While I'm still chasing him, I don't need amateurs possibly getting in the way. It's going to be difficult enough as it is," said Ish.

"That's true. Okay, let me see what the online chatter is saying, and then how about we touch base on it again?"

"Sounds like a plan," said Ish.

Chapter 54

Ish went to his room. He grabbed his iPod and set it to shuffle play his 'Soul Playlist.' The first song was The Five Stairstep's 1970 hit "Ooh Child (Things Are Gonna Get Easier)". He had always loved that song. It was one of the 45s that his mother used to play over and over again on the little box record player that they owned when he was a kid. Sometimes she and his father would get up and dance together to it, and they would all laugh like it was just the funniest thing in the world. He asked her once why she liked that song so much, and she said that the lyrics just gave her hope. Maybe it was a sign that this was the first song played at this particular moment, the darkest since they had begun this project.

Ish got undressed and stepped into the shower. It had only been a couple of hours since his last shower, but not only did he find the heat and the sound relaxing, it was also where he had always done his best thinking.

As the hot water rained down over his body, he mused about how quickly a situation could change. He had experienced it in combat many times. You'd go out on a mission with a certain game plan, and something would happen that made all those plans obsolete. It could be as simple as suffering a mechanical breakdown or as devastating as running into an ambush. But the difference between then and now was that in the army, more often than not someone else was responsible for making those plans, and for the safety and wellbeing of the men and women charged with executing them.

But here and now, notwithstanding the conversation he'd just had with Chad, he was the one who carried the majority of the burden of keeping this team safe. But what Chad said was true. The formation of PROPR had been Chad's idea. And to be honest, maybe that idea had saved Ish's life. Without the distraction of this group objective, he would probably have gone after the two Baltimore cops who attacked him, and there was a very good chance that would not have ended well for him.

He thought about Layla and wished that he could talk to her right now, just to get her opinion. Her mind worked differently than his did. She was often able to show him angles on things that he hadn't considered.

His thoughts shifted to Bird. It was like the man had become a cancer, and that cancer was starting to slowly spread to the rest of the team. He hated saying that about his friend, but it was undeniable. It seemed like Bird was never really fully invested in this fight. And from the comment he made yesterday, he apparently also had doubts about the Stanwick incident. But why wait all this time to bring it up? Why did Bird agree to go along back in Afghanistan if he wasn't 100% committed?

Maybe he was all-in at the beginning but had changed along the way. Ish should have cut him loose when he first saw that he was starting to unravel. But now the damage was done. His negativity, like some kind of airborne poison, had already begun to infect Ma'am. And with Ma'am as connected as she was to Jag, it was possible that he might also start to feel some of those effects. They were a string of dominoes, the three of them, all lined up and ready to fall.

After his shower, Ish got dressed. When he grabbed his phone to put it in his pocket, he saw that there was a missed call. It had to be Layla.

"Shit!" he said. He had meant to bring the phone into the bathroom with him while he showered but had forgotten. He was about to start cursing again when the phone sprang to life in his hand. He stabbed the button to connect the call.

"Babe!" he said, but then had to wait for the recorded announcement to finish.

"Hey, love," said Layla finally, her voice as warm and silky as ever.

"Sorry I missed you the first time," he said. "I was in the shower."

"Hmmm," she said seductively. "I know how much you love your showers. Are you standing there buck-ass naked and dripping?"

Ish smiled. "No, not exactly. But I could be if you want me to," he said.

"Don't you know it's cruel to taunt a starving woman with talk of a delicious five-star meal? You can get hurt doing that."

"Sorry. I'll try to control myself," he said, his voice a deep purr.

"You're a bad boy," she said.

"Only for you, baby." They both took a deep breath, each taking a couple of seconds to savor the moment and the memories it invoked.

"How are you?" he asked finally.

"I'm fine," she said. "But I'm feeling unsettled. My intuition is telling me that something is not right with you."

"I'm good. My only issue has to do with those stray dogs I was telling you about. We tried to capture one to take to the pound, but he got away."

"That makes me nervous," she said. "You know how I worry about the neighborhood kids. It's not safe for them with a crazy, possibly rabid, animal running around."

"I know," said Ish, his voice tightening a bit. "We're still going to get him. But things are a little more complicated now."

"What do you mean 'complicated'?"

"Somehow, someone gave my name to the dogcatcher. Apparently, the dogcatcher thinks that it was wrong for me to take it upon myself to go after this dog rather than leaving it to them. They're probably looking for me right now."

"You know how white people are about their dogs."

"Exactly," said Ish.

"What about your buddies that were helping. Is the dogcatcher looking for them, too?"

"Not that I know of. At least, not yet."

"Do you think it's possible one of them might be the one that dropped your name?"

Ish paused for a moment. "Anything is possible. But probably not deliberately. It may have come up in casual conversation."

"Casual conversation?" she replied. He could almost see her nodding her head in understanding. "I guess you never can tell who's listening."

"Yeah," said Ish. "Even now." He gave that a few seconds to seep in. "But enough about wild dogs. Tell me how you've been."

"I'm keeping my head above water," said Layla.

"Does that mean you're staying out of trouble?" asked Ish.

"You mean have I had to beat anybody's ass lately? No, everyone's been staying out of my way."

"Well, that's good news. Have you heard anything from the lawyers?"

"No, I think they've been trying to stay out of my way, too," said Layla. "The warden did come by the other day to tell me that they're still pushing to get the new charges filed."

"Assault or attempted murder?"

"They're still peddling the attempted murder charge."

"Shit, Layla," said Ish. "How badly did you beat this girl?"

"It wasn't my fault, Ish! She attacked me!"

"Sorry, babe," said Ish.

"It's alright. Anyway, it's not like she was left clinging to life or anything. She had a minor concussion, a busted eardrum and a few bruises. Trust me, she's alive and well. And talking shit already."

"Well, it would be a good thing if you could avoid having any more run-ins with her. Don't make the lawyers' job any harder than it has to be."

"Why? It's not like they're working for free. Last time I checked you had already paid them almost $300,000. And for what? That was money down the drain."

"I don't give a fuck about the money, Layla. Money can be replaced. No one can replace you. I need you. I need you here."

"Sumatra told me you were going to say that. She told me to be nice to you and to try not to cry. I don't know why she would say that. I've hardly cried at all since I've been here," said Layla. But Ish heard a quiver in her voice as she spoke the last couple of words, and she instantly began weeping. He gave her a moment to get it all out.

"Don't worry, babe. Everything's going to be alright. We'll get you out of there, one way or another."

"And then what?" she asked, sniffling. "Go from being a target in here to being a target out there? I've told you over and over again, Ish, I don't want to trade one prison for another."

"I'm working on it," said Ish. "Things are changing out here. You're not able to see it from where you are, but things are changing."

"Ish, America is a like an aircraft carrier, not a speed boat. Even when it does decide to change course, it takes a long time for it to happen."

"So, what if we were to leave America for a while?" he asked. "Get away from it until some of the changes are locked in?"

"Leave the U.S.?" she replied, then paused. "You know, it's crazy, but I never even considered that. Where would we go?"

"Anywhere we want," said Ish. "Money is not an object, so there's nowhere that's off limits. What about Paris?"

"Oh, Ish, we had such a beautiful time the last time we were there, right before Sumatra was born! I was already into my second trimester; big as a house and uncomfortable as hell. But in Paris none of that seemed to matter." She paused again, and he could almost hear her biting her lip the way she always did when she was really pondering some decision. "Okay," she said. "Maybe."

That's all Ish needed to hear. His heart began to soar at the possibility that this was something she could cling to until he could get her released. He heard something ringing in the background.

"I've got to go, babe. They're sending everyone back to their cells. I love you. Be safe, and I'll talk to you soon."

Before he could respond, she was gone.

After taking a moment to compose himself, Ish went to find Chad. He found him in the office. The desk he was sitting at held three separate computer monitors, and each was showing either video or streaming text. Chad's head hardly moved, but his eyes were constantly sweeping back and forth over the three screens, reading and comprehending the data in a manner that made him look like some kind of android. This was one of his many talents; he could multitask in a way that Ish had never seen anyone else do.

"Hey, Ish," he said without looking up, his eyes maintaining their focus on the screens. After a moment, he clicked the mouse and all three monitors froze. "You've got to see what's going on out there," he said, his voice full of excitement.

Ish grabbed a chair and sat down next to him.

"As I suspected," said Chad, "there's a ton of conversation online about what happened today. Right now, it's about 50/50 between those that think it was us and those that think it was probably copy cats. But the cool thing is that the people that support us don't seem to care whether it was really us or not. They appreciate the spirit of whoever it was that did it, even if it wasn't ultimately successful."

"Wow, that's huge," said Ish.

"Tell me about it," said Chad. "This is how I always imagined this would go; that the actions we took would be like setting spark to a small bit of brush that quickly grows into a forest fire." His eyes shone in such a way that Ish could practically see that fire in them.

"That's great news," said Ish. "What's all this?" he asked, pointing at one of the screens that was frozen on the angry face of a young black male. He appeared to be perhaps eighteen or nineteen years old with a light mustache and short dreadlocks. He had one of his fists raised in some act of defiance.

"Oh, that's the other cool thing," said Chad. "The protests are continuing to heat up across the country. This is from a university in Kansas, but the same thing is happening in schools all over the place; sit-ins, marches, even a few hunger strikes."

"And all this is in support of PROPR?"

"Not all directly," said Chad. "Some of them are rallying for lower tuition or equal rights for gays and lesbians, but there is a contingent of PROPR supporters at all of them. I've even seen people sporting their own handmade PROPR t-shirts and hats. It appears that when it comes to public conversations about minority justice, PROPR now has a seat at the table."

"That's beautiful," said Ish. "Based on all of this new info, what are your thoughts now about how we should personally respond to today's miss?"

"I've looked at all the angles," said Chad, "and I think you're right. Publicly admitting that Janssen was our target is only going to crowd the field with amateurs. If we can get him in the next couple of days, it'll be fine; we'll still have the momentum."

"Cool. Did you see those burner phones I left for you?"

"Got 'em right here," said Chad.

"Excellent. I also sent you the tracing app I've been working on. Let me know when you've loaded it on to one of the phones and it's ready to go, and I'll give this agent a call. It's time for the mouse to start chasing the cat."

Chapter 55

Half an hour later Ish was standing in the back yard, ruminating on the current situation, when Chad sent a text asking him to come to the office.

"That program you created was a beautiful piece of work," said Chad as Ish entered the room. "I've set up the tracing software on this prepaid phone and already tested it. Not only does it triangulate the location of the other phone, but it also prevents anyone from triangulating ours, just as you designed it. But as you know, you'll need to keep him on the line for at least ten minutes for a truly accurate trace. Less time will get us some data, but the longer you keep him online, the closer we'll get."

"It's such a shot in the dark," said Ish. "We have no idea where he'll be when he gets the call. But if we call him tonight, let's say about 3am, there's a better chance he'll be in his hotel room, in bed."

"Most definitely," said Chad. "I've got a fridge full of Mountain Dew, so burning the midnight oil is not a problem."

"Cool. So, what else?"

"Everyone checked in a few minutes ago. They're all set up in different hotels, all within fifteen miles of the house, awaiting instructions."

"My guess is that Ma'am and Jag are not quite fifteen miles from each other. Or if they are, they won't be for long," said Ish.

Chad laughed. "What, exactly, is up with that?" he asked.

"I guess they have a 'thing'. And it appears to be getting more and more serious by the day."

"Really?" said Chad. "I knew they were sharing some sheets, but I thought it was just, you know, 'battle boredom' or something. I never thought they'd ever get into a real relationship."

"Dude, it's already so far beyond that," said Ish.

"What do you mean?"

Ish took a deep breath and pondered how much he should tell Chad. It wasn't as if Jag or Ma'am had asked him to keep any of what they told him confidential. And there were practical reasons for Chad to know what was happening between them. They were all involved in highly dangerous maneuvers, and as Jag, and Bird, had already made glaringly apparent, how the team members felt about each other could dictate how they reacted in a crisis.

"Well," he began, "Jag confided in me the other day that he wants to marry Ma'am."

Chad's mouth literally fell open.

"Are you shittin' me?" he asked, incredulous.

"Not even. Trust me, I was as shocked as you are."

"Wow. They are like the epitome of the term 'odd couple'."

"You ain't never lied," said Ish, causing them both to laugh.

"It just goes to show," Ish continued, "that you can never judge a book by its cover."

* * *

At 2:55am Ish was standing over Chad's bed, shaking him awake.

"What's up, dude?" mumbled Chad.

"It's time," said Ish.

"Already? Shit, sorry. I'm up!" he said as he slowly rose to a sitting position and began rubbing his eyes.

"What happened to all that talk about Mountain Dew and burning oil?"

"Sorry, man. I had a couple of glasses of wine that I think counteracted the Dew. Ow!" he said, stretching. "Give me five minutes to get dressed, and I'll meet you in the office."

"No problem," said Ish as he walked out of the room.

"And please put on a pot of joe if you don't mind!" Chad yelled after him.

"Already done!" yelled Ish in reply.

Ish went to the kitchen and poured them each a cup of coffee. It was already his third of the day. He had been up since 1:00am. Actually, it was probably more accurate to say that he hadn't really been to sleep since he woke up yesterday, with the exception of a quick nap between midnight and one. Sleep used to never be a problem, but from the first day he went into combat, sleep had become something that he occasionally struggled with, especially if there was something on his mind.

His most recent conversation with Layla had been rattling around in his head ever since he hung up the phone with her. It was like one of those strange noises that you hear in the engine of your car but can never find the source of. And as is often the case with strange noises, Ish had no idea whether it was something benign or something serious that needed immediate attention.

It kept coming back to how different she was since they lost Sumatra. And it wasn't just the fact that she was talking to her dead daughter. That part was disturbing enough, but what was more troubling to Ish was how raw she had gotten. Of course, he knew that she came from the hood, just like he did, but until recently she had always been so refined, so sophisticated. He had seldom even heard her use profanity before she went to jail. It was one of the things he had always loved about her. She had always shown an ability to transcend her environment, just like Ish and Chad had been able to do. But now it was like she was morphing into a wilder version of the woman who he had met so many years ago.

Ish started to wonder if maybe he had really lost her. Losing Sumatra was hard enough. It was almost unbearable. He didn't think he could survive losing Layla as well. Of course, there was the issue of first getting her out of jail and then beating the case so she wouldn't have to go back. But after that, what? Would she ever again be the woman who he fell in love with? Or would she come back to him as this feral, wild creature with a tenuous hold on reality?

He had seen it enough times with men who he served with. Some of them suffered from PTSD, which was becoming more and more common. Most of those guys had the ability to heal over time, with the right kind of counseling and enough support from their families. Those were the people you read about in magazines or saw profiled on TV shows about the cost of the 'war on terror'.

But what was less spoken about were the people who were so traumatized by what they experienced in combat that they never fully recovered. These were men whose psyche was not just fractured, but broken. A friend of his, a fellow soldier, had once dubbed them 'The Lost'. They were a group that was growing in size every year.

Layla hadn't experienced war, but what she had experienced was in many ways much worse. That much he knew from personal experience, because while he had personally witnessed the death of many a comrade through an enemy bullet or bomb, none of them shook him the way the news of the passing of his daughter had. He couldn't even imagine what it would have been like to be there to see it first-hand. Layla badly injured the cop who did it. Ish was sure that had he been in her place, he would have ended the man's life long before any of the reinforcements showed up. Then he would have been the one sitting in jail.

Many a night he had lain awake, wishing that he could have traded places with her, wishing that he had been there when it happened. But if there's one thing you learn in Special Forces training, it's to improvise; to roll with the punches and deal with whatever situation fate gives you. So here he was, trying to change the world, ready to go toe-to-toe with the Federal Bureau of Investigation.

And for what? He felt the acrid taste of resentment bubbling up in his throat. Would people even appreciate what he was sacrificing for them? Would it all make any difference a year from now? Five years? Ten years? Chad clearly thought so, but he had always been an optimist. It was one of the things that Ish had always admired about him. But Ish wasn't nearly so optimistic.

However, he still held on to the dream that maybe this would be the tonic that would cure his wife. Like the kiss that awakened sleeping beauty, maybe these protests and sit-ins and marches would be the magic element that delivered Layla back into his arms. And not just any Layla, but the Layla he knew—not the stranger who was currently lying in a cell, talking to the dead.

"What's up, man?" asked Chad, entering the room. "You look like you're elbow deep in thought about something. Everything alright?"

"Yeah, it's nothing," said Ish as he handed his friend the second cup of coffee.

"Ahhh, this is exactly what I needed," said Chad as he took a sip. "And you made it just the way I like it!"

"We aim to please," said Ish. "I guess we'd better get this show on the road."

They brought their coffee with them to the room that served as the home office. Chad got right to work, firing up his laptop and manically punching the keys as he loaded software and initiated programs.

"Okay," he said ten minutes later. "We're set. Hopefully you can keep him on the line long enough for us to zero in on where he is."

"We'll see," said Ish as he dialed the number. It rang three times before it was answered.

"This is Madden," said the voice on the other end. He sounded completely awake, though somehow Ish instinctively knew that he had been soundly asleep when the phone rang. Ish wondered if he had served in the military or perhaps had been a fireman in a previous life.

"Agent Madden, this is Ishmael Carter. I understand you've been looking for me."

"Yes, Mr. Carter," said Madden without missing a beat. "Thank you so much for getting in touch with me. We just wanted to ask you a few questions." He conspicuously avoided mentioning anything about the hour of the call. One would have thought it was three in the afternoon as opposed to three in the morning.

"Certainly," said Ish. "Anything to help out law enforcement. What exactly is this about?"

"Are you familiar with the terrorist group PROPR? The one that has been leading attacks on various police officers?"

"I've heard about it," said Ish. "I mean, it's impossible not to if you turn on a TV or log into any website that reports news stories."

"Exactly," said Madden. "I'm heading up the FBI's investigation into the matter, and we have reason to believe that someone with a military background might be involved. Specifically, someone that is ex—or possibly even current—Special Forces. That makes for a long list, so we've been looking for people that might be able to help us narrow it down. Since you recently served in such a unit, we thought you might be able to provide some helpful information. Is there a time and place that we could get together to chat?"

"That would be kind of difficult," said Ish. "I'd love to help, but I'm a very busy man these days. Can't we just do this over the phone? I have a few minutes right now."

"I understand," said Madden, "and we definitely want to be respectful of your time, but we prefer to handle these matters in person. We can meet you anywhere; at your home, at your office, wherever is most convenient for you."

"I thought you just needed me to answer a few questions," said Ish.

"Yes, that's right."

"Well, all that requires is the ability to hold a conversation. And we're doing that right now. So, I don't understand why we can't handle this now and save us both a lot of unnecessary hassle."

"Mr. Carter, is there a particular reason that you don't want to meet in person?"

"Is there a particular reason that you do want to meet in person?"

Madden didn't immediately reply. Ish took a deep, cleansing breath as he waited. He couldn't tell if the man was trying to check his temper or if he was actually stumped for what to say next.

"I apologize," he finally said. "I think we've gotten off on the wrong foot. Sometimes I forget that it can be intimidating being interviewed by someone from the FBI. It's not our intention to make you feel uncomfortable in any way. If you give me a few moments to grab my notes, I think we can plow right through it pretty quickly."

"No problem," said Ish. He could hear the man rustling through some papers and the snap of something, maybe a briefcase, being opened or closed. It seemed unprofessional and disorganized, which felt out of character based on the little bit he had managed to glean about the man so far. He wondered if it were actually a ruse to cover up the fact that he was speaking to one of his associates and perhaps trying to get a trace on the call. After a bit more rattling, he returned to the phone.

"I'm back," he said. "Sorry about that. The list of questions I have is actually pretty short. So, let's start at the top with some basic information. Is your name Ishmael Octavius Carter?"

"It is."

"And what is your current address?"

"I don't currently have one."

"Are you saying that you're homeless, Mr. Carter?"

"You make it sound like a bad thing," said Ish, an impish half-smile on his face. "Just because someone doesn't have a place of permanent residence doesn't mean they're a bad person. Let's just say, for the sake of this discussion, that I'm 'between homes' right now.

"I guess that explains why you weren't home yesterday when we went to your last known address."

"That would explain it," said Ish dryly, though he wasn't sure why he was giving this guy such a hard time. The man was only doing his job, and Ish had already gotten the feeling that he was a pretty decent guy.

"Okay," said Madden, "let's back up a bit. I understand that you don't have a permanent place that you call home. But maybe you can start by telling us where you slept last night."

"At a friend's house."

"And could you please give me the address of that friend?"

"I'm afraid I can't do that. My friend is very shy about those kinds of things."

"How about this," said Madden. "For the purposes of my report, is it alright with you if I use your mother's address?"

"Somehow I doubt that I could stop you even if I wanted to," said Ish.

Ish heard Madden release a massive sigh and could imagine him straining to maintain an air of civility.

"Okay, Mr. Carter," he began. "Let me cut to the chase. As I said before, we believe that some members of this organization may have SOF backgrounds. I'm sure you would agree that if that is the case, the quicker we bring these guys to justice, the better. No one that's ever been a part of Special Operations Forces wants to see their group dragged through the mud by being associated with terrorists, especially of the home-grown variety. So, when we came across your name, naturally we were hoping that you could be of some help."

"I see," said Ish. "Tell me, how exactly is it that you came across my name in the first place?"

"Just typical investigative police work," said Madden. "A list was generated of people with recent SF experience and your name happened to be near the top of it. Carter starting with 'c' and all."

Ish nodded into the phone and somehow knew that Madden could sense it.

"What we were hoping to do is get together with you and have you look over a few lists we have, some with matching photos, to see if you might recognize anyone that you perhaps served with or came across out in the field."

"You mean lists like the one I'm on?" asked Ish.

"No," said Madden, "I mean lists of individuals we consider to be 'persons of interest'. Meaning, people that we think have the potential to be involved in something like this."

"And I'm not one of those 'persons of interest'?"

"Not yet," said Madden. "But the day is young." He smiled into the last word, indicating the joke, but Ish knew that neither of them saw the humor.

"I'm sorry, but I don't think I can help you," said Ish. "None of the Spec Ops guys I served with would ever be involved in something like this. Showing me names and photos isn't going to change that."

"I see," said Madden. "Well, thank you for your time and for contacting us. Please hold onto my card. If you think of anything that might help the investigation, we would very much appreciate you getting in touch with us again."

"Not a problem," said Ish.

"And by the way," said Madden. "If we have more questions for you, is there a number we can reach you at?"

"I'm in the process of changing cell plans right now, but you're more than welcome to leave a message with my office. I stay in contact with them fairly regularly."

"I've made a note of that. Thank you again for your time." They both hung up.

"That sounded, uh, tense but polite," said Chad as he took off the headphones he was wearing.

"You could say that. Was it long enough?"

"Hold on, one minute," said Chad as his fingers flew across the keyboard.

"Yes! I've got it narrowed down to a two-block radius, and there happens to only be two hotels in the area, and only one that I think the FBI would bother to stay in. They're ours."

Chapter 56

Madden hung up the phone and looked at Phillips, who had her own phone up to her ear. He was grateful that she slept as lightly as he did and had run to his room in response to his text about the incoming call.

"Did we get it?" he asked.

Phillips shook her head. "They said the signal was altered somehow. They've never seen anything like it."

"That's the same thing they said when they tried to track down the website."

"Exactly," said Phillips. "But I don't understand. Carter had to know that we were probably going to try to trace the call. By masking his signal with technology so advanced that we can't even crack it, he had to know that we would put two and two together. He's basically telling us point blank that he's part of PROPR."

"Maybe, maybe not," said Madden as he slowly bent his head from side to side, causing a cracking sound in his neck. "He still has plausible deniability simply because of the fact that he owns a company that deals in government secrets. Whether he is involved with this case or not, he would still have good reason to shroud his phones."

"You have a point," said Phillips. "So, where does that leave us?"

"We still need to find him, if for no other reason than so I can look him in the eye and ask him directly."

"Maybe we should have followed our first thought and driven out to his partner's house yesterday," said Phillips. "We might have gotten lucky and found him there."

"Perhaps," said Madden. "But at the time I believed we'd get more bang for our buck by going over the evidence from the crime scene. Besides, even if he was there, there's no reason he had to answer the door. And getting a warrant would have been a challenge."

"Do you think it's worth putting a surveillance detail on Yang's house?"

"It's an idea," said Madden. "But if we're going to do that, it would make sense to do the same to their office and Carter's mother's house, too. Right now, I'm not sure we can spare the manpower, but let's revisit it during our evening meeting."

"Got it," said Phillips. "Well"—she yawned, covering her mouth—"if there's nothing else, I'd like to catch a few more Zs before we get back into the thick of it."

"Sure thing, Phillips," he said distractedly. He barely noticed that she had left the room. His mind was already spinning, groping and digging at the problem, like an octopus looking for the weakness in a clam's shell.

Madden dosed off for a couple of hours, but he was up again by 6 after finally giving up the fight against this current bout of insomnia. Right after Phillips left the room, he had sent a message to the D.C. office to immediately have a file created and forwarded to him containing everything they knew about Ishmael Carter. With any luck he'd have something by breakfast.

In the meantime, he began crawling the internet, visiting all manner of blogs and news sites, including some that were known to be particularly subversive and militant in the name of black rights. As he read through the blog posts and articles, he felt torn, the way he always did. Yes, some of these people were preaching hatred and trying to incite others to commit crimes in the name of justice. Which was bad. No doubt.

But on the other hand, you could not ignore the fact that these people—his people—were struggling against a systematized history of discrimination that went back generations. Black people were dying in the street at alarming rates at the hands of both law enforcement and other citizens, and no one had an answer for how to stop it. So, people were pissed off. Understandably.

But as both a cop and a black man, he was caught in the middle. He would never forget once, early on in his career, when he went to interview a man who was suspected of transporting cocaine across state lines. After five minutes of scanning the brief, he instinctively knew that the man was completely innocent, but he still needed the interview for the files.

The man was black, probably about twenty-six or twenty-seven, with a conservative, close cut afro. He had a biology degree from Berkeley and worked in a research lab in Virginia. Someone had given his name. Could have been anyone; a scorned ex-girlfriend, a jealous work associate, maybe even a neighbor who thought he played his music too loud. The bottom line was that he had become a 'person of interest' and it was Madden's job to either move him to the 'suspect' list or rule him out.

They visited the man at his job, a common Bureau tactic meant to throw the suspect off balance. The interview was short and to the point, and Madden felt it had gone well, but as they were wrapping up to leave, the guy stood up, all 5'2" of him, and said, "Thanks for treating me like a criminal, you fucking Uncle Tom!" He then spat in Madden's face.

The older agent that Madden was with, a white guy with twenty years on the job, went to grab the kid, but Madden held him back. Madden was both stunned and disgusted, but he knew how the guy felt, and it was hard not to feel sympathy for him. He pulled a handkerchief out of his jacket, wiped his face, thanked the man again for his time, and left.

The other agent chewed him out when they got back to the car. He talked about how, as an officer of the law, you could not afford to ever show weakness; that you always had to come from a place of power and embrace the fact that you were the one with the upper hand. But as a white guy, he never understood that it was that very attitude that created the anger that drove the man to do what he did. And it was that same anger that was simmering inside black communities all over the country.

Website after website, page after page, Madden was seeing evidence of the rising level of frustration in the country among people of color. He was surprised by how bold some of the rhetoric was, though he knew he shouldn't have been. Most people assumed that because they weren't using their real name, they were anonymous online. Most didn't realize just how easy it was for the government, or anyone with half decent hacking skills, to find them.

He was also surprised at the number of racist trolls that were active in the comment threads on so many of the civil rights websites he visited. But again, he shouldn't have been. It was an election year, and not just any election year. The country was in the process of choosing a new president, at the end of the first black president's second term. The first black president of the United States had been a historic political event, but what was coming might prove to be even more historic.

The two front runners had already been decided: Democrat Kathleen Hamilton and Republican Trevor Gage. That's what made it so historic. America was either about to elect its first female president or its first openly racist megalomaniac. Regardless of who won, nothing in America was ever going to be the same.

Gage had started as a joke; someone that no one ever thought could possibly have a chance. And yet, here he was, basically neck-and-neck with the Democratic nominee. It made Madden's head hurt to think that this man could possibly one day run the country. It had been the source of many a heated debate when he and some of the other Bureau guys had gone out together for drinks after work. It would probably come as no surprise to most people that a high percentage of individuals who worked in law enforcement identified as Republican. Therefore, a remarkably high number of the people he worked with supported Gage, even some women, gays and officers of color.

It was mind-boggling to him that some people who should have been terrified of this man getting anywhere near a public office, let alone the most powerful office in the world, were willing and ready to vote him into that very role. Madden considered the man a danger to the U.S. as well as the rest of humanity. But of course, he wasn't the only one.

There had been a lot of 'protest' chatter online. Some people even openly pledging to assassinate him if he were ever actually elected. Again, most of these people were just talking out of their ass, standing behind the mistaken belief that no one could ever identify them. But the Secret Service had already determined some of these threats to be credible, and word around the water cooler was that a special SS task force had already been assembled and that it would be systematically investigating all threats, no matter how minor they might seem on the surface.

Supposedly, there were already people sitting in jail cells all over the country for making those threats. If that were true, Madden had no doubt that the majority of these people were of color, which would only serve to increase the rising anger in minority communities. It was similar to America's war on terror. By preemptively going after the people who we thought were a danger to our national safety, all we really did was turn them into martyrs and create even more enemies intent on participating in our destruction. It was like a dog chasing its tail; the stereotypical vicious cycle.

A lot of people who were disappointed with the way the presidential race was going thought that Gage was the problem. They believed that bringing back the status quo was simply a matter of getting rid of this 'racist', this 'charlatan', this 'crazy man'. But these people somehow completely ignored the fact that Gage would not have gotten as far as he did if he didn't have a lot of people behind him. In fact, millions and millions of people had voted for him and supported him in the primaries, allowing him to secure the Republican nomination.

So even if he were to do a *Jimmy Hoffa* and disappear tomorrow, his supporters would still be there. These millions and millions of people, people who agreed with his xenophobic, racist, sexist ideas, would still be out there, looking for a new leader and sadly showing the rest of America that we haven't progressed as far in our struggle for civil rights as some people might like to believe.

Trevor Gage was never really the problem. He was like Toto when he pulled back the curtain to reveal the lie that was the Wizard. In this case, the Wizard was the American people and the lie was that we live in a country that is progressively becoming more and more racially tolerant. It simply wasn't true.

Being a black man who was married to a white woman, Madden felt particularly disappointed. It was only fifty or so years ago that it was still illegal in some states for blacks and whites to marry. And yet, here he was, able to freely walk down the street hand-in-hand with his one and only, double-dating with their white friends and living in a beautiful house in a gentrified neighborhood where almost everyone looked more like his wife than like him. He had once believed that most of America, meaning at least 51%, accepted all this as not just okay, but as the ideal of what the society was working towards. He had since been disabused of that belief.

Of course, as an FBI agent, he knew firsthand that America was still full of crazies, including all kinds of white supremacists, with everything from skinheads to racist militia groups to card-carrying members of the KKK. But he had still held onto the idea that things were good and slowly getting better every day. The rabid enthusiasm of the Gage supporters burst that bubble for the foreseeable future.

So, depending on how you looked at it, this was either the absolute best time for PROPR to have appeared or the absolute worst time. It was probably good if you were a middle- to lower-income person of color, struggling to make ends meet and without the political or financial clout necessary to demand justice when you were treated unfairly.

But you would no doubt consider it to be terrible timing if you were in government, particularly law enforcement, and charged with maintaining the peace when people were fed up, enraged and finally being led by the example of a group that was showing that it was possible to take the fight for justice into your own hands. And here Madden was in the middle, one of the people with the job of trying to get everyone to just calm down and not do anything stupid.

When Madden heard the knock at the door, he glanced at his watch: it was 7:30am. Time had gotten away from him. He opened the door and greeted Phillips. She looked fresh as a daisy, but then, she always did.

"Did you not go back to bed?" she asked with concern.

"Not really," he said. "I spent some time trying to catch up on my reading. The internet is full of information related to this case. And none of it is good."

"What do you mean?"

"The tension in the streets continues to rise. I'm surprised Bainbridge hasn't called to chew my ass yet again. Things have got to be heating up for him, too."

"If he hasn't yet, you can be pretty sure he will soon," said Phillips.

"Ain't that the truth. You up for some breakfast?"

"I wouldn't complain if you threw a bagel at me," she said, smiling warmly.

"Give me a few minutes to freshen up," he said. "Meet you at the restaurant downstairs in fifteen?"

"You got it," she said.

Twelve minutes later he was sliding into the booth across from her. The waitress came around the corner smiling. She quickly took their orders and left.

"So, what did you find out online?" asked Phillips.

"Nothing that I didn't already know. But it was still depressing," said Madden.

"We'll get through it, like we have every other case."

"We will," said Madden, "but that won't exactly cure anything. The country is changing. Or should I say, showing its colors. Putting the members of PROPR in prison is just a stop gap measure. They've lit the fuse, and I don't think there's anything we can do to put it out. An explosion is imminent."

"That's why you need to stick around," she said. "We need people like you to help pick up the pieces when it all goes down. We're the warriors trusted to bring order to the war."

"You're right," he said. "This is war. But people don't seem to understand that it's a nuclear war. No one will win. And when all is said and done, there may not be many pieces left to pick up."

"You may be right," she said, "but I hope you're not."

The waitress returned with their food, and they spent the next ten minutes eating in silence.

"What's on the agenda for today?" she asked.

"I put in a call to HQ right after we got off the phone with Carter. They're putting together a dossier on him which should be ready any time now. Once we get that, maybe we'll have some clues on where to head next."

"Good," she said. "I touched base with the local office here before I came to your room. They have twelve agents they can spare for surveillance detail. I suppose if you were to sic Bainbridge on them, they might be able to cough up a couple more."

"They—" started Madden when his phone began to ring, cutting him off. He pulled it out of his pocket and looked at the display. It was Bainbridge.

Speak of the devil. "This is Madden," he said into the phone, his voice cool and even.

"Where are you?" asked Bainbridge without bothering to announce himself.

"Phillips and I were just finishing up breakfast."

"Finish faster and call me back in five minutes from someplace you can talk," said Bainbridge, and then hung up.

Madden pulled the phone away from his ear, looked at it and slowly shook his head.

"I see he's as polite as ever," said Phillips.

"Yeah," agreed Madden. "He wants some alone time," he said, smiling. "I've got to take it upstairs. Can you call in and see what the ETA is on my Carter file?"

"Sure," said Phillips. "Just buzz me when you're done."

Back in his room, he closed the drapes, took off his jacket and sat down in the most comfortable chair. He took a deep breath and closed his eyes. He could feel his heart beating a bit faster than normal. Most of the time he was able to remain pretty even-keeled during these conversations with Bainbridge, but every now and then the fear started to get to him, the way it was doing right now.

The fear wasn't about what Bainbridge might say or do to him. The fear was about what Madden might say or do to Bainbridge. He realized as he sat there trying to calm himself that this kind of fear was the same type of fear lots of black men experience during their encounters with police. A lot of them weren't really afraid of what the cops may do to them, either because of misplaced bravado or maybe just due to the blindness that frustration mixed with anger can sometimes create.

It was like the shy kid back in grade school that the bully kept picking on who was afraid that one day he was going to snap and strike out one way or another and end up getting the shit beat out of him in front of the whole school. With Madden and Bainbridge, his worry had always been that he'd finally get enough and say something that ruined his career. Bainbridge was an asshole and an idiot, but he was an asshole and an idiot with power, and he wasn't afraid to use it.

Madden had personally witnessed him politically beat down other agents who had tried to stand up against him. The ones who were still with the Bureau were often reduced, for all intents and purposes, to the role of male secretaries. But some were drummed out altogether. One, a good friend of Madden's, was now selling aluminum siding in

Florida somewhere. Another was running a failing private investigation agency, struggling to keep his house out of foreclosure.

He took another deep breath, then dialed the number. Bainbridge answered on the first ring.

"So, Madden, have you—"

"No, sir, I have not solved the case yet," said Madden, cutting him off. "But we're getting a bit closer."

There was silence on the other end of the phone. Madden knew that by interrupting his boss, he had raised the man's hackles. Interruptions were not something he was accustomed to. Especially from Madden. But today Madden was not in a mood to be fucked with. He waited patiently, letting the quiet between them breathe and giving Bainbridge all the time he needed to formulate a caustic response. But for some reason, the man decided to ignore the slight.

"Well, it's finally nice to hear a bit of good news for a change," said Bainbridge. "But before you go on, I have to ask. How is it that you just happened to be in the exact city that the current PROPR attack took place?"

"It was the result of solid police work by my team. They found intel that led us to believe that at least one of the suspects might reside here. But I have to admit, being here on that exact day was really just luck."

"Even a broken clock is right twice a day," said Bainbridge, a sneer in his voice.

Madden ignored the comment. "And to be clear," he said, "at this time we have absolutely no evidence that ties this attack to PROPR."

"Yes, I read your prelim report about this possibly being an imitator, but my gut tells me that this is them. These are our guys."

"I hope that you're right. We're continuing to follow up on several leads here and hope to have more info soon."

"Are you still alone?" asked Bainbridge, his voice dropping in both volume and pitch.

"Yes, sir."

"Listen, Madden. Over the last couple of days, I've been involved in some high-level meetings on this case. There are certain interested parties, who shall remain nameless, that have grave concerns about how this is all going to pan out in the end."

"What exactly do you mean?" asked Madden, but he already had a pretty good idea where Bainbridge was headed.

"I'm a history buff," said Bainbridge. "Always have been. The heyday of the civil rights movement in the 60s took place before I was even born, but I did my college thesis on that very movement. So, I've done a significant amount of research on the topic. Since I've been with the Bureau, I've watched quite a bit of confidential footage that was shot at the time; interviews, investigative pieces, surveillance videos, and the like. One thing I can tell you is that what's happening in this country now feels a lot like what was happening in the country fifty years ago. People were nervous then, and they're nervous now."

"They have every right to be," said Madden.

"Yes, but the wrong people are getting nervous now," said Bainbridge. "It's a much different world today than it was in the early 60s. Information travels at the speed of light. People are more informed. And information is power. People are getting uppity."

"Are you referring to black people?" replied Madden, his voice hard.

"I'm referring to the people clogging up the streets, marching on police stations, calling for resignations and creating all this fucking chaos!" said Bainbridge.

"Sir, we will crack this case. We're getting closer every day."

"This is about more than just cracking the case. The interested parties I mentioned are worried that once we have the offenders in custody, they'll be seen as martyrs, and perhaps we'll be in an even worse position."

"I don't think I'm following you, sir," said Madden.

"I'm saying that it's better for everyone involved if these people never see the inside of a courtroom," said Bainbridge, his voice edgy with frustration.

Madden paused.

"Are you asking me to fumble the case?"

"And let these fucking animals stay out on the street? No, I'm not asking you to fumble the fucking case!"

"Sir, I'm still not sure I understand what you're asking me."

"Jesus Christ," mumbled Bainbridge, "are all you people this fucking dense? When you catch these motherfuckers, you need to take them down and take them out!"

Madden took a deep breath.

"Sir, you're talking about a sanctioned hit. That's CIA territory."

"Don't give me this Boy Scout shit," said Bainbridge. "It's not like you've never killed anyone in the line of duty. As a matter of fact, if I remember correctly, you've been involved in at least four shootings. All fatal. These people are kidnappers, torturers and, if not for a quirk of fate, they'd be murderers by now! You'll be doing everyone a favor by deleting them from existence."

"Sir," said Madden, "with all due respect, I'm not an assassin, and neither is anyone on my team. We'll handle this case by the book, like we've handled all our cases, and we'll let a judge and jury decide what happens to these suspects."

"Let me put it to you like this," said Bainbridge. "If any member of PROPR ever gets in front of a jury, you can go sell siding with your friend in Tallahassee. Is that understood?"

"Perfectly," said Madden just before the line went dead. He sat frozen for a few moments, the phone still against his ear. He could feel a bead of sweat slowly rolling down the right side of his face. Finally, he pulled the phone away, looked at the screen and, after taking another deep breath, threw it across the room.

Chapter 57

Ish woke up in his hotel room. He had checked in early that morning, and after spending some time catching up on the news online, he had dozed off. He awoke with a start. He couldn't remember what it was he was dreaming, but he could tell that it wasn't anything fun. He looked out the window and saw that the sun was low in the sky. He had napped longer than he intended. He was supposed to meet Chad for dinner at six, so he needed to get moving.

They had decided to meet at a little Italian restaurant on the outskirts of Hollywood. It was once one of his favorite places to take Layla. It was a classy establishment with fantastic food. It was dimly lit, with heavy curtains separating the booths. It was a great location for anyone looking for a little privacy—romantic or otherwise. When he arrived, Chad was already seated. He was sipping on a martini.

"Hey, bro," he said as Chad stood, and they briefly embraced. "Getting started without me?"

"I gotchu', man," said Chad. "I already ordered you a *Camas*. Ahhh! Here it is now."

A pretty dark-haired woman approached the table and smiled as she sat Ish's drink in front of him. Both he and Ish placed their dinner order, and he waited for the woman to retreat before he began speaking again.

"So," he said, taking a sip of his own drink. "What did you find out?"

"Unfortunately, the rooms on both sides of these agents are occupied. And their rooms are right next door to each other, so miking them from an adjacent room isn't going to really be an option."

"I was afraid of that," said Ish.

"However," said Chad, "I had another idea. Do you remember those old femtocells that Verizon used to use a few years back?"

"You mean those wireless network extenders people were using to hack into phones?"

"Those are the ones."

"Yeah..." said Ish, his mind whirring. "If I remember correctly, not only could you listen to calls and intercept all the data, you could also turn the mic on and listen to surrounding conversations."

"That's exactly right," said Chad. "Of course, Verizon patched that hole, as did all the other carriers, but I was able to put something together that works pretty much the same way. It only has a range of about 50 feet from the target phone, but that's enough for us. There's a table in the hallway between both agents' rooms that couldn't have been more perfect if I had placed it there myself. A little double-sided tape and I was able to slap it underneath the table as I walked by; I didn't even have to slow my roll."

"Aren't you the clever boy," said Ish, raising his glass for a toast.

"Thanks," said Chad. "But of course, this only gives us access to what they say in the room. Anything outside that 50-foot radius will be dark to us."

"What about that TVC software? Maybe we could use that to tap directly into them 24/7?"

"I thought about that," said Chad, "but word on the Dark Web is that the FBI runs a daily bug sweep on their phones that would catch that every time. I don't know if it's true or not, but I figured we probably don't want to take the chance."

"You're right; we definitely don't want to show our hand if we don't have to," said Ish. Their food arrived and they dug in, spending the next few minutes enjoying their meal in silence.

"Have you spoken to any of the other guys? Or girl?" asked Chad between bites of ravioli.

"I did," said Ish. "I touched base with each of them on the way here. They're doing well, though getting a little antsy sitting around. That's the good news. The bad news is that the FBI has been around to see everyone's people, looking for info on their whereabouts."

"Damn," said Chad. "How do you think that happened? Do you think they found new evidence?"

"Nah," said Ish. "I think we were too careful for that. My guess is that they just started putting the pieces together, working their way backwards from where I've been and who I've been around for the last couple of years. Guilt, or at least suspicion, by association."

"And what did the families have to say?"

"Bird and Ma'am are black. You know my people are seldom eager to cooperate with the police. But Jag's mother was more than happy to tell them anything she thought they might want to know. Fortunately, she didn't know much, other than the fact that he told her he was working in L.A. somewhere."

"If they're putting clues together, that's not good,' said Chad.

"No, it's not, but it is what it is."

"Well, I'm glad to see they're holding up well. I meant to reach out to them myself, but I've been so busy. Are Bird and Ma'am still pissed off at you?"

"Hard to say. Ma'am tends to always be in a good mood, and Bird tends to always be in a shitty one, and those are the vibes they gave off when I spoke to them today, so I really don't know."

"Don't worry about it, man. They'll be there when you need them."

"I hope so," said Ish. "Speaking of need, I've had an idea brewing around in my head the last few days, but I need help with it, if you're up for it."

"Come on, bro. You know I'm always here for whatever you need. What can I do?"

"I've been thinking about this issue with Layla having this attempted murder charge hanging over her head. I feel like she's making some really solid progress towards changing her mindset about getting out, but this pending charge could fuck it all up. So, it occurred to me that maybe I need to try to do something to address that."

"What were you thinking?"

"Paying this woman off to drop the charge."

Chad whistled softly. "That could be quite a challenge to pull off, even if she is open to the idea. Forget for the moment that even if you're successful with this, the D.A. could still push the charge. The first thing you'd have to do is get her to agree to speak to you. Then you'd have to somehow make and negotiate the offer without any of the eavesdropping jail officials knowing what you're up to."

"Exactly. And that, my man, is where you come in."

"What did you have in mind?" asked Chad.

"I think the only way to get in touch with this woman is to go to the jail and meet her face to face. With the FBI looking for me, that's probably not the best place for me to be right now."

"You think?" asked Chad jokingly.

"Of course, they'd love to talk to you, too, but I don't believe that you're an actual suspect yet. So, I think you could probably get in and out without any problems, especially with a fake ID. But there's no guarantee, so if you're the least bit uncomfortable with that, just say the word. I'd totally understand," said Ish.

"I ain't worryin' 'bout no po-po!" said Chad, smiling broadly. "Let's do this thang!"

"Okay, gangsta', calm down," said Ish, returning the smile. "But seriously, this isn't without risk."

"I understand," said Chad, his smile fading as his mouth formed a grim line. "But this is for my homeboy and his woman. I'd give my life for you, man, with no second thought."

"Thanks," said Ish, his voice a bit croaky.

"So how do you want to handle it?" asked Chad.

"Well, you're right about communication being an issue. The phones are going to be tapped and there are guards everywhere. When Layla and I speak, we sometimes speak in code, but this woman isn't going to have a clue about that."

"Is there any chance Layla could speak with her first; let her know that we're coming?"

"Possibly. My concern is that they're not exactly on friendly terms, so if Layla approaches her, they could end up going at it again before she can even get a chance to deliver the message."

"Maybe Layla could get someone else to actually pass the word along? I could visit Layla first and tell her the plan."

"That's an idea, but it's probably best if you don't show up on both her visitor list and this other woman's, too. Even if you used different IDs, you'd have to try to disguise yourself so the guards wouldn't recognize you as the person that was there before. That's adding unnecessary risk to an already risky situation. What I can do instead is try to have her lawyer get a message to her to call me. Then I just have to figure out a way to get her to understand what I'm trying to say without tipping off the phone monitor."

Chad nodding his head in agreement. "And what is your proposal to this woman going to be?"

Ish paused for a moment, thinking. "One problem is that she's in jail, so there's only so much money she can have on her books. I'll have to find out the exact amount, but I'd be surprised if it were more than $500. So, what I'm thinking is that we offer to max out her account there, whatever that amount is, then give a lump sum to some trusted friend or family member of hers to hold for her, in addition to setting up a small trust account that drips money to her jail account."

"Sounds like a plan. How much were you thinking?"

"Dude, I'd give every penny I have on this earth to get Layla out," said Ish, his face set hard. "But I think $50,000 should be enough." Then he smiled. "But let's start at twenty and work our way up."

Two hours later Ish was just arriving back at his hotel when his cellphone rang.

After the recorded announcement that the caller was calling from a California correctional institution, Layla's voice appeared on the line.

"Hey, love," she cooed.

"Hey, baby." Suddenly he forgot about all the worries that were on his mind, gnawing away at him. All he could think about was the joy of being able to once again connect with the woman he loved.

"Is everything okay? Aquila told me you needed me to call right away."

"Yeah, everything is fine. It's just that I'm working on something, and I could use your help."

"My help?" she replied, her voice full of skepticism. "Okay."

Ish had spent a lot of time thinking about how best to get his message across to Layla in a way that only she would understand. He recalled once when they were still dating and they had taken a day trip up to Santa Barbara. It was a rainy day, but they were still able to get in some shopping and sightseeing.

They were thinking it was about time to get on the road and head home when suddenly the sun stuck its head out from behind a cloud and turned the entire scene golden. They were mesmerized by the glory of it all and spent a few more minutes walking around until they came upon an ice cream shop. By then, it was 6:10pm and the shop actually closed at 6:00pm. Ish knocked on the window, but no matter how he smiled, the man cleaning up inside continued to ignore them. That is, until Ish took out a $100 bill and held it up to the glass door.

The man still had an attitude, but his irritation didn't outweigh his desire for that hundred dollars, so he opened the door and served them both double scoops on waffle cones. Ish would have given him another hundred just to smile, but in truth another hundred might not have been enough. He had gotten the feeling that it wasn't just the fact that they were trying to get service after hours that bugged the man, but the fact that they were black and trying to get service after hours. Oh well, Ish had thought at the time, hopefully that crisp Benjamin Franklin he had just pocketed would help him feel better about it by morning.

"Remember that time we went to Santa Barbara?" he asked.

"You mean that weekend before my birthday, when it rained? Yeah."

"Remember that little shop we stopped at just before we headed back? I was thinking about how good that ice cream tasted."

"The guy had such a shitty attitude, especially considering how much you paid him for five minutes work," said Layla, "but you're right, that ice cream was the bomb. Artisanal ice cream is hard to beat."

"Right. I was thinking about maybe bringing some to the jail. Maybe giving some to that girl you had the fight with."

"LeAnn Wayne? What the hell would you want to give that b—"

"Hold up for a second," Ish said, cutting her off. "Think about what I'm saying. I was hoping that if I brought her enough ice cream, maybe it would squash the beef between you two."

"First of all," said Layla, her voice starting to rise, "I don't think—" She paused. Ish could hear the wheels turning in her head as she began to realize what he was really saying. "I'm not sure that's going to do much good. I'm sure the woman likes ice cream as much as anyone else, but she may hate me more."

"I don't know," said Ish. "Like you just said, it's artisanal. That's damn good ice cream. Enough of that goodness can put a smile on anyone's face."

"I suppose it's possible," she said slowly. "Then again, it might just be a waste of perfectly good ice cream. She could eat it all and still have a problem with me."

"Maybe, maybe not. Do you think you might be able to get a message to her, to let her know that the Good Humor man may be paying her a visit? Without pissing her off in the process, that is?"

"I think so," said Layla. "But I don't know how the hell you expect to get ice cream delivered to her in jail."

"Let me worry about that, babe," he said.

"Alright," she said, but she sounded skeptical. "Listen, I'm really not supposed to be on the phone right now, so I'd better go."

"Alright. Keep your head up. I love you."

"I love you, too," she said right before the line clicked and went dead.

Ish was putting the phone back into his pocket when it rang again. Again, it was a number he didn't recognize. He looked at it for a moment, debating whether to answer it or let it go to voicemail. Something told him that it might be important, maybe even Layla calling back, so he hit 'answer' just before it would have transferred over to the recorded message. He decided to let the caller speak first.

"Hello?" said a female voice on the other end.

"Yes?"

"Hi. I'm trying to reach Ishmael Carter."

"Who may I ask is calling?"

"This is Khadija Syed of #BlackForLife."

"Hi, Khadija!" he said. "This is Ishmael. How are you?"

"I'm fine, and yourself?"

"Good. What's up?"

"I'm actually calling to ask you a rather large favor."

"Sure. What can I do for you?"

"This is a bit awkward, but I came upon some information regarding your background with the police. Specifically, I'm referring to their involvement in the death of your daughter."

"Are you telling me that you've been digging around in my private life?" asked Ish, all the humor gone out of his voice.

"No, not at all! Well, not directly," she said, sounding a bit flustered. "What I mean is, we were doing research on African Americans that have died at the hands of police officers in the last three years, and your daughter's name came up. Then I saw your name listed as one of the parents and recognized it instantly."

"I see," said Ish quietly.

"I'm sorry. I don't mean to open old wounds," she said. "I really don't. And if you tell me that you don't want to talk about it, I'll hang up right now and never bother you again."

Ish took a deep breath. "No," he said tiredly. "It's..." He was about to say 'it's no big deal', but that just sounded absurd, given the circumstances. "It's okay. What is it that you need?"

"Thank you," she said with some relief. "I don't know how much you've been keeping up with the news, but there is more and more unrest brewing in the streets of our black communities. This group PROPR has everyone agitated, especially since that attempt on the life of that police officer in Los Angeles a few days ago."

"Yeah, I heard about that."

"We're worried that things are about to boil over. We believe that a significant number of people are getting close to being ready to take aggressive action, action that is only going to lead to more violence and more innocent people getting hurt. So, we're planning a major rally here in Baltimore tomorrow evening, marching in the name of peace and restraint. We'll have many people speaking, including some that have suffered personal tragedy at the hands of the police, but that are still willing to come out as advocates of a non-violent response. We hoped that you might want to join us as one of the featured speakers."

"Did you say tomorrow?"

"Yes. I know. I'm so sorry for the late notice. I had no knowledge of the situation regarding you and your daughter until about two hours ago. I know it's a ridiculously last-minute request, and I really debated whether or not to call you at all, but this is so important that I felt it was worth risking the embarrassment," she said, sounding almost out of breathing as she spoke the last few words.

"No, there's no need to feel like that. You're right, this is very important, and I'm truly glad that you called. I really feel honored that you think my voice could help you. Unfortunately, I'm in L.A. at the moment and it's just not possible for me to get away at this time. Believe me, if I could be there, I would be. But please, keep me in mind for future events. If I can manage to work it into my busy schedule, I will definitely be there to lend my support."

"Thank you very much. That's very generous of you. I'll definitely put you in our database. By the way, any progress on Nathaniel's case?"

"Not much," he said. "I believe the lawyers were finishing up some depositions last week, but I don't think the preliminary hearing is even on the calendar yet."

"Hang in there. You know the wheels of justice move slowly. And when black people are involved and threatening the white dollar, they move even slower still," she said.

"That is the truth. Thanks again for calling, and tell Marquita I said hello."

"I will. God bless," she said as they hung up.

He pulled the phone from his ear and stared at it, transfixed. He couldn't explain it, but something about the call felt ominous, like it was a sign of something bad to come. He only hoped he was just feeling paranoid. But somehow, he knew that wasn't the case.

Chapter 58

Ish spent the early part of the next day visiting the individual members of his team at their respective hotels. He could have reached them all by cell again, but he felt that he would make a better connection and get a better assessment of where everyone's head was by visiting in person. It was somewhat risky, but he reduced that risk by wearing a clever but subtle disguise consisting of thick, black-framed glasses and a light-colored wig, topped off by a baseball cap.

The first stop was the one he assumed would be the easiest: Jag.

"Hey, Ice-Man," said Jag, opening the door before Ish even had a chance to finish knocking. "Come on in, man. Let me get you a drink."

AC/DC's "Highway To Hell" was coming through the TV speakers, and the drapes were drawn. It looked like Jag had decided that the mini-bar was bullshit, because he had a counter covered in 750ml bottles of alcohol. There was tequila, scotch, vodka and gin. Most of them were at least half empty.

It was early for Ish to be thinking about alcohol, but he didn't want to be rude, so he waited while his friend poured him a scotch on the rocks. Jag handed him the glass and waited for him to take a sip. It wasn't *Camas*, but it was pretty high quality.

"That's delicious, thanks," he said before turning to look directly at the assortment of alcohol bottles.

"Looks like this is the place to be—be here or be square," he said.

"Just a little something to take the edge off," said Jag. The worrisome thing was that Ish had never known Jag to be a particularly heavy drinker. Considering the fact that they had only been gone a couple of days and that Ma'am did not drink, it was clear that something was wrong.

"What's going on, chief? You look a little bit rough around the edges."

"Is it that obvious?" asked Jag.

Ish shrugged as if to say, *Well, actually, yes, it is.*

"The truth is, Ma'am and I are having a bit of a quarrel. Ever since that day she bumped heads with you in the kitchen over that issue with Bird, she's been different."

"Different how?" asked Ish.

"I don't know how exactly to explain it. More distant. More closed off. More...aggressive."

"And have you asked her what's wrong?"

"Of course. But you know women. It's always the same answer: 'Nothin's wrong, I'm fine. I'm just tired.' But I know there's more to it than that. Also, she doesn't seem to want to talk about the wedding plans anymore." Jag was clearly trying to appear strong, but behind his eyes was something Ish had literally never seen there before: fear. Ish took another sip of his drink to give himself some more time to think.

"Has she been spending much time with Bird lately?" he asked.

"It's hard to say. I haven't been around her much the last 48 hours or so. But it wouldn't surprise me."

"Do you get the feeling she might be having second thoughts about marrying you?"

"I don't know what the hell to think!" he answered.

"Look, I'm going by there later today," said Ish. "I'll try to get her temperature on the matter and report back to you. How's that?"

"That's great! I'd really appreciate it. Just, uhhh, don't let on that I sent you."

"Don't worry," said Ish. "Your secrets are safe with me."

As Ish walked out of Jag's room on the way back to his car, he couldn't help but shake his head in wonder. This certainly wasn't the Jag he had met, what felt like a lifetime ago, back in Afghanistan. He would have never imagined that Jag showing the kind of emotion for a woman that this Jag was showing.

Maybe Ma'am felt that Jag had betrayed her by not standing with her and Bird in the showdown in the kitchen. But if she knew anything at all about Jag, she should know that he always stood up for what he thought was right and that he always spoke what he thought was the truth, regardless of how crass it might have sometimes sounded.

Ish vividly remembered one incident that happened shortly after he had arrived in Afghanistan. There was a guy in the unit named Lipinski. He wasn't a particularly large man, but he had a large mouth. He was one of those guys who was loud even when there was no reason to be. And he was a bully.

Ish had, of course, known lots of bullies when he was a kid. But it always struck him as odd when he met one in the service, in combat surroundings. It was one thing to get in someone's face on the playground when, more often than not, all the other guy had to defend himself were fists that he didn't know how to use. Getting in the face of someone who had been trained by the U.S. government to kill and who was either armed or had lethal weapons nearby was the epitome of stupid. But as perplexing as it was, it was also something that he saw on more than one occasion.

One day at chow, Lipinski was harassing one of the new guys, a baby-faced kid who looked like he had just finished boot camp. Whenever he was witness to things like this, Ish would give the guys some room to work it out between themselves as long as it didn't get too serious before he felt the need to intervene on the victim's behalf.

Getting involved in someone else's squabble was something he had been warned about time and again by his superiors, both in school and in the service. They told him that he was out of line and that it wasn't his place to play 'mother bear' to every snot-nosed kid who had his mashed potatoes taken from him.

And he knew they were right. Even though he had the best of intentions, things didn't always go as he would have hoped. He had made many enemies along the way by sticking his nose in. Sometimes he even attracted the hatred of the person he was trying to save, because fighting the guy's battle for him could make him look even weaker and cause more problems for him further down the road. But Ish had always found it difficult to sit back and watch people who were incapable of defending themselves be abused.

However, on this particular day, he had decided to use some restraint. This guy who Lipinski was bothering didn't seem terrified as much as he seemed resigned. He had probably dealt with people like Lipinski his whole life and knew that he just needed to weather the storm until the guy lost interest. But apparently, Jag had a different idea. Maybe he had witnessed the interaction between these two more often than Ish had, or maybe he was just in a bad mood. Whatever the reason, he decided he had seen enough.

"I'm tired of listening to you oink," said Jag to Lipinski. "Why don't you go roll in shit someplace else and leave this boy alone?"

The rest of the scene played out like something out of a comic book, and Ish could not help but laugh as did just about everyone else in the mess hall. After exchanging a few more words and ducking a flying fist, Jag had grabbed Lipinski by the nose with two fingers and started guiding him around the room while simultaneously kicking him in the ass. Lipinski literally began to cry, probably as much a reaction to Jag's fingernails digging into his sinuses as from the embarrassment of it all.

"You gonna cry, you little faggot? You gonna cry?" yelled Jag before sweeping the man's legs out from under him and slamming him into the floor. "This war ain't got no room for faggots, you hear me?" said Jag, standing over him and leaning down into his face. "Now get your sweet ass out of here, and don't let me find you actin' out again."

As far as Ish knew, the guy never again said an unkind word to anyone, nor did he report Jag. A couple of days later Jag and Ish were out on patrol together, leaning against a truck when Lipinski walked by. "Good evening, sirs," he had said, his head bowed respectfully.

"And they say you can't teach an old dog new tricks," said Jag, smiling. Ish just looked at him. "I'm talking about that Lipinski. I had to give him a stern talkin' to a couple of days ago."

"Yeah, I saw," said Ish.

"What's wrong?" asked Jag. "You don't have sympathy for that little butt plug, do you? Somebody needed to teach him a lesson."

"I suppose that's right," said Ish. "But I don't know if that was exactly the best way to do it."

"Are you one of those non-violent soldiers?" asked Jag, still grinning.

"I didn't have a problem with you giving him a good beating. But the gay-bashing was uncool."

"Gay-bashing?" asked Jag, looking puzzled. "Oh, you mean me calling him a faggot?" Ish just stared at him again. "Sorry if I hurt your feelings, dude. Are you gay yourself?"

"What if I am?" replied Ish, his tone a challenge. "Are you going to try to grab my nose, too?"

Now it was Jag's turn to pause. He took a moment; staring at Ish, sizing him up. Finally, he seemed to have come to a conclusion.

"Nah, I don't think you're gay," he said. "Not that it matters. I have nothin' against gay people. The more the merrier as far as I'm concerned. Let freedom ring!"

"Then what the hell was all that 'faggot' stuff about?"

"That was about demeaning a man; taking his pride away from him. Or as my mama used to say, showing him that he done got a little big for his britches," said Jag. "Calling him a faggot ain't no different than calling a black man a nigger, and I done that, too, a few times in my day."

At the word 'nigger' Ish's shoulders hunched up, and he quickly turned to stare at Jag, fire in his eyes and his muscles coiled to strike.

"Hold on, now," said Jag, raising his hands in defense. "At least give me a second to explain."

Ish had looked around. They were in the middle of enemy territory, with no idea who might be watching them. This was the wrong place to get into a fistfight with a fellow soldier if it could be avoided. He relaxed a little and returned to leaning against the truck, his blank expression giving Jag permission to continue.

"You see, what you got to understand is that these ain't nothin' but words. They're insults, pure and simple," said Jag. "It's like if I call someone a 'motherfucker', it doesn't mean I think that they've ever had sex with their mother. At least, not most of the time." His grin returned. "It's just an insult; something to be used to ruffle another man's feathers."

"It's the same with words like faggot and nigger," he continued. "They're insults because they represent handicaps. The truth is, no one really wants to be black or gay, if they don't have to be." Ish's eyes squinted into a frown.

"Come on now, I know all about 'black pride' and 'gay pride', and you should be proud of who you are, absolutely. But let me ask you this," said Jag, leaning a bit closer to Ish. "Imagine if, before each person was born, God were to appear before them and say, 'It's time for you to choose what you want to be in this world. You can be tall or short, fat or skinny, white or black, straight or gay, rich or poor, good-looking or ugly, etc., etc.' If he explained the consequences of each of those choices, how many people do you think would really choose to be gay? Or black? Or short? Or fat? I'd bet you dollars to donuts that the option most people would choose would be the tall, skinny, rich, straight, good-looking white man!"

Ish smirked and shook his head. "Man, you really think a lot of yourself, don't you?"

"This has nothing to do with me," said Jag. "This is simple logic. Short people are viewed in this world as just a little bit less desirable than tall people. Skinny versus fat? Skinny is gonna win every time. Rich versus poor? No question. And while you may love being black, and a gay guy may love being gay, neither of you can deny that in this world, you both face an uphill battle to be accepted as an equal. So again, I ask you, brother, given the choice, who in his right mind would choose to knowingly saddle themselves with a handicap?"

Ish shook his head again, in a motion of denial, but he had to admit that the guy had a point. What he said pissed Ish off, but it was hard to deny the logic of it. It was true; they did live in a society in which the white man was considered the ideal. It didn't matter what nation or what race of people you examined, all you had to do was look at their billboards, at their TV commercials, at their magazines and you could clearly see how wholeheartedly they worshiped the Anglo-Saxon aesthetic.

"You're one crazy fucking white boy," he said, unable to hide a slight grin.

"I know, right?" said Jag. "But I preach the gospel, brother! You know I do! I'm all about the truth! And just for the record," he said, dropping his voice slightly, "some of my best friends are black and gay. But don't tell my mama."

* * *

Next on Ish's list to visit was Ma'am. When he knocked on her hotel door, she opened it wrapped in a towel.

"Sorry," she said. "I'm just getting out of the shower. I'll be out in a minute. Help yourself to the mini-bar."

He watched her as she walked back into the bathroom and was suddenly struck by her beauty. She might not be everyone's cup of tea, but he could definitely see how Jag could be so attracted to her. There was a strength in the way she carried herself. Ma'am was one of those women who moved in a way that was casual but at the same time indicated to anyone who was curious that she was a woman with places to go and that it would take a lot to stop her from getting there.

She returned to the room wearing baggy, khaki-colored jeans and a matching Under Armor t-shirt. She may not be currently enlisted, but she still looked like she was. And Ish guessed that, in her mind, she probably still thought that she was. She sat on the edge of the bed to put on her socks and shoes.

"It's good to see you, my brother. How are you?"

"I'm good. You?"

"Fine. To what do I owe this lovely visit?"

"No particular reason," said Ish, shaking his head slightly from side to side. "Just wanted to check up on you, make sure you're holding up okay."

"That's nice. But I can tell by the vibe you're givin' off that there's something else."

Ish doubted that he was giving off any such vibe. He suspected that she knew he had gone to see Jag first and was guessing.

"Well, now that you mention it, there is a little something. I saw Jag a little while ago and he seemed uncharacteristically glum."

"You're the only nigga I know that uses words like 'glum'," she said, chuckling slightly. "Is that anything like sad?"

"More or less," he said. She just nodded her head in return, offering him nothing. "So how are things between you two? How are the wedding plans coming?"

"I don't know, Ish. I don't know if this is the right time for all that. I feel like there is still some wildness in me that I need to get out, and the only way to do that is out in the world."

"What kind of wildness?"

"I don't know," she said, pausing and turning her head to the side. "It's hard to explain, but I feel like I need some more time to be completely black."

Now Ish chuckled. "What the hell does that mean?"

"It's like...well...I feel that if I marry a white man, I'm dilutin' a part of my blackness, you know? I'm not sayin' that Jag ain't totally acceptin' of me the way I am, but I don't know that I'd exactly feel comfortable always being 'full black' around him. Like, I just used the word 'nigga' with you. I've used the word around Jag, but I've always been a little self-conscious about it, you know? I worry that I'll lose part of my soul, my ethnicity, if I mate myself to a white man for the rest of my life. I'm not sure I'm quite ready to do that yet."

Ish nodded and paused to ponder that statement. On the surface it might seem like kind of an odd thing for someone to say, but he knew exactly what she meant. He had gone through something similar in college.

Coming from a basically all-black inner-city school and moving into the inner circle of computer geeks was a bit of a culture shock. At first Ish told himself that he didn't really give a damn what any of these people thought about him and that there was no need to try to fit in with them. But over time, he felt himself developing a need to belong to something.

In high school, he mostly rolled with the jocks and was always considered one of the 'cool' guys. But in college, that no longer felt like enough. As his love for computer programming grew, he felt himself being distanced from the athletes. Of course, he still played sports, but it was no longer where his passion lay.

However, what didn't change was his desire to be around people of color; people who looked like him. The thing that surprised him most was that now, even the guys who were part of the crowd he ran with and who did look like him didn't act like him. These guys looked black, but they were what many in the neighborhood he grew up in would have called 'Oreos'—black on the outside, white on the inside.

Sometimes it was clear he had absolutely nothing in common with these guys. He listened to Jay-Z, they listened to Green Day. He wore Sean John, they wore Abercrombie. He watched The Bernie Mac Show, they watched South Park. Everything was different, including, of course, the way they talked.

Most of these guys were not 'from the hood'. They were not street smart. They were more likely to use vernacular common to the surf culture than the inner city. Sometimes it felt to Ish like they were actually speaking a different language. To fit in, he eventually began self-censoring his own language, not to copy them but just so that he didn't come off as quite so raw. In other words, so that he didn't come off as quite so 'black'. So yeah, he knew exactly what Ma'am was saying.

"I hear where you're coming from," he said. "I'm not here to try to change your mind. Who am I to be giving you advice, anyway? I'm not exactly an expert in love. You know your own self better than anyone else does. I'm confident that you'll ultimately make the right decision."

"Thanks, Ish," she said. "But tell me. If you was to give me advice, what would it be?"

Ish thought about that for a moment. Ma'am and Jag were more than just his friends. They were like family. He wanted both of them to be happy, but he wasn't sure they would find that happiness together.

"When it comes to love," he said, "I've always found a lot of wisdom in music. There are a bunch of old songs which tout some version of the adage 'love don't wait for no one'. And I believe that to be true. So, the only real advice I can give you is to treat time like an enemy. In the end, you need to do what feels true to you at the soul level, but remember that love requires nurturing—water, sunshine, soil. If you walk away today from something as alive and vibrant as what you and Jag have, and then one day change your mind, you may return to find nothing but a dead, dried up weed in its place."

"Thanks, Ish," said Ma'am as she walked over and wrapped him in a warm embrace.

"No problem," he said, returning the hug. "Well, I'd better get going. I still have to stop by your brother's spot to check on him, and then I'm meeting up with Chad for a late afternoon powwow."

"Hey, speaking of Bird," she said, putting her hands in her pockets, "about what happened earlier. I didn't mean to come off like a—"

"Don't worry about it," said Ish. "You were just standing up for your family."

"It's a little more complicated than that. Some of the stuff that happened to me on the street..." She bowed her head momentarily. "I think that people assume that recoverin' crackheads don't remember or maybe that they just don't care. But I remember all that shit. All of it. Every dirty, filthy ass thing I ever did, and ever had done to me," she said, ending the last few words almost at a whisper.

She cleared her throat, the sound echoing in the air between them. "In fact, I don't just remember it. I still experience it. At least once a week I wake up in a cold sweat from a dream in which I'm livin' it all over again. These dreams are so real, Ish, that I see and experience every tiny detail. I can feel the hot breath of some unnamed man on top of me. I can smell my own filth, a combination of sweat, drugs and my raw womanhood. I can taste the foulness of someone's unwashed body in my mouth."

Ish stared, not really sure how to respond.

"And you know the worst of it? Even though I've been clean for nine, going on ten years now, in these dreams I can feel the hunger. You know how your mouth waters when you're really, really hungry and you smell something really, really delicious cooking? My brain does that, Ish. In these dreams I'm a fiend all over again."

"I'm sorry, Ma'am," he finally said. "I'm sorry you're still going through this. I know you already know this, but I'll say it anyway. Those are just bad dreams. You've put all that behind you. That's just the past talking, trying to make you feel guilty for having been strong enough to have left it behind. As you know, I do battle with my own demons of the night, so I know something of what you're dealing with. Is Jag aware of these dreams you've been having?"

She nodded. "The funny thing is, since he's been in my life these last few weeks, the dreams are...fading? No, that's not really the right word. They're not exactly fading. It's more like they're becoming less...vivid. It's almost like they were in HD before, and then they went to regular picture...whatever that's called," she said sheepishly.

"Standard definition."

"Right. And now, they're whatever is below standard definition. It reminds me of when I used to watch shows on this gigantic, decrepit-ass TV set that my grandfather used to have. This thing was the size of a small horse and must have weighed a thousand pounds. Sometimes the picture was fine, but a lot of times it would get this interference that made the images kinda ghost-like, if that makes any sense."

"I know exactly what you mean," said Ish. "I had an uncle back in Chicago that had the same type of TV with the same type of problem."

"Yeah, well anyway," she said, shaking her head as though it were some kind of giant etch-a-sketch and she was desperate to erase the picture as quickly as possible. "Thanks again for everything. And tell Bird I'll give him a call later on."

"Will do," he said. They embraced again, and then he walked out of the room with her staring after him as if there was more she wanted to say but didn't know how.

Chapter 59

Ish was not looking forward to this visit with Bird. His friend had become more and more unpredictable since the beginning of this project. Ish had no idea which Bird he would find when he finally arrived at his hotel, and he was not a man who liked surprises.

He had to knock three times before Bird finally came to the door. "Hey, man," he said, giving Ish a dap, but failing to embrace him the way he normally did.

A Charlie Parker tune was blaring on a small boombox. Ish recognized it immediately—"Confirmation". There was also porn playing on the television, but the sound was muted. Bird saw Ish glance at it, but he didn't seem at all embarrassed or in a rush to turn it off. Ish noticed a half-empty bottle of cheap whiskey sitting on the desk, next to an empty pizza box and a small prescription bottle.

"Looks like you've been having a party up in here," he said cheerfully, trying to break the ice.

"I wouldn't exactly say that," said Bird. "I'm just relaxing a little."

"Sorry for disturbing," said Ish, "but I'm just checking in on everyone, making sure you're all okay."

"I appreciate that. I'm doing fine. A little bored, but I'm sure everyone is."

"True. I'm meeting up with Chad in a little while to go over some things. Hopefully, we can return to action in the next couple of days."

"That's great. So, I assume that means you haven't heard anything more from the FBI?"

"Nothing significant. I actually contacted them. We needed to know where they were staying, so Chad set up a tracer on a burner phone and I called the lead agent."

"That's original," said Bird. "What did he have to say?"

"Not a whole lot. Just that they thought that some of the members of PROPR could be Special Ops and wanted my help in identifying some possible suspects."

"So, in other words, they suspect it's you and want you to turn yourself in for questioning."

"More or less," said Ish.

"So that means it's only a matter of time before they have a bead on every one of us, if they don't already."

"I think that's a safe bet."

Bird's face was unreadable. Ish couldn't tell if he was pissed off, worried, or just didn't give a damn.

"What was the point of finding out where they were staying, anyway?"

Ish explained the device that Chad had planted to eavesdrop on the FBI's conversation and how they hoped to pick up some intel that would keep them one step ahead.

"That sounds like a serious long shot," said Bird.

"It is. But it's better than nothing," said Ish. Then, after a beat, he added: "Oh, by the way, Ma'am told me to tell you she'd call you later. I saw her right before I came here."

"How is she?" asked Bird, which, together with what Ma'am had said, made it clear to Ish that he and his sister weren't currently communicating much. He wondered if it had anything to do with the confrontation from a couple of days ago.

"She's fine," he said. He wasn't sure how much he should say about what was going on between Ma'am and Jag. "She seems to have a lot on her mind. But you know your sister; she always was a deep thinker."

"Yeah, she's a regular Penseur," said Bird, referencing the French name for Rodin's famous *Thinker* sculpture. It was a reference so obscure that Ish barely got it and had to wonder if Bird was purposely trying to insult not only his sister, but Ish as well.

He chuckled softly. "I don't think you give your sister enough credit," he said. "She may not be up on her French artists of the nineteenth century, but she's still a very intelligent lady. And she's always had your back."

Bird glared at him for a moment, then his faced drooped.

"You're right, man. I don't know what's gotten into me lately. Ever since we came back to the States, I've felt off, somehow. I think maybe I'm just missing the combat life. Even though I never thought myself the ideal soldier, at least I felt a sense of belonging there. To be honest, that was one of my main reasons for accepting Chad's proposal to join this little project. I thought it might fill the void. But it hasn't. Running these little missions is really nothing like being in-country, right up against it."

"I never thought you'd be one to experience homesickness for Afghanistan," said Ish.

"It's not so much the place as the lifestyle," said Bird. "I think it's really about the simplicity. Having someone else tell me where to be, when to be, what to do, had a certain appeal."

"Really?" said Ish, seriously shocked. "That is surprising. You, of all people, always struck me as so independent. What you're describing is what I've often heard people just released from prison say; people that have been inside so long that they're not sure they can survive on the outside."

Bird looked ashamed. "I know. People don't expect to hear this kind of talk from a 'college educated' black man. We're supposed to be forward thinking, militant, in control of our own destinies. But sometimes...sometimes I just feel lost out here."

Ish chuckled again, shaking his head. Bird glared at him again. "So, you're laughing at me now?"

"I'm sorry, man. I'm not laughing at you. It's just that what you just expressed is something that I've heard Layla say, in so many words, so many times since she's been locked up. I'm laughing not because it's funny, but because of how blind I can be at times. My parents were somewhat radical in their thinking, I guess, because I was basically raised on the 'be free or die' dictum. But I'm starting to realize that not every black person was raised the way I was. And it doesn't make one way better or worse than the other. Just different. I'd probably do well to learn to be a bit more sensitive to those differences."

Bird mumbled something that sounded like 'don't worry about it', but Ish couldn't be sure.

"Anyway, I'm going to get moving. If there's anything you need, even if you just need to talk, call me anytime, day or night. Seriously."

"Thanks, Ish," said Bird.

Ish was about to head towards the door, then turned back around.

"There is one more thing I wanted to chat about," he said. "The other day you mentioned Stanwick. What was that all about? Are you having second thoughts about how we handled that situation?"

"I just..." stammered Bird. "I just got caught up in the moment. My temper got away from me, I guess. Stanwick definitely deserved everything he got."

"We all agreed at the time that we'd never, ever mention that incident again, and then you go and bring it up in casual conversation," said Ish.

"I'm sorry, man. It won't happen again. You have my word," said Bird.

Ish didn't know what else to say, so he nodded once and left.

He stopped back at his hotel to shower and change clothes before he headed over to Chad's. It was almost 8:00pm when he finally arrived.

"What's up, brother?" asked Chad as he met Ish at the door. His face looked a bit tight. Ish sensed that something had happened.

"Did you get a hit on the FBI phones?" he asked.

"No, those have been silent all day. I suspect they're probably out trying to find us. But have you heard about Baltimore?" he asked as he walked over to his laptop.

Ish tensed. "No, what happened?"

Chad answered the question by tapping a few keys on his laptop and turning it so that Ish could see the screen. A video began to play. Off to the side of the screen was a middle-aged Hispanic man, a reporter. It was clearly shot at night, on a street somewhere in Baltimore, per the caption displayed below. Lights of various colors splashed across the display, and people could be seen running frantically to and fro. Almost all the people were either black or blue—African Americans or police officers. Chad turned up the sound.

"...started out as a peaceful rally has ended in tragedy," said the reporter. "Details are still sketchy, but what we know so far is that this was a peaceful march organized by the political action group #BlackForLife. It started about three miles from here, the marchers holding hands, chanting and waving banners as they made their way to City Hall. Once at City Hall, several people addressed the crowd, all telling stories of how negative encounters with the police had affected their lives but expressing a belief in hope and holding out the olive branch to these same police officers. Just as the last person finished speaking and the group was beginning to disburse, shots rang out as an unidentified person opened fire on the crowd.

"Here behind me," said the reporter, turning and gesturing, "is where most of the victims fell. Thirteen police officers and four civilians were struck by the shooter's bullets. The civilians all survived while all but three of the police officers were declared dead at the scene. The remaining seven victims, one of which is #BlackForLife co-founder Khadija Syed, have all been transported to a local hospital and have all been reported to be in serious to critical condition."

"And what do we know of the shooter?" asked an off-screen female voice.

"So far the authorities have declined to release his name. But it's been reported that he is a twenty-three-year-old African American man. The police gave chase, cornering him in a large commercial warehouse. Attempts to negotiate a surrender failed, and police finally sent in a K-9 unit to find and subdue the suspect. The suspect struggled with the dog, suffering injuries that proved fatal. The dog was reportedly unharmed."

Chad tapped a button, freezing the video.

"Shit," said Ish. "I should have been there."

"What do you mean?" asked Chad.

"Khadija called me yesterday to ask if I'd come speak at the rally. Somehow, she heard about what happened to Sumatra and thought my story would be a good fit. Of course, I declined. But if I had gone, maybe she wouldn't be in the hospital right now."

"That's a real stretch," said Chad. "I know you're upset, and you have every right to be, but what makes you think you being there would have at all changed the outcome of the situation?"

"I don't know," said Ish, sounding a bit lost. "The shooter waited till the last speaker finished. So, if I had been one of the featured speakers, maybe it would have delayed the shooting for a few minutes, and

Khadija might not have been hit. Or maybe I would have been close enough to pull her to safety once the shooting started. Hell, maybe my story about Sumatra would have been enough to change the shooter's mind."

Chad just stared at him.

"Okay, I admit, it is a stretch," said Ish. "But it's possible."

"I hear you, brother, and I'm sorry. I wish there was something we could have done to change the outcome of what happened," said Chad. "However, I do think this changes things going forward. I know we talked before about not going public with the Janssen story, but I think we have to now. People are going to be crediting PROPR with this attack. Hell, it's already started. There are twitter wars raging right now, where people are debating whether or not the shooter could have been one of us. If we don't set the record straight, it's only going to get more ugly, more complicated."

Ish took a deep breath, and then let it out. "Alright," he said. "Grab your video gear. Let's do this."

Chapter 60

Ish and Chad made a quick trip over to the Macrolox office. Ish ducked down in the seat, and Chad drove around the property for fifteen minutes to make sure no law enforcement was staking it out before they actually parked and went inside. As before, they set up the cameras in the War Room, after once again covering the walls in black material.

"Have you sketched out what you want to say?" asked Chad as he made some final adjustments to the equipment.

"I think I'm going to wing it this time," said Ish. "I'm feeling an urge to just speak from the heart."

"Good," said Chad.

Five minutes later the red light on the camera began glowing, and they were ready to begin. Ish was dressed in the now standard all-black PROPR regalia with Chad's audio equipment set to disguise his voice.

"Good evening, America," said Ish, staring into the camera. "Welcome back to PROPR TV. A lot has been happening in the world since last I reached out to you. A lot of it has been confusing, with both missing and inaccurate information as it relates to our organization and its actions.

"Before I go any further, PROPR would like to offer its deepest condolences to both the private citizens and members of the police department injured in the senseless shooting in Baltimore today. I also want to very clearly state that our organization had absolutely no knowledge or association with the shooter, and we categorically condemn his actions. He injured many innocent people that were marching for peace, as well as injuring and killing police officers that were there to protect them and to help preserve that peace.

"As we've said all along, we do not subscribe to the wanton attack of random police officers. Our organization was formed to dispense justice on those officers that have broken the law in their attacks on people of color, officers that seem to feel that they are above those laws.

"Having said that, we also want to publicly take responsibility for the botched attempt a couple days ago to deliver that justice to an Officer Janssen in Los Angeles. Officer Janssen has over 40 complaints of police brutality in his personnel folder. He's also killed eight people in the line of duty. Seven of those were unarmed black males. If his name sounds familiar to you, you probably saw reports of an incident early last year in which he shot and killed a young black man in front of his five-year-old daughter. This was a man that he stopped for failing to use his blinker while making a left-hand turn. The entire incident was caught on video. I'd like to take a moment to show you that footage right now."

Ish paused, knowing that Chad would add the footage later, during the editing process, before he uploaded their video online.

"As heinous as the crime you just witnessed was," Ish continued, "not only was Janssen not punished, he wasn't even charged. The only repercussions he suffered from this horrible crime was that he was restricted to desk duty—with pay—for three weeks while his fellow officers 'investigated' the incident. An investigation that clearly found him without fault.

"PROPR decided that we as a society could no longer afford to allow Mr. Janssen to be a part of it, to continue his bloodthirsty campaign of violence against innocent African Americans. I imagine what some of you may be wondering right now: Is it possible that some of the eight people that he shot were guilty? Maybe, maybe not. But what is undeniable is that all of these people were unarmed, and none of them had been convicted of any crime in a court of law. Even the crimes that Officer Janssen suspected them of didn't carry the penalty of death. But he dealt out that penalty anyway. Officer Janssen appointed himself judge, jury and executioner, and that's not something we could just turn the other cheek to.

"So, PROPR determined that Mr. Janssen himself was in need of judging. Our verdict: guilty. Our punishment, in accordance with the biblical principal of an-eye-for-an-eye, was death. We attempted to carry out that punishment a couple of days ago. Unfortunately, some unforeseen interference caused us to fail to deliver. But we are not discouraged. We will carry out that sentence. Officer Janssen, if you're watching, continue looking over your shoulder, because you will answer for your crimes. PROPR is coming for you.

"In conclusion, we would like to say to all those that support what we're trying to do, please keep the faith. We will continue seeking justice against those officers that feel they are above the law. And as always, we encourage you to also seek out your own justice in situations where the authorities are not listening to your pleas. But remember, make your weapon of justice a scalpel, not a sledge hammer. This isn't a war on all police officers, nor should we be asking innocent, upstanding officers to pay the debts of their dirty fellow officers. Make sure that if you feel the need to strike out in the name of justice, you do so in such a way that no innocent people are harmed. Because anything less than that is not justice. At least, not the kind of justice that PROPR supports.

"We also wanted to take a minute to thank you for all your emails and the flood of supportive comments on our site. We wish that we could respond to you all individually. We especially wish that we could respond to those of you asking for help with your own specific problems with predatory law enforcement officers. At some point we hope to be able to look into some of these cases, but right now our team is small and we have our hands full dealing with the targets we have already set our sights on. But we'll keep you updated on our plans as they continue to change and develop." Ish bowed his head for a moment, trying to think of anything he might be forgetting.

"We do have one request: we know that many of you are eager to get involved with our organization, and some of you may think it would be helpful for you to go after Officer Janssen yourself. Please, do not do so! You would only get yourself into unnecessary trouble, not to mention the fact that you may foul our own efforts. That's all we have for now. Thank you for your time, and we'll be posting an update again soon. Until then, good day and stay safe."

By 11:00pm Chad had the video completely edited and live on the website. God bless the internet.

Chapter 61

Madden sent Phillips a heads-up text to let her know that he was en route to her room. When he arrived, he found her bent over a laptop, her hands wrapped around a large cup of lemon-chamomile tea. He knew it was lemon-chamomile because that was all she ever drank. If they were back in the home office, she would have had stacks of files spilling off the desk around her, but when they were in the field it was safer and faster to have sensitive info transmitted digitally rather than shipped via messenger.

"How's Bainbridge?" she asked.

"Ummm," said Madden, pausing as he searched for the right words. "I would say he's a little grumpier than usual."

"Just a little?"

"Just a little," said Madden, smiling. "So, what do we have?" he asked, gesturing at the computer as he began to take off his jacket.

"Some good stuff," she said, putting her cup down and rearranging herself in the chair. "Carter served under a captain in Afghanistan that disappeared."

"What do you mean disappeared?"

"Meaning one day he was there, the next he was gone. No one saw him leave the base, but he was never seen again. Everyone in the squad was questioned, but Carter especially so, because they reportedly had a beef at one point, though apparently it had been squashed by the time of the disappearance."

"What was the beef over?"

"That we don't know, but it seems this captain was a real asshole, so it could have been over anything. There were some rumors that maybe he was abusing the native women, but nothing was ever proven."

"If Carter is part of PROPR, that would fit," said Madden, "because this captain sounds like the type of person they would want to go after."

"Exactly," said Phillips. "In fact, I think the army would agree. While they didn't find any evidence to charge him with the captain's disappearance, it appears they did 'highly recommend' a hardship discharge, using his daughter's death and wife's incarceration as the excuse. He accepted."

"Is that it?"

"No, I'm just getting started," she said. "Three of the guys he served with in the same platoon were also looked at closely during that investigation, but apparently only because it was known that they were close with Carter. They were Justin Anthony Gilroy, Damon Johnson and Nathaniel Bartholomew, affectionately known as 'Jag', 'Bird' and 'Blade', respectively. The especially interesting thing is that they all discharged at roughly the same time."

"That is interesting," said Madden.

"And," continued Phillips, "it also turns out that Johnson has a sister who served; Marines. Athena Johnson. They call her 'Ma'am'. No one knows why. Anyway, she was also recently discharged."

"Which potentially puts them all stateside when all this shit began," said Madden.

"It also accounts for the member of PROPR assumed to be female."

"This is starting to finally come together," said Madden, smiling again.

"Hold on. It gets better," said Phillips, her voice rising in excitement. "Nathaniel 'Blade' Bartholomew is currently deceased. You'll never guess what happened to him."

Madden shook his head in confusion.

"Killed by a cop in Baltimore about a month before the first PROPR video aired."

"Holy shit," said Madden. "So, it looks like we have enough players for a quorum. Do we know where any of these people are?"

"We've already sent agents to all of their last known addresses. All vacant. So, we reached out to the closest family members we could find. 'No habla ingles' from the Johnsons' people, but according to Gilroy's mother, who lives in Tennessee, he's been working out of state for the last few weeks. Right here in the beautiful city of angels."

"Holy shit, again," said Madden. "So that's potentially four assailants. The reports say there are at least five. Are you feeling Yang for the fifth? A rich Asian yuppie seems like a bit of a stretch for this team."

"I would have thought the same thing, but check this out," said Phillips, her fingers dashing over the keys to access another file. "Not only did Yang and Carter attend the same high school and college, but Yang was a member of the Black Student Union."

"The *Black* Student Union?" said Madden, raising his eyebrows skeptically.

"Exactly," said Phillips.

"That's not conclusive evidence, but it certainly paints the situation heavy with possibility. Does he have a record?"

"Several arrests for unlawful assembly, disturbing the peace and misdemeanor inciting a riot, all related to protest marches for one thing or another."

"A regular Chinese Martin Luther King. What about the others?"

"Gilroy also has several misdemeanor arrests, mostly for public drunkenness and disturbing the peace. He also had some assault and battery charges related to bar fights, but none of them ever got to trial," said Phillips. Her fingers deftly tapped the keys again.

"The Johnsons are a bit more interesting. Sister Johnson had a pretty colorful life before she joined the service. Several convictions for, among other things, prostitution and drug possession. She did a couple of years of jail time. Apparently, she's been on the straight and narrow since becoming a marine."

"Now the brother," she continued, "is another story. A college boy with two master's degrees and a PhD in literature. He was a college professor at a couple of universities in the Midwest before he joined the army."

"Why would a black college professor join the army?" asked Madden.

"I'm getting to that. He was charged with rape on three separate occasions. The last, when he was about twenty-two, was ruled a case of mistaken identity. But the other two, which happened a few years earlier, were more serious. One involved a fellow student at his high school; the other was apparently a complete stranger. Both went to trial. The jury deadlocked on the coed, and the other girl refused to testify so they threw the case out. Both cases looked pretty strong."

"But he skated on both of them," said Madden quietly, speaking to himself. "So, what does that have to do with him joining the army?"

"I guess the final straw was allegations of sexual impropriety between him and one of his students at the university."

"That sounds heavy," said Madden. "Was there a criminal investigation?"

"No, it appeared to be consensual, so no crime was ever reported, but of course it's still against the rules. During their internal investigation, the university discovered the previous rape charges. That was more than enough. They let him go. I guess he decided a change of scenery was in order and joined the army. Maybe he bought into the line about 'seeing the world'."

"Or he was just tired of being all he could be," said Madden. "And Carter?"

"Clean as a nun on Sunday morning. If anyone were ever going to be the poster boy for 'upstanding black citizen', he'd be it. Smart, good-looking, rich, successful—and a true patriot, putting it all on hold to serve his country. His life was like a Hallmark movie."

"Minus one daughter."

"Yeah, there's that," said Phillips.

"And the wife? Is she still incarcerated?"

"Yes, she's here in California. OCJ. Apparently, she's not adapting well to the life. She's already facing a new charge of attempted murder over a fight with another inmate."

"Why isn't she out on bail?"

"They offered. She refused."

Madden nodded slowly, his mind trying to fit the pieces together.

"Putting the situation behind the wife's plight aside, none of these guys look like cop-killers."

"What does a cop-killer look like?" asked Phillips. "They all have a motive, either directly or by association. And with the exception of Yang, they've all been trained to kill. I think this may be our team.

"So," she continued, "we have some idea who our culprits may be, but no idea how to find them. We could try staking out Yang's place, but I get the feeling none of the others are going to be visiting there anytime soon, assuming they ever did."

"I think you're probably right," said Madden. "And our resources aren't unlimited, so we need to use what we have wisely."

"Precisely," said Phillips. "That doesn't leave us a lot of options. I think we should put out a nationwide APB on all of them. Release their names and pictures to the media and go ahead and get this wrapped up before it gets any uglier."

"I don't think so," said Madden. "First of all, we barely have evidence linking Carter to this group, let alone any of the others. A mumbled word overheard in the midst of a traumatic attack? The D.A. would laugh in our face. And the only real connection that the others have to Carter is that they all served together. We can't pin any of them to PROPR without a hell of a lot more evidence."

"Okay then, let's at least put an APB out on Carter. If not nationwide, then just here in L.A. Certainly we have enough evidence for that."

"No, not yet," said Madden, rising from his chair and slowly walking toward the sliding glass windows. "We need to get closer to this. We need more ammo in our guns than just a mumbled word."

"And how exactly are we supposed to get that ammo if you won't even allow us to properly look for the guy?"

"You don't understand," said Madden, turning from the windows to look at his friend. "Have you not been watching the news? It's dangerous out there for black men—even the innocent ones. Cops are shooting blacks over the whiff of the *potential* of a perceived threat. The whiff! How itchy do you think their trigger fingers are going to be if they think that they've cornered someone suspected of the attempted murder of a fellow police officer? I'm not going to potentially give a guy a death sentence until I have stronger evidence that he's the right guy."

Phillips laughed abruptly. "Are you serious right now?" she asked, incredulous. "Everything we have points to this guy. I agree that it's not exactly a mountain of evidence. I wish we had a smoking gun and the whole thing on HD video with his name in the credits, but what we have should be enough. All we're trying to do is question the man!"

"Right! All we're trying to do is question the man! I'm not going to put his life in jeopardy simply because we want to ask him a few questions. We don't have enough evidence for that!"

Anger flashed in Phillips' eyes. "With all due respect, how have you done your job all these years if you're this worried about whether or not some suspect might be rough-handled during first contact?"

"And how have you done your job all these years without understanding that the scale is tilted in a way that doesn't allow for fair treatment across the board and that we sometimes need to take that into consideration? Or is it that you understand and just don't care?"

"Are you calling me a racist?" asked Phillips. The anger in her eyes was teetering on rage.

Madden was stunned. First of all, in all the years that he had known her, in all the cases they had worked together and all the stressful moments they had shared, she had never once raised her voice at him. There had been times when they had a difference of opinion about a procedure or tactic, but it had always been minor and something they were able to discuss, with one eventually bringing the other around to the alternate way of thinking.

Also, just a few days ago she had been defending the rights of the black man, but now she was doing the polar opposite. He took a second to gather his thoughts, not wanting to make her even more angry, while at the same time trying to suppress his own growing ire.

"No, Phillips," he said finally. "I'm not calling you a racist. I have never in my wildest dreams ever considered you to have a single racist bone in your body. Do you believe you're a racist?" he asked.

"No," she said, somewhat defensively. "It would be pretty much impossible for me to be a racist." Something in the way she said it struck a nerve.

"Impossible? What exactly does that mean?" he asked.

"It would be impossible for me to be a racist because I've actually been in love with a black man for years," she said.

"Really?" he asked, smiling warmly. "That's great. Who's the lucky guy?"

"You are," she said, looking at him like he was a complete moron.

His mouth literally fell open as though it were attached to his head with a hinge.

"What?" was all he could say, to which she answered by silently raising her eyebrows as if to ask, '*Why are you looking so surprised?*'

"Wait," he said, slowly shaking his head in disbelief. "You can't...me? I mean, I just...," he said as he grabbed the nearest chair and took a seat. "Are you...are you serious?"

Phillips' answer was an icy stare off into the distance.

"I'm sorry," he said. "I just...never knew. I mean this...this really complicates things."

"Love tends to sometimes do that," she replied dryly. "Don't worry, I know you could never feel the same way about someone like me."

"Someone like you? What are you talking about? I think...listen, Phillips. You're a very attractive woman, and I care about you a great deal. You're much more than a co-worker. You're like family. Besides, you know that I love my wife and that I'm completely dedic—"

"Completely dedicated to her. I know. I've heard it all before. It doesn't change my feelings. Though, god, I sure wish it would."

Madden didn't know what to say. The silence was awkward and growing more so with each passing moment.

"Listen," he said softly, "I know there's more that we probably need to discuss about this before we can put it to rest, but can we table it at least until we get through this investigation? Maybe when we get back to D.C., we can make a joint appointment with the department shrink to help us resolve it in a way that doesn't affect our working relationship."

"Sure, that's fine," she said curtly as she swung her attention back to the laptop. "So, ix-nay on the APB. Got it. What's the next move?"

Suddenly Madden became urgently aware of his bladder. He wasn't sure if it was just all the coffee catching up to him or if his subconscious was desperately reaching for some kind of diversion to give him a few minutes to catch his breath.

"Uh, do you mind if I use your restroom?" he asked.

"Not at all."

In the bathroom, as Madden urinated into the toilet, he arched his head back and took a breath. It felt like it was the first he had taken since arriving in Phillips' room. Instinctively, he knew that this was probably not going to end well. He was angry, and he was disappointed.

He was angry because, in spite of all the shit he had to take from Bainbridge, until two minutes ago he believed that he at least had a solid team behind him. Now, the foundation of the team had fractured and was threatening to crumble beneath his feet. He couldn't understand how a woman who had always been the epitome of control could have lost it so completely. He had often described Phillips as his 'right hand man', and now he felt like he had lost not just his right hand but also the arm it was attached to.

But he was also disappointed. He couldn't believe that Phillips, someone he cared so much about and felt so close to, would put him in such an awkward position. It was also disrespectful of his marriage and, more specifically, of his wife.

What could she have possibly hoped to gain by dropping this bombshell? If what she said was true, and she knew that her feelings were going to be unrequited, what was the point of her telling him? Was it just something that she blurted out without thinking? Again, that was so unlike her. She had always been so predictable; so reliable. He certainly didn't need any disruptions when they were finally making some headway on this case. But he'd have to deal with it anyway.

He flushed the toilet, washed his hands and took another deep breath.

"So, you were asking about the next move," he said as he exited the bathroom, trying to sound as casual as possible.

"Yes?" she said.

"I think the best option right now is to put Janssen under surveillance just in case they try to finish the job. But when I broached the topic with him yesterday, right before we left the scene, he was against it. Said he didn't want people following him around. I may have to push the issue."

"I think common sense would dictate that them coming after him again would be a long shot. I don't think they'd be that stupid," said Phillips. She was back to business as though the last ten minutes had never happened.

"I don't know if stupid is the right word. These guys have strong principles. It's completely conceivable to me that they may be willing to put it all on the line to complete what they originally set out to do."

"Anything's possible," said Phillips.

"I'll give Janssen a call tomorrow; see if maybe I can't convince him to listen to reason."

* * *

Madden and Phillips arrived back at the hotel late. They had spent the day interviewing various witnesses who had observed the chaos surrounding the attempt on Janssen's life. Their interaction had been professional. Phillips had been cold and distant, and though Madden felt that he should say something, he wasn't sure what, so he left it alone.

"Want to grab a bite to eat?" he asked as they entered the lobby from the parking garage.

"No, I'm beat," said Phillips, rubbing the back of her neck. "I think I'll just have something sent up to the room."

"Okay," said Madden. "I'll see you in the morning. I'd like to go over some of the interview results before we get started with the next names on the list."

"Sure," said Phillips quietly. "I'll see you bright and early."

Madden stood and watched as she walked down the hall to the elevator and waited till the door closed behind her. She never looked back. He glanced in the direction of the restaurant and considered dining there alone, but decided he'd eat in his room as well.

Madden was in his room, putting butter on a baked potato and wishing he had some seasoned salt for his steak when there was a knock at the door. He looked out the peephole and saw it was Phillips. Maybe she had decided she wanted to talk after all.

"Have you seen the news?" she asked when he opened the door. There was urgency in her voice, and when he stepped to the side, she entered the room before he could answer and went straight to his laptop sitting on the desk.

"I haven't had time to look," he said, joining her at the computer.

"I'm surprised no one from D.C. noticed it and thought to reach out to us," she said. She brought up a website, and when he saw the headline, he felt a chill run down his back. It read: *17 Shot, 10 Dead At #BlackForLife Rally.*

Madden skimmed the article quickly, but then immediately looked to Phillips for the details, ignoring the attached video for the time being.

"Who was the shooter?" he asked.

"Officially, we don't know. I put in a call to HQ, and someone is digging into it as we speak. But according to the news reports, it was just some crazy asshole. He was African American and was apparently shooting at the cops, not the protesters. He even yelled out that Janssen was next, which a reporter was lucky enough to get on tape and which all the media channels have been looping for the last twenty minutes. He died not far from the scene after cops cornered him."

"Any apparent affiliation with PROPR?" asked Madden.

"It's still too early to tell. Looks promising, though."

"Alright. Well, there's not really much we can do at the moment. Let's get some sleep and see where the local investigation stands in the morning. Hopefully, that will at least give us enough info to determine if it's worth a trip to Maryland."

"Thanks," said Phillips. "I think I could use a few winks. See you soon."

A couple hours later Madden was still reading through reports when his phone buzzed. It was a text message from one of the techs who was in charge of monitoring the PROPR website. Something new had been posted. When he pulled up the website on his laptop and saw what was there, he immediately called Phillips.

"There's been a development," he said.

"I'm on my way."

Chapter 62

Madden and Phillips watched the latest PROPR video twice through before either of them spoke.

"Do you think it's true?" asked Madden. "Do you believe this shooter wasn't part of the crew?"

"It appears so," said Phillips. "I ran his name when I went back to my room. He had never served in the military, and I haven't seen anything that would tie him to any of the current suspects. The guy was a barista at a Starbucks and worked weekends at a hardware store, for Christ's sake."

"Shit!" he said.

"I thought you'd be happy to know that they weren't involved," she said.

"I am," said Madden, "but this is probably just the beginning. The whole world now knows about the assassination attempt. They also know that the shooting of that motorist was the impetus for it. Now there's just no telling how many crazies, in addition to PROPR, might take it upon themselves to go after Janssen. Damn. We need to move this guy into a safehouse. Right now. Tonight."

"That's easier said than done," said Phillips. "It'll take at least a few hours to get it approved and set up. It would probably be early morning at the earliest before we'd be ready to actually move him."

"You're right," said Madden. "But maybe I can call in a couple of favors. I'll get on the horn to Washington and start the clearing process. Please get a couple of local agents to park in front of his house and sit on him until we can get there. Tell them to keep a sharp eye out for anyone in the area that looks even the least bit suspicious."

"Will do. But don't forget to eat," she said with a smile, glancing at his half-finished meal as she rose to leave. "You're the boss. It's okay to talk with your mouth full."

He smiled in response, shoving a forkful of potato in his face as he grabbed his phone and started scrolling through his contacts.

Madden made several phone calls. Half of the people he called were sleeping and none too happy for the disturbance, but the plan for setting Janssen up in protective custody ASAP began to come together. He did all this without first contacting Janssen himself. The man was not just an ass, he was a macho ass. There was a good chance he would reject the offer, making all of this a waste of time.

Madden was about to call room service to see if someone could possibly nuke his cold steak and potato when his cell rang. It was Kelly.

"Hey, honey," he said.

"Hi. Am I interrupting?"

"No, not at all," he said, sighing. "What are you doing up at this hour?"

"Something woke me," she said. "I had the feeling that something was wrong. What is it?"

"Nothing. It's just a tough case that's really got us on the run."

"Is that it?"

Madden knew that his wife would pick up on the underlying issue whenever he next spoke to her. No one knew him like she did. All day he had been thinking about whether or not he was going to tell her about his argument with Phillips—and about her big reveal. He was a bit nervous about how she might react. In all their years together, she had never shown any signs of serious jealousy. And God knows she'd had many opportunities.

Phillips had been right when she made the statement that women often seemed to throw themselves at him. But while Phillips might have thought it was because he was so irresistibly handsome, he knew that was not the case. Yes, he would admit that there were certain women who genuinely found him physically attractive, but he knew that there was also another factor at play in many of these scenarios.

He never understood it but, for some reason, there was something especially enticing for some white women when they saw a black man out with another white woman. It reminded him of the 'wedding ring attraction' phenomenon. When he was in college he had a good friend, a handsome white guy named Jeff. Jeff was a true ladies' man and was notorious for the number of women he was able to pick up. When they first met and started hanging out at bars together on the weekends, Jeff had shown Madden one of his tricks of the trade: he would slip on a gold wedding band before he got out of the car.

He explained to Madden that there was a faction of women who found the challenge of a married man very attractive. Madden had called bullshit at the time, but one night they went bar hopping and Jeff had proven it to him by taking the ring off and putting it back on throughout the night. The difference was undeniable. The women who migrated to Jeff when he was wearing the wedding band weren't necessarily the kind of women you'd want to take home to Mother, but neither were they in short supply.

Madden had experienced something similar when out with Phillips or Kelly, but instead of a wedding ring, it was the white woman that was the allure. Something about white women seeing him with another white woman drew them like flies to honey. He would have been flattered if he didn't know the source of all the admiration. As it was, it was simply annoying.

"There's something going on between Phillips and me," he said finally. "We had a bit of a blowout a little earlier."

"I'm sorry," she said. "That doesn't sound like her at all. Is it the pressure of the case?"

"I think that's part of it. The racial element is causing an issue. She's actually accused me of perhaps not being able to be impartial in this investigation."

"Because you're black?" asked Kelly. "That's ridiculous. This isn't the first case that you've had in which the suspects were black."

"No, but this is different, Kelly. This group is all over the media, the public outcry is going all the way up to the President, and Bainbridge has been pushing me to resolve this anyway I can, even if it means going against protocol."

"What do you mean, 'going against protocol'?"

"I don't really want to get into it on the phone," said Madden, "but he's drifting into a dark place right now. He's a politician, masquerading as an FBI Associate Director, and he sees this case as either a stepping stone or possibly a career-ender."

"This sounds dangerous," said Kelly.

"It could be."

"And Phillips is onboard with this? I always pegged her as 'strictly by the book'."

"That would be a pretty good description," said Madden. "I haven't clued her in yet to what Bainbridge is proposing."

"So then why does she think that you being black could have an effect on how you handle the case?" asked Kelly.

"Well, we have a suspect. A strong suspect. He might even be our guy. She's ready to put out a full APB on the guy, but I refused, because I think there's too great a risk that he'd never make it into custody alive."

"Sounds like maybe that's something Bainbridge could live with," said Kelly, starting to get the real gist of the matter.

"Perhaps," said Madden, not wanting to say too much.

"I'm surprised Phillips isn't more sympathetic. Hon, this is going to probably sound like a strange question considering how many years you two have worked together, but do you think it's possible that she has a problem with black men?"

"Problem as in racist?" asked Madden. "No, I'm pretty sure that's not the case."

"I only mentioned it because I've known several Caucasians in my life, one in my own family, that can work with, socialize with and even be great friends with blacks, but behind the scenes, when they think no one is around that matters, they're no better than rednecks."

"Well, actually, in the course of our discussion, she asked me if I was calling her a racist and took it upon herself to submit proof that she wasn't."

"And what was the proof?" asked Kelly.

"That she couldn't be racist because she was in love with a black man."

"Phillips is in love with a black man? I didn't even know that she was...wait a minute—you?"

"Yeah," muttered Madden sheepishly.

"Wow. I didn't see that coming. I'm sorry, hon. I know this is probably the last thing you need to be dealing with on a case like this."

Madden smiled. He loved how his wife always had his back; how strong her faith in him was. He couldn't ever remember a time when she showed any doubt in him, no matter how difficult or challenging the situation. It was inspiring, but sometimes it was humbling, too.

"Thanks," he said. "Don't worry. I'm sure it'll all work out in the end."

"Okay. I'd better let you go. I'm sure you still have some work to do," said Kelly. "I miss you."

"I miss you, too. I'll talk to you soon."

Madden was just dozing off in front of his laptop when his phone buzzed. It was D.C. The approval for the safehouse had come through. He checked the clock. It was 3:00am. He could have waited till sun-up, but he felt that the sooner they put Janssen under wraps, the better. Besides, truth be told, he was kind of looking forward to dragging the asshole out of bed.

Phillips was dressed and ready to go within fifteen minutes of his call. Sometimes he wondered if the woman ever really slept at all.

"Are the chaperons in place?" he asked.

"Yes. Two agents arrived there a little before midnight. Of course, there was no way to confirm whether or not Janssen was actually home without alerting him to the fact that he's being watched. But I just confirmed with them that no one has gone in or out of the premises since they arrived, and they've observed no suspicious activity."

"Beautiful," said Madden. "Everything has been set up on my end. We have a safehouse reserved in Culver City. It's near the beach, not far from here. Janssen'll love it."

"I'm sure," said Phillips.

Madden took a gulp of coffee from a mug that had been sitting since dinner. It tasted like cold dishwater, prompting him to make a mental note to stop at a drive-thru on the way for a fresh cup.

"You ready?" he asked Phillips. She responded with a curt nod. "Alright. Let's go wake sleeping beauty."

When they arrived at Janssen's place, Madden immediately spotted the surveillance detail. They were parked a ways down the street, under the shadow of a large tree. Phillips called them on their cell, and they confirmed that the status hadn't changed. Madden pulled up into the driveway, parking in front of a small garage, and he and Phillips got out.

Janssen opened the door both bare-chested and barefoot, wearing nothing but a pair of sweatpants. His hair was sticking up at an odd angle on his head, and he had what looked like two days of scraggly, black and gray beard growth. He frowned at Madden, but his face softened into a slight smile when he saw Phillips standing behind him.

"What time is it?" he asked.

"It's just after 3:30. Do you mind if we come in?" asked Madden.

Janssen stuck his head further out the door and looked around. Madden wasn't sure if he was looking for other agents or to see if any of his neighbors were watching.

"Sure," he said gruffly, his sour breath almost forcing Madden to take a step back. "Make yourself at home."

He led them into the living room, where he plopped down into a recliner as Phillips and Madden took a seat on the adjacent sofa. Madden was surprised at how neat and clean the room was. Either Janssen was a deceptively tidy person or the place had seen the benefit of a woman's touch.

"What can I do for you fine people?" he asked, scratching at his beard with one slim-fingered hand.

"We're here in response to a video that was posted online—" began Madden.

"Yeah, I saw it," said Janssen. "My niece in Texas called me a little before midnight to tell me about it. She was all worked up into a frenzy. But the guy's dead as dog shit now, so all's clear, right?"

"I think we're referring to two difference incidents," said Madden.

"What do you mean?"

"First, there was the shooter that attacked the rally in Baltimore, which is what your niece was probably referring to. I imagine she saw the news footage, as it was on every channel," said Madden. "Yes, that suspect did publicly threaten you, and yes, he is now deceased. However, we don't believe he is the shooter that made the attempt on your life or that he is in any way associated with the group that did."

"So then who was he?" asked Janssen.

"He appears to just be some pissed off citizen that got pushed over the edge by who-the-hell-knows-what. The original shooter is still out there. And as proof, there was also another video released earlier tonight—the second incident. This one was from PROPR directly, posted on their website and shot after the Baltimore attack. Not only did they disavow any knowledge or association with the Baltimore shooter, but they claimed responsibility for the earlier attack on you. And pledged to finish the job."

Janssen sunk back in his chair, his face dark with concern. He ran his hand through his hair. "So, you came all this way at three o'clock in the morning just to tell me that?"

"No," said Madden. "We're actually here because we want to move you into a safehouse. We think it's the only way to guarantee your safety until we catch these people."

"A safehouse?" said Janssen, scratching his beard again. "For how long?"

Madden shrugged. "It's impossible to say. Hopefully, not long."

"I don't know. I'm pretty comfortable here," said Janssen, running his hand through his hair again, clearly trying to appear unconcerned. "And I'm extremely well-armed. I have a closet full of guns and a truckload full of ammo."

"Do you also have the ability to sleep with one eye open?" asked Madden. "Because these guys are professionals. Don't underestimate them just because they missed the first time. They're nothing like this disgruntled java jockey in Baltimore, opening fire on a crowd of marchers with a rusty .22."

"How do you know this wasn't the guy? The news reporters seem to think he is. I even heard he had a tattoo: 'Live PROPR or Die'. I saw a picture of it."

Madden and Phillips exchanged glances. "That's the first we've heard of that," said Madden. "We'll look into it, but anyone can get a tattoo of anything. It's early in that investigation, but my gut tells me that our current take on this is correct. Besides, ultimately, it doesn't matter whether he's an official part of the group or just a wannabe, because other members are still out there. That means your life is still in danger. We just want to try to keep you alive until we can alleviate the threat."

Janssen ran his hand over his stomach as he mulled over the request.

"Alright, I guess I can stand to get out of here for a little while. Where is this safehouse?"

"We'd rather not say," said Madden, "but it's not too far away."

"Okay. When do we leave?"

"Right now, if you're ready," said Madden. "We have two agents parked down the street that can escort you."

"And how do I know that someone from PROPR isn't also out there, ready to follow me to the safehouse?"

"Don't worry," said Phillips. "Our guys are very good at detecting tails. No one is going to follow them that they aren't aware of."

"Alright," said Janssen, exhaling deeply as he extricated himself from the easy chair. "Let me throw a few things in a bag."

Madden and Phillips patiently waited as Janssen busied himself packing for the move.

"So, I heard a K-9 ate his ass, is that right?" he asked from somewhere in the next room.

Madden waited until he walked back into the room to answer. "Yes, the reports are that they sent in the dog and that the suspect later died from injuries sustained in the struggle."

"Good for him," said Janssen. "Maybe the dog's developed a taste now."

"A taste?" said Phillips tersely. "A taste for what exactly?"

Janssen paused to look at her, a slight smile on his face. He had found a t-shirt to put on and had exchanged his sweatpants for a pair of chinos.

"For bad guys," he finally said. "We spend way too many tax dollars in this country hauling these social deviants into court and then paying to warehouse them for years on end. That 'dog justice' was much more economical, not to mention efficient."

"That guy was a murderer and he certainly deserved to pay a price for what he did, and maybe that price would have ultimately been death," said Madden. "But that decision should not have been made in the street. Those cops should have figured out a better way to take him down."

Janssen tilted his head and shrugged. "We'll have to agree to disagree. But in my opinion, he was a lowlife and a waste of oxygen."

"Well, there's one thing about the guy that I do admire," said Madden.

"What's that?"

"The reports are that in addition to the long rifle, he was also found with several fully loaded handguns and a hunting knife. It's believed that he could have taken the dog out, but chose not to. Apparently, he had more respect for the animal than he had for the police officers. Sometimes I think I know exactly how he felt."

Chapter 63

The first thing Ish did when he awoke the next day was to call the hospital to check on Khadija's condition. He was relieved to discover that her injuries were non-life-threatening and that she was expected to be released within the next 24 hours. He had barely hung up the phone when a call came in from Chad inviting him to an early meeting over breakfast. They decided it was safer to have the meal served in Chad's hotel room rather than going to a restaurant.

"You look tired," said Ish after they had exchanged greetings, the usual small talk, and placed their meal orders with room service.

"Yeah, I've been up all night. I still haven't been to bed."

"Then I imagine you must have some news."

"I definitely do," said Chad. "First things first. I went to see LeAnn Wayne this morning. I was the first person in the visitor's room."

Ish held his breath. "So, she accepted your visit?"

"She did," said Chad. "She bitched a little about how early it was. Apparently, she's gotten used to sleeping in. But she changed her tune when she knew I was the one bringing her wet 40."

"Wet what?" asked Ish.

"Wet 40, dude," said Chad, laughing. "It's what they used to call it in the old days when you brought a prisoner money, because the limit was $40 and the jailers ran it through water to remove any residue of drugs. Of course, it's all digital now, directly deposited to their accounts. No more water."

"Got it," said Ish. Sometimes he forgot just how 'up' Chad was on the customs and rituals of urban culture.

"Anyway," Chad continued, "Layla had already spoken to her, so she knew someone would be coming to see her. Though, to be honest, it seemed like she had almost forgotten already. She came across as a tweaker to me. I think maybe she burned a couple brain cells too many when she was on the outside. She might even be using now, considering how easy it is to get drugs in and out of jail these days."

Ish frowned. "That sounds like trouble. Did she agree to the deal?"

"She did. It was like some kind of Abbott and Costello comedy routine watching her trying to communicate with me without tipping off the guards. I hope they're all as stupid as they look, because she was way too obvious for my tastes."

"My concern," said Ish, "is that if she's that far gone, she might betray us at some point without even being aware of it."

"Yeah, that did occur to me," said Chad, "but it's all we have."

"Right. So, what was the amount she agreed to?"

"Fifteen thousand," said Chad, smiling proudly. "Five thousand now, delivered to a girlfriend of hers on the outside, five deposited into an online account in her name once she's talked to the D.A., and the final five once the charges have officially been dropped. I started at ten thousand and let her 'force' me up to fifteen."

"Good job, man. I hope it works. Because otherwise..." said Ish, letting the thought trail off.

"Don't worry, dude. Fifteen thousand dollars buys a lot of fucking meth. She's motivated."

Ish nodded. "Did she give you any idea of how long she thought it would be before she's able to meet with any officials?"

"No, but I took the liberty of sending a lawyer to speak with her later on today to get the ball rolling. The lawyer's a 'personal' friend of mine, so she'll keep my identity protected. She's also a beast in the courtroom. She'll get this thing handled for us, quickly and quietly."

"Good man," said Ish. "Thank you."

"No problem."

There was a gentle knock at the door.

"Thank god," said Chad. "I'm starving."

Ish and Chad waited in silence as the guy from Guest Services set the table for their meal. Ish gave him a generous tip, and Chad waited until he left and the door was locked securely behind him before he continued.

"Check it out," he said as he sat down and began sprinkling salt and pepper on his eggs. "The exciting news isn't the druggie jail chick. It's the femtocell. It paid off! I linked it to a laptop and set it to record via voice activation. It's picked up several conversations since, which I'll play for you later, but the important one took place last night in Madden's room. They freaked when they saw the video we posted and decided that Janssen needed to be moved immediately."

"Safehouse?" asked Ish.

"You guessed it."

"Did you get an address?"

"Not from them," said Chad. "It appears they didn't get the address until they were actually on the way to Janssen's place to pick him up, at about 3:00am."

"Shit," said Ish.

"But—" said Chad excitedly, "one of the toys I bought at the beginning of this project was a high-tech drone, but until now I hadn't had an opportunity to use it. Ish, this thing is freakin' amazing! Built-in GPS, camera, mic and it even automatically tracks moving objects. It's the reason I was up all night. I was worried that maybe another team would pick Janssen up, and that these two agents might never get the address. So, last night I quickly pulled this unit out of storage, practiced with it for a couple hours to get comfortable with the controls, then set it up in surveillance mode, circling Janssen's house."

Ish smiled. "That's genius."

"I know, right?" said Chad, his face animated. "And I didn't have to go anywhere near Janssen's neighborhood to get this in place. I didn't even leave the hotel. I sat out on the balcony with a pot of coffee, dialed in the GPS location and sent it on its way. Once it arrived, I was able to visually monitor the house from all sides, streaming video to the laptop. It was up so high that no one could see it or hear it. There's also a phone app, so even if I'm not close to the laptop I can still control and monitor everything from wherever I am."

"That's very cool," said Ish, shaking his head in wonder. "Were Madden and Phillips the ones that picked him up?"

"No, but they were there. I checked their head-shots thru DMV yesterday so that I'd know what they look like, and the camera on this thing could read a book at 1000 feet. They were the ones that entered Janssen's house, but another car, with two unidentified males, actually transported him. Madden and Phillips shadowed them the entire way, no doubt looking for tails."

"That's great work, Chad," said Ish. "This actually works out well for us. Him being stashed in a safehouse means we don't have to worry about stumbling into someone else trying to make a move on him when we make ours."

"That's the good part. The bad part, of course, is that he's now directly protected by the fucking FBI."

"Getting by them shouldn't be a problem," said Ish. "The real issue is getting to Janssen without harming them in the process."

"Do you have any ideas?"

"I do, but it's going to require a bit of luck and a lot of timing. However, we do have the element of surprise on our side. They probably think that no one knows where they're stashing him."

"Right," said Chad. "How soon did you want to do this?"

"As soon as possible," said Ish. "Let me contact the rest of the team and let them know what's going on. Then, it will be time to serve some justice."

Chapter 64

The plan had been that they would all meet in Ish's hotel room for lunch the next day at 12:30pm. Ish looked at his watch. It read 12:49. He was irritated. Chad was on the computer, catching up on some office work, and Bird was sipping a cup of coffee and tapping his foot, but Jag and Ma'am were nowhere to be found. He had gotten a text from Ma'am twenty-five minutes ago stating that they were running five minutes late. Obviously, that wasn't quite true. He was about to call them again when there was a knock at the door.

After looking through the peephole, he opened the door, and Ma'am and Jag waltzed in, smiling and looking much too relaxed. Ish could imagine what probably held them up.

"Hey, boss, sorry we're late," said Jag. "We, uh, got sidetracked."

Well, thought Ish, at least they didn't try to blame it on traffic. He took a deep breath.

"Don't worry about it," he said. "It's not like any of us have anyplace we need to be." Which was true. The rest of their day after this meeting would be more or less free. He was letting the stress get to him, and it was causing him to overreact a bit.

They had already ordered lunch: an assortment of cold cuts, bread and salad, with lemonade and coffee. It would be delivered at 1:30, so they still had some time to chat before everyone started stuffing their faces.

"Thank you all for coming," said Ish once everyone had found a seat and gotten themselves settled.

"Our video spooked the FBI, and they moved Janssen to a safe house. However, boy genius here," he said, smiling at Chad, "was able to track them when they transported him, so we now know the location. I have a plan on how to get to him, but it's simple enough to be a one-man operation. I think me going in by myself might be the safest way."

"Safest for who?" asked Ma'am. "We've been in all of this together from the start. How does it make sense to start changing that now?"

"Things are changing whether we like it or not," said Ish. "Take you, for example. You're in a completely different head-space than you were when we began this thing. Same with Jag," he added, consciously forcing himself not to glance in Bird's direction. "I think we've all been changed a little, if for no other reason than the simple fact that we have been part of altering the perception of what so many people believe is possible. What's been going on in the streets the last couple of weeks is testimony to that."

Bird was nodding his head. "You're right," he said. "No thanks to me."

"Don't beat yourself up over minor bullshit," said Ish. "You're as important to this team as any of us."

"Thanks for saying that, Ish," he said. "I appreciate it, especially after the way my sister and I jumped all over you the other day. I want to make it up to you. Let me do this run with you."

"That's not really necess—" began Ish.

"Me too," said Ma'am, cutting him off. "You never can tell what might go wrong. You've been on enough FUBAR missions to know that. Three heads is always better than one."

Ish looked at Jag, who looked concerned but didn't say anything.

"Um, alright. I can see you're not going to be easily deterred—" began Ish when he was interrupted by a knock at the door. Room service was a bit early. "Let's eat first, and then we can get into the plans."

* * *

The next morning, Ish walked into Chad's hotel room. The TV was on and the sound turned up to a comfortable level.

“Dude, you’re just in time. Check this out! I’ve been following it for a couple hours now.”

Ish took a seat in one of the overstuffed chairs and turned his attention to the broadcast. There was a woman being interviewed, and unless he was mistaken, it was Marquita from #BlackForLife.

“...so how would you say that this is different than the Million Man March?” asked the reporter holding the microphone in front of her face.

Marquita chuckled. “Well, in case you haven’t noticed, for one thing, I’m a woman, as are the majority of people walking with me today,” she said, motioning to the huge mass of people milling around in the background behind them. Some were mugging for the camera, some flashing the two-finger ‘peace’ sign, some thrusting out the clenched ‘black power’ fist.

“Another difference,” she continued, “is that we’re walking the entire way, not traveling in buses or some other motorized transport. And finally, our goal by the time we reach D.C. is to have quite a bit more than a million people with us.”

“In case any of you are just joining us,” said the reporter, turning to look into the camera, “I’m speaking to Ms. Marquita Valdez of #BlackForLife, the civil rights organization that grew out of recent protests against what they consider to be the mistreatment of people of color by police officers in this country. Ms. Valdez has most recently organized a cross-country walk, yes, I said walk, called the ‘Black March For Peace’, where she’s inviting people of all nationalities, races, sexes and colors to join her as she marches from here in Los Angeles all the way to Washington, D.C.”

“Ms. Valdez,” he said, turning to once again face Marquita, “what about the logistics of moving that many people? The challenge of feeding them, finding them places to sleep, even dealing with rest room breaks, must be enormous.”

“True, it won’t be easy, but nothing worthwhile ever is. While we do expect to march into D.C. well over a million people strong, most of the way we’ll probably be a group of no more than a few thousand at a time. Of course, the number will constantly ebb and flow. Some people will join us for a while to show their support as we pass through their area, and then return to their lives as we move on. We’ll constantly be picking up people and losing people along the way. Besides that, we have thousands that have donated funds, time and the use of facilities along the way which we're using to support the marchers."

"What kind of support exactly?"

"We have a team of people that are pacing us in vans and RVs, riding ahead when necessary to make arrangements for food and places for us to pitch our tents or get an occasional room for the night. They will also supply us with medical support for anyone that might suffer an injury or fall ill along the way."

"Well," said the reporter, "it seems like you have everything under control. I wish you the best of luck, and I'm sure the nation will be following this story closely."

Chad muted the sound. "How crazy is that? That's us, dude. We helped start that!"

"I don't know if I'd exactly say that. They were here first, and #BlackForLife and PROPR are not what one might call 'simpatico'. But I understand what you mean. We did help shine a brighter light on the issue. But I think what they're doing is even more important than what we're doing. In fact, why don't we make a donation?"

"I was thinking the same exact thing," said Chad. "A million sound good?"

"Let's do it."

An hour later, Ish and Chad were still in Chad's room, talking about the finer points of the modern civil rights movement when Ish's phone rang.

"Mr. Carter? This is Manuel Aquila, Layla's attorney."

"How are you, Mr. Aquila?"

"I'm fine, sir. And yourself?"

"Good. What's going on?" asked Ish, anxious to get to the business at hand.

"Are you sitting down, sir?" asked Aquila.

"As a matter of fact, I am."

"Well, I don't know how it happened, but the woman that made the assault charges against your wife has suddenly withdrawn the complaint! It's miraculous. The D.A. still wanted to pursue the case, filing its own charge against Layla, similar to the way they often handle domestic abuse cases when the wife has a sudden change of heart. But the complainant not only said that Layla wasn't the one that attacked her, she actually identified another inmate as the real attacker."

"Wow," said Ish, unable to hide the joy in his voice. "That's fantastic news! So, what does all this mean in regards to Layla's case?"

"I don't want to get your hopes up too soon, but that charge really was the fly in the ointment. We felt that we had made a lot of progress in building a case for getting the original charges thrown out—or at least reduced to time served—until this woman filed her charge. That not only ground everything to a halt, but actually began pushing us backwards."

"So, we're back on the fast track?"

"Yes, sir, I believe so."

"And exactly how fast is this track?" asked Ish.

"When you're dealing with judges and all their inherent personality quirks and idiosyncrasies, it's impossible to predict with any certainty. But assuming there are no other hiccups," he said cautiously, "it's possible this matter could be successfully concluded in a matter of a few weeks."

"That is definitely the best news I've heard all day," said Ish.

"However," continued Aquila, "I regretfully have to remind you that getting the court to release her is only half of our battle. I spoke to Layla about an hour ago, and she told me she's still not quite ready to leave jail, regardless of the outcome of this case. Of course, once the orders come through, the jail will force her to leave, but all she has to do is attack a guard or another inmate at any point in the process, and she would be re-arrested, new charges would be filed and we would be back at square one before she even made it outside the jail walls."

Ish sighed. "I know. I'm working on that part of it. But in the meantime, I want to thank you again for hanging in there for the long haul and keeping things moving along."

"It's my pleasure," said Aquila. "As my beloved grandfather was so fond of saying, '*Las cosas buenas vienen a aquellos que esperan.*'"

"Good things come to those that wait," translated Ish.

"Exactly," said Aquila.

After they hung up, Ish sat there for a moment, smiling to himself as he slowly put the phone back in his pocket. As the seconds ticked by, his reverie was broken by the gradual awareness that Chad was staring at him expectantly. Finally, Ish glanced in his direction.

"It worked, dude," he said. "The woman recanted, and those charges against Layla have been dropped."

"Are you serious?"

"I guess it's like they once said about O.J. Simpson: you're entitled to all the justice you can afford."

"Whatever fucking works!" said Chad, rushing over and giving him a 'high five'. "Whatever fucking works! So, does that mean that she'll be getting out soon?"

"Maybe, maybe not, but at least the wheels of justice have been greased and are turning once again. Speaking of grease, do you mind taking care of the rest of the payments we promised this lady?" asked Ish.

"Gladly," said Chad. "I'll take care of it today while I'm out."

Ish's phone immediately rang again. Somehow, even before he got it out of his pocket and saw that the number was blocked, he knew who it was.

"Hey, love," she said after the robotic voice identified the caller as an inmate at a California correctional facility. He could hear her smiling.

"Hey, babe," he replied. "I just got off the phone with Aquila."

"I figured. He told me he would be calling you," she said. "I only have a few minutes, but I just wanted to hear your voice."

"As always, I'm glad you called," said Ish. "You sound good. How's everything going?"

"Everything is good. No fights, no headaches. Everything is good except..." She paused.

"Except?" he asked.

"Except I haven't seen Sumatra in the last couple of days."

Ish nodded, even though he knew she couldn't see him over the phone. "And how does that make you feel?"

"Anxious. And like I think I lost something, something vital. I don't mind being in here, but being in here without her is another matter. I imagine it's probably how women feel when they look down at their hand and suddenly realize that their wedding ring isn't there and they're not sure they know where they last saw it."

"I understand," said Ish gently. "But wherever she's run off to, I'm sure she's safe."

"I have no doubt of that," she said quietly, her voice distant, as though she were fading into the background.

"Hey," she said, suddenly back in the present. "I saw on the news today that there was a big dog fight and a bunch of pit bulls got hurt. Were you there?"

"No," said Ish. "That had nothing to do with me. And to be honest, it really bothered me the way it went down."

"Why is that?"

"Babe, you know I don't like to see innocent animals being hurt."

"Innocent?" said Layla. "Ish, there wasn't anything innocent about those dogs. At least, not the pit bulls. We've already talked about how dangerous pit bulls can be. Any one of them could have gone rabid and attacked some innocent citizen at a moment's notice."

"I've known a lot of pit bulls, Layla, and some of them are the kindest creatures you'd ever want to meet. Yeah, there are definitely some bad ones out there, like the ones we were trying to round up, but that shouldn't be a blanket condemnation of them all."

"I thought you were supposed to be making the streets safe for me?" she asked, the volume of her voice starting to rise. "That's why I'm keeping my behind right here inside these walls! And you say you want me out," she scoffed.

"Babe," he said again, sighing heavily, "of course I want you out. But not at the expense of taking innocent lives."

"See," she said, her voice full of venom, "that's exactly why I'm in here, and that's exactly why we no longer have a daughter! You were more interested in protecting the lives of some people you never met before instead of being there for your own goddamn fam—" she began, then caught herself.

"I'm sorry, Ish! I'm sorry! I didn't mean it!" she said through a flood of sobs.

Ish felt like a knife had been plunged into his chest. It took him a moment to get his breath back and find the words to respond.

"It's okay, babe," he said softly. "I understand."

"No, it's not okay," she said, fighting to get her emotions back under control. "You're absolutely right. I never would have fallen in love with you if you were the kind of person that could turn your back on those in need. I didn't mean any of that shit I just said."

"I know," he said.

"Listen," she said, her voice nasally and full of congestion. "If you still want me, and you can get me out, I'll come. I'll come and I'll spend the rest of my life with you."

"Thank you," he said heavily, exhaling for what felt like the first time in weeks. "That's all I wanted to hear you say. Don't worry, I'll fix this. We'll get you out of there soon."

"Okay," she said, then paused. An uncomfortable silence began to fill the space between them.

"So," she said, then paused again. "Oh! By the way, how are things going with that one particular pit bull you were after?"

"It's coming together," he said.

"I would have thought you'd have wrapped it up by now."

"So would I," said Ish. "But you know, once these dogs learn how to navigate the streets and that certain people will protect them, they become really good at staying out of sight when they don't want to be seen. But one of the neighbors spotted him, hiding under some old house. So, we know where he is; we just have to find some time to go get him. We'll catch up to him soon."

"I hope you do," said Layla. "But be careful. The last thing you need right now is to get bit running after some feral animal."

Ain't that the truth, thought Ish. Ain't that the truth.

Chapter 65

After finishing his call with Layla, Ish spent another hour with Chad hashing out some preliminary plans for the next assault, then left to return to his own hotel. On the way to his car he dialed Jag's number.

"What's up, Ice-Man?" asked Jag when he picked up the line. Ish immediately noticed an odd tension in his voice.

"I'm just checking in. Everything alright? You sound a little off."

"I'm okay. It's my goddamn mother. She and I just had a falling out."

"Over what?"

"Over Ma'am. Mama's been leaving me messages for the last couple of days. I've been kind of ignoring her because I knew I wasn't going to be able to keep my mouth closed about me and Ma'am's relationship. But today I was in such a good mood that I decided to risk it. Bad move," said Jag.

"I take it she didn't take too well to the idea?"

"That's the understatement of the fuckin' year. I told her I wanted to bring Ma'am home in a couple of months to meet the family. Once she found out the particulars, she went totally ballistic. Called me a 'nigger lover' and said in no uncertain terms that she never wanted to see me again."

As long as Ish had known Jag, he had never seen him this upset. He'd seen him involved in fist fights, in firefights, in screaming matches with some idiot fellow soldier, but Jag had always taken it all in stride. This was clearly a blow to the man's heart.

"I'm really sorry to hear that, man," said Ish. "But you know how some people are about race. Sometimes it passes with time, though. People cool off and later become a bit more open-minded. Give her a little space."

"You're right," said Jag. "But it's hard. I'm just super pissed right now. And Ma'am was here and heard the whole thing."

"What did you say to Ma'am about it?"

"I basically told her the same thing that I told my mother—that Mama's reaction don't change the way I feel about Ma'am and don't change the fact that I aim to marry her."

"That's good. How did Ma'am react?"

"She actually got a little teary. I think it touched her, maybe in a way that I haven't been able to connect with her before. I don't know. Maybe she never believed that I was completely ready for this until now."

"I guess you have to look at the glass as half full. There's distance between you and your mother now, but maybe it will work to ultimately bring you and Ma'am closer together. That's huge."

"Yeah," said Jag, "I guess you're right. Anyway, I know you didn't call to hear my blubberin'. What's goin' on?"

"I'm just leaving Chad's. We kicked around some ideas for this next move, and we wanted to run it by you guys. Are you free tomorrow?"

"I'm free every day," said Jag, chuckling. "Just give me a time and place."

"Cool," said Ish. "I'll see what works for Ma'am and Bird and get back to you."

* * *

Ish and the team were all in Chad's room, gathered around his laptop. What they were watching was live action footage of a street scene. A lady was bending down, cleaning up the poop of some large, mixed-breed dog.

"What exactly are we lookin' at?" asked Jag.

"This is the safehouse," said Chad. "Janssen is inside."

"Where do you have the camera hidden?" asked Ma'am.

"It's in a drone that we have stationed in a tree across the street. It's a tiny thing, and I painted it a camouflage green. You wouldn't know there was a drone there even if you knew exactly where it was. I have another drone set up to watch the back door."

"How long have they been perched there?" asked Jag.

"Since dawn this morning."

"And how do you know he's still in there?" asked Bird. "How do you know they haven't already moved him to someplace else?"

"I also planted a femtocell nearby. It picks up all adjacent cell phone reception. Trust me, he's still inside."

"That's some sweet gear you've got, son," said Jag.

"Thanks. It gets the job done."

"So how are we going to do this?" asked Bird.

"My plan," said Ish, "is to wait for an opportunity to drug their food with a sedative, then just go in while they're sleep and make Janssen's nap permanent."

"That's pretty smooth," said Bird. "I can see why you thought it would be easy enough that you could do it alone. But I still stick by what I said. I'm going in with you."

"Me three," said Ma'am.

"As you wish," said Ish. "But in the meantime, you could both help by hanging out and helping with surveillance duty."

"You mean Chad's fancy equipment can't do everything a real man can?" asked Jag, smiling.

"Almost," said Ish. "He actually does have an algorithm programmed in that will sound an alert when anyone other than the two agents we identified come out of either the front or back door, but nothing is foolproof. Nothing beats a set of human eyes, especially when you can do it from the comfort of a plush hotel room with room service on tap."

"Speaking of food," said Jag, "I'm getting a little tired of the hotel chow. Who's up for a grub run?"

"I'm down with that," said Ma'am.

Moments later they had all decided on where they were getting the food, and Ma'am had taken everyone's order.

"We'll be back in two shakes of a lamb's tail," said Jag as he and Ma'am flitted out the door.

Ish and Chad were in the living room going over some specs related to a project one of the Macrolox development teams were working on, when a distinctive and familiar scent wafted into Ish's nostrils.

"What the hell..." he sniffed. "I'll be right back," he said to Chad. He found Bird—and the source of the offending odor—on the balcony. Bird was gazing reflectively into the distance, a fat joint pressed delicately between his right thumb and index finger.

"What the fuck are you doing?" Ish hissed. Bird looked at him nonchalantly.

"It's just a joint man, relax. It's legal. Don't worry, I have a medical card. It's my back," he said, smiling slyly.

"I don't give a fuck if it's legal or not, Bird. We're supposed to be keeping a low fucking profile! You don't do that by smoking dope in the room, even if you do have a fucking permit for it!"

"Yeah," said Bird, nodding to himself, "I guess you're right. My bad." He stubbed the joint out on the balcony railing and slipped it into the breast pocket of his shirt.

"I'm worried about you," said Ish, walking over to the balcony to join him. "Ever since we started this PROPR thing, you've been different. I've said it before and you don't seem to be hearing me, but it's true. You're not the guy I served with. You're sloppy, you're distracted and you act like you want to be anywhere else but here. So why are you?"

"Why am I what?"

"Why are you here? Why aren't you back in Afghanistan? Or at least in some civilian job where you aren't on call 24 hours a day?"

"I don't know, man. I honestly don't. I'm feeling kind of lost these days."

"Listen, I don't want to be the one that's the cause of you dying out here," said Ish. "You fought in some serious battles over there, kicked a bunch of ass and came out without a scratch. After making it through all that, I don't want to see you come back to your own country and get hurt on a humbug."

"You worry too much, papa bear," said Bird, patting Ish on the chest as he walked past him and back into the suite. "I'm going to live forever. Come on, I'll buy you a drink."

Ish watched him walk towards the mini-bar and wondered if maybe Bird was right. Maybe he was just being paranoid. But then again...what was the old saying? *Just because you're paranoid doesn't mean they aren't out to get you.* Amen to that.

* * *

For two days they watched the safe house and listened to all incoming and outgoing phone calls. Janssen and his two protectors had quickly fallen into a predictable pattern. Watching these three men stuck in that house reminded Ish of what one element of war was like—not the exciting, fear-inducing, adrenaline-rushing part of being shot at and bombed, but the time-dragging, mind-numbingly boring part of waiting around hour upon endless hour for something to happen. At least Ish and his team could get out and go for a ride when the stir-craziness began to feel overwhelming. Janssen and his protectors were not so fortunate.

Ish gathered everyone into the room for an announcement.

"It's been a couple of days, and I think we've seen everything we need to see. I think tonight is as good as any to make our move, especially since Chad heard them talking about maybe ordering Chinese for dinner."

"Sounds good," said Jag. "How do we intercept the food to spike it?"

"We intercept the call," said Ish. "Instead of going to the restaurant, it goes right to us. That way we don't have to worry about dealing with a delivery driver. We pose as the restaurant, take their order, then immediately place an identical order with the restaurant they thought they were calling, so that we can pick up the food and add the sedative."

"Who's going to deliver it?" asked Ma'am.

"I will," said Chad, smiling. "I mean, come on, I'm the most obvious choice. I'll wear a disguise and cover my fingertips with clear epoxy so that I won't leave any prints. It'll be a piece of cake. Certainly, the easiest part of the entire operation."

An hour later Ish passed by the open door of the bathroom and saw Chad trying on a long, dark wig in the mirror. He stepped into the doorway.

"Looks good on you," said Ish. "Maybe you should wear wigs more often."

“You think?” asked Chad, smiling as he made some adjustments. “What about these glasses?”

He had several pairs of eyeglasses with clear lenses on the counter before him and began trying them on one by one.

“Not bad,” said Ish, when he donned the first pair. “Those are about the same,” he said in response to the second.

“Now those make you look like Charlie Chan,” said Ish, laughing at the third pair. “A disguise is supposed to draw less attention, not more. You need to just toss those in the trash. Seriously.”

“Alright, alright,” said Chad. “But here’s the piece de resistance.” He grabbed something out of his pocket, turned away from Ish for a moment, and when he turned back around, he was wearing a small fake mustache. Ish laughed out loud.

“That works. Even your own mother wouldn’t recognize you now. And even if she did, she’d probably pretend that she didn’t.”

They laughed together as Chad put the glasses, wig and mustache back in a bag. As Ish watched his friend’s face, almost unchanged from when they met so many years ago, his eyes still burning with that undeniable sense of wonder and curiosity, he thought again about how much he loved this man. His brother from another mother. It had been awhile since he had seen Chad’s parents. He missed them. Maybe after they wrapped things up with Janssen, he’d pay them a visit. After this, everyone would probably need a break.

Ish and Chad were in the large bathroom of Chad’s suite preparing the sedative when Ma’am walked in.

“I thought you two were computer nerds. Where did you learn about drugs?” she asked.

“The same place we learn about everything else—the internet,” said Chad, flashing his boyish grin.

“This guy could find online instructions to build a goddamn nuclear bomb if he needed to,” said Ish.

Ma’am watched them in silence for a moment as they weighed and divided the powder they were working with.

“Tell me,” she said. “How do you know how much of the food they’re going to eat? How do you know they’re not going to overdose? Or under-dose?”

“That’s the tricky part,” said Ish. “Once we thought about it, we realized that we have no idea if they’re going to eat a couple of bites or a whole plate full. But we do know that every time they order a meal, they always order three drinks, so spiking the drinks is the way to go. But even then, we don't know if they're going to drink the entire drink at once or nurse it all night, so we had to choose our drug carefully. We needed something with a lot of room for error. And that was tasteless."

"And we figured that would be the hardest thing to research online," said Chad. "You'd think there wouldn't exactly be a lot of blogs talking about what drugs are best for knocking people unconscious without killing them. But we were surprised how many sites there were dedicated to date rape and how to get laid without ending up a murder suspect. There are some seriously sick motherfuckers out there."

"You ain't gotta tell me," said Ma'am.

Ish declined to mention that he had already previously done a little research on date rape drugs—back in Afghanistan.

"Anyway," continued Chad, "we were able to find a couple of compounds with a lot of leeway regarding dosage. Based on the data we found, we were able to come up with a single serving that will safely put a baby to sleep just as easily as a 400-pound man. It's extremely reliable."

"That's amazing," said Ma'am. "How long do you expect it to take this wonder drug to do its thing?"

"It's slower acting than most drugs," said Ish. "But that was the only way to keep it safe. The last thing we want is to put these two innocent agents in a coma or something. This drug will probably take 60-90 minutes to be fully effective, but the effect will last for about three hours, so we'll have a ton of time to get in and do what we need to do."

"You brothers never fail to surprise me," said Ma'am. "I mean, y'all are on some serious James Bond shit with this one. That's one of the reasons I'm so proud to be a part of this team. It's always good to work with muthafuckin' professionals!"

"We love you too, Ma'am," said Chad.

"I don't think you and Jag are going to have very much to do on this mission," said Ish. "Seriously, if you want to hang back that's perfectly cool. If this goes off as planned, it'll be a walk in the park. I'll be in and out in under two minutes."

"And if it doesn't go off as planned? Don't worry, brother, we got your back," said Ma'am, nodding at him before she turned and walked away.

Chad rented a car for the delivery and crafted a fake license plate for it, just in case someone in the safe house was taking note. Ish watched him getting ready.

"How're your nerves?" he asked.

Chad held his hand out. "Steady as a rock."

"That's a curious thing," said Ish. "I don't think I've seen you nervous at all during any of these maneuvers. How is that?"

Chad stopped what he was doing and cocked his head to the side. "I'm not really sure. I don't think I ever thought about it. Maybe it's just because I believe so much in what we're doing that I'm not really worried about the consequences. Crazy, huh?"

"Passion is good," said Ish, and he left him to finish preparing.

* * *

Jag, Ma'am, Bird and Ish gathered around the laptop in Chad's room and watched him drive up to the safe house. He got out of the car holding two plastic bags heavy with food and drink and skipped up the stairs to the home's front door as if he didn't have a care in the world. It was the perfect way to deflect any suspicion, and the best thing was that it was all natural for Chad.

One of the agents opened the door and came outside to pay for the food, closing the door firmly behind him. Ish wouldn't have been surprised if the other agent locked it for added security. There was no audio, but Ish could tell by Chad's gestures that the agent gave him a decent tip. Moments later he was in the car and on his way back to the hotel. Now all they had to do was wait.

Chapter 66

As usual, Madden was up early the next morning and went downstairs to the lobby restaurant for a coffee and a copy of the L.A. Times. He found a comfortable table for two near the back. He could have made coffee in his room and gotten his news from one of any number of online newsfeeds that he was subscribed to, but this morning he had an urge to get out of the room by himself for a bit.

There was something very nostalgic about reading the newspaper while drinking a cup of coffee. Growing up, it was something that he had watched his father do almost every morning, right before he left the house for what was regularly a twelve-hour day. He missed his father, more than he could possibly express to anyone.

Madden's father had been dead for thirty years now, but sometimes it still seemed like it had only happened yesterday. The simple act of reading the paper while drinking a cup of coffee somehow always made him feel just a little closer to his dad. Sometimes, when he did it at home on the rare occasions when he visited his mother, he could feel her staring at him from the corner of her eye. She never said anything, but he was sure that she was thinking about his father, and maybe about how much they looked alike in that moment. He made a mental note to call her soon.

He hadn't spoken to her in several months. They weren't as close now as they once were. It wasn't any one particular thing that had come between them, but a variety of things over the years; some big, some small. He had made some decisions that had disappointed her, and vice versa. One of the biggest things was that she had never liked, nor ever gotten used to, the idea that he worked in law enforcement.

His mother had a history of conflict with the law. When he was a kid, she had committed petty crimes like writing bad checks and minor drug use, but never anything she had ever gone to jail for. Yet, like many in the black community, to her the cops always represented the 'them' in the "Us vs. Them" equation. Always. And when he joined the Bureau, Madden had instantly become one of the 'them'. She still loved him. He didn't think that would ever change. But he had the feeling that she didn't completely trust him anymore.

It hurt him to know that his job was one of the factors responsible for creating the rift between them. However, it wasn't just that. It's not as though everything in their relationship had been sunshine and roses before he joined the FBI. His mother could be a challenging personality at times. However, no matter how many times they had drifted apart, they had always managed to drift back together. Joining the FBI had simply made the drifting back together part more difficult.

The news in the paper was both inspiring and depressing all at the same time. The #BlackForLife organization had announced some kind of Black March For Peace that sounded promising for possibly helping to quell some of the brewing discontent in the streets, but another unarmed black man had also just been shot dead the previous night by a police officer in New Hampshire. He was stopped for a traffic violation, and the cop shot him when he mistook his wallet for a gun. The streets were getting to be like a bad TV show.

His reading was interrupted by a beep from his phone. It was a text from Phillips.

PHILLIPS: I knocked on your door. You okay?

MADDEN: Couldn't sleep. Grabbing an early bite. I'm actually just finishing up. Would you like me to bring you something?

PHILLIPS: Maybe just a bagel. I'm trying to cut back. We still meeting at 7:30?

MADDEN: Yes. See you in ten.

Madden was knocking on her door moments later. She answered wearing a set of earplugs that were connected to the laptop. She was frowning, and held up a finger to let him know she was almost done.

"Sorry," she said, pulling the buds out of her ear.

Madden handed her the bag with her bagel. "No problem," he said. "You looked disturbed. Are you listening to rap music again?"

"Not hardly," she said, rolling her eyes as she got up and poured herself a cup of coffee. "I was listening to the jail call recordings, and there was some interference on the line."

"What jail call recordings?"

"Oh, that's right, I forgot to tell you. The other day when you were still down at the station, I finished up early and had the idea of checking out any phone recordings between Carter and his wife, so I submitted a formal request to the warden. They emailed me a copy this morning."

"Oh, okay. Good job. Anything interesting on there?"

"Not really," she said. "Just some silly stuff about some dogs that are running around loose in the neighborhood."

This time Madden frowned. "Let me take a listen," he said.

As the recording ended, he was still frowning. Something was tugging at his mind, but he couldn't quite put his finger on it.

"Please get me a copy of these," he said once he finally looked up.

"Did something pique your curiosity?"

"I don't know," he mumbled. "It just strikes me as odd that Carter would be interested in some stray dog and, in the midst of all that is going on in his life right now, would take the time to actually try to capture it."

"Doesn't seem so odd to me," said Phillips. "I mean, assuming he is part of PROPR, his whole shtick is saving the helpless. If they're worried that this mutt is going to run up on some innocent kid, I can definitely see them making it a priority to go after it."

"Maybe," said Madden, staring off into the distance above her head. "Anyway, what else do you have for today?"

"Not much. I checked on Janssen a little while ago. He's settling in comfortably, and is only being a *slight* pain in the ass."

"That's good to know."

"Tell me," said Phillips, "what are you going to do if we haven't caught these guys in a couple of weeks and he starts getting antsy to leave?"

"I don't know. I guess we'll have to cross that bridge when we come to it. But let's hope we never come to it."

"From your mouth to God's ear," muttered Phillips.

"There are a bunch of files of potential suspects that are being delivered to us this morning via email, so I guess I'd better order some more coffee," said Madden. Phillips gave him a look that was slightly rude, to the point of being just shy of insubordinate. She didn't say anything, but he knew exactly what she was thinking: *Why are we looking at other suspects when we already know who the perps are?*

Madden and Phillips spent the rest of the day reviewing files and investigating phone tips. The FBI had received over a thousand calls from individuals claiming to have some knowledge of the people behind PROPR. The majority of them were no doubt false, but all leads needed to be explored, no matter how ridiculous some of them sounded.

There were several leads in the L.A. area that could best be followed up on face-to-face. To cover more ground, Madden and Phillips had mutually agreed to split up. For Madden, it was a simple matter of efficiency, but he had the feeling that Phillips wanted to have some time away from him. For the last couple of days, they hadn't shared any meals, and their conversations were cordial, even pleasant, but definitely more business-like that what Madden was used to.

Driving around solo gave him a lot of time to think. Some of the time was spent thinking about this thing with Phillips, but mostly he pondered the enigma that was PROPR and what he was going to do about the way Bainbridge was riding his back. One thing that kept drifting back and forth from the background to the foreground of his mind was the jail phone call that Phillips had played for him.

It sounded innocent enough, but he kept getting the sensation that something about it was wrong. He checked his watch. It was 7:30pm. Phillips had sent him a message that she was headed to dinner almost an hour ago, so there was no rush to get anywhere. He pulled the car over to the curb and turned off the engine. He needed a minute to just be able to focus on the issue at hand. He started back from the beginning and took it one logical step at a time.

Carter and his wife were having a conversation about stray dogs. There were some stray dogs in the neighborhood that had been causing a problem, and he and some friends were going to apprehend them and...what? Turn them over to animal control? Kill them? He was having a hard time picturing a black, multi-millionaire, possible fugitive from the law spending his afternoon chasing after a misbehaving pooch.

Okay, so if that wasn't what he was talking about, then the conversation about the dog had to be code for something else. That sounded like a logical possibility. But what? Was there some package that he needed to pick up from somewhere? And what kind of package could he not speak about on a tapped line? A weapon? Could PROPR be picking up some kind of bomb, perhaps? No, that didn't make any sense.

Wait. What if it wasn't an animal or a package they were referring to, but a person? A bad person? He paused. Could 'dog' be code for 'cop'? It was a little far-fetched, but what if they were talking about finding a cop that had gone wild? What if they were talking about Janssen?

He knew he was stretching, yet he couldn't deny that it was a possibility. If it were true, it meant that perhaps they knew where Janssen was being stored. He couldn't imagine how they could have gotten that information without there being some kind of leak at the Bureau, but he knew it was a fool's errand to ever underestimate this group.

He thought about calling Phillips to run the idea by her, but he didn't want to disturb her dinner. He looked up and realized that he was only a few minutes away from the safe house. It couldn't hurt to drive by to make sure everything looked alright. Maybe even drop in and have a quiet chat with the two agents there to give them a heads up. He pulled away from the curb and used the voice-control option in the car to speed dial one of the agent's numbers. There was no answer, so he tried the second number and got the same result. He could feel his pulse quicken and his forehead start to sweat.

Madden dialed 911 as he turned onto the street where the house was located and was put on hold. As he slowed down and came to a stop in front of the house, he heard three gunshots and saw matching flashes of light behind the house's closed blinds.

"911, what is your emergency?" asked an operator's voice that had just come on the line.

"Shots fired. Possible officer down!" he yelled at the speaker, followed by the address. He was opening his car door when he saw three figures run by the open space between the rear of the safehouse and the house next door. They were heading down the alley that ran behind the back of the homes. He jumped back into the car, started the engine and roared off down the avenue toward the entrance to the backstreet.

Chapter 67

Ish, Ma'am and Bird, each clad all in black with black ski masks in their pockets, were ready to go. Chad had already swapped out the previously rented car for a different one. He and Jag were going to man two separate vehicles to give them two separate avenues of escape, just in case.

One of the vehicles, the one Jag was using for the drop-off, was a utility van painted to look like a plumbing truck. They had decided at the last minute that Ma'am would exit the truck and ring the doorbell as Ish and Bird approached the rear of the house to make sure no one was awake to answer.

Everyone had in-ear intercoms, and Chad was also monitoring the femtocell, though it had been experiencing some kind of intermittent interference all afternoon, which was causing dropouts and static. Besides the occasional burst of white noise, he hadn't heard any sounds in the house other than the TV for the last hour.

Jag pulled the van into the driveway as close to the house as he could get while Ish and Bird donned their masks. Ma'am got out with a clipboard in hand and sauntered up to the door while the two masked men slunk around to the back of the house. Ish knew there was a slim possibility that they could have been seen by one of the neighbors, but they'd be in and out so quickly that it wouldn't matter.

Standing at the back door, Ish could hear the doorbell being rung in front by Ma'am. He kept watch while Bird picked the lock. It was a skill that he had only recently acquired, so it took a bit longer than it does in movies. Finally, Ish heard the click on the second lock and Bird cracked the door open as the doorbell rang for the fourth time.

"Okay," he whispered into his mic. "We're a go."

They were just swinging the door open when they heard the voice:

"Will one of you guys get the damn door? I'm still in here on the toilet!"

Ish recognized the voice. It was Janssen. He and Bird froze. Bird gave him a questioning look as if to say '*What do we do?*' Ish quickly stepped into the doorway, which put him in the back part of a darkened kitchen. Bird followed suit and quietly closed the door behind him as they both crouched down.

Ma'am heard the voice in her headset as well and stopped ringing the doorbell. She didn't have to ask the question. Ish knew that she was doing what everyone else was doing: waiting for direction from him. He raised his fist as a signal to Bird to hold their position. The seconds ticked by agonizingly slowly as he waited for some other sound to give him a clue as to what was happening. He and Bird had both drawn their weapons, Beretta .380 automatic pistols, and screwed on silencers.

They heard some soft grunting, followed a minute or so later by the sound of a toilet flushing. A faucet was run for about two seconds, after which they felt as much as heard someone lumbering from the back of the house towards the front.

"Sorry I've been in there so long," they heard Janssen say, "but my stomach is seriously fucked up. I'm still not hungry, but I'll take that drink now." The footsteps stopped. "Guys?" There was concern in his voice. "Guys!"

Ish signaled Bird, and they quickly advanced towards the sound. Moments later they stepped into the brightly lit living room where they found Janssen trying to wake the two unconscious agents, who were sprawled out, one on the sofa and the other in a leather recliner.

As Ish and Bird entered the room, Janssen had just figured out that something was amiss and had pulled the service weapon out of the shoulder holster of the agent in the chair. When he saw Ish and Bird, he quickly ducked behind the chair, using the agent's body as a shield as he pointed the gun in the general direction of the two intruders and fired off five rounds.

Ish and Bird both deftly stepped back behind the wall, wood splinters raining down around them. Bird raised his weapon and prepared to advance, but Ish held a hand out to stop him. "Wait! You could hit the agents!" he hissed.

"So, you assholes are finally coming to finish the job, huh?" said Janssen as Bird looked at Ish and shrugged, awaiting instruction.

"Fine," said Janssen. "You may take me out, but I'm not going alone. At least one of you motherfuckers is going with me! Who's it going to be? Who's ready to die tonight?"

Neither Ish nor Bird responded. Ish knew that Ma'am was right on the other side of the front door, listening to the conversation and trying to decide whether or not to kick it open. Ish stuck his head out as far as he dared and surveyed the area, looking for options. He signaled for Bird to cover him while he made a dash for the other side of the room.

Just as they made their move, Janssen made his, his hand flicking out as he hit the light switch and plunged the room into darkness. He fired three times, each deafening blast exploding like a roman candle in a black, country sky and driving the two soldiers back. It was followed by the sound of running footsteps and Ish knew that Janssen was making a break for the back door.

"You hit?" asked Ish.

"I'm good," replied Bird.

"Let's go! We're in pursuit!" he said aloud, for the benefit of the rest of the team. He ran through the back door without slowing, betting that Janssen wouldn't be posted up on the other side of it, waiting to pick him off as he came out. His bet paid off. Janssen was already halfway down the alley, huffing and puffing as he ran. He was making good speed but clearly was not in the best of shape, so Ish knew he wouldn't be able to keep it up for long.

"I'm in the car with Jag," said Ma'am in his ear-piece. "We're headed in your direction."

As Ish got to the end of the alley, he saw Janssen run across the street and drop down behind a parked car. "Incoming!" he yelled to Bird, and they both hit the ground as several rounds zipped by inches above their heads, shattering car windows and setting off alarms.

Ish and Bird barely had time to peak their heads up before Janssen was on the move again.

"He's headed to a park west of the house," he said into his mic. "Chad! See if you can cut him off!"

"I'm on it!" said Chad, and Ish could hear the wheels screeching in the background.

By running into the park, Janssen had made a tactical error. Not only was it well-lit and with a lot of open space, but the only structure in the vicinity was a small cinder-block restroom building. Janssen ran across the baseball diamond, heading in the direction of the bathroom. Ish only had moments before Janssen would be able to put the restrooms between himself and them, so he stopped, pulled a .38 revolver out of an ankle holster and quickly fired three shots into the air.

As he had hoped, Janssen assumed that the shots were aimed at him, and instead of running past and around the building, he ran into the open door to the women's restroom. Ish silently thanked his lucky stars that he had thought to carry a backup weapon. Janssen wouldn't have heard the silenced .380 that was in Ish's hand, and Ish didn't want to take a shot at this distance for fear of it possibly going wide and hitting an innocent bystander who might be hiding in the area.

"Check out the back," he said to Bird as they approached the short, rectangular building. Bird ran around the building and out of sight.

"No windows," he said into Ish's ear-bud before appearing seconds later on the other side. Their luck was holding. Janssen had trapped himself.

"It's over!" he yelled, facing the open door of the restroom. "Throw your gun out and we'll take care of this quickly. It'll be practically pain-free, which is more than you deserve!"

"Fuck you!" answered Janssen. "If you want me, come get me!"

Ish looked at his watch. Time was ticking. Surely the police were on the way.

"You don't have a chance!" he yelled. "There's two of us out here, with more arriving any minute. I don't know exactly what those agents were packing, but you've already fired twelve rounds. At most, you've got four or five shots left. We have several magazines of ammo. If we have to come in, it's going to be a gut shot instead of a head shot. That's a slow, very painful death! Do yourself a favor and throw the gun out!"

He was answered with silence. He could almost hear the gears of Janssen's mind spinning as he weighed his options. He was probably hoping that some cops would show up in time to rescue him, but Janssen had been a cop in this city for many years. He was well aware of the average response times, even for reports of shots fired, and he had to know that a rescue was extremely unlikely.

"Kiss my ass!" he said, finally. "I'm not going to let you motherfuckers film yourselves shooting me down in cold blood and posting it on YouTube for my family to see." His voice faded as he spoke the last couple of words. "I...I couldn't do that to them. So, fuck you all. I'll see you in hell!"

There was the sound of a single shot, which sounded like an explosion as it echoed around the tiled walls of the bathroom. Ish and Bird looked at each other briefly before they both began cautiously walking towards the open door, guns at the ready.

They inched their way into the bathroom, with Ish in the lead. One of the overhead fluorescent bulbs was flickering sporadically, but the remaining lights provided plenty of illumination. They could clearly see the red pool that was slowly creeping out from under the stall at the far side of the room. Ish put his gun away and walked forward. The stall door was closed, so he couldn't immediately see Janssen's body, but he could see the tips of his shoes in the middle of the crimson tide.

The door creaked when he pushed it open with his gloved hand, and there was the renegade cop. He was seated on the open toilet. His right hand hung by his side, still gripping the pistol he had taken from the FBI agent. His eyes were open and staring directly at Ish, but he wasn't seeing anything due to the fact that most of his brain and the back of his skull were plastered against the back wall of the stall.

"Janssen is no more," Ish announced aloud so that the entire team could hear him. "Chad, where are you?"

He heard Chad's voice in his ear-bud. "North side of the park."

"Stay there; we'll come to you," answered Ish.

"It's not quite as satisfying when they do it themselves," said Bird as he unscrewed the silencer from his weapon and put them both away.

"In the end," said Ish, "it doesn't matter who breaks the egg as long as the omelet gets made. Let's get out of here."

Ish looked around to make sure there were no witnesses, then removed his ski mask and stuffed it back into his pocket, with Bird following suit. As they emerged from the restroom, they saw the vehicle Chad was driving, a white Jeep Cherokee, parked about 200 yards away at the curb. The headlights flashed on and off briefly.

"Ma'am, where are you?" asked Ish.

"We're about a block down from you."

"You okay?" he asked.

"I'm fine," said Ma'am. "We'll rendezvous with you once you're en route."

"Roger that," said Ish.

"Thanks for the backup, bro," he said to Bird as they began walking. "I told you it was going to be pretty tame, but I'm still glad you were there."

"You call that tame?" asked Bird, scowling. "That didn't exactly go 'as planned'. We're damned lucky neither one of us got shot." Then he smiled. "But I'm glad I was there to cover your ass."

"Yeah, it was—" began Ish, but stopped when he saw the smile suddenly disappear from Bird's face.

"Ish, three o'clock," he said quietly before shifting his gaze straight ahead.

Ish slowly turned his head to the right, trying his best to appear casual. There was a dark-colored sedan creeping down the street, pacing them. He couldn't see the face of the driver from the distance they were at, but he had no doubt that they were being watched.

"You think it's FBI?" asked Bird.

"Could be. Could just be another Zimmerman, suspicious of two black men in hoodies, especially in the midst of all this gunfire. Chad. We don't want to lead whoever this is back to you. Stay where you are. We're going to angle off till we lose the lookie-loo, then we'll either circle back or give you a new rendezvous point once we're clear."

"Roger," said Chad.

Ish and Bird changed direction, heading toward the center of the park. At that point the car sped up, turning left at the end of the block.

"Let's go!" said Ish. He and Bird both broke into a sprint, heading towards a group of commercial buildings just beyond the far edge of the park.

Ish looked over his shoulder and saw that the sedan had jumped the curb and was barreling down on them, slipping and sliding across the park's grassy field, which was still wet and soft from a heavy rain the night before.

"He's gaining on us!" he yelled to Bird.

They both broke to the right just as the car slid past them and slammed into a park bench. The car was now in front of them, with the engine gunning and one spinning tire kicking up mud, but it wasn't moving, having become lodged against the concrete bench.

As they altered their course to go around the car, the door opened and a man jumped out. Ish instantly recognized him from the file. It was FBI agent Dexter Madden. Suddenly Bird stopped and turned, pulling his pistol from its holster. Before he had a chance to aim, Ish grabbed him by the back of the collar and yanked him off balance.

"What the fuck are you doing?!" he yelled. "You know better than that. Let's go!"

Bird gave him a look that was as cold as death, but followed the order and they continued running, with Madden now in pursuit on foot.

They ran down another alley, at the end of which was a dumpster positioned against a wall. With one giant leap, Ish was atop the dumpster, and with his second leap he cleared the wall and landed with a forward roll, softly rising to his feet. As he stopped and pivoted, he could hear Bird hit the same trashcan, and heard him grunt as he climbed up moments before he also sailed over the wall, stumbling as he hit the ground.

"Come on, man!" said Ish as they ran into an adjourning parking lot. They both ducked down behind the cars. Ish was hardly breathing heavy at all, but Bird was huffing, sweat dripping down his face. Seconds later they heard Madden leap onto the same dumpster and then heard his feet hit the ground as he cleared the wall.

Still in a crouch, Ish began to slowly move through the maze of cars. Bird followed him as they navigated away from the place they had last heard Madden. They moved quietly for a minute or two until they heard a sound that caused Ish to freeze. He looked back at Bird as he strained his ears to identify the direction of the sound, but all he could hear now was silence.

Ish and Bird began moving again and found themselves at the end of a row of parked cars. Directly across from them was a grouping of individual self-storage buildings. Ish looked around then quickly scrambled across the lighted area, stopping in the shadow of the nearest building to wait for Bird, who appeared seconds later.

They began to navigate around the buildings, but they could hear that Madden was still somewhere close behind. Ish stopped, signaling for Bird to wait, and then scurried across another brightly lit area into waiting shadows. Again, Bird followed.

Ish could see a street beyond the next cropping of buildings. He silently pointed it out to Bird, then quickly made a dash to the next building and began scanning the street for any signs of police or other agents. Everything looked clear. Suddenly, he realized that Bird was no longer behind him. Alarmed, he rapidly backtracked, trying to be as quiet as he could.

As Ish came around the corner of the next building, he saw that Bird had stepped into the light and was in a Weaver stance, gun in hand and aimed point blank at Madden, who was also carrying a gun but was moving with his back to Bird. Without thinking, Ish ran forward, his feet kicking up gravel. Madden quickly turned at the sound, just in time to see Ish slam into Bird, knocking the gun from his hand.

"I said stand down!" yelled Ish. Both turned to face Madden, who seemed stunned to the point of being frozen. Time was reduced to slow motion as Ish locked eyes with Madden for what felt like an eternity. Then it suddenly sped up again as Madden yelled "Freeze!" and began running towards them.

Bird ran left, scooping his gun up off the ground as he passed it, and disappeared between two buildings. Madden was so close at that point that Ish had no choice but to turn and run right. As he ran, he heard Madden reach the point they were just at, and he could tell by the way his footsteps were fading into the night that Madden had decided to follow Bird.

"Fuck!" said Ish as he skidded to a stop. He paused for a moment before he turned and began running after them.

Chapter 68

Madden spotted the two men as soon as he turned the corner. They were the only people in the park, and although they weren't wearing ski masks now, they were otherwise dressed exactly like the two people he'd seen chasing Janssen.

He had already called his location into the local PD, which had two units en route, but he knew these two guys would be long gone before they got there. He wished he could have tailed them back to wherever they were going, but he knew they had already made him. With nothing to lose, he slammed his foot down on the accelerator, looking for an opening in the fence that would allow his vehicle access.

The two suspects began running, and with no place to hide, he quickly began gaining on them. But the field was muddy, and he was having trouble maintaining control of his car. He was right behind them when he slammed on the brake, but his tires had no traction and the car began to slide. With a curse and a prayer, he spun the wheel and began tapping the brakes, narrowly avoiding the pair and slamming into a bench.

He pressed on the accelerator again and felt the car shudder as one of the rear wheels got caught up on the bench. The other wheel spun aimlessly for a few moments before he made the decision to abandon the vehicle and continue his pursuit on foot.

Both suspects were only about forty or fifty yards ahead of him, and he was maintaining the distance. He kept them within eyesight until they jumped a wall and disappeared. When he landed on the other side of the wall himself, there was no sign of them, but instinct told him that they were still in the vicinity. Madden drew his weapon and began to slowly creep forward, listening carefully for some evidence of their location.

Hc found himself in the middle of a group of low storage unit buildings, which gave the suspects a lot of places to hide. He thought about trying to climb up on one of the buildings to get a better view, but the risk of making himself too easy a target caused him to think again.

Dex, what the hell are you doing? he thought to himself as he crept from one building to the next. He had no backup—even the local cops didn't know exactly where he was—and somewhere around here were two armed suspects who had already made at least two attempts on the life of a police officer. For all he knew, Janssen was already dead, and if these two did it, they certainly had nothing to lose by killing him as well.

He saw Kelly's face in his mind's eye and thought about how devastated she'd be to receive the news that he had been killed in the line of duty. He had never been one to shy away from a fight and had been the first one through the door on many a raid, but what he was doing here was stupid and selfish. Suddenly, he felt extremely exposed.

"Fuck this," he muttered quietly. He was about to begin walking back the way he came when he heard a noise behind him. He spun just in time to see one of the suspects crash into the other, who had drawn on him and had just had the weapon knocked from his hands. He finally got a look at their faces and recognized both of them. It was Ishmael Carter and Damon 'Bird' Johnson.

Time instantly slowed down, but a single thought flashed through his mind like a bolt of lightning: *I think this guy just saved my life.* The shock of that realization caused him to pause momentarily, but he quickly recovered.

"Freeze!" he yelled. Both men reacted by running in different directions. He could have fired on either of them, but couldn't bring himself to be responsible for another black man being shot in the back.

"Fuck!" he muttered as he took off after the one he recognized as Johnson.

Normally in this type of situation, Madden would have been concerned about the suspect behind him circling back around so that the two of them could catch him in a cross-fire. But he had just seen suspect number two stop suspect number one from shooting him, so he didn't think a cross-fire was a major concern.

Still, the suspect he was trailing had already tried to kill him once, so he knew he needed to be extra careful. After every couple of steps, he paused to listen for any stray sounds, but all he could hear were crickets and the slight rumble of traffic from a nearby street.

He kept walking until he reached the last crop of buildings. Cars were driving by on the adjacent street. If Johnson was smart, he was long gone. It would have been easy for him to casually walk down the street and blend into the neighborhood while Madden was still creeping around these buildings. But something told him that was not what this man had chosen to do.

Chapter 69

Ish rounded the next corner, and neither Bird nor Madden were in sight. He stopped and rested in the shadow of a building.

"Bird," he said into his mic. "The agent is somewhere behind you, but he'll probably be moving cautiously. Keep running south, and you'll hit that back street while he's still tiptoeing around the storage units. Jag can be there to scoop you up in ninety seconds."

There was no response.

"Bird! Are you alright?"

"I'm good," said Bird, his voice a whisper.

"Where are you?" asked Ish.

"I'm close by. Give me about ten minutes and I'll meet you at the rendezvous point."

"Bird!" said Ish, his voice rising in anger, in spite of him trying to keep in down. "What the hell are you doing?"

"I've got to take care of this guy," replied Bird. "He saw our faces. I can nip this in the bud right now, before we end up all over the news."

"Bird," said Ish, "he already knows who we all are. And if he knows, his friends at the Bureau know, too. If we're not on the news yet, it's because they're holding the info. You're talking about taking a life for no good reason. Let it go!"

"I can't talk right now," said Bird. "I'll meet you in ten."

"Fuck!" said Ish as he pushed off the wall and began running in the direction he had last seen the two men headed.

"Bird!" he heard Ma'am say in his ear-piece. "Do what Ish said! Let it go!"

Again, there was no answer.

"Bird!" she said again. He could hear her cursing under her breath.

Tracking someone in this maze of buildings was not like tracking someone in the bush. The gravel-covered dirt was noisy and didn't leave much in the way of footprints. Ish moved as fast as he dared while still trying to be as quiet as possible. He maintained radio silence, as he knew the rest of the team would also be doing, for fear that if Bird hadn't turned off his radio, their voices in his ear-piece could be enough to give away his position to the FBI agent that was hunting him. Or that was being hunted by him, depending on your perspective.

Suddenly the silence was broken by the sound of gunshots.

"Come on, man, we don't have to do it like this!" said a voice. Ish instantly recognized it as Madden's. He sounded exactly as he had over the phone. "Throw your weapon out, and we'll go in peacefully. There's no need for anyone to die tonight."

Ish quickly began moving in the direction he thought the commotion was coming from, but the sounds were echoing around the buildings and making it harder to pinpoint.

"Fuck that! If you didn't want to dance, you never should have come to the ball!" he heard Bird yell, followed moments later by more shots. He continued moving toward the sounds, praying he would get there in time, and having no idea exactly what he was going to do once he did.

Chapter 70

Madden was about to turn around and backtrack when his attention was drawn to a particular shadow on the other side of the path. He was already running for cover when the shadow morphed into Johnson, who immediately began firing.

"Come on, man, we don't have to do it like this!" he yelled. "Throw your weapon out, and we'll go in peacefully. There's no need for anyone to die tonight."

"Fuck that!" said Johnson. "If you didn't want to dance, you never should have come to the ball!"

"Shit," muttered Madden. He inched his head out from around the building and quickly pulled it back as Johnson squeezed off three quick shots. They all missed but they were close—too close. He needed to find a better position.

Madden stuck his head out again, and this time when he drew fire, he fired a few shots in return as he sprinted across the open pavement and slammed against the wall on the opposite side of the building that Johnson was using as cover.

He was certainly closer, but now he had to watch both sides of the building, since he knew Johnson could come at him from either direction. But Johnson had the same dilemma. He didn't know how Madden was going to move either. Madden quietly bent down and picked up a handful of pebbles, then, walking loudly enough so that he could clearly be heard, he deliberately moved down to the far end of the building and then quickly crept quietly back. He tossed the pebbles overhead and in the direction that he hoped Johnson was expecting him to come from and dived from the other side.

Johnson quickly figured out the deception, but he was a half second too late. He had time to fire two rounds in Madden's direction, but both were high. Madden followed Johnson's two shots with two of his own, but neither missed. One grazed Johnson's ear, taking the entire earlobe with it, and the other hit him point blank in the chest, knocking him onto his back.

Madden scrambled to his feet and kicked Johnson's gun away, which had fallen about six inches away from the wounded man. He patted him down and found another gun, which he also tossed away. He pulled out his phone and hastily dialed 911, putting the phone on the ground with the speaker activated. As it rang, he frantically took his jacket off, balled it up and pressed it against Johnson's chest as hard as he could. Sweat was glistening off both their faces.

"911, what's your emergency?"

"Someone's been shot!" he yelled. "I need an ambulance immediately!"

After giving the 911 operator his location and identifying the victim as a downed officer, which he knew would get a faster response, Madden un-balled his now bloody jacket and pulled a large, plastic evidence bag from the inside breast pocket. He quickly spread the bag open and placed it over the wound, then repositioned the jacket over it and once again began applying pressure.

Johnson's eyes had been open during the 911 call, but now they closed and his head lolled to the side. Madden felt for a pulse and found it faint. He stopped and looked closely at the man's chest, but couldn't see it rising.

"Come on, goddamn it, don't die on me!" he muttered. He turned Johnson's head to the side and reached into his mouth with his fingers to made sure that the tongue wasn't obstructing the airway. There was blood pooling in the wounded man's mouth and Madden used the sleeve of his jacket to wipe the blood out. He then spent about two minutes pumping on his chest.

He felt for a pulse again and it was still faint. He was just about to place his mouth over Johnson's bloody lips and begin mouth-to-mouth resuscitation when the man coughed suddenly, spraying a mist of blood and mucus into the air. He took a massive breath and then his body relaxed as he began breathing again.

"Thank God," mumbled Madden. Johnson had opened his eyes and began blinking and trying to lift his head.

"Just relax," said Madden as soothingly as he could. "You've been shot. An ambulance is on the way. You just need to hang on till they get here."

Johnson began working his mouth, opening and closing it as though he was trying to speak, but nothing came out.

"I'm sorry, man," said Madden. "But when you fired on me, I had no choice. Believe me, the last thing I wanted to see was another brother lying in a pool of blood." His voice expressed his sadness and frustration.

Johnson closed his eyes, and Madden feared he was about to pass out again.

"Come on, man, try to stay awake," he said. "We need to keep you as conscious as possible until the paramedics get here." As if on cue he suddenly heard a siren in the distance.

"See?" he said. "They're almost here."

"Listen, I know you're scared," he continued, trying to think of things to say to keep the conversation going, "but I've seen people with far worse injuries than yours pull through. You just have to want it."

Johnson's eyes fluttered open again. "Sister," he muttered weakly.

"What's that?" asked Madden, bending down so that his ear was closer to Johnson's mouth.

"Sister...sorry," he whispered.

Johnson passed out again just as an ambulance came barreling down the driveway. It skidded to a stop and two medics jumped out and ran to where Madden was kneeling over the fallen man.

"What's the officer's name?" asked one of the medics as he began taking Johnson's vitals.

"Huh?" said Madden distractedly as he moved back out of their way. "Oh. Johnson. Damon Johnson."

Madden sat on the ground for the next six minutes as the blood on his hands dried, watching the two paramedics try to revive the injured man. Finally, one looked up and sat back on his haunches.

"I'm sorry, he's gone," he said.

Madden simply bowed his head and said a prayer. He wasn't sure if the prayer was for Johnson or himself.

Chapter 71

There were more shots fired, and Ish could tell it was from two different guns. They were louder now, and he knew he was getting close. He continued in what he hoped was the right direction. Moments later, there was another exchange of gunfire just as Ish rounded the corner.

Three buildings away he saw Madden dive as both he and Bird fired almost simultaneously, and saw Bird collapse, falling backwards. For a moment, he thought that maybe they were both hit until Madden jumped up, ran over to Bird and began trying to stop the bleeding.

Damn, mouthed Ish, hanging his head. Madden wasn't aware that Ish was there, so he quietly stepped back behind the building. He peeked his head around the corner, his heart breaking as he watched from the shadows as the FBI agent tried to save his friend's life.

Ish continued watching as the ambulance arrived, then quietly crept away once they pronounced Bird dead. He made his way to the street, where he had Jag pick him up. Ma'am was in the front passenger seat, and as he climbed in the back, he placed his hand on her shoulder. She turned her head to acknowledge him, but didn't speak.

"I'm sorry, Ma'am," he said solemnly.

"You say this FBI dude's name is Madden?"

"Yeah," said Ish.

"He's a dead man walkin'," she said. Her voice was calm and level, her tone one of resolution.

"It wasn't the agent's fault," he replied quietly. "I was there. And we all heard what happened. Your brother was itching for a fight. He was intent on murdering that agent. And in spite of it all, I watched the man try his best to save his life."

At that, Ma'am bowed her head, and he watched her shoulders shudder as the first sob escaped her. Jag drove in silence, staring straight ahead.

Ish's hand was still on her shoulder, and now he leaned forward and awkwardly wrapped both arms around her from behind as best he could.

"Why didn't he just let it go?" she asked as she looked up and caught his eyes in the rear-view mirror, her face wet with tears.

"I guess Bird had his own demons," said Ish. "His spirit had been restless ever since we arrived back stateside. I don't know that he was ever as comfortable here as he was in-country, fighting as a soldier for the U.S. government. But I guess he didn't find peace there, either."

Ma'am didn't answer, but her tears slowed and finally stopped.

"Chad, are you there?" asked Ish into his mic.

"I'm here," he answered. "I'm three cars behind you, checking for tails. You're clean."

"Thanks," said Ish. "Let's all meet up back at your hotel."

The rest of the ride was conducted in total silence. Ish struggled to stop emotion from overwhelming him. One of his worst fears had finally come to life, and still he felt like he could have done something more to prevent it. He knew it wasn't his fault, and yet he felt keeping order was his responsibility. And he had failed.

When they arrived back at the hotel room, Ish immediately grabbed a small bottle of scotch from the mini-bar and poured it over a glass of ice. By the time he walked out to the balcony, everyone had already given him their condolences at least twice. He didn't think he could take any more. He wanted to scream at them to leave him alone. He wanted to punch someone. Anyone. He wanted to throw his glass and everything else in the hotel room off the twelfth-story balcony.

But he didn't, because he knew that now, more than ever, the rest of the team was looking for him to be strong. Though exactly for what purpose he wasn't sure. Was it just to be strong in their grief over the loss of a good friend and brother? Was it to be strong as they attempted to avoid capture and conviction for what they had done? Or was it to be strong for forthcoming missions, of which they had yet to even consider or discuss?

Maybe it was all of the above. Maybe his job now was to do all of these things and more. But these were topics to be contemplated more thoroughly tomorrow, when the sun was shining and the future didn't look quite so dark. He finished his drink and left the balcony in search of Ma'am to see if there was anything he could do for her tonight.

Ish, Chad and Jag all drank more than they should have that night. Ma'am was the only one who abstained, and Ish worried about her the entire time. He wondered if her pain, along with their drunken display, would cause her to fall off the wagon. But even in her time of grief, she proved to be stronger than the three of them combined.

They all slept in Chad's suite that night. They could have each taken Ubers back to their own hotels, but no one was eager to leave. They were all hurting, and the pain felt easier to suffer through with someone beside them who shared the same pain. But Ish knew that this was only the beginning. There was no doubt much more pain on the horizon.

Chapter 72

Phillips arrived at the crime scene fourteen minutes after the paramedics called the time of death. Madden wondered how she had avoided an accident, even with siren and flashing lights, racing there as fast as she had.

"Are you alright?" she asked, dodging paramedics and uniformed officers to get to him.

"I'm fine," he said, looking down at his clothes and noticing all the blood for the first time. The paramedics had given him some sanitizing solution and large wipes for his hands, but there wasn't much they could do for the blood on his shirt and pants.

Five minutes later several other FBI agents arrived, joining the PD officers who were already there and making the area an even busier beehive of activity. Phillips quickly transformed from concerned friend to full-blown Bureau agent. She took over the position of quarterback, sending agents and PD officers into the surrounding neighborhood to canvass for witnesses, while doing her best to secure whatever evidence might be in and around the crime scene.

Madden could only sit back and watch her work. It wasn't that he was in shock exactly. This wasn't his first on-duty shooting, nor was it the first black man who had died at his hands. But for some reason, it felt like the most tragic.

It was 4:00am before they wrapped everything up and headed back to the hotel. Phillips had asked him a few perfunctory questions, but he had deferred the majority of them, telling her that he would put everything in his report the next morning.

As the elevator reached their floor and they began walking towards their rooms, Phillips stopped and turned towards him.

"I think you need a drink," she said. "I have something that's a step up from the mini-bar. Come on." He silently followed her to her room. He took a seat while she prepared drinks for both of them. From where he was sitting, he couldn't see what she was pouring, and he really didn't care as long as it was strong.

"I don't remember you being this affected by the last shooting you were involved in," she said as she handed him his drink.

"Maybe," he said.

"Don't forget that the guy tried to kill you," she said.

"I'm aware of that. It doesn't make it any easier."

"That I don't get," she said as she kicked off her shoes and drew her legs up under her in the oversized chair. "If you were going to be this upset over the guy dying, why go after him with a gun in your hand in the first place? And while we're on the topic, why did you describe that scumbag as a 'downed officer'?"

"See, this is part of the problem with how peace officers are trained in this country," said Madden, feeling his temperature begin to rise. "So many of us believe that if lethal force is necessary, the desired outcome is always the death of the suspect. The truth of the matter is that the use of lethal force is only meant to eliminate the threat. Once that threat has been eliminated, we should give that suspect's life the same value we'd give any other life—including that of a downed officer. That's why I described him that way. I wanted to make sure that he got the fastest, most qualified medical attention available at the time."

"It was disrespectful," said Phillips, looking off into the distance as she took another sip of her drink. "There's a line between them and us, and you're blurring it," she added, bringing her eyes back to focus on his.

"Maybe I am," said Madden, "or maybe you're blurring the line between 'suspect' and 'convict'. There is a difference, you know."

Phillips answered by massaging her bad leg with one hand and stretching her neck. "You said you didn't recognize the other suspect," she said after a few moments of silence, changing the subject. "And you didn't give a very detailed description."

"It was dark," said Madden. "They were moving quickly. Are you suggesting that I'm not being forthcoming?"

Phillips shrugged and took another sip of her drink. "I'm just asking the question. Since we both recognize the dead guy from our files, I thought it was a little odd that he was rolling with someone we haven't come across yet."

"Sounds like you're hinting again at me recusing myself from the case."

Phillips just stared at him.

"But maybe it's not me that should be recused. Maybe you're the one that needs to walk away from this."

Her mouth dropped open, and her face twisted in shock.

"Based on what?" she exclaimed.

"You know," said Madden, placing his drink on the table as he stood up, "it's late, and I need to wash this blood off before I hit the sack. We can discuss this further in the morning."

He walked out of the room as she silently watched him go, her mouth still a gaping hole in her face.

Madden went to bed with a headache and woke up two and a half hours later with the same headache. He stood in the bathroom looking hard at his face in the mirror. Some might say he was aging well. His skin was still tight and wrinkle free. But every year he had lived was now fully displayed in the puffy bags under his eyes. It was the result of more than just a lack of sleep; it was a lack of peace.

He brushed his teeth and then stood staring at his face again. What the hell was he doing? Why hadn't he told Phillips that he had ID'd Carter as the second suspect? Sure, he was worried about what Bainbridge would do with proof like that. It was all he would need to start a shoot-on-sight nationwide manhunt. But there was something else. He felt a kinship with the man, and he somehow believed he could bring him in safely, if he just had enough time.

His mind drifted back to his most recent conversation with Phillips. She was continuing to surprise him and to show him that she was so different than the person who he had thought she was all these years. He considered putting her in for a transfer. She was no good for this investigation. The only thing stopping him was that he knew that doing so would probably irreparably damage her career, and he still cared for her too much to do that.

He walked back into the bedroom area and flicked on the TV to CNN as he began getting dressed. Almost immediately, a story appeared about last night's shooting. After listening for a few moments, he froze, one leg in his pants and one leg still out. He sat down heavily on the bed.

"Here," said a pretty, dark-haired female reporter, "is where officials discovered the deceased body of police officer Thaddeus Janssen." Madden recognized the structure she was standing in front of as the restroom building in the park where he had first made contact with Carter and Johnson.

"Officer Janssen was able to avoid PROPR's first attempt on his life," continued the reporter. "However, despite being taken into protective custody by the FBI and secured in a secret FBI safe house, PROPR was able to track him down and finish the job. Members of the terrorist organization incapacitated the agents who were guarding the officer, and after chasing him into this park restroom behind me, shot him to death inside one of the women's bathroom stalls."

"What the fuck," muttered Madden, feeling like he was about to start frothing at the mouth. He grabbed his phone and finished putting his pants on as he called Phillips.

"Good morning," she answered.

"Have you seen CNN?" he asked, louder than he had intended to.

"Uhhh, no, I haven't. What's wrong?"

"They just ran a story claiming that PROPR killed Janssen!"

"Ummm, okay."

"No, it's not okay! You were there. You know damn well that Janssen's wound was self-inflicted. How the hell did they get this story?"

"Chief, you know as well as I do that these days the news agencies don't exactly run their stories by us before they go to press with them," replied Phillips matter-of-factly. "Maybe one of the officers on the scene explained it to a reporter this way. Maybe they made the entire thing up themselves. Who the hell knows?"

"This investigation is turning into a real clusterfuck," said Madden, his defeat apparent in his tone.

"Speaking of clusterfucks," said Phillips, "has Bainbridge called to explain how disappointed he is that we lost the safe house?"

Now Madden remembered what had caused his headache.

"No, not yet," he said, sighing heavily. "But I'm sure my phone will be blowing up any minute now. You up for some breakfast before the madness starts?"

"Sure," she said, "but I don't think we can eat that fast."

Madden chuckled softly. "Let's try."

Chapter 73

Chad had given Jag and Ma'am the bedroom. He'd offered Ish the sofa sleeper, but Ish refused, choosing instead to squeeze his large frame into the recliner. He awoke the next morning with a crook in his neck and something worse in his back. Everyone else was still asleep, so after going to the restroom, he slipped on some shoes and crept out onto the balcony.

It was only 5:00am, but the city was buzzing already. From his twelfth-story perch, the gleaming streets stretched as far as the eye could see. The sky showed very little smog this morning, so visibility was breathtaking. Even in the glow of the early morning sun, the buildings and traffic lights twinkled like a blanket of stars at his feet. There was a chill in the air, with a slight breeze blowing, but it felt good on his skin.

Ish wasn't sure how long he had been out there, but suddenly his peace was interrupted by the sound of the glass door sliding open. It was Ma'am. She was wearing a fluffy white hotel robe, but he could see that under it she still had on the jeans she was wearing the night before. Her eyes were red and swollen.

"You're up a lot earlier than I thought you'd be," she said, her voice soft but strong.

"I could say the same for you," he countered.

"Yeah, but I didn't drink a bottle and a half of whatever it was that y'all was guzzlin'."

"*Camas,*" said Ish, smiling at the memory.

"Yeah, that," she said.

Ish turned his face back towards the warmth of the morning sun, basking in it for a few moments before he spoke again.

"How are you holding up?" he asked without looking at her.

In his peripheral vision he could see her slowly shake her head from side to side.

"You know, it's funny," she said. "I always thought it was ridiculous when people would be devastated at the news that their enlisted brother or husband or son had just died in combat. I mean, they had to know, right, that their person was going to live in a war zone; a situation where they was regularly gonna to be shooting at folk and folk was regularly gonna be shooting back. Right? So, you do the numbers, right, and you know that the odds are fairly high that they're going to get caught in some shit, right? I mean, at least higher than walking down the street in their own neighborhood."

Ish turned to face her but didn't say anything.

"But now I understand. No matter how much you know it can happen, somewhere deep inside your soul you tell yourself that it ain't gonna happen to your people. That you know a lot of soldiers make it home safely, and that somehow, some way, yours is gonna make it home, too."

She paused, taking a moment to compose herself. Ish's weight shifted from one foot to the other as he prepared to move to comfort her, but she reacted with a slight, almost imperceptible shake of her head, so he stood his ground.

"He was an asshole, my brother," she said. "But he was mine. I—"

There was a knock on the glass door, and they both looked over to see Chad staring at them. He slid the door open.

"Sorry to interrupt you guys," he said, "but you may want to see this."

As Ish and Ma'am followed Chad into the living room area, they saw that he had connected his laptop to the auxiliary input of the room's flat screen TV, and the image of a male news reporter was frozen on it. Chad waited for them both to take a seat before he pressed the 'play' button.

"Details are sketchy, but here's what we know so far," said the reanimated reporter as he glanced down at some papers in front of him. "Earlier in the week, the FBI had taken Officer Janssen into protective custody, fearing another attack on his life. They secured him in a safe house somewhere in the vicinity of Springley Street.

"Sometime late last night two masked men overpowered the agents that were guarding the policeman. Officer Janssen ran from the house but was pursued by the two men and chased into the public restroom of this local park," continued the reporter, glancing at the still photo of a red brick building that appeared beside him, "where eyewitnesses say he was cornered and shot to death by the two men."

Ish thought he heard Ma'am's breath catch in her throat.

"Those same two men were then spotted by another FBI agent that arrived on the scene. A gunfight ensued, and one of the men escaped and is still at the large. The other was wounded and pronounced dead at the scene. That was this man," said the reporter as a mugshot of Bird appeared on the screen beside him, "identified as Damon 'Bird' Johnson."

Ish glanced over at Ma'am to see how she was reacting, but her face was now completely impassive, as though she were listening to someone recite a grocery shopping list.

"Johnson was a veteran of the Special Forces, having most recently been deployed in Afghanistan. He has a record of being arrested for rape on several occasions, though he was never convicted. A source in the police department that asked not to be identified described him as a career criminal and 'a sexual predator that was somehow able to always stay one step ahead of the law'. Authorities are still trying to ascertain the identity of the second man and have yet to officially link either of the men to the terrorist organization PROPR. We'll have more as this story develops."

Chad froze the video again, then closed the laptop, causing the TV screen to go black. No one said anything. Chad coughed, and Ish wondered if it was because he was coming down with something or just because he was feeling uncomfortable.

Ish looked at Ma'am again and saw that she was now staring at the floor.

"This," she said without looking up, "is all some bullshit." Her voice was low, but so intense that it sounded like a growl. "My brother wasn't...he was...my brother was a good man."

"We know that," replied Ish. "We served with him. We would never have invited him into this if we believed anything less than that."

"I need a minute," she said suddenly, and just that fast she was up and out the door. Jag jumped up to follow her, but Ish waved him off.

"I think you should let her go," he said. "She's okay. She'll come back when she's ready."

Jag looked around the room, an expression of helplessness on his face. Finally, he nodded and returned to his seat. The air in the room was thick with tension. Ish noticed that both Chad and Jag were looking around like they were lost. Chad excused himself to the restroom, and Jag started examining the snacks in the mini-bar. Not knowing what else to do, Ish picked up the remote and turned on the TV. TCM was on, playing *The Maltese Falcon,* one of Ish's favorites.

He barely paid attention to what Chad and Jag were doing during this time, but as the minutes ticked by, he became more and more concerned about how Ma'am was. As the credits began to roll on the Bogie film, he looked up and noticed that Chad was doing something on the laptop and Jag was preoccupied with his phone.

"You heard from her?" asked Ish, hoping that perhaps he had at least gotten a text.

"Nah, not yet," said Jag, shaking his head. It was clear that he was also worried.

"I'm getting stir-crazy sitting here," said Ish, "but I don't want to miss Ma'am when she comes back, in case she needs us. Plus, we don't know when the news is going to break with our names and pictures, and I'd hate to be casually running around the city not knowing that we made the cover of the L.A. Times."

"Actually," said Chad, "it would only take me a few minutes to set up a Google alert that would text us when our names appear anywhere online. And this laptop camera has motion detection. I can point it at the door and we'll know if Ma'am, or anyone else, comes in while we're gone."

"That's a good idea," said Ish, "because these stale donuts aren't doing it for me. I need real food."

"I hear you," replied Chad. "Give me ten minutes and I'll be ready to go."

Ish began idly clicking thru channels on the TV while he waited for Chad.

"Ready," said Chad moments later.

Ish turned the TV off, and they all rose to leave when there was a knock on the door. Ish opened it and Ma'am slowly walked in.

"You guys on the way out?" she asked.

"Just thought we'd grab a bite," said Ish.

"Are you alright, babe?" asked Jag.

"Yeah, I'm okay," she said.

"You hungry?" asked Ish.

"Starvin'," she said, "but I'd like to say something before we go."

The men all looked at each other and then each took a seat, following Ma'am's lead.

She looked nervous. She rubbed her open palms on her jeans, then began.

"This rape stuff? I, uh, knew all about it," she said. "Or at least, I knew about two of 'em. They both happened at a time that I was still usin', but somehow I was lucid enough to make it to both trials, which were both eventually thrown out. He always said he was innocent. He swore to it. And I believed him. He was my brother. Besides, I knew bitches out on the street that were shakin' dudes down with similar bogus claims. But when that reporter mentioned it this morning, a memory came back to me." She stopped to grab a tissue off the table and wiped her nose.

"We were teenagers. I was probably like fourteen, fifteen. Maybe sixteen. Anyway, I came into the house one day and heard a ruckus upstairs. I opened his bedroom door and there was a girl in his bed. She was dressed, but her hair and clothes were all messed up. She was crying and begging him to let her go. I asked him what the fuck he was doing, and he told the girl to get the hell out." She paused and looked around at each of them, licking her lips nervously.

"I never saw the girl again, and he and I never spoke about the incident. But I now know in my soul that if I hadn't showed up that day when I did, he would have raped that poor girl. And he probably raped the two that he went to court over, too."

"Bird," said Ish, choosing his words carefully, "was his own man. He, and he alone, was responsible for whatever it was he did during his life. And if there is an afterlife, he's probably atoning for it all right now. And maybe it doesn't matter, but I had a conversation with him, just a few days ago, that gave me the impression that at some point he had seen the error of his ways and was a changed man in that regard."

"Thanks," said Ma'am. "But you know how the press is; they're going to spin this to make us all look like the devil."

"They'd be doing that anyway," said Ish, chuckling softly. "Believe me, they are not lacking ammo in that fight."

"I know," said Ma'am. "I just wish that I had told you earlier. Maybe it would have made a difference. Maybe you would have never invited him to join the group."

"Maybe," said Ish. "But it is what it is. Onward and upward."

Ma'am stared at him, frozen for a moment. Then he saw something shift in her eyes, as though she had made a decision. Or perhaps just put something to rest.

"Okay, now I'm ready," she said, clapping her hands together softly. "Where the pancakes at?"

At the restaurant, Ish kept his phone on the table. It was set to both chime and vibrate if any of their names got a Google hit, but he was paranoid and wanted it where he could see it as well. No such alerts were received.

Chad drove, and on the way back to the hotel, sitting in the backseat and wearing an ear-bud, Ish began checking some of the newsfeeds from his phone. The headline for a video looked interesting, so he pressed play.

A white man in a suit sat beside a low wooden table, his legs crossed, and stared into the camera.

"I'm Carl Hornsby. We have with us today Bull Stemway, the campaign manager for Republican presidential candidate Trevor Gage. Welcome, Mr. Stemway," he said as the camera pulled back to reveal a man sitting beside him.

The man looked like one might assume someone with the first name 'Bull' would look. He was a large man, his girth made up of more fat than muscle. He had a puffy, walrus-like mustache, a bulbous, shaved head and his skin was more red than pink, as though he had fallen asleep sunbathing somewhere.

"Thank you, Carl. Happy to be here," he responded. He had a thick New York accent.

"So, let's get right to it," said Hornsby. "Mr. Gage made headlines earlier today when he condemned the FBI for failing to protect Officer Janssen. He called for a complete restructuring of the Federal Bureau of Investigation, including the immediate firing of Associate Director

Wesley Bainbridge. He even went so far as to call the killing of Officer Janssen part of an intricate plot by Democratic presidential candidate Kathleen Hamilton to prevent the leaking of information that could be damaging to her campaign. Those are some astounding allegations. Can you tell us what evidence Mr. Gage has that would lead him to such conclusions?"

"Listen," said Stemway, "Mr. Gage has a lot of connections, not only in the business world but in many political circles as well. Just like people come to you as a reporter and offer you information in confidence, many people do the same with Mr. Gage. Probably more than you could ever imagine. Mr. Gage is not at liberty at this time to reveal those sources, but believe me, he will when the time is right."

"I assume that time would be sometime after the election?" asked Hornsby.

Stemway shot him an icy stare. "I said when the time is right."

"Fair enough. Let me ask you about another comment. Mr. Gage also went on record today to say that the rape allegations against suspect Damon 'Bird' Johnson prove that not only is PROPR nothing more than a vicious gang—a 'criminal collective'—but that anyone that supports their cause is equally criminally liable. He added that when he becomes president, one of his first jobs will be to round up as many of these supporters as humanly possible and prosecute them all en masse. His detractors have called that not only a fantastic overreach of authority, but also a reaction rooted in racism. What is your response to that?"

"Mr. Gage only said what so many good citizens in this country are already thinking. Most politicians are too politically correct to tell the truth. My candidate isn't bound by such malarkey."

"So, you deny that these comments are racist?"

"Just because you tell the truth about someone and they happen to be black, or Mexican or whatever, doesn't mean you're a racist."

"Well, he also tweeted on the topic a while later, saying that his previous comments weren't racist because that's 'just the way black people are'."

"No," responded Stemway. "He said that's how 'some' black people are."

"Actually, no," retorted Hornsby, "I have a picture of the actual tweet right here. It says, 'I'm not...'"

“Listen here,” said Stemway, interrupting him and leaning closer to the camera. “I’m not going to get into a debate with you about whether or not someone may or may not have photo-shopped this document you have here. What I will say to you unequivocally is that America is waking up today and smelling the coffee on the group PROPR. The polls show their support dropping off more than thirty points since this story broke, and they are continuing to plummet. Mr. Gage stands on the side of justice, and when elected president, he will see justice done.”

“On that note,” said Hornsby, turning to face the camera, “I’m afraid we’re out of time. Thank you so much for joining us. We’ll see you next time—”

Ish shut down the webpage. He felt his stomach cramp. Listening to Gage’s nonsense always had the ability to do that.

Chad dropped Ma’am and Jag off at Jag’s hotel. It was obvious they had some things they were anxious to discuss in private. Ish considered going back to his own hotel but decided at the last minute to go back to Chad’s instead. A change of scenery would do him good. Or so he hoped.

Chapter 74

To give himself a break from the heavy thoughts that were swimming around in his head, Ish decided to return some of the phone calls he had been neglecting the last few days. He went into the bedroom and dialed Marquita's number.

"Ishmael!" she said when she answered. "How are you?"

"I'm good. How are you?"

"I'm blessed, thank you. And thank you—and Chad—for the donation. I mean, a million dollars! I don't even know what to say. I've tried calling you probably a hundred times. Did you get my gazillion messages?"

"I did," said Ish. "Sorry I haven't been able to get back to you sooner. But life has been a bit hectic lately."

"I figured," said Marquita. "And I apologize if my constant calls were an annoyance. It's just that we've just never had anyone make such a gigantic expression of support for the cause before. I mean, the things we can do with this money!"

"It's no problem at all," said Ish. "We were happy to do it. I've been following the march in the news. How is everything going?"

"The last 48 hours or so have been rough," she said, sighing. "I suppose you heard about the killing of that police officer over in Amster Park?"

"I did," said Ish.

"Yeah, that really caused the winds to shift for us. Even some people that made monetary pledges have reneged. If it weren't for you and Chad, we would probably not be able to afford the support team that we have now. It wouldn't matter for me, because I'm going to complete this march even if I have to do it by myself on my knees. But a lot of the people choosing to march with us couldn't do it without that financial support. Without you, we'd probably be dead in the water right now."

"We wouldn't let that happen," said Ish. "As long as we can help, we will. By the way, how is Khadija? I read that she was injured in that Baltimore shooting."

"She's doing great! She's been going through a series of physical therapy sessions which, thank God, are almost over. When she was shot, the bullet hit her in the ankle. It broke the bone, so she's wearing a cast now, but other than that the damage wasn't too bad. She's actually flying to meet me at the next rest stop, and she'll be marching with me the rest of the way to D.C."

"With a broken ankle?"

"She's going to be in a wheelchair. I know, it's crazy. I tried to talk her out of it, but once Khadija gets her mind set on something, it's going to happen one way or another," said Marquita, laughing.

"I'm glad to hear it," he said. "And don't worry about the movement. I'm sure things will turn around soon, and your poll numbers will start to go up again. Keep me updated on how everything is progressing. I might even fly out and walk with you for a few days if I can possibly get away."

"We would love that! Just let us know."

"Will do. Tell Khadija I said hello and that I hope to see you both soon."

"I will. Take care of yourself, Ishmael. And thanks again."

Once back in the living room of the suite, Ish flopped into a chair and kicked off his shoes. His leaned his head back and ran his hands through his hair.

"What's up, dude?" asked Chad.

"Oh, nothing really. I just got off the phone with Marquita."

"How is she?"

"She's good. She just wanted to thank us for the donation."

"Cool. So, what's bothering you?" asked Chad, knowing his friend well enough to know there was something more on his mind.

"I was checking headlines on the way back here, and so far, my name still hasn't been mentioned."

"That's a good thing, isn't it?"

"Maybe, maybe not. It depends on the reason. Perhaps it's time to check in with our friend at the Bureau and try to see what we're up against," said Ish.

Chad nodded. "I'll grab you a new burner." Ten minutes later Ish had a brand new, freshly unwrapped prepaid cellphone with their cloaking technology uploaded to it. The encryption software was so good that they could have simply used their own phones, but you could never underestimate the resourcefulness of the FBI's hackers, which were some of the best in the world. Better safe than sorry.

Ish dialed the number. He had only seen it a couple of times, but he had already memorized it. It was part of his gift for math.

"Madden," said the voice that answered.

"Why haven't you come after us yet?" asked Ish.

"Hey, babe," said Madden, after an almost imperceptible pause. "I was just in the middle of breakfast. Give me a minute." There was another pause. Ish could tell that the phone receiver was covered, and then he was back.

"Are you seriously asking me to give you some details of our investigation?" asked Madden, incredulous.

"Call it 'professional curiosity'," said Ish. "You're free to say no, but my mama always said 'nothin' beats a fail but a try'."

"I have some questions for you, too," said Madden. "So maybe we can exchange some information. But not right now. My vicinity is too crowded. Give me a number, and I'll call you back when I can cut myself loose."

Ish just chuckled softly in response.

"Alright," said Madden. "Call me back tonight at 10:00pm."

"10:00pm," said Ish, and hung up.

He placed the phone on the table and began tapping it with an index finger.

"That was awfully short," said Chad, looking at him expectantly. "Did we learn anything?"

"It wasn't a lot of words, but it may have been a ton of information," said Ish. "I've got to call him back later tonight. In the meantime, I'll dig around and see what else I can find out."

Ish spent the rest of the day surfing the web, reading various media reportings on PROPR. Eventually, he found himself on Facebook, something that he had previously never really been into.

He had never understood people like his mother who would log onto Facebook and say they were going to 'check in real quick' and the next thing you knew, two hours had passed and they were still scrolling. That is, until now. Now he understood what that compulsion felt like. He kept telling himself he would only read one more article, watch one more video, but four hours later he was still there, reading various strangers' opinion of PROPR, both pro and con. Chad had left him alone for most of the day, but it was his interruption that finally broke the spell.

"You learning anything useful?" he asked.

Ish looked up, frowning as he rubbed his eyes. "I'm learning that a lot of people don't like us."

"That's not news, dude."

"People are wondering where we are; why we aren't answering the rape allegations. I think we need to issue another broadcast. We owe them that much."

"I think you're right," said Chad. "It's actually been on my mind all day. I don't know that it's going to do much good, but it's the thought that counts."

"Alright," said Ish. "I guess I'll get started on the script."

"Cool. I'll order some coffee," said Chad, picking up the room phone.

"And another bottle of scotch," added Ish. He felt he was going to need it.

Chapter 75

After he hung the phone with Carter, Madden unlocked his briefcase and pulled out a small stack of notes. They were notes of the report that he should have already electronically filed regarding last night's incident and that Bainbridge was no doubt chomping at the bit to read. But he wasn't sure of what exactly he wanted to report. Or even what was right to report.

Should he out Carter? He just didn't know. He'd been struggling with the question ever since the moment he realized that Carter had saved his life.

Why would the man do that? It didn't make any sense. Madden could have easily shot both of them. If he had been the typical white FBI agent, he probably would have. Then Madden reminded himself that this is what it was all about. It wasn't about allowing this group to avoid justice. Quite the opposite; it was about getting them all to the courthouse alive so that they could stand properly before a judge and plead their case rather than have justice meted out to them via a pistol held by an unsympathetic peace officer.

He thought about the look he had seen in Carter's eyes after Carter had knocked the gun from Johnson's hand. It was only the briefest of moments, and maybe his vision was affected by the adrenaline surge, but he thought he saw hope and compassion. And maybe a bit of resignation. But no fear. In that split second, Madden saw a man who was not afraid to die and, furthermore, who was actually ready to forfeit his own life to save that of another.

The question Madden needed to ask himself now was what was *he* ready to sacrifice. His job? His conscience? They were both on the line right now. If he filed this report stating that he could not identify the second suspect, there was no going back. Sure, no one could ever prove what he did or didn't see that night, but he'd know the truth. He'd know that while he might be saving another black man's life, he was betraying everything that he had taken an oath to protect so many years ago.

The reality was that this was only delaying the inevitable. Phillips was gathering her own pile of notes and would be filing her own reports. Of course, they had to go through him first, but that was just a formality. He couldn't force her to alter her report. At least, not unless he had something that the Bureau would consider to be a damn good reason.

And there was something else. He wasn't exactly sure when he had first noticed it, but he was starting to suspect that Phillips was communicating with Bainbridge behind his back. It was little things that came up in meetings, subtle comments that hinted that she knew more about what was going on back in D.C. than he did. If that was true, then it was definitely only a matter of time before Bainbridge figured out that there was a possibility that Madden was withholding evidence. And when that happened...well, he didn't want to think about that right now.

He sat down in front of his laptop, organized his notes in several distinct piles, and began writing his account of the events that took place the night of the shooting of Damon 'Bird' Johnson. Carter's name never once appeared anywhere in it.

Chapter 76

Ish and Chad were in the War Room and Chad was setting up the cameras.

"How did the script turn out?" Chad asked as he plugged a cable into a lighting unit.

"It didn't," said Ish. "No matter what I wrote, none of it felt right."

Chad stopped and looked at him. "So, what are you going to do?"

"I'm going to do what we did in the military when things got way fucked up. I'm going to improvise."

Chad nodded his head. "Maybe that's the best way," he said. "Speak from the heart, and you can't go wrong."

"We'll see about that," said Ish. He already had on his PROPR uniform of black jeans, hoodie and gloves, with the masks perched on the top of his head.

He didn't want to admit it to Chad, but part of the problem he had writing the script had to do with the fact that he was preparing to defend someone who very well might have been a serial rapist. Probably was. And when you defend the indefensible, you share in some of the guilt. PROPR didn't deserve that, but Bird was still a member who died in battle, and in a lot of ways that made him a hero. A flawed hero, but a hero nonetheless.

Ish slowed his breathing and tried to clear his mind of everything but the task at hand. He tried to remember only the best things about Bird and the time they had spent together, watching each other's backs in foreign lands.

"You ready?" asked Chad.

"Yeah," said Ish. "Let's do it." He positioned the masks and shades over his face, pulled the hood up over his head, checked himself in the mirror and walked to the center of the room.

"Three, two, one, go," said Chad.

Ish stood there, frozen in place. He could feel the heat from the lamps raining down on him, and he could feel sweat beginning to form at the back of his neck. A moment passed. And then another. He still had not moved.

Chad turned the cameras off. "Are you alright, dude?" he asked. "We can do this later if you like."

"No, I'm good. Let's get it over with," said Ish, shaking his head and flexing his shoulders, trying to force his body to loosen up.

Chad restarted the cameras as Ish mentally reset himself. Chad gave him the countdown again.

"Good evening, America," said Ish, staring directly into the front camera. "Welcome back to PROPR TV. Today—" He paused and cleared his throat.

"Today we come to you with a heavy heart. We've lost one of our own. Damon Johnson. Better known to friends and family as 'Bird'. If you've been following the news, then I'm sure that by now you've heard the reports of how we made good on our promise to continue our attempts to mete out justice to the murderous Officer Thaddeus Janssen. But there are a lot of lies in the press surrounding that event, and I'm here to set the record straight."

"First, contrary to what the media has reported, we didn't kill Janssen. We chased him and cornered him in a park restroom, but he committed suicide before we could get to him. He chose to shoot himself in the head rather than face us." Ish began to slowly pace back and forth, looking at the ground.

"Perhaps that was for the best. He checked out of this society on his own terms, and we don't care how he left so long as he's no longer a threat."

"Bird and—" Ish paused, then tried again. "Bird and another of our colleagues were chased from the scene by an agent of the FBI."

"I believe—" Ish paused again and turned to stare into the camera. "*We* believe that Bird got spooked in the heat of the moment, and when he felt cornered, he opened fire on the FBI agent. The agent returned fire, fatally wounding Bird who, as you know, died at the scene.

"It's important to make special note of the fact that we don't condone what Bird did, firing his weapon at, what we must assume to be, an innocent member of law enforcement. We're not anarchists. We are not waging war on the police, as so many media pundits have claimed. We are simply righting individual injustices as we find them and trying to hurt as few innocent people in the process as possible.

"Now, this next bit is particularly difficult. But as you may or may not have also heard, Bird had some trouble with the law some years ago. He was accused of rape on a couple of different occasions, although he was never convicted of any of those charges. We want to go on record as stating that we were not aware of these charges before the press reported them. This same press has been calling him a thug, a sexual predator or worse. They are using these charges as one more justification for labeling PROPR as a criminal organization.

Ish took a deep breath. "I don't know whether Bird raped the women that filed charges against him or not. I wish that he was alive so that I could at least look him in the eye and ask him myself. But as human beings, we encounter each other in slivers of time, and the windows into our lives during that time together often have a limited view. Rape is a despicable crime, which we of PROPR have no tolerance for. Perhaps the best evidence of that is the fact that rape is also the crime that sent us after our last target, Officer John Ratcliff.

"At the end of the day, regardless of whether the rape charges against Bird were legitimate or not, we knew him as we knew him: a man of strong conviction that believed in our cause and was willing to give his life for it." Ish paused again and shook his head back and forth.

"What I would like to ask of you, the viewers, is that if you supported us before, please don't abandon us now over this scandalous news. Our mission statement is still the same; to deliver justice to those that can't find it themselves, and we'll keep doing this for as long as we can. But your support means everything, and we hope that you can understand.

"In conclusion, I would also like to ask you to remember that no one is perfect, and just because someone is flawed doesn't mean they can't do great things. A great example is Martin Luther King, Jr. He was strongly rumored to have been unfaithful to his wife on multiple occasions, but no one ever questioned his loyalty to the fight for civil rights. Thank you for your time and, hopefully, your continued support. We'll speak to you again soon. Until then, good day and stay safe."

"That's a wrap," said Chad.

Ish walked over to the nearest chair and lowered himself into it. He took off the masks and bowed his head. He wondered if what he had just done was a good thing or a travesty of justice. All he knew for sure at that moment was that he probably was not going to find the answer to that question tonight. Not unless it appeared at the bottom of a bottle of whiskey.

Chapter 77

When Ish called Madden, he answered on the second ring.

"10:00 on the dot," he said, his tone friendly. "Punctuality is an asset. I suppose it comes in handy as a soldier?"

Ish didn't respond.

"Okay," said Madden. "I guess it's straight to business. So, what is it that you wanted to speak about?"

"There are a few things on my mind," said Ish. "But let's address the elephant in the room first: Why haven't you turned me in?"

"I'm not even sure who you are yet," said Madden. "You could be a ghost for all I know. But that does beg another question: How do you know I haven't turned you in?"

"I know because if you had," said Ish, "my face would be plastered over every media screen in North America, and that's just for starters."

"You have a point," said Madden. "So, what are we doing? What exactly is the point of this call?"

"I just wanted to touch base with you," said Ish. "See how you were doing."

"Like two old friends, just hanging out at a bar?" asked Madden.

"Yeah, something like that," said Ish. "As a matter of fact, I have a drink in my hand right now, so that's quite an apt comparison."

"Nice," said Madden. "What's your poison of choice?"

"Scotch," said Ish. "*Camas an Staca.*"

"I'm a scotch man, too," said Madden. "But I've never heard of that. I imagine it's probably fairly high-end stuff?"

"One might say that," said Ish, taking a sip. "But it's worth it. It's good for the soul. Maybe when this is all over, I'll send you a bottle."

Madden chuckled. "Let's wait till we get to that point, and see how you feel then." There was a moment of silence between them. "You know, I've been a good boy this week, and it's Friday. I think I'll join you in a little nightcap. Let's see what the mini-bar has. Hmmm. Surprise, surprise, no *Camas an Staca*. I guess it's Johnny Walker Red for me."

Ish heard him screw the cap off the bottle and ice cubes dropping into a glass.

"So, I have to ask," said Madden. "Why did you stop your partner when he was about to fire on me?"

"For the same reason that you tried so hard to save his life," said Ish. "Because the death of either of you was not the mission. It was never our intention to harm innocents. And obviously it was not your intention the needlessly kill a suspect."

"How do you know I'm the one that tried to save his life?"

"I was there. I saw the whole thing."

"I see," said Madden. "Something else has been bugging me for a few days now. Let me know if I'm getting too personal, but I have to ask. You went after Janssen because you felt he deserved it. I understand that. The guy was an asshole, and then some. But how is it that you chose him over the cop that killed your daughter?"

Ish froze. Of all the things he imagined they might discuss, the death of Sumatra wasn't one of them.

"I'm sorry if I crossed a line there. You don't have to answer—"

"No," said Ish, pausing to take another sip of his drink. "It's actually a fair question. For one thing, I was too close. Not just because I would have immediately been a prime suspect, but because I was still too close emotionally. That wound was still fresh—*is* still fresh." He paused again.

"But more important," he continued, "is the fact that although that cop was directly responsible for the death of my daughter, and was probably a racist piece of shit for shooting at a black man trying to get into his own house, the reality is that he wasn't aiming at Sumatra. He didn't even know she was in the back of the house."

"I see your point," said Madden. "Sometimes intent is everything."

Ish took another sip in response. Suddenly he was feeling very tired. A weariness had crept into his bones that he did not think was associated with either the scotch or his recent difficulties sleeping.

"It's been great hanging out," he said, "but I think it's past my bedtime."

"Same here," said Madden. Ish could tell by the way he said it that there was something else he wanted to add, so he waited.

"I don't mean to spoil a great conversation," said Madden, "but you do know that eventually I'm going to have to bring you in, right?"

"I know you're eventually going to try. Goodnight, agent," said Ish as he hung up the phone. The game was heating up.

Chapter 78

Madden could feel his body starting to relax from the scotch. The stress was melting away as the buzz increased. He had always been a bit of a lightweight when it came to alcohol. Usually one drink was his limit, but after hanging up with Carter, he stared longingly at the mini-bar and decided he'd have another. What the hell; it was on the Bureau's dime.

Half an hour later he was staring out the window at the lights twinkling in the distance, when his phone rang. He looked at the number. Shit, it was Bainbridge—the call he'd been dreading all day. Something told him not to answer it, but he knew that would not go over well.

"This is Madden," he said as he answered, hoping that his words weren't sounding slurred.

"Bainbridge. Did I wake you?"

"I'm FBI. You know we never sleep," said Madden.

"That's what I like to hear. I meant to call earlier, but I've been in meetings with POTUS and his cronies all day. Anyway, I read your report and just called to say congratulations on capturing the first member of PROPR. That's one down and what, about four to go?"

"Well, it's hard to say exactly how many there are, but I think four sounds like a reasonable guess."

"By the way," said Bainbridge, his voice dropping a bit in volume, "that was a great job, making it look like you were trying to save him. It was great press for the department."

"What are you talking about? That wasn't an act. That man didn't need to die! If I could have brought him in alive, believe me, I would have."

"You listen to me!" Bainbridge hissed. "We already discussed this. I thought you understood the arrangement. I told you none of these people are to see the inside of a courtroom. You need to get your priorities straight and stop fucking around. Stop trying to be the white knight. You have no idea what you're messing with."

"Meaning?" asked Madden.

"Meaning the n—," said Bainbridge, catching himself. "Meaning the natives are getting restless. They're marching across the fucking nation in droves!"

"Natives?" Madden chuckled sarcastically. "Go ahead and say the word. Tell me how you really feel!"

"I'm sorry," said Bainbridge with feigned sincerity. "Did I hurt your feelings? Get the fuck over it! Either you solve this case by delivering me four more body bags, or your career is as dead as the 'nigger' that you just put a bullet in!"

The line went dead as Bainbridge hung up. Madden was actually trembling with rage. He had never really believed that Bainbridge was serious about killing the members of PROPR. And while he always knew that Bainbridge didn't care for blacks, he never imagined that he would actually say something like that out loud. He was now seeing the man with fresh eyes.

He looked down at the phone in his hand. He wanted to call him back, to cuss him out, to...to...he didn't know what. Something! He felt like throwing the phone out the window, packing his stuff, getting on a plane and going home to his wife. For good. He didn't need this shit! He could be working with her, relaxing by making things grow instead of watching things die.

No, he thought as he hung his head in defeat. He at least needed to finished this case. If Bainbridge wanted these guys this badly, Madden was probably the only one in the Bureau with a chance to keep them alive. But that was tomorrow. Right now, he needed another drink.

Chapter 79

Ish called for a meeting in Chad's room the following afternoon. There was a heaviness in the air. Even Jag was uncharacteristically subdued. It felt wrong, having the meeting without Bird present. But here they were.

"Before we get started," said Ish as he cleared his throat, "I'd like to have a moment of silence for Bird." Everyone nodded, then bowed their heads. A few moments later Ma'am's "Amen" ended the silence.

"I wanted to give you all an update on what we know," said Ish, "and go over some possible options for the path forward."

"First, I wanted to let you know that the FBI agent that, uh," he paused, bowing his head. "The agent that chased Bird and me is the agent that I've been speaking by phone with. He saw my face. He knows I'm the second suspect, the person that the news keeps reporting is still at large."

"So, if he saw you," said Ma'am, "why haven't they started a public manhunt?"

"I asked him that," said Ish, "and he failed to answered the question. But he's a brother. Maybe on some level he believes in what we're doing."

"So, you're saying the FBI agent has a conscience?" asked Jag, incredulous.

"I don't know. Maybe," said Ish. "But if that is the case, there's no telling how long his conscience will last. At any moment he could release my name, as well as all of yours, to the press. Chad has set up a Google alert so we'll know exactly when that happens. In the meantime, we need to forge some plans for where we go from here."

"What did you have in mind?" asked Ma'am. "We're open to whatever you'd like to do."

"Chad and I have come up with an idea. We want to offer you and Jag the opportunity to leave the country."

"Leave the country?" asked Ma'am, her voice sounding anxious. "Why? How?"

"Chad has checked the national databases, and as of an hour ago, none of our names were on any 'no fly' lists and our passports contain no restrictions. But we don't know how long that's going to last. So, if anyone is going to leave, now would probably be a good time."

"I can get any of us phony passports if need be," said Chad, "and I would recommend that anyway, just in case. But that's going to be a lot less of a hassle if they aren't already looking for us."

"What the hell would we do outside the country?" asked Jag. "And where would we go?"

"Well, we'd wire you some money into offshore accounts. Enough for you to live on for years, maybe even the rest of your life if you're careful. With that kind of money, you could go anywhere and do almost anything."

Ma'am and Jag stared at each other, and Ish could hear their minds calculating the possibilities.

"Ummm, well, do we have some time to think it over? Have a private discussion about it?" asked Jag.

"Absolutely," said Ish. "But remember, the clock is ticking. Once the FBI goes public with our names, they'll be looking for our faces at the airports, so even with fake passports, things could get a little dicey."

"What about you and Chad?" asked Ma'am. "Are you leaving, too? Is this the end of PROPR?"

"We're still a little bit undecided at this point," said Ish. "We have no idea if, or maybe I should say 'when', we'll become the subject of an all-out FBI pursuit. So, it's hard to plan the next move. I will say that we're not ready to close shop on PROPR just yet."

"Ish and I have a little bit of a difference of opinion on this," said Chad. "As far as I'm concerned, the only way I'd let PROPR die is if I'm killed or thrown into prison. I started all this with the idea that it was a cause worth dying for. Not the way Bird did it...no disrespect, Ma'am...but honorably, as a warrior on the front lines."

Ma'am stared hard at Chad, an intensity in her eyes. Ish couldn't tell what she was thinking, and for a moment it looked like she might attack him. Then her face visibly softened and she looked away.

"So, tell me, Chad," she said, still not looking at him. "What do you think is the ideal plan of action now, considering the situation?"

"I think we should continue what we've been doing: going after bad cops. There are hundreds and hundreds of people that have emailed us through the site, begging us to help them. There is no shortage of criminals dressed in blue uniforms, and there probably never will be. I say we keep bringing the war to the fuckers for as long as we can."

"I like a little piss with my vinegar too, son," said Jag, "but we're only four people. How much do you think you can get done? I joined this outfit with the understanding that we'd go after these first three targets and then reevaluate the situation. We've finished the third mission. Now the reevaluation needs to begin. Things are different now. Ma'am and I are...well, Ma'am and I are both in different places than we were when we started this thing."

"Yeah," said Chad, "I can see that you both have different priorities now, and that's cool. I mean, hey, I'm glad you found each other. You're good people, and I think you can create a great life together. But PROPR is my life now. I'm finally doing something that matters. A long time ago I thought that making a lot of money creating software for the government was the 'dream come true'. I was wrong."

Ma'am suddenly looked resolved, like she had just woken up from a dream herself.

"Jag is right," she said, looking at each of them in turn. "He and I need some time to discuss what we think would be the right move for us, but we can't do anything until after I bury my brother."

"Of course," said Chad. "Use the credit card I gave you for whatever you need. I can get you the numbers of a couple of places that can handle all the details. No one will ever be able to trace it back to you."

"What are you talking about? I have to be there when my brother is laid to rest. My family will be there. It's where I belong."

"I don't think that would be a good idea, Ma'am," said Ish. "Even though they haven't publicly released our names yet, there's a damn good chance that the FBI will be at the funeral, hoping to snatch us up nice and quietly."

"I don't give a damn about that!" said Ma'am, her voice rising as her eyes became glassy. "I can't let them put my brother in the ground without me being there, even if it means going to prison!"

Ish began rubbing his chin thoughtfully, then got up and walked to the sliding glass doors and looked out across the city.

"Ma'am is right," he said as he turned around to face the group. "Bird wasn't perfect, but he gave his life for the mission, and he deserves to be honored for it." Chad and Jag began nodding.

"You can count on me, Ma'am. Regardless of the consequences, I'll be there," said Chad.

"Babe, you know I go where you go," said Jag to Ma'am, smiling.

"The question is," said Ish, "is there a way for us to be there without delivering ourselves into custody?"

"I don't see how that would work," said Jag. "Disguises? I think the FBI would be able to figure that out within the amount of time a funeral service lasts."

"Ma'am, how many people do you expect to attend the funeral?" asked Ish.

"Not too many. Most of our people live outside California and won't travel this far. Plus, my brother and I have burned a few family bridges over the years. But he did have a few military and old college friends. I'd say probably somewhere around 50."

"Maybe with that amount of people, the FBI will be reluctant to approach us during the ceremony, for the safety of the other mourners. If so, then we'd only have to worry about getting out of the cemetery without being captured," said Chad.

"That's possible," said Ish, "but we can't count on that. Remember Ruby Ridge and Waco. They don't always care too much about collateral damage. No, we have to assume that if they have enough personnel there, they'll try to grab us as soon as they spot us."

"What if we could reduce the number of agents that are there?" asked Ma'am. "What if we could create some kind of diversion?"

"That'd be some huge fuckin' diversion," said Jag. "It would have to be bigger and juicer than capturing PROPR, and right now, what's bigger than PROPR?"

Ish began pacing back and forth across the room, rubbing his chin again. Everyone was deep in thought, apparently all working through the problem in their heads, frantically searching for a solution.

"Hold on," said Chad suddenly as he jumped up and ran to his laptop. "I saw something just yesterday..." He pecked rapidly at the keys for a few moments. "Yeah, here it is. What's considered an even bigger threat in this country than PROPR? How about ISIS?"

He smiled, looking around at everyone as he raised his eyebrows in giddy anticipation.

"I like it so far," said Ish. "What did you have in mind?"

"I remembered a headline yesterday that the mayor of Los Angeles is going to be visiting the VA hospital here next Thursday morning. Some kind of campaign push or something. Ma'am, could you arrange to have the funeral that same day and time?"

"Yeah, I don't think that would be a problem."

"Cool," said Chad, getting excited. "What if we could create the illusion that the hospital was being attacked by ISIS during the mayor's visit? Do you think that would be enough to get all the FBI agents in the city to make a bee-line there?"

"That might just be crazy enough to work," said Ish. "But it would take a hell of a lot of convincing to get the FBI to take the bait."

"I could intercept some police radios," said Chad. "Make it sound like an officer was calling it in."

"That's a start, but I don't think it would be enough," said Ish. "To get the entire Bureau's team to converge on one spot like that is going to take more than a couple of flatfoots calling in a few reports."

"What if we added some explosives?" asked Jag. "I could rig some timed charges in the parking lot around the hospital, maybe even get a couple in the lobby trashcans."

"Hmmm, we're getting warmer," said Ish. "But remember, we don't want any innocents getting hurt. But if you used flash bang charges..."

"Aren't those still kind of dangerous if they go off really close to someone?" asked Chad. "What if a kid is putting something into a trashcan at just the moment that it detonates?"

"True," said Jag slowly. "But one thing I could do is equip all the charges with a heat-activated sensor to create a proximity safety switch, which would cancel the detonation if a warm-blooded body is too close. Those sensors aren't cheap though."

"That's alright," said Ish. "I think we can afford it. What else?"

"I could send last minute alerts to all the major news services in the area," said Chad, "as well as 911 and the police and FBI 'hot tip' lines. All that chatter, combined with the explosions, and they won't be able to ignore it."

"You guys are geniuses," said Ish, smiling. "I think this just might work. We may be able to pay our respects to Bird and still keep our asses out of prison. At least for one more day, anyway. What do we need to get started?"

"I need to go on a supply run," said Jag. "Some of the stuff I can have mailed to me overnight to one of your anonymous mailing addresses. Some of it I may have to pick up in person. I'll also need to do a couple of recon runs out to the hospital. I could use a spotter."

"I'm down," said Chad. "I need to get out of here anyway. I'm starting to get antsy."

"And I'll get started on the funeral arrangements," said Ma'am. "I've been dreading making these phone calls to some family members that I haven't spoken to in years, but it's time."

"If there's anything that I can do to help you, Ma'am, you know you only have to ask," said Ish.

"Ish, you've already done so much. But thank you, brother."

"Hey, I'm not saying these meeting always have to be catered, but I'm starving," said Chad. "Who's up for some food?"

Ish gave them his order and then walked out onto the balcony for a moment of solitude. His thoughts wandered to Layla. He wondered what she was doing right now and what her current state of mind was. He hoped she'd be proud of him for what he had helped create with PROPR. Suddenly, he had some additional ideas that might give them some extra insurance at the funeral. He couldn't wait to go over it with the team during breakfast.

* * *

The funeral arrangements went off without a hitch. Ish, Chad and Jag decided it was safer to skip the viewing, but Ma'am threw caution to the wind and spent the week congregating, socializing and commiserating with many different friends and family members who were in town to pay their respects. She told Ish that if the FBI was looking for her, she wasn't going to worry right now about trying to make herself too hard to find. So far, her luck was holding.

On the day of the funeral, everything was ready. The explosives were set and all plans were in motion. Ish and Jag found the perfect recon spot at the top of a small, tree and bush-covered hill conveniently overlooking the cemetery. Using high-powered binoculars, they closely examined the area.

"Check out the guy raking leaves at six o'clock in the blue shirt," said Jag.

Ish adjusted his sight. "You're right. He looks a little too clean to be a grounds keeper. Plus, I can just make out the ear-bud in his ear. What is that now, ten?"

"Yep," said Jag. "Ten little FBI Indians, all in a row, waiting to grab little ol' us."

Ish and Jag both had their own ear-pieces, which linked them in two-way communication to both Ma'am and Chad.

"Chad," he said, "have you been able to tap into their radio signal yet?"

"Yes, I'm in," said Chad. "They've counted off. I can confirm that ten is the number in the immediate area. There are also two full SWAT teams and a helicopter two miles away, all just waiting for the order to move in on the cemetery."

"Perfect. And the stand-ins?"

"All suited and booted and waiting for us in the SUVs."

"Excellent. We have twenty-two minutes till blast off. Better send out your alerts to the news and police. We'll meet you at the spot."

"Roger that," said Chad.

It took Ish and Jag nine minutes to drive down the hill and join Chad and Ma'am at the meeting place, which was the underground parking lot of a nearby mall about twelve blocks away. There, they had gathered together twelve identical black SUVs, all with dark tinted windows and identical temporary paper license plates. Each SUV had a driver who they had hired. In the back of eight of the SUVs were the stand-ins—actors they had also hired, each bearing a striking resemblance to a member of the PROPR team.

The actors were body doubles, and there were two of each. They had the same physical build and skin tone as Ish, Jag, Chad and

Ma'am, and they were all wearing the same exact matching outfit and had the same hair styles. All of them, including Ma'am's two doubles, were wearing black business suits with white shirts, black ties, and matching dark shades.

Ish and Jag got out of the car to meet Ma'am and Chad, and they all embraced.

"So, are we all set?" he asked.

"Locked and loaded," said Chad.

Ish looked at his watch, where a digital countdown timer was showing T minus three minutes. "Alright," he said. "Let's move out."

They were still several blocks from the cemetery when Ish's ear-bud beeped.

"The explosive charges have started going off," said Chad, "and the team at the funeral are all getting new instructions. Hold on."

A moment later he began speaking again.

"They're calling off almost everyone, including the SWAT teams, but are still leaving two agents and the helicopter there. The two agents were told to follow you, Ish."

"That doesn't surprise me," said Ish. "But two agents, we can deal with."

The service was beautiful. Ish kept one eye on the two agents the entire time, while Chad continued to monitor the radio chatter. As the service was ending, Ish gave the signal to Chad to have the doubles exit the vehicles and join the crowd.

Suddenly, there were three Ishs, three Chads, three Jags and three Ma'ams all moving through the crowd in various directions. Moments later Ish heard the helicopter appear overhead.

"Let's hit the road," he said, and on that signal Ish, Jag, Chad and Ma'am, plus their eight doubles, all entered a separate black SUV. The SUVs moved out together, driving at a moderate speed, but constantly changing position so that in the event that someone had been able to spot which vehicle the 'real' Ish had entered, they would now be thoroughly confused. At a pre-determined intersection, the twelve vehicles split up, all moving in different directions. From the air it must have looked like a black rose that had suddenly blossomed. The two agents and the helicopter that was trying to follow them didn't have a chance.

Chapter 80

"How difficult can it be to follow one fucking guy?" asked Madden. He was driving, with Phillips in the passenger seat beside him, and he was so pissed he could feel the heat emanating from his body.

"Technically, it wasn't just one guy," said Phillips. "It was at least three. And all we had were two sedans and a chopper. The truth is, they planned this very, very well."

Madden knew that it was unfair to direct his anger at Phillips, even as he was in the process of doing it, but his frustration level was in the red.

"What did the bomb squad have to report?" he asked, exasperated.

Phillips cleared her throat. "Unfortunately, not much. All those explosions were simple flash bang grenades. There were thirty-six devices altogether, but only twenty-three of them actually detonated," she said as she read a report on her laptop.

"So, a third of them were duds?"

"No. Apparently they were set to self-deactivate if a body triggered an attached heat sensor within a certain window of time."

Madden looked confused. "Why the hell would the perps do that?"

Phillips shrugged. "Public safety?"

Madden nodded solemnly and returned his attention to the road. He was tired. They had just spent nine hours at the VA. For all the manpower they had diverted there, which was probably half the law enforcement available in the city of Los Angeles at the time, they didn't have shit to show for it. No fingerprints, no surveillance photos, no witnesses. They didn't even have any suspects. But only a blind man would fail to see that it was more than coincidence that this hospital 'attack' happened at the same exact time the gang from PROPR were attending a funeral service on the other side of town.

"Have you heard from Bainbridge?" asked Phillips.

Madden sighed heavily. "Not yet, but I'm expecting his call at any minute." He didn't add that it was the last phone call in the world he wanted to answer right now.

"If you don't mind, I'd like to go over the incidence reports over dinner, while it's still fresh in my mind," he said to Phillips as he pulled into the parking lot of their hotel.

"That's fine. I'll order dinner now so they can bring it up when it's ready. Would you like the fish again?" asked Phillips.

"Sure."

Ten minutes later they were in his room, and he was rolling up his sleeves as Phillips started pulling up documents on the laptop when there was a knock at the door.

"That was fast," he said as he walked to the door. "We must have missed the dinner rush."

When Madden opened the door, he was shocked to find not room service, but A.D. Bainbridge, in the flesh. He involuntarily took a step back.

"Good evening, Madden," said Bainbridge, stepping into the room without waiting for an invitation.

"Sir?" said Madden. He turned to look at Phillips, who appeared equally confused.

"Ummm, to what do we owe the honor?" asked Madden after a moment of waiting as Bainbridge stared back and forth at the two of them.

"Oh, I don't know," said Bainbridge, an evil smirk playing at the corner of his mouth. "Your incompetence?"

Madden was stunned into silence. He literally did not know what to say.

"Relax," said Bainbridge, his smile broadening as he patted Madden on the shoulder. "I'm just here to have a little chat." He began unbuttoning his jacket as he turned to face Phillips. "Can we have the room, please?"

"Sure," said Phillips. She gathered up her laptop and a stack of notes and headed for the door.

"Thank you, Agent Phillips," said Bainbridge as she pulled the door open. Phillips just nodded, but something in the exchange gave Madden the impression that Bainbridge wasn't just thanking her for leaving the room.

"Can I get you something to drink?" asked Madden. "I have water, juice..."

"Water is fine," said Bainbridge as he took a seat, crossing his legs and folding his hands in his lap.

"You should have told us you were coming. We could have ordered you some dinner," said Madden as he grabbed a bottle of water from the mini-fridge and poured it into a glass. "Are you staying here in the hotel?"

"Yes," said Bainbridge. "As a matter of fact, I'm in the suite right next door."

Madden handed him his water and he took a sip.

"Ahhh, that's refreshing," he said as he sat his glass down on the table. "But you know what isn't refreshing? Getting a report that you had the chance to catch the rest of these clowns and that you let them all get away."

"With all due respect," said Madden, pausing to let the words sink in, "it wasn't quite that simple. We got a call that there was a possible terrorist attack in progress at a location in which the mayor of Los Angeles and other prominent city officials were present. Protocol dictated that we offer all possible assistance."

"I don't want to hear about protocol!" screamed Bainbridge. "You were in charge here. It was your job to carry out the orders you had been given. Priority one should have been the 'containment' of the people we've identified as suspects in the PROPR investigation."

"I understand that," said Madden, who was starting to recover from the shock of the surprise visit. "But you have to remember, these people are not even hard suspects. They're just persons of interest at this point. If they were hard suspects, we'd have already issued nationwide APBs on them."

Anger flashed in Bainbridge's eyes. "That is not the reason that we haven't issued APBs, and the fact that you aren't acknowledging that is evidence that either you're a complete fool or that you're consciously choosing to blatantly disobey the directives that I gave you regarding this case!"

"If you're referring to your order to shoot these people on sight, then yes, sir, I have blatantly chosen to disobey that directive! Or have you conveniently forgotten our last conversation?"

Bainbridge's face blanched briefly before color sprung to his cheeks. He took a deep breath and smiled slightly, shaking his head as he stared at the floor.

"Now is not the time to deal with your insubordination. We'll handle that back in D.C. once this investigation is over. I'd send you back now, but we're shorthanded enough as it is. At any rate, you clearly no longer have what it takes to handle this case, so I'll be taking over, effective immediately," said Bainbridge. He rose from the chair.

"Understood," said Madden.

"Meeting in my suite, 5:00am. Alert the team. I want everyone in attendance," said Bainbridge, and without another word, he exited the room.

Madden was still sitting in his seat and staring at the wall, fuming and trying to calm himself down when he heard a knock at the door. He opened the door to find Phillips standing there, her face dark with concern.

"Is everything alright?" she asked.

He stepped aside to let her enter and flopped into a chair. "No, I don't think things have been alright with this job for some time now."

"Is there anything I can do?" she asked.

Madden shook his head, while making a mental note that although she was saying all the things that a concerned friend or colleague would say, there was also a strange look in her eyes, and several times she avoided meeting his gaze.

"Oh, by the way, I'm no longer the head of this investigation. Bainbridge is taking over. Please send a text to the rest of the team that we are to meet with him tomorrow, 5:00am."

Phillips pulled out her phone and began to type deftly with her thumbs.

"So, I take it he blamed you for Carter getting away?"

Madden paused, wondering exactly how much he should be saying to her.

"You could say that," he said. "Look, I'll admit that Carter probably organized the VA stunt, but we had no alternative but to respond the way we did. No one could have guessed at the time we began receiving the reports that the terrorist attack was a decoy," he said.

"True," she said. She again avoided looking him in the eye.

"But?" he asked.

"You're right, there was no way for you to connect the two. But you already know that I think you've been going a little easy on Carter from the beginning."

"Jesus Christ, not this again," he said.

"I'm speaking to you as a friend," she said. "I don't want to see you end your career like this, over something silly. If you just follow orders, we can get through this."

"Something silly? Just follow orders? You don't know the half of what's involved with this," said Madden. "For example, do you know that Bainbridge ordered me to make sure that none of our suspects in the case make it to court alive?"

She seemed frazzled by the question. Her mouth dropped open. "I, uh, did not."

"So, you say I should follow orders. Are you prepared to gun these guys down in the street to comply with Bainbridge's 'orders'?"

"No," she said, shaking her head from side to side. "We're not...assassins. I just want to do my job, that's all. Anyway," she added, lightly slapping her hands on her thighs and rising from the chair, "I'd better go get some sleep. I'll see you in the morning."

As she rushed out the door, Madden stared after her. Her behavior had continued to be increasingly odd and out of character. His instincts told him that someone was communicating with Bainbridge directly, feeding him inside intel on their investigation. Could it be Phillips? Could she have betrayed him? It was hard to imagine, but anything was possible. What was undeniable was that Bainbridge was clearly out to destroy him, and a showdown was coming. He couldn't help but wonder what side Phillips would be on when it arrived.

Chapter 81

After the success of the funeral diversion, Ish and the gang decided it was time for each of them to change hotels. Ish and Chad had some work from the office that needed catching up on, so while they dealt with that, working out of a Santa Monica coffee shop, Ma'am and Jag handled getting them checked out of their current hotels and set up elsewhere.

Ish was swigging the last dregs of a stale *Americano* when Ma'am and Jag sauntered into the shop and slid into the seat directly across from him and Chad. The coffee shop they were in was a very modern affair, spacious and spotless. It was well lit and appointed with tasteful art on the walls, some of which was apparently for sale. It was decorated with several sofas, love seats and plush leather chairs, situated around sturdy art deco tables. There was enough room between them that it gave the customers a sense of some degree of separation, if not real privacy. It was one of the reasons Ish and Chad liked it so much and were regulars there.

"You're all set," said Ma'am, sliding two room keys across the table. There was one for Ish and one for Chad, each with a post-it note attached to it. On the notes were addresses. Ish smiled when he saw his.

"What?" asked Ma'am.

"Nothing," said Ish. "It's just that I know this hotel."

"You want me to switch it?" she asked.

"No, it's cool. I haven't been there in years, but I have fond memories. It'll be nice to spend some time in a place that's somewhat familiar for a bit."

"Hey, check this out," said Chad, angling his laptop so that they could all see it better. He leaned forward and lowered his voice. "That last video we released was a real hit. I created this little bit of code, a data scraper that scours the net looking for comments related to PROPR and determining whether those comments are positive or negative. Before the video, we were down twenty-seven points from where we were before Bird's death. Now we've totally reversed that and we're actually up eight points!"

"Thank God," said Ish. "The people at #BlackForLife are going to be happy to about that, because if our numbers are up, it means their numbers are up."

"That's good to hear," said Ma'am. "After this week, I need some good news."

Ish reached across the table and patted her arm and gave it a squeeze. His phone rang and he excused himself to go outside and take the call. When he returned a few minutes later, he was smiling widely.

"I have a bit more good news," he said. "That was Virginia Goldberg, Blade's sister. I guess all this news coverage has gotten the Baltimore PD lawyers nervous. They just offered the family $3.2M to settle the lawsuit, and they're going to accept."

"That's awesome!" said Jag as everyone exchanged high-fives.

"They even offered to give me half the settlement, but I asked them to donate it to #BlackForLife instead. They need it more than we do."

"You're a good man," said Ma'am.

"Thanks," said Ish and then looked around to make sure he wouldn't be overheard by anyone else in the cafe. "But listen, this doesn't change the fact that we're still prime targets of a massive search. Our identities haven't hit the news yet, so that makes us harder to find, but still, I think we should spend at least the next week or so laying low."

"And doing what?" asked Jag.

"Whatever," he said. "You don't necessarily have to stay indoors. Go see a movie. Eat something other than take out or room service. Go for a bike ride on the beach. Anything that keeps you out of trouble while we make plans for where we're going from here. You can even do some traveling if you like, though I'd restrict it to places you can drive to. We probably want to stay out of train stations, bus stations and airport terminals. Just to be safe."

"Roger that," said Jag.

"By the way," said Ish, "are you two still considering our offer to leave the country?"

"We are," said Ma'am. "I'm sorry, but it was so hectic planning the funeral that I haven't really had a moment to be in the right headspace to talk about it with Jag. Can we have another few days? I swear we'll have an answer for you by the end of the week."

"No problem," said Ish. "We don't want you to rush. We want you to be sure. But don't take too long." He stretched his arms and stifled a yawn.

"If there's nothing else, I think I'm about ready to get out of here," he said. "Anyone up for going out for a drink?"

"No, I think we're going to call it an early night," said Ma'am. "Jag and I have laundry to do, among other things."

"She means I've done run out of clean drawers!" said Jag, grinning.

"I'd love to join you, Ish," said Chad, "but I still need to spend a few more hours tonight on my part of this project if we're to meet our DoD deadline next week."

"You need my help?" asked Ish.

"Thanks, but no. I should have been working instead of cruising social media."

"Well, let me know if you change your mind," said Ish.

"Will do, but there is something I just heard that I'd like to play for you before you take off. I'll walk you to your car. You two might want to join us," he added, nodding at Ma'am and Jag.

Fifteen minutes later they were all packed up and sitting in Ish's rented Range Rover in an empty parking lot across from the coffee house. Chad began connecting his laptop to the car's wi-fi so they could hear the audio through the car speakers.

"It had been a few days since I was able to check the recordings picked up by the femtocell," said Chad, "but I started playing it in the background a few hours ago, and this is what I heard."

He played two conversations between Madden and Bainbridge. The first was from the night that Madden and Ish shared their 'virtual' drink, and the second was from a few nights later, when Bainbridge arrived at Madden's hotel.

"Muthafucka," whispered Ma'am. "They don't even wanna give us the fairness of a court trial! I guess I shouldn't be surprised. After all, it's the exact kind of behavior that got us started down this road in the first place."

"At least we know what we're working with. More importantly, though," said Ish smiling, "is that we now have some leverage. This recording gives us the kind of power that a bullet never could. Chad, get this to the lawyers, please. Make sure they know what to do with it should anything ever happen to us."

"I thought you'd say that," Chad answered. "I already started drafting an email. I'll send it as soon as I get back to the room."

As Ish drove back to his hotel, with Dexter Gordon's *Don't Explain* playing on the stereo, he should have felt relaxed. The recordings of Bainbridge's assassination order should have given him a sense of relief. But instead, he just felt emotionally exhausted. He was thinking about Bird. He missed his old friend, regardless of what the news reports said about him, and was again wrestling with his guilt. He also missed his girls—Layla and Sumatra.

He had almost made it to the hotel when he hit a U-turn and drove to his favorite liquor store. He bought two bottles of *Camas*. The cashier wasn't the regular guy, and Ish could feel the suspicion coming out of the man's pores in waves as he ran Ish's credit card twice to make sure it was valid. Ish was too tired to even be pissed off.

He ran through a drive-thru a few blocks from the hotel and grabbed a burger and some fries, but somehow, he felt he was probably going to be doing more drinking tonight than eating.

Ish was sitting on the floor of his hotel room, gazing at a half-empty bottle of *an Staca* and marveling at how the light in the room reflected off the amber color of the liquid when his phone rang. It was a blocked number. He took a deep breath before he answered it.

He took another deep breath as he patiently waited for the recording to finish announcing the fact that the call was from a California jail.

"Hey, love," said Layla.

"Hey, babe," he replied.

"What's that I hear in your voice?" she asked. "Is that *Camas*?"

Ish chuckled. "Damn, nothing gets by you. I've been thinking about you all day. How are you?"

"I'm..." she began, before sighing heavily. "I'm fine. I'm fine."

"What's wrong?" he asked, sitting up straighter and putting his glass on the floor beside him.

"It's just that I spoke to the lawyers today. Aquila. Actually, we spoke twice, once yesterday and then again this morning."

"What happened?" said Ish.

"He came by yesterday to say that the 'order to dismiss' was on the brink of being signed, and that I'd probably be out within the next two weeks. He said he had spoken to the judge personally, and that they were just waiting for his clerk to gather all the paperwork."

"That's great news, babe!"

"Well, yeah, I guess it was," said Layla. "But he came back today and said it was all off."

"What do you mean off?"

"Off. Done. Canceled," said Layla. "In his words, it was 'summarily voided'.

"What the hell happened?!"

"He has no clue. He can't even get the judge to speak to him. His best guess is that maybe some local politician got wind of it and decided to make a political statement by pulling some strings to get it denied," she said, sighing again.

"But fuck it," she continued. "It's obvious I was meant to stay right where I am. I wasn't even sure I was totally ready to be released. For a moment, I thought it might be worth a try, but I was just fooling myself."

"Babe, don't say that—"

"No, it's true," she said. "You know, Sumatra came to me last night and she was crying; sobbing. I couldn't get her to stop. I'm surprised it didn't wake up my cell mate."

Ish felt the tears begin to stream from his eyes.

"I'm so sorry, babe," he said. "Don't worry, we'll figure something out. We'll get you out of there, one way or another. You just have to stay strong."

"Ish, I know you mean well, but I don't need to hear that shit right now. I need to stay focused so I can cope with the rest of my life here. Or, at least, the next few years."

"I know. I'm sorry," he said. He got up and walked to the window, taking in the spectacular view before him.

"You know," he said, "one of the things that got me thinking so much about you today is that I was thinking about the night that Sumatra was born."

"Yeah?" she asked. "What brought that on?"

"I can see the hospital from where I am," he said as he took a large swallow of scotch. "I'm looking down on the parking lot as we speak. I still remember how worried I was that something was going to go wrong. And how Mama spent two days in this same hotel just so she could be close in case it did."

"Those were better times," she said wistfully.

"We'll get it back," he whispered.

"Hey, I've got to go. It's almost 'lights out'. I just wanted to give you an update. Aquila said he would call you but I told him I'd rather do it myself."

"Thanks," said Ish. "I love you."

"I love you, too."

"Layla?"

"Yeah?"

"If you see Sumatra tonight...give her a kiss for me and tell her Daddy said 'hi'."

"I will," she said.

Chapter 82

Ish woke up with a massive headache. One bottle of the expensive scotch was laying empty on its side on the nightstand. The other was in much better shape but had survived a serious attack. He stumbled into the bathroom to relieve himself, then walked back to the living room and turned on the TV.

He didn't know if it was serendipity or if it was just a reflection of how much media attention they were receiving, but the first three news channels he turned to showed either pictures of Khadija and Marquita or scenes from #BlackForLife's 'Black March For Peace'. He paused on CNN.

"So what, then, is #BlackForLife's exact relationship with PROPR, if any?" a pretty female Asian reporter asked Marquita, who was standing behind Khadija, who was sitting in a wheelchair.

"Let me be perfectly clear," said Marquita, looking directly into the camera, "#BlackForLife has never had any kind of relationship with PROPR. Not only that, but as we have publicly stated many times before, we categorically condemn all of their actions and everything they stand for."

"But isn't it true," asked the reporter, "that both of your organizations claim to be primarily concerned with justice for minorities?"

"Just because we have the same end goal doesn't mean there is any kind of association between us. #BlackForLife Is. Non. Violent," said Marquita, slapping her fist into her palm to emphasize each word. "We don't know how else to say it. You media people love to paint us all with the same broad brush because it gets you ratings to do so, but it is not the truth, and we will not be misrepresented!"

"Thank you," said the reporter as she turned to the camera, smiling. "We have been speaking to—"

Ish changed the channel. It was MSNBC displaying a night scene, showing a throng of people moving down a street. Most of them were people of color. Some were wearing bandanas as masks. Some were yelling and laughing, others looked somber and serious. Many of them were holding signs or waving banners, some of which had the phrase "#BlackForLife" with a red circle around it and a diagonal line through the circle.

"...and since the wheelchair-bound Khadija Syed joined the cross-country trek, the popularity of the #BlackForLife movement has been once again growing by leaps and bounds," said a young white man who was holding a microphone and standing on a street corner, watching the crowd flowing past him.

"It's a story that has captured the heartstrings of the American public," the reporter continued, "and every day the crowd of supporters joining them on their 'Black March For Peace' grows. However, as you can see behind me, there is a more militant segment of the black community expressing themselves in competing protests. They claim to have no faith in a non-violent solution to the problem of racial inequality.

"In spite of the differences between these two groups of protesters, they had managed to keep things fairly peaceful. That is, until last night, when things turned violent in three separate cities simultaneously as police and protesters clashed. Many witnesses at the scenes stated that the police were the cause when they began attacking protesters for no reason, often targeting the phones that the protesters were using to shoot videos. The police tell a different story, one of protesters that were out of control.

"To show you just how complicated and chaotic things got, here is footage from San Francisco of an incident in which, right in the middle of a fight between protesters and police, several officers were filmed stripping off their uniform shirts to the white undershirts beneath and joining the protesters! Yes, officers were actually walking off the job to become one with the mob. It's one of the most fascinating things I've ever seen."

* * *

Ish was about to walk out the door on his way to the hotel's gym to sweat some of the previous evening's alcohol out of his system when his phone rang. It was his mother calling.

"Hey, Mama."

"Hey, baby, how are you?"

"I'm fine. How are you?"

"Fair to middling."

"I've been meaning to call you," said Ish, "but things have been hectic as usual."

"That's okay," said his mother. "The reason I'm calling is that another FBI agent showed up asking questions about you yesterday."

"Really?"

"Yes. He left his card. His name was Bainbridge. Associate Director Wesley Bainbridge."

"What did he want?" asked Ish.

"Same as the other one. Asked if I had seen you or knew where you were. He said he needed to ask you a few questions, but wouldn't say about what."

"Don't worry, Mama. I have everything under control. I'm sorry these agents keep bothering you. I'll see what I can do about that."

"Just be careful, Ishmael," said his mother. "The first two agents that came by, the man and the pretty girl with the limp, they were friendly. I got a good vibe from them. But this Bainbridge is different. There's something dark about him. Having him here with me, alone in my house, scared me a bit."

"Did he do something to you?" asked Ish, his voice sharp.

"No, nothing like that. It was just a vibe. Just a feeling," said his mother. "All I'm saying is be careful. Watch yourself out there."

"Thanks, Mama. I will," said Ish. "And I'll come see you soon. Maybe we can grab lunch or something."

"I'd love that, son."

After hanging up with his mother, Ish sat on the couch and began weighing his options. He needed some more data. He dialed Madden's number. When Madden answered, Ish said five words: "I'll call back at midnight," and immediately hung up. He spent the rest of the day running errands and working on office business. He purposely avoided all alcohol so that he'd be at his most coherent when he and the agent spoke.

Ish called at exactly 12:00, and Madden answered on the first ring.

"I didn't expect to hear from you so soon," said Madden.

"I didn't expect to call so soon," said Ish. "But something's come up. Another FBI agent went to see my mother. His name was Bainbridge. Is this guy with you?"

"Yes," said Madden. "Actually, he's my boss. I had no idea he had gone to see your mother. He's kind of frozen me out of certain aspects of the investigation. Without having a lot to go on, he must be retracing my steps, gathering his own information."

"My mother said she felt frightened when he was there."

"I can understand that," said Madden. "Bainbridge is intense. And relentless. It's only a matter of time before he starts to get more aggressive, begins making some hard moves."

"Like what?" asked Ish.

"I don't know," said Madden. "Maybe he'll charge your mother with harboring a fugitive."

"How can he do that when I haven't even seen her in weeks?"

"He doesn't care about that. It's not about sending your mother to jail. It's about smoking you out into the light."

"You can't do anything to steer him away from her?" asked Ish.

"I wish I could," said Madden. "If it were up to me, the man wouldn't be working in law enforcement, period. But he runs the show right now. It's out of my hands."

"Then I guess I'm going to have to see what my hands can do with it," said Ish.

"Don't go getting yourself into worse trouble," said Madden.

"What kind of worse trouble?" asked Ish. "I'm not going to go do a drive-by on the man. But I do have a couple of tricks up my sleeves. Quiet, non-violent tricks, but they might prove effective."

"I don't know what that means," said Madden, "but what I will tell you is this: Bainbridge is a major asshole, but he's also really, really sharp. So, watch yourself out there."

"You're starting to sound like my mother," said Ish, smiling.

"Alright, alright," said Madden. "Is there anything else?"

"No," said Ish, "I think that's about it."

"Are you sure you don't want to change your mind about surrendering to me? It's the surest way I know to avoid all this nonsense and keep you, and the rest of your family, safe."

"I wish I could but..." said Ish.

"I know, I know. It's not in your nature. Have yourself a good night. And stay in touch."

"Will do," said Ish.

After he hung up with Madden, Ish called Chad.

"Hey, dude," said Chad when he answered. "How'd it go?"

"Pretty much as I expected," said Ish. "There's nothing he can do. The guy is his boss. We're going to have to rein this dude in ourselves. Is the recording safe?"

"Safe and sound on a flash drive in the safes of three different attorneys. If any one of them don't hear from either you or I once a week, they'll automatically turn the recording over to the Los Angeles D.A. as well as the editors of several newspapers, including the good ol' L.A. Times. Are you ready to make contact with Bainbridge?"

"Not quite yet. I don't want to show our hand too soon," said Ish. "We need to make sure all our ducks are in a row before we make the big reveal."

"Makes sense."

"There's also a new wrinkle to the narrative," said Ish. "I didn't mention it to Madden, but I suspect that this guy Bainbridge might be behind the cancellation of Layla's appeal."

"Serious?" said Chad. "It seems to me it would make more sense to let her out and then follow her, if his main objective is to find you."

"True, except that we already embarrassed them at the funeral. He probably doesn't want to risk it," said Ish. "Hell, for all we know, he may have been the one that originally pushed the appeal through, and then changed his mind once he saw how easily we eluded them at the cemetery. Anyway, on to other business. What's the rest of the week looking like for you?"

"Pretty packed," said Chad. "Remember, we have that meeting with the DoD team Wednesday, and Friday is the deadline for the testing on the Protocol G program."

"That's right. I almost forgot. But that's great. It'll keep us busy and give Ma'am and Jag a few more days to make a decision about our offer. I'll let them know that we want to meet, let's say Sunday morning, to finalize everything."

"Sounds good," said Chad. "I'll reserve us a table for breakfast at Clementine's."

Little did Ish know at the time that none of them would make it to that reservation.

Chapter 83

Madden walked into his hotel room, kicked off his shoes and fell back onto the bed. His feet hurt and he was exhausted. For the last couple of days Bainbridge had kept him busy with the VA hospital investigation. Of course, they all now knew that it was a hoax and were convinced that it was orchestrated by PROPR, but what Bainbridge had him doing was just 'busy work', assigned for the primary purpose of keeping him out of the loop and in the dark on whatever it was Bainbridge was ultimately planning.

Phillips had been spending her time with Bainbridge and the team of agents he had brought with him. So far, Madden wasn't privy to whatever it was that she was doing with him. He had passed her in the hallway and casually asked her about it, but all she would say was that she was reading through 'tons of reports', whatever that exactly meant. Madden was pretty sure there was more to it than that, but now wasn't the time to try to push her.

He used the room phone to order dinner then walked into the bathroom and splashed some water on his face. He scrutinized his face in the mirror.

"This is crazy," he said to himself out loud. "Are you sure you really want to do this?" He shook his head. The truth was that he wasn't sure, but he was going to do it anyway.

He walked out of the bathroom, sat down on the edge of the bed, and pulled the new phone out of his briefcase. He stared at it intensely for a moment before he even took it out of the packaging. It was a prepaid cellphone that he had picked up on his way back to the hotel and paid for in cash. It was probably safe for him to use his Bureau-issued phone, but with Bainbridge sneaking around, the only way he could be absolutely sure of his privacy was to use a throw-away.

It came fully charged, so he was able to use it immediately. He opened the web browser and navigated to the PROPR website. He clicked on the 'Contact Us' button and a dialog box popped open. He left the 'name' and 'email' fields blank and scrolled down to comments section. He paused again, then began typing.

"Carter, it's your old drinking buddy. Loved our chat the other night about your forthcoming hunting expedition. I may be interested in tagging along. I also have info on some new changes to the poaching restrictions that are going into effect very soon. Give me a call tomorrow at midnight @ 555-684-3766. We'll talk turkey."

He stopped and stared at the 'submit' button, willing himself to press it while at the same time trying to convince himself to delete the entire thing and throw the phone away.

A knock at the door gave him a start. He placed the phone in his briefcase, locked it and answered the door. It was room service. After signing the receipt and thanking the server, he turned on the TV, sprinkled a bit of salt and pepper on his food and began eating, but his eyes kept being drawn back to the locked briefcase that was sitting on the bed.

Finally, he stopped what he was doing, walked over to the bed and retrieved the phone. The message was still there on the display, waiting for him to make a decision.

"Fuck it," he muttered as he pressed 'submit'. He set a password on the phone, powered it off and, using a chair, hid it in one of the room's ceiling tiles. As he sat back down to eat, he realized that his appetite had suddenly disappeared.

The next night, Madden retrieved the prepaid phone from the ceiling at 11:50pm, and it buzzed at exactly 12:00 midnight.

"I'm glad to see you monitor your emails closely," Madden said by way of greeting. "I thought I might have to wait days for you to get the message."

"I've missed you, too," said Ish. "What's going on?"

"Remember I told you that my boss, Bainbridge, had taken over the investigation?"

"Yeah?"

"Well, there's a little more to it than that. This man has a real hard-on for you and your group. You're familiar with the phrase 'wanted dead or alive'? Well, he'd very much prefer the former."

"I see," said Ish. "I asked you once before why you're helping me, and you didn't answer the question, so I'm asking again. Why?"

"I'm just doing my job, man, which is simply to deliver suspects to a courtroom so that they can be fairly judged. I failed with your friend, but I did my best."

"Understood. So, what exactly are you expecting me to do with this news?" asked Ish.

Madden paused briefly before he answered. "I'd like you and your group to turn yourselves in. To me."

Ish chuckled softly. "Turn ourselves in? Are you serious?"

"As I said before, it's the best way I know to keep you all safe," said Madden. "Bainbridge is a dangerous man. He will stop at nothing to get you, and get you his way, and he has a lot of resources at his disposal to do so. So far, I've been able to keep your name out of the press and the rest of the law enforcement community, but as his frustration continues to mount, it's only a matter of time before that changes. With a nation of pissed-off 'boys in blue' gunning for you, your chances of becoming the victim of an 'incident' are greatly increased. I don't want to see that happen."

"I'm touched by your concern," said Ish. Madden couldn't tell by his voice whether he was being sincere or sarcastic. "But I can't do that. I'll have to take my chances in the street."

"I thought you might say that," said Madden, "but I had to at least ask. Just remember that you're not the kind of person that can easily blend into the background. Physically, you stand out like a sore thumb."

"You're right," said Ish. "But rolling over isn't in my nature. We started this for a reason, and that reason hasn't changed. The need is still there. We still have work to do."

"You're not going to be very productive from a grave."

"And how much more productive do you think I'd be from a prison cell?"

"At least you'd be alive."

"Alive is not necessarily the same as living."

Madden nodded in response, even though he knew the other man couldn't see him. "Well, watch yourself out there," he said, "and if you need to reach me in the future, use this number. It's private. You can leave a message."

"Thanks," said Ish. "I appreciate the heads up."

They said goodbye, and as Madden placed the phone back in its hiding place, he couldn't help but feel that he should have said more.

Early the next morning, the first thing Madden did upon waking was contact L.A. County Jail and OCJ and have the last three months of Layla's recorded phone calls uploaded to a secure FBI cloud server, where he could access them.

As soon as he heard the latest call, in which Carter mentioned that he was gazing at the hospital in which his daughter was born, he knew what he needed to do. He quickly logged into a database, and within minutes knew the name of the hospital. He pulled out his phone and quick-dialed a number.

"Robinson, it's Madden," he said when the phone was answered. "I need a favor."

Patrick Robinson was an agent that Madden went back years with. They had hung out with each other's families, and Madden knew he was not only a great guy, but someone that could be totally trusted to be discrete. In addition, along with another well-trusted agent, Bill Derry, they were both conveniently in L.A. as part of the team working on the PROPR case.

"Sure, Chief," said Robinson. "What can I do for you?"

"I need you to burn some shoe leather for me," said Madden. "I need some hotels checked out here in town. Basically, any hotel with windows that offer a line-of-sight with Holy Lutheran Hospital. We're looking for anyone at the hotels or adjacent businesses that might recognize a picture of one of the PROPR suspects. But Pat, I need you to keep this under your hat. Not even Bainbridge can know about it right now. So, there's a possibility you might catch a little heat from it later."

"As many times as you've helped me out, I'd be glad to do it," said Robinson. "How quickly do you need it? It could take some time."

"As quickly as possible," said Madden. "I'll be calling Derry next, and hopefully he'll be up for helping you. I'm also going to send you two locals that can help share the load."

"Got it," said Robinson. "Text me the info, and I'll get right on it."

"Thanks," said Madden before he hung up and began scrolling through his contact list for Bill Derry's number.

The two locals he was referring to were Stephen Provsky and Richard Welborn, the two agents who had been guarding Janssen. They had both caught a lot of shit from their bosses due to how that situation had gone down, and Madden had felt bad about it because they both seemed like good guys. His instincts told him that they would be open to the possibility of making amends by helping with this operation, and they didn't report to Bainbridge, so it would be easier to keep their involvement quiet.

Three more phone calls and he had a four-man team on the way to canvas the areas around the hotels, looking for anyone who might recognize Carter as a guest, past or present. He was holding his breath that one of them would get a hit, and that they'd find Carter staying at one of the hotels. If they could locate him, he felt pretty confident that the five of them could take him into custody without incident. It might be the only way to save the man's life.

Two hours later his phone buzzed. Welborn already had a match.

Chapter 84

Before he had a chance to act on the hotel lead, Madden was summoned to Bainbridge's room, which had become the de facto communications center. The first thing Madden noticed was an espresso machine set up on the desk, and the A.D. was sipping from a small white cup. It was all he could do to stop himself from smiling and shaking his head in disbelief.

"You wanted to see me?" he asked.

"Yes, I did," said Bainbridge, taking another sip of his drink and dabbing his mouth with a cloth napkin. "What have you been working on the last couple of days?"

"Just running down leads on the VA bombing, as per your instructions," said Madden.

"And?"

"Nothing so far. I have yet to come across anything promising or anything that we didn't already know."

"I see," said Bainbridge. "Then I think it's time to pull you back from that. As I'm sure you can imagine, pressure has continued to mount from above. I've been ordered to release the names of all suspects that we currently have interest in."

Madden, who had been standing, walked over and took a seat across from his boss.

"When is this going to happen?"

"Probably this afternoon sometime," said Bainbridge. "As you know, it's not my preferred course of action, but I can't keep resisting the powers that be. Once the story breaks, we'll need every able-bodied agent, even if it's just to follow up on tips and sightings."

"Understood. Anything else?"

"No, that is all," said Bainbridge. "Let's hope this thing gets wrapped up quickly. You and I have business to conduct back in D.C." Their eyes locked for a moment before Madden nodded curtly and left the room.

Thirty minutes later he was pulling into a parking area under a freeway overpass. The area was empty with the exception of a dark blue SUV. As he pulled up to the other vehicle, Robinson and Derry exited that vehicle and climbed into his.

The two agents couldn't have looked more different. Robinson was rail-thin, about 6'1" and 140 pounds with jet-black, neatly trimmed hair, brown eyes and a clean-shaven, boyish face. Derry, on the other hand, was about 5'8" and 190 pounds of chiseled muscle. He had red hair and blue eyes, with a neatly trimmed handle-bar mustache. One would be hard-pressed to guess that they were both thirty-nine years old. But each of them was a solid guy that Madden would trust with his life.

"Hey, guys, it's good to see you," said Madden after they were in and seated.

"So, I want to give you both one final chance to walk away from this," he continued. "I know you're both grown men, but this is potentially career suicide."

"Look," said Derry, "based on what you've told us, Bainbridge has basically issued a 'kill order' on this guy. That's not what we do here. Whether it hurts my career or not, this is my job. This is what I joined this organization to do. So, let's have at it."

Robinson nodded his head. "I'm all-in."

"Great," said Madden. "So, here's where we stand: I just had a meeting with Bainbridge, and he said he's prepared to publish the names of all suspects later today. Once that happens, there's not a whole lot we're going to be able to do. So, if we're going to make a move, we need to do it now. Are Provsky and Welborn still sitting on the hotel?"

"Yeah," said Derry. "One in front, one in the rear. They're shooting pics and grabbing license plates of everyone going in or out, but so far, our boy hasn't shown. They've been there since 11:00am. We can only assume he's still inside, based on when the hotel clerk last saw him."

"Perfect. Let's go knock this out real quick so we can finally put this thing to bed."

"We'll be right behind you," said Derry. Madden waited until they were back in their vehicle before he pulled away.

On the way to the hotel Madden called Provsky and Welborn and told them to meet him and the other two agents about a block down from the building in a Starbucks parking lot where they still had a line of sight to the front of the hotel. They all parked, and everyone squeezed into Madden's vehicle.

"Any news?" he asked once the two L.A. agents were seated.

"No, all quiet," said Provsky. "We spoke to the night manager. He believes he saw Carter enter the hotel at about 11pm last night but hasn't seen him since. Of course, we told him to keep this all in the utmost confidence. He was happy to oblige."

"Good," said Madden. "Maybe we'll get lucky today and get to avoid any overtime. I've already had 'the talk' with Robinson and Derry, and now I get to have it with you two. You could both end up in a barrel of shit over this, so if you want to walk away now, I'd definitely understand. I don't want to see any of you getting jacked up because of my actions."

Madden thought he saw something flash in the eyes of Welborn. He wasn't sure what it was. Maybe it was nothing, but the man just looked a little shifty. The fact was, Madden didn't know Welborn or Provsky. He'd read their personnel files, which were both spotless, but that didn't necessarily mean anything. Maybe Welborn was always like this. Maybe it was just nerves. Every agent experienced their jitters in their own unique way. Some got excited, some got twitchy. Some just needed to take a few deep breaths, some needed to barf up their breakfasts. He had never kicked in a door with these two, so he didn't know what to expect from them.

However, what he did know is that they were experienced, fully trained FBI agents, and that they knew how to handle themselves in these kinds of situations and had done so many times in the past. So then why was he feeling so uneasy? He mentally shook his head, clearing away the distracting thoughts and bringing his attention back to the present.

"We wouldn't have agreed to do this in the first place if we had any issues with it," Provsky was saying.

"Excellent," said Madden. "Let's get this show on the road. Robinson, you and Welborn ride with me. We'll take the front. Derry and Provsky, you've got the back."

Madden was just pulling out of the parking lot with Derry and Provsky right behind him when six black SUVs suddenly came roaring down the street. The lead vehicle stopped in front of the driveway, blocking Madden's exit. Robinson, in the seat beside him, immediately reached for the service weapon in the holster under his jacket, but Madden touched his arm.

"Hold on," he said.

The rear passenger door to the vehicle that was blocking their way opened, and the first person that emerged was an agent that Madden vaguely recognized from the D.C. office. The second person that emerged was Agent Phillips and the third was Associate Director Wesley Bainbridge.

"Fuck," said Madden.

Bainbridge began walking toward him, leaving Phillips and the other agent waiting beside their vehicle. Madden exited his own and met him half-way. As they came together, Bainbridge stopped and, clasping his hands in front of him, smiled smugly. Madden glanced at Phillips, who looked away, before he spoke.

"What's going on?" he asked.

"It's a beautiful day," said Bainbridge looking up at the sky. "As I heard in a movie once, it's a great day to die. I think that was Clint Eastwood. Is that Clint Eastwood?"

Madden shook his head. "I'm not much of a movie buff. I prefer to read the book."

"No matter," said Bainbridge, shrugging. "I hate to actually say this, because it sounds like something out of a bad B-movie, but did you really think that anything goes on in this organization that I don't know about?"

Madden shook his head again, "I guess not."

"I have to say I'm surprised that Derry and Robinson went along with this. Those other two assholes, well..." Bainbridge trailed off. "They already proved their worth, didn't they?"

Madden assumed the question was rhetorical, so he didn't attempt to answer.

"But back to you," said Bainbridge. "What am I going to do with you? I mean, I should simply tell you to go back to the hotel, pack your bags and wait for me back in D.C. But Phillips here," he said, turning his head in her direction, "reminded me that we can use as many hands on this as possible. And since you have a bit of history with the subject," he continued, pausing to lock eyes with Madden, "I'm going to let you accompany us on this. Just remember what side you're on."

Madden nodded. "How big is the team?"

"Twenty, including Phillips and me," said Bainbridge. "I guess that should be enough to bring down one 'ghetto soldier', right?"

Madden nodded. "I would imagine so. But just so I'm clear, what did you tell them the mission was?"

Bainbridge smiled again. "To subdue and capture the suspect, of course. What else?"

"Subdue?" said Madden, returning the smile.

"Well," said Bainbridge, "some of the agents with me do tend to be a bit more aggressive than others, so they may have a bit of a different definition than you do of the word 'subdue'. These are 'A' players, Madden. My advice to you is don't get in their way. Sometimes they're like sharks in a feeding frenzy. They see blood and don't stop attacking until nothing else is moving."

"I know the type," said Madden.

"Good," said Bainbridge. "I'm glad we have an understanding. And since you're the one that found him, I'll even let you take point. You can lead us into temptation, so to speak," he said, smiling smugly again.

Madden paused for a moment, then turned and walked back to his vehicle.

"What's happening?" asked Robinson.

"I think the shit has hit the proverbial fan," said Madden as he put the car in gear. "Let's go get dirty."

Chapter 85

Madden looked in the rear-view mirror and saw that Derry and Provsky had taken up a position directly behind him, screeching into the gap between Madden's vehicle and Bainbridge's convoy. His phone rang and he answered with the SUV's hands-free option, piping it into the speakers.

"What the hell is going on?" asked Derry.

"Looks like someone tattled," said Madden.

"Looks like," replied Derry. "So, what's the new plan?"

"It's going to be one big happy party, and everyone's invited."

"Maybe I'm just old," said Derry, "but this looks like a lot of firepower to bring down one solitary man."

"To say the least," said Madden. "Listen, all of you: Bainbridge has a couple of his attack dogs with him, and my guess is that they're not going to be happy unless there are fireworks. I know that I told you I recruited you into this so we could grab this guy peacefully, but that's all scrubbed now. Bainbridge is hosting this event, and if you get in his way, he will have no problem adding you to the casualty list."

"Hell," said Robinson. "Let's be realistic. If Bainbridge has a shit list, we're already on it, so there's no advantage to smiling and playing nice now. In for a penny, in for a pound, as my gran-gran used to always say."

Madden caught Welborn's eyes in the rear-view as he pulled up to a red light. The man still looked nervous—even more so now than before. Could he be the one who had alerted Bainbridge? It really wouldn't be too surprising. He had no allegiance to Madden, and who could blame him if he had tried to hedge his bets? Madden had taken a chance, hoping that Welborn and Provsky were stand-up guys who wanted to make amends the right way, doing the right thing. But he knew all along that it was a gamble, and it looked like it was a gamble he had lost.

"Just watch yourselves out there, all of you," he continued. "There's no need to get Bainbridge any more pissy than he already is." Madden's phone began to beep. Another call was coming through. Speak of the devil. "I've got to go. Stay close," he said as he hung up one call and answered the next.

"You and your team wait in the front," said Bainbridge. "We'll go see what the front desk knows."

As the phone disconnected, Madden saw three of the SUVs speed past him, headed for the rear of the hotel. He pulled into a spot at the curb, marked for valet. Derry and the vehicle carrying Bainbridge pulled in behind him. Another member of the caravan double-parked alongside. He watched Bainbridge, Phillips and the third agent exit their vehicle and enter the hotel.

Robinson looked across the seat at him. "Do you really think Bainbridge has the balls to drop this poor bastard, unprovoked, in front of a group this large?"

"Bainbridge's ambition knows no bounds," said Madden. "He sees this as his ticket—or, at least, one of them." He glanced at Welborn in the back seat again and wondered to himself if he was digging his grave deeper by talking so much. "Besides, the more people, the more chaos, and chaos can conceal a lot of impropriety."

A few moments later, Phillips walked out of the front of the hotel and over to Madden's window.

"They're not positive, but management is pretty sure he's still in his room," she said. Madden noticed that agents in the other SUVs were exiting their vehicles. They were all wearing bulletproof vests, and one was carrying a steel battering ram.

"Why are we forcing entry?" he asked. "Why can't we use the hotel's master key?"

"Bainbridge is worried that the latch could be on the door, ruining the surprise."

Madden wanted to say that his boss would have blown the door whether or not he knew there was a latch on it, but he held his tongue.

"Alright, guys, I guess we're up," he said to the men in his car. Phillips stepped back so that he could exit, and stood there watching him, as though there was something she wanted to say or something she was waiting to hear.

"You okay?" he asked.

"Yeah, I'm just," she began, then shook her head. "It's nothing."

"I know you're not worried about entry, as many doors as you've kicked in."

"No, it's not that. It's just..." She looked nervously at Robinson on the other side of the vehicle. "Maybe we can talk later."

"Sure," he said. He was about to say more, but Derry interrupted him, handing him a vest.

"Thanks," he said as he slipped it on. That's when he noticed that Phillips wasn't wearing one. "Why aren't you vested up?"

"Bainbridge wants me to wait down here. Be his 'eyes on the ground'," she said.

"What?" he asked, incredulous. "He was just talking about how he needed all hands on deck."

Phillips just shook her head, a strained look on her face.

"Okay, well, keep your eyes open. You know anything can happen in these situations," he said.

"You're the one that's going to be wrestling with a perp," she said, smiling. "I'm just out here listening to the radio. How dangerous can that be?"

Madden returned the smile. "Hey, after this I'd like to take the guys out to grab some drinks. Maybe you'd like to come with?"

"Sure," she said.

"Alright. See you in a minute." He and Robinson had to walk briskly to catch up to the rest of the group. To the hotel guests, they must have looked like Stormtroopers, marching into the lobby dressed all in black. People literally scurried out of their way to give them room. They stopped right inside the door, directly across from the bank of elevators, where Bainbridge was waiting and staring at his watch.

One of the agents had brought him a vest, and as he slipped it on, he turned to address the men.

"Listen up everyone. Let's make this fast and clean," he said. "We don't know what this guy is packing. He could have a rocket launcher up there for all we know, so please, nobody try to be a hero." He paused and scanned the faces for effect. "Let's move out."

Just as Bainbridge turned, one of the elevators opened and a man walked out. *Holy shit,* thought Madden. *It's Carter!*

A split second later, Carter spotted the group at the same exact moment that Bainbridge recognized him.

"Freeze, FBI!" yelled Bainbridge as he reached for the 9mm in the holster that was hanging from his shoulder. By the time the words were out of his mouth, Carter was already disappearing through the door that led to the parking garage.

Bainbridge sprinted after him with the rest of the group following close behind. Madden began shouldering his way to the front of the crowd as he ran, and a couple of the agents shoved him back in annoyance. As they emerged into the parking structure, Carter was nowhere in sight.

"Spread out! Let's find this asshole!" yelled Bainbridge. The men began to systematically search the nearby cars. Bainbridge tapped a headset that was in his ear.

"The suspect is on the run. Have you seen him?" he asked. He was obviously speaking to the agents that he had stationed in the front and back of the hotel. He nodded his head. "Well, stay sharp." He tapped the headset again and then looked at Madden.

"Let's go make the news," he said. He walked a few yards into the garage, and Madden followed. Bainbridge stopped, looked around and tilted his head back.

"Carter! I know you're in here!" he yelled, his voice bouncing around the concrete structure in echo. It was amazing how much sound such a small man could generate. "Why don't you make this easy on yourself and give up! Otherwise, we'll have to do it the hard way, and you really don't want that!" He paused and cocked his head to the side. When he heard no response, he shrugged and then smiled at Madden.

"Let's go," he said.

Madden began walking with Bainbridge, scanning the area, but still had yet to draw his weapon. He was the only one who hadn't. He couldn't see Derry, Robinson or Welborn, but Provsky was 50 yards ahead of him and was moving with his gun held straight in front of him, just like they taught in FBI training.

"Freeze!" he heard someone yell, followed by the sound of two shots being fired. It sounded like they were coming from the other side of the garage, which was separated by a wall.

"Man down!" someone else yelled.

"Man down!"

"Man down!"

Madden and Bainbridge broke into a run and moments later arrived at a spot between two parked cars where four agents were kneeling, attending to their fallen comrade. One of the agents was Welborn.

"What happened?!" exclaimed Bainbridge.

"He's alright," said an agent that was checking the fallen man's pulse. "The suspect must have got the jump on him. He's out cold."

"Where is his service weapon?" asked Bainbridge.

"I think it's..." said the man, looking to the sides and behind him.

"It's gone; I already checked," said Welborn.

Bainbridge looked at him and paused ever so slightly before he continued. "Alright!" he yelled. "We have one man down! If our suspect wasn't armed before, he sure as hell is now! Watch yourself, and don't take any chances!"

Madden and Bainbridge began slowly advancing further into the garage when Bainbridge stopped abruptly and scowled at Madden and then down at his still holstered weapon. Madden pulled the gun out, and they continued walking. Moments later the silence was once again broken by gunfire as two shots echoed through the structure.

"Man down!" yelled two or three voices.

Madden and Bainbridge both, again, ran toward the sounds. As they turned the corner, they found one agent helping another off the ground. The agent getting up was rubbing the back of his neck and shaking his head. A third agent picked a gun off the ground and handed it to the previously downed agent.

"What the fuck are you people doing!?" screamed Bainbridge. "Pair up and stop acting like a bunch of fucking Walmart security guards!"

Derry was standing nearby, and Madden walked over to him. "Come on," he said. "Let's go find this guy."

They began trotting down the driveway, past numerous agents, many of which were bending down, looking under parked cars.

"Two agents down. This guy is good," said Derry.

"Yeah, so good someone is going to end up putting a bullet in his head," said Madden. As if on cue, a chorus of gunshots rang out. It sounded like they were on the level below.

"Stairway!" said Madden, heading in the direction of the shots.

As they came out of the stairwell, he saw six agents standing in a group with their guns all pointing in the same direction while two more were lying on the ground, searching beneath the cars.

"What do we have?" he asked one of the men.

"We saw him running between this group of cars," he said. "He's down here somewhere."

There was a sound of running behind them, and they all turned to see Bainbridge and six or seven other agents emerge from the stairwell.

"Do you have him?" asked Bainbridge.

"Not yet," said one of the other agents, "but he's close."

"How many people does it take to find one fucking guy?" he screeched. "There aren't that many fucking places to hide!"

The two men who were lying on the ground got up, shaking their heads. The group began fanning out again.

"Do we know what car he's driving?" asked Derry.

"No clue," said Madden. "He has several registered to him, but Welborn and Provsky canvassed the entire garage several times and couldn't find any matches. So, he could be in a rental. Or a vehicle registered to someone else."

Madden was cut off by more shots fired.

"Shit!" he said as he, Derry and several other agents took off in a sprint.

"I got him!" said an agent who was staring intently at a cluster of cars in the corner of the garage.

"Is he down?" asked Madden, taking control of the situation.

"I don't know. I don't know if I hit him, but he's in there."

Madden looked behind him and saw Bainbridge and several other agents approaching at a fast jog.

"Listen! Carter!" he yelled. "My name is Dexter Madden of the FBI. Come on out, man, it's over. There's nowhere else to go. If you've been hit, we'll get you immediate medical attention, but first we've got to know that it's safe to approach." He paused, waiting for a response.

"Agent Madden," said a deep, commanding voice from somewhere behind the parked cars, "I'm not the one that's shooting at people. That's your team."

"Point taken," said Madden. "And we appreciate that you haven't fired at any of our agents. Now if you'll just toss your weapons out and come out with your hands above your head, we can end this peacefully." He could feel Bainbridge staring hard at him from ten feet away, but he refused to acknowledge the man.

"I don't have any weapons," said Carter. "You guys caught me on the way to a late lunch. The places I go to dine don't usually require firearms."

"Bullshit!" said Bainbridge. "We know you at least have the weapon you took off that first agent you attacked."

"You're mistaken," said Carter. "I didn't take anyone's weapon. I did defend myself, barely preventing one of your men from shooting me in the face. But I did not take his weapon. Maybe he was ashamed of himself and threw it away."

"You're real funny, asshole!" yelled Bainbridge. "How about this for humor: You have thirty seconds to toss the weapons out and walk to us with your hands up, or we're coming in after you."

"Again, I have no weapon!" yelled Carter. "And to be honest, you guys seem a bit trigger happy. I have the distinct impression that I'm going to suffer the same fate whether I come out unarmed or not."

Bainbridge scowled in frustration. "Enough of this nonsense. Schneider, Gomez, Barnet, go get this asshole." Three agents that Madden recognized from the D.C. office began to move forward.

"Hold on," said Madden. "Let me go in and try to talk to him. I'm probably the one here that's most familiar with his file."

Bainbridge tilted his head to the side and looked at Madden from the corner of his eye. Madden could see he was thinking; doing some kind of calculation, the nature of which Madden could only guess.

"Alright," he said, finally. "You've got three minutes, starting now, and if you're not out by then, we're coming in hot."

In response, Madden handed his gun to Derry. "Carter!" he yelled. "This is Dexter Madden again. I'd like to chat with you in private. I'm unarmed and I'm coming in."

"Alright," said Carter.

Madden walked into the mass of cars, zig-zagging through the maze of parked automobiles, until he soon lost sight of his fellow agents. There must be some kind of car rental agency using the building, he guessed, because cars of similar makes and models were parked three- and four-deep in an arc that followed the curved wall of the garage. Abruptly, he came upon Carter. So abruptly, in fact, that he almost stumbled into him.

"So," Madden said as they stood staring at each other, "finally, we meet face to face. Are you hurt?"

"No," said Carter, his voice quieter now, but just as resonant. "Your guys are not very good shots."

"I'm glad to hear it."

"By the way," said Carter, "were you the one that tracked me down?"

Madden nodded.

"How'd you do it?"

Madden shrugged. "Just good old police work."

"No, seriously. The curiosity is killing me. Besides, we're old friends," said Carter, smiling. "You at least owe me that."

Madden nodded again. "Okay. It was your phone call with your wife. You mentioned that you could see the hospital where your daughter was born."

"Shit," said Carter, smiling. "I always knew that scotch would one day be my downfall."

"There are worse ways to go," said Madden.

"So, what are we doing here?" asked Carter. "Do you really expect me to just walk out there with you?"

"I don't think you have much choice," said Madden. "My boss gave me three minutes to get you to surrender, or he's sending in the dogs."

"Isn't this the guy that you told me wasn't trustworthy? The guy that went to see my mother?"

"Bainbridge. Yes, that's him. But again, my back is against the wall here. And so is yours. You're surrounded. You don't have a whole lot of options. I don't think he'll give the order to shoot if I bring you out in cuffs as my prisoner."

Carter seemed to think it over for a moment.

"Why should I?" he finally asked. "There's no future here. Why not just go out in a blaze of glory?"

"First of all," began Madden, "if what you said is true, you're not armed. So, any 'blazing' would be one-way. And second, you still have someone in jail that needs you to be strong for her and that expects for you to be waiting for her when she gets out."

Carter chuckled, and shook his head. "When she gets out," he scoffed. "Who knows when that will be, if ever? You know, she was almost out. The judge had agreed to dismiss the case. But then someone killed it. Could that be your man Bainbridge?"

Madden looked thoughtfully back toward the direction he had come from. "I don't know," he said. "It's possible. If you come out with me, I promise I'll look into it. And if he was the one, I'll see what I can do to reverse the damage."

"You've got ten seconds!" came Bainbridge's voice, as if on cue.

"Hold on, we're coming out!" yelled Madden in response. "So, what do you say, my man? Are we ready to do this?"

Carter paused again. "Fuck it," he said, apparently finally coming to a decision. "I might as well."

"Good," said Madden. "Thank you for making this easy on me." He pulled out a pair of cuffs and Carter extended his arms to him. He was about to cuff the man when he had a thought and stopped.

"Wait a minute." He slipped the cuffs into his pocket and quickly took his bulletproof vest off. "Here, put this on," he said as he helped the larger man squeeze into the protective garment. "Damn, you're a big dude."

"It's that army food," said Carter, smiling.

Once the vest was in place, Madden grabbed the cuffs again, cuffing Carter's hands in front of him.

"Are you ready?" he asked, locking eyes with his captive.

"Man, I was born ready," said Carter.

Madden nodded. "Alright, we're coming out!" he yelled. "The suspect is secure! Everyone stand down!"

Madden took up a position on Carter's right side. He grabbed his prisoner by the back of the vest, then reached toward his holster before he remembered that he'd given his 9mm to Derry to hold. "Damn," he muttered.

Carter stared at him, seeing the worry on his face. "Your friends really don't play nice, do they?" he asked.

“Sometimes they’ve been known to bend the rules a bit,” said Madden in response. “Let’s hope today isn’t one of those days.”

Madden retraced his steps through the maze of cars with Carter at his side. They emerged to see every agent in the garage waiting for them, with each man aiming a gun in their direction. Most lowered their weapons when they saw that Carter was cuffed.

“Good job!” said Bainbridge, who was standing about fifty yards away. “By the way, did you frisk him?”

The question caught Madden by surprise.

“Well, um, I…” he said, stumbling over his words.

“Gun!” someone yelled. It sounded like Welborn’s voice.

At that same instant, Madden caught a flicker of something to his right. It only took a split second for him to register it as the glint of light off a rifle scope.

“No! Don’t shoot!” he yelled as he turned, grabbing Carter in an embrace to shield him from harm.

A barrage of gunshots rang out. It sounded to Madden like the loudest 4th of July party he had ever heard. Pain exploded in his back, and he felt himself and Carter falling. Like it always happened in situations like this, everything slowed down, like a slow-motion scene in one of those great, big-budget Hollywood action movies. The last thing he remembered as their intertwined bodies bounced on the hard concrete of the garage was that Carter’s face was covered in an awful lot of blood. Then everything went black.

Chapter 86

The darkness slowly began to clear until suddenly it was all gone and Madden's vision was assaulted by an overwhelming light. He felt himself wince and turned his head to try to escape it, but it was everywhere.

After a few moments, some shapes began to materialize, and the first image he recognized, as it slowly took form in front of his eyes, was Bainbridge's face. The man looked like he had just swallowed someone else's saliva. Madden licked his lips, noticing how dry his mouth felt, and wondered to himself if this was a dream—or, more to the point, a nightmare.

"So, you're still with us?" asked Bainbridge. Madden's head felt like someone had stuffed it full of cotton and banged on it with a wooden mallet for several hours, so he wasn't sure whether his boss was showing concern or contempt. But the sour look on his face was probably a clue.

Bainbridge slowly shook his head back and forth. "You've certainly got balls. I've got to give you that. After that fiasco, I would have thought you'd at least have the decency to die. But here we are."

Madden opened his mouth to try to speak, but nothing came out, so he licked his lips again. He tried to lean forward, but that set off an explosion in his chest and shoulder, so he laid back again.

"I'm glad I was able to be here when you woke up," Bainbridge continued. "I wanted to be able to tell you personally to your face, in case you had any lingering doubts, that your career is over. In addition, we found the phone that you hid in the ceiling of your hotel room, and that, along with your laptop, gives me more than enough evidence to file charges against you for concealing evidence and obstruction of justice, which I will be doing first thing Monday morning. And you can believe that I will do everything I possibly can to prosecute you to the fullest extent of the law."

Madden slowly blinked, hoping that this really was a dream, and that when he opened his eyes again Bainbridge would be gone, but it didn't work. It did, however, cause Bainbridge's face to break into a smile; an evil, cruel, cold-blooded expression reminiscent of some giant, deadly snake.

"Have a nice day," he hissed, and then he was gone.

The void he left was quickly filled by Phillips, her eyes red, glossy and full of concern.

"Are you alright? How do you feel?" she asked, her voice husky and cracking.

Madden shook his head slowly, remembering not to move too much lest he reignite the fire that was still smoldering in his upper torso.

"What the hell happened?" he finally managed to whisper.

"You were shot," she said.

"Shot by who?"

Phillips looked away briefly before returning his gaze. "It was chaos. The slug passed straight through, in and out, so we may never know exactly what gun it came from. But it really doesn't matter. It was just a case of friendly fire."

"Friendly fire?" asked Madden, wincing as he felt another stab of pain in his head. "Friendly fire from who?"

"From the other agents that were present," she said.

"Why were they shooting at me to begin with?" he asked.

"They weren't shooting at you, they were shooting at Carter."

Madden froze, his eyes searching the space above her head, trying to make sense of what she was saying. Then it all started slowly coming back to him. She patiently watched him go through the process. Finally, he understood.

"Shit," he muttered. "Okay. Now I remember."

"It's the anesthetic and the pain meds—and the shot of Ritalin," she said. "It's a stimulant. The doctor wanted to let you sleep, but Bainbridge ordered him to do whatever he could to wake you."

"Since when are doctors bossed around by government agents?" he asked.

"Since Bainbridge told him it was a matter of national security and threatened to put him and his entire family on a no-fly list if he didn't cooperate."

"That sounds like Bainbridge," said Madden. "Now everything makes sense. When he was talking to me, I thought I was in a dream. You know, one of those dreams where you don't understand what's going on, but you go along with it anyway because you don't know how to wake yourself up."

A look of discomfort appeared on Phillips' face.

"Well, I just wanted to check on you and see how you're feeling. I'll let you rest."

"Thanks," said Madden, still working on clearing the cobwebs from his mind.

"Oh, by the way, I called Kelly."

"I wish you hadn't done that," said Madden. "You know how she is. She's probably on a plane on the way here right now."

"No, I told her it was just a flesh wound and that they were only holding you for observation. I wanted to let her know that you were alright, so that she didn't panic in case she heard about the shooting on the news. Turns out that wasn't something I needed to worry about."

"What do you mean?" asked Madden.

"Bainbridge suppressed the entire incident. Froze out the press and threatened anyone present that might be thinking about leaking it, including the other agents."

"Really? So, wait," he said, trying to piece it all together in his head, "are you saying the press isn't aware of Carter?"

"Not last time I checked," she said. "And for some reason, Bainbridge seems to be intent on keeping it that way."

"What happened to him—Carter?"

"They have him in custody, in a detention center somewhere downtown."

"How badly was he injured?" asked Madden. "The last thing I remember was falling on top of him and seeing him covered in blood."

"That was your blood," said Phillips. "He was hit several times but survived with nothing more than a few bruises. It's no wonder, seeing as how you gave him your vest." There was a hint of snideness in the last comment.

"It was the right thing to do, considering the situation," he said.

Phillips shook her head in frustration. "Now's not the time to go into all that. I just wanted to make sure you were okay. I think the nurse is waiting to take your vitals, so I'm going to take off. I'll try to come check on you again in the morning."

"Thanks," said Madden. "I appreciate it."

As Phillips was turning to go, Madden said: "One more thing. Were you the one that told Bainbridge that we were going to be at the hotel?"

"No. I didn't know anything about it. From what I overheard, I believe it was Welborn."

"I figured about as much. Thanks again."

Phillips nodded and then walked out of the room, leaving him to his thoughts.

As soon as Phillips left the room, a nurse entered. She had a kind face and smiled in a way that immediately relaxed Madden and reassured him that everything was okay. As she was taking his blood pressure he thought to ask her what day it was, but before he could open his mouth, he was already asleep.

He awoke sometime later in a room that was now dimly lit. This time it only took a few seconds for him to realize where he was and what had brought him there. He felt rested, and all the fuzziness that had surrounded his brain when he spoke with Phillips had faded away. He looked for a buzzer to call the nurse and pressed it. A few moments later the door opened.

"Hi, can I help you?" It was the nurse who had been attending him right before he fell asleep.

"Yes. Can you tell me where my cellphone is?"

"Oh, it's right over here," she said, walking over to a tall, narrow closet and rummaging through a large plastic bag.

As she handed him the phone, he opened it and checked the battery. It was down to 13%. He also saw that it was 5:27am.

"Thanks," he said. "Any chance you might have a charger around that I could borrow?"

"I'm sure we do," she answered. "We try to keep a few on hand. I'll be right back."

As she left, Madden opened an app on his phone and checked the date. It had been two days since he had been shot. His first thought was that he needed to call Kelly and reassure her that everything was fine. His next thought was of Carter. Phillips had said that Bainbridge had thrown a blanket over the entire situation. The fact that he wasn't taking public credit for the capture and wallowing in photo ops could only mean one thing: that he was making good on his threat to avoid courtrooms on this case, and was most likely planning on having someone get to Carter from inside the jail.

After the nurse delivered the charger, he made a few phone calls. The first was to his wife, even though he knew she was probably sleeping and hardly ever heard the phone. He got her voicemail and left a short message.

Next, he needed information. He considered calling Phillips, but even though she apparently wasn't the one who had sold him out at the hotel, he still didn't entirely trust her. So he called Derry instead. He knew the man was an early riser and a fitness nut, and was probably up doing some kind of calisthenics in his room.

"Good morning, sir!" said Derry when he answered the phone. "I dropped by to see you yesterday, but you were out like a light. How are you doing?"

"I'm good. I feel like I was hit by a truck, but the nurse says I'm mending quickly."

"That's good to hear, my friend. When you went down, I thought it was all over. It was truly a miracle that you were only hit once. The entire situation was unbelievable. Have you seen Bainbridge?"

"Yeah," said Madden. "He came by yesterday. The verdict is that I'm pretty much out. And I may even be going to prison before it's all said and done."

"Shit, I'm really sorry, man. I can't believe that asshole is actually going through with it. If there's anything I can do, just let me know."

"Actually," said Madden, "there is. I need to get in to see Carter, and I'm worried that Bainbridge may have already put me on a 'denial of entry' list. But if you could get in, maybe I could be your 'plus one'?"

"Sure, just let me know when to come pick you up."

"Thanks. But you know, Derry," said Madden, "this is not without risk. You could end up in Bainbridge's cross-hairs over it."

Derry chuckled. "I already am. I punched one of the assholes that shot at you and he's bringing me up for disciplinary action. So, fuck him. Let's do it."

Madden checked himself out of the hospital against his doctor's advice. The nurse, the one with kind face, echoed the doctor's concern. Kelly had returned his call as he was getting dressed, and they even ended up having a small argument over the issue. She was so mad that she hung up on him, but then immediately called back and apologized. While he appreciated all the concern, he knew that the business he had to attend to simply couldn't wait.

He felt fine as he left the hospital with Derry, but by the time they arrived at the jail, he was literally limping from the pain in his shoulder.

"You look like you need to take a knee for a minute," said Derry, his face etched with concern.

"Yeah, maybe just a minute." Madden grunted as they took a seat on a concrete bench that was located right outside the jail entrance. They had picked up a pain prescription on the way, and he popped two of the pills in his mouth and chewed them dry. The chalky bitterness almost made him gag, but he didn't care. He closed his eyes and took a deep breath. Moments later he could feel them working.

Derry hadn't spoken much during the ride. He seemed to somehow sense that Madden needed the silence to gather his thoughts. But now that he could see how much Madden was struggling, it was clear that he wanted to say something.

"Are you sure this is a good idea?" he finally blurted out. "I mean, you could have just given me the message and I would have delivered it."

"I know you would have," said Madden, patting his friend on the shoulder, "but I felt like I owed it to him to tell him myself. I don't know why. It's not like it's my fault that he's here. But still. He saved my life once. This might be my only chance to return the favor."

"I understand," said Derry as he leaned back and stretched, patiently giving Madden as much time to rest as he needed.

"Okay," said Madden a couple of minutes later as he sighed and flexed his shoulder. "Let's get this over with so I can go lie down somewhere."

He was surprised to see that they were able to gain admittance to the jail so easily. To be honest, he didn't think he was going to get in at all. He was sure that Bainbridge would have created a list of people with permission to see the prisoner and that the cop at the desk would have cross-referenced his name against that list. But instead, their FBI badges worked like all-access passes at a Rolling Stones concert. They were welcomed with reverence and immediately shown to a private meeting room.

"I'll wait out here," said Derry as they were approaching the door to the room. Madden nodded, a movement that caused him to wince.

The room was empty when he entered. It was barren except for a medium-sized table and two matching chairs, all of which were bolted to the floor. There was no mirror, which meant no two-way glass, but there were cameras in two corners of the room. Both exhibited red lights, showing that they were functioning and probably recording. It wasn't the ideal situation, but at this point he didn't have much choice.

Carter shuffled into the room, his movement restricted by the fact that both his wrists and his ankles were shackled and then chained together. He was escorted by two very large guards. However, he appeared remarkably at ease, and not at all surprised to see that it was Madden who was waiting for him. Madden refrained from speaking until after the guards had left the room, even though he realized that with the cameras, it was all just a formality.

"How are you?" he asked.

Carter shrugged. "As well as can be expected. You look none too worse for wear."

"That's a matter of opinion, but at least I'm alive."

Carter responded with silence, leaning back in his chair in a way that said, *Well? What can I do for you?*

"Anyway," said Madden, pushing through the awkwardness, "I'm here because I wanted to warn you to be especially careful."

"Careful of what?" asked Carter.

Madden glanced up at one of the cameras before answering, making sure that the prisoner was aware they were likely under surveillance.

"Remember in one of our conversations how I told you that a certain individual had it out for you?"

Carter nodded.

"Well, I think he's going to try to get to you in here. I'm not sure exactly what his move will be, but everything I'm seeing points to some ultimate plan to...end this prematurely."

Carter seemed to consider this information for a moment before he answered. "Thanks for that. I appreciate it. I can see that you probably dragged yourself out of a hospital bed to tell me this. And before I forget, thanks for what you did back in the garage. If you hadn't, I wouldn't even be here to be having this conversation, so you've already put me ahead of the game."

"You're welcome. Is there anything I can get you? Anything I can do to make your stay a little more comfortable?"

"I don't think so. Remember, I'm special ops. I'm used to bad food, uncomfortable beds and occasionally battling some asshole in a winner-takes-all death match."

"I could try to get you put into isolation, to try to protect you from whomever may be coming," said Madden, "but I don't think it would last very long. I wish I knew someone in here that I could trust to watch your back. Who knows, I may be able to watch it myself pretty soon."

"What do you mean?" asked Carter.

"I'm washed up at the Bureau. I might even be facing prison time."

"Over what happened in the garage?"

Madden chuckled. "To be honest, that was just a small part of it. I've been dealing with some 'managerial difficulties' for quite some time now. It was probably bound to happen sooner or later, even if you and I had never met."

"Brothers helping brothers," said Carter, shaking his head. "That's not something you see a lot of these days. And law enforcement helping brothers? Even rarer. I appreciate what you stand for."

Madden shifted his weight in the hard metal chair and winced.

"I think you'd better get back," said Carter.

"You're probably right. I suspect you already have a lawyer on this?"

"One of the best in the world," said Carter.

"Good. If there's anything I can do to help while I'm still an official employee of the U.S. government, have him get in touch."

"Will do," said Carter.

"Guard!" yelled Madden. He waited until the guards had led Carter from the room before he popped another pain pill into his mouth and slowly rose to his feet. It was going to be a long, painful trip back to his hotel room.

Chapter 87

Ish sat on the edge of his bunk, chin resting on the pyramid created by his arms and interlocked fingers. The visit from Madden was a welcome one. It was good to know exactly what he was facing.

The jail officials had refused him his phone call; he supposed that had been by order of Bainbridge. His saving grace was that one of the guards in the holding area, a brother, had balked at the injustice of the order and had let him sneak in a call to his attorney. The attorney wanted to immediately storm the jail and file a complaint, but Ish told him to concentrate his efforts on getting prepared for the bail hearing, though they were both sure that bail would be denied. However, it would likely give them time to confer and determine how best to use the ace up their sleeve.

Ish had to admit that he was kind of surprised that this is how it all ended. If he was being honest, he would have guessed that the final play would have had him falling under a hail of gunfire. He certainly never would have imagined that his life would be saved by an FBI agent.

He wondered how Chad, Jag and Ma'am would react when they got the news that he had been captured. Ish had instructed the lawyer to contact Chad, and he knew that Chad would immediately alert Jag and Ma'am. Hopefully, they could keep the news from Layla for as long as possible. Her situation was stressful enough as it was. The last thing she needed was more bad news. It was bad enough that—

"Alright, Carter, let's go!" said a guard, interrupting his meditation.

"Go where?" he asked, scowling up at the man standing on the other side of the bars.

"Visit."

"I already went to my visit less than an hour ago."

"Well, you've got another one, Mr. Popularity. Get the fuck up. Let's go!" he said as he slid the door open.

As two guards came in and re-shackled his hands and feet for transfer back to the visitor area, Ish wondered to himself who the hell this was who wanted to see him. If it was the attorney disobeying his orders, he would be transferring his business to another firm at his earliest opportunity. Hopefully, it wasn't Chad, Jag or Ma'am. Surely, they had enough sense not to walk into the lion's mouth just to chat with him for five minutes.

If they had any sense at all, and of course they did, they'd all be taking evasive maneuvers, putting as much extra distance between themselves and him as possible, while he figured out exactly how tight the case against him was. More to the point, he needed time to figure out whether the secret weapon they had was going to be enough to allow him to wiggle free.

The guards took him to the same visitation room that he had been in earlier. As the door opened, he immediately recognized the man standing before him, though they had never been introduced. His had been the face Ish saw first when the elevator doors opened at the hotel. He was wearing an impeccable blue pinstriped suit. The white shirt looked freshly starched, clearly some kind of expensive linen, and it was capped off with a beautiful tie of the most amazing shades of teal. The brown leather shoes he wore were equally impressive.

He had a handsome face, with thick graying hair that looked like he had just left the salon. In fact, though he appeared to be in his late forties now, he looked like he could have been a model when he was younger, except for one thing: he was only about five feet tall. Maybe 5'2" on a good day. But none of that was what most identified him to Ish. What did was the smirk on his face; the look of total and complete domination and satisfaction. This could only be one man: Bainbridge.

"Mr. Carter," said Bainbridge, slowly drawing out the first syllable of 'mister' in a long hiss that comically reminded Ish of the snake from the animated movie *Jungle Book*. "I'm Associate Director Wesley Bainbridge of the FBI. I led the team that captured you. What a pleasure it is to see you again," he continued, the smile never leaving his face.

"I wish I could say the feeling was mutual," said Ish as he took his seat. Bainbridge continued standing, and Ish was amused to see that they were now about the same height.

"I can understand you feeling a bit vexed," said Bainbridge. "I must admit, you had a good run." He stepped forward to lean on the back of the chair on his side of the table, still choosing not to sit. "But all things must come to an end."

Ish nodded. "Why are you here?" he asked.

"I have a bit of news for you, regarding your two partners, Justin Gilroy and Athena Johnson. I believe you call them 'Jag' and 'Ma'am'? Such colorful names. Anyway, we have them both safely in custody. One of my agents recognized them entering the hotel through the lobby just as we were heading out. What luck, right?"

Ish's face showed no reaction. "I have no idea who you're referring to," he said, his expression deadpan.

Bainbridge chuckled. "Is that really how you want to play this? You're going to deny knowing a man you served with and the sister of yet another man you served with who just happened to walk into the same exact hotel you were staying in?"

Ish starred at him silently, his face still blank.

"Okay, let's cut to the chase," said Bainbridge, his smile fading a bit. "Of the five of you that made up PROPR, one is dead, three are in custody. I'm anxious to get this case fully bow-tied so that I can move on to more important matters that require my attention back in D.C. So, in the interest of expediency, I'm willing to cut you a deal. You tell me where I can find the fifth person, and I'll put in a word for you with the D.A."

Ish tilted his head back and looked casually at the overhead lights as though he were considering the proposal. When he turned his gaze back to the FBI Associate Director, his eyes showed a hint of humor. "I appreciate the gesture, I really do," he said, his tone mocking, "but I think I'm good."

"You're good? I'm glad to hear that," said Bainbridge. "What about your wife, Layla? Is she good, too? No response? I was saddened to hear that she was having a difficult time. Something about a denied appeal hearing? If you help me out, maybe I could be of assistance with her case as well. No?"

It was only the fact that Ish held a trump card that he had yet to play that allowed him to stop himself from lunging across the table and breaking the man's neck. Even though he was still fully shackled and both guards were standing against the wall behind him, he and Bainbridge were only separated by about three feet. In one fluid motion he could have sprung out of his seat, leaped across the table and snapped Bainbridge's vertebrae before the guards even knew what was happening. But now was not the time for that.

"Alright," said Bainbridge, fidgeting a bit as though he could somehow feel the danger he was in. "I'll let you sleep on it for a day or two, but this is a limited time offer. It expires Tuesday at midnight. If you change your mind, tell one of the guards, and they'll get in contact with me."

Bainbridge nodded at the two sentries, indicating that the meeting was over.

The next morning Ish was up early. An orderly brought him some cold oatmeal and two small, over-cooked sausage patties along with a plastic cup containing what tasted like watered down Sunny Delight. But beggars couldn't be choosers, and he finished every bit of it. He needed the energy. He then began moving, starting with 500 push-ups and 500 sit-ups. He was just finishing his 200th burpee when the same two guards from yesterday appeared at his cell door.

He had yet to learn either of their names, so he had begun to think of them as "Burp" and "Slurp", characters from a show about sea monsters that he used to watch as a kid. Both men were massive, with bodies that had obviously spent a lot of time in the gym. Burp's short-sleeve shirt revealed arms fully covered in tattoos. Slurp was ink-free, but had crepe-like skin that reminded Ish of a lizard that had spent too much time in the sun. Both were Caucasian, mid-thirties, blond-haired and blue-eyed. They also made it abundantly clear that they didn't care for Ish in the least. The feeling was mutual.

"Let's go, pretty boy," said Slurp.

"Where to now?" asked Ish, trying to catch his breath from the burpees.

"Visitation," Burp answered.

Ish considered telling them to fuck off, just to see what they would do, but then decided against it. He didn't know how long he was going to be in here, so it was silly to start provoking the local idiots for no good reason. Instead, he silently toweled some of the sweat off his body and pulled a t-shirt over his head. He then turned around and assumed the position, allowing them to come into the cell and shackle him as they had done each time he was allowed to leave it.

Ish wasn't expecting anyone, so he had no idea who could be waiting for him in the visitor's room. His best guess would have been that Bainbridge had returned to have another pass at trying to get him to talk. What he saw when the guards opened the door and escorted him into the room was so shocking that he almost stumbled. Sitting at the table, smiling, was none other than Chad. As Burp and Slurp exited the room, slamming the door shut behind them, Ish settled into the chair across from his friend. He folded his hands together atop the table, the chains from the shackles making a grating sound as they raked across the edge. He glanced up at one of the cameras near the ceiling, and cleared his throat before he spoke.

"What are you doing here?" he asked, trying to keep his face neutral and his voice as low as possible.

"It's good to see you, too," said Chad, much louder. "And don't worry about the cameras. We have attorney-client privilege, so they aren't allowed to film this." But there was a twinkle in his eye. This let Ish know that Chad had entered under the guise of being a lawyer and that he understood completely that the entire session was definitely being recorded.

"I guess I'm just a little surprised to see you here," said Ish, trying to match Chad's casual tone.

"Well, getting on the FBI's approved visitor list was certainly no small effort," said Chad, still smiling. "They're keeping you locked down pretty tight here." He then leaned forward and lowered his voice conspiratorially. "To be honest, I think they're a little afraid of you," he said. "But no worries! I have everything under control and I'm sure we'll soon be able to get them to see that this has all been a big mistake. In fact—"

Ish's keen ears had heard the keys jangling in the lock seconds before the door flew opened. This time he was somehow not at all surprised when in walked none other than FBI Associate Director Wesley Bainbridge.

Ish immediately glanced at Chad and saw a flash of concern on his face as his body tensed for flight, followed quickly by a look of stern resolve as he settled back down, leaning back in his chair and trying as best he could to appear nonchalant.

"What, may I ask, is going on here?" asked Bainbridge, his voice annoyingly cheerful.

"I'm having a meeting with my client, if you don't mind," said Chad.

"Oh, that's right, you're the attorney. Mr. Lee, is it?"

"That's right," said Chad.

"I think maybe you're confused," said Bainbridge, walking over to the side of the table to stand between the two men, "because according to my records, your name is actually Chad Yang. And last time I checked, Mr. Yang, you had yet to pass the bar."

Chad smiled and raised his hands, palms up, in a sign of silent resignation. But his expression was more smug than alarmed.

Bainbridge returned the smile. "I'm glad you're taking this so well. It makes my job so much easier. Now that I have the complete barrel of monkeys, I can get back home early and surprise my wife. So, thank you for that. Alright guards, take them away," he said, waving in the direction of Burp and Slurp.

"Actually, you may want to hold off on that for a moment," said Chad as the two hulking men approached him.

Bainbridge raised his hand, causing both guards to pause.

"And why would I want to do that?" he asked, seeming genuinely curious.

"Because we haven't had a chance to negotiate our deal yet," said Chad.

"Deal?" scoffed Bainbridge. "To make a deal, you have to have something to deal with. And I don't see any evidence that you have anything I want. But I'm a reasonable guy, so I'll humor you for a moment. What do you have to offer me that's better than the joy of seeing you both thrown into a dark, damp prison cell?"

Chad gazed at Ish for a split second before answering: "Your life."

Bainbridge slightly chuckled. "My life? You certainly have large balls for a Chinaman. I don't think you're in a position to be threatening the FBI."

"It's not a threat," said Ish.

"Really? Okay, what is it?"

Ish nodded his head in the direction of the two guards. "You might want to get rid of the bookends. I don't think you want either them or the cameras to hear what we have to say."

Bainbridge looked back and forth between Ish and Chad, seeming unsure of what to do.

"Don't worry," said Ish, "we're not going to attack you. We don't need to."

Bainbridge took another moment to consider Ish's comments before finally addressing the two jailers. "Give us a moment. And kill the recording," he said as they both walked out of the room.

Bainbridge waited for the sound of the door being locked from the outside before he shrugged his shoulders. "Well? What is it that you want to say?"

"Do you have a cell phone on you?" asked Chad. "They made me leave mine at the desk."

Bainbridge sighed impatiently but reached into his pocket and withdrew an iPhone.

"May I?" asked Chad, extending his arm.

Bainbridge looked skeptical. "If anything happens to this phone, you'll be spending your first three months here in the jail hospital on a liquid diet," he warned as he entered the code to unlock it and handed it to Chad.

Chad dialed a number from memory and gave the ringing phone back to Bainbridge. Bainbridge watched the two men warily as he placed the phone to his ear. From where he sat, Ish could hear Bainbridge's voice coming through the phone, which he instantly recognized as the recording they had made of the conversation at the hotel in which Bainbridge had given Madden the kill order. After about thirty seconds, the Associate Director's lips tightened, and it appeared that every trace of blood had just drained out of his face.

Bainbridge snorted like an enraged bull as a spot over his right eye began to visibly twitch.

"You motherfuckers," he muttered as he disconnected the call and put the phone back in his pocket. "How many people know about this?" he demanded, his head swiveling back and forth between the two men.

"Only those that need to," said Chad. "Only the people on our team have actually heard it, but copies are stored in the safes of several prominent attorneys around the country. They've been instructed to release the recordings to the D.A. and several news outlets once we give them the command. They've also been instructed to release it automatically if they haven't been able to contact either Ish or myself for a maximum period of seven days. It's a pretty simple arrangement, but very effective, if I do say so myself."

Bainbridge's hands balled into a fist as they rested on the table, his knuckles turning white. He gazed at each of them with such hate that Ish thought to himself that if looks could kill, both he and Chad would be stone cold dead right now.

"So, what is it that you want exactly?" asked Bainbridge, through clenched teeth.

Chad nodded at Ish.

"I think you know," Ish replied. "I want out of here—an immediate release, with all charges dropped. And I want my friends, Jag, Ma'am and Chad released as well. Oh, and my wife, Layla. I think you're fairly familiar with her case. She gets out, too."

"Oh, is that all?" asked Bainbridge, his voice heavy with sarcasm.

"Actually, there is one more thing. I want Agent Madden reinstated and given a raise and a promotion, along with a commendation for his work on this case."

Bainbridge looked at him as though he had lost his mind.

"Who the fuck do you think you are? And who the fuck do you think I am? I'm not a miracle worker! If I let you all go, how the hell do you expect me to give Madden a commendation when the fucking case is still unsolved?"

"I'm not going to try to tell you how to do your job," said Ish. "You either get it done or you suffer the consequences. I guess it depends on how much you love the current life that you have." Ish smiled faintly. "Maybe you're tired of all this, and ready for a change? I wouldn't blame you, really. I imagine working for the FBI can sometimes be kind of a thankless job anyway."

"And what if I said 'fuck it', and let you go but hired some snipers to put a bullet in your head and in the heads of everyone you know?" snarled Bainbridge.

Ish shrugged. "That's a lot of bullets, but it's definitely one of your options if you're okay pissing away your life, career and freedom. Besides," he said, leaning back in the chair and stroking his chin absentmindedly, "my guess is that your plan all along was for our prison life to be cut prematurely short, anyway. So, when you look at it that way, we really don't have much to lose."

Bainbridge scowled up at the ceiling for a moment, before turning back to Ish. "So how many days now before you have to check in with your attorneys?"

Chad glanced at his watch. "About two and some change," he said.

Bainbridge looked down at the floor, tapping his foot, before walking over and pounding twice on the door.

"I'll give it some thought," he said, turning his back to Ish and Chad as the door was being unlocked. Both guards walked in and stood at attention.

"Take this one back to his cell," said Bainbridge, pointing at Ish. "And arrest this one for falsification of ID."

"What?!" yelled Chad, this time fully springing up out of his chair.

Ish gave him a slight nod. "Don't worry, we'll fix this," he said calmly as he watched one of the guards place his best friend in handcuffs and lead him from the room.

It was hard watching his friend being taken away. He hoped that Chad believed that they would be able to get themselves out of this. The truth was, he wasn't absolutely sure he believed it himself.

Chapter 88

That night, sitting in the tiny cell all alone, seemed to Ish to last a lifetime. He didn't care much about himself, but he couldn't sleep worrying about his friends and how they might be suffering.

The next morning, he was up at what he could only assume was around dawn, doing push-ups, jumping jacks and the like. It was impossible to know exactly what time it was because there were no windows, but the activity that he heard outside as the ward began to wake was a good gauge.

A guard brought his breakfast about two hours later. He recognized him as the same one who had allowed him to sneak a phone call when he first arrived.

"Thanks, man," said Ish as he pulled the tray from the slot in the door.

"Hey," he said as the guard was turning away. "Any chance I could make another phone call?"

The guard just looked at him, tight-lipped and sullen. His eyes were a mix of sadness, sympathy and maybe just a little bit of anger. He simply shook his head from side to side and walked away.

Bainbridge must have gotten to him, thought Ish. Clearly, this asshole had big ears and even longer arms. With power like that, there was really no telling what he might be capable of. He and Chad had been pretty confident when they first listened to the incriminating recording that they had an ironclad 'get out of jail free' card, but now doubt was starting to fester deep within his soul.

Maybe Bainbridge really didn't care about the recording. Maybe he no longer cared about his job. Maybe he had a few million stored in offshore accounts and was ready to retire in some foreign country without an extradition treaty. Maybe Ish and his friends would all be dead within a week. He was starting to drive himself crazy going over all the possibilities in his mind, so he lay back in his bunk and began meditating. He started by concentrating on his heartbeat. He could feel the pulse of it beating in his chest, even as the distant screams and yells of other inmates threatened to break his concentration.

Slowly he began to descend into his own consciousness. The noise of the jail faded away, and he could physically feel the stress bleeding out of his muscles. Before long, he felt himself begin to disconnect from his body. He was no longer in the jail. He was walking through a dense forest, the trees so thick that there were only patches of the sky visible overhead. But there was still enough light to wonder at all the vivid colors that surrounded him; rich browns and golds and various shades of orange and red, all on a background of luminescent green.

He could feel the dry leaves crunching under his feet and a slight breeze blew against his skin. He began to smile, and then he heard something. He wasn't sure if it was a cry or a laugh, but it sounded like a child; probably a little girl. His first thought, of course, was of Sumatra.

"Sweetie, is that you?" he called out. The sound stopped, and moments later he saw a flash of white streak across the path in front of him. He ran after it, pushing through the brush, oblivious to the branches pulling at his clothes and tearing at his skin.

"Sumatra!" he called as he broke into a large clearing. He looked around, but there was no one there. Then he heard a rustling behind him and turned to see his daughter standing about twelve feet away, calmly staring at him.

Ish tried to run to her, but suddenly his entire body felt like it was encased in cement. The only thing he could move was his mouth and his eyes. He felt beads of sweat break out across his back from the effort.

"It's okay, Daddy," said his daughter. "Everything is exactly as it should be."

"As it should be?" asked Ish. "What do you mean, baby? What's going on?"

"I don't have long," said Sumatra, "but Mama thought you might be able to use some reassurance that everything was going as planned."

"I don't know what you mean," said Ish in frustration. "What plan?"

"It's not important," said the little girl as she tilted her head to the side and smiled warmly at her father. "I don't have a lot of time before I have to leave, so please listen carefully."

Ish wanted to say more. He wanted to interrupt, to ask more questions, to yell and scream for whatever was holding him back to let him go to his little girl. Instead, he forced himself to shut his mouth and allow her to continue.

"I know you have doubts that what you did was right. But know that the universe has been keeping track, and the scale is heavily weighted in your favor. People may not completely understand the value of what you've done today. Maybe Mama doesn't even fully comprehend it," she said, pausing to gaze momentarily somewhere off in the distance, "but one day they'll all know your sacrifice, and they'll remember you in song and verse."

Ish felt his eyes begin to fill with tears. "I'd give all that up for just one more day with you," he said, his voice breaking.

"I know, Daddy, but all this was destined. It happened exactly the way it was supposed to. We all have a role to play."

"You sound so wise for such a little girl," he said, sniffling and smiling through the tears. "How do you know all this?"

"I'm one with the universe now," she said, "and the universe is one with me. So are you, but you just aren't aware of it in your present state. But one day the veil will be lifted, and you'll see the truth in all its splendor."

"And will I be with you then?" he asked.

"If the wise ones deem it so."

Ish tried to shake his head, but he still couldn't move.

"Okay. I guess I will have to accept that answer for now. Thanks for telling me all this."

"You're welcome. But I have to go now. Take care of yourself, Daddy. And take care of Mama, too. She needs you more than the sun needs the moon."

Sumatra's face broke into a wide smile so bright that her entire face glowed. The light became brighter and brighter until Ish had to squint to continue staring at it. His daughter started walking backwards as her image began to fade, and the light began to fade with it.

"Wait!" said Ish. "Just one more minute! Just one more—" but then she was gone, like a puff of smoke caught in a harsh wind.

Whatever was holding him in place suddenly released him, and Ish fell to his knees. He placed his head on the ground and began sobbing. He wasn't sure how long he was in that position before a loud sound caused him to jerk with a shudder, and he found himself sitting upright in his bunk, back in his jail cell.

"I said get the fuck up, Carter!" said Burp.

Ish touched his face. His eyes were dry, but his hand was trembling. He swung his legs over the edge of the bunk and slid his feet into his slippers.

"You won't need the slippers," said Slurp.

"What do you mean?" asked Ish.

"I mean you don't need the fucking slippers," snarled the guard. "Or any of the rest of that shit. Strip. All of it." A smile played at the corner of his mouth.

Ish wondered what in the world could be behind this. "Fuck you," he said, "I'm not taking my clothes off for you freaky motherfuckers! Get your jollies somewhere else!"

"Carter, you can do this the easy way or the hard way. If we have to come in there, things are going to get messy. They'll be lots of soft tissue flying around, especially if you fit the stereotype," said Burp, grinning devilishly. "I think the last person we had to disrobe lost a testicle, didn't he, Joe?" he asked, looking over his shoulder at one of the six additional guards who had just joined them in front of the cell.

"I don't know if he actually lost it," said the guard called Joe, chuckling and shaking his head, "but it sure was fucked up!"

Ish stood facing them and weighed his options. There was a total of eight guards. He could probably fight them all off for a while, hand-to-hand. But if they used pepper spray or tasers, it would be all over in seconds. And even if they didn't, it was only a matter of minutes before backup arrived, at which point things would get much worse. He did the math. There wasn't a whole lot of choice.

Ish locked eyes with Slurp, and continued to stare at him as he slowly began taking his clothes off. He didn't know what they were up to, but he wanted to silently let the guard know that this indignity was not something he was going to soon forget. There was a price to be paid, and one day he was going to collect.

"Turn around and back up to the bars," ordered the guard, once Ish was completely undressed.

Ish did as he was told. Based on the temperature of the jail, he should have felt a bit chilled, but he was so furious that he was actually starting to sweat a bit. Once both his arms and legs were secured, someone radioed for the cell door to be opened, and he was escorted away. There were three guards in front of him, three behind him and one on each side. As he passed the other cells, he found all the other prisoners standing and staring with intense interest. Ish could tell by the look in their eyes that they were all wondering exactly what he had done to deserve such treatment. Ish wondered the same thing himself.

Finally, they arrived at a brown metal door. It looked very much like the door to the room he had met with Bainbridge in, except that it was in a different part of the jail.

"Stop," said one of the guards, directing Ish to stand before the closed door. "We're here," he said into a radio. There was a click and one of the other guards pushed the door open.

Ish wasn't sure what he expected to see, but this surely wasn't it.

He was still trying to take in the scene before him when he was shoved into the room and the door was slammed behind him. He barely noticed. The shock of what he was seeing overrode everything else. Sitting on a concrete floor in the corner of what he now realized was a cell, was Jag, Ma'am, Chad and Layla. They were all nude, and they were all shackled by their hands and feet, just as he was. They were also all wet, with water dripping from their hair as though they had just stepped out of the shower. Chad and Jag were covered in red welts, and he could see traces of bruises on Ma'am and Layla as well.

Ish barely had enough time to register the significance of this before he was hit by a blast of icy water straight from a fire hose. It was only his lightning fast reflexes that allowed him to remain on his feet, but he was still slammed into the far wall. He turned his back to the water in an effort to protect as much of the more delicate areas of his body as possible, but it still felt like punches on his back, buttocks and legs.

After what felt like ten or fifteen minutes but what couldn't have been more than two or three, the water shut of abruptly. Ish looked over at his friends, who all watched with a combination of sympathy, fear, anger and sadness. He shook his head and ran his hand over his face to clear his eyes as he turned around and stood defiantly, ready to go head-to-head with his attacker. What he saw was that he and his friends were the only ones in the cell. On the other side of the bars stood Burp, grinning and holding the water cannon at the ready. Standing next to him, hands in the pants pockets of a perfectly tailored gray pinstriped suit, was Bainbridge. He was also smiling.

"Good morning, Carter," he said. "You look cold. Let me get you a towel. Can you get him a towel?" he casually asked the guard holding the fire hose. The guard carefully laid the hose on the ground and left the room.

"I know you're uncomfortable," said Bainbridge with feigned kindness, "but before he gets back with that towel, there are a few things I'd like to discuss. This," he said, taking a hand out of his pocket and waving it at the cell, "this is just an example of the power that I have. You want to kill me right now, don't you? I bet that if these bars weren't between us, you'd rip my spine out before I could even blink, wouldn't you? I don't blame you. I'd want to do the same to a man that had just done this to me.

"But listen to me carefully. I'm not just a man. I am the U.S. government. That means I'm something akin to God. In other words, I'm everywhere; seeing all, knowing all. You thought you could hustle me? You can't hustle God. It's just not that fucking easy." He paused, apparently waiting for Ish to reply. When none came, he continued.

"You're right about one thing: there's not much I can do about these attorneys that you gave the recordings to. But fortunately, you're not the only person with access to attorneys. So, here's the deal, you fucking monkey," he said through gritted teeth, taking a step forward towards the bars. "I'm going to do as you asked, and let you and your friends go, but not before getting you all to confess on video to all the PROPR crimes. I'll send copies of those videos to several of my own attorneys, and I'll let them know that if anything happens to me—if I mysteriously disappear, have a stroke from too much cholesterol or get hit by lightning—they're all to be immediately delivered to the head of the FBI, upon which time you'll all be hunted down like the animals you are. This agreement is non-negotiable. If any one of you refuses to confess, you'll all be arraigned and you can do whatever you like with that illegally-obtained recording of yours. So, what'll it be?"

As he stood there, Ish began to shake with rage. He didn't give a fuck anymore. Here he was, along with some of his closest loved ones, naked and dripping wet, standing before this arrogant white man and feeling like a slave just off the ship from Africa. All the 'coolness' that he had gained a reputation for was gone. In that moment, he would have done anything to get his hands on Bainbridge and beat him until he was simply an unrecognizable puddle of body fluids.

But he knew that if he did that, it wouldn't only be him who suffered, but it would also be his friends and his wife. He had to acknowledge that he had responsibilities that prevented him from selfishly giving in to his base whims and desires. However, there was no way he would ever cower in front of this poor excuse for a human being.

This man was enjoying the fact that he was treating him like chattel, but like Kunta Kinte from *Roots*, Ish refused to let the man take his dignity. He closed his eyes and took a deep breath, letting it out slowly and literally begging his body to relax. Bainbridge cleared his throat impatiently, but Ish ignored him. Finally, he opened his eyes and once again felt in control.

Without saying a word to Bainbridge, he turned and walked over to his friends. He kneeled down and put one arm around Layla and one around Chad, forgetting his nakedness.

"Is everyone okay?" he asked.

"We're alright," said Layla, but her voice cracked a bit as a tear fell from one eye. "A little bruised, maybe, but it'll heal." The others nodded.

"I'm so sorry you all had to experience this," he said. He took another deep breath before he continued. "So, I guess you've heard his offer. What are your thoughts?"

"We don't have a lot of choice," said Jag. "Possession is nine tenths of the law, and we're in his possession. There is a ton of shit he can do to us, both legally and illegally."

"Yeah," said Ish. "If it weren't for that recording, we'd probably all be dead by now."

"So, if I'm understanding this right," said Ma'am, "we can take him down, but it'll be a suicide mission. Or we make the deal, and hope this muthafucka sticks to his side of the bargain?"

"That's pretty much it," said Ish.

"If we give him these confessions, it's like we'll have our own little Cold War," said Chad. "We're the U.S. and this asshole is Russia. Neither one can launch without suffering lethal retaliation from the other."

Ish bowed his head. Chad was right. They were at a stalemate.

"So, we're all in agreement that we want to do this?" he asked.

Everyone nodded, but Layla was the only one willing to look him in the eye while she did it. "Alright," he said as he rose back to his feet and returned to his previous position in front of Bainbridge.

"We'll do it," he said to Bainbridge, "but we have a few conditions. First, if we do this, we get out today. Next, this protection extends to everyone we know. That means family, friends, anyone who we care about. You don't fuck with any of ours. Also, we want a signed confession from you, that what we have on the audio recording is true."

"Are you out of your fucking mind!" exclaimed Bainbridge. "I'm not giving you a fucking confession!"

"Then you may as well call your water boy back in here, and then bend over and kiss your own ass goodbye, because we either exchange confessions or we have no deal."

Bainbridge yanked his phone out of pocket and began quickly walking towards the door, as if he was going to storm out of the room.

"By the way," Ish called after him, "this is a limited time offer! It expires in five minutes."

Bainbridge froze and stood staring at the phone in his hand for a few seconds. Finally, he put it back in his pocket, straightened his tie and slowly walked back over to Ish.

"Alright. But since you wanted to make a point of treating this as a 'friends and family' plan, understand that if it ever goes sideways, I'm coming after everyone that you've ever known."

"Go get our fucking clothes," said Ish in response. "And some goddamn towels."

Bainbridge glared at him, but once again fished his phone out of his pocket. He speed-dialed a number.

"Get these people dressed," he said. "I want them all in Room 17 in fifteen minutes."

Chapter 89

It took almost three hours for Ish and his friends to record their confessions and begin to be processed for release. It probably could have happened faster, but they had to wait for one of their lawyers to arrive with a cell phone to record Bainbridge's confession and upload it to a secure server. Until it all actually happened, Ish wasn't sure that it really would. He felt certain that Bainbridge would change his mind at the last minute or come up with some angle that he thought would get him out of the predicament while still protecting his future. But fortunately for everyone involved, Bainbridge excluded, that didn't happen.

Ish was the last one to arrive in the holding cell that was the final place they were all parked before being allowed to walk out the front doors.

He ran to Layla as soon as he saw her and wrapped her in a long, suffocating embrace. "How are you, baby?"

"I'm alright now," she whispered into his ear. Her tears against his face were warm and sweetly comforting. He hadn't touched her since she had been locked up, and the reconnection felt simultaneously alien and completely familiar.

He realized that, although he had never been consciously aware of it, he had dreamed of this moment a thousand times since he had learned that she was in jail. It was not something he had ever allowed himself to acknowledge, because to do so would have created a hope that came with a certain amount of desperation, and for the things he needed to do, he couldn't afford the luxury of feeling desperate.

After what felt like both forever and the most fleeting of moments, he let her go, kissing her briefly on the lips as he touched her face and gazed lovingly into her eyes. Only then did he turn his attention to the rest of the group, warmly embracing each of his friends in turn.

Once the greetings were concluded, Jag was the first to speak.

"I can't help but feel like someone is going to pop that door open any minute now and toss a grenade or something in here," he said. He smiled, but the usual humor was not present in it.

"Don't worry," said Ish. "Our ace is still safely in the hole. Actually, it's safely in multiple holes. They're just dragging it out to be assholes. We'll be out before you know it."

"And then?" asked Ma'am. "Where do we go from here?"

Ish put one hand in the pocket of his jeans, and ran the other through his hair.

"Well," he began, "I think at this point we can do whatever we want."

"What exactly does that mean?" asked Jag.

"Like Chad and I said earlier, we'll take care of you all financially, so money won't be an issue."

"That's great, because we have a small wedding to plan," said Jag, winking at Ma'am. "But then what? Sit at home all day watching reality TV and ordering stuff off the Home Shopping Network?"

"If you like," said Ish, smiling for the first time since he entered the room. "Or..." he shrugged.

"Or what?" asked Ma'am.

"Well, you said you wanted to learn to be a computer programmer. You can do that, if you like. Chad and I will work with you and teach you everything you need to know."

"Absolutely," said Chad, chiming in.

"That would be kind of cool," said Ma'am. "And what about you? What are your plans?"

Ish absently scratched at the hair on his chin and walked over to one of the benches and sat down. Layla sat beside him, snuggling so closely up against him that it looked like they were one person instead of two.

"The first thing I'm going to do," he said, taking a deep breath, "is spend some serious quality time with my lady. It's been far, far too long."

"Yes, it has," she cooed.

"Then, we'll sit down and decide together what we want to do next. There's some healing that needs to take place," he said, taking one of Layla's hand into his own, "and that will take time. After that..." He shrugged again, glancing up at the camera that was perched overhead. "Chad and I have a company that we need to get back to. And there are other business opportunities he and I have been discussing that we need to look into further."

Jag nodded. "Onward and upward," he said.

"Onward and upward," said Chad, smiling.

Ish took a moment to look closer at his oldest friend. He expected to see some evidence of the strain of this journey in his face, but Chad's eyes twinkled with the same fire and excitement they had when they first embarked on this crusade. Clearly, he was thinking about what Ish was cautiously refraining from saying aloud in a place that was most certainly devoid of privacy: This wasn't over. Not by a long shot.

Of course, he hadn't had a chance to chat with Layla about it yet, and he had to weigh her opinion as well. But he hoped that she would agree that they still had work to do. He hoped that she understood that the war was not over and that there were still battles to wage; that they owed it to their community to keep up the good fight.

But what if she didn't? What if she was tired of fighting and just wanted to ride off into the sunset and try to forget that any of this ever happened? He didn't know how he would react to that. It was something he didn't want to think about too much; a bridge that he would cross when he got to it—it he ever did. But considering Sumatra's place in this equation, he couldn't imagine that Layla would ever be able to just walk away if she knew there was more they could do.

There was a loud metallic clang, and the door swung open. Standing in the opening was Burp. He was alone, his better half, Slurp, conspicuously missing, as was Bainbridge. "Let's go, ladies!" he yelled, tapping his foot impatiently. They all filed out of the room, Ma'am first and Ish bringing up the rear. Ish paused at the doorway and locked eyes with the guard.

"Where's your boss? He too busy to come kiss us goodbye?" he asked.

"You're a real funny guy," Burp grunted. "If you're not careful, one of these days you and I will meet again inside these walls, and you'll be smiling out of the other side of your fucking face."

"Maybe so," said Ish, "but it may not go exactly the way you think it will." They stared hard at each other for a few long moments until Ish shook his head, smiled, and walked out of the jail to join his friends.

The sun surprised him as he exited the final door separating the jail from the real world, like rounding a corner and running smack into an old, dear friend that you haven't seen in years. He paused for a minute, closing his eyes and angling his face up to fully accept the warm kiss that it had been holding for him. Once he had taken a couple of deep breaths, he opened his eyes, smiled, and began following the rest of his group.

They were heading towards a black SUV limo parked at the curb that Chad had arranged as transportation, when he noticed another car parked in front of it. Leaning against the passenger door was FBI Special Agent Dexter Madden. He looked slightly amused.

Ish stopped in his tracks, then called to Layla. "Babe," he said, walking over to her. "Go on and get in. I'll be there in a minute."

She looked past him and gave Madden a good once-over. "Is everything okay?" she asked, frowning.

"It's fine," he said as he walked away. "He's a friend." He could feel her stare after him for a few seconds before she finally headed to the SUV to join the others.

"That's some vehicle," said Madden, smiling and pointing with his thumb. "What's that get, like three miles to the gallon?"

Ish turned to look at the limo. "Probably something like that," he said.

"Not exactly environmentally friendly," said Madden.

"I'm a black man in America," replied Ish, his eyes twinkling. "I have more pressing matters to worry about right now than the fucking effects of my mode of transportation on climate change. Not that it's not important," he said, shrugging slightly, "but you know...priorities and all that."

"I can't argue with you there, my brother," said Madden. He paused as though trying to find the exact right words for what he wanted to say. "Listen, I want to thank you. Bainbridge told me what you did. I don't know what possessed you—or what kind of skeletons you found that would put this kind of pressure on an asshole like that—but thanks."

"It was nothing," said Ish. "My daddy once told me that if black people stopped acting like crabs and started acting like water, maybe one day we'd overcome."

Madden face registered momentary confusion, then he nodded knowingly. "Right. The crabs in the barrel versus the rising tide that lifts all boats. My father said something similar to me when I was a kid, but it wasn't nearly as eloquent."

"Daddy was a poet," said Ish.

"Clearly," said Madden. He paused. "I don't mean to come off as ungrateful, but I have to ask. I'm not sure how you did it, but you somehow dodged a bullet here. Is this it? Are you done with all this madness now?"

Ish looked off into the distance, beyond the horizon. "There are people still out there hurting. Our people. And there are going to be more hurting tomorrow, and more hurting the day after that," he said.

"And you have to be the one that saves them?" asked Madden. There was a hint of sadness in his voice, but also a hint of something that sounded like respect. "What about other groups, like #BlackForLife? That cross-country march they started is really picking up steam. There are other ways to do this; ways that don't involve breaking the law."

Ish just looked at him and smiled.

"Okay," said Madden, shaking his head in resignation. "But know that just because you saved me from the unemployment line doesn't mean that you have a permanent get-out-of-jail-free card with me. If we cross paths on the job, I'll do what I'm being paid to do."

"I wouldn't expect anything less," said Ish.

"Good. As long as we understand each other. Well," Madden continued, pushing off the car and straightening his jacket, "you take care of yourself." He stuck his hand out.

"You do the same," said Ish, taking the hand and shaking it warmly. As he turned and headed back to the limo, the golden glow all around him, he couldn't help but feel like the cowboy hero of an old western movie, walking into the sunset, alive to fight another day. It felt good.

<<<<>>>>

ACKNOWLEDGEMENTS

I would like to take a moment to give very special thanks to my Oh So AMAZING editor, Kit Duncan! Kit didn't know me from Adam when I initially contacted her, asking her to edit this novel, yet she approached the task with a kindness, thoughtfulness and generosity that touched me deeply. Her knowledge of writing styles, language and the literary arts is astounding, but I believe that she went above and beyond the call of duty of an editor in the care and attention that she gave my manuscript. Not only did she make this novel infinitely better than it could have ever been through my efforts alone, she made me a much better writer in the process. Thank you, Kit!

I would also like to thank all of the dedicated, caring, understanding and downright *cool* police officers that I've met throughout my life. It is these officers that have allowed me to bring what I hope is a clear sense of balance and fairness to a story centered around a very sensitive and polarizing topic. I sincerely appreciate you and all the great work that you do and the sacrifices you make to keep us all safe and protected.

R.A. St. James

www.ingramcontent.com/pod-product-compliance
Lightning Source LLC
Chambersburg PA
CBHW081130300726
48982CB00005B/920

* 9 7 8 1 7 3 6 1 0 7 9 0 4 *